Adam Kennedy is novelist of remarkable versatility whose previous novels range from the highly successful thriller *The Domino Principle*, which inspired the international hit movie of the same name, to *In A Far Country*, an enthralling family drama set in the 1960s. His most recent titles include *Love Left Over*, a collection of bitter-sweet love stories, and *Passion Never Knows*, the first novel in the Kincaid Trilogy. He lives in Connecticut with his wife, Susan.

Also by Adam Kennedy

The Bradshaw Trilogy
No Place to Cry
The Fires of Summer
All Dreams Denied

Novels
Debt of Honour
The Domino Principle
The Domino Vendetta
In a Far Country
Passion Never Knows

Stories
Love Left Over

The Fires of Summer

The Bradshaw Trilogy Volume Two

Adam Kennedy

HEADLINE

First published in Great Britain in 1987
by W. H. Allen & Co. PLC

First published in paperback in 1988
by Star Books

Published in this edition in 1991
by HEADLINE BOOK PUBLISHING PLC

10 9 8 7 6 5 4 3 2 1

All characters in this publication are fictitious and any resemblance to real persons, living or dead, is purely coincidental.

ISBN 0 7472 3527 9

Printed and bound in Great Britain

HEADLINE BOOK PUBLISHING PLC
Headline House
79 Great Titchfield Street
London W1P 7FN

I'm lucky to have good friends. This book is dedicated to some of those friends

Frank Billerbeck	Don Jones
A. C. Brocki	Tom King
John Connell	Art Long
Egon Dumler	Tom Madigan
David Echols	Angelo Malaperdes
Philip Gould	Angelo Palikaris
Jess Hahn	Charlie Ross
Bob Hixon	Doc Savidge
Tony Jackovich	Bob Stephan

Star-crossed, ill-met
creatures adrift,
senses impaired, eyes softly bandaged,
stumbling ahead, call it love.
Deaf to sirens and whistles,
blind to directional arrows,
sensing no smoke trails,
heeding none in any case,
scarred by the flame-tongues, consumed
by the cruel and blood-coloured
fires of summer.

Jean-Louis Dorfinant

Book One

Chapter One

[1]

The gods were surely smiling the night Floyd Bradshaw was conceived. Light-hearted and careless perhaps, carousing a bit. On the other hand there is evidence to suggest that their mood was more sombre than gay. But in any case they surely knew at last that they had presided over the beginnings of a unique and contrary creature.

His mother, Helen Bradshaw, who never saw him or spoke to him till he was twenty years old, felt at first that this unusual circumstance alone might have moulded him. But as she came to know him, as she marked traces of his father in him, of her father also, and of herself, she began to believe that Floyd was simply the sum of his genetic inheritance and had no more control of his ultimate structure than she had of hers.

From the naval station in San Diego where he was stationed, just after the start of the war with the Japanese, Floyd wrote a letter to Lowell Simison, the man who had adopted him as an infant, telling him in detail about his first meeting with his natural mother.

> She told me she'd been to see you in South Dakota so you know what she looks like. She's a snappy-looking woman, all right. And smart, I think. And she was damned nice to me. Trying to be particularly nice. I could tell that. Feeling guilty, maybe. Figuring she owes me something after all this time. And maybe she does.
>
> You remember how I acted when you first told me I was adopted, two or three years ago, when I found out you and Mom weren't my real folks. I was sore as hell. Couldn't believe you when you said you didn't know who my real parents were. But now, since I talked with *her*, I can see what happened. I understand the way things work at adoption agencies.

He had seen his mother twice. The second time, when they were having dinner, she told him she planned to stay on in San Diego so she could see him as often as possible. But he told her all future liberties had been cancelled and he'd be shipping out within a week.

> We talked a lot those two evenings I saw her. Mostly she talked and I listened. She showed me some snapshots and told me all about the Bradshaw family.

Helen told him she was never married to his real father. 'I'm afraid we didn't know each other very well and he died not long after you were born.' Later she married a man named Wilson but when they divorced she took back the name Bradshaw.

> As far as she's concerned, that's my name too. Floyd Bradshaw. We'll see about that. Looks like I'm a bastard no matter how you slice it. But maybe I'll be a rich bastard. She says the Bradshaws are an English family and they have piles of money. Would I like to be rich? You bet I would. I'm not crazy.

She told him about her father, Raymond, who had died when she was only seventeen, about her grandfather, Angus Bradshaw, her aunt Clara, and her cousins, Nora and Hugh. And she told him in detail about Jesse. 'He was like my brother. After he left his own parents in Chicago he came to live with us in Fort Beck and Raymond raised him as if he was his son. When Raymond died, Jesse went with me to England to meet my relatives. He loved all the Bradshaws and they loved him. Angus decided to adopt him. So Jesse changed his last name from Clegg to Bradshaw. After Nora divorced her husband and went to live in Paris with her daughter, Valerie, Jesse and Nora got together and they've been together ever since. Not married, just together. And Nora's brother, Hugh, lives in Scotland.'

> She says her father left England when he was about my age and came to America. And his family never saw him or heard from him again. He married an Italian girl from New York. That means I had an Italian grandmother and an English grandfather. He was a teacher like you, Pop, at some college in Illinois.

'I knew nothing about my father's family in England till after he died,' Helen told Floyd. 'Everyone who knew him thought he'd been born in Maine. Even my mother didn't know the truth. I found out later that he'd had a tragic love affair with a married woman before he left England. He blamed Angus for the ways things turned out so he abandoned his whole family and started a new life here in America.'

I'm telling you all this so you'll know as much as I do about these new relatives of mine. And because I want you to know that nothing has changed between you and me. You're still my dad and you always will be and if Mom was still alive she'd be my mother. I know this other lady, Helen Bradshaw, gave birth to me but that doesn't cut much ice as far as I'm concerned. I'll never *know* her the way I know you and Mom and she'll never know me the way you do. Not that that's been a lot of fun for you. I know I've been a real jackass the last two or three years. I can't think of any good excuse for the way I acted but I want you to know it had nothing to do with you. It was all a question of me being fed up with myself and not knowing what to do about it. You know what I mean? I felt rotten about Mom dying and I didn't know what to do about that either so I just got into the habit of breaking things. And after I'd been in jail two or three times it got worse. It looks like I'm not too good at following other people's rules, especially when they don't make sense to me. So what the hell am I doing in the Navy where you can't take a leak without doing it by the numbers? Well you know the answer to that one and so do I. The judge in West Virginia gave me a choice. Go to the reformatory in Wheeling or join the Navy. If I had to do it over again I'd go to jail. As it is I expect to be in the brig most of the time I'm in the service. That means I'll be getting the short end of the stick both ways. But who gives a damn? I'll sweat it out. Either they'll get used to me or they'll court-martial me. And if that happens I'll come up there to South Dakota and you and I will start a little truck farm together. We'll sell fruit and vegetables in Yankton and live like a couple of kings.

[2]

A few weeks before Floyd's letter to his adoptive father, Jesse Bradshaw had accompanied Helen on a trip to Crawfordsville, Indiana, and then to Yankton, South Dakota, where they had at last sat down with Lowell Simison and learned where they could contact Floyd. When Helen went on to San Diego, however, she'd insisted on going alone. So Jesse returned to New York and explained his future plans to Nora.

'I can't believe it,' she said. 'If you'd come home and said you were going to marry Helen I wouldn't have been surprised. But *this* sounds like some sort of idiotic joke.'

'It's not a joke. You've mentioned it yourself quite a few times. You said you thought Valerie and I would make a good pair.'

'When *I* mentioned it, I *was* joking,' Nora said. 'I'm still not sure you're serious.'

'I'm serious all right.'

'She's my *daughter*, for God's sake. And you helped me raise her. You took care of her when she was little more than a baby.'

'That's right. I've reminded her of that,' Jesse said. 'But it doesn't matter to her so why should it matter to me?'

'Well, it matters to *me*,' Nora said.

'No, it doesn't. You just care about how it might look to other people. When I left here to go out to the Midwest with Helen you made it clear that I wasn't welcome back.'

'I didn't mean that and you know it. I was mad. I say all kinds of things when I'm angry. Or when I'm jealous.'

'There was no reason to be jealous. I told you that.'

She smiled. 'It seems to me there was plenty of reason to be jealous. How long have you and Valerie been planning this?'

'We haven't planned anything. She doesn't know I'm talking to you.'

'I don't believe that.'

'It's the truth. I was going to Boston from Chicago but I decided to come here first.'

'What are you telling me . . . that you and Valerie are going to get married but she doesn't know it yet?'

'That's right,' Jesse said.

'Well, in that case, maybe I still have a chance. Maybe she'll turn you down.'

'I don't think so.'

'No, I suppose not. You've certainly had plenty of time to get to know each other.'

'That's right. We've been friends for a long time,' he said.

'When did you stop being friends and turn it into something else? I might decide to write a book about this and I want to be sure I get my facts right.'

'Not funny, Nora.'

'I didn't say it was funny. It's not funny at all. But it's damned bizarre. Very few women get to share a man with their daughter. Most of them don't *want* to. *I* certainly didn't want to.'

'You haven't.'

'Don't insult my intelligence. You don't have to lie to me.'

'I'm *not* lying. Valerie's no more a virgin than you were at her age but she's never slept with me.'

'Stop it . . .'

'It's the truth. Why would I lie about it? We're all grown-ups.'

'Maybe. But some of us are more grown up than others.'

'That's right. Valerie's more grown up than either one of us.'

'Oh, my God. Spare me that. "The child is father to the man" and all that rot.'

'You raised her,' Jesse said. 'You should be proud of her.'

'I feel as if I raised you, too. But I'm sure as hell not proud of *you*.'

'I don't blame you. I never said I was perfect.'

'Don't give me that. You can't wait to father a few children so you'll have some reasonable copies of yourself toddling about. That's what this marriage is all about, isn't it?'

'I expect we'll have some kids but that's *not* what it's all about.'

'We'll see,' she said. Then, 'When's the big affair to be?'

'Soon.'

'Before Christmas?'

'I wouldn't be surprised.'

'What part will I play in the ceremony? Will I be giving *you* away or Valerie?'

'Neither. It will be a small affair I should think. Just the two of us and the judge.'

'Not bloody likely, Jesse. You can make it as small as you like. But don't try to keep *me* away. If you think I plan to miss my daughter's wedding, you're gravely mistaken. I'd be there even if she'd chosen a Turk. Since she's marrying the best man I know, nothing could keep me away.'

'*I* have no objections to your being there. But I think we have to consider Valerie's feelings.'

'I *am* considering Valerie. And I assure you she would never get married without her mum in the hall.'

'Of course she must be there,' Valerie said when Jesse saw her next day in Boston. 'We can't have a wedding without Nora.'

'Sounds awkward to me.'

'That's the point. We mustn't *let* it be awkward. I don't expect to be my mother's enemy for the rest of my days. Nor will she be mine. I admit the circumstances are nutsy but everything about Nora's life has been that way. Whatever else the three of us are to each other, we've all been friends. And there's no reason for that to end.'

'You're awfully matter-of-fact.'

'Not about you, I'm not. Not matter-of-fact in any way. But I know my mother.'

As it turned out, she did not know her mother at all, not in matters of vengeance and self-vindication. Nora was indeed a member of the very small wedding party and she managed in the process to appear both sedate and glamorous, filling both her roles admirably — loving mother of the bride and long-time loving mistress of the groom. The judge and his wife, knowing none of these particulars, were mesmerized by her; they found her both gorgeous and gracious. They thought the bride, as lovely as she was, a pale copy of her mother.

The groom, of course, was ill at ease. As though he alone was aware of the fires that were crackling inside Nora, of the patience she would show as she waited for her moments of retribution. Not against her daughter — she held her blameless — but against Jesse. And very specifically, for reasons clear only to her, against Helen. Since their first meeting twenty years before, she had seen her cousin as a kind of hateful catalyst in everything that related to Jesse.

Watching the marriage ceremony, however, she felt a soft wave of something almost benevolent towards Helen. Nora knew suddenly that *she* was the key to her problem, that somehow, through Helen, she would find the weapon she needed to recapture the things that had been wrenched away from her. These diabolic feelings unquestionably produced the madonna-like glow that so impressed the judge and his wife.

[3]

Jesse was Helen's only confidant in the matter of Floyd Simison Among her family, only he knew that there was such a person with such a name and that he was Helen's son. And Jesse, of course, had helped her to follow the paper-chase that led her at last to San Diego and a face-to-face meeting with a tall young man in Navy whites whom she had given birth to but had never seen. She was most eager, therefore, as she rode the train later towards home from California — the crew and passengers around her totally occupied with news of the just-declared war — eager to see Jesse again and tell him the details of what had transpired since he'd put her on the train for San Diego and bought himself an east-bound ticket.

When she stopped for a few days at her home in Illinois, however, where she had lived as a young girl with her father and Jesse, she found the announcement of his marriage to Valerie. Inside was a note:

> We're off on a short wedding trip. And Christmas in Quebec. Hope you can come to Boston for a long visit in January or February.

She had not gone to Boston that winter. Bad weather, travel restrictions because of the war, and a heavy schedule of volunteer work she had taken on in Fort Beck — all these prevented her from leaving. It was midsummer before she made her way east and saw Jesse again.

'Of course I was surprised,' Helen said. 'You and Nora had been together for a very long time. Twenty years, wasn't it?'

'More like eighteen, I think,' Jesse said. They were sitting in the garden of his house in Boston. Valerie was sleeping in a hammock not far away.

'How did she react?'

'Smooth and cool. She's a tough-minded lady. Besides, she and I knew we wouldn't stay together for ever. And even if she had been bothered, Nora heals quickly. Once she's handled the public aspects of a situation, once she's decided what she'll *tell* people, then everything else falls into place. In this case she came up with Slayback.'

'Who's that?'

'Her new house-guest. He plays drums in a jazz band in Greenwich Village. He's tall and black and handsome as hell. From Jamaica, I think. I'm not saying she had him standing by but he moved in a few days after I moved out. So she made her public statement well before our wedding.'

'And you're not too concerned with what happens to her now? Is that what you're saying?'

'Of course I'm concerned. I was in love with Nora for a long time. And she's Valerie's mother. Both of us care about her. But things don't *happen* to Nora. *She* makes things happen to other people.'

'I'm not sure she'd agree with that right now.'

'Maybe she wouldn't. But it's true nonetheless. Besides, I don't think she's thinking much about Valerie and me right now. She's got her hands full with Slayback.'

'How do you mean?'

'I've seen them together a few times. He's crazy about her. When she decides to move on, he may not be as amenable as she might like.'

'Maybe she won't want to move on.'

'Of course she will,' Jesse said. 'She can't help it. It's her nature.'

'She stayed with you.'

'I know she did. And I've never understood why.'

'Have you turned modest?' Helen said.

'Not me. I know she liked me. Maybe she even loved me in her self-absorbed fashion. But even love is no guarantee of longevity with Nora. As a matter of fact she's scared of all that tender stuff. Makes her feel vulnerable, she says.'

'The fact remains you were together for years.'

'I know. I've thought about that. And I think maybe Valerie had something to do with it. We had a sort of father-daughter relationship when she was growing up and I don't think Nora wanted to break that up.'

'A little irony in the atmosphere, it seems to me.'

'There always is if you look for it,' Jesse said.

'How does she feel about becoming a grandmother?'

'I don't think that bothers her at all. She's only forty-two and she could pass for thirty. She says she's going to be the youngest and best-dressed grandmother in New York. And after the war she'll be the best-dressed grandmother in Paris.'

'And how do you feel about it?'

'Can't wait. All my life I've been trying to find something I'm good at and I think maybe this is it. I expect to be a world-class papa.'

'Well, you've had some experience. You helped bring *me* up.'

'Not a chance,' he said. 'We brought each other up.'

'Only after Raymond died,' Helen said.

'That's right. Before that *he* had all the answers.'

'What kind of marks do you think he'd give us if he came back for a visit?'

'I don't know. Pretty good, I expect. All his students said he was an easy grader.'

'I'm not sure. I think he had higher standards for us. I think he might give you a B minus . . .'

'That's not so great,' Jesse said.

'It's not so bad either. I think he'd say you've handled yourself pretty well but you could have done better.'

'Not fulfilled my potential . . . is that it?'

'Something like that,' she said.

'How about you? He never saw any flaws in you. I figure you'd be good for at least a B plus.'

'Never,' she said. 'A D at best.'

'Not possible.'

'Sure, it's possible. Think it over. I didn't finish college. That's a big mark-down right there. I was married and divorced. Then I was widowed by a man I never married. And I have a son more than twenty years old whom I'd never seen till last December. I'm not at all sure what happened to all the years and I don't have any particular plans for the ones that are coming up. So that's my record.'

'You're being hard on yourself.'

'Not, I'm not. I'm not singing the blues. I just paused for a moment to take an objective look at the old girl and that's what I saw.'

'That's not what *I* see. I see a great-looking young woman who can do whatever she wants.'

'Ahhhh . . . but that's the catch. Outside of taking care of Chet, looking after him when he was sick and we both knew he couldn't get well, outside of that and trying to find Floyd, there's never been anything I really wanted to do.'

They had talked about Floyd the day after she arrived. Jesse had driven her to Boston College to show her the campus and his office. 'Valerie and I are stuck here till the war's over and we can go back to England, so I thought I might as well teach. The Army's not much interested in old birds who were in the last war, especially one like me with a stiff leg. And half the young teachers here in Boston were drafted or they enlisted, so I decided to fill in as well as I could.'

'You were a terrific teacher at Foresby.'

'Maybe I was. I don't remember. That seems like two lifetimes ago. I feel as though I'm struggling now just to keep up with the students.'

After they'd talked for more than an hour about Helen's meeting in San Diego with Floyd, she said, 'I feel as if we're keeping some big secret from Valerie. Did you tell her about all this?'

'No. You know I wouldn't tell anyone.'

'But I think you *should* tell her. Now that you're married . . .'

'That has nothing to do with it. This is something that concerns you and Floyd. No one else. If this fracas with the Japanese lasts as long as I think it might he could be in the South Pacific for quite a while. After he comes back and you two can see each other on some sort of regular basis, there'll be plenty of time then to tell people about it. We're not hiding anything from Valerie. I *know* her. She would expect you to do exactly what you're doing. You kept it to yourself for more than twenty years. There's no reason to make public announcements now. The main thing is for *you* to know how you feel about what you've done. Now that you've found him, do you think it was a good idea or not?'

'Oh, I've never questioned that. It was something I had to do. No matter what happens from now on, whether it turns out that he likes me or not. Even if he decides he doesn't want to *see* me, even if he wants nothing to do with me . . .'

'Why would he decide that?'

'I don't know, but he might. And I'd understand it if he did. But still I wouldn't be sorry I found him.'

'I'll bet he was as glad to see you as you were to see him.'

'I hope he was. But I don't count on anything. I talked so much when we were together and he talked so little. He just sat across the table from me and *looked*. And *listened*. I felt as if he was asking himself why I had finally turned up after all these years, why I hadn't come sooner, and why I didn't keep him with me when he was a baby. I was actually hoping he'd ask me those hard questions but he didn't. So I tried to give him the answers anyway. I told him how difficult it had been to get the information, that finally Chet and his friends in Maine had found a way to bribe someone to slip the records away from the adoption agency. But all the time I think he was wondering why I hadn't done it sooner. When he was five years old, or six, or ten.

'But he didn't *say* any of those things?'

Helen shook her head. 'No, he didn't. But still I had the feeling he was studying me, making some sort of judgement, filing things away in his head. He seemed very cool and quiet and grown up, and I felt like a ten-year-old girl babbling about her trip to the zoo. He was terribly polite but I kept expecting him to say something really nasty to me. He has a wonderful face, a very sweet look sometimes, but behind it I sensed there was a terrible temper waiting to explode. He's very thin, no weight on him at all, and his hands look as if he's worked hard. They're all bones and tendons. Heavy veins and callouses.'

'Who does he look like?' Jesse said. For a moment then Helen almost told him the complete truth, something she'd never told anyone except Chet. 'Does he look more like you or more like his father?' Jesse went on.

Again she hovered on the edge of telling him everything. But then she said, 'It's hard to say. As I told you, I hard! remember his father. But I suppose Floyd resembles him in some way. Mostly, I guess, he just looks like himself. He's a fine-looking boy . . .'

'No resemblance to you or Raymond or any of your family in England?'

'Nothing I noticed particularly. Nothing that jumped right out at me. But as I said, I was so crazy nervous I couldn't see straight. Maybe the next time I meet him I'll notice a striking resemblance to someone straight away.'

'I admire you,' Jesse said then. 'I think it took a lot of courage to do what you did.'

'I don't know. After we said goodbye to each other I thought of a thousand things I wanted to say, things I wanted to ask him.'

'I can't imagine what it would be like, walking into a room and sitting down to dinner with a grown-up person you'd never seen before who just happened to be your own kid.'

'I know it will be a lot better the next time I see him,' she said. 'At least I hope it will.'

'How did you leave it with him?'

'I wanted to kiss him but we shook hands instead, like two people at a school reunion who don't really remember each other. He gave me his Navy post-office number when I asked for it and I said I'd write to him. He said he'd probably be pretty busy but that he'd write, too. And that was it. He walked away and I just stood there and watched him go. I felt like crying but I didn't.'

'*Does* he write to you?'

'I've had a few letters, but not many. And he never writes more than a page. He was on a destroyer but now he's on what he calls a "bucket". It's some kind of a junky supply ship, like a freighter. Or at least that's how he describes it. He said, "The Navy has ships like this so they'll have some place to put guys like me." What do you suppose that means?'

'I don't know. How often do you write to him?'

'I started out at once a week but when he didn't answer very often I decided I'd better not smother him. So I cut back to two or three times a month, usually just two.'

'Did you talk about what will happen when the war's over?'

'I told him the truth about the Bradshaws. I said there was a lot of money there and that I'd be able to give him whatever help he needed after he got out of the Navy.'

'How'd he react to that?'

'He grinned and said he hoped I wouldn't forget I'd said it because he was sure he would *need* a lot of help.'

'I'm not sure I like the sound of that.' Jesse said.

'I'm not sure either. But I don't care. I'll give him whatever he wants.'

After a long moment, Jesse said, 'Can I ask you a question?'

She smiled. 'You *always* ask me questions.'

'Do you like him?'

'Of course I like him. He's my son.'

'I mean — do you *really* like him?'

She looked away. 'I don't *know* him, Jesse, and he scares me a little bit. But that's not his fault. I *want* to like him and I want to love him and I will if he lets me.'

[5]

Jesse was in no way an ingenuous man. But there was a directness about him, a willingness to accept people at their own evaluation of themselves that made him appear at times to be less perceptive than he was. He felt that he himself was in fact what he seemed to be and he preferred to believe that other people were the same. Since he was both intelligent and aware, he knew of course that they were *not* but he persisted in his original judgements till hard evidence proved him wrong.

Nora had once said to Clara, her mother, 'It would be no fun to deceive Jesse. There would be no point to it. Either he wouldn't notice or he wouldn't believe it. And if he finally came to believe it he would simply leave and you'd never see him again. He is what he is. No hidden chambers. Damned rare if you ask me. And damned appealing. No wonder women fall all over him.'

It was not a planned pattern of behaviour with him. It was a reflex, an instinct, a natural rhythm that he felt comfortable with. It was a way of relating to the world that made sense to him and he was willing to accept the occasional shocks, detours and surprises that came with it. Valerie's reaction to Helen's visit to them in Boston, for example, was a total surprise to him. When he came from delivering Helen to the railway station for her return to Fort Beck, Valerie said, 'It was nice to see her, wasn't it?'

'That's hardly the word for it. For years she's been my closest friend. Until she and I went to England together more than twenty years ago and came up the driveway of Wingate Fields and met the Bradshaw family I felt sometimes that she and her father were my *only* relatives.'

Valerie said, 'I've never had a chance to spend much time with her but *I* like her too.' She smiled. 'But I won't like her at all if she thinks she's going to go on being your cosy friend.'

He put his arms round her. '*You're* my only cosy friend.'

'I know that and *you* know it but it's very important that Helen should know it too.'

'She's crazy about you. She'll end up being your best friend. You'll see.'

'I already have a best friend. *You*. It's nice if she likes me. But I'm more concerned with how she feels about *you*'. 'She loves me,' he said.

'That's what I mean.'

'And *I* love her. We're like sister and brother.'

'I know that's what you keep saying. But you're *not* sister and brother. She's *my* second cousin but she's not related to you at all.'

'You know what I mean,' he said.

'No, I don't. That's what we're talking about. I only know what you *think* you mean.'

'You're serious about this, aren't you?'

'Absolutely.'

After a moment he said, 'All right, let's start again. What exactly are we talking about?'

'We're talking about a very attractive woman who's been in love with you all her life . . .'

'That's what I just said.'

'No, you didn't. You said she loves you like a sister and I say she doesn't. I say she loves you like I do. Like Nora did. Like any woman loves any man.'

'Oh, for God's sake . . .'

'Do you think I'm the only one who sees that?' Valerie said.

'No, I don't. Nora had the same idea. She couldn't get it out of her head. But you're certainly nothing like Nora.'

'Don't be too sure of that. Nora's very good at seeing around corners. Maybe I'll be good at it, too.'

'What does that mean?'

'It means that practically any woman in the world who saw you and Helen together would assume there was something *there*. Or else there had been at one time. Or else there would be sometime later.'

'*You* don't assume that, do you?'

'Of course I do. What do you think we're talking about?'

'I don't know *what* we're talking about. I don't recognize you. I've never seen you like this before.'

'I've never had to *be* like this. Now I do. I'm protecting my interests.'

'There's nothing to protect,' he said.

'Of course there is. As long as you keep telling me, and telling yourself, that Helen simply sees you as a big brother . . .'

'What's wrong with that?'

'Nothing's wrong with it if it's true. But it's *not* true. And if you insist on keeping your head in the sand . . .'

'You've been talking to Nora, haven't you?'

'No, I haven't. I don't need Nora or anybody else to tell me what I think. And I don't need you to tell me I'm crazy when I know I'm not.'

Again he sat looking at her for a long moment. 'Are we going to have a quarrel about this?'

'I don't know. That's up to you.'

'Why should we even have a discussion?'

'Because it's necessary. If we don't deal with this now we'll have to settle it later. It won't go away.'

'What is it exactly that we have to settle?' he said.

'I hate for it to sound as if I'm giving an order. Making some kind of demand.'

'Go ahead.'

'I'm just saying that whatever that special relationship is that you had with Helen, no matter what you call it, it has to change now.'

'Do you think Helen and I have been having a steamy love affair all these years?'

'I don't know. I'm not accusing you of anything. What I'm saying is that Helen's been having a love affair with *you* whether you've been having one with her or not. And she still *is*.'

'That doesn't make sense.'

'Oh yes, it does. It would make sense to any woman. It made sense to Nora and it makes sense to me.'

He walked across the room, sat down beside her and put his arms around her. 'Are you feeling bad today? Is that what this is all about?'

'No, damn it. That's *not* what it's about. It's not a prenatal symptom. This is a serious discussion about something that's important to me.'

'I can see that. What is it you want me to do?'

'I want you to be honest with yourself. Try to see things as they *are*. You can do that if you try. And if you do then you and I won't have any problem. But if you don't, or if you *won't*, then we'll have the same problem from now on. It won't go away till you deal with it in your head.'

He pulled her close to him again. 'I'm surprised you never brought this up before.'

'I didn't want to. I thought it wouldn't be necessary. Until she came here, till I saw the way she *is* when you're around. I thought . . . I don't know what I thought.'

'I'll be honest with myself. I promise. And nothing's gonna screw us up. I promise that, too. Before you know it, we'll have two or three kids, the war will be over, and we'll be living at Wingate Fields. You'll be the finest lady in Yorkshire and I'll smoke cigars, drink claret with every meal, and get fat.'

'Good. That's what I want. I'll like that.'

[6]

The news of Valerie's marriage to Jesse, when it came to Wingate Fields, triggered an explosive device inside Ned Causey, Nora's father and Valerie's grandfather, that seemed to have been waiting for many years to be set off. It gave him an excuse, it appeared, for a tirade against all the Bradshaws, living and dead, not excluding Clara, his wife. And a particularly venomous outburst against the late Angus. And of course Jesse.

'The day that Jesse Clegg came striding into this house, that milksop grin on his face and Raymond's daughter, Helen, draped on his arm, that was a sad and sorry moment for all of us, all of us included — think back on it — from Angus and Louise right down through a third generation to our granddaughter.'

'You never liked him from the start,' Clara said.

'Not for a second. I'm proud to say it and history has proved me right. Look at your family, one by one. Would Angus have come apart the way he did, adopted that scallywag and changed the whole structure of the family if your fancy Jesse hadn't given him some sweet potion of lies and put him into a stupor? And do you imagine that Angus's strange behaviour had no effect on your mother? Why do you think Louise hated him so before he died? Do you think she'd have gone on that crazy spin of hers and ended up as she has in a convalescent clinic if Angus had minded his affairs, if he'd stayed at home here and kept himself on course the way a man of his standing is expected to? It's all Jesse at the foundation when you look at it closely. You think things have been the same between you and me since he came here? Not by any means. You defended him from the start, thought he was a fine chap whatever he did. Enticing your daughter into his bed right here under our own roof . . .'

'Not true, Ned. You've gone off there. Whatever may be wrong with Jesse, there was certainly no enticement needed where Nora was concerned. If anyone took the lead it was our daughter.'

'You're back at it again, as I've said, defending him at every corner. You know as well as I that Nora would be married to Edmund Bick today if it weren't for Jesse.'

'I don't believe that. Jesse was in America when Nora married Edmund. And he was back in England for quite a time before Nora and Edmund separated.'

'The details don't matter. The fact is that if Jesse had never come here in the first place, Nora would be a contented woman living a decent life in a fine house and looking after her children. But instead, after she was free of her husband, what did she do? Lived like a woman of the streets in a house in Paris. With your hero, Mr Jesse, as her permanent house-guest. And her daughter, pretty little Valerie, a witness to whatever went on there between those two. But all the same I don't hold Nora responsible. She was taken in, just as Angus was and just as you are to this day, taken in by that second-rate opportunist from America. If he'd been born in England, he'd be a gardener or a groom in some poor stable. He fooled you all, did his little dance and took you all in, Angus included. Look at your son. Do you imagine there's no connection between Jesse's being named lord of the manor and Hugh's high-tailing it to Scotland like a man bent on killing himself with isolation and whisky.'

'Isolation? Hugh's not isolated. He's buried among that brood of children his wife brought him for a dowry.'

'That came later. When he left here he was fleeing Wingate Fields and I say it was because of Jesse and Angus and all those little tricks. Turning a drifter from Chicago into the head of a fine old family! It was a scandal. There's no other word for it. Ask some of your neighbours if you don't believe me. They all thought Angus had gone off the rails. They still think so. And I agree with them.'

'You're hopeless, Ned. You're simply frustrated and envious and you have been for most of your life. You were almost fifty years old before you ever set eyes on Jesse and you were as angry and confused and dissatisfied then as you are now. You didn't need help from Jesse to make you despise yourself. You've been trying to blame your own shortcomings on someone else for longer than I can remember. Before Jesse arrived it was Angus who was to blame for everything. He didn't appreciate you. He didn't give you enough responsibility. He didn't praise you. He didn't reward you.'

'And it was all true.'

'You don't know how fortunate you were to have Angus looking after you, patching you together, trying to turn you in the proper direction. If you'd been left to yourself, God knows what a mess you'd have made.'

'I've been waiting a long time for this. I knew that sooner or later you'd say what you really thought of me.'

'You know what I really thought of you. I thought you were the most wonderful man I'd ever met.'

'But you were mistaken. Is that it?'

'No. I wasn't mistaken. But the man you *were*, the man I married, disappeared. By the time Hugh and Nora were born you were unrecognizable and you know it. You'd turned into a quivering mound of self-pity. Your horses and your dogs, claret and brandy — that's what you settled for. And those sad, fat little girls in the village public houses. Everyone knew what you were about. And Angus knew better than all of us. If it hadn't been for me and the children, he'd have put you out long ago. But instead he gave you responsibility, more responsibility than you could handle.'

'You think so, do you? Ask the tenant farmers and they'll tell you how I've handled things.'

'I'd be afraid to ask them. They think you're a joke. They think you're lazy and incompetent and cruel to your horses.'

'I've never seen a horse I couldn't handle.'

'You've never owned a horse that wouldn't kick you to death if it had the chance.'

'You're clever, Clara, always have been, I'll give you that. But you don't fool me. All this attack on me is to get us off the subject of your precious Jesse and his latest adventure among the Bradshaw women. He's had quite a time of it. Starting with Raymond's daughter, using her to get Angus and having a bit of fun on the side as well . . .'

'What a second-rate mind you have.'

'Just sharp eyes, my lady. Those two didn't fool anyone when they arrived here all bright-eyed from the Colonies. Ask your daughter. She knew what was happening. But, as we all know, it didn't take Jesse long to discard Helen and take up with Nora. And, as I've told you before, I always thought he had his eye on you as well. I never accused you of responding to him but he was taking you in all the same, sizing you up. If you'd said the word, you might have been allowed to take your daughter's place.'

'You're disgusting.'

'Disgusting is the word. I agree with that. But I'm not the person it should be applied to. You can't deny that your granddaughter has now taken your daughter's place. Defend him as much as you wish but you'll never make me believe that you're not put off by the turn of events. We won't be calling the bishop in Newcastle to pass along the news, will we? No parties planned for the tenants, I'm certain. You can find whatever fault you like with me — I'm almost happy to sit here and hear you list my shortcomings. Because I know in my heart, no matter how contemptible I may be in your eyes, that no little misdeed of mine could begin to compete with this latest adventure of Jesse Bradshaw.'

[7]

From the time when Helen was eight years old, her mother, Anna, and her father, Raymond, had been separated. Until she was thirteen, Helen lived in New York with her mother. From then on, until Raymond's death in 1918, she lived with him in their house in Fort Beck.

Anna's second husband was Joseph Buscatore. With him she had three children: Paul, Maria and Nina. When Nina was born, Anna died in childbirth. A year later Helen had received a printed card in the mail announcing that Joe had married again.

On her way home to Fort Beck from Boston, Helen stopped in New York to see her half-brother, Paul, and her two half-sisters. When she called Joe at his house on Staten Island to make a date for that visit, he suggested they meet next day in Manhattan.

'Why don't I just come there?' she said. 'So I can see the kids at the house? I don't have so much time in New York.'

'First we'll have to talk,' he said.

They met in a Ukrainian café on Tompkins Square. Joe seemed ill at ease from the moment he sat down at the table. He was heavier than Helen remembered and he wore a moustache now. The first thing he said was, 'I don't have much time. So I'll just have some coffee. I'm doing a big job at a house on West End Avenue. Two men working under me. I have to get back.'

'I'm sorry. I thought it would be better if I just came to the house. That's what I said on the phone. So I could see the children.'

'They're not such children now. Paul is twenty-one, the two girls not a lot younger. They haven't seen you for a long time. They don't remember you much.'

'I'm sorry. I had some difficult years after Anna died.'

'You wrote that you got a divorce,' he said.

'That's right. I tried to write to you as often as I could. And I sent cards and gifts to the children. But no one answered. I was never sure that you got my letters.'

'I don't write letters much. I never had time. Lots of people to feed. Pauline and I have four babies now — four boys.'

'Are Paul and the girls still living with you?'

'Paul comes and goes. In and out. He's got big ideas.

Handsome Harry. Thinks he's too good to work. Too good to go into the Army. One of his street-corner friends gave him a pill to take so he flunked his physical and they gave him a 4-F card. I thought he'd be ashamed to be a reject but he thinks he pulled a fast one. He drinks too much and fights in the streets, wears fancy clothes and sleeps with other men's wives. Pauline doesn't even want him around but he comes around anyway.'

'What about the girls?'

'They're at home. They go to convent school and behave themselves. But they've got big ideas too, like their brother.'

'When can I see them?'

'It's hard,' he said. 'They go to school all day.'

'Then why don't I come in the evening? We'll go out to supper together.'

'We don't do that. We eat at home every night.'

'Then I'll come after supper. Or I'll eat with you if you want me to.'

Joe looked at his watch. 'You know how young girls are. Always busy with one thing and another. Running back and forth. And like I say, they don't really know who you are.'

'Then I'll *tell* them who I am. We're sisters.'

'Half-sisters,' he said.

'It doesn't matter. We had the same mother.'

'To tell you the truth they don't remember Anna much either. It's Pauline who's been a mother to them.'

After a long moment Helen said, 'When can I come?'

'It's hard. Sometimes the girls sleep over at my sister's place down by the ferry landing. She's by herself since her husband died and she likes to have the girls around. She's close to their school so sometimes they're there with her at night. They just sleep over and go to school from her house the next morning.'

'You mean if you told the girls I was coming to see them on a particular night, let's say next Thursday, and you told your sister it was important for them to be at home that night, they still might not be there.'

'Oh, if I told them to be home, they'd be there all right.'

'Then what's the problem, Joe? Are you saying you don't want me to come to the house?'

'No. I didn't say that. It's not *me*.'

'Then who is it?'

'Well, you may not like to hear this but we don't talk

about Anna much. Pauline's my wife now and she has been for a long time. She got tired of hearing Anna's family talk about how terrific their daughter was, how beautiful she looked, what a good mother she was. So after a while Pauline stopped going there. And she wouldn't invite them to our house. When I took the kids to see Anna's folks I had to go alone. You see what I'm talking about? Pauline's a good wife to me but she's just a regular, plain woman. She'd take one look at you and she'd decide it's Anna all over again. She wouldn't be fit to live with for a month.'

'My God, Joe, I'm no threat to anybody. I'm here in New York for a few days and I want to see my mother's children. What's the problem? If you don't want me to come to your house, then I'll meet them at your sister's house. Or if that's no good, I'll meet them at a restaurant on Staten Island. I'd like you to come too but if that's going to upset your wife . . .'

'Don't say anything bad about my wife.'

'I didn't. I'm just trying to . . .'

'Don't think you can stop by in your fancy clothes any time you feel like it and tell everybody what to do.'

'I'm *not* telling you what to do. I just think it's wrong . . .'

'Who are you to say what's wrong? You'd better take a look at your own life. Getting a divorce and running around the country with this one and the next one. And back and forth to England. I know something about the Bradshaw family. Anna told me a few things about your father and those people he comes from. Sure, they have money and they live fancy and they make up their own rules as they go along. I guess they buy and sell men like me every day, men that work with their hands to put food on the table. What they don't know is that I don't *want* a life like they got. And I don't want my kids to live like that. I don't want them to get a lot of crazy ideas in their heads, thinking a woman like you is their sister so maybe they could dress like you some day and run around and be rich and not have to earn a living or raise a family.'

'What are you saying? You know me from before. I'm not a terrible woman.'

'I don't know *what* you are. You're a stranger to me. And you're a stranger to my children.'

'But they're not just *your* children. They're Anna's children too.'

He went on as though he hadn't heard her. 'Anna should

never have left this city and her neighbourhood and her family. She was never happy till she came back to the things she knew. She wouldn't want her children to make the mistakes she made and I don't want it either.'

'For God's sake, Joe, I'm not trying to . . .'

'Don't talk to me about God. Don't talk to me about anything.'

He stood up suddenly. 'My family don't need your money or your fancy presents. You're not your mother's daughter and she knew it. You belong to your father's people. There's no Italian blood in you. The best thing you can do for us is to go back to wherever you came from and leave us alone.' He took a crumpled dollar-bill out of his pocket and dropped it on the table. 'That's for my coffee.' Then he walked, slow and stiff, out of the restaurant, climbed into his truck parked at the kerb, and drove away.

[8]

It seemed to Helen that she had spent endless tormented hours on trains travelling west from New York to Illinois. Except for the one time when she had left her mother to live permanently with Raymond in Fort Beck, she remembered those trips as defeats, each of them, in one way or another. She had no memories of returning to Fort Beck in triumph. Always, it seemed, she was in flight from some painful experience or from some internal chaos that could not be quelled.

Travelling home from her visit to Jesse and Valerie, however, and from her agonizing session with Joe Buscatore, she couldn't recall any time or any trip when she had felt she had so little to look forward to. Her frustrations were intensified by glancing at her ticket as the train rolled, late afternoon, out across the marshes of New Jersey and realizing that the next day was her birthday, that at midnight she would be forty-one years old.

If the other train rides she remembered were associated with particular calamities or disappointments, this time there was no such specific event or feeling to deal with. Instead, as she looked out the window of her compartment at the wasted landscape she felt stifled by something spongy and without definition. She felt a general sense of loss.

The war itself, of course, made her uneasy. Its beginning had made her sharply conscious of the ending of the last war, of the day in 1918 when it had been declared officially over. Her father had hosted a victory party that he had planned for months. He had believed, as had many of his friends at the university, that the end of that war might indeed mean the end of all wars. So celebration was in order. But that night as he sat alone in his library, very late, after all the guests had gone and Helen was asleep upstairs, he had closed his eyes, his head resting against the side of his wing chair, and stopped breathing.

So Helen thought of her father, still, as a war-connected loss. And Chet Comiskey, although he had died only three years ago, was unquestionably a war victim. Mustard gas had begun the poisoning that had finally destroyed his bone marrow and impelled him to speed the process by destroying himself. And Jesse's poor stiffened leg, souvenir of the Somme, although it had not ruined his life, might very well have changed his conception of himself in ways that were invisible to her, perhaps even to him.

Now a new war had begun, one that was sure to be bigger and longer and more destructive, one that would affect more people, more countries, more lives. She felt as if she had opened a thick book with blank pages, one which would inevitably tell a tale of loss and heart-break.

Her personal future, too, seemed to have no armature. Angus was dead, his wife was institutionalized, and Clara, Raymond's sister, as well as Wingate Fields itself, were not available to her until some time, months or years ahead, when the fighting stopped and she would be able to cross the ocean again. Nora was in New York, of course, but Helen had made no effort to contact her. There had been a time, when she first went with Jesse to Wingate Fields, when she thought that she and Nora, because they were first cousins and close in age, would become permanent friends. But the contretemps, real and imagined, that developed because of Jesse, had pushed them far apart and kept them there.

Chet's death had been the ugliest calamity of her adult life, more agonizing in some ways than the death of her father. Its inevitability had made the pain worse, not better.

Her father's death, by its quickness and its surprise, had shocked and shattered her but it had not deadened her entire system, had not numbed her abilities to feel and react over a long period of time. Only Chet's death had done that.

At last, however, that numbness had begun to pass. After her many solitary months in Maine, there in the house where she had lived with Chet, she had begun to respond again to that life in the woods, a world of birds and animals and trees and plants. Then, suddenly, the surprise of the new information about Floyd, the prospect of finding him, of seeing him and talking with him, had brought her back to a path that led someplace other than to Chet's grave.

Jesse had helped, of course. He had been the engine that moved her ahead. He had asked the proper questions and persisted till he found the answers. He had forced her to come alive and use herself. By the time they had learned Floyd's adoptive name, by the time they had seen the house where he grew up and talked with Lowell Simison, by the time they found out that Floyd was in the Navy, at a specific address in San Diego — by that time she had reclaimed her senses and her rhythm, had re-entered her skin, and was able to decide, by herself, that she herself would go to San Diego and complete the circle begun before Floyd was born in 1920.

Now, however, as she had indicated to Jesse in Cambridge, that exciting plateau of discovery was behind her. She had achieved the impossible, had solved the Chinese puzzle that had obsessed her adult life. She had found her child, seen him, talked with him, touched him. Now she was forced to admit to herself that, having had that reward, she would not have it again. It was a triumph that could not be repeated. She could never see him again for the first time. Nor could she pursue him for her entire life. If it turned out when he was home again — she never allowed herself to imagine that he might not survive the war — that he was eager to see her, to establish some sort of continuing pattern that would give security and satisfaction to each of them, then of course she would be delighted. But she had no assurance that such a pattern would develop. She'd had no hint from Floyd, either in person or from his letters, that his being found by her had meant to him what it had meant to her. So she had forced herself to deal with uncomfortable truths. If he didn't like her, if he didn't love her, if he didn't need her, if he saw no reason to clutter his life with this woman who had suddenly appeared on a bright day in San Diego and identified herself as his mother, if any or all of these were true, then she must accept the fact that she, by herself, could not make a life between them. After all the years that had passed she admitted to herself that the *idea* of parenthood, of *being* a parent, or of being the child of a particular person was *only that* — an idea — until it was vitalized by some unit, small or large, of shared experience. She was determined to find a way to *know* Floyd, to know *about* him, to have the best possible relationship a grown-up parent can have with a grown-up child. However, as she told herself that such a thing was not only possible but, with the proper determination, inevitable, a small voice reminded her that everything was not in her hands, that only time and patience would provide the answers. She had her son at last and yet she *didn't* have him. Like all children, he owned himself and he would give over as little or as much of that self as he chose to.

And what about Jesse? All through a tiresome Illinois winter she had looked forward to her springtime trip to Boston, to her visit to Jesse and Valerie in their fine house. She told herself that their marriage was a splendid happening. And when she found out that they were expecting a baby, that too delighted her. 'It's about time someone got Jesse on the right track,' she said to Valerie. 'I hope you'll have enough children to fill all the bedrooms at Wingate Fields.'

'Not *that* many, I expect. But we do hope to have a big family.'

'And the first one will be a boy, of course,' Helen said.

'No question about it,' Jesse said. 'Angus wouldn't have it any other way. He'd come back to haunt us.'

As she sat in her train compartment and reviewed the days she had spent with Jesse and Valerie, Helen found nothing but pleasant memories. It was a solid old house with dark panelling, large windows, well-used furniture and a walled garden. 'We fit well here, don't we?' Valerie said. 'We decided to leave it just as it was when we bought it. It reminds us of Wingate somehow. There's even a pretty nursery and a nanny's room upstairs.'

Normally, Helen did not consider herself a graceful house-guest. She didn't like the process of fitting into another rhythm. Nor did she enjoy being entertained or catered to. With Jesse and Valerie, however, she discovered that she was free to come and go as she wished, to join them for breakfast before Jesse went off to his lecture or to have breakfast brought up to her room on a tray, to lunch at home with Valerie or to meet Jesse for lunch at the college. Or to walk and read and spend the day alone. At dinner of course, and in the evening, the three of them were always together. They played cards sometimes, or Valerie played the piano, or they listened to the radio, to musical programmes or to news broadcasts about the war in Europe and in the South Pacific. The Japanese had invaded Burma and the Dutch East Indies, Mandalay and Corregidor; Rommel's troops were sweeping across North Africa; and in Russia the Germans were moving swiftly toward Stalingrad.

'It's doesn't look good, does it?' Helen said.

'Of course not,' Jesse said, 'but in a year, or even six months, you'll see a different picture. Don't forget . . . Hitler said he'd have troops in England by now. Instead, England's getting stronger all the time.'

'Clara writes that morale is very good now,' Valerie said, 'even with all the bombing. Churchill promises that Montgomery's the man to stop Rommel and there are rumours that a great many American troops will be in North Africa soon as well.'

'The Germans made a serious mistake by taking on Russia. They've spread themselves too thin. No army can fight on three major fronts hundreds of miles apart.'

'What about the South Pacific?' Helen asked them.

'That's another matter. Another problem altogether. But it can be handled. Once our Navy's in place and we have the planes and pilots and ground forces to do the job, things will start to turn around. But it won't be an easy victory.'

There was a gentleness, a calmness about the house in Boston that made time seem to pass slowly. Even the two dogs and three lazy cats seemed peaceful together. In the mornings when Jesse was away at the college, Helen and Valerie often spent hours together. Valerie was warm and open and candid with her but all the same Helen sensed that there were walled-off areas, soft partitions, and bolted doors. If she had hoped for the kind of relationship she had enjoyed with Clara she realized quickly that it could not be that way between her and Valerie. She sensed a wariness in the younger woman, a watchfulness that brought out, *began* to bring out, the same qualities in Helen. As they reassured each other, by their voices and their manner, that they were guileless and trusting, their guile and lack of trust became more and more visible. Or so it seemed to Helen. She drew no conclusions from these observations. She did not like Valerie less because of them. But she found herself longing for those lovely idle hours with Clara in the morning room at Wingate Fields.

One day with Valerie it came to Helen as a mild shock that she herself was now precisely the age that Clara had been when they met. And Valerie was only a bit older than Helen had been.

That particular crystal moment stayed with her persistently, Helen found, for the rest of her visit. And on the train as she headed for Fort Beck. It didn't speak to her of age or ageing, it spoke to her of *change*. Jesse, she realized, as the end of her visit came near, was no longer available to her in the way he had been for all of her adult life. Even during their periods of misunderstanding or mistrust, times when they had gone for months, or even years, without seeing each other, the connecting cord had never been frayed. Now, however, for the first time, she knew that it had been. Whether *he* knew it or not, whether he admitted it to himself, Jesse didn't need her now. Those many years, since she was thirteen, of shared confidences, of interdependence and, most important, of a common relationship with Raymond, that strong three-cornered sense of animal and intellectual kinship that had sustained them all — all *that*, she sensed, was altered now. Not ended perhaps, but rendered less important, less immediate, less pertinent when one was making current choices. In Jesse's present time of marriage and children-to-come and a carefully charted future that would centre around Wingate Fields, all previous years and previous lives, Helen's along with them, had to be given less weight, less power, less voice. Jesse could not and would not be the person he had always been, not in relation to the world, to himself or to her.

Anyone who knew Helen well — Clara, for example — would have said that probably no circumstance could have upset her more than a disruption of the emotional contract — how else can it be defined? — between herself and Jesse. And that was true, of course. But it was also an area, in theory at least, that allowed for self-deception. Or for varying interpretations of the facts at hand. Even as Helen painted the darkest possible picture for herself, she was able to remember the pleasant details of all the time she and Jesse had known each other; to remember even more clearly the hours they had spent together just days ago in Boston; and, if she pushed herself far enough, to conclude that the future might take all sorts of unforeseen turns that, while depriving no one else, might quite possibly and agreeably benefit her.

Her more immediate pain, one she could not escape, involved her meeting with Joe Buscatore. His words echoed in her mind as though they had been recorded there. Word by cruel and idiotic word. As she told herself over and over that the judgements of this man, of all people, should not matter to her, they *did* matter, she found, and they continued to disturb her.

First of all, the idea of being cut off from any contract with her mother's children was hard to accept. The guilt she felt for not having seen them during the years since Anna's death was tempered somewhat by her recollection of the number of letters and cards she had sent, and the gifts. And she had *tried* to see them whenever she was in New York. Bu' each time there had been an excuse. This last encounter with Joe had made it clear that those excuses were scraps of the same fabric of contempt and rejection he had spread out before her in the café on Tompkins Square. He had made up his mind a long time ago.

As with her thoughts about Jesse, however, she told herself that the future was not frozen in place. The situation in the Buscatore house might change, the children would soon be away from home, working and living on their own premises. Contact could be made with them that would have no effect on Joe and his wife. She would be able to give them the chance to judge her for herself, to accept her as a sister or not accept her at all. It was a situation she could think about and make plans about. There was still a role for her to play.

Joe's angry and vindictive judgement of her, however, was another matter. It had left no room for self-defence, no place to hide. He had swiftly painted a portrait of her that seemed to have real meaning for him. Then he had stood up, walked away, and left her with it, the colours raw, the paint still wet.

She was not shocked by his words or his conclusions. It

did not surprise her that someone with Joe's background, with his particular set of beliefs and circumstances, would not admire her. What really struck her and made her tremble was to hear a description that so closely resembled her own evaluation of herself. Not theoretical. Not vengeful. Not at all. On the contrary, it had been a simple listing of habits, actions, past performance and present circumstance that sickened her because she saw in it nothing but truth. Having always believed, as Raymond had taught her, that broken things can be fixed, she had suddenly been confronted by an entire tableau of things past fixing, of behaviour that had become character, of facts and incidents that had become history, of deep scratches in the bronze that could not be polished away.

She saw the past more clearly, suddenly, than either the present or the future and in that instant, for the first time, she felt old. Not the age of failed vision or muscles that respond slowly but the kind that corrodes the consciousness, the recognition of meaningless goals, careless values and lost oppotunities, of mistakes that need not have been made but cannot be corrected.

Always before, in any such crisis of self-esteem, Helen had taken refuge in Raymond. Referring to *his* evaluation of her, *his* sense of her importance, she was able to refute any negative views of herself, whether they were hers or someone else's, to stabilize herself and live in the moment till the passing days and her own resiliency got her through the squall. This time, however, for the *first* time she could remember, she was afraid to call up Raymond, afraid to refer to him, afraid to risk the possibility that even her controlled re-creation of him might tell her things about herself that she could not absorb.

So she left the compartment, walked to the club car, ordered a drink there, watched the fields and forests slip by, and had a long conversation with a man from Fort Wayne about his company that had manufactured steering-gears for Studebakers but was now converting to military ware of a secret and complex nature. Then she had a short talk with the man's wife; she believed that her four-year-old granddaughter had powers of extrasensory perception inherited from her grandmother, a farm woman living in Red Wing, Minnesota, who had predicted in 1918 that Germany's next ruler would be a man with an odd moustache.

Helen ate a light supper in the dining car before she returned to her compartment. By then it was dark outside. She closed her window-shades and started to read a copy of Upton Sinclair's *Dragon's Teeth*, a novel she had bought at the station in New York. Her eyes, however, kept turning away from the page, and finally she began to cry. Unwanted and unbidden, the tears slid down her cheeks and spotted the cover of her book.

[9]

On the night of November 5th, 1943, the lights in Lowell Simison's house went out during a windstorm. As he opened the basement door, carrying a flashlight and a box of electrical fuses, he tripped, fell to the concrete floor at the bottom of the stairs and fractured his hip. He lay there until the following night when a neighbour, seeing no lights in the house, came and found him. He was taken to the hospital and placed in an intensive-care unit but he died of pneumonia the following morning at six o'clock.

On November 9th, Hugh Causey, Nora's brother, walked out to his stable after breakfast, shot his favourite stallion, Hector, then put the barrel of the gun to his own forehead and killed himself.

A week later, Louise Bradshaw, who had celebrated her ninety-fourth birthday the month before, and who had not been told about her grandson's suicide, died quietly in the solarium of the convalescent home where she was a patient. Her detailed obituary in the London *Times* identified her as the wife of the late Angus Bradshaw, mother of Clara Causey and the late Raymond Bradshaw. The names of her grandchildren were also listed: the late Hugh Causey, Nora Causey and Helen Bradshaw.

A week after Lowell Simison's death, Floyd was notified by the Red Cross. Three weeks later he received the old man's last letter, postmarked the afternoon of the day he fell and broke his hip.

Dear Floyd

I've done quite a lot of reading lately. Japanese history.

Fascinating. Culture and violence. It astounds me how often the two go together. I wish I could send these books on to you but I know I can't. So I've paperclipped notes to specific pages, directing your attention to certain passages. They'll be waiting here for you when you get back. Don't misunderstand me now. I'm just as much against the Japanese as anybody. But when you adjust to a longer view, the newspaper stories take on a different meaning. Wars come and go. Soldiers die, and politicians. But some little metalworker spends ten years working on a brass serving-tray and it lasts for ever. People keep looking at it and admiring it and learning from it as long as there are any people around. The work survives. The man who did it is unknown. The men who ruled him are dead and forgotten, and the battles they fought, the intrigues that engaged them, go all unmarked and unremembered.

Most human activities we discover at last are written on water. No tracks are left in the sand. As you know, I always thought of teaching as a high calling, perhaps even a noble one. Now I'm not so sure. I'm beginning to suspect that it's an activity like any other, a way for a man to earn his bread and pass the years. In my mind when I was a young man, education was an end in itself. The goal of a fine school was to develop minds that would question and reflect and reach conclusions. On the other hand if one simply wanted to learn a craft one was apprenticed to the proper journeyman or enrolled in a trade school. One explored life in all its variety or one learned how to earn a living. Or so it seemed to me when I was seventeen years old and entering university. I was idealistic of course and dogmatic, as are all seventeen-year-olds. But still, my notions about the purpose of learning were not unusual at the time. Now, however, I see that education has become a means to an end, an entrée to a lucrative profession, a tool of commerce, a guarantee of a certain level of comfort and recognition. Someone has painted a moustache on the Mona Lisa.

You will see from all this that I don't regret that my teaching career is over. Nor do I regret the years I spent in the classroom. Fortunately my illusions and self-deceptions stayed with me almost till the day of my retirement.

You will note from the above, however, that I do have a continuing envy of the nameless artisan who hammered out that brass serving-tray. And all those others who are able to make objects not on an assembly line but by themselves, in a quiet room. The ability to paint a good picture and hang it on the wall and look at it must be one of the great joys a man can have. Recently I found one of your old botany textbooks and I've been trying to make copies of the line drawings of plants and trees and flowers. I've made a sorry mess of it in every instance but I continue to try. It gives me great pleasure.

After Hugh Causey killed himself, it was discovered that he had left no message of love or regret or explanation to his wife, to his parents, Clara and Ned, or to anyone else. The photograph of Helen that he had kept hidden for many years in his bureau drawer was discovered by his wife but she bundled it up with his other papers and family pictures, and thought nothing more of it.

A week before his death, however, Hugh had written to his sister, Nora, in New York.

I don't regret anything, do you? What a waste of energy to follow yourself about with a willow stick, cracking yourself on the buttocks and upper legs as punishment for sly thoughts and misdeeds. I can proudly say that I have never tried to atone for Tuesday's actions on Thursday. Sufficient to the day is the pleasure thereof. How's that for a retooling of the gospel according to somebody or other?

Enough philosophy. How are you? Do you revel and prosper? I expect you do. I should have visited New York. All the nasty things I hear about it make me think I would have liked it there. I would perhaps have been well liked there. Lauded maybe. Written about. Pursued by long-legged women with chancy backgrounds and scarlet mouths. A verse narrative might have been written about my life as a rake.

Am I a rake in your eyes? I am not in my own. Far from it. Remembering my childhood, I think of myself still as a timid fellow, an in-turned little chap hoping for approval. I never had your hunger for combat, your instinct for battle. I was destined, I'm sure, to be where I am now, among my gillies and grooms, surrounded by my dogs and horses. Even my wailing stepchildren are off somewhere now, violating local laws, violating each other perhaps. Who cares? I don't.

They tell me there's a war going on but I'm having none of it. Had no interest in the last one. Less in this version. I've hoarded a great deal of ammunition during the years so nothing interferes with my bird-shooting or stag-hunting. Only lethargy and good brandy keep me by the fireside. I've had excellent new locks made for my rooms so sometimes I am able to avoid my hateful wife for weeks at a stretch, a task made easier by her outspoken desire to avoid me, *and* her frequent trips to Glasgow to sit at her father's knee and help him sort through his cartons of pound notes.

So much for all that. By the time you get this letter you will undoubtedly have heard some ugly news about me. Distasteful reports. Distasteful to others but not to me. I look upon it as a triumph, a great adventure. Having discussed the matter at some length with Hector, my incomparable grey stallion, I have decided — more accurately, he and I have decided together — on a joint venture, a suicide pact I believe it's called in the tabloids. He is as dissatisfied with *his* paddock as I am with mine so we're about to try something new. Since he's the only creature that I truly care about and since I've never questioned his feelings for me, it seems totally appropriate that we should chance this thing together. We'll simply canter out in a direction we've never tried before and see what happens.

You're the only person I'm confiding in because you are my only human friend and because I know you will not weep for me any more than I would weep for you under similar circumstances.

In a letter to Helen just after her mother's death, Clara wrote:

After the ugly shock of Hugh's suicide, the senseless horror of it, I imagined that nothing worse could happen to me. But then a few days later my mother died and I saw that I'd been mistaken. In Hugh's case, I had felt a terrible tormented mixture of anger and bewilderment, guilt and heart-break. But when Louise died, it was pure sorrow. I felt absolutely weak and lost and helpless. And totally female. Do you know what I'm saying? I've always told myself, and I believed it, that the natural rhythm of our lives includes, it *must* include, the death or our parents. It's a kind of chronological truth that we're all prepared for. An unbearable tragedy, I always believed, would be the loss of one's child. Nothing could be worse, I felt. But I was mistaken. As lonely and forsaken as I felt when Angus died, when I heard of Raymond's death, when the horrid news about Hugh came to me, those blows were no preparation at all for the news about Louise. Since then I've spent a great deal of time by myself, sorting through her things, sorting through my memories of her, trying to see her clearly again the way she was when I was a child. Finally, after many hours I began to understand my feelings. Louise was a woman who had everything, absolutely everything, in her lifetime. She had natural gifts, high intelligence, remarkable beauty, and the power to attract people to her. She loved her husband and loved her children. And God knows she was loved in return. When Raymond and I were small we believed there was nothing she couldn't do. No one thought much about heroic women in those times but that was what she seemed to be. Nothing, it appeared, had been denied her. Nothing ever would be. Then, like the sea washing away a great headland she lost everything; not material things, not people or possessions or wealth, but all the internal force and stamina and humour and resilience and leadership that had made her what she was. I know Angus believed that it all happened when Raymond went away, that she pulled back inside herself then and never came out again. When I was younger I rejected that notion. I didn't have that kind of belief in cause and effect. I still don't. But all the same I couldn't push it away. And at last I accepted it completely. Not until then, when I realized what the loss of her son had done to *her*, did I finally allow myself to admit what the loss of Hugh has done to *me*.

Through the years since Floyd's birth, Helen had been tempted many times to tell Clara about him, in the clearest and truest possible way, sparing no details, leaving out nothing. But each time some fear, some sense of guilt had held her back. Now, as she reread Clara's letter, all hesitation left her. As soon as circumstances permitted, as soon as she was able to go to England again, she would tell her everything.

[10]

Floyd did not, as he had anticipated, spend all his Navy years in confinement. During his first months at sea, however, on a destroyer, he was twice threatened with court martial and spent more than half his time locked in a detention area on a lower deck. At last he was transferred to a small ship that ran a haphazard schedule of deliveries from whatever supply centres had been set up in the islands to the combat vessels. An hour after his arrival on that ship he found himself in a small office below deck with a hard-looking, ginger-haired man with a torso like a tree trunk.

'I'm the first mate. My name's Jack Flowers. This ship is called the *Osceola* but the men call her *Asshole*. We've got a captain, a lieutenant and an ensign on board but *I* run things. This is a simple operation. Nothing like that faggot destroyer you just came from. If you can get along with me you've got it made. If you don't you'll have a tough go of it. Sometimes we work our asses off and lots of times we don't turn a tap. There's not much spit and polish here. We just try to keep the rust chipped away or painted over. Since we haul a lot of food we eat good. And we even get decent movies once in a while. But we ain't had a shore liberty in over a year so things get a little nutsy sometimes in the crew's quarters. I see you've got a broken schnoz and I notice in your papers here that you like to fight. So you ought to be happy on this tub. Plenty of hard noses on board. But if you decide to choose somebody, you better know what you're doing. Cause nobody stops fights here unless sombody picks up a wrench or pulls a knife. I mean you fight till the other guy can't cut it any more. Or till you drop. Do you follow me so far?'

'Yes, sir.'

'It also says here that you won't take orders. Say you don't like to work. How about that?'

'I had a problem with an ensign where I was before.'

'Everybody has problems with ensigns. But this business about *work* bothers me. You see, I don't like to work either. There ain't a guy on this ship that *likes* to work. You see what I'm getting at?'

'Yes, sir.'

'And if you're thinking about bucking for a court martial so you can get locked up stateside and maybe even get sent home, forget about it. You'll never be in the brig here and I'll never send a bad report on you to the old man. We *got* a brig below decks like every other tin can in the Navy but ours never gets used. Don't ask me why. I can't tell you. It just seems to me that when a man gets assigned here he takes a look around. He sees we got a small crew and we're all living in tight quarters and he just decides to make the best of it. What we got here is a fuck-up crew and fuck-up officers. That's why they're here. But we get the job done. If you keep your nose clean, people will let you alone. I've got a hunch that's all you want anyway. Any questions?'

'No, sir.'

'You look like a decent kid. If you play straight with me you've got a friend. If you cock me around I'll make you so fucking miserable, you'll wish you was dead. Got it?'

'I got it.'

Years later, when he and Jesse were comparing their times in service in the two wars, Floyd said, 'I hated the Navy from the first day I put on a uniform. I don't mean I thought it was silly or a waste of time. I don't mean I didn't *like* it. I mean I *hated* it. Everything about it. All the rules and the games and the traditions, the fucking *romance* of being a Navy man and going down to the sea in ships and all that storybook crap. I hated it when I was still on *land* in San Diego. Before I'd ever set foot on a ship. Then when I ended up on a destroyer I hated it even worse. It reminded me of summer camp at the YMCA in Crawfordsville. All those bastards were really *enjoying* themselves. Strutting up and down, learning all that salty talk, polishing their shoes, drinking coffee by the gallon, saluting anything that moved. I thought, "Man, this is a floating nut-house I've got myself on." And it *was*. Everybody playing some kind of a *part*. Like they were making a movie about life in the Navy. Like every single one of those guys had wrapped his real self in a bundle with paper and string, and mailed it home with his civilian clothes from San Diego.'

'But after you got transferred, it was different,' Jesse said. 'Right?'

'Night and day. The funny part of it was that I liked the ocean. I liked being on the water. But on the destroyer I felt as if I was below decks all the time.'

'In the brig,' Jesse said.

'That's right. But even when I wasn't, it was like being inside a floating hotel with no windows. So when I saw the *Osceola* it was a whole new piece of cheese. I could stand forward on the main deck and look all the way aft and take in the whole ship. I could stand at the rail when I wasn't pulling a work detail and spit in the ocean. And the sky at night came down over us like an umbrella. It was all the right *size* for me. It was like a hunk of life I could handle. And Jack Flowers was right. It was a good crew. Crazy misfit bastards most of them, all ages and all colours, most of them sluffed off from some other ship. They all cussed and bitched and moaned but they liked it just the same, as much as anybody can like being shut up with a bunch of men in the middle of nowhere and not knowing when you're liable to swallow a torpedo or take on a kamikaze freak. Or how long it will be before you walk on solid ground again. But they all stayed on the rails, those guys. And mostly because of Flowers. He was right. It *was* his ship. He ran it kind of loose but he ran it. He knew when to look the other way and when not to. And if he had to he'd take off his shirt and tangle with any guy on the ship. Nobody could handle him so he didn't have to fight very often. He was right about the officers, too. If they weren't on the bridge they stuck close to their quarters. The three of them and the ship's doctor played a lot of poker together and guzzled alcohol from the dispensary. And once in a while they'd show up, spic and span, for an inspection or an announcement, or just to prove they were alive. But the whole thing worked. We knew we were in a war all right but it was a war of nerves, of shipments and schedules and deliveries, of waiting and doing the same things over and over and trying not to get so bored you wanted to cut somebody up. It was Jack Flowers's war and he got us through it, all us guys on the *Osceola*.'

After Helen received one of her infrequent letters from Floyd, telling her about Lowell Simison's death, she tried to imagine his reactions. Knowing nothing of life on a naval vessel, she assumed he would have long periods of time alone, times when he would grieve about Simison's death, think about his two meetings with her in San Diego, and make plans, perhaps, for what he would do with himself after the war ended. When she first began to write to him, she had hoped he would confide in her, tell her something about his thoughts and his feelings. But there were no such insights or revelations in his short, staccato messages, all of which seemed to be jotted notes for longer letters that were never written. Her assumption that he was either unable or unwilling to confide in her was not correct. The fact was that Floyd, from the time his ship sailed south-west from San Diego, made a strong and specific effort to live in present time. It was as though he had decided to put a cap on his personal life and, for the moment at least, to keep the past *in* the past. As far as the future was concerned, he made no plans. First he wanted to make sure he had one.

[11]

When Valerie received a letter from Clara telling her of Hugh's death, and of Louise's, she and Jesse had just celebrated the first birthday of their son, Raymond Angus Bradshaw, and they were expecting another child, due to be born in May of the following year.

As soon as she read the letter she tried to call Nora in New York but there was no answer at her home. At her office a cleaning woman answered and said no one would be there till Monday. During the weekend Valerie called Nora's home repeatedly but there was still no answer. At last, early Monday morning, Sam Slayback answered. 'I've been trying to reach Nora for three days. Is she all right?' Valerie asked.

'Yes, I believe she'll be fine now.' He spoke in a deliberate, almost scholarly Jamaican accent.

'What does *that* mean? Has she been sick?'

'Not really sick. A bit of an accident.'

'What sort of accident? What do you mean?'

'I think she would rather tell you about it herself.'

'Is she there?'

'No. She's not here just now.'

Valerie turned from the phone to Jesse. 'God, this man is exasperating.'

'What's going on?' Jesse said.

'That's what I'm trying to find out.' Then, into the telephone, 'But where *is* she? It's very important that I talk to her.'

'She asked me not to give out information to anyone. You must forgive me. I must hang up now. I have to go to visit her. I'll tell her you telephoned.'

When the line went dead she hung up the receiver and turned to Jesse again. 'Some sort of accident, he said. It sounds as if she may be in hospital. Who's that doctor friend of hers? You know him, don't you?'

'Dave Guthridge.'

'Can't we call him?'

Jesse looked at his watch. 'He won't be in for another hour. I'll call him at ten. The main thing is I don't want you to get yourself worked up. If there were anything serious the matter with Nora, Dave would have let us know. I see him at the Century almost every time I go into New York. He has our number here and he knows Nora's antics as well as we do.'

'I just hope she's not . . . I mean she and Hugh were so close. And for her grandmother to die almost at the same time.'

'Nora won't go to pieces. You know that. You just finish your breakfast and after a bit I'll talk to Guthridge and we'll see what's going on.'

At ten o'clock Jesse went into his study to call New York. Half an hour later he came upstairs to Valerie's sitting room, where she was waiting for him. 'Nothing to worry about. Not only did I speak with Dave, I called Nora.'

'Where is she?'

'She's in the hospital but she's fine.'

'What happened?'

'She called Guthridge late at night to tell him she'd accidentally taken too much of a prescription drug he'd given her.'

'Oh, my God . . .'

'Wait a minute. It turned out she was crying wolf. As soon as the ambulance picked her up and the doctor examined her in the hospital he saw there was nothing wrong with her.'

'What do you mean?'

'Just what I said. She was shamming. When I asked Guthridge why, he gave me her number at the hospital and said I should ask her.'

'How'd she sound?'

'A little sleepy but fine otherwise. I asked her what was going on and she said she's trying to get rid of Slayback but she's having a difficult time of it. So she decided to have herself put in hospital with no visitors allowed. That's where Slayback was going when you talked to him today. He sits in the waiting room all day till it's time for him to go to the club where his band plays, but he never gets to see her.'

'What good does *that* do? She'll have to go home eventually.'

'Not according to her. When she leaves the hospital she's going to a hotel.'

'Which one?'

'Doesn't know yet,' Jesse said. 'Or if she knows she's not telling. She said she'd call in a few days so we'll know where she is.'

'What if she doesn't call?'

'She'll call. Why shouldn't she? She's not hiding from *us*.'

'Did she say anything about Hugh and Louise?'

Jesse nodded. 'She feels awful. She must have got a letter the same day you did.'

'She always told me how close she and her brother were when they were children. It must have killed her to hear . . .'

'I'm sure it did. But you know Nora. If she's suffering she won't let anybody see it. When I asked her about Hugh, she said, "What a senseless way to die. What a beautiful man he was and what a stupid thing to do." '

[12]

Helen's earliest memories were of her father's house, the great stone pile at the edge of the Foresby campus in Fort Beck, its lawns and gardens sprawling about on four sides, the carriage house with its mysterious loft under the elm trees at the end of the driveway. Every corner of the house and its surrounding property held a sharp girlhood memory for her, many of them specifically redolent of Raymond and Jesse and those electric years the three of them had spent together.

After Raymond's death, when she had gone to England, and when she had travelled around her own country later, working and educating herself and trying to forget that she had a child now, a boy she had given up to strangers, during all that time the house in Fort Beck remained a symbol of solidity and permanence in her life, a place that would always be there, warm and unchanged, for her to think about, remember, or return to.

During the war years, however, after her return that springtime in 1942 from Boston and New York, the magic of the house and her relationship to it was changed somehow. Without any decent period of transition the rooms that had been havens became, in her eyes, something quite apart from that. Where everything had been warmth she began to feel cool draughts. She sensed dampness where in fact everything was as snug and dry as before. She imagined she heard sounds at night. The house where she had been mistress since she was thirteen seemed somehow to have taken her captive. It echoed and creaked, and when it grew silent that silence was oppressive.

It was not simply loneliness she felt. It was a gnawing dissatisfaction with herself, with the things she had done and had failed to do, and with the person she, in her own eyes, had become. She kept herself as busy as possible with charity work, war committee work, and two afternoons at the hospital as a volunteer. She played bridge one evening a week, listened to the radio, and went by herself to the movies. She read popular novels simply to distract herself. And she wrote long letters to Clara in which she held back almost nothing about herself and her feelings.

> Do you ever get disgusted with yourself? Tired of yourself and bored with yourself? I don't imagine you do. You're too busy always. Managing Wingate Fields and taking care of other people's problems. And now, of course, you're occupied with the war projects you've told me about. I wish all that could work for me but it doesn't. I'm not idle, God knows. I seldom have a free minute during the day. And I know I'm doing things that need to be done. But it's all mechanical with me.

My brain keeps steering its own course, making its own statements, and none of them make me feel good about myself.

I still feel like a young woman. I *am* a young woman but I find myself surrounded every day by women who are old enough to be my mother, women whose children are grown, whose husbands are either working long hours or are dead. I hear them chattering to each other about their ailments and their hobbies and their grandchildren and I keep thinking, 'What am I doing here? What kind of life is this?' I start to feel as if every choice I've made since I was eighteen years old was a bad one.

When I'm really low I try to imagine what you would say to me if we could sit down and talk the way we did when I was in England. It's hard to believe those days were so long ago. It's more than ten years since we met the last time in New York.

I also try to practise the things that Raymond used to preach. He was a great believer in self-reliance. And so am I. Or I always have been. But I can't help thinking that I've carried it too far. The sad and silly fact is that apart from you I have *no one* to confide in. How is that possible? I've certainly met a lot of people and known a lot of people but I feel as though none of them really *knows* me. I can see your face as you read this and almost hear you saying, 'If that's true then it's because you didn't allow them to know you. You didn't *want* them to.'

If you're thinking that, then I'm sure you're right. I think it myself but I don't know how to fix the situation. I'm not even sure that it should be fixed but I certainly don't like things the way they are now. At my age I should have some of the best years of my life ahead of me. Or am I mistaken about that? Am I just finding out what everybody else already knows? That the whole business is just a process of gradual loss, of scattering things here and there along the way and then trying to make do with what's left? Even if that *is* true, I certainly don't want it to be true for me. On the other hand, I don't want to spend the rest of my days (according to the longevity charts, my life is only about half over) feeling sorry for myself. In the first place it's a full-time activity (lesson number one from Raymond), and in the second place it doesn't get you anywhere, and in the third place it's magnificently boring. But all the same every word I'm writing to you seems to be soaked in self-pity.

Am I just lonely? Of course I'm lonely. But it's more than that. I've never felt alone before. When I was young and at home, I always had Raymond. And for years Jesse, in a way, took Raymond's place. Then I was married to Frank. And after Frank I was with Chet for all that painful, lovely time. You see, I've had only men friends. It seems that way and it *is*. Apart from you, my dear aunt and friend and kindred spirit, I've never had a really warm and close friendship with a woman, not even my own mother. Nor have women, other than you, had any impulse to confide in me. I didn't plan it that way. It just happened. When I was younger I always thought of myself as independent and strong because that's what I wanted to be and that's what I thought Raymond wanted me to be. So maybe that pulled me toward certain men who seemed to be stronger than me. But whatever the reason . . . God I'm tired of moaning about myself and my problems.

For whatever it's worth, the people who see me every day here in Fort Beck would be stunned to know that I feel the way I do about myself. The creature I present to them, all clean hair and bright teeth and straight seams in her stockings, is quite different from the one you know. And *altogether* different from the poor stumbling soul I'm describing in this letter.

This is not the last time I will unburden myself to you. I'm sure you realize that just the simple act of writing like this helps me a lot. Admitting to some of my stupid flaws gives me a leg up towards correcting them. Describing myself as helpless makes me determined to be otherwise. Out of the ashes the phoenix will rise. Or it won't. But if it doesn't it won't be for lack of trying. By the time I see you again, and that will be as soon as possible after the war ends, I promise you that I will be a whole person again. By hook or by crook.

Later, Helen would try very hard to remember what, exactly, had brought Frank Wilson into her mind again. It was not the process of rediscovering an old friend. It was more complex that that. Their marriage had not been painful or chaotic and their divorce had been peaceful and by mutual consent. No accusations, no guilt, no resentment. At least none of these had surfaced. But when they parted after the divorce, when he had driven her to the railroad station in Chicago and they had said their civilized good-byes, it was clearly understood, though unspoken, that they would not see each other again. They would not write, would not telephone, would not communicate through mutual friends. The door was closed and bolted, and would not be opened again.

Not long after her letter to Clara detailing her state of mind, when she and Frank finally saw each other again, when they had lunch near his office on Lasalle Street, Helen said, 'I didn't *plan* this. It was pure impulse. I was in Chicago for the day and I just picked up the phone and called you. It was as simple as that.'

It was not, of course, as simple as that. It was not simple at all. Clara, who knew from her letters exactly how Helen was feeling, would not have been surprised to learn she had called her ex-husband. And in fact she was *not* surprised when Helen told her. Frank Wilson, of course, was genuinely surprised and Helen herself pretended to be surprised. But she was not.

'I half-expected not to find you at your office,' she said. 'You always said you wanted to retire at thirty-five.'

'I *did* retire at thirty-five. I sold my company and played golf for a year. Played on every great course in the world. Then I collected antique cars. Then I collected primitive sculpture. And on my thirty-seventh birthday I went back into business again.'

When she wrote to Clara the next day telling her what she'd done, Helen said she'd had second thoughts as soon as she and Frank made a luncheon date.

> Even when I walked into the restaurant I wasn't convinced that I could go through with it. But as soon as I saw him, when I sat down and we started to talk,

it was all easy and relaxed, the way I remember it when I frist knew him, those three years when I was travelling around the country, just after I'd spent that summer with you in Wingate Fields. He was already working in Chicago then and he used to come to visit me wherever I happened to be. It was all very light-hearted and platonic and I had no idea at all that it would become serious or that we would ever get married. I just enjoyed being with him and hearing him talk. He was a fantastic talker then and he still is.

He's married, of course. I knew that. Someone sent me a clipping at the time. He got married a few months after we divorced. He and his wife live in Lake Forest, north of Chicago, and they have two daughters. But he didn't talk much about them. He just told me stories about where he's been — he's travelled a lot — and what he's done. Not boasting. He never does that. He usually makes a joke out of things. And we talked about things we use to do together when we first met. We were like two people who'd never been married. After lunch he kissed me on the cheek and put me in a taxi and said I should let him know next time I'm coming to Chicago so we can have lunch again. I'm not sure that's a good idea but it was nice to see him once.

As though she was testing herself, when Helen was in Chicago two weeks later she didn't call him. But the next time she was going she called him the day before. He sounded gruff and abrupt on the phone but they made a date to meet in the Drake bar at one o'clock.

He was late. She was waiting when he got there. He sat down and ordered drinks and she said, 'I thought maybe you weren't coming.'

He looked at his watch. 'Ten minutes late. That's not bad.'

'As a matter of fact, *I* almost didn't come,' she said. 'You sounded very cross on the phone.'

'I was in a meeting with a man who is so stupid he thought I was stupid. I was straightening him out when you called.'

'If I remember right, you never took calls when you were in a meeting.'

'I always took your calls,' he said.

'That's right. You did.'

'I still do.'

'But you still sound cross,' she said. 'Why is that?'

'I've got a lot on my mind.'

'Would you rather skip lunch?'

'That's up to you.'

'I've got a lot on my mind, too.'

'Like I said . . . it's up to you.'

'Then I say let's skip it.'

'Whatever you say.'

She finished her drink and set the glass down. 'Thanks for the drink.'

'You're welcome.'

After a moment she said, 'All right. I give up. What's the game? Did we come all the way up here to the Drake just to have a drink and a little spat?'

'No, we came to have lunch. But I don't want to play ping-pong with you like we did last time. If you want to have a serious lunch and have a serious talk like a couple of grown-ups then I'm all for it.'

'That depends on what you mean by *serious*.'

'Serious means whatever I want it to mean. Right now I'm talking about two people who used to be married to each other talking about where things stand now.'

'You're going too fast for me.'

'No, I'm not. You're the one who called. I didn't call you.'

'You mustn't read anything into that.'

'Why not?' he said. 'We had lunch three weeks ago. Then you called again. Why'd you call the second time?'

'You asked me to.'

'People ask *me* to do things all the time. But I don't do them. I just do what I want to do.'

'So do I.'

'Now we're getting somewhere,' he said. 'You called me because you wanted to.'

'That's right. What's so strange about that? We're friends, for Pete's sake.'

'No, we're not. We're two people who used to be married to each other.'

'Aren't you and your wife friends?'

'Not at all. Not for a minute. We're just married.'

They walked down the street to a restaurant on Pearson Street. As soon as they sat down he said, 'Since you brought up my wife, let's get her out of the way.'

'Why should we do that?'

'Because I want to. And so do you or you wouldn't have brought her up in the first place. Here's the situation. Carol and I are married and we have been for quite a few years now. Unless one of us gets run over by a train we're going to stay married. We're not just a family. She and the two girls and I are a corporation. We're a whole cluster of corporations. Lots of money involved, lots of legal documents and accountants working long hours. Real estate. Horses and boats and annuities and stock options, and all of it woven together like a Persian rug, a very expensive, museum-quality rug. Guards standing in front of it and hand-lettered signs saying "Do not touch".'

'I understand,' she said.

'No, you don't. I'm not finished.'

'God, what an ego! Do you really think I came after you like a lady with a butterfly net? Is that why you're so testy and disagreeable? Do you think I'm a naughty woman who's going to steal you away from your wife and kiddies?'

'No, I don't think that. I'm just trying to be honest with you. I thought it might be contagious.'

'It *is*. I'm telling you the truth. I think you're an egomaniac. That's something new. When I knew you before you didn't have such magnificent delusions about yourself.'

'All right,' he said then, 'I'm willing to drop it if you are. Let's have some nice wine and a fattening lunch, and talk about whether or not you like Roosevelt.'

'I *love* Roosevelt.'

'Good. So do I.'

After they finished eating, when they had ordered coffee and brandy he said, 'As far as I'm concerned we no longer have any proposals on the table so there's no reason for you to raise your voice. But since I have a mania about unfinished business I want to finish what I started to tell you before. I'll keep it brief.'

Their coffee arrived then. After testing his brandy, Frank said, 'What I wanted to tell you is this. Other than my marriage contract I have no ties to anyone. I have no love-life, secret or public. When I saw you again I knew I wanted to keep on seeing you. Whatever you and I had together I wanted to have it again. That's my entire case. I had hoped to present it in a little more persuasive way but things took a bad turn and it couldn't be done.'

'You want me to be your mistress. Is that it?'

'I wouldn't use that word. I wouldn't put any label on it.

I just want to see you and talk with you and sleep with you and make love to you. I want to spend time with you and see you wake up and have breakfast and a glass of wine in the bathtub. I want to buy you things if there's anything you want and take you on trips and feed you fancy meals. I want no promises, no contracts, no guarantees. I just want to give you whatever I have and take whatever you're able to give. And if you think that's an unselfish declaration of love, you're crazy. I've always wanted all I could get. You know that. I still do.'

She sat looking down at her brandy glass. 'I don't know what to say,' she said.

'You're not supposed to say anything. As I said, there are no longer any proposals on the table. What I just said to you was said after the fact. I was able to be so forthright because I knew where I stood before I started.'

'I don't understand you.'

'Of course you do. You always have. From the beginning, *you* understood me perfectly and I didn't understand you at all. I thought I did but I didn't. That's not really true, either. Actually my very first impression was correct but I decided to ignore it. As soon as I met you all those years ago, I told myself you were already taken. You were sweet on somebody else, as my mother used to say. But I kept after you for some reason and finally I decided that there wasn't anybody else after all, that there was just this withdrawn quality about you that made it difficult for you to show your real feelings.'

'I'm really not interested in learning this.'

'Of course you're not. But I'm interested in telling you anyway.'

'Are you saying I wasn't an affectionate wife?'

'No, I'm not. It turned out that you were not only affectionate, you were demonstrative. Passionate. All the things a woman is supposed to be. But I never could get over the feeling that it wasn't for me. I was there *with* you, like a lucky lottery winner, but all that love and affection had somebody else's name stencilled on it.'

'I can't believe what I'm hearing.'

'I'm not trying to hurt your feelings. I'm telling you the truth.'

'What truth?' she said. '*Whose* truth?'

'That's only one kind.'

'Why didn't you leave me?'

'What do you mean?' he said.

'If you felt that way, if you thought *I* felt that way, why did you stay with me?'

'Why wouldn't I? We're not talking about how *I* felt about *you*. We're talking about you in relation to yourself. I felt sorry for you.'

'Why, for God's sake?'

'Why wouldn't I? Why do you think we had the most peaceful and civilized divorce in history? Because neither of us was giving up anything. It wasn't because we lost the baby. We could have got past that if everything else was in place. We didn't really get a divorce like most people do. We just documented the fact we'd never been married. At least *one* of us had never been married.'

'You bastard. You're really trying to punish me. I damaged your bloody ego and now you're trying to get even.'

He sat looking at her and didn't answer.

'Admit it,' she said. 'That's what you're doing, isn't it?'

'If that's what you want to hear then I'll say it. You damaged my bloody ego and now I'm trying to get even.'

She stood up very deliberately then, picked up her purse and walked slowly through the restaurant to the exit. When the waiter came to his table with a silver pitcher of hot coffee, Frank said, 'No, thank you. Just bring me the check.'

Almost a month later a special delivery letter arrived at Helen's home in Fort Beck. It was from Frank.

> I'm driving down to St Louis next Friday morning. I'll be there for a week or ten days and I'd like you to come with me. I have a little business to take care of but most of the time I'll be free. St Louis is a good town. We'll have some fun. If I don't hear from you, I'll assume you're coming along. I'll be at your house at eleven on Friday.

Helen read the letter, carefully reread it, then slowly tore it in tiny squares and dropped it into the leather basket by her desk. Then she checked her calendar to make sure she would be away from home Friday morning.

When Frank pulled into her driveway, however, precisely at eleven, two pieces of luggage were sitting on the steps just outside the entrance. When he rang the bell, Helen came to the door wearing a blue travelling suit, her fur coat over her shoulders.

'Today I'm not late,' he said.
'That's right. Today you're right on time.'

Chapter Two

[1]

Unlike Helen and Jesse and Valerie, Nora did not see the war's ending as an opportunity to return to Wingate Fields, the family estate in Northumberland. The end of her marriage to Edmund Bick, Valerie's father, had allowed her to leave the north of England and settle in Paris; she had no desire now to go back. As soon as de Gaulle re-entered Paris on August 25th, 1944, she began to plan for her own return there.

During the years she and Jesse had spent together in France, they had founded, edited and published a literary quarterly called *Icarus*. In its pages, Jesse had first established himself as a shrewd critic of painting and poetry and the novel. And Nora had become a courageous publisher, able and willing to present writers who had not been published elsewhere and to promote the work of young painters who had not yet found markets for their efforts. She not only collected pictures herself but opened an art gallery on the Rue de Seine, which exhibited young, unknown painters. And at the social centre of her activities was her regular Thursday evening salon. The artists and writers and critics called it *Nora-Jeudi*, and they gathered there faithfully. For some of them it was their only proper meal of the week.

This life had come to an end, of course, when the war began. Along with Valerie and Jesse, she had reluctantly transplanted herself to New York, had bought a house on lower Fifth Avenue, and had continued to publish *Icarus*. But always she longed for her home on L'Ile St-Louis and her country place in the forest north of Paris. And most of all she missed the busy and productive life she had fashioned for herself there. Without Jesse, of course, she knew it would be a different life altogether but she reasoned that it was better to be without him in Paris than in New York.

Just after Christmas, in 1944, she announced, in an interview in the book section of the *New York Times*, that she was returning at once to Paris and that the first post-war edition of *Icarus* would be published there in June. When reminded by her interviewer that the war had not ended yet, she said, 'I've always regretted that I wasn't the last one to leave Paris. So now I intend to be one of the first ones back.'

'What's she talking about?' Valerie said to Jesse when she read the interview. 'She can't travel to France, can she?'

'Officially, she can't. But with money and determination, all sorts of things are possible. And Nora has plenty of both.'

'I think it's insane. She'll get herself killed.'

After attempting, without success, to reason with her mother on the telephone, Valerie went to New York to see her.

'I'm delighted you've come down,' Nora said. 'If everything goes according to plan I'll be leaving in about ten days. So this is the last time we'll see each other for a while.'

'That's what I want to talk to you about.'

'I've cancelled all my appointments for the rest of the day and I made no plans for dinner so we can have a proper chat about anything we like.'

'You know what *I* want to talk about. I mentioned it to you several times on the telephone.'

'You mean Christmas? I told you already I was sorry I couldn't get up there. Everything was too frantic here. I still haven't decided if I should sell this house or keep it. Do you and Jesse want it?'

'No, Mother . . .'

'You know, it's the strangest thing. All your life you've called me Nora. But as soon as you started to have children of your own, you started calling me *Mother*. Do you realize that?'

'I still call you Nora.'

'Not very often. Mostly it's *Mother*. I hope we won't be getting to the *Mummy* stage.' Then, 'Did the children like the presents I sent?'

'We all liked your gifts. We were just sorry *you* couldn't be there.'

'So was I. But it couldn't be helped. And you'll have to admit I've been an exemplary grandmother so far. I mean, I know you don't expect me to do the nappies and feed them that atrocious baby-food. And I don't get sick and throw up when Rab calls me *Nanny*. So I'm quite proud of myself. Two granchildren and a third on the way. I feel that I'm handling myself quite well. When's the next little bugger due?'

'Not till the summer. The doctor says sometime in July.'

'If you had a caesarean it could be born in May, on my birthday.'

Valerie smiled, 'I don't believe my doctor would think that's such a good idea.'

'I guess not. Not fair to the other children, really, if one of them is born on Nanny's birthday and the others aren't.'

'I thought you didn't like being called *Nanny*.'

'I don't. I hate it. Makes me feel like a goat. With great dugs hanging down.'

'You really don't like being a grandmother, do you?'

'Of course not. I love your little children. But I don't like the idea of a big *grandma* sign being pasted on me. I don't like *any* signs, to tell you the truth. *Wife, mother*. All those labels bore me. They seem to require certain costumes, a particular sort of behaviour. You know what I'm saying? I just don't seem to fit easily into any of those moulds. I mean, I don't have any preconceived rules for behaviour. Never have had. How can a person know how she's going to behave on a particular day before she's had a chance to see what that day consists of? Doesn't that make sense?'

'I know it makes sense to you,' Valerie said, 'but it would never work for me. I have to have guideposts. I'm not good at handling surprises. Jesse laughs at me. When I'm driving a car I never explore country roads. I always stick to the big roads that take me straight to where I'm going.'

'What if you don't know for sure where you're going?'

'Then I stay home.' She smiled. 'I guess I take after my father, don't I?'

'There's nothing wrong with that. Edmund's still the best-looking man I've ever seen. And he's a solid citizen. He's just not adventurous.'

'Neither am I. Once I get back to Wingate Fields, I don't think I'll ever leave it.'

'How does Jesse feel about that?'

'He feels the same way.'

'Well, good for you,' Nora said. 'Sounds like a match made in heaven.'

That evening, as they sat at dinner in Nora's house,

Valerie said, 'How can you manage to get back to Paris when the war's not over yet?'

'Aaah, now we're getting somewhere,' Nora said. 'Now we're getting to the reason for your trip to New York. We're going to talk some sense into the old lady. Is that it?'

'No, that's not it. I'm just scared to death at the thought of your making the trip just now. I'm worried about you and so is Jesse.'

'*Jesse's* worried about me? No kidding.'

'Of course he worries. Why not?'

'That's right. I forgot,' Nora said. 'I'm the grandmother of his children now. Isn't that amusing?' She filled her glass from the wine decanter. 'I notice a certain expression on your face every time I pour myself some wine. I hope it's not disapproval. Just because you don't drink any longer, you mustn't shun those who do. It's quite a common habit among grandmothers. We all sit with our needlework in the afternoon and sip a bit of wine.'

'You're making fun of me, aren't you?'

'No, I'm not. I'm making fun of myself. But I'm going to stop it now because I don't like it. You asked me how I can manage to get to Paris. I wondered that myself. Then I remembered that people have been getting *out* of Europe ever since the war started so why shouldn't I be able to get *in?* So I worked it out. I'll go to Miami and take a clipper from there to Rio. Then I'll either fly or take a ship from there to the Azores. Or all the way to Lisbon. I have lots of friends in Portugal and Spain. I'll either go overland from Lisbon or I'll get on a freighter that's going from Lisbon to Marseilles. Once I'm inside France, I'll have no problem making it to Paris. Odette, my housekeeper, has been in my house all during the Occupation so I'll move in, get myself settled, and take up a civilized life again.'

'Does that mean New York's not civilized?'

'Not at all. It's just a different *kind* of civilization. I've had a reasonably good time here, all things considered, but if I thought I had to stay here for the rest of my life . . . I just couldn't do it.'

'I feel the same way about France,' Valerie said.

'I know you do. Which only proves again that we like different things. New York is a city of decisions and conclusions. Paris is a city of details. New Yorkers discover something they like to do and then they do it a *lot*. In Paris, one does a great many different things. You put your life together every day. Brand new. It's never quite the same as it was the day before. New York is Middle European, German, English, Scandinavian. All those cultures have something in common, something solid and respectable and predictable and dependable. France is Latin. If you like it there, you'll never like it so much anywhere else. And I *like* it. I *need* it. It nourishes me, makes me sing a little, makes me like myself better. So I'm going back. If there's a risk it's one I'm willing to take. The prize is worth it.'

'I had a lot of arguments prepared to throw at you but you've already handled them all.'

'Good.' She poured herself some more wine. 'Now we can finish dinner, I can drink my wine, and we can have a jolly time together, nothing to win, nothing to lose.'

After a moment, Valerie said, 'Do you think of me as a happy woman?'

'I stay away from that word. It's all worn out. It has no meaning any more. Besides, I try not to nose around into other people's lives. It's none of my business whether they're working out their problems or not. I just try to feel good and I assume that's what everybody else is trying to do. What do you think?'

'About what?'

'About yourself,' Nora said.

'I think I'm lucky. I'm twenty-five years old, I have two children and another one on the way, before too long I'll be able to go home to England, and from then on I'll be able to have everything I want. Or so it seems to me.'

'That's nice. Good for you.'

'You said you just try to feel good. Do you feel good now?'

'I'd feel a lot better if we got off this subject.'

'Why?'

'Because I don't want to talk about it and I don't think you do either.'

'Yes, I do. You said before that being in France makes you like yourself better.'

'Did I say that?'

'Yes, you did. Does that mean you don't like yourself much now?'

'You don't really want me to answer that, do you?'

'Why do you keep saying that? Of course I want you to answer.'

'All right. I will. But you won't like what I have to say. I promise you that. If it gets to be too much for you, just stop me.'

'I don't understand any of this.'

'Of course you don't. And when you do it will be too late for me to take it back.'

'Why would you want to?' Valerie said.

'Because I don't want to hurt you.'

'Why do you have to hurt *me?*'

'God, what an innocent daughter I have.' She sipped from her glass. 'You're asking me if I like myself. How shall I put it? I know very well what people think of me. I know my public image. I designed it and produced it so I should know all about it, and I do. People see me as unassailable and impregnable, all the facets of my life under control. I'm still young and I look younger than I am, I'm successful at what I do and I have a lot of money whether I'm successful or not. I can go wherever I like and do whatever I want to do. I own my own life. I control my own destiny. Some people hate me for what I seem to be. A lot of people envy me, too. But I've always thought that envy was just a coward's word for hate so I lump all those people together. Then there are a few people, ten at most I should think, who genuinely wish me well. But all of them, whatever else they think about me, think that my self-esteem is carved out of marble, that I was born with it and I'll die with it.' She paused. 'I see you're smiling. I must have touched a nerve. That's what *you* think of me, isn't it?'

'I guess it is. Something very like that. And I guess I've always envied you a little. But there's no hate in it. I'm one of those people who wishes you well.'

'I know you do. Are you sure you won't have a glass of wine with me?'

Valerie smiled and shook her head. 'Go ahead. I interrupted you.'

'Self-esteem,' Nora said. 'That's the topic. Quite apart from other people's judgements, do I truly like myself or not?' She looked at Valerie for a long moment. 'All right, sweetheart, I hope you can handle this. Since the day Jesse sat here in this same room and told me that you and he were going to get married, since that particular afternoon, I have had no self-esteem at all. None. Not a shred. Not a particle. It had never occurred to me once, never in my life, that not being liked by someone, by some particular person, *liked, loved,* whatever we call it, could completely alter the way I felt about myself. But it happened. And it's still happening. That never occurred to you, did it?'

'Of course it *occurred* to me . . .'

'But you put it aside. You said to yourself, "Nothing could shoot her down. She's too strong. And besides, she and Jesse wouldn't have stayed together anyway." '

'I really did think that. And so did Jesse.'

'And so did I. I admit it. But the fact was, we were still together. And then he came to see me, the day he got back from Chicago or wherever he'd been on some wild-goose chase with Helen and he told me about his plans, told me I was about to become his mother-in-law . . .'

Valerie broke in. 'But you *wouldn't* have stayed together. You know you wouldn't have.'

'No. I don't know that. I know that's not what you want to hear but I'm telling you the simple truth. We certainly had our problems together, Jesse and I, but we were together for nearly twenty years, half my life, practically *all* of my grown-up life. I can't be sure that he wouldn't have left me. You know I always felt there was something between him and Helen. But I *never* would have left him. He thought I would and I threatened to more than once but I wouldn't have done it. I *couldn't* have done it.'

Valerie sat very still in her chair, her eyes looking down at her plate. At last she said, 'God, I feel awful.'

'I'm sorry. I told you you wouldn't like it.'

'It's all *my* fault, isn't it?'

'It's nobody's fault. Not now. It's all over. It's been over for a long time.'

'But I feel miserable. How can I look at myself? I was so sure. So smug. I knew Jesse wanted to have children and I knew you'd decided you didn't want any more . . .'

'It wasn't that,' Nora said. 'I *couldn't* have children. I *can't*. I had an operation after your father and I broke up.'

'Does Jesse know that?'

'No. I didn't want him to know. And I still don't. I didn't want him to feel sorry for me. So I lied to him. I told him I didn't *want* to have children.'

'Oh, my God, it just gets worse and worse.'

'No, it doesn't. It doesn't matter now.'

'It matters to *me*. How can it not *matter*? No matter how much I loved Jesse, do you think I'd have married him if I thought I was taking him away from you? I thought you were just going through the motions. Sometimes I thought you were just staying with him because of *me*, because I'd grown up seeing you two together. Even in Paris, a lot of people thought you and Jesse just had an understanding, some sort of arrangement, that your work on the magazine was all that kept you together . . .'

'I know what they thought and I know what they said. But they were wrong.'

'I don't know what to do,' Valerie said. 'What am I going to do?'

'You're going to forget we ever had this conversation. And so am I.'

'How *can* I forget it?'

'I don't know. But you have to try.'

'How can I *look* at you? How can I look at myself?'

Nora got up, walked to the other end of the table and put her arm around Valerie's shoulder. 'You think this won't go away but it will. I'll be in France and before long you'll be back in England and by the time we see each other again, things will be all right. I won't always feel the way I do now and neither will you. You're my daughter and I'm your mother and nothing will change that.'

'We get hurt and Jesse doesn't. Is that the way it goes?'

'It's not Jesse's fault. It's nobody's fault.'

After Valerie went back to Boston, their conversation stayed with Nora as though it had been recorded inside her head. Valerie's torment had not given her mother pleasure. The memory of it nagged at her. All the same she could not ignore the tiny notes of vindication that trumpeted faintly in her ears, prelude to the orchestral din of vengeance she hoped some day to orchestrate for the benefit of Jesse and Helen.

[2]

From the time he started grade school in Crawfordsville, Floyd had been in the same class with Jeannette Kinsman. The house where he lived with the Simisons was just adjacent to Sycamore Meadows, the elegant section where Jeannette lived with her parents and her twin brother, Tom. Her father, Herbert Kinsman, was an investor who owned a dozen farms between Lafayette and Terre Haute. He was also a powerful and generous alumnus at Wabash College, where Lowell Simison was a teacher. It was because of Kinsman that Floyd quit high school and left Crawfordsville in 1938. Two days after Kinsman had made a surprise visit to his river house and found Floyd and Jeannette there in bed, Floyd was picked up by the local police on suspicion of burglary. When he was led into an office at the station house the man waiting to interview him was Herbert Kinsman. 'You could be in a great deal of trouble here. I want to help you if I can,' he said.

'Like hell you do. You just want to make sure I stay away from Jeannette.'

'That's right. Her mother and I have other plans for her. We're sending her off to a private school in Canada. She left last night.'

'That won't do you any good. She'll have to come home some time.'

'Yes, she will. That's why you and I are having this talk. When Jeannette does come home, it would be better if you weren't here.'

'Better for you, you mean?'

Kinsman nodded. 'Also better for you. If you insist on staying in Crawfordsville, two things will happen. Your father will lose his job at the college and you will go to the reformatory at Pendleton for burglary.'

'Who says so?'

'*I* say so.'

'I didn't steal anything. I never stole anything in my life.'

'That doesn't matter. When the police search your father's garage, they'll find at least a dozen articles from my house on the river, some of them quite valuable. A total value of over two thousand dollars, I would guess. Neighbours have seen you around the property and if the police decide to check for fingerprints, I'm sure they'll find some of yours in the house.'

'You know why my fingerprints are there.'

'Of course I do. But no one else does. Except Jeannette. And she won't be here to testify, in case you decide you want to go to trial.'

'Are you saying it's up to me?'

'Exactly. If you and I reach an agreement, I will simply tell the police that since all my possessions have been returned to me, I'm withdrawing my complaint. I'll tell them it was a mistake on my part.'

After he left Crawfordsville, Floyd tried to write to Jeannette, sending the letters to her friend Amy Briscoe to forward. But he never had an answer. When he was in the South Pacific, he wrote to her several times at her father's house but again no answering letters came.

When he was discharged at San Pedro in October, two months after the Japanese surrendered, the discharge officer said to him, 'Now what? Where's home?'

'No place,' Floyd said. 'Both my folks are dead.'

'That's too bad. I guess you'll have to do what all the rest of us are doing . . . look up an old girlfriend.'

'That's it. That's what I plan to do.'

'How long since you've seen her?'

'Long time. Seven years, I guess.'

'*Seven* years? Forget it. She's probably married. Two or three kids maybe.'

'I guess so. But I want to see her anyway.'

When he got to Crawfordsville he discovered that she'd married Glen Tillis. His father owned an automobile agency and their house was on the same block as the Kinsman house. When he looked up Jeannette's phone number he saw that she and Glen were living in the same neighbourhood.

'I can't believe my ears,' she said when she answered the telephone. 'Where are you?'

'In a phone booth just outside the Kroger store on Romig Street.'

'You're crazy, calling me here like this.'

'I want to see you.'

'I want to see you too, I'm dying to see you, but . . .'

'Come on. Make an effort.'

'Let me think,' she said. Then, 'Here's what you do. Remember the Red Top cabins where we used to go?'

'No questions asked.'

'That's right. They tore the old cabins down but there's a new motel there now. It's called the Elms. You got a car?'

'I'll get one.'

'Well, *rent* it. Don't steal it. Go check in at the Elms and I'll meet you there at . . . what time is it now?'

'Ten-thirty. Halfway between breakfast and lunch.'

'I'll meet you at noon. Is that all right?'

'That's just fine. I'll be there.'

When he checked into the motel he left his door slightly open. When she came in, he was in bed, smoking a cigar. An open whisky bottle, a bucket of ice, and two glasses sat on a table by the bed.

'You crazy nut,' she said. 'You haven't changed a bit, have you?'

She locked the door behind her, slipped out of her dress, and said, 'How do I look?'

'You haven't changed either. You still don't wear any underwear.'

She stayed in the room with him till four o'clock. The next morning she arrived at nine-thirty, brought lunch with her, stayed till five.

'What do you tell your husband?' Floyd asked her.

'I don't tell him anything.'

'Where does he think you are?'

'He never asks me. He knows I'm all over the place. I go see my mother a lot. Or I'm at my cousin's house in New Richmond, or visiting Tom's wife down in Greencastle. Or over in Lebanon at Amy's. That's where she lives now. And I go into Indianapolis to shop whenever I feel like it. I just pick up Betsy, after she's had her breakfast, and we take off, sometimes for the whole day. Or I leave her with the housekeeper and go off alone.'

'How old is she?'

'Three last month. She was born when Glen was in the Aleutians. She's a great little kid. Smart as a whip. And pretty. You ought to see her.'

'You planning on a big family?'

'I don't think so. Two or three maybe. I didn't want to have one too close to Betsy. I wanted to enjoy her.'

'Maybe you got pregnant yesterday,' he said. 'What about *that?*'

'I hope I did. I checked the calendar when I got home last night and it could happen.'

'You're serious. I was just kidding.'

'Men are always kidding. At least *you* are. I'd love to have a baby with you. I always wanted to. You remember that. We used to try to pick out names. You wanted a girl named Tracy and a boy named Duane. After Duane Purvis, the guy who played halfback at Purdue.'

'I don't remember that.'

'Of course you don't. But *I* do. I'll tell you what. If you hear later on that I had a little girl named Tracy or a boy named Duane, you'll know you're the daddy.'

The third morning they met at a motel on highway 43, just south of Lafayette. The motel had a restaurant so they ordered their breakfast from room service and ate it sitting up in bed. When they ordered lunch at two o'clock, Jeannette said, 'These people will think we never get up.'

'We never do.'

Later in the day, lying with her head on his shoulder, she started to cry.

'What are you doing?' he said.

'You're not supposed to notice. Just don't say anything sweet to me or I'll really come apart.' After a while she said, 'I can't see you any more. It kills me to say it but if we don't stop now I won't be able to.'

'We could get in the car and just start driving,' he said.

'I know we could. Don't you think I've thought about that?'

'California's a nice place. You'd like San Francisco, I'll bet.'

'I can't, Floyd, and you *know* I can't. Don't make it worse than it is. I'm locked in. All the years haven't changed how we feel about each other but it's changed what we can *do* about it. There's always somebody who thinks it's not good for you to have what you want. And finally you start thinking that way yourself. Look at my dad, for instance. He doesn't think of himself as a mean guy. He's just used to making decisions for other people. Telling them what's best for them. When he caught us in bed that time I don't think he was so shocked at what we were doing. He just realized his baby daughter had been making some decisions that he'd had nothing to do with. So he had to straighten things out. That's how he's made all his money, by straightening things out. He said to himself, "Here's my daughter who's gonna be rich some day. And she's with a young hot-shot who doesn't have a dime, who probably won't even go to college . . . " Did you ever go to college, by the way?'

'No. Didn't finish high school.'

'There you are. My dad just figured we were a bad match and it was up to him to break it up. And he did. It didn't matter how *we* felt about it. And that's the way it goes, I guess. Some people have money or muscle or whatever it takes so you can decide about your own life. And some people don't. Most people don't. I don't give a damn for such things. I don't want to run somebody else's life for them. But I know things would be very different for me if it wasn't for what my family has and what Glen's family has. I don't have to worry or plan ahead because somebody already did that for me. I don't have to fret about what might happen to Betsy . . .'

'Unless she gets mixed up with a guy like me.'

'I'm serious.'

'So am I,' he said. 'It sounds like you're saying you can't afford to go off with me.'

'I know it sounds like that but that's not what I'm trying to say. I guess I'm saying that love isn't enough. It seems like it is at first. But the older you get the more complicated things get. When I was eighteen I'd have followed you anywhere. You know that. Now I can't, because no matter how much I love you I can't do something that's bad for my daughter. I can't break a lot of people's hearts to make myself happy. I just don't think *I'm* that important any more. Every minute I spend with you is like some shining thing that I can put in a box and keep for ever. I feel as if I can remember everything we've done, every place we've been together. And that's like some kind of a foundation for me. I always feel right when I'm with you. I don't feel as if I'm cheating on Glen. When I'm with him I feel as if I'm cheating on *you*. But those are just feelings. They're real for me and I know they're real for you but to the rest of the world all that matters is what I do, how I act, how I behave. After a certain point in your life, the only time you can do what you *feel* like doing is when there's nothing else you *have* to do.'

'I came here to see you because I *had* to,' Floyd said.

'I know you did. Just like I came running to find you that first day and every day since because *I* had to. That's why we'll always feel good about it. That's why I'll always be crazy about you no matter what.'

[3]

During his twenty-five years, Paul Buscatore, who was not a good student, a serious reader, or a deep thinker, had spent his time on more important things. He was infinitely curious about the way things *worked*. He knew every intricacy and contradiction, for example, of the New York subway system, the precise routes, where they started, where they ended and where they intersected. He knew which stops on each line were express stops, whether the express tracks were above the local, below them, or just across the platform. He knew which cars of any given train to board so that when you reached your destination you were just at the exit stairs. He knew which stations had rest rooms and when they were locked and unlocked. He also carried a counterfeit employee's card, which allowed him to ride without paying.

His head was packed with the lore of New York City. He knew where to find the best bagels, the best egg creams, the least expensive glass of beer. He knew all the rest rooms in midtown buildings that were left unlocked during the day. He knew where to find a cab at a moment's notice, even on a rainy day, and he knew how to leave a cab without paying. In any neighbourhood he could tell you where to find the best cup of coffee and the best pastrami sandwich. He knew which doormen and bell-hops and bartenders were hustling women or cocaine, and which cops were on the take.

These things he had learned gradually as he grew up in Manhattan and on Staten Island. He took that knowledge for granted and felt no particular pride in having accumulated it. He was vain about his appearance, he knew he was able to attract attention, but that, he felt, was simply a gift from his mother's family, the Bardonis, for which he could take no credit.

His intuition about people, however, his instinct about their capabilities, their strengths and weakness, these particular talents he felt he had developed himself. He had observed, made mental notes and comparisons, listened, queried, made secret predictions, and gone to great lengths to compare his silent assessments with the concrete observable results. More and more he felt his strength in these areas, more and more he felt capable of penetrating a man's character, or a woman's, in a matter of seconds. His future, he sensed, was rooted in this ability to outguess and outmanoeuvre his opponent, whoever that opponent might turn out to be.

Before he left high school in his third year, he'd played

football. He was fast and quick and he'd been an elusive runner. If he'd stayed in school, he felt, he could have gone to Fordham or Columbia, played football, and become a well-known athlete. But only that side of college life appealed to him. All the rest of it, the conformity and the discipline, were in direct conflict with his basic instincts. So when he watched the New York Giants play their games, he simply imagined that he had gone to college and had become a professional. From his seat in the stands, he identified with particular players. Their exploits, week after week, became *his*. By some miracle he had become a famous performer in a game he hadn't played since his school days. This, at least, was his private illusion.

Illusions made up a significant part of his life. He had learned to trust them. As a small boy, when his mother was still alive, he had envisioned himself, sometime in the future, as a male replica of her, tall and handsome. And it had come to pass. Idolizing the dark and slender young men who sang with orchestras — Jack Leonard, Ray Eberly, and Al Martino — he saw himself in that role, wearing sleek jackets, standing in a magenta spotlight with the saxophones and trombones moaning behind him. And that too became a reality. He sang and sang, for himself and for whatever girl he was with at the time. And one of those girls, it turned out, was the sister of a bandleader. So Paul, calling himself Buddy d'Angelo, ended up singing for two years during the war, at the Knickerbocker Ballroom on Fourteenth Street in Manhattan. He turned down offers to go on the road with Jan Garber and Charlie Spivak, and at last he turned away from singing altogether when he came to realize that his true talent lay elsewhere. His uncle, Vinnie Bardoni, finally convinced him. 'You're a nice singer. You get lucky, you could end up with a couple of grand a week. Somebody puts you in a movie, you might really rake it in. But we're talking long shots. That's something you know something about. As soon as the war's over, next week maybe, a few hundred beautiful young guys that sing like canaries are gonna be fighting each other for every job in the country. What you gotta do is go with what you're really good at. You got a nose for the horses like nobody I ever met, you roll dice like you own them, and I never saw you come out losers at black jack. All the amateurs think it's luck. It *ain't* luck, believe me. Some guys got it and some ain't. And you got it, Paulie. You'll have people standing in line to back you. Trust me. I know what I'm saying. You can get rich playing with other people's money. You can't ask for a better deal than that. You could sing your brains out for a month and not make half of what you can pick up in one night at the tables or one afternoon at the track. Get wise to yourself, baby. You got a gift. If you don't use it, you're crazy.'

His father had taken another position altogether. Almost a year after Paul had left his job at the ballroom, Joe Buscatore cornered him one Sunday at a family picnic, walked him down to the beach and said, 'All right, you're twenty-five years old and you got the world in your pocket. Right? You live uptown on the east side, a nice big apartment, they tell me. Fancy foreign rugs on the floor.'

'Why don't you come see it, Pop? I've asked you a hundred times.'

'You can ask me a hundred more and I still won't show up. I've got no business up there and neither have you. The only difference is I'm smart enough to know it and you're not.'

'What difference does it make where a man lives? I pay rent like everybody else.'

'Don't tell me. I don't even want to know how much rent you pay.'

'I can afford it. That's all that matters. I earn my way just like you do.'

'Not like me, you don't. I sweat for my living and I'm proud of it.'

'I know you are but there are all kinds of jobs where a man doesn't *have* to sweat. What if I worked in a bank or at Macy's?'

'You don't work in a bank. You don't work anywhere.'

'There's all kinds of work.'

'No, there ain't. There's just work and not-work.'

'What about Vinnie?'

'What about him?' Joe asked.

'He runs a candy store on Ninth Street. He's not sweating.'

'He's not working either. He's taking bets and selling numbers. He's playing with fire. That's what Vinnie's doing. He's dealing with people who'll break your arms just for fun. And unless I miss my guess you're mixed up with the same crowd.'

'That's where you're wrong. Ask Vinnie. He'll tell you.

I'm on my own. I run my own action. Two guys from Cleveland backed me at first but I bought them out. Fair and square. They made a profit and everybody was happy. I work with my own money. I keep what I win and I eat my losses.'

'Don't give me that. Just cause I got callouses and work with tools don't mean I've got my head under my arm. This year I'm sixty years old. I grew up with wise guys. I seen them come and go. And most of them *went*, a long time ago. There's no such thing in this town as running your own action.'

'Sure there is,' Paul said. '*You* do.'

'That's 'cause I'm small potatoes. I'm a little contractor. Most of my jobs I don't even get a city permit for. Nobody's gonna bother with me. The pay-off ain't worth it.'

'That's what I'm trying to tell you. That's *my* angle. Those two guys from Cleveland I told you about . . . when we split up, one of them gave me some good advice. And this guy's been around, believe me. He knows the ins and outs. You've seen his name in the papers. He knows *everybody*, if you know what I mean.'

'I know what you mean. Those are the guys I'm talking about.'

'I know that. But this guy's out of action now. He's retired and nobody's mad at him. He always paid his taxes and he's clean. He lays a few bets here and there, and that's it. What I'm trying to tell you is that he gave me this very good advice. He said, "All the guys I knew who wanted to make a killing are dead now. The ones that are left are the ones who settled for making a living. You make a little money, the next guy makes a little. Just live your life and run your little operation and don't be a hog. Then you'll die of old age with a smile on your face." '

'Are you telling me that's what *you're* doing, just making a few dollars to pay the rent?'

'No. I make a lot of money. But I play straight. There are plenty of people who want to shoot craps or play cards and almost all of them are amateurs. That's who I play with and that's where I make my money.'

'They may be amateurs but that doesn't mean they like to be cheated.'

'I don't have to cheat, Pop. I just try to be the best man at the table and usually I am. When I'm not, I lose, just like everybody else.'

'You don't live like a king up there on Madison Avenue by *losing*.'

'That's right. I play to win and I usually do.'

Three months later, the next time Paul saw his father, they met in the same Ukrainian café where Joe had sat with Helen.

'I don't have much time,' he said as soon as he sat down.

'Neither do I,' Paul said. He picked up his hat and stood up.

'Wait a minute,' Joe said. 'What's to get so hot about? I just said . . .'

'I know what you said. It's what you always say. I never see you at my house. I never come to your house. And when I manage to get you cornered in some lousy coffee-shop, I'm lucky if you give me five minutes.'

'Sit down. Everybody's looking at you,' Joe said. He turned towards the counter and ordered two coffees. After the waitress brought them over, he said to Paul. 'All right. You don't come to my house. Why is that? You act like you're not invited or something.'

'I'm not welcome there and you know it.'

'Who says so?'

'*I* say so. Pauline looks at me like she's never seen me before. And you're like somebody I don't recognize when she's around.'

'She doesn't like what you're doing.'

'She doesn't even know what I'm doing except what you tell her. Do you think she'd like me better if I drove a bread truck for a living? It has nothing to do with what I'm doing. She's looked at me the same way since I was a little kid. Since you and she got married. And Maria and Tina the same. They feel the same as I do. Why do you think they're at Stella's house so much? You think Stella doesn't know what's going on?'

'How do you know so much about what everybody knows?'

'I know, that's all. What do you think it's like, growing up in a house where nobody ever says your mother's name?'

'Well . . . it's hard. Pauline's a woman. I'm her husband. She has her own boys.'

'I'm not talking about her. I'm talking about you. Once you brought Pauline home it was like Mama had never lived there, like she never lived at all. All the pictures put away. Everything she liked put in boxes in the attic or given to one of her sisters.'

'A man can't live with two wives at once.'

'That sounds like something Pauline would say.'

'Don't say anything bad about Pauline.'

'Why not. You're not saying she never says anything bad about *me*, are you?'

'She never talks about you.'

'Don't lie to me, Pop. It's not your style.' Then, 'Look, I'm not trying to hurt your feelings. Something just set me off.'

'Why are you bringing all this up now?' Joe said.

'I've tried to talk about it a dozen times, and you know it. When I was a little kid I used to try to talk about Mama at the supper table and you'd hush me up like I'd said a dirty word.'

'Pauline was embarrassed to have to explain everything to the little boys.'

'Why, for God's sake? She knew you'd been married before. She knew you had three kids. All your family knew, the neighbours all knew. The only house on the block where nobody could mention Anna Buscatore was *our* house. *Her* house. Does that make any sense to you?'

'Maybe not. But Pauline wanted it that way.'

'I don't give a damn what Pauline wanted. What about Tina and Maria? What about what they want? What about what I want?'

'What *do* you want? You're a grown-up man now. Living your own life. What do you want from me?'

'I'll tell you exactly what I want. I'd like you to admit once in a while that there *was* such a woman as Anna Buscatore, that she was your wife, that you had a good time together. Don't you remember anything nice about her? Was it all terrible? Did you have such a rotten life that you don't want to talk about it?'

'Don't talk like that. I never said anything like that.'

'You never say anything. That's the problem.'

'I've got my own problems to take care of,' Joe said. 'I've got to keep some peace in the house.'

'Are you telling me that you're so scared of Pauline, that you're so pussy-whipped . . .'

'Don't talk to me like that.'

'I'll talk any damn way I want to. Are you saying that you can't just sit here alone with me and talk a little bit about my mother?' He sat there looking at Joe for a long beat. Finally he said, 'No, I guess you can't.'

Joe looked at his watch and Paul said, 'Yeah, I get it. I know you're in a hurry. Go ahead.'

'No, I can stay a little longer. You want a sandwich or something?'

'No, thanks. I'm not hungry.'

'How about some more coffee?'

'No, thanks,' Paul said. He sat across the table not saying anything as his father ordered a buttered roll and drank a second cup of coffee. Finally Paul said, 'I'm sorry I yelled at you. That doesn't make things any better, I guess.' When Joe didn't answer he went on. 'The reason I wanted to see you is that I have to go to Chicago for a few days and while I'm there I thought I'd try to look up my sister. I know she's in Illinois. I thought you might have her address.'

'What do you mean?'

'I mean Mama's daughter when she was married before. Her name's Helen. Helen Bradshaw. Remember?'

'I don't know anything about her. Who's been talking to you about her?'

'Rosa.'

'Don't count so much on what Rosa says. She doesn't always get things straight.'

'You're not telling me you don't know Helen Bradshaw, are you?'

'Well, I knew Anna had a daughter when she was married before . . .'

'Rosa said she came to stay with us one winter in Staten Island when I was just a baby.

'What's the point of dragging all this up now?'

'There's *no* point. We don't have to talk about her at all if you don't want to. I just said I was going to try to see her in Illinois and I thought you might have her address so I can let her know I'm coming.'

'Why would I have her address? She's nothing to me.'

'OK. Let's drop it. I'll look her up when I get there.'

'I don't know why you'd want to bother. She ran away from your mother, you know. I never noticed that she ever treated Anna so great when she was alive. She's nobody I ever want to see again, I'll tell you that. Nobody I'd want you and your sisters to associate with if I had any say in the matter. She's nothing like us. Nothing like your mother at all.'

'Maybe not. But she's my half-sister all the same. I think I ought to see her at least once in my life. All Rosa knows is she lives in a town called Fort Beck. At least that's where she used to live.

'You couldn't prove it by me. I don't know anything about her. If I was you I'd just leave her alone. Once you dig her up, you might be stuck with her. This way you've got nothing to worry about.'

As it turned out, Paul did not see Helen in Fort Beck. When he drove down there one afternoon from Chicago, he found that she was in Chicago for a few days. Her housekeeper couldn't tell him where she might be staying. He left a note for her, however, and a few weeks later he had dinner with her in New York. She was on her way to England.

[4]

In early autumn of the year after the war ended in Europe, Ned Causey fell unconscious one afternoon in the pig shed of one of the Bradshaw's tenant farmers, and died there. When a small private service was held a few days later, only Clara, Valerie and Jesse, and their three children were there. Nora was in Florence and could not be reached, and Helen, of course, was unable to come from America at such short notice. Clara wrote to her the day after the burial.

> Only you, I suspect, *know* how complicated my feelings were, and *are,* regarding Ned's death. But we will discuss all that when I see you. And that *must* be soon. I insist. I realize that you are for ever young but I am not. Nor do I wish to be.
>
> Here's what I've done. I've scheduled a proper memorial service for the first week in December. All of Ned's relatives and friends who could not come for the burial will be there. And our neighbours and tenants. And, of course, Nora will come over from France to join Jesse and Valerie and myself here at Wingate Fields. And *you* must come. The results of our difficult war years are still with us. Many things in short supply.

But I began hoarding weeks ago so we'll be able to have a fine Christmas for Valerie's children and ourselves. The old house will be warm and smelling of good things to eat, as it used to be.

I want you to stay with me for as long as you can. All through the war I hoped that after it was over, you would come here to live. I still hope that. But for now let's just say that you must arrive by December 1st and you must stay through the Christmas season. We will grieve properly for Ned and then we'll rejoice for ourselves and the children, and for our blessed peace.

When Helen told Frank about her plans, he said, 'I'm not sure I like the sound of that. Is this some way you've found to abandon me?'

'That's right. Enough is enough. For months I've been looking for some excuse.'

He put his arms around her. 'The king is not amused.'

'I have to go, Frank. I had planned to go before now. I can't say no to Clara and I don't want to.'

'I know it. But I don't have to like it.'

'I don't like it either. But it won't be for long. We never see each other during Christmas week anyway. You know that.'

'But we see each other New Year's Eve and plan what we're going to do for the next year.'

'We can still do that,' she said.

'That's a promise.'

'No, it's not. I can't guarantee it. But I'll be back as soon after the first of the year as I can. And whenever that is, we'll pretend it's New Year's Eve. You'll meet me in New York and we'll have a fine celebration.'

'All right . . . *that's* a promise.'

She nodded her head. 'That's a promise.'

It astounded her that after all the time she had longed to go back to England, to settle into one of the lovely rooms at Wingate Fields and luxuriate, she now felt little enthusiasm for it. So many circumstances seemed to have reversed themselves. Although she had seen Floyd only twice since his discharge from the Navy and she was never quite sure how or where she could contact him, she was still not eager to be so far away from him. Nor was it easy to leave Frank now. However one defined their relationship, and she avoided defining it too carefully, it had become a constant. Each month as she scheduled her days and weeks ahead, the days or weeks that she and Frank would be together had become the backbone of that process. And it was as vital, she knew, perhaps *more* vital, to him. The fact that they were bound by no formal commitment to each other, no restrictions, no contract, made each of them more conscientious, it seemed, about being fully responsible to the unspoken needs of the other.

So she was unquiet about what she was leaving behind. But she also had reservations about what she would find at Wingate Fields — the place itself, and the people there. She had visited Jesse and Valerie in Boston as often as she was able to during the war and had last seen them there just ten days before they left to return to England with their three children, Rab, Polly and the baby, William. Only after they were gone and she was back in Fort Beck did she begin to admit to herself how disturbing those visits had become. It seemed to her that with the birth of each child Valerie and Jesse had withdrawn a bit further into their own small fortress, where the details and rhythms of their lives occupied them totally. Valerie, in particular, was almost unrecognizable as the vibrant young woman Helen had met and talked with at the time of Angus's funeral. She seemed now to function exclusively in relation to the three small creatures she had given birth to. And Jesse, when he was with her and the children, was much the same. Only when he and Helen spent time alone together did he seem to relate to other worlds and other notions, to become curious and articulate, to become himself. Consequently, Helen's instinct was to steer him away to a corner or to a private lunch, where they could have a conversation or make some connection that did not centre on educational playthings and three-o'clock feedings. The stronger that instinct became, however, the more she resisted it. While Jesse, she suspected, welcomed opportunities to talk with her alone, Valerie, she sensed, had other feelings about it, feelings that were unspoken.

Helen found herself retreating to her room for naps and trying to find ways to avoid having six-o'clock supper with the children. She chided herself for being inflexible and intolerant but all the same she could not help thinking that Valerie's rigid regime, which was designed, it seemed, to turn adults into infants, bore some relation to her attitude towards Helen. There was a genial coolness in the air. All seemed didactic and prearranged and unalterable. Helen felt almost as if she were being deftly punished, as though the guest-room sheets were deliberately not quite fresh. Was Valerie saying, 'If you're not totally contented here, perhaps you won't be eager to come back.'? Helen did not believe that to be true. But all the same there was not, from Valerie at any rate, an overwhelming rush of acceptance and hospitality. She seemed to be saying, 'If you're determined to share our lives for a few days you are of course welcome. But we, as you can see, are both occupied and preoccupied. So don't be offended if you have to fend for yourself a bit more than usual. Perhaps if you had children of your own you'd see that things must be as they are.'

All of this was fantasy of course; Helen realized that. But whatever the foundation of her present feelings towards Valerie, or if indeed those feelings had a foundation, she was not eager to immerse herself once again in Valerie's world of porridge and coddled eggs. Nor was she looking forward to seeing Nora. If Nora had been vain and unpredictable before, there was no way of knowing how she would behave now, in the company of Jesse and Valerie and Helen.

All these negative and unknowable considerations, however, in no way lessened Helen's enthusiasm about seeing Clara again. That prospect eclipsed everything else and made her impatient suddenly, as her departure day drew near, to be on her way.

[5]

As had been the case at Angus's funeral, the details of Ned Causey's memorial service, the preparations, the plans to be made and the great numbers of relatives and friends to be dealt with, postponed interpersonal relations between the gathered members of the Bradshaw family. All contacts were pleasant and a bit perfunctory; everything was deferred, it seemed, until the major event, the church service, was attended to. Even in the earliest stages, however, it was hard to miss the strained relations between Valerie and Jesse and Helen, and between Nora and almost everyone. She had arrived, all sleekness and high energy, with a young Italian man on her arm. 'His name is Rodolfo but I call him Raoul. Isn't he divine? Doesn't understand a word I say. That's the best thing about him. He looks very young, doesn't he? He likes to tell people he's only twenty but actually he's almost twenty-two. Soon he'll be of no more use to anyone.'

Clara, however, saw no evil, heard no evil and spoke no evil. Unmistakably the mistress of her house, she moved steadily forward like a handsome ship, handling minor squalls as they arose and ignoring for the moment any disturbance that promised to be major. Nora, she knew, had only allotted three days to her trip, two before the memorial service and one after, so she could postpone dealing with her.

This is not to say that Nora was more flamboyant than expected. Her gowns were more striking than the occasion warranted perhaps. And the inclusion of Raoul had been a questionable choice certainly; but apart from these gaffes she behaved, for her, quite well. At least at the beginning. Raoul was kept, for the most part, in Nora's apartments in the west wing, and she, too, spent most of her time there. They drank a great deal of wine, according to the butler, and on one occasion a short rendition of a Neapolitan love song floated faintly into the central part of the house. But from that wing, for the most part, there was only silence. And Nora, when she ventured forth, was, in appearance at least, the essence of a lady. Some of her words, however, though spoken softly and intended exclusively for the ears of the person she addressed, were often quite extraordinary. To Helen she said, 'Don't you think it's in rather bad taste to continue pursuing Jesse now that he's married and having what promises to be an enormous family? I realize you two have been having a bit of a romp together since you were in your nappies but even the *best* things have to end sometime. You should give up on Jesse, just as I have.'

She managed such penetrating comments always when the social situation prevented any reply. She believed, apparently, that once the moment had passed she would be free from any retort or recrimination. Jesse, however, made a point of going to her rooms later, accosted her in front of Raoul, and said, 'What's happened to you? You're an embarrassment to yourself and everyone else. Can't you think of anyone except yourself?' She replied, 'When I knew you, you had a sense of humour. Fatherhood has turned you deadly serious. You laughed a lot when we were together. You never got cross just because I teased you a bit.'

She had prompted Jesse's reaction by sidling up to him the evening after the memorial service, in a room crowded with friends and relatives, and saying, *sotto voce*, 'You should be ashamed of yourself, Jesse, still carrying on with Helen after all these years. Awfully tiresome by now, I should think. I'm not surprised, of course, that Valerie turned out to be something less than you bargained for. A woman who gives so much attention to her babies doesn't have much left for a man.' When he tried to edge away from her, she followed, smiling sweetly, having, it seemed, an innocuous drawing-room conversation. 'If you want to stray a bit, I suggest you pay a visit to Paris. I'm sure you haven't forgotten your pleasant life there.'

To Valerie, one afternoon in the nursery, she said, 'I'm very proud of you. You and Jesse have made a fine marriage and you have absolutely beautiful children. And I must say I admire your tolerance toward your cousin Helen.'

'She's very sweet and kind to us,' Valerie said. 'There's no need for tolerance. We all love her.'

'A very nice speech, sweetheart. But you know very well what I'm talking about. An old flame never dies. Isn't that the way the song goes?'

'There was nothing between Jesse and Helen.'

'Is that what he told you?' Nora said.

'Yes. And I believe him.'

'That's what he told me as well. But I didn't believe him. And I still don't.'

'I don't think you and I should discuss Jesse like this.'

'Neither do I,' Nora said. 'I'm sorry.' Then, 'I just don't want you to get hurt if I can help you avoid it.'

'Jesse won't hurt me.'

'I'm sure you're right.'

If Nora had planned her stay at Wingate Fields like a military campaign she might very well have concluded, as she and Raoul prepared to leave, that she had won every battle. Her final skirmish, however, with Clara, was one she had not planned on or prepared for. As she waited for her car in the hallway by the carriage entrance, having said goodbye to the family in the morning room, her mother appeared and said, 'Can you come into the library for a moment? There's something I need to say to you.'

They went into the library and Clara closed the door behind them. Going no farther, standing with her back to the door, Clara said, 'I never expected to see such a moment as this. I never thought I could say what I'm about to say to you.'

'What do you mean?'

'You're no longer welcome here, Nora. Somehow you've turned yourself into a person I don't recognize. You've behaved in a way these past three days that I cannot forgive. For many years I overlooked everything because I thought you were just young and wilful. You're still wilful but now you have a grown daughter living in this house and she has children of her own. If you have no regard for me or for yourself then I would hope you might consider them. But you haven't. You've considered no one except yourself.'

'Are you telling me I can't come back to this house? Does Valerie know what you're saying to me?'

'She will as soon as you've gone. If she wants you to come here then that is up to her. It's her home as well as mine. But I am still the mistress here and I say you're not welcome. If you choose to come regardless of my wishes I will simply arrange to be away whenever you're here.' She opened the door, then turned back. 'I'm sure this is painful for you. I hope you never realize how agonizingly painful it is for me.'

[6]

If Nora had assumed that neither Helen nor Jesse nor Valerie would repeat the things she said to them she would have been correct. In fact, after she left, it was as though she had not been there. She was discussed, when her name came up, in only the most general and circumspect way. Almost at once, the memorial service past and Helen now the only guest in the house, the regular rhythms of Wingate Fields were evident once more. Having feared that everything would be totally changed, Helen was struck now by how much remained from other times. She felt again that easy personal freedom inside a solid daily structure. Everything was there as needed. On the other hand, if nothing was called for, nothing would be provided. She strolled through the gardens, walked across the deer park and along the river, went riding across the moors and drove one of the cars along the twisting roads bordered by rock walls or thick hedges. And almost every day she sat after breakfast in the morning room, talking with Clara, bringing to life again the relationship with her father's sister that had been a foundation stone for her ever since his death.

From conversations the two women had had when Clara visited New York fifteen years earlier, Helen knew that Clara's marriage to Ned had been, at best, unsettling. And she expected that his death might prompt a re-examination of their years together. It would be a natural reaction, Helen felt, an understandable reflex from a woman long-married who now found herself alone.

No such dialogue, however, took place. It was as though the memorial service was the final act of their lives together, more final than Ned's burial. Clara did not avoid speaking about him if someone else brought him up, but apart from that, it seemed as though, in her eyes, the fabric, whatever its original colour and pattern, had at last worn thin, grown discoloured, and unravelled. The shredded pieces could perhaps be wrapped in tissue and kept in a cupboard as a remembrance but there was no daily use to which they could be put. And no words to describe the appearance or the quality of the fabric when it had been fresh and bright and new.

Clara's curiosity about Helen's life, however, was inexhaustible. When Helen told her she had seen her half-brother and her two half-sisters in New York she was eager to hear all the details.

'Paul had left his New York address and telephone number at my house when he tried to see me in Fort Beck,' Helen said. 'So when I knew I was coming here I called and told him when I would be in New York and we made a date to have dinner, the four of us.'

'And you hadn't seen them since they were children?'

'That's right. And Tina, the youngest, I'd never seen at all. That's when my mother died, when Tina was born.'

'I suppose it happens all the time but I can't imagine having a close relative like that and not meeting them until they were grown up.'

Helen smiled. 'Your memory's going, Clara. That's how you and I met. I was almost eighteen and I'd never seen any of Raymond's family until Jesse and I came to Wingate that summer.'

'That's right. Of course you hadn't. It seems now as if I've known you since you were christened. But at the time it was a new experience for all of us.'

'Of course it was,' Helen said. 'And it was strange for me sitting there at dinner with these three gorgeous young people and knowing we had only one thing in common, but a very important thing. We all had the same mother. But because they were all so tiny when she died, I'm the only one who remembers her well. So the questions came thick and fast. You can imagine. What did she look like? How did she dress? Was she a good cook? What kind of music did she enjoy? They'd had some information from my mother's family but they wanted to hear it fresh from me.'

'How odd that their father . . .'

'Of course it's odd. But as I told you, he's not a brilliant man. How anyone could be married to two men as different as Raymond and Joe Buscatore . . .'

'That's his name?'

Helen nodded. 'He was a friend of Anna's brother. You know that she and Raymond never divorced even though they were separated for years. Her family is Italian. Strict Catholics. Divorce was never a possibility. So she didn't get married till after Raymond died. Then . . . for some reason that I've never understood, she married Joe. But she was happy with him. I saw them together and there was no doubt about it. And they were both delighted with their children.'

'But he didn't want them to see you. Isn't that correct?'

'He had some idea in his head. God knows what he thought. He thinks I'm some sort of fast-and-loose lady, I suppose. But even that is mixed up in his head with all sorts of other things. As I said, he's not exactly a clear thinker. Still, I'm sure he thought he was doing the best thing. I deserve part of the blame, too. As you know I was having problems of my own during those years when Anna's children were growing up. But I could have been more insistent, I guess, about seeing them. I'm not sure it would have done much good because Joe's hard to budge once he gets a notion in his head. But perhaps I could have tried harder. When I was married to Frank, however, and later during all the happiness and heartbreak with Chet, I just . . . I guess I just took the easy way out. But anyway . . . better late than never . . . I'm glad I've met them now.'

'What are they like?'

'They're attractive kids. All in their early twenties, and full of beans. And they were staring at me, of course, trying to find some resemblance to themselves. But as you know, I look like Raymond and these three are dead ringers for Anna and her family. Black hair, dark eyes, lovely brown skin. They're sweet kids, but they're Joe's kids too, as well as Anna's. He raised them, and it shows, particularly in the two girls. It's hard to know if they're intelligent or not. But it's easy to see that they don't *know* anything. I mean, a lot of little everyday things that Anna would have taught them got lost in the shuffle. I don't mean to be cruel or judgemental, I'm just trying to tell the truth. They didn't finish high school, for example. I don't think they'll ever try to stretch themselves. They'll get married and have children and become consumers. And there's nothing wrong with that, I suppose. But sometimes you see a young girl and you say to yourself that she could have *seen* a lot more, experienced more, known more about the world and about herself, if somebody had just given her a little nudge at the proper time. Don't misunderstand me. I'm not presenting myself as a role model. Anything negative I'm implying about Maria and Tina could also be said about me. More so. Because I had Raymond to tell me things. But you know what I mean. Raymond used to say that waste is the worst sin of all. I knew that and I believed it but that didn't stop me from wasting a lot of things, including myself. So when I make judgements of my sisters I'm not speaking from a position of superiority. They're nice young women and that's the important thing. I'm proud to be related to them. I just hope they'll be proud of themselves some day, but I'm not sure they will be.'

'What about your brother? Paul, is it?'

Helen smiled. 'Now Paul is something else again. He's the one who looks the most like Anna. Tall and elegant. Something sleek about him. He's learned some silly tricks about how to be charming, but he's charming anyway. When you catch him off-guard. He was a singer, the girls said, and there's some of that sort of performing surface to him. But it's clear that he doesn't think of himself as a finished product and that's what saves him. He knows how to conduct himself in a good restaurant, he's very anxious not to make a mistake, but if he did, you get the feeling he could handle it. He seems to have a sense of humour about himself, too. He makes a great deal of money — Tina calls him "our rich brother" — but no one says what he does. He made some reference to "presentations and promotions" but he didn't go beyond that. If someone told me he was presenting and promoting himself I would believe that. There's enough menace to him to make him damned attractive but I'd be surprised if he's involved in anything truly dishonest. He wears well-tailored conservative clothes and only his cufflinks give him away. They sparkle more than they should. And he wears a ring that seems to give him self-confidence because of the size of the stone. But those things, I suspect, are holdovers from his days as a singer. You'd like him, I think. He's a work-in-progress and it will be interesting to see how he turns out.'

'I take it you'll all be seeing each other again.'

'I hope so. I asked Maria and Tina to come see me in Fort Beck when I get back, but I'll be surprised if they come. I doubt if they'd like Illinois any more than Anna did. They're New York kids. The Midwest seems halfway round the world to them. Also they're working. They both have jobs. And there was a great deal of giggling when I asked about their boyfriends so I suspect that's another reason they wouldn't be eager to leave the city. But that's all right. If they can't come to me I'll see them when I'm in the East. Now that we've made contact and now that they're living away from home, there should be no problem.'

'And Paul . . . what about him?'

'I'm sure I'll see *him*. And I don't think I'll have to pursue him. I think he's fascinated with the idea of having a presentable older sister. My guess is that he thinks I know some things he doesn't know. I've been to places he hasn't seen. All that is catnip to Paul unless I'm mistaken. Also he asked a lot of questions about life in England, what London's like, what it's like here in Northumberland. He has no real education but he wants to be a polished man, I think. He's already come a long way from Staten Island, where he grew up, and I think he wants to go much farther. I have a notion he won't be wearing that flashy ring or those shiny cufflinks next time I see him. I'm sure he thinks that if he gets the wardrobe and the manners and the small talk all worked out, a new world is going to open up for him. And he's probably right. Certainly he doesn't suffer from a lack of feminine companionship and I don't think he ever will.'

Clara had known from Helen's letters that she had discovered her ex-husband, Frank Wilson, again. When his name came up soon after Helen arrived at Wingate, Clara said, 'I know so little about him, only what you told me that time I saw you in New York, and by then, as I remember, you were already separated or divorced. Which was it?'

'Divorced.'

'But all the same,' Clara went on, 'when you wrote that you'd begun to see him again, it didn't really surprise me. We all have a tendency to look back to some other time, when there's something or somebody we need. I was very taken with a young man called Arthur Melvin when I was only sixteen years old. He was a school chum of your father. It never came to anything — those were very proper days, at least for *me* they were — we never even kissed. But, still, when things started to go so much off-course for me and Ned, I found myself thinking quite often of Arthur. It was as though he'd been hiding there in the back of my mind waiting to come out and do his little dance. It made no sense, of course. I had no idea where he came from or where he'd gone after university. And I would never have contacted him even so, under any circumstances. But all the same, he made regular appearances in my head. He still does.'

'I don't think my seeing Frank again was as romantic as that,' Helen said. 'After we broke up I rarely thought of him. I was in such a state about all sorts of things. Also it wasn't that much later before I met Chet and then I was totally occupied. But quite apart from that, I'd never had any nostalgia for the time I spent with Frank. We had a pleasant enough marriage, we were kind and loving to each other, but when it ended, there was no doubt in the mind of either of us that it was over. When I lost the baby I must have felt that our only reason for staying together was gone. But whatever was churning around in my head I saw no future for Frank and me. Didn't see one, didn't want one. And I know now that he felt the same. We weren't angry with each other. It was just as though we got tired of each other. Or tired of ourselves. Or bored to death. God knows what we really felt.'

'Now I take back what I said. If *that's* the way it ended I don't know *how* you managed to find each other again.'

'We didn't find each other. I found him. And not because it made sense to me. It didn't. But I was so desperately lonely I didn't know what to do with myself. I felt as if the war and all the other circumstances of my life had pushed me into a corner I'd never be able to struggle out of. I didn't want a boyfriend or a lover. I just wanted *somebody* I could talk to and spend time with. Even after I'd called Frank and seen him and had lunch with him, I had no thought of luring him into my bed or allowing myself to be lured into his. Nor did he have any such ideas. Or so I thought. But I was wrong.'

'Sometimes people don't stop liking each other. They just stop liking being married.'

'Maybe that's it,' Helen said. 'But whatever the reasons, for *now* everything works fine. We have no future whatsoever and we never ever talk about the past. We just paddle around in the present, like children in a wading pool. I know him better than I ever did and I like him better. And love isn't allowed to spoil things. I don't fool around with that word any more.'

'You're too young to talk like that.'

'That's why I *am* talking like that. I feel as if I've been old all my life. Now I'm planning to be young for a while. I may decide to be young till I die.'

[7]

Contrary to the premonitions she had felt before coming to England, Helen found, as the holiday preparations began in the great house, that she was enjoying every detail of the life there. The return to Wingate Fields that had been in her mind throughout the war years was now a reality for her, fully as satisfactory as she had hoped it would be. Every morning she got up rested and full of plans for the day ahead. At night, she got into her soft canopied bed with a book and read till the house grew quiet. Occasionally, outside, she heard a far-off dog bark or the sound of a night bird. Then black silence again. And at last she would turn off her light and go to sleep.

The atmosphere she remembered from Jesse and Valerie's house in Boston had not travelled across the ocean with them. Or so it seemed to Helen. Jesse prowled the house and grounds, romped with the dogs, led the conversation at dinner, sang bawdy songs to Valerie's accompaniment, read Marlowe and Spenser and John Donne to the three assembled ladies, made toasts at dinner that rang with humour, sarcasm and wisdom, and reminded everyone of Angus Bradshaw at his best. He behaved like a man who was truly and finally at home, a musician's son from Chicago who had transformed himself. He seemed, in appearance and actions, a true member of the Northumberland gentry.

Valerie, too, seemed to have arrived at the destination she had long planned for. She still occupied herself primarily with her three small children, ignoring the nanny's complaints to Clara that she was perfectly capable of overseeing the nursery and caring for her charges. But the note of frenzy that Helen had either noticed or imagined in Boston had apparently been left there. There was, in fact, once Nora was gone, no tension at all in the house. The four residents — not counting the children — Clara, Helen, Jesse and Valerie, came and went, joined and parted, gathered in groups of two or three or four, or followed their solitary courses, sometimes for hours at a stretch. With certain exceptions, all persons were privy to all conversations. There were no intrigues or dark secrets, there was no sudden hush when a third person entered a room occupied by two others. Helen did not hesitate to ride out with Jesse, to talk with him in the library, or to walk beside him in the garden or the deer park. And Valerie, when she and Helen were alone together, or with the children, or with Clara, was gracious and at ease.

With Jesse, however, when *they* were alone together, Valerie was often less gracious, and seemingly not at ease. She had begun to say things that seemed out of character for her, provocative statements, surprising observations or requests. Emotional *non-sequiturs*.

Late one evening after Helen and Clara had gone to their rooms, when she and Jesse were in their upstairs sitting room, Valerie said, 'Do you ever feel we made a mistake, leaving Boston and coming back here to live?'

'God, no. Do you?'

'I don't know. But I do think about it sometimes.'

'What do you think?' he said.

'Mostly about our house there. It was cosy and nice, wasn't it?'

'*Too* cosy. If nothing else, we'd outgrown the nursery.'

She smiled and said, 'That's true.' Then, 'What would you say if I said I wanted to move back there?'

'I'd give you a glass of warm milk with a bit of brandy in it and tuck you up for the night.'

'I'm serious.'

'So am I. Since the day we got married we've been planning to come back here. Every day we talked about it, all through the war.'

'I know that.'

'It was the centrepiece of our lives. Boston was nice, we said, but once we got home to Wingate Fields, everything we'd dreamed about and planned for would fall into place. Don't you remember those conversations?'

'Of course I do. But . . .'

'But what?'

'I don't know, Jesse. I just find myself thinking about that nice house in Boston.'

'We *sold* that nice house in Boston. The Tollivers are living in it now. They love it as much as you do. They don't want to sell it back to us.'

'I mean a house *like* that. There are lots of fine old houses not far from where we lived.'

'I can't believe what I'm hearing.' Jesse said. 'You're serious, aren't you?'

'I don't know what you mean by serious. I'm just telling you how I feel and it doesn't help when you keep trying to make me feel like a monkey.'

Jesse got up, walked to the table by the window and poured himself a whisky. When he came back to his chair he said, 'Do you realize that this is the strangest conversation we've ever had?'

'It doesn't seem strange to me. Do you expect me never to change my mind about anything?'

'No. But there are some things I don't expect you to change your mind about. And living here is one of them.'

'I don't know why I feel the way I do. Maybe it's because we were so happy where we were.'

'We're happy here, for God's sake. I'm certainly happy. I've never felt better in my life.'

'I know you like it here,' she said. 'And I thought I would. And I do like it. But it's different from the way I remembered it. It's so huge.'

'It was always huge.'

'But I didn't remember it that way. It seems as if we're never by ourselves.'

He set his glass down. 'You're really not making sense, do you realize that? We're by ourselves *now*. We can be by ourselves any time we want. One thing you can be sure of at Wingate Fields is privacy. A platoon of the Queen's Guards could be stationed here and nobody would ever have to *see* them.'

'That's what I mean. It's so big it's not like a house. It's not like a *home*. I'd forgotten how many servants it takes to run this place.'

'What difference does *that* make? You've had servants all your life.'

'Not in Boston.'

'Of course we did,' he said. 'We had a nanny, and Mrs McBain, the housekeeper, and the men who did repairs and looked after the garden.'

'But it all seemed cosy and private to me. It belonged to us. This place seems to belong to itself. Or to all the people who've lived here for three hundred years.'

'Not true. It belongs to *us*. To you and me.'

'But other people can live here if they want to. Clara lives here. And if Nora wanted to come back, she could. It's not *our* house. It belongs to the Bradshaws, the living ones, the dead ones, and the ones who aren't born yet.'

'What's wrong with that?' Jesse said.

'There's nothing wrong with it, I suppose. It just doesn't make me feel comfortable, that's all.'

Jesse got up then, walked across the room and sat down at the foot of Valerie's *chaise-longue*. 'Is all this about Helen?' he said. 'Is that what we're talking about?'

'What do you mean?'

'Just what I said. Are you thinking that maybe Helen is planning to move back here and live at Wingate?'

'No. Is that what *you* think?'

'I have no idea. She hasn't mentioned it to me. But she could if she wanted to. She's a Bradshaw. It's her home too, if she wants it to be.' He sat looking at her. 'That's it, isn't it?'

'No, it's not. Why do you insist that it is?'

'It isn't as though we'd never discussed her. I'm sure you remember some talks we had about Helen when we were in Boston.'

'Yes I do. But things were different then. I was expecting one of the children, I don't remember which one . . .'

'William, I think.'

'That's right. And I guess I was feeling sorry for myself. Some sort of chemical maladjustment. You know about those things. You're smart.'

'Then you don't think she's trying to steal your husband?' he said.

'I think everybody's trying to steal my husband. So why should Helen be an exception? As a matter of fact, she and I have had some nice talks since she got here. She's very nice to me. And awfully sweet with the children. Rab's very fond of her, I think.'

'Well, that's good news. If you decide to move back to America, maybe we should ask her to come live with us.'

'I know you're teasing me, but I don't think that's such a terrible idea. I've thought of it, in fact. Now that I know her better, I think it would be nice if we could see her more.'

'I think I'll take you to see Dr Schuyler next week. I don't believe your head's working just right.'

'Oh, yes it is. I've meant everything I said tonight.'

'I'm sure you have. But if you don't mind, I won't ask for my bags to be packed tomorrow. I don't expect to be leaving here soon. I don't expect to be leaving here at all.'

She went on talking as though she hadn't heard him. 'And there's something else I want to say. I think we should have another baby.'

'All right.'

'No discussion about *that?*'

'Not tonight,' Jesse said.

'Later maybe?'

'We'll see.'

She sat looking at him for a moment. 'I'm serious, Jesse.'

'I'm sure you are.'

'That's one reason I'm thinking about moving away from here. I can't imagine having a baby here.'

When he didn't answer, she said. 'I know you're going

to remind me of what we said after William was born.' Again he didn't answer. 'I meant it then,' she said. 'I thought three children was a nice-size family for us. Two boys and one girl. But now I feel differently about it. I feel like I did when we got married. I think I'd like to have lots and lots of children. Do you think I'm crazy?'

'No. I think you're full of surprises tonight.'

'Nora always told me men like to be surprised.'

'Nora's wrong about all sorts of things.' Jesse said. 'That's one of them.'

'You're not disappointed that I want to have another baby, are you?'

'No, I'm not. I'd just hate to see you get into a frame of mind where you started to feel that was your only function.'

'Why would I think that?'

'I don't know,' he said.

'Do you think that?'

'No, I don't. But I know it's not unusual for a woman, when she's had her children close together as you have, to start having doubts about herself the moment she's not pregnant or doesn't have an infant to take care of.'

'I'm not emotionally disturbed,' she said. 'I just want to have some more children.'

'I didn't say you were emotionally disturbed. I'm just saying I think it's important for you to understand what your reasons are.'

'Why can't we just say, "Let's have a houseful of kids and to hell with it"?'

'We can. But I'm not going to.'

'Why not?' she said.

'Because it's too important to me, that's why.'

'You're angry with me, aren't you?'

'No.'

'Yes, you are. You hate it when I talk about leaving Wingate Fields.'

'I don't hate it. Because I don't take you seriously.'

'Maybe you should,' she said.

'Maybe I should, but I don't. Not on that subject.'

[8]

'What was it like to see him again?' Jesse said. Helen had just told him about Floyd's coming to see her in Fort Beck.

'Better than the times in San Diego,' she said. 'He seemed more grown up. Everything was just easier because we'd met and talked before.'

'What's he up to? What's he planning to do now?'

'Well, the first time I saw him was over a year ago. He'd only been discharged a few weeks before. The first excitement of being out of the Navy was over and I think he was a little confused about what he should do next. He'd been to Crawfordsville just before he came to see me. We didn't discuss it but I got the feeling there's an old girlfriend there. I also got the feeling that maybe she's somebody else's girlfriend now. Floyd's not a big talker. If you have any secrets I think they'd be safe with him.'

'How long did he stay at your house?'

'Three nights and most of three days. He was on his way to South Dakota, where we saw Simison. To Yankton. After Simison died, all his furniture and clothes and personal stuff were put in storage. So Floyd was going there to sort through everything and see what he wanted to keep and what he'd have to get rid of.'

'Did he seem glad to see you when he showed up?'

'I think so. It's hard to tell. We're still like a couple of tennis players in the first game of the first set. Sizing each other up. Playing a careful, defensive game. But he was nice. And sweet. Although *sweet* is not a word most people would use to describe him. If he was in the movies I think he'd play tough guys. I cooked him dinner two nights and we went out one night, to that catfish place down by the river. I never can remember the name.'

'Stiney's,' said Jesse.

'That's right. Anyway, he liked my cooking, he said. He ate as if he did. We drank some beer with dinner and listened to some radio programmes afterwards. And the night we went to Stiney's we went to a movie later. That Hitchcock picture *Lifeboat* was playing at the Mars. Since he'd been in the Navy I thought he might like it but I don't think he did. He said he liked it but he squirmed around in his seat a lot.'

'Those tight sailor-pants,' Jesse said. 'Was he still in uniform?'

'Yes, he was. Maybe you're right.' Then, 'I don't want to forget to tell you . . . while we were in the restaurant we saw Dr Pressman, who used to be Dean of men at Foresby before he retired. Do you remember him?'

Jesse nodded, 'I remember him, all right. He should have been a prison warden. And that peculiar wife of his. No lips.'

'She was with him. She smiled her no-lips smile at us as we passed their table on the way out. I chatted with them for a minute or so while they stared at Floyd, and just before we walked away I said, "I'd like you to meet my son, Floyd." Then we sailed out of the restaurant. When I looked back from the door, they were still staring, their eyes popped out like hard-boiled eggs.'

'You'll be a scarlet woman in Fort Beck from now on.'

'I doubt it. A bad report from Alice Pressman very seldom gets passed along. You only lose friends if she says something *good* about you.'

She said she'd seen Floyd twice since that first time, both times in Chicago. 'Once when he was there to catch a bus for California and another time when he came to check up on an art school he was thinking about entering.'

'Is he an artist?'

'I guess the school didn't think so. They turned him down. He was in a camouflage unit in San Diego before they reassigned him so I guess he got sort of interested watching some of the camouflage artists' work. But it didn't seem to bother him when the school didn't accept him. The two of us had dinner together, we got a little tight on Manhattans, and then he caught the night train to Yankton.'

'He's still there?'

'He was then. But now he's in California. That's where he was heading the second time I saw him in Chicago. That was two or three months ago and I haven't heard from him since. He has a friend who lives in a cabin in the woods somewhere north-east of San Francisco and he said he thought he'd spend some time with him.'

'Was he working when he was in Yankton?'

She shook her head. 'He was living in a boarding-house and reading a lot, he said. The window of his room looked down on the Mississippi. He said he sat there in front of that window and read a dozen books by Mark Twain.'

'Did you give him some money?'

'No. I offered to but he said he didn't need it. He'd saved all the money he made during the war, his discharge guaranteed him twenty dollars a week for a year, and he sold a lot of furniture and books and things that belonged to the Simisons. Also, the old man had some life insurance, apparently. Not a lot, but five thousand dollars maybe. So Floyd says he's fine for now. If he needs any money, he'll let me know.'

'If he's not going to work and he doesn't plan to go to school, I'm sure you'll hear from him. Did he graduate from high school?'

'He took some courses in Yankton while he was there and they gave him some credits for his Navy training, so he got a high-school equivalency diploma. He can go to college if he wants to but I don't think he will.'

'Why not?'

'I don't know. Just a feeling I have. I just can't see him sitting in a classroom for four years. He'd be twenty-eight or twenty-nine when he graduated.'

'Lots of young guys are doing it.' Jesse said.

'I know they are. But I don't think Floyd will be one of them.'

'Maybe he's decided to live off his mother.'

'Why do you say that?'

'Didn't you tell him when you met him in San Diego that there's plenty of money if he needs it.'

'Not exactly. I told him there would be money in his name whether he needs it or not. It's his money, Jesse. Just like yours is yours and mine is mine. It's Bradshaw money and he's a Bradshaw.'

'Not quite. Not technically,' Jesse said.

'He most certainly is. Technically and actually and every other way. I'm a Bradshaw and he's my son.' Then, 'You resent him, don't you?'

'I've never even met him. Why would I resent him?'

'I don't know, but you do. I can tell it from your voice. From the questions you ask.'

'I don't resent him at all. I'm delighted you found him. I just don't want anybody to make you unhappy.'

'Floyd won't make me unhappy. He's not like that. You'll see.'

'Have you told Clara about him yet?'

Helen smiled. 'No. I'm saving that till the holidays are over. It's going to be Clara's main gift.'

'How do you think she'll react?'

'I know how she'll react. And so do you. She'll be thrilled and delighted. Especially since Hugh . . . I mean . . .'

'What does Hugh have to do with it?'

Helen hesitated. Then, 'I just mean that losing him was such a terrible loss for her. She'll be happy to have a new young man in the family. She'll be happy for Floyd, happy for me, happy for all of us.'

After a moment Jesse said, 'You always expect the best of people, don't you?'

'What does that mean?'

'It means you never expect to be cheated or deceived. In your world there's no deception.'

She smiled. Then she began to laugh.

'Did I say something funny?'

'Very funny. I'm the queen of deception, Jesse. Don't you know that? My life is like a Chinese box. Secret compartments concealing all sorts of other secret compartments.'

'Not a chance,' he said. 'I know you like I know my pocket. In a world of takers, you're a giver. That's your constant. It's the most unchangeable thing about you. Do you remember a few years ago when I said you had to stop loving people who don't love you back.'

'Sounds familiar.'

'And you said, "I can't stop doing that. I don't even want to." '

'So there we are,' she said. 'Am I a saint or am I just dumb?'

'I can't decide.'

'Neither can I.'

Chapter Three

[1]

For years Helen had planned and replanned the moments when she would sit down at last with Clara and tell her about Floyd, about his existence, the circumstances of his birth, why he had lived apart from her for all of his life, and how they had, at last, come back together. It was a story she had needed, from the beginning, to share with Clara. Once before, when they had met in New York, she had intended to tell her but something had held her back. At that time she knew nothing of Floyd's whereabouts. Looking back, she felt the fact that the story was so sadly incomplete had kept her from confiding in Clara. Also, the true identity of the boy's father, something she had told no one other than Chet, was something she wanted to present carefully. That, still, was the part of the story that gave her the greatest concern as she rehearsed it in her mind. At last she concluded that it could be told only as it happened, as simply and honestly as she was able to remember it.

She had planned to create some circumstance whereby she and Clara would be away from the house, in Newcastle perhaps, or having tea in the nearby village. She wanted to proceed from beginning to end without interruption.

One afternoon, however, when Jesse and Valerie had driven off somewhere with the children, Helen found herself sitting with Clara in her upstairs parlour, and she said, 'I have a secret to tell you, something that no one else knows.'

Clara smiled and said, 'Shame on you. I thought you'd told me all your secrets.'

'I believe I have. And I wanted to tell you *this*. A long time ago. But the time never seemed right. I fully intended to tell you that time we met in New York but for some reason the right moment never presented itself. I just couldn't get it out.'

'That's a long time ago. This must be an old secret.'

Helen nodded. 'Almost as old as our friendship. It goes back to that first summer when Jesse and I came to Wingate Fields.'

After a moment, Clara said, 'If you've kept it to yourself this long, maybe you shouldn't tell it now.'

'No. I must tell you. If I didn't I'm sure you'd find out anyway and I don't want it to be like that. I want to tell you myself so you'll understand everything that happened.'

'It all sounds quite mysterious. Is this something that will make me terribly upset?'

'Not at all. I think it will make you extremely happy.'

Clara smiled. 'That's good. I like a bit of cheerful news sometimes. When you reach my age there always seems to be too much of the other kind.'

'Those months here that first summer were filled with all kinds of new experiences for me. I'm sure you remember that. Most of them were good but some of them were disturbing. As you know I almost didn't come at all. After my father died and I found out that everything he'd told me about his past was untrue, that was disconcerting enough. But then when I learned that he had come from England and that I had a whole family here whom I'd never even heard of, I didn't know how to react. I was eighteen years old and I worshipped Raymond. It was very difficult and painful for me to learn that for some reasons of his own he'd covered up his entire background, including who his parents were and where he came from. Later, when you told me everything that had happened before he left England, about the woman he was in love with and how she died, I began to understand. But before, when I was still at home in Fort Beck, I just felt confused and betrayed. And Jesse felt the same way, I think. He wasn't actually a member of the family but he'd lived with us since he was sixteen and Raymond was more of a father to him than his own father had been. When we found out about you people, and you began to write to me, Jesse and I reacted quite differently. My first thought was that if Raymond had chosen to leave his family then I didn't want to be with them either.'

'I remember that,' Clara said. 'Jesse started to answer our letters long before you did.'

'That's right. He thought it was my obligation to have *some* contact with you, to *see* you, to see where Raymond was born and how he had lived. At last he wore me down. I agreed to go with him to England that summer of 1919.

'Thank God you did. It meant a lot to us. I always thought my father lived ten years longer because of you and Jesse. All those years of knowing nothing about Raymond, where he'd gone or what he was doing, whether he was dead or alive, had changed Angus terribly. But seeing you and Jesse, even when he knew at last that Raymond was dead, was like a tonic to him. It was clear evidence that his son had lived a good life, that he had a lovely young daughter and a sort of foster son in Jesse. Angus was neither sentimental nor romantic. He was a tough old cock. But all the same, whether he realized it or not, he couldn't help fixing on Jesse. Here was a young man, very nearly the same age his own son had been when he saw him for the last time. Also Jesse had known Raymond as a man in a way that I think nobody else did, not even you perhaps.'

'That's true. Whether Raymond intended it or not, he made Jesse a carbon copy of himself. Or perhaps it was the other way around. Jesse worked very hard to make himself a duplicate of Raymond. So did I, of course, as much as any girl can emulate her father. We were an odd little triptych. Raymond in the centre and crudely painted copies of him on either side. When he died, however, and the centre panel disappeared, Jesse and I were hinged together even more strongly than before. Not as sweethearts, the way a lot of people assumed, but as emotional survivors, clinging to whatever scraps of wreckage we could find. The reason I finally decided to come here to England — I'm not sure you ever knew this — was because I realized that Jesse was planning to come whether I did or not. And I wasn't ready just then to try to get along by myself. I'm not sure Jesse knew how dependent I was on him. And once we got here to England, where everything was strange to me and I was suddenly in the midst of Raymond's family — and mine — I was even more inclined to turn to Jesse for his reactions, his assessments of people, for everything. As you remember, he was much more at home here than I was, certainly at the start. I felt comfortable with you, thank God, from the very beginning. But I was frightened by Angus and Ned, I didn't know what to make of Louise, and Nora made me feel like the village milkmaid, dressed in her mother's clothes . . .'

'I think you're exaggerating.'

'I am. Of course I am. But I did feel a bit like a pigeon among the swans. Jesse, on the other hand, seemed to put on his swan feathers from the first day. To my eyes it appeared that he had an instant relationship with every person in the house. Male and female, animal, mineral, and vegetable. I admired him for his amazing social courage, and at the same time I resented it. It's like when you're an eight-year-old girl in school and you discover your very best girlfriend has two other best friends. She's your best friend but you're not hers. It was as childish as that. But I *was* only eighteen and I had an unusually strong attachment to Jesse. He was half brother, half father, half God-knows-what to me.'

'And you suddenly saw it floating away.'

'Something like that. All at once I seemed to be sharing him with everyone in the county. I hardly saw him at all and when I did see him he was full of stories about what he'd done and where he'd been. He'd gone shooting with Hugh, and fishing with Angus, and driving to the coast with Nora.'

'I always wondered if that was a problem for you. Nora and Jesse, I mean. Ned thought that the reason you left for America so suddenly that late summer was because he'd announced one night at dinner that Jesse and Nora were going to be married.'

Helen smiled. 'That *was* a problem, and it's a part of this whole story I'm telling you, but not the sort of problem you might have imagined. Jesse and I lived in the same house for a number of years. One of the most frequent topics at dinner during that time was a discussion of one or more of Jesse's girlfriends. You have to remember . . . when I was sixteen, still playing field hockey, Jesse was twenty. He was a grown man. He'd been to the war and back, and he'd had some sort of a sashay with half the pretty girls in Fort Beck. Every time he started a new romance, Raymond would say, "There he goes again," and we'd drink a toast to Marcella or Diane or Mildred, or whoever the current little gumdrop happened to be. He always made sure that Raymond and I met these girls and afterwards the three of us would discuss them thoroughly at the table. Raymond was cruel. He'd say things like, "She seems like a perfectly acceptable young woman but she has no neck. Never trust a girl with no neck, or a girl whose waistline is just below her armpits, or a girl who takes unusually small steps. No neck is a sure sign of a bowel disorder, high waistline means that kidney and bladder problems are on the way — such women are often incontinent by the age of thirty — and women who take small steps are inevitably prosecuted sooner or later for snitching small items from clothing shops." '

Clara smiled. 'That sounds very familiar. He used to give lectures like that to his chums when he was still at school. He once told *me* that Ned had the exact skull measurements of an axe-murderer named Poliakoff who killed twenty-seven women in Marseilles.'

'What I'm saying,' Helen went on, 'is that I grew up with Jesse's romantic adventures. He changed girlfriends like other men change their shirts. He was a popular fellow. Lots of women liked him. Young women and women who were not so young. So I was certainly not surprised to see him and Nora fall all over each other. I predicted it, in fact. The day we arrived I said to him, "How nice that they've provided you with a female companion for the summer." He played innocent but I'd seen the two of them looking at each other and I knew it was just a question of time.'

'Is that really the way things were between you and Jesse or are you just telling me this now because of everything's that's happened since?'

'If I'd been in love with him why would I lie about it now? Especially in view of what's happened since. We've both gone our own ways but we're still friends, the same as we always were. When I'm in trouble he's the first person I try to get in touch with. It's always been that way and I guess it always will be.' She paused as if she'd come to a crucial point and wanted to be sure to select the precise word. 'That *connection* we've always had, if that's the proper word, was the thing that got me in trouble at the end of the summer here at Wingate Fields. Not the *existence* of it, but the feeling I had that it had ceased to exist. Not overnight. It happened gradually through the summer. Little by little I felt that the young man I had come to England with had disappeared. In his place was someone who strongly resembled the original but who in all other respects, especially in relation to me, was changed. I was no longer his confidante and he had no impulse, it seemed, to be mine. Our conversations together, which had always been private and personal and funny, spiced with specific memories and images, were strangely general now, hurried sometimes, careful, and insultingly polite. Every time I talked to him alone I felt offended, as though he was anxious not to reveal himself to me and just as anxious that I should not tell him what I was thinking or what I'd been doing. I don't know what had come over him just then. I didn't know then and I don't know now. He had simply become secretive in a way he had not been before. He seemed to have a strong impulse to keep me away from whatever it was he was thinking.

'As you can imagine I was pretty put off by all this. But I told myself that we'd be going back to America at the end of the summer and by then he would come out of whatever fog he'd allowed himself to slip into. So then I felt better. But not for long. The next thing I knew he said we'd have to delay going back for a few weeks because he had to do some research in London for a monograph he was planning to write about della Francesca. He was all excited about it. Angus was going to back him and see that it was published. So I decided a few more weeks wouldn't matter. At least I felt as if he was letting me in on what was happening. So again I felt better about things. But then came the big evening you mentioned before. I'll never forget that dinner till the day I die. First your husband stood up and announced that Jesse and Nora were going to be married right after Christmas. Then as soon as we'd drunk a couple of toasts to that, Angus stood up and made his own announcement. He'd decided to adopt Jesse as his son, he'd had all the proper papers drawn up and signed and it was an accomplished fact. Jesse Clegg was now Jesse Bradshaw.'

'I know what you mean,' Clara said. 'That was a lot for all of us to absorb in just a few minutes.'

'That's true. But for me especially. Because the way I saw it, I was the only one who was surprised. Maybe a couple of people didn't know about the adoption process but I was convinced that everyone except me knew about the engagement.'

'It was a hectic few days as I remember it. I'm sure we all thought Jesse had told you.'

'But he hadn't. And that's what made me crazy. I remember sitting there at the table that night, everybody laughing and talking and drinking champagne, and thinking, "Why am I the outsider here? Why would Jesse make these elaborate plans, things that will totally alter his life, and never breathe a word of it to me?" I couldn't find an answer to that question and to this day I don't know the answer. He must have known I wouldn't have had any objections to his marrying Nora. And I would have been delighted about Angus deciding to take him officially and legally into the family. I would have encouraged him. After all it was my family he was joining, both by marriage *and* adoption. Since I'd always felt as though he was part of Raymond's family and mine, what reasons could I have had to object? But he obviously had some sort of bug in his head, some reason for keeping everything secret. So he did. And it almost killed me. I sat there drinking champagne and smiling, knowing I was drinking too much and not giving a damn, but inside a cold wind was blowing through me. I wanted to get up and run outside and bay at the moon. But I didn't. I sat there like a proper family member taking part in a family celebration. But I felt as if a part of my life, the best part, was over. Jesse, for reasons of his own, had abandoned me. When I went back to America, I realized suddenly, I would be going by myself. But some toughness in me said, "All right, if that's the way it is then the sooner I go, the better." So I knew, there at the table that night, that I'd be leaving for home as soon as I could make the arrangements. That decision helped me through the rest of the evening. But when I got to my room later, when everyone was laughing and half-drunk, whatever determination I'd found in myself quickly disappeared. I took off my clothes, had a bath, and tried to go to sleep. But I couldn't. Too many trolls dancing in my head. So I got up — the house had gone dead-quiet by then — put on my dressing gown and sat in a chair by the window looking down on the gardens. There was a decanter of brandy by my bed. I had never touched it in all the weeks I'd been there. But now I poured a small glass for myself and sat by the window with the lights turned down, sipping it. I may have had a second glass, perhaps even a third, I don't remember. I just recall that suddenly the autumn garden looked very inviting to me. I knew that your mother sometimes walked there at night and it seemed like a lovely idea to me. So I got up, left my room, and walked along the upstairs corridor. I passed several bedroom doors on my way to the great staircase. But when I got there and looked down into the entrance hall below, I stopped. I hadn't changed my mind. No idea seized me. I simply stopped. Then suddenly I started back towards my own room. But when I reached the door to Hugh's room I tried it and found it open. I went inside, took off my dressing gown and my nightdress and got into his bed. I stayed there with him all night. In the very early morning, before anyone was up, I got up and went back to my own room. And a few days later, you went with me on the train to Liverpool and I took the ship back to America. You remember that.'

'Of course I do,' Clara said. 'Is *that* your secret?'

'That's the beginning of it. By the time I got to New York, when I'd been there for a short time, I wasn't feeling well so I went to the doctor. He told me I was going to have a baby.'

'Because of that one night?'

'Yes.' Helen said.

'You poor thing. What did you do?'

'I decided I wanted to go ahead and have the child.'

'Did you tell Hugh?'

'No. I didn't tell anyone.'

'I wish you'd told me.'

'I wanted to. God, how I wished you were there. But you weren't. And I saw no reason to get you mixed up in it. I didn't want it to be a whole family disturbance. I decided it was my problem and I'd have to deal with it myself. So I did. The doctor in New York told me about an organization in Maine, a reputable group that takes care of unmarried girls during pregnancy and then arranges to put the babies in good homes.'

'Oh, Helen, I hope you didn't . . .'

'Yes, I did.' She told her the details then, of how she'd given birth to a boy but had never seen him. She'd been assured that he'd been placed with a fine couple but wasn't told their name, where they lived, or anything else about them.

'How horrible,' Clara said. 'How awful for you.'

'I thought it was the only thing I could do. And when I began to have second thoughts it was too late. I pleaded with the head of the institution but he wouldn't tell me anything. Finally he told me my boy's first name was Floyd. That's all the information he would give me. He said he was a normal healthy boy and his name was Floyd.'

'And that's all you knew?'

'That's all I knew until 1941. Then some friends of mine in Maine found a way to pay off a young woman who worked at the adoption agency. She smuggled Floyd's file out and we got some additional information.'

She told her then how she and Jesse had followed the clues in the file. They'd gone first to Crawfordsville, Indiana, where Floyd's adoptive father had been a teacher at Wabash College and then to Yankton, South Dakota, where he had moved later. 'He told us Floyd was in the Navy, stationed in San Diego. So I went on to California and saw him.'

'You say Jesse went with you. So he knows everything you're telling me?'

'All except for one thing. He doesn't know that Hugh is Floyd's father. I told him I met a young man on the ship between Liverpool and New York. I said he was the boy's father. I told Floyd the same story when I saw him in San Diego.'

'Why did you tell him that?'

'I'm not sure. I was ashamed, I guess. And frightened a little. Hugh and I were first cousins, after all. All during the months I was pregnant I was afraid . . . you know . . . that he might not be . . . that there might be something wrong with him. That's why it meant so much to me when I finally learned from the agency that he was a normal child.'

'So now you've seen him.'

'Several times. He was in the South Pacific all through the war but I've seen him three times since he came home.'

'What's he like? How does he feel about all this?'

'It's hard to tell. He's not very open. But he's awfully nice to me. It's just . . . I suppose we're still a bit wary with each other. I explained to him as well as I could why I did the things I did and he seemed to understand, but I'm sure he thinks I had other choices if I'd only decided to take them.'

'Do you think that now?'

'No, I don't. I still think I did the only thing I could do at the time. Hugh and I scarcely knew each other. I didn't see how I could . . . you know what I mean. And I didn't have either the courage or the maturity to take a baby back to Fort Beck and raise it by myself. It wasn't today we're talking about. Floyd was born in 1920.'

'What date?' Clara said. 'When's his birthday?'

'March 20th.'

'Isn't that odd? Hugh was born on March 13th. Did you know that?'

'No.'

'He was just twenty-three when your boy was born.' She was silent for a long moment. Then, 'I never thought Hugh particularly *liked* children. I know he wasn't fond of his stepchildren. But all the same, I think he might have been pleased to know he had a son.'

'I hope so,' Helen said. 'Are you pleased?'

'This is all coming at me so fast, but of course I'm delighted to know that you have a son, Raymond has a grandson, and I have a grandson. And when I've accustomed myself to the idea that you and Hugh produced a child . . .'

'I know what you mean. I've never really got used to the idea myself.'

'Does he look like Hugh?'

'I don't think so. But perhaps you'll see him differently.'

'When will that be?' Clara asked. 'When *will* I see him?'

'I don't know. Soon, I hope. But I can't guarantee it. He seems to do things when he's ready to and not before.'

'Sounds like a genuine Bradshaw.' Then, 'Is this still a secret or are we going to announce it to the rest of the family?'

'I don't want to keep it a secret any longer. But I want to tell people the same story I told Floyd. About who his father is. You and I are the only people who know it's Hugh. I'd like to keep it that way.'

After a moment Clara said, 'I think you're right. The real story might put a lot of pressure on him in some way.'

'In many ways, I'm afraid.'

'So his name is Floyd Bradshaw?' Clara said then.

'It is if he wants it to be. I wasn't married and my name is Bradshaw, so he's entitled to it. Or he can use the name he's used all his life, Floyd Simison. That's the name of the people who adopted him.'

'To us he's a Bradshaw no matter what we call him.'

'That's right,' Helen said.

Clara got up and walked to the table by the bay window looking out across the deer park. 'It's a bit early in the day but I think you and I should have a drink.' She poured sherry into two glasses, carried them back to the sofa and sat down. 'I've had some unpredictable and memorable experiences in this house but this is an afternoon I'm certain I will never forget.'

[2]

Among the Bradshaws, when there was some news that affected the whole family it was customary to make an announcement at the dinner table. Clara insisted that the news about Floyd should be handled in that way.

'I'm not sure,' Helen said. 'All of us know now except Valerie. I don't want her to feel the way I did that other time.'

'This is an altogether different circumstance. It's far too important to be discussed over tea in the drawing room. It *is* an occasion so we must treat it as an occasion. Nora won't be here, of course, but she, too, will be informed in a proper way. Jesse's the head of the family now so I'm sure he will want to write her a letter telling her about Floyd. The Bradshaws have a long history of producing many more females than males. Several times the line has been in real danger of dying out. Now, all of a sudden we're in excellent shape. Jesse and Valerie have two healthy sons and now we have your son as well. It's truly a cause for celebration and we mustn't fritter it away.'

Clara's spirit had unquestionably carried the day. It was a joyous dinner. The announcement of Floyd's existence was celebrated with enthusiasm and true emotion. And the feelings of that evening carried forward through the two weeks that Helen remained at Wingate Fields before flying home. Even Nora's cable in answer to Jesse's letter was warm and spontaneous.

> What glorious news. Can't wait to meet newest member of the Bradshaw clan.

Helen returned to America, therefore, in high spirits. As she waited to change planes in New York, she tried to call Paul at his apartment but the servant who answered said he was in Los Angeles for a few days.

As she flew on to Chicago and as she drove from the airport later to Port Beck she began making plans for the future, starting with another trip to Wingate Fields, perhaps in the late spring, this time taking Floyd along with her.

At home in Fort Beck, as though she'd willed it there, she found a long letter from Floyd, the first one she'd received in more than six months. And he enclosed some snapshots of himself, each one posed with, as he put it, 'a different vagabond dog'.

> It's a long time since I've written but I won't apologize because by now I guess you're used to my drawbacks. I've never been much good at writing letters and I've never tried very hard to get good at it. Abe Rettberg, the guy I've been staying with here in California, says I'm too easy on myself and I guess maybe he's right. He says any blockhead can write a letter. All you have to do is sit down and do it. So here I am. that's what I'm doing.
>
> Abe's an interesting guy. He's about fifty, I guess. A big belly and not much hair left. He was in the Navy during the First World War and lost most of his right arm. So he taught himself to do everything left-handed. When I met him in S.D. he was a bartender. He could throw a drunk out of the place quicker with one hand than most guys can with two. He had a big reputation with the navy guys. Nobody wanted to start anything with him. I got to know him because he had a couple of dogs, a mutt named Sadie who was part Shepherd and part Collie, and an Irish setter named Jake. I've always been nuts about dogs and those two dogs of Abe's decided they liked me. So that made Abe think I was all right too. I used to look him up when I had some free time and we'd go fishing or go to a ball game. Or his girlfriend, a big red-head called Billie, would cook us up a bunch of clams or a batch of lasagna. I wanted to get in touch with Abe when I got my discharge so I called the bar where he'd worked in Diego. They said he wasn't there any more but they gave me a number where I could reach him. It turned out he was living in the woods about seventy miles north-east of San Francisco. He and Billie had split up and he was by himself, he and the dogs, and he was working as a repair man and rough carpenter. I promised to come see him as soon as I left Yankton but a lot of time went past and by the time I got to California,

he was living at the north edge of Los Angeles in a place called Topanga Canyon. Lots of weirdos and winos and nutsy people there. But some good people too, folks without much money, raising chickens and growing their own vegetables, and getting by the best way they can. And quite a few vets and their wives, people my age. Abe got himself a bunch of bees and he's making out pretty well, selling combs of honey to fancy grocery stores in Santa Monica and Beverly Hills. He's also got some goats and he makes quite a bit of goat cheese. He sells that, too.

I've got a steady girlfriend now, a Mexican girl named Luisa. She came up here from Sonora three years ago to try to get some work in the movies but she hasn't had any breaks so far. She works as a waitress and sings a couple of times every night at a place called Las Hamacas in Culver City. She knows the two guys who own the place and she fixed it so I could work there too. I wear a suit and tie and a white shirt and I pretend I'm a host. Standing around smiling at the customers. But I'm really a bouncer. I guess you know what that is. When customers get crazy-drunk and start breaking things or slapping their wives around, this other guy and I, his name's Pulver, throw them out. As you can see, I'm taking myself seriously, preparing myself for the future. Joke! You probably won't believe it but I really like what I'm doing. Maybe I should say I like what I'm not doing. I hear other young guys talk about their work, about their jobs, and I think, 'Jesus, I'd go nuts if I had to sit behind a desk all day, nodding my head and saying "Yes, sir" to some dumbhead just because he happens to be my boss.' Or walking around with a sample case trying to sell things to people. Everybody seems to be selling something. That's the ticket. If you can sell enough stuff then you're in good shape. If you can't, you're out in the street. Nobody likes those jobs, I found out, but they all tell themselves they're working up to something, that *later on* everything's gonna be great. But when I ask them *when*, when I ask how *much* later, they just smile kinda funny and say they don't know. So *I* say those poor bastards are selling *themselves*, a little bit at a time, like a panful of meat. Somebody's kidding them about the big payoff down the line. But mostly they're kidding themselves. And I don't want to do that. I say if it's no good today, what makes you think it'll be worth a damn tomorrow? When somebody promises me something great my first question is, 'Oh yeah? What do I have to do to get it? What do I have to give up? Who do I have to turn into?' Nobody ever wants to answer those questions so I just keep walking down the street.

Do you know what I'm talking about? Most people don't. Even Abe, who's as independent as a hog on ice, thinks I'm nuts. When I showed him that picture of you, the one you sent me, he said, 'You're crazy. Go live with your mother. If I had a mother like that I'd still be at home, raking leaves and taking out the trash.' He said, 'Tell her when she gives up on *you*, there's a one-armed carpenter she can adopt.' He didn't mean it in a bad way. He just thinks you look nice and he knows you've been good to me whenever I showed up so he thinks I ought to give a little something in return.

That's why I'm writing. I may be screwed up and lazy but I'm not dumb. I know without being told that you thought once you found me, once we found each other, after all these years, that things would be different than they've turned out to be. I mean you'd be a regular mother to me and I'd be whatever a son is supposed to be to his mother after he's grown up. Stuff like that.

Now we both know that hasn't happened, not the way it might have. And I'm the one that has to take the blame. I don't know how much you've figured out about me but I don't change very quickly. It's not that I think I'm great the way I am. I just think I *am* the way I am. That doesn't mean I'll be the same the rest of my life. I've sure changed since I left home in Crawfordsville when I was eighteen. But it does mean I have something in my head about doing things my own way. I never expected to have an easy life but I'd like to have some say about it. I don't want to lose my vote. I'd rather have less and feel as if I was in control of it than have a lot more and no control at all. I need to run my own life even if I wreck it. How does this apply to you? I'm not sure. You've never made any demands on me at all. Not in any way I can remember. All you've done is *offer* things. And not asked for anything in return. But that's the problem. Right there. At least in my head. I just don't believe there are any free rides. I don't think anything comes without a price tag. That doesn't mean I don't trust *you*, I do. After I've spent some time with you I really come away feeling as if there really is a great, comfortable, free-wheeling life available to me. All I have to do is nod my head. And don't think that doesn't sound good to me. Of course it does. I'm not crazy. Even Abe doesn't think I'm crazy. He just thinks I'm stupid. But I'm not. I want most of the things that everybody else wants. I'd like to have nice wife and some kids and a big house and a couple of cars and a boat maybe and six dogs. But not if I have to give up too much for it. And here's the important thing. I need to know what I'm giving up before I make the leap. Abe tells me that's impossible. He says you have to take a chance. I don't mind that. I've taken lots of chances. But I don't want to find out when I'm thirty-five or forty years old that I gave something away that I can't get back. Abe says to me, 'What the hell have you *got* that's so important? As far as I can see, you've got nothing to lose.' Maybe he's right but I don't see it that way.

Now here's the hard part. I hate the idea of your not knowing what I'm up to or when I'm going to write or when we're going to see each other again. I don't *want* you to be waiting to hear from me. I don't want to foul up your life. So for now, maybe a year, maybe two, till I get some things straightened out for myself, till I've had a chance to shake off all that Navy crap and some of the bad stuff that went before, you're not going to hear from me. I mean, I'm not going to forget about you, not at all, but you shouldn't *count* on me. That's too much pressure for both of us right now.

I hope you understand what I'm trying to say. I'd hate to make you feel bad or hurt your feelings. Don't think it doesn't mean a lot to me that you went to the trouble of finding me. I'm not saying I didn't have some funny feelings about it at first but I never wanted you to go away, and I still don't. I've never written a love letter in my life and I wouldn't know how to start. But one thing I want you to know is — I'm *not* trying to get rid of you. If you wrote to me tomorrow and said to meet you in Denver or Kansas City or anywhere in ten days, then I'd be there. If you said things had to be *your* way or no way, then I guess I'd give in. But I don't think you'll feel that way about what I'm saying. At least I hope you won't.

When she finished reading the letter, all Helen could think of was the atmosphere she'd left at Wingate Fields, the excitement about Floyd, the eagerness to meet him, her own plans for taking him there, for driving him around Northumberland, for showing him things and places, for making him slowly aware of his identity and his heritage, as she had been made aware of hers when she was eighteen.

She sat down, read his letter again, tried to sort through her feelings about it, and found only bitter disappointment. She went into the library, sat down at her father's big desk took out a piece of stationery and quickly wrote a note.

Dear Floyd,

I've just read your letter and I want to give you my immediate reactions when they're still fresh.

I think you are being unbelievably selfish. As you know, as you said yourself, I have gone out of my way to make no demands on you. You're my son, my only child, and I love you. I've tried to show you that in the few times we've been together. I'm proud of you. I'm proud to be your mother. And I'd like to make you proud of me. But for God's sake, let's not talk about long periods of silence as though they were some sort of spiritual necessity. They're certainly *not* necessary for me. I'm hungry to see you whenever I can. Whatever may be lacking between us will certainly never be supplied by our not seeing each other. You're a very young man and I'm only eighteen years older than you are but *please*, let's not wait until one or both of us are doddering old creatures before we're able to look at each other with some kindness and understanding, and acknowledge that we love and respect each other. Don't spend years trying to anticipate what price you may have to pay. We've already paid the price. Both of us.

She put the note in an envelope, addressed it and stamped it. Heading for the post office, she was in her car, backing out of the driveway towards the street before her original flow of energy and decision subsided. She turned off the engine and sat looking across her garden trying to remember the exact words she'd just written. At last she got out of the car and went back into the house. At the desk in the library she slit open the envelope, took the letter out and read it carefully several times. At last she put it aside on the desk, took out a fresh sheet of paper, and began to write.

> I don't like the idea of not seeing you or hearing from you but I understand what you're saying. I'm glad to know that you have some standards and some principles and I'm proud of you for trying . . .

She sat staring at what she'd written. Then she put her pen down suddenly. 'Jesus, what am I doing?' she thought. '*That's* not the way I feel at all.'

She tore up the page she'd been writing on. Then she reread the first note she'd written, put it in a fresh envelope, and addressed it to Floyd. Before she could change her mind again she drove downtown to the post office and mailed it to him.

[3]

The day Floyd dumped his clothes and books in the back of a pick-up truck and moved from Topanga Canyon to an apartment on Motor Drive in Culver City, his friend Abe said, 'Mark this date down in your day-book, pistol-head, because sooner or later you're going to say to yourself, "That's when I made my big mistake." '

'Come on, Abe, don't give me that stuff. You always said you'd be glad to get rid of me.'

'I *am*. Ever since you fell in with that little Mexican bonbon.'

'She's got a name, Abe. *Luisa*. You know it as well as *I* do.'

'That don't matter. I'm just saying that ever since you started up with her you ain't been worth a damn to anybody, including yourself.'

'Like I said, if that's the way you feel, you'll be glad to have me off your hands.'

'We're not talking about what's good for *me*, knucklehead. We're talking about *you*. I just hate to see you get your tail in a crack.'

'I can take care of myself. Don't worry about me.'

'I know that old song,' Abe said. 'I've heard it over and over. I'll bet over a hundred guys have said those exact same words to me. And over half of them are dead now.'

'What's that have to do with anything?'

'It might have a lot to do with *you*. All those guys were just as cocksure as you are.'

'Listen, Abe, let's face it. You don't like Mexicans. I'm working in a Mexican gin-mill and living with a Mexican girl so you think I'm going to hell in a hand-basket. Isn't that it?'

'No, that's not it. You think I never crawled into the sack with a Mexican chick? I lived in Tampico for three years when I was younger than you. I like Mexicans and they like me. But I like them in Mexico. The ones that come up here to live in California are a different tribe altogether. And that gang in Culver City is the worst of the bunch.'

'What are you talking about? You've been to the club where I work a dozen times. You've sat down and had a drink with the people I work for. What's the problem? What are you talking about?'

'I'm talking about a club that's crowded two or three nights a week and the rest of the time you could fire a shotgun in there and not draw a drop of blood. There's more owners and waiters and bouncers and bartenders than there are customers. So I say how are all those cats making a living? They all dress good and drive big cars and a lot of money gets flashed around. Nobody made that money from selling tacos and a few bottles of Carta Blanca. Think it over.'

'I don't have to think it over. It's none of my business. I just work there. I put in my hours and I go home and that's *it*. I'm not moving into the club, for Christ's sake. I'm moving into an apartment.'

'Don't get hot with me, buddy. I'm not telling you where to live. I'm just telling you to keep your eyes open. Why do you think they hired you there in the first place? You're the only guy in the joint that don't have brown skin and brown eyes . . .'

'There you go again.'

'Listen to me. What do they want with a blue-eyed hayshaker from South Dakota or Indiana or wherever you came from? What do they need with you?'

'You tell me.'

'I *can't* tell you. That's my point. And you can't tell *me*.'

'Sure I can. They hired me because Luisa introduced me.'

'No, she didn't. Her brother took you in there. Estéban, the pretty boy. And does anybody know what he does for a living?'

'He's a printing salesman. Sells all kinds of business cards and stuff.'

'My ass,' Abe said. 'If he can read English, I'll kiss your foot. He's a hustler. I guarantee it. A little something going here. A little something going there. Everybody's friend. Handing out cigarettes. Always a handful of tickets to the ball game. He's trouble. I'm telling you. Turn your back and he's sold your suit.'

'I'm not living with Estéban. I'm living with his sister.'

'That's another problem. Those Mexicans don't like guys doing naughty things with their sisters. They're the only people I know of that don't pray to God. They pray to the Virgin. Does that tell you something?'

'No. Who do *you* pray to, Abe?'

Abe grinned. 'I think I'm part Navajo. I pray to the Rain God for a good corn crop so there'll be plenty of cheap bourbon in the stores. And I pray there'll be plenty of aspirin so I can doctor my headache after I drink all that bourbon.' Then he said, 'Forget it, kid. Don't pay any attention to me. I don't want you to leave here with a bad taste in your mouth. You want a dog to take with you? Take Jake. Jake'll follow you straight to hell if you scratch his head once a day.'

'Thanks, Abe. I wish I could take him but Luisa already has a dog.'

'That's not a dog, for Christ's sake, that little squirt of a thing she carries around with her. That's a rat in a dog suit.'

'You're right. I don't like it either. But she likes it.'

'Jake would eat that yippy little mutt in one bite. One gulp and that little pain-in-the-ass would be gone.'

'I know it,' Floyd said. 'And so does Luisa. That's why I can't take him with me.'

Just before Floyd pulled away in his truck, Abe said, 'You're wrong about me wanting to get rid of you. It was good to have you around here and you're welcome back any time. Luisa's a pretty little girl and I hope you two have some fun together. And don't get the idea I'm trying to steer you off Mexicans. I'm not. You're a decent kid with more guts than sense and I just don't want to see you get burned. Fair enough?'

'Fair enough, Abe.'

'You keep in touch now.'

'I'll do it. You'll be hearing from me.'

'Maybe I'll come over to the club some night and get drunk and raise hell. Then you can throw me out. I've been tossed out of lots of joints but never by a buddy.'

'That's a deal, Abe. I'll throw you clear across Washington Boulevard.'

[4]

When Helen told Frank about the letter she'd received from Floyd and what she'd written in reply, he said, 'Are you asking me for advice?'

'No. I was just telling you what I did.'

'Oh, I see. I thought you wanted me to tell you you did the right thing.'

'What's the matter with you?' she said.

'Nothing. What do you mean?'

'You know what I mean. What's going through your head? It's like you're thinking one thing and saying something else.'

'I never do that,' he said.

'I know you don't. But you're doing it now.'

'You're awfully edgy, aren't you? What's the matter with *you?*'

'I'm reacting to you. If I'm edgy you're making me that way.'

'I don't think so,' he said. 'You're upset about your son.'

'You never call him Floyd. Are you aware of that?'

'Well, we're not exactly on a first-name basis. I've never set eyes on him.'

'You could have,' Helen said. 'I asked you to have dinner with us one time.'

'I know you did. I couldn't make it.'

'That's not what you told me then. You said you thought it wasn't such a great idea. *Awkward*. I think that's the word you used.'

'Did I?'

'Yes. You thought it would be awkward, you said.'

'Well, be that as it may . . .'

'You never made clear if it would be awkward for you or Floyd or me.'

'All of us, I imagine.'

'*I* didn't think it would be awkward,' she said. 'I wanted you to meet him and I wanted him to meet you.'

'Well, it doesn't matter now, does it?'

'I suppose not. What matters is that I think you resent him.'

'Why would I resent him?' Frank asked.

'You'll have to answer that. You've been strange about it ever since I first told you about him.'

'I wasn't aware of that.'

'It's as though you think if we never talk about him he'll cease to exist.'

'It seems to me we talk about him quite a lot.'

'And you resent it. That's what I'm saying.'

'I know what you're saying but I don't think it's true.'

'Is it because I never told you about him when we were married?'

'I didn't know it then so it couldn't bother me.'

'But it bothers you now,' she said.

'I don't think so. You just surprise me every now and then and I suppose I react without thinking. You can't pretend that your life is filled with simple open relationships. You have Jesse who's like a brother but who's not *quite* your brother, you have a half-brother in New York who *is* a brother in a sense. But on the other hand you barely know him. And then there's Floyd. He *is* your son but he's *not* your son.'

She smiled. 'And I have a darling, attentive lover who just happens to be my ex-husband.'

'You see what I mean? All the men in your life have dangling participles and qualifying clauses. None of us are exactly what we seem to be.'

'Speak for yourself,' she said.

'And I won't even begin to diagnose *you*.'

'I appreciate that.' She leaned over and kissed him. 'I

guess maybe I'd understand it if you resented Floyd. But I hope you don't.'

'Resentment's not the word. I think he acts like a jackass toward you.'

'How do you expect him to be?'

'That's beside the point,' Frank said. 'How do *you* expect him to be?'

'I try not to expect too much.'

'Then you should be happy. Because that's what you're getting.'

'We all settle for less than we want, don't we?'

'That sounds like a trap to me. I don't think I'll fall into it.'

'You think I'm about to discuss *our* situation?'

'I didn't *say* that,' he said.

'You didn't have to. That was the message I got.' Then, 'The fact is I think you and I have exactly what we bargained for. I never complain, do I?'

'No. You never do.'

'You manage to make *that* sound like a complaint.'

'Not at all. Any guy I know would be happy to have what I have.'

'You mean a wife and children at home and a nice girlie on the side?'

'No, I don't mean that. I'm just talking about us. I meant any man would be happy to have a woman like you.'

'Warm and loving. Available when needed and never complaining.'

'That's a pretty good description,' he said.

'Never mind what *any* man would be happy with. How about you?'

'You want the truth?'

'Of course I do.'

'Sometimes I wish you'd say you want more,' he said.

'That wasn't our deal.'

'Did we have a deal?' he asked.

'Not a signed document. But a clear understanding. You made quite a speech about it. Your life was like an intricate corporation, one that couldn't be dissolved. Wasn't that it?'

'Something like that. Sounds pretty stuffy to me now.'

She smiled again. 'It sounded stuffy then. But it did the job. It made our ground-rules very clear. And it's a tribute to both of us that we've never tried to change them. That's why we've had a good time together. That's why we're still having a good time. We made a grown-up choice and we've stuck to it.'

'A kind of limited partnership.'

'I guess you could call it that. Limited in some ways. Totally unlimited in others.'

'Free to come and go. Always welcome back. No questions asked.'

'That sounds a little more libertine than I like. I've never assumed that you and your wife lived like strangers when you're home but I'd be mad as hell if you thought I had other men lolling about when *you're* not with *me*.'

'I don't think that,' he said.

'But all the same, that wasn't part of our understanding.'

'Of course not.'

She kissed him on the cheek. 'Character is fate.' Then, 'We got off the subject of Floyd.'

'Yes, I guess we did.'

'I don't want to beat this to death but you're the only person I can ask. After I sent that letter off to him, answering *his* letter, I had a lot of second thoughts. I thought maybe I was too tough. What do you think?'

'I think you should forget your second thoughts. What you wrote *wasn't* too tough. If anything it wasn't tough enough.'

[5]

As Clara had suggested he might, Jesse did indeed write a letter to Nora telling her about Floyd. Including discreet details about the circumstances of his birth, the identity of his father, and the adoption process, explaining that Helen had just now chosen to tell the family of his existence. Since it seemed to have no relevance, Jesse did not reveal in the letter that he himself had known of Floyd's existence for several years.

Because of some flaw in her own character perhaps, Nora assumed as she reread Jesse's letter that Helen had lied, not about the fact of her son but about the identity of his father. Noting Floyd's birthdate in the letter she counted backwards and came to the immediate conclusion that Jesse was the father of Helen's son. No other scenario made sense to her. Certainly not the shop-girl's tale of a romantic interlude on board ship with an unidentified young man who had since died.

On the other hand, some quirk in her nature made Nora take pleasure in the assumption that while Jesse was welcoming *her* into his bed every night at Wingate Fields he was also managing somehow to continue his affair with Helen, one that had started, Nora believed, long before their coming to England, sometime during Helen's adolescent years in Fort Beck, either before her father's death or after. She believed also that this relationship had continued all through the years she herself had lived with Jesse and that it continued still, as a kind of melodramatic backdrop to the marriage of Jesse and Valerie.

Another woman might have been enraged by this development which, in Nora's mind at least, proved that her suspicions through the years were in fact true. She, however, felt vindicated and triumphant. And her condescension towards Helen turned suddenly to a kind of admiration. The woman she had always called Baby Helen had become someone altogether new and different. A worthy adversary. And Jesse, of course, took on new outlines also.

Jesse's letter, in fact, redefined everything for Nora. Even the fact that the letter came from *him*, in his handwriting, seemed to have significance for her. It was as though, with this announcement about Floyd, he was telling her that he was about to re-enter her life. And Helen, in some odd and unpredictable way, was making it possible. Nora's assumption that Floyd was Jesse's child, her further assumption that Jesse and Helen had been lovers for as long as she had known them, also put Valerie's marriage in a new light. Nora told herself that Valerie would very probably draw the same conclusions that she herself had drawn about Floyd. And even if she didn't she was certain before long to see the truth about Jesse and Helen. In either case, her marriage to Jesse would founder. Having made that assumption, Nora quickly made another one. For her daughter's sake, the sooner her marriage ended, the better off she would be.

Having chosen a long-term strategy, however, Nora was content to bide her time. She sent off the cable acknowledging receipt of Jesse's letter. Then she contemplated, at leisure and with a great amount of joy, her future. A few weeks after receiving his note she dictated a crisp and businesslike letter to her secretary and sent it off to Jesse.

> I know how involved you are with your life at Wingate Fields so I think I already know the answer to the question I'm about to ask. But I will ask it anyway.
>
> As I mentioned to you when I saw you in England, as soon as I began to publish *Icarus* again in Paris I began getting mail asking when your critical pieces would resume in the magazine. A few people asked if you had been killed during the war.
>
> As you know from the copies I send regularly to Valerie, I have not replaced you with a permanent critical voice. Instead, I've had a number of people writing those articles. Now, however, I have decided that we need someone who will give us a consistent tone, someone whose style is as snotty and hateful as yours.
>
> I have several people in mind but before I make a choice and a long-term commitment I want to be absolutely sure that you've truly given up the ghost. As I've said, I assume that you have. If by some miracle you *haven't*, then I would welcome you back on whatever terms might seem proper and reasonable to you.
>
> Let me emphasize that your presence here in Paris would not be required. There are plenty of people who can handle the local art and theatre scene for me. You would write, as you always did, from a wider perspective, as a kind of contemporary historian, if you will, of the arts.
>
> This is not a matter that requires a fast decision. After you've had some time to think it over let me know how you're leaning. I won't go ahead with someone new until I've heard from you.

[6]

Soon after the family celebration of Floyd's newly announced existence, as the matter was discussed in detail, it came out, of course, that Jesse had played a key role in helping Helen find her son in San Diego.

'I'm surprised you never told me about it before this,' Valerie said to him one evening.

'I wanted to but I'm sure you can see why I couldn't.'

'I suppose I can see why you thought you couldn't.'

'I really couldn't. It was Helen's secret. It was a vital and painful part of her life. There was no reason for me to tell anyone. And I had no right to in any case.'

Valerie smiled. 'Do you have all sorts of other little secrets that are going to pop up through the years?'

'I don't think of this as a secret. Helen never swore me to secrecy. I just thought of it as a piece of information that had been entrusted to me as a friend.'

'That's what a secret is,' Valerie said.

'Maybe you're right. But what I'm saying is, it wasn't my secret. I had no personal stake in whether it became known or not.'

'Did you think it would become known if you told me?'

'I never even thought about that. I simply never considered telling you or anyone else.'

After a moment she said, 'Do you think I have secrets that you don't know about?'

'I've never thought about that either.'

'Well, think about it for a moment.'

'Let me put it this way. I have certainly never expected you to recite to me all the actions and thoughts of your lifetime, and if you volunteered to do so, I think I would prefer that you didn't. So whether we call them secrets or information gaps, I'm sure there are some. I don't *need* to know every single thing about you, past or present. I love you but I have no impulse to dissect you.'

'I think you're manipulating me.' she said.

'Not deliberately.'

'Of course not. You're just clever. You can't help it.'

'You know what I think of clever people,' he said.

'Of course I do. And you're usually not clever at all. You're smart and wise and concise. But sometimes you're clever in spite of yourself. I think it's a defence mechanism with you.'

'What am I defending?'

'I'm not sure. Helen, I suppose. You often get quite defensive when the conversation turns to her.'

'Why do you think I would do that?' he said.

'I don't know.'

'Neither do I. I don't see her as someone who needs to be defended.'

'Neither do I,' Valerie said. Then, 'Do you believe that story about some young man she met on the ship — that he's Floyd's father but she never saw him or heard from him again, and now he's conveniently dead.'

'Why wouldn't I believe it?'

'I mean, did you believe it when you first heard it, when she first told you about it?'

'I don't see what you're getting at. Why would she lie?'

'I don't know,' Valerie said.

'And what's the difference if she did? It doesn't really matter who the boy's father is, does it?'

'I guess not. I was just wondering if that's a secret, too. I thought maybe Helen told you a different story from the one she told us.'

'Why would you think that? Why make a mystery of something that's very simple?'

'I don't *want* to,' Valerie said. 'I hate mysteries. I like to know the way things really are.'

'It's an old story, it seems to me. A young girl is going to have a baby and she's not married. What does she do about it?'

'That's exactly what I'm talking about. Don't you think Helen made some strange choices?'

'Of course I do,' Jesse said, 'but hindsight makes a genius out of everybody.'

In her conversation with Clara, Valerie came more abruptly to the point. 'Can I tell you something in total confidence?' she asked.

'Of course you can.'

'What would you say if I told you that I think Jesse's the father of Helen's son?'

Clara smiled. 'I'd say you've been listening to your mother too much. Nora always believed there was a great romance going on between Jesse and Helen.'

'I believe it, too. Not now, but some time.'

'Well, I was never able to persuade Nora and I'm sure I couldn't persuade you. All I say to you is — what if it were true, what difference would it make now?'

'It shouldn't make any difference,' Valerie said, 'but it does. Some people say things like that never end.'

'Only unmarried people say things like that. And they're

wrong. If that were true, then a lot of married women would still be in love with their husbands.'

Valerie smiled. 'Shame on you. Are you saying they're not?'

'I'm saying a few lucky ones are. Most of them are not.'

'I think you're trying to change the subject.'

'No, I'm not,' Clara said. 'I've had this conversation with your mother a dozen times so I'm an expert at it. I don't believe that Helen and Jesse were ever in love in the way you mean, but *if* they were, what difference does it make?'

'It would make a difference to me if I knew they had a child together.'

'Why?'

'I don't know. It just would.'

'You know that Jesse's a great deal older than you are. He hasn't lived in a monastery all his life.'

'I know. He lived with Nora.'

'Apart from that,' Clara said, 'it must have occurred to you that somewhere, in America or England or France, there might be a few toddlers who look like Jesse.'

'That's not what I'm talking about. This is different.'

'Because it's Helen?'

'Maybe,' Valerie said.

Clara shook her head. 'You and your mother seem to have the same extraordinary attitude towards Helen. I've never understood it. She's an attractive young woman, civilized and kind. But in Nora's mind she seems to walk around in silk nightgowns and bare feet with gold loops in her ears, scarlet lips and great daubs of rouge on her cheeks.'

'There's nothing like that in my mind,' Valerie said. 'I just know that she and Jesse are very close, they've always been close, and I can't help wondering sometimes how close they are.'

'Do you honestly believe that since you've been married, Jesse has been having a fling with Helen or with anyone else?'

'No. I don't think that. If I thought that I couldn't stay with him.'

'Well, maybe you could and maybe you couldn't. I don't think you'll ever have to make that decision,' Clara said. 'But getting back to your original question, I guarantee you that Jesse is not Floyd's father.'

'Clara, you're darling. I know what you're trying to do,

but how can you guarantee that? How do you know Helen told the truth?'

'I know things about Helen that you don't know, things that would mean nothing to you if you did know them. And I absolutely know, as surely as I know my own name, that Helen's child is in no way connected with Jesse.'

[7]

Paul Buscatore's protestations to his father that he was a solitary operator, that he had no connection with any organization of any description, had been absolutely true. But since that conversation he had become more prosperous than he had ever imagined. Inept but enthusiastic gamblers with great sums of money to lose had his name and telephone number tattooed on their wrists, it seemed. And since the war he discovered there were games and betting parlours to be found in every large city, many of them in private clubs that were allowed to operate outside the local laws, or with the approval of the local law enforcers. These games were like social affairs, by invitation only. Usually he was the only professional gambler there. He never asked why, but one time a member of the Pickwick Club in Chicago explained it to him. 'You make it fun. We all know you're a pro and we're out to beat you. When we lose, at least we know we lost to somebody good. It's all a write-off anyway. We're gambling with government money.'

A weather-beaten wildcatter in Wichita, a man who'd made several fortunes in oil and lost them all playing cards, had a better explanation. 'These birds in Kansas know that when they go to New York, all they have to do is call you and you'll find them some clean action. So they're returning the favour when they ask you out here. None of us likes to lose but if we have to we don't mind it so much if it's you who's winning.'

So Paul was travelling a lot and he was winning a lot. But he stayed away from Reno and Las Vegas and all the hot games in New Jersey and New York. Remembering his friend's advice, he made a handsome living but never tried to make a killing. After a successful two or three months he always took a vacation. He'd telephone a charming lady and they'd go to Havana for three weeks. Paul would dance and drink and play the wheel like a tourist. But he made money there too.

In New York he dressed like a broker, stayed away from night-clubs, and drove a Daimler. He treated whores like ladies and ladies like whores so he was loved and respected by both whores and ladies. He avoided big parties. He hosted only small, quiet dinners at his home or in a private dining room of an elegant restaurant. He never socialized with the people he gambled with and the people he did socialize with were too well bred to wonder where he got his money. When he couldn't avoid a bridge game in someone's town-house or during a Connecticut weekend he always played badly and lost. This annoyed his partners but delighted Paul.

He was proud of his achievements, of course, and pleased about his social success. But most of all he was proud of his anonymity. He truly believed that he had carved out a double life for himself with two totally separate lists of acquaintances; each group knew him and accepted him, but neither knew anything whatsoever about him. In every niche of his life he was, as he had told his father, a private contractor.

In the fall of 1949, however, on a flight from New Orleans to New York, a grey-haired man sitting beside him on the plane said, 'I'm Mike Rosenthal. I'm an attorney from New York.'

Paul shook hands with him and said, 'I'm Paul Buscatore.'

'I know who you are,' Rosenthal said. 'That's why I'm sitting here.' Then, 'I'm not going to play games with you, Mr Buscatore. I know exactly what you do for a living and I have a pretty good idea how much money you make every year.'

'You're not with Internal Revenue, are you?'

'No, but I know you're clean. You pay your taxes like a good citizen.'

'I have an expert accountant,' Paul said.

'George Klein. I've known him for years.'

'Did he put you on to me?'

'No. And I'd appreciate it if you didn't tell him I've talked to you.'

'Why not?' Paul asked.

'Just a personal thing. Nothing that involves you.'

'I think it does involve me. I don't like to sit down on a plane beside a stranger and find out he knows things about my business life that I don't want people to know.'

'None of us lives in a cocoon, Paul. *Somebody's* got a tap on everybody. When you start to succeed, when you come up in the world, people notice. People pay attention. And sometimes they like what they see and want to help out.'

'No, thanks.'

'What does that mean? I didn't offer you anything.'

'I know you didn't. But I didn't hatch out of an egg. I know what you're leading up to. And I don't want any help. I don't need it and I don't want it.'

'Everybody needs help.'

'Not me,' Paul said.

'Well, maybe you're right.' Then, 'Let me ask you a question. Do you mind if I ask you a question?'

'I don't promise to answer.'

'Of course not,' Rosenthal said. 'No promises expected.' He lit a cigarette, taking his time. 'If I said your net income the past six months was about a hundred and twenty percent higher than it was the six months before, what would you say?'

'I'd say, "So what?" '

'What if I said that your income for the next six months was going to be four times higher than it was for all of last year, what would you say to *that?*'

'I'd say you know more than I do.'

'That's right. I do.'

'Good for you. You should open a booth out at Brighton Beach and tell old ladies' fortunes.'

Rosenthal smiled. 'A couple of years from now, when you and I are having a drink together at the Sherry Netherlands, I'll remind you that we had this conversation.'

'And what will I say?'

'I don't know. Let's wait and see.'

'That's fine with me,' Paul said. 'I'll meet you in the Sherry Netherlands bar two years from today.'

'I think I'll see you before then. I plan to get in touch with you in six months to see if my prediction comes true.'

'What if it does?'

'Then maybe we can talk business. I have some important clients I'd like you to meet.'

Paul shook his head. 'I don't like to meet important people and I don't like to talk business with a stranger.'

'Then you don't have to. I get paid to persuade people, not to pressure them.'

'Good. In that case we'll get along fine.'

'I'm going to take a nap now,' Rosenthal said. 'I fly all the time but planes scare me to death. The only way I can lick it is to take a couple of pills and put myself out for the whole trip. But before I go to sleep I want to say just one more thing. There's no such thing as a one-man business any more. Maybe if you're living in Topeka or Seattle you can go it alone. But even there, once you start to take off, once you get successful, you need help. You need people to back you up, handle details, count the money, all sorts of little things like that. A man who tries to do it all by himself is sure to fail, one way or the other. You know what I mean? I guess you don't. But six months from now, you will.'

[8]

On his birthday, in January of 1950, Jesse sat quietly in the library after everyone else had gone to bed. He did not methodically list his many good fortunes. He simply sat with his brandy in the dimly-lit book-lined room and felt very good about himself and his life. If he *had* made such a list, if he'd written it fully and candidly for his own eyes only, it might very well have read like this:

> I am fifty-three years old today, in excellent health and fine spirits, truly in the prime of my life. When I look at this handsome house, when I walk through its magnificent grounds and realize that this is my home and will be the home of my children and *their* children, when I compare all this with the upstairs flat in Chicago where I lived with my parents when I was a boy, when I compare *my* life now with the petty, small-minded lives *they* led, I feel fortunate indeed.
>
> I have proved to myself that I'm capable of earning my keep. If things had gone in a different direction I

believe I could have become quite prosperous from my own efforts. I was never attracted to the world of commerce but I think I could have functioned successfully there. Consequently, I feel no guilt about my present circumstances. I became wealthy by the stroke of a pen. When Angus Bradshaw adopted me he freed me from any previous concerns I may have had about making my way. I am rich, my wife is rich, and my children will be rich. However that money was accumulated through the centuries, by whatever means, it is now simply there for us to use, depend on, and enjoy.

My greatest wealth, however, is this family. Here among the Bradshaws, I've found my closest friends, perhaps my only friends. Raymond first, of course, and Helen. Then Angus and Clara and Nora and Valerie. And now my three children, Rab and Polly and William. If someone accused me of living in a cocoon, of separating myself from the outside world I would plead guilty. My only defence would be that everything I need or want is here. In this house, in these gardens, and on the moors. I've never imagined that I could escape old age or death but I have no fear of being old or dying at Wingate Fields.

No man's life, of course, can be encapsulated. But such an entry in some ledger would have told no lies. Jesse did indeed consider himself fortunate. He loved the facts and the foundations of his life and all its small details. The people who lived with him and people who met him for the first time were strikingly aware of his state of well-being. He wore it like a garment, not a bright costume calling attention to itself but a comfortable well-worn thing that had lasted through the years and would continue to last and be worn for as many years as it might be needed.

So much for Jesse's assessment of himself and for the image he presented to others. Cynics and psychiatrists tell us there is no such thing as a truly contented man. Gogol said, 'Men who pretend to be happy should be confined to an appropriate institution.' Luther Elfant, a psychologist specializing in marital relations tells us, 'All husbands believe their wives are content. Those wives, who are seldom content, believe that their husbands are as discontented as *they* are.' Whatever the truth of these observations, the second one, in particular, seems to have some relevance in Jesse's case. It was Valerie who called to his attention that he was not so contented as he believed.

'I have no idea what you're talking about.' he said.

'Of course you do. You may not want to discuss it with me or even admit it to yourself but it's very obvious, not to everyone perhaps, but certainly to me, that the Garden of Eden we were determined to create by returning to Wingate Fields has become something quite different for you.'

'You're really amazing sometimes. You were the one who suggested we should leave here and go back to America.'

'I know I did. But that was a temporary thing with me. A little emotional snowstorm. Right after the memorial service for Ned, when Nora had been acting like such a pill . . . you know what I mean.'

'No, I don't. You were determined to move back to Boston and have twenty more children.'

'I know I was. But I've discovered that raising three is quite a handful. Besides, I'm only twenty-nine. Perhaps in a year or two we'll decide to have a second brood. But not, I think, if you're still in the state of mind you seem to be in now.'

'We're back to that,' Jesse said.

'It seems to amuse you.'

'It doesn't amuse me at all. As I said, I don't know what in God's name you're talking about.'

'I've mentioned this before and you know I have. I think you're too stubborn to admit it to yourself but you're not cut out to be a country squire. I think you're restless and bored and you don't know what to do with yourself.'

'I'm busy from morning till night,' he said.

'Of course you are. You're very good at making activities for yourself. But it's all a sham.'

'Do you think this place runs itself?'

'Yes, I do, as a matter of fact. It operated quite well before we came back and it would continue to operate if we were not here.'

'Is that what this is all about . . . you'd still like to move away?'

'No. I told you, that was a temporary thing. I don't ever want to leave here now. But if it's not good for you . . .'

'It's exactly what I expected when we came back here. It's what we talked about. It's fine for us, it's fine for the children, and I've begun writing again.'

Valerie smiled. 'Not exactly, darling. A little critical essay every month or so for *Icarus*. That's not really extending yourself.'

'What are you suggesting I do?'

'I'm not suggesting anything. You asked me why I feel you're discontented and I'm trying to tell you.'

'I think this is a frustrating and pointless discussion. Why don't we stop it before one of us gets angry.'

'*I* won't get angry. We needn't talk about it if you don't want to. But it's a discussion we'll have to have sooner or later.'

'Later is better as far as I'm concerned. And *never* is best of all.'

She shook her head. 'You can fool yourself if you like. But you can't fool me. There's something storming about inside your head and until it comes out things will be difficult for us.'

'Nothing's difficult for *me*,' he said. 'Only this ridiculous conversation is difficult. I don't know what it's all about.'

'Of course you do, Jesse. Of course you do.'

He did know, of course. He knew precisely. But he was unsettled by the fact that she sensed something he had tried very hard to keep from her. The truth was he was eager to be as contented with his life as he told himself he was, and as he had indeed been until recent months. Even now he felt that his unquiet moments were transient, that everything was basically as it had always been and so it would remain. But his restlessness, his uneasiness, grew heavier and more persistent. If his thoughts had occasionally wandered before, he now went through long periods where he barely heard the conversations at table between Valerie and Clara, when he found himself standing in the garden for long empty moments, staring out across the fields, when he rode his horse for hours across the moors, the wind in his face, his mind as blank as the terrain around him.

If he could have put a label on what he felt or what it was he was unable to feel, it would have helped him. If he could have branded Valerie as an inattentive wife, one who had involved herself with her children to such a degree that she had forgotten his existence, if he could have told himself that country life and country society had become tiresome and repetitive, if he could have coughed and wheezed and cursed the Northumberland winters — any of these things would have given focus to his malaise. But his fundamental integrity would not permit him to so deceive himself. He could not find fault with what he had, he could not pretend that he loved his wife or his children or his home less than before. He could only say, when he saw an occasional flash of light through the haze, that he wanted *more*, that he craved something else, that he needed to identify himself in new ways, to *use* himself. To be better than he was.

While they were living still in Boston, planning ahead to England, he and Valerie had discussed endlessly the projects he would take up once they were settled in at Wingate Fields. They had agreed that he should embark on the books and surveys and anthologies he had planned to do for years. Now at last he would have the time and the peace and the freedom to begin and to finish those ventures.

He had indeed had the time, as it turned out. And the handsome office and private library that Clara had fitted out for him years before were still waiting for him. But just as no tangible work had come out of those rooms before, none came out now. He discussed ideas and projects and concepts with Valerie now, just as he had once discussed them with Clara. And Valerie listened as patiently as Clara had done. Only when he mentioned one day that he was considering a monograph on Piero della Francesca did she say, 'Do you realize you've been toying with that notion since before I was born? I think perhaps you may have gone a little stale on *that* one.' Only that one time did she say anything to him that was less than encouraging. But all the same, after that, he was slow to discuss his ideas with her, perhaps in part because his ideas became fewer and fewer. His hours at the desk produced pages of scratches and squibbles but very little more.

When he responded to Nora's suggestion that he write again for *Icarus*, he had a flurry of energy that lasted a few weeks but then began to subside. He managed to turn out an occasional respectable review or a skilfully disguised rehash of something he had written before the war but it was a struggle for him. And the results, he knew without being told, were feeble. The cutting edge that had characterized his work before was gone. The acid had turned to porridge. Nora, however, wrote to him regularly, praising his work. And Clara and Valerie read each piece carefully and discussed it positively in Jesse's presence. But he knew that what he was writing was tiresome and empty, and he was aware that *they* knew it.

After his conversation with Valerie a great amount of his solitary time was spent in trying to find answers to a problem whose existence he had previously refused to acknowledge. His dissatisfactions with his work were only a part of his general discontent but they were, he concluded, an integral part. As he reviewed the time, years before, when he had lived at Wingate as a bachelor, recently adopted and elevated to the role of young master of the manor, as he remembered those months of solitary work which had produced nothing concrete or in any way worthy of the time spent, he compared that time with his present inability to function and concentrate in any worthwhile way. Then he compared both those periods with the days in Paris and New York when he had found a subject everywhere he turned, when he had also found the energy and the curiosity to develop it and finish it. Where was that energy now and why couldn't he tap it at will?

Like many creative people who are not truly creative, Jesse was a tireless reader and a memorizer of the details of other writers' lives, their personal quirks, their sources of inspiration, and their work habits, especially their work habits. He devoured all the material he could find about Shaw and Henry James, Thoreau and Thomas Paine, trying to find parallels with himself and his own critical voice, trying always to isolate his shortcomings and overcome them. At last, applying a system of deductive reasoning that served his needs better than it served the truth, he began to draw conclusions. Thoreau was a man who functioned well in isolation. Shaw, on the other hand, had left Ireland and gone to London, had thrust himself into the centre of the life there and had found a stimulus for his plays and his criticism. Henry James, too, had deliberately transplanted himself into a turbulent and foreign society, and had profited from it, it seemed, in both the quality of his work and impressive productivity. Paine, Jesse decided, was a different case. But there was a parallel. His political and social convictions, and the turbulence they supplied in his life and in his thinking, had stimulated his work and had in fact *become* his work. Without trying to put too fine a point on it, Jesse concluded that he was not a man who worked well in isolation, however benevolent the circumstances might be. He believed now that the energy and the turmoil of cities like Paris and London and New York, the quality of life in such places, the frustrations and pressures of meeting deadlines, facing challenges, simply surviving in such communities, had provided the stimulus for his best work. He had built his professional reputation by puncturing inflated egos, by questioning the true value of acknowledged masterpieces, by daring to go against accepted credos. He'd been accused of using acid in his pen, and other critics had begun to emulate him. But as he stood in the peaceful fields of Northumberland, he felt no such impulse to flail about him and draw blood.

Telling himself that the answer, as it related to him, could not be that simple, he continued to examine and question the proposition. But examination only strengthened it. What had been a kind of general unrest now became a specific discomfort. He had gone from a vague suspicion that he was wedged into an escapeproof box to a certain knowledge of it. Since, in his circumstances, escape was out of the question, he had only one option: to accept his circumstances and live with them as peacefully and quietly as possible.

These were not instant conclusions, of course. They came to him, slowly and painfully, over a period of time. He tried in fact to prevent them from becoming final and irrevocable in his mind. But at last the strain of trying to suspend himself between what he wanted to be true and what he *knew* was true was something he was no longer willing or able to deal with. He sat down one morning and wrote a note to Nora in Paris.

> I've given my situation a lot of thought lately and I've come to the conclusion that my interests and duties here at Wingate Fields do not leave me the time to write the way I want to. So I feel that I must stop trying to ride two horses. If I felt my retirement from the field would in any way damage *Icarus* I would, perhaps, try to find some different solution. But I *don't* feel that way. There are dozens of angry and hungry young buckos, I'm sure, who are standing by, eager to annihilate Stendhal, Maillol, Camus, or anyone else who seems to have an unassailable reputation. I remember those days in Paris with fondness, when we were struggling to bring out our first issues. But now, I feel, it's time for me to bow out.

Valerie, when he told her what he'd done, said, 'I hope you know what you're doing. In my opinion you don't cure a broken leg by deliberately breaking the other leg.'

When Nora received his letter she cabled him a two-word reply: *You're bonkers.*

[9]

In early April of 1950 a late snowstorm fell in Chicago. After dark it turned to freezing rain. Driving south on Lake Shore Drive at eleven that night, returning with Helen from a week in Milwaukee, Frank's car hit a patch of ice, sideswiped the car heading south in the lane beside him, ripped across the highway divider and smashed head-on into a light delivery truck.

The driver of the truck was killed instantly. Frank and Helen were taken to Passavant Hospital a short distance down the Drive. Frank with a fractured skull and a shattered pelvis, Helen with a broken ankle, a broken wrist and concussion.

The following morning an item appeared on the business pages of the *Chicago Tribune*, reporting that Frank Wilson, a prominent real-estate investor, had been injured in an automobile accident. It described his injuries as multiple fractures and said he was being treated at a near northside hospital. It gave the name of the dead truck-driver and went on to say that a passenger in Wilson's car, Helen Bradshaw of Fort Beck, Illinois, was also being treated for multiple fractures.

Either by chance or because someone so instructed the hospital, Helen and Frank, following surgery, were put in private rooms, on different floors, in separate wings of Passavant. As soon as he was able to be moved, an ambulance took Frank to another hospital not far from his home in Lake Forest. Helen, whose injuries were less critical, had been transferred, at her request, to the Fort Beck Hospital three days earlier.

Her housekeeper, Irene Clay, came to the hospital to see her the morning after she was brought back to Fort Beck.

She brought letters and a list of telephone calls that had come since Helen left for Milwaukee.

'And there was another call from California,' she said.

'Who was it?' Helen asked.

'He didn't leave his name. But then he called again yesterday. Seemed anxious to talk to you. This time he did leave his name.' She took a slip of paper out of her purse. 'Abe Rettberg. He said he'd call again today.'

'Be sure to get his number if he calls. And give him my number here at the hospital.'

Later that day Mrs Clay called her and said the man had called again. This time he'd left his telephone number.

'Did he say what he wanted?'

'No. Just wants to talk to you.'

As soon as she hung up the receiver she picked it up again and dialled the California number. When a man's voice answered she said, 'I'm Helen Bradshaw.'

'My name's Rettberg. I'm calling about your boy, Floyd Simison.'

'Is he all right?'

'He ain't sick if that's what you mean. But he's a long way from being all right. He's in jail and unless somebody moves pretty fast they're going to send him upstate for a long vacation.'

'What did he do?'

'*I* don't think he did anything. But the police say he's been passing bad paper.'

'What does that mean?'

'Counterfeit money. They found a bundle of phoney twenties on a shelf in his closet. And another package under the seat of his truck. How soon can you get here?'

'I can't get out there at all. I'm in the hospital. I can't walk.'

After a long silence Rettberg said, 'Well, I guess that does it.'

'What do you mean?'

'I mean we're fightin' the clock here. They'll handle this case in about thirty seconds once it gets in front of a judge. As far as the law's concerned, they caught him with his pants down. Unless I miss my guess they'll talk him into pleading guilty so he'll get a shorter trip.'

'But if you say he didn't do anything . . .'

'That don't mean *zip*, what I say. Nobody's coming out here to Topanga Canyon to get my opinion. I just know something about the set-up he was involved in and I think I got a good idea what they did to him.'

'God, I feel so helpless. What can I do?'

'If you can't get out of bed, you can't do anything. He needs a wad of money to bail him out of the can and a lawyer with a lot of smarts to get him off the hook. And he needs it all now. Like yesterday.'

'I'll call you back in an hour. Will you be home?'

'I'll stay here till I hear from you.'

As soon as she broke the connection she called Paul Buscatore in New York. Ten minutes later Paul put in a call to Mike Rosenthal. His secretary said he was in Phoenix.

'I don't care where he is. I need to talk to him. Right now.'

'I'll do my best,' the woman said. 'Hold on.'

A few minutes later she came back on and said, 'I have Mr Rosenthal for you.'

'This is Mike Rosenthal,' a man's voice said.

'This is Paul Buscatore. I need a favour.'

'You got it.'

Book Two

Chapter Four

[1]

At the time of the memorial service for Ned Causey, no one believed that the conflict between Clara and Nora would continue. When Clara told her daughter that in future she was not welcome at Wingate Fields, it was assumed that this banishment was temporary. And so it turned out to be. Nora did not, however, visit England again for more than a year, but that was her own doing, a matter of her own schedule rather than a response to Clara's words.

Not long after returning to Paris, Nora had written a note of apology, an unusual gesture for her.

> I behaved like a consummate ass when I was at home with you and I'm sorry. There's no explanation for the way I acted so I will offer none. I may try to appear independent and self-sufficient, and perhaps I am. But not in relation to you, Clara. If I thought you truly didn't want to see me again I don't know how I could deal with that. So I accept the banou've put on me only because I know it's temporary. I know you're angry and I don't blame you, but please forgive me as quickly as you can. Your disapproval is a heavy load for me.

Clara answered her at once.

> Yes, you did behave badly, and yes, I was angry but I didn't handle the situation correctly myself. A permanent estrangement between you and me is no answer to anything. There was a great deal of strain on all of us when you were at home. For a number of reasons. None of us was at our best. But whatever I said, it was never my intention that you and I should have an ugly long-time separation from each other. Perhaps we've both learned a lesson, but whether we have or not, let's pick up the pieces and go on.

Valerie, of course, had never expected that the situation between her mother and Clara would not right itself quickly. She knew, from a lifetime's experience of Nora, that it was impossible not to get angry with her, to be offended by her. But it was also impossible not to forgive her. Watching her own children grow up, Valerie realized more each year how much like a child her mother was. Wilful and unpredictable, quick to anger, and quick to subside. As she understood her more, she was able to love her in a new way. She discussed this often with Clara. 'It took me ever so long to solve the puzzle but little by little it came to me. One must never expect things from Nora. It destroys her. She hated being a wife and although she was a lovely mother to me, especially when I was little, I don't think she ever liked being labelled a mother. She needs to feel that she's inventing everything as she goes along, including herself. Especially herself, I suppose. So being classified, being put into any category, makes her frantic. She doesn't choose to behave the way she does. I'm sure she feels she has to.'

'You're right, of course,' Clara said. 'It's taken me a long time to admit that to myself but at last I've done it. Nora can't be changed, not in any significant way. One must either accept her as she is or get along without her.' She smiled. 'And neither of us is prepared to do that, are we?'

Responding to suggestions from Clara, from Nora, and even from Jesse, Valerie had begun to make occasional trips by herself to visit her mother in Paris. At first she said, 'I can't just go away from the children for days at a time,' but Clara replied, 'Of course you can. It will be good for them. And it will be very good for you.'

To Valerie's surprise she had been delighted to be in Paris again, to be in the house by the Seine where she had grown up. Some of her pre-war sweaters and skirts were still hanging in her closets and she was pleased to find they still fitted. 'Why wouldn't they?' Nora said. 'You're as slender as a snake. No one would ever see you as a mother of three. You still look like a Sorbonne student.'

In some ways it was a different Paris from the one she remembered. Five years after the war's end, the city was still recovering. Old women complained about the quality of bread, many buildings were pockmarked still by bullets, new money had not been printed and the franc notes were stiff with strips of paper tape. But the vitality of the place had returned in full force. The cafés and restaurants were crowded and the schools were filled with students, many of them from other countries. Montparnasse and St-Germain-des-Prés were a babel of foreign tongues and alien faces, all assembled there to live cheaply, to sleep with lonely strangers, and to recreate the splendour and lunacy of the twenties.

Valerie walked for miles in her old precious clothes, through the Luxembourg Gardens and the Tuilleries, up Boulevard Raspail and down St-Michel. She sat at the Select, the Dome, the Kosmos, and the Coupole, at Les Deux Magots and Le Flore. She saw again poor painters and poets she had first met in Nora's house, artists who had survived the war and were now struggling to survive the peace. She went to neighbourhood cinemas where she had first gone as a girl with Jesse. The films they had seen, with Arletty and Gabin, Raimu and Harry Bauer, were being shown again in small theatres all around the left Bank. She went to the flower market and the bird market, St-Chapelle and Notre-Dame, and haunted the book stalls along the *quais*. Each time she visited Paris in those years, the times when she went alone, she found herself repeating the same walks, eating in the same student restaurants, visiting the same tiny art galleries, stamping it all in her memory.

And in the evenings she spent long private hours with Nora, who said at the end of Valerie's first visit, 'We've spent more time alone together this week than any other time I can remember.'

'Except when I was very little.'

'That's right. Then, we were always together. I think of those days a lot. Your father and I were having an absolute war but it didn't affect you and me. We had our own fine life in our own wing of the house, with your nanny and our lovely servants and our cats and dogs. How nice it was. I was dying to get away from Bick House but at the same time I was enjoying every moment I spent with you.'

At the beginning they talked about everything under the sun except Jesse. But at last he began to creep into their conversations and they spoke of him as easily as they did of Clara or Ned or Hugh or Valerie's father, Edmund.

'I'm sorry he stopped writing pieces for *Icarus*,' Valerie said one evening.

'So am I,' Nora said. 'At least I was at the time. But finally I came to realize that he just doesn't *need* that kind of activity any longer. He has a full life with you and the children and all the details of Wingate to occupy him.'

'Ah, but he does need that activity. That's what I'm talking about. He tries awfully hard to pretend he's a fireplace cat, that he's a born member of the gentry who can clump around feed-lots in heavy boots and oversee the horses and the livestock, but that's alien territory for Jesse. He enjoys it but it doesn't occupy him.'

'But it must or he wouldn't . . .'

'Yes, he would,' Valerie said. 'He's a stubborn beast. There's a strong strain of German in him, you know, on his father's side. You see, Jesse decided what was best for him and best for us, and he feels now that he can't back away from that decision even in the slightest way. He's not a flexible man, you know. He'd be quite testy with me, I expect, if he heard me say that, but it's true.'

'He didn't invent that attitude, sweetheart. Almost all men, at least the ones I've known, treat their lives as if they were great steamships. They put them on course, then they stay on the bridge and keep them on that course for life. Any slight change in course they regard as a failure of purpose or a serious character-flaw. Why do you think I've spent so much of my time in the company of artists? They're never on course. Such a thought never occurs to them. Most of them, the really good ones, never plan beyond the piece of work they're doing at the moment.'

'But Jesse's an artist in his way, isn't he?'

'Not an artist,' Nora said. 'But he was capable of being a fine craftsman. He was on his way to becoming an artist among critics. He's intelligent and he had discipline and a respect for the language.'

'But what happened?'

'Who knows? That was some time ago. Before the war. Once we went to New York he began to lose steam.'

'And after he married me . . .'

'Not true,' Nora said. 'It has nothing to do with you. If he wanted to work he could have done it in Boston and he could do it in the North Country.'

'I'm not sure. I've read that some people work very well in one atmosphere and not well at all in another.'

After a moment, Nora said, 'Does all this matter so much to you?'

'Of course it does.'

'I mean if it doesn't matter to him . . .'

'But it does. He just doesn't know what to *do*.'

'What do you think he should do?'

'I don't know either. I just thought maybe if he could be more involved with *Icarus*. Like he was when we were here in Paris.'

'But we're not here in Paris. I am, but *you're* not. You and Jesse are in England, where you always planned to be. Besides, you saw the letter he wrote me. He doesn't want to write for the magazine any more.'

'It's not that he doesn't want to. He can't. Clara says he was never able to accomplish anything at Wingate.'

'That's true. But that's where he is. Unless you're telling me you're planning to move your family to Paris.'

'No,' Valerie said. 'Nothing like that. I just thought that if I can make occasional trips to Paris why couldn't Jesse do the same thing? Didn't he do that when you first started the magazine, before he came here to live?'

'Yes, he did.'

'I'm just saying if he could get involved, the way he was then, in the whole process of publication, it might help him to shake himself loose so he could write some good things again. Doesn't that make sense?'

'That depends,' Nora said. 'Does he know we're having this talk?'

'God, no. He'd be furious.'

'You haven't discussed it with him at all?'

'Not the idea of his coming here occasionally.'

'Then what makes you think he'd do it?'

'I'm not sure he would. But if he did I think he'd like it.'

Nora sat looking at her. Finally she said, 'Are you and Jesse having problems?'

'How do you mean?'

'I mean *problems*. Man and woman, male and female.'

'Why would you ask that?'

'Because I'm curious. It sounds as if you may be trying to get him out of the house. Cabin fever, I think they call it.'

Valerie smiled. 'Not *me*. From a selfish standpoint I'd love it if he never was away for a day. But I'm trying to think of what's best for him. I don't want him to realize all of a sudden that he's sixty years old and hasn't done any of the things he wanted to do. I don't want him to end up hating himself the way Ned did.'

'I don't know,' Nora said. 'It seems to me as if all this is in your head. I don't think wild horses could drag Jesse back to Paris.'

'Maybe not. But I think that if he thought you had a problem with the magazine, that you really needed his help or his advice, he wouldn't say no. Then maybe you could work something out where he could be here one week a month.'

'Then what?'

'I think he'd start feeling better about himself.'

Again Nora seemed to think it over. Then, 'Has it occurred to you that I might not want to have Jesse around?'

'We wouldn't be having this conversation if I thought that.'

'I just wondered,' Nora said.

'It's nine years now since you and Jesse broke up. I've never heard a word from either one of you to make me think there are hard feelings. Did I miss something?'

'No, sweetheart. You never miss anything.' Then, 'Let me try it another way. There are a lot of people here, people I still see and do business with, who saw Jesse and me together for a long time. They might think it's a little bizarre if he suddenly shows up again.'

'*I* don't care what anyone thinks. Do you?'

'Usually I don't. But this is an unusual situation.'

'Only if you *think* so. I don't see anything unusual about it. I'm not suggesting that Jesse come here to go to bed with you. I never slept with him when he was with you and I certainly don't think *you're* going to sleep with him when he's married to me.'

Nora smiled. 'That's putting the cards on the table.'

'Those cards have always been on the table. That's what you meant when you said, "What would people think?" Because that's the only thing that concerns most people . . . who's in bed with whom?'

'How did you get so smart in twenty-five years?'

'Twenty-*nine* years,' Valerie said.

'I know, but I always lie about your age. Otherwise I can't lie about my own.'

[2]

During Helen's last days in hospital, with a light cast on her wrist and a walking cast on her ankle, when it was almost impossible for her to think of anything except Floyd, she spent most of her daytime hours in the sun room on her floor, reading magazines or listening to the conversation in the room around her.

Early in the afternoon of the day before she was scheduled to go home one of the floor nurses came into the room, accompanied by a young woman in a sable coat. When they stopped in front of Helen the nurse smiled and said, 'You have a visitor, Mrs Bradshaw.' The young woman held out her hand and said, 'Hello. I'm Prinny Kellogg.' As the nurse turned and moved away she pulled up a chair and sat down, caressing her coat as she spread it around her.

'I'm sorry,' Helen said. 'I didn't catch your name.'

'Mrs Albert Kellogg. People call me Prinny.'

'Prinny?'

'My sister called me Princess when she was small. She thought I was very pretty. Then she shortened it to Prinny and I've been called that ever since.' There was an awkward silence, then she went on. 'I'm Frank Wilson's daughter.'

'Oh, I see.'

'I know you were wondering.'

'Yes, I was,' Helen said.

'We've never met.'

'I know.' After another silence she said, 'How is your father? Is he still in the hospital?'

'Yes, he is. He's had two operations and he's scheduled for still more surgery.'

'I'm sorry to hear that,' Helen said.

'I'm sorry to come here on such an ugly errand. I'm sure it must be as embarrassing for you as it is for me.'

'As a matter of fact I'm not embarrassed at all. Why should I be? And it's good to have some news about Frank. I haven't talked with him since the accident.'

'That's one of the things I have to say to you. I don't believe you'll be hearing from my father again.'

'Oh? Did he ask you to tell me that?'

'Not exactly. I don't know how well you know my father . . .'

'I know him very well,' Helen said. 'I was married to him for six years.' Then, 'Does everyone call you Prinny?'

The young woman's face turned slowly pink. 'Yes,' she said.

'I'm sorry if I interrupted you, Prinny. You were about to say something about Frank.'

'I started to say that he did *not* send me here. It was a family decision.'

'Your family or Albert's?'

'What?'

'Didn't you say your husband's name was Albert?'

'Yes, I did. Albert Kellogg.'

'Right,' Helen said. 'Now, what is it your family asked you to say to me? Since Frank didn't send you, I assume you're speaking for you and your sister and your mother.'

Prinny nodded. 'And Albert.'

'Of course. Did Albert drive down here with you?'

'Yes, he did.'

'Where is he?'

'He's downstairs in the waiting room. He has a terrible temper and he didn't trust himself to come in.'

'That's too bad. I have a nasty temper myself. We could have had a good battle.'

'Are you making fun of me?'

'Not deliberately.'

'You seem to think this is all quite amusing.'

'I don't know what to think,' Helen said. 'So far you haven't said anything. All I see is a very flustered young woman who doesn't seem to know what to say.'

'I know exactly what to say. We want you to know that you're not fooling anyone.'

'Am I trying to fool someone?'

'Mummy's had some inquiries made . . .'

'You mean your mother?'

'Of course. Why would I . . . ?'

'Do you still call her Mummy?'

'Don't try to distract me. Inquiries were made and we've discovered that you've been seeing my father for quite some time.'

'Worse than that. Not only have I been seeing *him*, we've been seeing each other,' Helen said.

'In other words, we want you to know that you're not getting away with anything.'

'How old are you?'

'What?'

'I said, how old are you?'

'I'm nineteen. But don't be fooled by that. I'm very old for my age.'

'That's true. No one can become as pompous as you are in only nineteen years.'

'If you're going to insult me, I'll have to bring Albert upstairs.'

'Only if you promise me that he's as pompous as you are. Is he nineteen too?'

'Albert is twenty-six and the president of a large corporation.'

'And he has an uncontrollable temper.' Helen said.

'You're really a common woman, aren't you?'

'Extremely. I've never understood what your father sees in me.'

'I wish you could see my mother.'

'I'd like to,' Helen said. 'You should have brought her with you . . . She could have helped you control Albert.'

'Mummy is the most beautiful woman in Lake Forest.'

'I'm sure she is. Now . . . was there something else you had to say?'

'You're very difficult to talk to.'

'I apologize,' Helen said. 'Just keep on talking and pretend I'm not here.'

Prinny squared herself in her chair, stroked her fur coat, and said, 'You can't be surprised at my reason for coming. I simply want to ask you in a nice way to stay away from my father.'

'Whatever you say.'

'Pardon me.'

'I said of course I'll stay away from your father. You should have said that when you first came in. Now all you have to do is get Frank to stay away from *me*. Or have you already talked with him?'

'About what?'

'About coming here to see me. He knew you were coming here, didn't he?'

'No, I told you, it was just . . .'

'You mean you came here and risked humiliating me in the town where I live, and Frank didn't even know you were coming?'

Trying to compose herself, Prinny said, 'We thought it would be better if it was just between the family and you.'

'*You* thought. Isn't Frank a member of the family? How do you think he's going to feel when he finds out you came here without telling him?'

'Now that you've agreed to stay away from him there's no reason to tell him.'

'You mean you won't be asking your father to stay away from *me?*'

'I couldn't do that. He'd kill me. And besides, once you tell him you won't be seeing him again, everything will be fixed.'

'Oh, I see. Well, I hate to disappoint you. But *you* have to tell him I'm not going to see him again. You arranged it, so I think you should take the credit. When he stops calling me and coming to see me I'll assume you've given him the message. Until that happens I see no reason for me to hurt his feelings. Now . . . do we understand each other?'

'No. I don't understand at all. You *promised*.'

'That's right. And I never go back on a promise. If Frank doesn't get in touch with me, I promise I won't get in touch with him.'

That night, as she sat reading in her room after dinner, her telephone rang several times. But she didn't answer it. When she finally got into bed she lay awake a long time, staring up into the darkness and listening to the squeak the nurses' shoes made on the polished floor of the hallway.

[3]

When Floyd flew from California to Chicago, it was near the end of May. Helen met him there at the airport. When he walked out of the tunnel into the waiting room he put his arms around her and said, 'I love you. I love you a lot. I'll never forget what you did for me.'

As they headed South towards Fort Beck, Floyd driving Helen's car, he said, 'Mike Rosenthal. Quite a guy. I've heard of lawyers like him but I've never seen one in action before. Where'd you find him?'

'I didn't. My brother . . . my half-brother knew him. They're friends, I guess.'

'Is that Paul? He mentioned that name a few times.'

'That's right. He's your uncle. He's four years younger than you but he's your uncle all the same.'

'Well, it looks like I owe him one too. Because his friend, Rosenthal, is really an operator. He came to see me at the jail in Los Angeles one morning and that afternoon I was out on the street. Out on bail. He drove me up to Santa Barbara and put me in an apartment just next door to the Biltmore Hotel. He said, "I don't want your friends in LA to know you're out of jail so just stay here till you hear from me." He gave me a roll of money and said, "Stay out of trouble. I'll have this whole business straightened out in a few days." Sure enough, a few days later, he came back and said, "Here's the picture. They've got you cold on possession of counterfeit money but they can't prove you passed any so they've got no felony case. If you want to go to trial I guarantee I'll get you off. If you want to plead guilty to misdemeanour I can get you sixty days suspended. The only problem with that is it goes on your record as a conviction. Does that bother you?" I told him it didn't matter because I had two previous convictions in the East before I went into the Navy. Did you know that?'

'When I met Lowell Simison, he told me you'd been in some trouble after you left home.'

'Yeah, I was. Nothing heavy. Just a few odds and ends here and there. Anyway, a few days after I had that talk with Rosenthal, the one I just told you about, a driver picked me up in Santa Barbara and drove me back to Culver City. I pleaded guilty to misdemeanour, I got my sixty days suspended, and here I am. Rosenthal had it fixed so I could come here to you and make my weekly appearance at the probation office in Springfield. Is that far from you?'

Helen shook her head. 'An hour's drive.'

Floyd grinned at her. 'So now you're stuck with me. At least for sixty days.'

'Longer than that, I hope.'

When they stopped for lunch on the way home, Helen noticed that two of the waitresses were looking at Floyd from across the room. He was wearing a bright blue shirt and a tan jacket, his hair was sun-bleached and his skin was very brown.

'I think you've made a hit with those waitresses,' Helen said.

'I don't think so. They're probably wondering what an elegant lady like you is doing with a beach bum like me.'

'Shall we tell them I'm you're old, broken-down mother?'

He shook his head. 'They'd never believe it.'

When they'd finished lunch and were having coffee, Floyd said, 'Remember when I wrote you that stupid letter saying I didn't want you to be depending on me because I wasn't dependable or some such crap like that?'

Helen nodded and he went on, 'Well, that was a terrific letter you wrote back to me. It was so simple and logical it made me feel like an idiot. If I'd had any sense I'd have left California right then. I thought about it but I had some sort of idea in my head about what I was going to do with myself so I decided to hang on out there. Also, I won't lie to you, I was really hung up on Luisa. Did I tell you about her?'

'You mentioned her in your letter.'

'Yeah, well, I met her at that club where she was working and the next thing I knew the two of us had set up housekeeping in a little motor court apartment. Curtains on the windows, a new electric coffee-pot, and paper roses in a vase on the TV set. I thought it was really hot stuff. I was crazy about her and I thought she was crazy about me. And I *still* think she was, in her way. But . . . she's got this problem. She has an idea in her head that she's . . . I mean she's very ambitious. Some place along the line she convinced herself that she's gonna take the movie business by storm. She had pictures of Lupe Velez and Dolores del Rio all over the joint. Mexican girls who came to Hollywood and made a big splash. And she was determined that she would be the *next* one. So that's the main thing in her life. Everything else has to take a back seat to *that*. But still she was very good to me. I mean she was a beautiful little thing, *tiny*, like a Siamese kitten, and she was always very sweet and nice to me. But Rosenthal said she was setting me up. From the beginning. And when I look back on it I guess he was right. But even if I'd known it, even if I'd been smart enough to see what was going on, it wouldn't have changed how I felt about her. I was really drowning. I saw a movie with Orson Welles and Rita Hayworth where she was really taking him for a ride, and in one scene he said, "Everybody's somebody's fool." That was me when it came to Luisa.'

'How do you mean, she was setting you up?'

'I should have listened to Abe. He had the whole deal pegged from the start. When I left his place and hauled my stuff into Culver City, he told me I was sticking my head in a buzz-saw. He said, "What do they need with a guy like you?" Well, as it turned out, they *did* need a guy like me. They needed somebody who looked halfway decent, somebody who wasn't scared to deal with rough trade, and somebody who wasn't Mexican. What they had was a boat-load of counterfeit twenty-dollar bills. Beautiful stuff, Rosenthal said. They'd shipped it up in a fishing boat from Baja and now they were trying to lay it off in big bundles, twenty-five cents to the dollar. Five *good* bucks for a phoney twenty. The problem was that the customers they wanted to contact wouldn't do business with them because they were Mexican. So they needed a guy like me. They hired me as a bouncer so they could size me up, and then Luisa and I got together. So I guess they thought they had me surrounded. But things never worked out. Either they decided I was a bad risk or somebody told them the police were onto them and they needed a patsy. That's what Rosenthal thought happened. He thought they stashed the phoney money in my garage, in the tool-box of my truck, and then tipped off the police. Then they could say, "You see, it's not us. We're clean. It's that gringo kid who works for us." '

'You mean they never even approached you about passing any of the money?'

Floyd shook his head. 'It never came to that. But I think I made some deliveries. Several times I took liquor cartons from the club to houses in Beverly Hills or Bel Air. Heavy cartons all taped and tied up. But I never knew what was in them. Rosenthal said that was part of the plan. If they had come to me with a proposition to front for them in Orange County where no one would deal with them, they'd have told me I was already *in* because I'd made deliveries in the past. All this was going through my head when I was sitting in jail. Before I talked with Rosenthal I figured I was good for a twenty-year trip.'

'And you think Luisa was a part of the whole thing.'

'I don't *like* to think that. But she had a brother called Estéban, who was one of the partners at the place where I worked and he was in and out of our apartment all the time. Now I'm not even sure he was her brother but I know that whatever he knew, she knew. She must have been involved in something because just before they sent me here from California, the police arrested Estéban, the other two guys who owned the club, and half a dozen more people. And Luisa was one of them. Abe told me they had them on dope charges, blackmail, prostitution . . . you name it.'

'What a mess,' Helen said. 'Thank God you're out of it.'

'Thank *you* I'm out of it.'

When the waitress brought their check, Floyd said to her, 'Would you believe that I own one of the biggest movie studios in the world?'

The girl giggled and Floyd went on. 'All I have to do is say the word and you could be having a screen test and signing an exclusive seven-year contract. What do you say to that?'

'I know you're just teasing me. But you do look like some of those people out there in the movie business.'

'Floyd Bradshaw,' he said, 'remember that name. When my secretary calls you long-distance, you be ready to fly out to the coast at a moment's notice.'

The girl giggled again and looked at Helen. 'Is he always like this.' When she hurried back to her friend across the dining room, Helen said, 'That poor girl. You've redirected her whole life.'

'No, I haven't. She knows I'm kidding. But all the same, when she gets married she'll have a club to use against her husband. She can say that if she hadn't married him she could have gone to Hollywood and acted in the movies. And her girlfriend over there will back her up.'

When they got into the car and pulled out of the restaurant parking lot, Helen said, 'You told that girl your name is Floyd Bradshaw.'

'That's right. How does that sound to you?'

'Sounds fine.'

'I had it changed legally just before I left California.'

'I thought that was a long involved process.'

'Not for Mike Rosenthal.'

[4]

Later that night, when she was in her bedroom, Helen called Paul in New York and they talked for half an hour.

As soon as she hung up, her phone rang. It was Frank Wilson.

'Now I know what's the matter with you,' he said.

'What do you mean?'

'I know why I haven't seen you since the accident, why I haven't heard from you, why I have so much trouble getting you on the phone.'

'It's been a difficult time, Frank.'

'I knew there was something screwy going on. Tonight I finally got my daughter to admit what she did.'

'Don't blame her,' Helen said. 'I'm sure she thought she was doing everybody a favour.'

'Not everybody. Just the bloody Kelloggs. When she married into the Kellogg family she and her mother died and went to heaven. That's what got them crazy. They saw my name in the paper with yours and all of a sudden they were scared to death the Kelloggs might be humiliated.'

'I think it's more than that.'

'No, it's not. It's *just* that. I'm surprised you let Monica get around you like that.'

'Who's Monica?' Helen asked.

'My daughter. She's the one who came to see you.'

'She said her name was Prinny.'

'I know she's says that but *I* never call her that.'

'Are you all right?' Helen said then.

'No. I'm mad as hell.'

'I mean how do you feel? Is your therapy coming along?'

'Sure. I'm walking fine now. I'm leaving this monkey-house hospital tomorrow.'

'I guess you'll be glad to go home. I certainly was.'

'I'm not going home. I'm going to my apartment on the south side.'

'I don't think that's such a good idea.'

'Yes, it is. I've got my houseman. Charlie knows how to take care of things. And my knock-kneed therapist will come in every day. She's the one who needs therapy if you ask me. I've never seen a pair of legs like that.'

'You sound like you're back to normal.'

'Well, I'm not. And I won't be till I see you again. If I live to be two hundred I'll never understand why I haven't seen you all this time I've been in the hospital.'

'I was in the hospital, too.'

'But you've been getting around since the second week.'

'Did you really think I'd come cruising up to Lake Forest

and fight my way past Prinny and Mummy to pay a sick call?'

'Why not? Who cares what they think? You don't, do you?'

'Not particularly,' Helen said. 'I just didn't think it was a brilliant idea.'

'Well, after tomorrow I'll be in the apartment so you can come there. How soon can you make it?'

'I'm not sure.' she said.

'What does that mean?'

'Just what it sounds like. I'm not sure. Floyd is here now. He just got here today.'

'How long will he be there?'

'Where?'

'At your house. How long's he staying?'

'He didn't say. I hope it will be for a long time.'

Frank didn't answer.

Finally Helen said, 'Are you still there?'

Another silence. Then, 'We've got a lot to talk about, Helen. What the hell did Monica say to turn you off like this?'

'I'm not turned off. I'm just . . . I don't know . . . it's very late, Frank, and I've had a long day. Call me tomorrow and we'll . . .'

'I don't want to talk on the phone. I want to see you. When can you come to Chicago?'

'I don't know. We'll have to see what happens.'

'If you won't come here then I'm coming there,' he said.

'I don't think that's a good idea.'

'Maybe it's not. But it's the best one I've got. I don't know what sort of butterflies you have in your head but whatever's going on you owe me some kind of explanation.'

'We don't owe each other anything, Frank. We both understand *that*'.

'I knew I'd said the wrong thing as soon as it came out of my mouth. I'm sorry. But try to see things my way for a minute. All I know is that we were spinning along down Lake Shore Drive and we hit a patch of ice. Both of us got broken up a little. But did something else get broken that I don't know about? You may not owe *me* anything but I certainly owe you an apology for the visit my daughter made to you.' When she didn't answer he said, 'Are you just tired of me? Is it as simple as that?'

'No,' she said. 'It's not simple at all. And you're right.

We should see each other. I'll come to Chicago as soon as I can.'

'That's better. I'll talk to you in a couple of days and we'll make a plan.'

'That's a promise.'

Lying in her bed then, waiting for sleep, she thought, 'What am I doing? Why am I making Frank suffer? Why am I complicating things?' Those questions and several others danced back and forth in her head. But they were not followed by answers. Her last thought before she went to sleep at last was another unanswered question.

[5]

The morning after his call from Helen, Paul Buscatore called Rosenthal. Late that afternoon they met for a drink at Rosenthal's club on Forty-fifth Street. They sat in the member's bar surrounded by dark panelling, leather chairs, and walls lined with books.

'My sister called last night. Her son arrived from California yesterday and she wanted me to tell you how much she appreciates everything you did.'

'I had some luck,' Rosenthal said. 'It worked out well.'

'She would have written you a letter but she had no idea how to reach you.'

'Tell her I appreciate the thought but it's not necessary. If somebody goes to jail I don't take the blame. If somebody gets off easy I don't take the credit. There's no sentiment in my office. No apologies and no thank-you cards.'

Paul smiled and took a card out of his pocket. He put it on the table and said, 'Nothing sentimental about this. Here's where you can send your bill. It's her address in Illinois.'

Rosenthal looked at the card and handed it back to Paul. 'No bill.'

'What do you mean?'

'I mean your sister didn't hire me. If she'd tried to I'd have told her I was too busy.'

'What's the difference who hired you? *I* hired you.'

'No, you didn't. Nobody hired me. You called me up and said you needed a favour. You remember what I said?'

'You said, "You got it." '

'That's it,' Rosenthal said. 'Case closed.'

'Not a chance. The favour you did me was to handle the case. That didn't mean you were working for nothing. My sister's a wealthy woman and she wants to pay you.'

'I'm sure she does. But I'm not interested in what she wants. I am almost exclusively concerned with what I want.'

'All right. Since I called you, then I'll pay you.'

'Grow up, kid. Nobody's going to pay me. Not this time. I charge most of my clients a lot of money. That way, when I decide to work for nothing I can afford to do it.'

Paul sat looking at him across the table. Finally he said, 'What you're saying is that I *owe* you now. Is that it?'

Rosenthal smiled and said, 'This isn't a George Raft movie. I'm not trying to put you in a corner. You asked me for a favour and I delivered. If you want to clear your account with me, all you have to say is, "Thank you".'

'There are all kinds of ways to say "thank you".'

'There you go again. I'm not playing hopscotch with you. Take a chance for once. Just put those two words together and see what happens.'

'I told you what my sister said and that goes for me . . .'

'Thank you,' Rosenthal said.

'I wouldn't know how to repay you if I tried . . .'

'Thank you . . .'

They looked at each other like smiling contenders in a game without rules. Finally Paul said, 'Thank you.'

'You're welcome. That completes the transaction. I owe you nothing and you owe me nothing.' He signalled to the waiter for fresh drinks.

'Where'd you grow up?' Paul said then.

'I wasn't a tough slum kid if that's what you're thinking. My father was a dentist in Brooklyn Heights. He made a good living. He sent me to Brown and the Yale law school.'

'Did you have a lot of fights when you were a kid?'

'Every day. I still have lots of fights.'

'I mean fist fights.'

'So do I. A lawyer who won't fight should never walk into a court room. It's no place for a gentleman. How about you? Are you a fighter?'

Paul shook his head. 'I took piano lessons when I was a kid. If I came home with bruised knuckles I got my ass kicked.'

'That's not the way I heard it.'

'What do you mean?'
'Somebody told me you had a reputation for throwing guys downstairs at that ballroom where you used to sing.'
Paul smiled again. 'You asked me if I was a fighter and I said no. That doesn't mean I don't know how to fight. I grew up on the tough end of Staten Island.'
'Good. That makes me feel better. I get nervous around guys who won't fight.'
It was a soft spring evening when they left the club. 'Which way you heading?' Rosenthal said.
'Uptown.'
'Me too. You want to walk a little?'
'Why not?'
After they'd walked a couple of blocks up Fifth Avenue, Rosenthal said, 'You still think I'm a recruiting officer for the mob?'
'What gave you that idea?'
'Wasn't that what you thought when we talked on the plane that day?'
'I don't remember what I thought,' Paul said.
'Don't play cool with me. I *invented* that game.'
'You tell me. What *was* that whole conversation about?'
'Just getting acquainted. Killing time on the plane.'
'You mean you were just blowing smoke? If I hadn't called you to bail out Floyd, I never would have heard from you again?'
'No. I don't mean that at all.'
'Keep 'em in the dark,' Paul said. 'Is that your game?'
'Just the opposite. I play all my cards face up.'
'I think I'll catch a cab here,' Paul said.
'No more questions?'
'Nope.'
'You surprise me.'
'Let me put it this way: I don't like the answers I'm getting.'
Rosenthal grinned. 'You want to fight?'
'Not me. I'm wearing my best suit.'
'That's a good answer.' Then, 'Just walk me to Rockerfeller Centre. You can catch a cab there.'
'I don't think so. I have to get uptown. Dinner date.'
'Good for you,' Rosenthal said. Then, 'All right, let's leave it this way. The impression you got the first time wasn't right on the mark and the one you're getting now

probably isn't either. But eventually it will all get straightened out.'

A taxi rolled up beside them and as he opened the door Paul said, 'You think so?'

'No question about it,' Rosenthal said. As Paul's cab pulled away he stood for a moment at the kerb. Then he turned and walked back down Fifth Avenue.

[6]

When Jesse received a long letter from Nora describing in detail the crisis she faced with her magazine, Clara took no part in the evening discussions between Valerie and Jesse. When she first learned about the letter, when Jesse read it to her at breakfast the morning he received it, she assumed from the things he said that there was no possibility he would fly to Paris and spend a week or ten days there helping Nora out of her difficulties. 'I'm sorry I *can't* help her,' he said. 'We had a similar problem with the printers before the war and it got pretty sticky. But I can't jump into that whole business again. Besides, it wouldn't be just one trip. I'm sure of that. And I can't be running back and forth between here and France. It wouldn't be fair to Valerie and the children, and I'm not anxious to do it in any case. Nora will come out of it all right, I'm sure. If she can't get help from me, she'll get help somewhere else. She's nothing if not resourceful.'

Clara was surprised, then, during the next few days, that the subject continued to surface. And each time, whether they were at table or in the drawing room after a meal, it was Valerie who brought it up. 'I can't get Nora off my mind,' she said. 'It's not like her to call for help. I wish there was something we could do.' Each time she mentioned it, it seemed that her discomfort had become more specific. At last, perhaps a week after the arrival of Nora's letter, Valerie said, 'I know it's a sacrifice for you, Jesse. In some way it's a sacrifice for all of us. But it's a sacrifice we're able to make and I think we should make it.' Two days later Jesse flew from Newcastle to London and from there to Paris.

The following morning at breakfast, while Clara and

Valerie sat alone in the morning room, Valerie said, 'You think I'm being a fool, don't you?'

'Why in the world would I think that?'

Valerie smiled. 'Don't try to put me off, my darling. It can't be done. I know you too well. For the past week you've been as silent as a stone. Very unlike you. In your case silence always means disapproval of something or of someone.'

'There are all sorts of things I might disapprove of before I got down the list to you.'

'Perhaps. But let me be more specific. If I'm on the mark will you tell me?'

'No promises.'

'You thought it was a mistake for Jesse to go skipping off to France and you thought it was foolish of me to encourage him.'

Clara sat looking at her for a long moment. 'I'm not sure that foolish is the word I would use. Ill-advised, perhaps.'

'Why?'

'Since I didn't enter into the discussions before, what makes you think I'll do it now?'

'Because the discussions are over. It's after the fact. He's already gone. I'm not going to quote you to Jesse or anyone else. But I really need to know what you're thinking.'

'All right. I'll admit I was a bit surprised at the position you took. I would have expected precisely the opposite.'

' "Please don't go and leave me here alone with my children" . . . that sort of thing.'

'Of course not,' Clara said. 'I just felt you weren't being as levelheaded as you normally are. There was an element of catastrophe about Nora's letter that didn't ring true to me. And your swallowing it and expanding on it didn't ring true either.'

'You mean you think Nora's pretending, that she really has no crisis at all?'

'That thought entered my head. And I was surprised that it didn't enter yours.'

Valerie laughed. 'What a wise and noble bird you are. You saw through the whole business. Thank God Jesse didn't. There *was* no crisis and there *is* no crisis, unless Nora has managed to patch one together since she learned Jesse was coming.' She told Clara then about the conversation she and her mother had had about Jesse. 'And all that talking we did led to this.'

'At least now I understand what you were doing. But I'm not sure I understand why.'

'As I said, I think it's something he needs right now.'

'You think, or Nora thinks?'

'Both of us. We agree,' Valerie said.

'You mean you came to a simultaneous decision?'

'Pretty much so.'

'Let me put it another way. Who brought up the subject in the first place?'

'I did. No question about that.'

'Are you absolutely certain of that?'

'Of course I am. How could I not be?'

'I can't say. But I'm sure it will come as no surprise to you when I say that you have a very clever mother.'

'I'm well aware of that,' Valerie said. 'But if you're implying that she mesmerized me with a cup of strong tea and then planted ideas in my mind, you're mistaken. The entire scheme hatched in my own brain and I passed it along to Nora.'

'How did she react to it?'

'She was negative at first. But she came round. I can see that something still bothers you. What is it?'

'There seems to be a piece missing somewhere. Some hidden motive. In Jesse's case, I think he was truly persuaded to go. You persuaded him. With Nora, one never knows what she's up to. But still, let's give her the benefit of the doubt. Let's say she is simply performing a selfless act.'

'It's not selfless exactly. I think she's doing it for me.'

'Maybe she is. At least we'll assume that. The motive that gives me trouble is yours. Not only did you contrive to have Jesse go away on this journey but, if I understood you correctly, you hope it's something he'll do on a regular basis, perhaps one week every month.'

'That's right.'

'In other words, this is a sacrifice you're making for his benefit?'

'Yes.'

'You're doing it for his own good?'

'Exactly,' Valerie said.

'Angus used to say when someone tries to do something "for your own good" the best thing you can do is run off and hide.'

'Angus was a cynic. I don't agree with that. Anyway,

Jesse doesn't know what I've done and I don't plan to tell him. Neither will you, and neither will Nora.' She sat quietly, studying her grandmother. 'Something still disturbs you.'

'No, I don't think so.'

'You're not a good actress, Clara. What is it?'

'I think you're being ingenuous.'

'Maybe I am. But I love Jesse. I've always loved him. And I think I know him. I want him to feel good about himself. That means more to me than having him here inside the house every hour of every day. If he wants to be a house-cat that's fine with me. But if he has other things to do that prevent him from being a house-cat, then I have to accept that too.'

'I admire that. But there are some practical problems about it that disturb me.'

'Like what?'

'Let me put it this way. History is not filled with stories of women who loved their husbands in that particular way. Hardly anyone recommends sending your husband back to a woman he lived with for twenty years. Even if it's only for a week every month.'

Valerie laughed. 'Shame on you. Now you sound like Nora.'

'Is that what she said?'

'Not exactly. But she said people would assume things when they saw Jesse back in Paris.'

'What did you say?'

'I told her I don't care what anyone thinks and she shouldn't either. You know as well as I do, Clara, that if you can't trust a man when he's away you can't trust him when he's at home either.'

'I've heard that theory but I've never totally subscribed to it.'

'Besides, if Jesse wanted to be with Nora he need never have left her. I didn't shanghai him. He came to me voluntarily. That's the only way I'd want him. It's the only way I'd want anybody. If he left me it would kill me. But if he stayed with me when he wanted to leave, that would be worse.'

[7]

After the death of Helen's father in Fort Beck, when she and Jesse went to England to meet the Bradshaw family, Angus, her grandfather, who was seventy-four years old that summer, took her for a long drive one day. They had lunch at an old inn west of Haltwhistle, and he carefully explained to her some of the long and intricate history of her family, and the extent of their wealth. Then bit by bit he described her own financial circumstances as a new-found adult member of the family.

Finding herself in a similar situation now with Floyd and remembering that particular day with her grandfather, she decided to duplicate it as much as she could, in spirit if not in detail. They drove along the Boone River one summer morning and stopped for lunch at an old frontier block-house that had been converted into a restaurant.

During her recent trip to Wingate Fields, after Helen had told Clara about Floyd, Clara had given her the latest financial report of the Bradshaw holdings and had clipped it to an addendum specifying the precise value of the investments that would now be catalogued under Floyd's name, as well as the annual income those monies would earn.

'Holy God,' Floyd said. 'I can't believe it.'

'I gave you some idea what to expect the first time we talked in San Diego.'

'I know you did. But it all seemed very general to me. I was sitting there in my sailor suit, drawing an able seaman's wages so it didn't really sink in.'

'I know how you feel,' Helen said. 'I'm sure it's very close to the way I felt when my grandfather told me what I'm telling you.'

'What does anybody do with all that money?'

'Most of us don't do anything with it. A large percentage of the income goes back into the trust. That's why so much has accumulated over the last two or three hundred years.'

'So the less you spend the more you accumulate. Is that it?'

'That's always true with principal. But it's particularly true when you're talking about the amounts that exist in the Bradshaw fund. All of us together could not possibly spend the annual income from the principal.'

'What if everybody decided to go on a big spending spree?'

Helen smiled. 'People don't seem to do that when they have all the money they need. And even so, the liquid funds, the monies that come into your hands, are a small percentage of your total income. As Angus explained it to me, it was structured so that all the family members would live extremely well, that capital could be made available when needed, but a great percentage of the income would continue to flow back into the fund, guaranteeing that your children and your children's children would always be splendidly provided for. In practice it works like this:

'Each January the amount of liquid funds that my shares have earned during the past year are deposited in my name at the Chase Bank in New York. If I wanted to withdraw that entire amount I could, but since I could never possibly spend that much in a year I have a certain amount per month deposited in my chequing account in Chicago.'

'And if you don't spend that money in New York, it goes back into trust at the end of the year. Right?'

'No. That's all liquid money. That's always available to me. And the same goes for the account in your name. Whatever you don't spend stays there at Chase.'

Floyd looked down at one of the pages in front of him. 'And this is how much I have in a chequing account in Chicago?'

'That's right. I opened the account for you right after I came back from England the last time. Next time we go to Chicago you'll meet the bank manager, and when we're in New York I'll introduce you to the man who'll handle your account at Chase.'

'I feel like Tom Sawyer in the cave with all that gold.'

'You'll be surprised how quickly you get used to it. I can live any place I want to in the world, in any sort of house I want to buy, but you see I'm still living here in Fort Beck in my father's house. I have a nice car and two fur coats but I don't have ten cars or twenty fur coats.'

'I guess I could buy a car if I wanted to, couldn't I?'

'Of course you can. You should have a car. And you can get yourself some clothes . . .'

'Don't tell me you're getting tired of my sweat shirts and blue jeans,' he said.

'I'm not tired of them but I thought you might be.'

He smiled and said, 'You certainly know how to treat a

guy, I'll tell you that. And on top of everything else, you're buying my lunch.'

'No, I'm not. *You're* buying *my* lunch.' She took a cheque book out of her purse and slid it across the table to him, his name printed on the cover. 'As Raymond used to tell me when he gave me a quarter to go to the movies, "Don't spend it all in one place." '

He started to laugh then and she said, 'You look about twelve years old right now.'

'Why not? I told you . . . I feel like Tom Sawyer.'

The next day she received a box of three dozen roses from the local florist, no card enclosed. She carried them with her through the house till she found Floyd in the second-floor sitting room. As soon as he saw her he said, "Ah-ha . . . you *got* them.'

'I've never seen so many roses in one box.'

'What do you think . . . I'm a cheapskate? Next time I'll really lay it on. If you're gonna be *my* mother, you have to get used to a lot of attention.'

[8]

'You feel like a stanger here, don't you?' Frank said.

'I don't think so,' Helen said. 'Why do you say that?'

They were sitting in his South Shore apartment, the one they'd selected together when they began to see each other again, where they'd had meals together and slept together and looked out across the terrace toward Lake Michigan as they were doing now.

'I say it because it's true. You've been here for two hours but you're *not* here. You look at me but you don't see me. If I touched you I feel as if you'd pull away.'

'Why do you say that? You *haven't* touched me.'

'I'm not crazy,' he said, 'and I'm not blind. You've got a *No Trespassing* sign plastered on you that nobody could miss.'

'What's the point of saying *mean* things? If you're just trying to hurt my feelings . . .'

'I wish I *could* hurt your feelings. Any response would be welcome.'

'You're really mad at me, aren't you?'

'No, I'm bewildered and I have been since we had that accident months ago. I told you all this on the phone. Or at least I tried to tell you. But I didn't make much progress then and I'm not making much progress now.'

'I don't know what to say to you.'

'Well, at least you're honest about that. That's what *I* just said to *you*. You feel like a stranger here.'

'I feel funny, that's all. I don't know why. And you're not making things any better.'

'I'm not *trying* to make things better. You're the only one who can do that. I feel exactly the way I did before we both went to the hospital. But I can't make contact with you. You're on the moon.'

'No, I'm not, Frank. I'm trying just as much as you are to straighten things out but I don't know where to start. I'm just as bewildered as you are.'

'Let's start with the accident and go on from there,' he said.

'All right. Let's do that.' She sat silent for a moment. Then, 'I'm not a physical coward. At least I never thought I was. But I'd never been in a crash like that before. I'd never broken a bone, never been knocked unconscious, never even been a patient in a hospital. So when I came to in the emergency room with tubes up my nose and nurses running all around, I was scared to death. I didn't know where I was. I wasn't sure what had happened, and I didn't know if you were alive or dead. When I was back in my room the next day and feeling a little better I kept thinking that someone would tell me something or that I'd hear from you . . .'

'I was so doped up I didn't know where I was.'

'I know that now but I didn't know it then. So I just kept waiting. And after the first two days I was afraid to ask anybody about you. I was afraid they'd tell me you were dead. Then after they'd moved me to the hospital in Fort Beck, I finally heard something. My doctor told me you'd been moved to the Lake Forest Hospital. He also told me there'd been an item in the Chicago paper so I decided I'd better not call you in Lake Forest.'

'I called *you*. As soon as I could. As soon as I found out where you were.'

'I know you did. But by then I'd spent a lot of hours in a hospital bed, looking up at the ceiling. First I was happy to hear that you were all right, then I was mad as hell because I hadn't heard from you. And I was mad at myself for being upset. I began to feel like a terrible movie version of "the other woman", someone with all sorts of privileges but no rights. All I could think was, if you *had* been killed, I'd have found out by seeing it in the paper.'

'I doubt that,' he said.

'You do? Who do you think would have told me? We're shadows. We don't exist in each other's lives. Not in anyone else's eyes.'

'Who cares about that? What difference does it make?'

'It makes a lot of difference when you don't know if someone's alive or dead. It certainly made a difference to me. It *still* does. I start to get angry just talking about it.'

'Listen,it was a tough time. I know that. I wish it could have been handled differently too. But it wasn't and it's over now. Thank God we're both all right.'

'I'm not sure I am all right.' Helen said. 'I mean my bones are healed but I still get the quivers inside. Have you ever felt like a nonperson?'

'No. And neither have you.'

'Oh, yes, I have. That's what I felt all through those days in the hospital, like a miscellaneous passenger in your car. I'm surprised they even bothered to print my name.'

'That's ridiculous.'

'Not to me. It wasn't then and it isn't now. I felt like an idiot because I'd put myself in such a position. It made me feel different about myself. Then I couldn't help feeling different about us.'

'I don't follow all this,' he said.

'I know you don't. That's the most disturbing thing of all. You act as if I should take an aspirin or drink a martini and put the whole thing behind me. But I *can't*. When your daughter came sailing into the hospital . . .'

'What does that matter? Monica's a tiresome brat.'

'I know that. I knew it before I'd talked to her for two minutes. But all the same, I felt like a butterfly on a pin. I realized I'd been *discussed*, thoroughly discussed and categorized in *two* families, the Wilsons *and* the Kelloggs . . .'

'You don't even know those people.'

'That's true. And they don't know me. But all the same they'd drawn conclusions about me, they'd discussed how to handle the situation, how to handle me. After your daughter flounced out that day I felt as if someone had spilled food all over me. I felt like a used tablecloth.'

'Is that my fault, Helen? I didn't send her there.'

'I know you didn't. And I *don't* blame you. That's what I'm trying to explain to you. I blame myself. And that's worse.'

'Listen,' he said. 'Don't think I don't understand. I do. I'm sure you were upset. But what I'm trying to say is that it won't last for ever. It will go away and you'll feel good again. I promise you.' When she didn't answer he said, 'I made a reservation at *McNamara's*. We'll drive over there and have a nice dinner . . .'

'I can't Frank. I can't stay.'

'Sure you can.'

'No, I can't. Floyd came in with me.' She looked at her watch. 'I have to meet him at the Ambassador East at six.' When she looked at him he turned away. She turned too then, and looked out through the glass doors. They sat there silent in the still afternoon, looking out across the lake.

[9]

That evening, having dinner with Floyd in the splendour of the Pump Room of the Ambassador Hotel, towering waiters costumed like Sikhs moving about the room and small black boys in turbans and red jackets standing at their stations, Helen told him about Frank. She had told him the first time they met in San Diego that she'd been married and divorced, now she told him in more detail, including their relationship of the last few years and the disturbing meeting they'd had just that afternoon. After she finished, she said, 'I suppose you're wondering why I'm telling you all this. I'm not sure myself. But I think it's because I feel guilty as hell and I'm hoping somebody will tell me I shouldn't.'

'Maybe he should feel guilty,' Floyd said.

'I know. That's what I tell myself. But he doesn't and I do. There's no logic to it. God knows, we're both grown-ups. And since he's married and I'm not, I suppose most people would say that I'm the one who's been sinned against. But I *haven't* been, certainly not by Frank. I don't feel that way at all. It's just that all this time, these last few years we've been together again, I've felt comfortable and easy about the whole arrangement. And now I don't. I always thought it was one of those rare situations where both people win and nobody loses. But I guess I was wrong. Since our accident, since I started to see things from a different perspective, I feel awkward with him. It's not his fault, it's nothing he's done. I just feel as if everything's been twisted around and broken up. But Frank doesn't know what I'm talking about. He just sits there looking at me and I know he's hurt and I don't know how to fix it. That's what makes me feel guilty.'

'What was it like when you got a divorce? How did he feel then?'

'I don't think I could answer that question in a million years. I was in such a turmoil myself, I was too crippled by my own feelings to know what was happening to him. I've always told myself that we felt exactly the same, that we got a divorce because we'd reached a completely mutual decision, but now I'm smart enough to know that *nothing* is ever mutual between two people, between a man and a woman. Somebody always loves a little bit more, somebody has more at stake, and somebody loses more if things don't work out.'

'When I was sweating it out in the South Pacific I read an article in an old magazine. Some psychiatrist had written it. He said people always feel sorry for the wife when a couple get a divorce but the truth is that husbands suffer more when a marriage breaks up than their wives do. And it takes them longer to get over it. Do you think that's true?'

'I don't know. In Frank's case he was married again less than a year later, so I always assumed . . .'

'That's what the article said. A guy who's really shot down after a divorce gets married again as fast as he can.'

She shook her head. 'I still think Frank and I split up because we simply couldn't stay together any longer.'

'Then a few years later you got together again,' Floyd said.

'I know. It doesn't make sense.'

'What do you plan to do now?'

'I don't know,' she said.

'Does that mean you don't know? Or you do know but you don't know how to do it?'

'What do you mean?'

'I mean a lot of people stay together just because they don't have the guts to say goodbye. Are you trying to get away but you don't know how to tell him?'

'I don't think so. It's not that black and white in my mind. I feel as if I'm being pulled in all sorts of directions. Has that ever happened to you?'

'What do you think? I'm stupid about women. I fall in love like people catch a cold. And I have a tough time getting over it. I had a girl when I was in high school — she's the one I went to see after I got out of the Navy — and I don't think I'll ever get *her* out of my head. She's nothing very special, I guess, but she sure put a tattoo on me. I thought maybe if I saw her again I'd get her out of my system — she's married now, for Pete's sake, with a couple of kids — but it was no different from before. I'm still crazy about her. And Luisa, the girl in California, the same thing. My head tells me I'm lucky to be rid of her but the good stuff keeps coming back to me. If I had it to do all over again, I'd probably do it all over again.'

Helen smiled. 'You mean you never learn from experience?'

'Never,' he said. 'Don't even want to, I guess. I go right into the deep end of the pool every time.'

'Well, I don't think I'll worry about you. I've always believed that people who fall in love a lot don't get damaged as much as the ones who fix on one person and never get over it.'

'It's a nice idea but it doesn't work. Not in my book. It stands to reason that if you're shot five times you'll bleed more than if you're only shot once.'

'That depends on how fast you get to a hospital,' Helen said.

'There aren't any hospitals for what we're talking about.'

'You're pretty smart, aren't you?'

'Not me. I told you. As far as women are concerned I'm dumb as hell.'

'Does that mean you can't give me any advice?'

'Sure I can. I say, have pity on the poor bastard. If you're tired of him or if you just don't want to see him any more for some reason, tell him so. However you feel, even if you don't know how you feel, you have to tell him something.

Just hanging on a hook, having no idea what's liable to happen next . . . that's the worst thing you can do to a guy.'

The next morning, sitting in her bedroom in Fort Beck, Helen wrote a letter to Frank.

> I've felt awful ever since I left you yesterday afternoon. You had such a strange look on your face, an expression I'd never seen before. I wanted to *say* something but nothing came out. And you weren't saying much yourself. All through dinner last night I wanted to go to a phone and call you but I didn't know what to say then either.
>
> This morning my head is working a little better. So maybe I can make some sense. First of all, I want you to know that after we were divorced I never said to myself that we would have been better off not to get married in the first place. I never thought that, not for a minute, and I don't think it now. I never blamed *you* because we didn't stay together. Just the opposite. I always felt that *I* was to blame. I wasn't altogether sure what I had done or failed to do but, all the same, I felt guilty and rotten about it. And the feeling never completely left me. Maybe that's why I looked you up later. Maybe I thought I could make up for something I should have done before.
>
> I know you're impatient and aggravated with me now and I wouldn't be surprised if you've decided to throw in the towel and never see me again. *If* that happens, once again I say I would have no regrets that we got together again when we did. I regret nothing except my own inability to deal with things that need to be dealt with.
>
> So where are we? What does all this mean as far as you and I are concerned? I'm not sure. I don't think we should yell and scream at each other and I don't think we should assume that everything's gone to pot and we'll never see each other again.
>
> Here's what I think we *should* do. Let's declare a truce. I have to go to England. I promised my family that I would take Floyd there to meet his new relatives. So we're going now. As soon as I can make travel arrangements. This is not a contrived trip. It has been planned for some time and has nothing to do with our

present difficulty, yours and mine. But still I think it can work to our advantage. I'll be gone for only a few weeks and when I get back I have a feeling you and I will be able to make more sense when we talk to each other. Perhaps we'll be able to just put aside this whole time since the accident and go back to where we were before. I'd like it if we could. Whatever happens we've always been civilized with each other and I see no reason for that to stop. If I don't hear from you before I leave, I will assume that you agree with me that it's best to let things lie dormant till I come back. I'll write to you from England and I will definitely let you know the exact date of my return.

[10]

During the days when Valerie was attempting to persuade Jesse that he should answer Nora's appeal for help, he was never for a moment convinced that her only motive was to help her mother. At first he was as baffled by her persistence as Clara seemed to be. But bit by bit he began to sense what was in her mind. Only at the last moment, as they lay in bed the night before he was to leave for Paris, did she say anything to support his suspicions. Just before they went to sleep she said, 'You're doing a very nice thing, I'm proud of you.' He switched off the light and she settled in beside him, her head on his shoulder. 'My nanny used to tell me that when you do something for someone, particularly if it's something you don't really *want* to do, you'll get something back, like bread on the water.'

'Your nanny was a nice lady,' Jesse said. 'but she didn't have a very clear idea of how the world works.'

'Oh, I think she *did*. People don't like to believe it works that way but I believe it does. You're doing something good, so something good will certainly happen to you.'

'I hope you're right,' Jesse said. 'I haven't won a prize for a long time. What do you think I'll get for being a kind person?'

'I have no idea. But you'll see.'

'Give me an example. Give me several examples so I'll have something to look forward to.'

'You might meet the love of your life.'

'Too late. I've already done that,' he said.

'You might find a beautiful fountain-pen to replace the one you lost in York two years ago.'

'That would be nice. I'd like that.'

'Or you might . . . let's see . . . what else could happen? You might get all excited about working again.'

'What's good about that?' he asked.

'I mean, you might get angry at something you read, or some bad paintings you see, and decide to write a blistering critique like you did in the old days.'

'I see. You think I'm turning into a stodgy old person and you want to re-create me as an angry young man.'

'Not me,' she said. 'I think you're swell the way you are. You can sit in your study and drink claret till you're eighty and I'll find no fault with you.'

'That's good. I thought maybe you were designing a programme for my declining years.'

'Not at all. I was simply listing some of the rewards that might come to you from doing Nora a good turn.'

Jesse arrived in Paris with no expectations whatsoever beyond the immediate task that Nora had outlined in her letter a week before. He would do what he could to untangle the problem with the printer and then he would be gone. And if it appeared that the problem would take too long to solve then he would be gone *before* it was solved. But the things Valerie had said were still with him. The trip by taxi from the airport to the centre of Paris gave him a sense of adventure that he hadn't felt in quite the same way since he'd left France before the war.

As soon as he saw Nora she said, 'I feel such a fool. You've come all this way for nothing. At one o'clock this morning I had a call from Monsieur Pignot, that idiot at the Syndicate. He insisted I meet him this morning at ten o'clock. You know me. At ten o'clock I'm just turning over and thinking about ringing for my first cup of coffee. But I made the supreme effort. I struggled out of bed at eight-thirty and met Pignot at ten. He stormed and ranted for fifteen minutes, then he laid out in front of me what he called his final proposal. It was a three-year firm agreement granting us every single concession we'd asked for.'

'That doesn't sound like Pignot,' Jesse said.

'Of course it doesn't. I was stunned.'

'You must have done *some* manoeuvre you're not telling me about.'

She smiled. 'I did. But I didn't think it would work. Last week I sent notice to the whole staff, editorial *and* production, that because of impossible demands by the printers, I was moving the entire operation to Brussels at the end of the month.'

'There you are. Looks like you've done it again.'

'Done it again for the first time, you mean. This is the first battle I've ever won with Pignot. Now I'm going to celebrate. I'm off to Rome tomorrow with my gentleman friend. He's a fashion photographer from New York. He has to shoot a layout for *Elle*. So I'll tag along and make all those skinny models look sick. Like I said, I'm sorry you made the trip for nothing but all this just happened this morning so there was no way I could stop you in time.'

'No, I guess not.'

'I expect you'll turn around and fly straight back, won't you?'

'Well, not today, but I'll probably go tomorrow.'

'I put you in that hotel you used to admire in Place St-Sulpice. They have a nice suite on the top floor and it's really quite cosy. I'm sorry I can't invite you for dinner but I have to meet Martin this afternoon and then we're having dinner in the Bois with Verna, the fashion editor of *Elle*.'

'Don't worry about it. I'm sure I'll find a place to eat. It'll be nice to wander around the streets a little.'

'If you decide to stay over a little longer, drop into the office. It's still on Rue de Seine where it used to be. You'll see some familiar faces and a few new ones. But they all know who you are.'

Valerie had given Jesse *her* impressions of post-war Paris after her visits there. But the splendid shock of being once again in the centre of those quarters where he had spent so many vital and creative years was something he could in no way have anticipated. The art of living in the moment, which the Italians had created and the French had refined, was evident everywhere he looked, and nowhere more strikingly than in the street markets. They seemed to insist that if you bought the proper *pâté de campagne*, a crisp *baguette*, radishes and sweet butter, celery, tiny carrots, onions and new potatoes, a plump chicken perhaps, or *lapin*, tomatoes, lettuce, salami, and wedges of Port Salut and Roquefort, sardines to begin, or *maquereaux*, a fruit *tarte* from the *pâtisserie*, and two or three bottles of wine . . . if you carefully placed all this inside your straw basket lined with pink cotton and carried it home to your kitchen, closing the door behind you, no chaos or catastrophe, no illness or anxiety could possibly touch you till that food had all been prepared and seasoned, and served and eaten. And by then, or shortly thereafter, a new supply of equally diverse and succulent food items would have been carefully selected and carried home and the climate of contentment and security would be created again. Years ago, Jesse and Nora had often said to each other, 'In England, a woman says, "Tonight I'll cook a joint of mutton, roast potatoes and spinach." In France, a woman says, "How do I know what I'm going to eat till I see what's in the market?" '

All these old impressions and many new ones occupied Jesse's senses as he walked through the streets of the 7th arrondissement after checking into his hotel. He stopped at a *bureau de voyage* and booked a return flight to London the next day. Then he telephoned Valerie from the *bureau de poste* and told her he was coming. He explained to her what had happened and why he was coming home so soon and she said, 'I'm delighted. Can't wait to see you.'

That evening he stopped for a pint of lager at Lipps. Then he walked to Montparnasse, drank a Pernod at Kosmos, and ate dinner at Chez Rosalie.

Later he walked back to St-Germaine-des-Prés along the side of the Luxembourg Gardens, and had a coffee and calvados at Les Deux Magots. When he returned to his hotel at midnight, he had met and talked with seven people he had known well before the war. One of them, a very old Hungarian painter named Mazsy, was having the first post-war showing of his work, with the vernissage scheduled for the following Thursday, in three days time. When Jesse telephoned Valerie again the following morning, she said, 'I remember him. What a fine man he is. Of course you must stay for his show. And bring me one of his landscapes.'

Each day he stayed, Jesse met more people he knew. And widows and children of men who had not survived the war. And the Mazsy vernissage was like a replay of one of Nora's Thursday evening salons.

Even men whose work he had criticized harshly seemed delighted to see him. All of them still saw Nora, of course, and they knew that Jesse was married now to Valerie. They showed photos of their children and grandchildren and were disappointed that Jesse carried no pictures of his own family. Each person he met had concrete and powerful reasons why Jesse should extend his stay in Paris. That failing, they scribbled specific dates on scraps of paper reminding him of events that he must come back to attend in the near future.

'There are no fine critics here now,' Mazsy said, 'Only failed poets who review expositions because they are paid so much per line. When you read their odd comments it is clear why they are failed poets. Michel Seuphor still writes well, of course, and Michel Tapié, and Barnett Conlan is still with us, writing for the London *Daily Mail*. But we need another strong voice. You must come back. Bring your babies with you. When a child grows up in Paris he understands the world.'

Jesse stayed in France for eight days. When he left, Nora had not yet returned from Italy, but he was in the *Icarus* office one day when she telephoned so he talked to her. 'Since you're still there, go and see the Post-Impressionist show at the Orangerie. And they've rehung everything at the Jeu de Paume. You'd better see that too.'

When he flew home, Valerie came down to London to meet him and they stayed three nights at Claridge's. 'Isn't Paris fantastic now? I told you it was. I knew you'd stay longer. I'm delighted you did. Otherwise I wouldn't have my fine new picture by sweet Mr Mazsy. He's still moving ahead, isn't he? Before the war he never would have painted a mauve sky. I love it.'

The day after they returned to Wingate Fields, Jesse went from the breakfast room to his office and began to work. Ten days later he had completed three long articles: *Déjeuner Chez Camus*, *Picasso: The Occupation Years* and *Zadkine: Genius in Exile*. The first two he mailed off to Nora, the third he sent to his friends at *Le Figaro*.

'Suddenly you're a phantom,' Valerie said one evening. 'I never see you.'

'You wanted me to get fired up, didn't you? Well, I'm fired up. Next I'm going to deal with Sartre and the Café Flore. And a long piece on the American novels that came out of Montparnasse. And then I'm going to put a few arrows in Seurat, something I've been wanting to do for years.'

She smiled. 'Looks like I've created a monster.'

'I wouldn't be surprised.'

[11]

'When we stop in New York on our way to England I want to meet my sweet old uncle Paul,' Floyd said.

'I wouldn't describe him as sweet,' Helen said. '*Nor* old. He's four years younger than you are.'

'I know. You told me. I was making a joke.'

'I'm sure he wants to meet you too. So we'll make a date. The three of us.'

Before they left Fort Beck to fly to New York, Helen called Paul and they arranged to meet for lunch the day before she and Floyd were to fly to London.

'I think you'll like each other,' she said to Floyd. 'You're very different. At least to *me* you are. But we're all descended from my mother in one way or another. So we're *connected*.'

Some sense of order, some sense of family, or the feeling of a debt to be paid to her mother perhaps, had made Helen eager to arrange the meeting between Floyd and Paul. But as the time drew near, she had an inexplicable sense of foreboding. She envisioned herself as the moderator of a silent luncheon, sitting between two young men neither of whom knew each other and neither of whom, for all her blood connection with them, *she* knew very well.

As it turned out, circumstances prevented her from being present when they met. An hour before they were to leave their hotel for the restaurant, she called Floyd's room from the hairdressing salon downstairs. 'They've had some sort of assinine power failure on this floor,' she told him, 'and I'm sitting here, angry as hell, with wet hair. If I'm not upstairs at 12.45 will you go along to the restaurant? It's right down the street between Madison and Park. Just ask the captain for Paul Buscatore's table. You two have a drink and I'll be along in a few minutes.'

Perhaps if Helen had been present the first time Floyd and Paul met each other, there would have been a different result. As it was, from the moment Floyd walked into Angelino's and was shown to the table where Paul was waiting, some strong chemical reaction seemed set in motion. They shook hands, of course, and smiled, and sat down opposite each other. Floyd started to explain Helen's tardiness but Paul said he already knew about it. She'd called him at his apartment right after she called Floyd. When the waiter came, Floyd ordered Scotch and Paul asked for cassis.

'What's that you're drinking?' Floyd said. Studying Paul, he decided his uncle had chosen to dress down for the occasion. Surrounded by extremely sleek customers, all expensive-looking and fragrant, he wore a tweed jacket with a brown tie and a tan shirt, grey slacks and loafers. Floyd, on the other hand, wore a chalk-stripe navy-blue suit, a crisp white shirt and a grey silk tie. He looked and acted, Paul thought, very much at home in Angelino's.

'Cassis,' Paul said, 'It's a light drink. An aperitif. I almost never drink at lunch.' He seemed ill at ease, Floyd thought.

'Do you come here often?' Floyd said.

'It's on my regular list. I never have dinner here but I come for lunch twice a month or so.'

'But never for dinner.'

'No.'

'Why is that?'

'No reason. I just have dinner at other places.'

Their drinks arrived. 'We're waiting for a lady,' Paul told the waiter. 'We won't look at menus till she arrives.'

There was a long, rather scratchy silence while they tasted their drinks, glanced at each other, then glanced away.

'I want to thank you for helping me out when I was in California.' Floyd said.

'I couldn't say no to Helen. As soon as I heard from her I got in touch with Rosenthal.'

'I really appreciate it. I could have been in a real mess if it hadn't been for him.'

'I know. He told me about it,' Paul said. 'I've made the same mistake you did a time or two. At least I came close to it.'

'How do you mean?'

'Picking the wrong woman. There always seems to be one around.'

'Yeah . . . well, it wasn't as simple as that.'

'Rosenthal thought it was. He said that little lady was really bad news. What was her name?'

'It doesn't matter,' Floyd said. 'It's all over now.'

'I'm sorry for bringing her up. I can see why you wouldn't want to talk about her.'

'It's not that. I just don't want to discuss her with somebody who doesn't know anything about her.'

'You're right. I *don't* know anything about her except what Rosenthal said. And like I told you . . .'

'I don't give a *damn* what Rosenthal said. He's a smart lawyer but he doesn't know everything. Nobody does.' He took a long drink from his glass. When he set it down, he said, 'While we're on the subject of Rosenthal, Helen said she never got a bill for his services. Why is that?'

'I don't know.'

'Helen said you told her there wouldn't be a bill. Does that mean you paid it?'

'No. There was no bill to pay.'

'Are you saying a sharp-shooter like Rosenthal works for nothing?'

'I don't know. You'll have to ask him.'

'I will,' Floyd said. 'He did a lot for me. He deserves to be paid. And I'm the one who should pay him.'

Paul smiled. 'That's right. Helen tells me you're a Bradshaw now. Changed your name and everything. I guess that means you can pay any bill that comes along.'

Floyd nodded. 'Yeah . . . it does. But not because I changed my name. I did that because I thought it would mean something to Helen.'

'I'm sure it did.' He looked at his watch. 'I thought she'd be here by now.' Then, 'What do you think of New York?'

'I like it. I lived here once for about six months when I was nineteen or twenty. Had a place down on Broome Street with a couple of other people. Helen says you grew up on Staten Island.'

Paul nodded.

'She said you lived clear out at the end of the island, where that narrow-gauge railroad goes. I know the area. Nice people around there. I used to go out there to the city dump with a friend of mine and his eight-year-old kid. We'd spend a whole Sunday afternoon digging in the dump. All kinds of great stuff we found. I'll bet you know the place I'm telling about.'

'No. I don't think so. Shall we have another drink?'

'Sure. Why not?'

After he signalled the waiter Paul said, 'You were in the Navy, weren't you?'

'That's right. Four bloody years.'

'You didn't like it?'

'I hated it. You didn't miss a thing.'

'What do you mean?'

'I mean you sat it out, didn't you? Some physical thing, Helen said.'

'Hypertension, they said, every time I went for a physical. But I'd never had it before and I've never had it since.'

'I met a guy in jail had the same problem. Only he brought it on himself. Every time they called him up he pumped himself so full of black coffee and amphetamines they had to pull him down from the ceiling to take his blood pressure. He told me lots of guys beat the draft that way.'

After a moment, Paul said, 'Are you trying to get a rise out of me, kid?'

Floyd grinned. 'Don't call me *kid*. I'm old enough to be your uncle.'

'I don't like it when somebody hints around that maybe I dodged the draft.'

'I wasn't hinting anything. I was just telling you about this guy I met in jail.'

The waiter brought them fresh drinks then and Paul looked at his watch again. Then he said, 'I've never heard a man talk about being in jail as if he was proud of it.'

'I'm not proud of it, not ashamed of it. It's a fact of life. It can happen to anybody. But not if you have a lawyer like Rosenthal.'

'He's not my lawyer.'

'Your lawyer or your friend, whatever he is.'

'I don't need a lawyer,' Paul said.

'I just thought maybe he was your business lawyer.'

'No, he's not.'

'What kind of business are you in?' Floyd said then. 'I asked Helen and she was sort of vague about it.'

Paul smiled but not a warm smile. 'Maybe *you* should be a lawyer. You ask a lot of questions.'

'That's the only way to have a conversation with somebody. You ask a question and you get an answer. Then it's the other person's turn. There's no other way to talk. But if you don't want to talk about your business that's all right, too.'

'I do promotions,' Paul said.

'That's right. That's what Helen said. But that didn't

mean anything to me. She didn't seem to understand it either.'

'I have certain projects that I work on, programmes that I originate, and I promote those things.'

'You mean you raise money so you can finance these ideas of yours?'

'Something like that. But there's more to it than just the money part. It's a certain skill. People say you either have it or you don't.'

'And you *have* it,' Floyd said. 'I'd bet on that. How old are you now?'

'I was twenty-six in January.'

'I was thirty in March. But I'll bet if we asked a few people sitting here in this restaurant, they'd say that *you're* older than *I* am. I don't mean you *look* old. You just have a certain way of talking like a man who's used to giving orders. You look dependable. But I don't have that look. I know I don't. When I run into people I used to know, they tell me I don't seem much different from what I was at twenty. Why do you suppose that is? Maybe it's because I don't take myself seriously enough? What do you think?'

'I couldn't answer that. An hour ago I'd never seen you before.'

'That's right. You hadn't. But all the same, when I walked in here and sat down you looked at me as if you had me all figured out. And after we'd talked for a few minutes your eyes started to glaze over as if everything I said was something you'd already heard. Am I getting warm?'

'I don't know what you're talking about.'

'I think you do. I've been watching you and listening to everything you said and I'm sure I'm right. You think I'm some kind of a hard-rock kid with a big mouth, and you're right about that. You think maybe I'm gonna raise my voice any time now and embarrass you in front of these waiters, and you're right. I'm capable of that too, but today I'm not planning to do it.'

'What brought all this on?'

'I'll tell you what brought it on. As soon as I sat down here I could tell you were looking down your nose at me. First you looked surprised that I'm wearing a good suit. You looked like you were expecting a Sears and Roebuck number right off the rack. Or one of those cardboard suits they give a guy when he gets out of the can.'

'I still don't know what you're talking about,' Paul said.

'The hell you don't. I've got you nailed and you know it. You took one look at me and clicked off like a flashlight with a dead battery. You decided I was taking Helen for a ride, didn't you?'

'Why would I think that? She's your mother. She's crazy about you.'

'That's right. She is. At least I hope she is. Because I'm crazy about her. Not because she's a Bradshaw. Not because it turns out she has a lot of money. I just *like* her. I liked her the first time I *saw* her. But I didn't want to show it. I didn't even like to admit it to myself. I figured if she went away once, she could do it again and I didn't want to set myself up for a big fall.'

'I don't know why you're telling me all this.'

'I'm telling you because I want to set you straight. I don't think you and I will be seeing much of each other so I don't want to miss this chance. While you were looking down your nose at me and sipping your sissy drink I was looking you over good. And I've got you pegged. You're a hustler. I've known a dozen guys like you and they all wear the same kind of shaving lotion. They talk slow and they keep looking around and they never lose their tempers. That's you, Uncle Paul. I don't know what you're hustling but I'll bet you're good at it. But don't ever try to hustle *me*. I've seen some places you're never gonna see and I've got a terrific memory. As soon as I met Rosenthal I thought I had your number. And as soon as I met you I knew I was right. But when Helen asks me I'm gonna tell her I think you're the greatest guy I ever met.'

After they finished lunch, after Helen had arrived and the three of them had laughed and chatted and had a bottle of champagne to mark the occasion, when she and Floyd were walking slowly back to their hotel, she said. 'What a nice thing to see you and Paul at the table together when I came in. I'm sorry I was late but I'm glad the two of you had a chance to get acquainted. Did you have a good talk?'

'We sure did. We covered everything we could think of.'

'That's terrific. I think he likes you a lot. I hope you like *him*.'

'No problem. I like him just as much as he likes me.'

[12]

No one had ever questioned the depth of Clara's emotional currents. At times in her life it had seemed that she was composed exclusively of tenderness and compassion. But she had no speck of sentimentality in her. The mention of Christmas did not bring tears to her eyes. She did not weep at weddings and christenings. She did not find all pets lovable or all children acceptable. Her emotions were neither general nor seasonal. Almost all annual occasions she held suspect. Family relationships were revered in direct proportion to the amount of reverence each specific relationship deserved. Most birthdays, anniversaries and all religious holidays she simply suffered, smiling, deferring, and providing nourishment to those whose entire emotional resources were reserved for such occasions.

About her own birthdays she had always been particularly unmoved, not for the classic reason that she hesitated to call attention to her age but because she thought it a foolish occasion for celebration and self-aggrandisement. 'Every day, every single person in the world is one year older than they were on that same day the year before. Either we should celebrate constantly or we should let it all pass.' This was her credo. Everyone who knew her had heard it many times.

As her seventy-fifth birthday approached, however, although she had no more appetite than usual for celebration, she could not, in her private thoughts, tell herself that it was just another year passing. It was indeed a milestone. She had lived for three-quarters of a century and she knew there was no way she could avoid reflecting on that long time, remembering the people who had come and gone, evaluating what they had meant to her and she to them.

It was not her way, of course, to lock herself into her sitting room one evening with a glass of port, imagine a sort of distant drum-roll, and begin, on cue, to chronicle her life to date. Rather, as she went about her daily routine, she recalled the years as she had lived them — in scraps and pieces, not chronologically, she found, not in any discernible order, not at all. Many people and events that logic told her should spring to the fore made no appearance at all. While other faces struggled endlessly, it seemed, to gain a front-line position and stay there.

Another surprise: whereas Clara's life had been characterized by balance and reason, by her need to find a way through any thicket no matter how tangled or thorny, by her ability to make a floating craft out of any wreckage, suddenly, now that many of the crises she had to go through were unquestionably behind her, she found that those moments of turmoil and pain and death and heartbreak were the things that had clung to her like burrs. No triumphs came to mind. No sweet memories or bright scenes of children and pets and blossoming trees. All her pictures were in earth colours, all their subjects were people in strife or collision.

Angus, for example, her father, who, whatever his faults, had always been a kind of regal figure in her mind, a monument to the achievements, past and present, of the Bradshaws, seemed reduced now in stature. Clara's assessment of him in fact began to resemble his own final assessment of himself. Without going so far as to say that life has no meaning, he had come quite close to that conclusion. He came to believe, without question, that the pursuit of land and capital, the attempt to preserve a family lineage and tradition, however valid those goals might seem, were not enough in themselves. His prediction late in his life, that Jesse would live to see the wind blow through the broken windows and ruined walls of Wingate Fields, was a symbol of his state of mind and his evaluation of himself and his life's work. He said, 'There was a lot more out there, more to be seen, more to be done, more to be understood, and I missed a great deal of it.'

Clara's mother, too, seemed to her now a failed person. Not in the early years, of course, when Louise had been an exemplary mother and a guiding force for both Clara and her brother, Raymond. But her values had not held up, Clara felt. Or perhaps, as Angus had hinted, her more questionable values had held up too well. Her loyalty and devotion to a nineteenth-century way of life, which had, in Northumberland, been passed down from even earlier centuries, had dimmed her vision, confused and aggravated her, and had contributed in a very real sense to her eventual retreat to some cloister inside herself, to a gentle pastel madness.

In her mother's case, however, Clara never forgot or

underestimated the effect that Raymond's disappearance had had on her. It had shocked and stunned the entire family, of course, but for Louise particularly the loss of her son had been more than just that. It was as though a keystone of her own structure had been removed. During the twenty years that passed between his disappearance and the news of his death, she lived in a kind of limbo, a condition of emotional stasis, obvious only to those who had known her intimately, who had been nurtured by her vitality, her humour and imagination, and her compassion. Those individuals — Angus and Clara, Clara's husband, Ned, and some of the older servants — sadly watched her subtle deterioration and pretended not to notice.

Raymond, too, Clara's brother, had heretofore occupied a sort of unassailable ledge in her system of things. When she reviewed his turbulent love affair with Emily Callison, her subsequent death and her husband's suicide, Clara had always criticized herself, had always felt that she, more than anyone else in the family, might have been capable of somehow averting that whole tragic series of events. Since they were close to her in age, both Raymond and Emily were accessible to her. She alone might have influenced Angus when he decided to abort the affair by sending Raymond off to Ireland, to university. And she alone might have had a chance to break through the walls that Raymond put up around himself when he sat for months in a private clinic after watching Emily die of a gunshot wound in a hotel room in Holyhead. But Clara had slavishly followed her father's lead when he insisted that their only recourse was patience. 'Raymond's a stable young man. This is something he must solve for himself.'

Soon after, of course, Raymond vanished from the clinic and from their lives. Only years later, when they received news of his death, did they realize he had gone to America, married there, become a university professor in Illinois, and fathered a daughter, Helen.

For years, then, for all that time since she had last seen him, up until the present moment, Clara had thought of Raymond as a victim, as someone driven to the course he had followed because no other course was available to him. Now, however, she realized that she had begun, gradually, to question her brother's choices. Whatever sins his family might have committed in trying to protect him from the consequences of a liaison with a young woman married to an unstable and dangerous man, however bitter and angry he must have felt after her death, all the same, at some period in his life he should have realized that no one in the Bradshaw family was in any way responsible for that final meeting between Raymond and Emily in the inn at Holyhead, or for Callison's knowledge of it, or for the struggle that ensued and ended in Emily's death. Surely some flash of reason, some time during all the years that followed, must have told Raymond that his family had been sufficiently punished, that his silence had lasted long enough.

But no such revelation or change of heart had taken place; it seemed that in Raymond's mind his family's crime deserved eternal punishment. Clara saw *that* decision now as a greater cruelty than any that had been visited on Raymond, a decision that had critically divided and redefined the Bradshaws, including, she sensed, her own children, who had never seen or spoken to Raymond but had memorized the details of his tragic passion for Emily Callison more thoroughly than they had learned their school lessons.

Those children, too, Clara felt, had failed themselves, although in quite different ways. Poor stormy Hugh, who had raced and roared and wenched his way through his early youth, forming no human relationships that anyone could see, except with Clara and his sister, and who then, shortly after Nora's marriage to his friend, Edmund Bick (a ceremony he had witnessed and helped to engineer), had withdrawn abruptly to a shooting estate in Scotland, on the Oykel; except for short and infrequent trips to Edinburgh or Inverness, he had remained there, alone with his dogs and horses and a few servants, until at last he had married an older woman with no apparent qualities, a common and unattractive person with five children from a previous marriage. Then, for no more profound reason, it seemed, than boredom, Hugh had simply shot himself in the head and died in the box-stall of his favourite stallion, having shot and killed the horse seconds before.

If Clara had ceased to feel responsibility for Raymond, she could not in any way disassociate herself from Hugh's fate. Nor did she want to. She felt, and would continue to feel, she knew, for as long as she was alive, a kind of living connection with him, something that exists only between a mother and her son. She forgave him his death, just as she had forgiven all the senseless and careless passions of his life. Even when she told herself that such loving forgiveness, which had characterized her relations with Hugh since his infancy, had been, very possibly, a key factor in his becoming whatever it was that he became, she never had the slightest impulse to regret it. She had loved him in the only way she could. Totally. Whether she understood him or approved of him had nothing whatsoever to do with it. Her failed attempts to guide him, to instruct him, to bring him closer to some more acceptable forms of thought and behaviour, in no way affected, influenced, or diminished her love for him.

Clara's husband, Ned, who had no relationship at all with his son, except when he and Hugh drank together, often said to Clara, 'Of course he loves you. That's plain to see. He doesn't give a damn for anyone on earth except his sister and you. But what good is *that* to you? What good is Hugh to anyone? He's as irresponsible as a raven and always will be.'

'But none of that matters to me,' she said.

'Well, it matters to me. He's careless and reckless and he has no sense of morality. And I'm held responsible because he represents me.'

'He doesn't represent you at all. Or me. He simply represents himself as we all do.'

Nora was another matter. Her flaws and failures, Clara felt, were more numerous and profound than Hugh's. But whereas his were public and flagrant, Nora's were carefully concealed. She had in fact, since childhood, presented to the world a façade of perfection. Her voice was soft, her movements graceful, and her eyes, unlike her brother's which were grey and angry, were soft and brown, as warm as chocolate. All visitors to the Bradshaw house went away praising Clara's daughter. She was, they declared, an absolute paragon of young womanhood. Only those who stayed behind when the carriages pulled away, only her immediate family and two or three perceptive servants knew the stubborn determination and monumental sense of self that lay beneath that exterior of honey and rose petals.

Nora had always had a strong and specific sense of direction. Clara, when she thought about her daughter, more often than not came to the conclusion that she had, on the surface at least, achieved everything she'd set out to do.

There had been early disappointments, of course. She and Jesse had been engaged to be married that first summer after Raymond's death, when Jesse had accompanied Helen to Wingate Fields. But Nora had married Edmund Bick instead, had enjoyed, albeit briefly, being the mistress of Bick House in Cumberland, and had given birth to a lovely daughter, Valerie. The marriage to Bick had ended, of course, with what seemed to most people a civilized, if mysterious, annulment. Only a few family members knew the ugly details of that separation. Since then, however, nothing, it seemed, had been denied Nora. She'd lived where she chose, in Paris and New York, she'd had a fine career as a publisher and dealer in paintings, and she'd had Jesse. They had lived together for many years in her house on the Seine and during the war years in New York City. Whatever the reasons for their parting, their friendship had survived it. Jesse's subsequent marriage to Valerie had apparently been a happy event for Nora as well as for them. So, Clara told herself, she had no reason to grieve for her lovely, strong-willed daughter, who slipped through the years, slim and lovely, seeming never to age, to fret or to suffer. But at the same time she remembered that Angus had often said, 'God help the poor souls who seem to have everything.'

If Clara had doubts about unquiet currents that might be coursing through her daughter, Nora's behaviour at the time of her father's memorial service turned these doubts into convictions. Seeing her now as an adult, with a grown daughter and grandchildren, Clara often thought of what Mrs Wiswell, her first governess, had said about her. 'With little Nora it's never quite clear what she proposes to do. But you can always be absolutely certain she's going to do *something*.' In that respect, Clara believed she hadn't changed. She remembered that Ned had often repeated Mrs Wiswell's remark and everyone had found it amusing. It no longer amused Clara. It made her uneasy.

As Valerie had become increasingly proud of Jesse's work, delighted by his reawakened productivity and by his trips to Paris, which took place now on what seemed to be a once-a-month basis, Clara found she could not share in that delight. She kept her reservations to herself, of course, because she was unsure about them. She told herself, in fact, that she was being hopelessly old-fashioned, that she was showing her age, if only to herself, in a most unattractive way. She went so far as to scold herself in the pages of a journal she had kept since the birth of her children.

> You must put a damper on yourself. You're running the risk of becoming a truly tiresome person. This is a time when acting your age is not apropos. If you look about, you'll see that even in this conservative and sheltered county some of the old habits and conventions don't hold any longer. People have greater freedom of movement now. It's accepted. It would also benefit you to remember some scenes from your own life. If you recall, Angus was away from Wingate Fields in the late twenties and early thirties as much as three or four months a year, travelling all around the world. And very often, particularly after 1930 till the war started, you travelled with him. It was business, necessary travel, you told yourself, but someone as hidebound as you're threatening to be would have said, 'Nonsense. You should be at home with your husband,' or to Angus, 'Why aren't you at home with your wife, minding your estate and looking after your interests?' So don't pretend, in this day and age, that there's anything extraordinary about Jesse's trips to France.

Clara had been the first person in England to encourage and support Jesse's ambitions. When he'd returned to Wingate Fields, to live there as Angus's son, she had provided him with a sumptuous and private place to work, had listened and counselled and tried to give him the confidence to go forward with some project, *any* project. She had continued to encourage him and believe in him when there was no production from him to justify her confidence, when Ned sneered at Jesse's apparent inability to produce anything more substantial than notions, when even Angus, though he never spoke of it, seemed to sense that his new son was deceiving himself about his call to literature.

When it came to Jesse, Clara had always been a believer. Consequently, when he finally began to produce substantial work, some time after the launching in Paris of *Icarus*, when his name appeared in print, not as the original and provocative writer he had hoped to be, perhaps, but as a strong and suddenly respected critic, she felt proud and fulfilled herself, not proud *of* herself but marvellously proud of him and fulfilled a bit also, in her own right, because she had continued to have faith in him when he had so little faith in himself.

His recent achievements, then, his new productivity, were as gratifying to Clara as they were to Nora. Different sorts and colours of gratification undoubtedly, but equal in volume and intensity. She had enjoyed hearing him read passages to her even in those other days when he couldn't write at all, coudn't even think or react like a writer, when three days' struggle might produce a limp and wandering half-page. So to hear him read an entire article now, or a piece of criticism, and to see it later in print for herself, was thrilling indeed. Like any person who lives in the house of a working writer, she felt there was some small shred of her in whatever he wrote. And she was correct of course. So it was a pleasure, a sensual one, to have him working again, to feel that the house was producing something vital that would float out through the walls and end up God-knew-where in all sorts of receptive brains.

So what was disturbing her? She couldn't say precisely, even to herself. She was a widely read woman and she was familiar with the classic complaints of women who live with painters or poets or composers . . .

> It's a tiny, private world. Just room for him and his work. But somehow I'm squeezed into it. Just at the edge. Through some little door that nobody uses but me. I go in and out by myself. But if *he* goes out, the work goes with him.

In Jesse's case, however, *his* wife seemed to have no such feelings of insecurity or second-class status. On the contrary, Valerie was enthusiastic about everything he was doing and she was light-hearted and outspoken about taking credit for her part in it.

'Here you are,' she said to him, 'scribbling away, happy as a schoolboy, and you owe it all to me. If I hadn't urged you to go to Paris again it would never have happened. I would like some praise, please.'

'I praise you,' he said. 'If you like, I'll even celebrate you. You are a giant among women.'

Monitoring Valerie's positive feelings and reactions, Clara felt even more foolish about her own nagging doubts. But they persisted nevertheless. At times she told herself she was too attached to her granddaughter, that she had become, in truth, a *daughter* to her in a way that Nora had never been. Valerie seemed to have taken her absent mother's place in the generational fabric of Wingate. There was also the fact that Clara and Valerie were very like each other. In appearance, in temperament, in the whole rhythm and texture of their womanhood. There had been a genetic leap across one generation and a particular woman had been duplicated, not in her daughter, but in her daughter's daughter.

Clara was very aware, of course, of this linkage between herself and Valerie. She was proud of it. It gave her joy every day. But it also led her to suspect that perhaps Valerie had fallen into a pattern that she herself had followed as a young married woman. Looking back on those days, Clara knew that for a critical period, from her marriage to Ned until well into her thirties, she had chosen, in the name of love perhaps, to subjugate herself totally to him and to her children. She had done it willingly and had taken a great deal of pleasure from it. Self-sacrifice, living entirely for others, all such labels and slogans that aid so greatly in the art of self-deception, had been key parts of her self-image in those years. Later, of course, she realized it was indeed a sort of hypnosis she had practised on herself, a kind of subtly disguised ego-gratification. By seeming to relinquish stature she had in fact gained greater stature in her own eyes.

All of these things crystalized in Clara's mind after her children had grown and gone. And particularly after she began to see her marriage to Ned for what it was rather than for what she had always told herself it was. Then she regretted those years when she had chosen to subjugate herself to a point of non-existence, when she had identified herself with roles and functions rather than feelings and needs and convictions.

Clara did not, however, in her ruminations about her own life, draw a direct parallel between her own marriage and Valerie's. She had only to see her and Jesse together day after day, to mark the easy flow of thought and affection between them, and she knew that she was witness to a kind of relationship that she and Ned had never had. Having known Jesse for so long, since before Valerie was born, Clara sensed that this particular warm quality of their day-to-day, back-and-forth style of living together was a more direct projection of his make-up than it was of Valerie's. And Valerie substantiated this. 'It's all Jesse,' she said. 'He must be the world's easiest man to live with. That doesn't mean he's not in charge. Because he is. But he doesn't have to be in charge of everything. He just goes along. Sometimes he's like the invisible man. But when something needs to be decided or planned, or when you just need somebody to put their arms around you, you never have to go far to find him. And you usually don't have to tell him what you need. He's a good guesser.'

Perhaps the apparent perfection of their marriage made Clara uneasy. Not the suspicion that it was something less than it seemed to be, but a fear perhaps that any tiny flaw or imperfection might develop in it. She was at the same time, however, aware, as she approached her seventy-fifth birthday, that her mind was beginning to function like the mind of a seventy-five-year-old woman. She found herself looking for shadows where no shadows, in fact, existed. Counting clouds. Predicting thunderstorms.

But all the same she was truly worried that Valerie, who was barely thirty years old, had fallen into the life-pattern of a much older woman. Of a country wife and mother without dreams or surprises in her life. And . . . however she ridiculed herself for her suspicions, Clara was aware each time Jesse left for Paris that Nora was waiting there.

Chapter Five

[1]

If Clara had known the precise nature of Jesse's relationship with Nora she would perhaps have had less apprehension about his trips to Paris. Or perhaps she would not have believed it if she'd been told. She might very well have assumed that Nora was playing some intricate game. But whatever conclusions she might have drawn, the simple facts would have surprised her. The facts were these. Outside of a few short meetings in the offices of *Icarus* and a chance encounter from time to time at a theatre opening or at a vernissage, Jesse and Nora had not seen each other at all during the months he'd been making his regular trips to Paris. She went her own way, *toujours occupeé* as usual. And when she wasn't busy with matters relating to the magazine or her gallery she was usually with Martin Vuko, her photographer friend from New York. For his part, Jesse stayed at his small hotel in Place St-Sulpice, dined with artist friends, and gathered information and interviews for his articles and critical pieces. He did not attend Nora's Thursday evening salons and he never visited her home. Furthermore, he found nothing unusual about this arrangement. In fact he liked it. And so, apparently, did Nora.

In late July of 1951, however, he found a note from her at his hotel.

> Need some advice. Hope you can meet me for dinner. 8.30 at La Petite Provençale?

'I was surprised to hear you were here,' she said when he joined her at her table by a window looking out across the *quai* towards Notre-Dame. 'I thought this was the week Helen was arriving with her grown-up baby son.'

'It is. But she had to change the date a couple times and we all got screwed up. When it was finally settled, it turned out she was coming just when Valerie had promised to take the kids to Bick House for ten days with Edmund. And I had to be here for the Vermeer opening at the Petit Palais.'

They had mulled it over one evening, Clara and Valerie and Jesse, but had not made much progress. Finally Clara said, 'We'll leave matters as they are. It will be good for Helen and Floyd to have some days to settle in before they're surrounded by people. I'll be here, and you'll be back in a week, Jesse, is that correct?'

'That's right.'

'And the children and I will drive down from Cumberland a day or so later,' Valerie said.

'Fine. I'm sure it will all turn out just right. Then on that first night you're back, Valerie, when the two of them have begun to feel at home, we'll have a nice family celebration. Like the old days.'

'Well, anyway,' Nora said to Jesse. 'I'm glad you're here. As I said in my note, I need your advice about something.'

'I solve all problems. Free of charge.'

'None of that. I don't trust free advice. So I'll buy your dinner.'

'That seems fair enough.'

'I've got a chance to sell *Icarus*. What do you think of that?'

'I didn't know you were trying to get rid of it.'

'I wasn't,' she said. 'But some people approached me, a couple of young Americans with more money than sense, and they made me a really splendid offer. Not only that, but I think if I shake my head for a while, they're ready to go a bit higher. What do you think?'

'Well, you and I have never agreed on the subject of money. Since you don't *need* the money, I can't see that it matters how much they're offering. On the other hand, if you're tired of being a publisher, if it's no fun for you any longer, then by all means sell it. Or give it away.'

'In other words, you have no feelings about it, one way or the other?'

'I'm surprised. But like I said, it's your investment, you made the magazine whatever it is, so if you decide you want to sell it, then you should.'

'Now *I'm* surprised,' she said. 'Before the war, and even during the war years in New York, you were as much part of the whole operation as I was. You and I did everything except set type that first year or so. You remember those frantic all-night sessions trying to make our printer's deadlines.'

'Sure I do. It was a lot of fun.'

'You didn't think so then,' she said.

'Sure, I did. I think about those days a lot.'

'That's what I mean. That's why I wanted to discuss it with you before I decided anything. I've always thought of it as *our* magazine, yours as much as mine.'

'Well, that's nice of you,' he said, 'but when it comes to making a decision like the one you're talking about, then you've got all the votes.'

'You're no help.'

'All right, let me ask you this. If you *do* sell it, what do you plan to do with yourself?'

'I've still got the art gallery.'

'You don't spend three hours a week in that gallery.'

'That's true. But I have other interests. And I spend a great deal of time with Martin now. I might even decide to get married. If I did that, then I'd have to be in New York a lot.'

'Well, that's a different situation. Then I think you should sell the magazine. Get the best offer you can and kiss it goodbye.'

'I thought maybe you'd like to take it over. Move Valerie and the children to Paris and have a fine time.'

'Not me. I don't have the patience for executive decisions and production details. Besides, I'm up to my ears in assignments now. I do a long piece every month for *Le Figaro*, another one for the *Observer* in London, and Arthur Wyndham wants me to do a monthly column on the European art scene for *Harper's*. Plus the junk I can't get rid of any place else that I palm off on you.'

She smiled. 'I made you what you are today.'

'That's right,' he said, 'but I forgive you.' Then, 'When are you planning the big event?'

'What do you mean?'

'You said you were getting married.'

'I said I *might* get married. No guarantees. When you're dealing with a Polish-American cuckoo bird who changed his name from Vukovich to Vuko, who drinks a quart of slivovitz every night and spends his days taking pictures of beautiful, skinny women accustomed to getting in and out of their clothes a lot, a mature and wise lady like me has to proceed carefully.'

'That's all right,' Jesse said. 'That's what you're good at. You wrote the book on proceeding carefully.'

'My mother doesn't think so. She thinks I proceed recklessly.'

'She's right. You proceed very recklessly up to a certain point and *then* you proceed carefully.'

'I have a feeling you're humouring me.'

'I have to. You're buying my dinner. Isn't that what you said?'

'Yes, it is. But I'm cheating a little. You see, they never bring me a check here. I send them so many customers they let me eat free.'

'There you are. That's what I mean by proceeding carefully. You've got everything covered.'

After they'd ordered dessert, Nora said, 'You know this may surprise you but I've always had a guilty conscience about Helen.'

'That *does* surprise me.'

'I always felt as if I wrecked your friendship or whatever it was.'

'It *was* a friendship, it still *is*, it's not wrecked, and I don't think you and I should discuss Helen.'

'Why not?'

'Because you don't like her and I do.'

'I don't dislike her. I just used to be jealous of her. But now I'm not.' Then, 'What's she really like?'

'No comment.'

'I'm serious. All these years I've known her and I realize I don't really know her at all.'

'Then why don't you leave it that way?'

'Because it makes me feel stupid. Just because I've never acted like a grown-up doesn't mean I'm not capable of it. I've done all kinds of things in my life that I'd like to take back but I can't. So the next best thing is to have some sense *now*. That's what I'm trying to do.' Then, 'I'm looking forward to meeting her son. I really am. What's he like?'

'I don't know. I've never seen him.'

'Valerie said . . . didn't you help Helen to locate him back at the beginning of the war?'

Jesse nodded. 'That's right. But after we found out he was in San Diego she went there by herself.'

'I can't imagine what it would be like, never seeing your child till he was grown up. Can you imagine that?'

'I wouldn't like it much. But strange things happen to people.'

'I always saw Helen as a young woman who had her whole life planned. A dependable husband, a nice comfortable house, and three or four beautiful children. But she fooled us, didn't she?'

Jesse sat looking at her for a moment. Then, 'It's not a case of *fooling* anybody. None of us have things work out exactly the way we plan. There's always somebody rolling boulders onto the railroad tracks.'

'Maybe. But still there are some people who manage their lives better than others. And Helen looked like one of those people. At least to me she did. She's the last woman in the world I'd have expected to have a secret like *she's* had all these years. Maybe she has more than one secret, but I mean the one about her son. Didn't it surprise you when you heard it first?'

'Yes, I guess it did,' Jesse said.

'Did you believe it?'

'Of course. Why wouldn't I?'

'I mean the part about the young man she met on the boat and never saw again. Did you believe that?'

'Why wouldn't I believe it?'

'Cause you're not a woman, I guess.'

'What does that have to do with it?'

'You could tell that story to fifty women and I guarantee you not one of them would swallow it.'

'Valerie believes it and so does Clara,' Jesse said.

'Valerie believes it because *you* believe it. And no one on earth has ever known precisely what Clara believes or does not believe. There's also a very good chance that Clara knows more than the rest of us.'

'What makes you think that?'

'Female intuition, old cock. Helen is closer to my mother than I have ever been or will ever be. And every woman tells *somebody* the truth.'

Jesse smiled. 'I feel as if this may be an earth-shaking moment,' he said. 'Who do you tell the truth to.'

'You.'

'I'm flattered.'

'Don't be. It's just an old habit. And old habits are hard to break. While we're on the subject, who do you tell the truth to?'

'Everybody. Liars have to have good memories and as you know I have a terrible memory.'

She reached over to a small service table, picked up the leatherbound wine list, placed it on the table in front of Jesse, and said, 'Put your right hand on this and pretend it's a Bible.'

When he did it, she said, 'Do you swear to tell the truth, the whole truth, and nothing but the truth?'

'Oui, bien sûr.'

'I'm serious.'

'So am I. When a man swears on a wine list, he can't fool around.'

She seemed to hesitate, then she said, 'Do you swear that Floyd is not your son, that you're not his father?'

Jesse took his hand off the book and said, 'Court's adjourned. The game's over.'

'It's not a game to me,' she said, and suddenly there were tears in her eyes.

'I can't believe what I'm seeing. You never cry.'

'Oh, yes, I do. But not if I can help it.'

He put his hand on the wine list again and said, 'Floyd is not my son. Helen and I are not in love and we've never slept together. And this is the last time you and I are going to discuss this.'

He sat there looking at her. 'You don't believe me, do you?'

'No. But that's all right.'

The waiter brought their dessert then, and coffee. After they'd finished the dessert and were sipping cognac with their coffee, she said, 'You and I are going to make a small wager. Fifty thousand francs. When I finally see Floyd I will know if you're his father or not. If I see you were lying to me I will send you a bill for fifty thousand francs. Otherwise *I* will send you a gift of fifty thousand francs. That way we'll both understand and we'll never have to talk about it again.'

Outside the restaurant, when he put her in a taxi, she said, 'I'm sorry I cried all over you. You're a good chap, no matter what anybody says.'

[2]

When Helen and Floyd arrived at Wingate Fields, as they drove across the moors and dales and saw it at last in the distance, and as they drove up the long curving and tree-lined driveway towards the great momumental buildings, she felt the excitement she had felt the first time she visited there.

'Holy God,' Floyd said as they approached the house. 'Do people really live here?'

'The Bradshaws live here. And that's us.'

'I can't believe it. Who are all those people waiting outside?'

'That's the staff. They're waiting to meet you. And that lovely woman in the centre is Clara. She's your great-aunt. My father's sister.'

All through lunch and through the full tour of the house and gardens with Clara and Gerald, the butler, Helen was seeing everything through Floyd's eyes and it was a thrilling experience for her. Only later, when she was alone in her room and Floyd had been taken to his, did she begin to feel let down. Although she understood the reason for Jesse's absence, and for Valerie's, she was still disappointed. She had particularly looked forward to the meeting between Jesse and Floyd. She told herself that Jesse's absence could in no way be interpreted as a lack of interest on his part but all the same she was disturbed that he wasn't there.

She was disturbed also by what seemed to her a radically changed quality of life at Wingate Fields. As they walked through the rooms and corridors earlier, although everything was as spotless and well cared for as ever, it all seemed strangely silent and uninhabited to her. She felt as if she were on a museum tour and she suspected by her careful monitoring of his reactions that Floyd felt the same way. When she asked him that early evening, however, when he came to escort her downstairs for drinks, he said, 'It's a fabulous place. I mean I don't know what I was expecting, but *this* is magnificent.'

'I was afraid it might look cold and empty to you.'

'It's not over-populated, that's a cinch, but who cares about that? I've lived in enough crowded places to last me a lifetime. Anybody who ever spent the night in a holding cell isn't likely to complain about too much space.'

'I'm glad you like it. I want you to feel at home here. And so does Clara.'

'That'll take some time, I guess. I'm not used to having somebody put all my clothes away and run the water in the bathtub for me.'

'You can do those things for yourself if you want to. Nobody expects you to turn into an Englishman overnight. Or ever.'

'What *do* they expect?'

'Nothing. You're a part of the family. They just want to meet you and make you feel at home.'

'How much do they know about me?'

'Nothing. They just know you're my son.'

'Do they know I've been in jail a few times?'

'No. I haven't told them anything,' Helen said. 'You can tell them as much or as little as you want to.'

'I'm not ashamed of anything I've done,' he said then. 'If somebody asks me a question I usually tell them the truth. Can I do that here?'

'Why shouldn't you?'

'I don't know. I just wouldn't want to embarrass anybody. Mostly I wouldn't want to embarrass you. I mean when I've met all these people I hope they'll like me but I don't think I'll be very good at turning into something I'm not.'

'Nobody expects that. *I* certainly don't expect that.'

'Good. In that case I think I'll have a great time. If you see me acting like a boilermaker in a perfume shop give me a high sign.'

Helen smiled and shook her head. 'Not a chance. You're a perfectly civilized man. Nobody has to coach you or keep an eye on you. You're not only acceptable, you're a social asset. Don't forget that.'

'Don't you forget it if you catch me eating my peas with a spoon.'

'You're a fake,' she said. 'Do you know that? You've decided apparently that you were brought up by aborigines in a straw hut. But you don't fool me. I saw where you lived and I met the man who raised you. Lowell Simison would have been very much at ease at Wingate Fields and so will you be. Just remember, it's your property. You own it, as much as anyone else who lives here. The man who drew your bath and laid out your clothes is working for *you*. *He* knows it, so it's important for *you* to know it too.'

Floyd held out his hand to her and grinned, 'In that case let's go downstairs and see if I've laid in some good booze.'

[3]

At the time of Clara's birthday, through that period of listing the catastrophes and mishaps of her years, of attaching guilt to people who had always before seemed guiltless, through all the moments of those particularly unpleasant and uncharacteristic days, she had only to contemplate the imminent arrival of Helen and Floyd and her thoughts took on a different colour. Logic would have told her that Helen's life had been as flawed in its way as had that of any of the other family members but logic and objectivity had never entered into Clara's judgement of Helen. There never had been, in fact, any such judgement. She had simply accepted her from the start and through the years she had continued to. Each time she saw her she hoped that Helen would not return to wherever she had come from; and the older Clara became, the more she treasured the hours they were able to spend together. This time, of course, there was the additional and mysterious pleasure of meeting Floyd, Helen's son and Hugh's son, her grandson. The fact that she would be unable to present him as a grandson in no way lessened the anticipation she felt. She remembered in detail when Helen and Jesse had arrived, that early-summer day in 1919, and she envisioned this new arrival as a joyful reprise of that occasion.

For that reason, perhaps, because she compared the remembered splendour of *that* day with the late-morning arrival of Helen and Floyd, she did not feel the exhilaration she had hoped to feel. The weather had turned abruptly cloudy for one thing, she was suddenly conscious of the fact that she was the only family member waiting on the porch at the south entrance, and the tousled young man in a sweater and corduroys who untangled himself from behind the steering wheel, took Helen's arm, and strode across the driveway gave her none of the shock of recognition she had hoped for. Studying him closely as he approached she saw no resemblance to Raymond, his grandfather, nor to Hugh, his father. He was simply an angular and long-legged young person she had never seen before.

'What do you think of my son?' Helen asked her later that afternoon when Floyd had gone out to inspect the stables and they were alone together.

'He's a fine-looking young man. Strong. I can tell you're very proud of him.'

'I am. I'm crazy about him.'

'And I like the way he treats you.'

'He's darling to me,' Helen said.

'He treats you like a friend.'

'I know. I love that about him.'

'I look forward to spending a lot of time with him and getting to know him. He's the second American young man you've brought into the family. First Jesse. Now Floyd.'

'They're very different,' Helen said.

'Of course. Why shouldn't they be?'

'When we arrived this morning I was thinking of that other time. Were you, too?'

Clara nodded. 'Yes, I was.'

'It seemed very different today.'

'Of course. You were eighteen then.' She smiled. 'Even I was younger then.'

'It's more than that. Why is it so different now?'

'The world has changed and Wingate Fields has changed with it. The biggest change is that all the men are gone. Only Jesse is still here and even he's away a lot. When you came to us that first time, Angus was here. And Ned. And Hugh. And all their friends were constantly in the house. And young men who came to court Nora. There were always plenty of those. And of course, once you'd arrived, we had Jesse as well. So it was a house filled with men. Now it's a house of women.'

'But as you say, I've brought you one more man.'

'So you have. And I'm delighted.'

'I couldn't help thinking this morning, when I saw him here in the house for the first time, how different he is from Jesse, from the way Jesse was when he first came here. You remember?'

'Of course I do. I hadn't known what sort of person to expect. But when he arrived he seemed very much at home and quite like us. He seemed almost English.'

Helen nodded. 'That's the way he *wanted* to appear. He

had learned a lot from Raymond, of course. Raymond never lost his British manner, for all his efforts at pretending he was an American born in Maine. I never realized until I came here how English Raymond was. And as I say, Jesse emulated him in every way he could. Once we'd decided to come here, when I saw him choosing the clothes he would bring, I knew he wanted to conform, to be a part of the fabric. He never wanted to be pointed out as an American. He still doesn't.'

'I have a feeling that Floyd is not so eager to conform.'

Helen smiled. 'I don't think it's ever occurred to him to be anything other than what he is. I don't mean that it's a conscious thing. He simply doesn't think much about himself, how he should dress and how he should behave. He's not trying to be accepted. He told me once that he prefers to have people like him but he says he's found that some people do and some people don't and there's very little he can do to influence them one way or the other.'

Clara smiled. 'I wish I'd known that when I was his age.'

'So do I. I still find myself trying to ingratiate myself to fools I don't care anything at all about. It's a characteristic I can't do much about, I guess. Jesse has it and I have it. We're like two dogs. Always looking for someone to scratch our heads.'

'And Floyd's not like that, I take it.'

Helen shook her head. 'Not at all. He seems content to scratch his own head.'

'He's not the first Bradshaw man to feel that way. Angus used to say he tried to alienate everybody and the people who couldn't be driven away were truly friends.'

'Seems like a severe test of friendship.'

'Of course. But Angus didn't really need friends. He certainly didn't need casual friends. So I guess that approach worked for him. He may not have had a legion of friends but he certainly always found strong allies when he needed them.'

'Most of us don't have his self-assurance,' Helen said.

'That's true. But I have a feeling that Floyd has at least some of it.'

'You're right. He has a great deal of it. He doesn't seem to be afraid of things like the rest of us cowards.'

Abe Rettberg, too, had dwelt at length on what he felt was Floyd's inordinate self-confidence. 'The trouble with you,' he said, 'is that half the people you meet want to take a punch at you. They take one look at you and they say to themselves, "What does that ass-hole have to feel so good about?" I don't mean you're stuck on yourself or bragging about how great you are in the sack or stuff like that, but you just have that calm look about you. Makes people think that nothing's gonna get you nervous. And since most of us are nervous as hell nothing gets us crazier than some dude who's just skating along with the wind at his back, not giving a damn about anything.'

'That's not me,' Floyd said. 'I give a damn about all kinds of things.'

'Not so anybody could notice it,' Abe said.

'Nobody has to notice it. Who says I have to wear a sign on my back that tells everybody what I'm thinking?'

'Nobody says you have to. But you're living in a world filled with jaybirds who can't stand to keep anything to themselves. If they got nobody to tell it to they talk to strangers on the street. Everybody trusts that. Everybody recognizes trouble. They sympathize with it. What they don't trust is a guy who looks as if he *has* no trouble. Or if he has, he knows exactly how to handle it. You look like a winner and nobody likes a winner. Unless maybe it's another winner.'

'Let me tell you something,' Floyd said. 'I had enough crap in my life before I was twenty years old to last me a lifetime. I'm not talking about my folks or the fact that I was adopted or anything like that. I'm talking about stuff I brought on myself. By my own stupidity. Always trying to look around corners, trying to figure out tomorrow when I hadn't taken a whack at today yet. You know what I mean? I had myself tied in knots trying to keep from making a mistake. So all I did was make mistakes. From the first night I ever sat in a jail cell all I wanted to do was stay out of jail. But I couldn't manage it. Not till I was in the Navy, when I was stuck on the rust-bucket down in the South Pacific, did I start to get things together in my head. Did you ever go to bed with a girl who can hardly get out of her clothes she's so scared she's gonna get pregnant? Well, that's a girl you have to get away from, because five'll get you ten she's gonna end up pregnant. A girl like that can get pregnant from taking an aspirin. You know what I'm talking about?'

'No. And neither do you.'

'Yes, I do. I mean people get so scared about screwing things up that they can't do anything else. All they do is screw up. So like I say, I thought a lot about that and I decided that what everybody's really scared of is making an ass of themselves in front of people. It's not that they mind screwing up, they just don't want people to see them doing it. So then I thought about that for a while but it didn't help me much. And then one day it hit me. I was working on the fantail, doing some kind of horseshit job, and I said to myself, "What's the difference. Nobody's looking anyway." And the more I thought about it, the more sense it made. All those people we worry about are busy worrying about themselves. They're all looking at their own belly-buttons. They don't care if you succeed or fail or get drunk and fall down. They've got their own fish to fry. So I said, "Screw it. I'm gonna do what I *want* to, whatever makes sense to me." So that's what I've been doing, ever since I got out of the Navy. And it's worked out fine. At least it's worked for me. I just tackle one day at a time, a little here and a little there. Then I wait to see what happens. If I fall on my can, I try something else. If something works out, so much the better. I'm an ordinary guy. I figured that out a long time ago. So I don't shoot for the moon. I go for things I think I can get. Some I get. Some I don't. But I keep on trucking.'

'I think you're nuts,' Abe said. 'You're on the moon.'

'No, I'm not. You asked me why I don't get nervous about things and I'm telling you. I'm not afraid to try anything because it's all right with me if I make an ass of myself. What I mean is that nobody can shoot me down or steal anything from me. I got nothing to lose.'

'Only a dead man has nothing to lose.'

'That's because he's already lost everything,' Floyd said. 'In my case I decided there's nothing I have that I couldn't give up if I had to. And since I decided that I've never had to give up anything.'

'All that means is you're lucky,' Abe said.

'Maybe you're right. But I'd rather be lucky than smart any day.'

[5]

'In the first place there's nothing to discuss,' Jesse said, 'and in the second place, even if there were something to discuss, it's nothing that you and I have to concern ourselves with.'

'Of course it is,' Helen said. 'I decided when I was fifteen years old that *everything* that concerned you would concern me too.'

They were driving home from the airport outside Newcastle. She had gone to meet him there when he flew in from Paris.

'Not this time,' he said.

'We're pretty cranky today, aren't we? Here I come all the way from America to show off my handsome son, I drive all the way to Newcastle to fetch you from the airport, and all I get is a cranky reception.'

'Not true,' he said. 'I'm tickled to death to see you.' He reached over and squeezed her hand. 'I just said I don't want to talk about Nora.'

'I didn't say anything about Nora, did I?'

'You were leading up to it.'

'Not only cranky, but touchy,' she said.

'Weren't you leading up to that?'

'Not necessarily. I said I felt neglected because you weren't at Wingate to meet me. Then I said I imagine Valerie and Clara feel neglected too when you're away so much.'

'Valerie and Clara did everything but chase me out of the house to get me to go to Paris again. Ask them. They had some idea that it would be good for me, get me started working again. And they were right.'

'Maybe it started you working again but that doesn't mean it's good for you.'

'It's *good* for me,' he said. 'Everything's working out fine.'

'Are we going to pretend that you don't know what I'm talking about?'

'I know exactly what you're *about* to talk about but I don't want to hear it.'

Helen looked at her watch. 'It's almost an hour before we'll be home so unless you plan to stop the car and throw me out, I'm afraid I'm going to talk about it.'

'Go ahead. But it won't do you any good.'

'Maybe not. But it might do you some good.'

'All right. Maybe I can save you some trouble. If you've got an idea that Nora and I have taken up where we left off ten years ago, if you think that's the reason I make these trips to France, you can forget it. I almost never see her when I'm there, I haven't been inside Nora's house since Valerie and I got married, and three or four nights ago was the first time we've had dinner together since she left New York after the war and came back to Paris.'

'All right. Now I'll tell you a story. When Frank Wilson and I got a divorce in 1930, I never expected to see him again. But I did, twelve years later, and we've been together, as the old expression goes, ever since.

'Good for you. But what's that have to do with me?'

'Nothing maybe. I'm just saying that when you've lived with somebody for a long time . . . how long were you and Nora together?'

'What's the difference?'

'How long? Fifteen years? Twenty?'

'I guess. About that,' he said.

'I'm saying that all that time together doesn't just dissolve and disappear. Things happen. Suddenly there's a pull back and there you are.'

'You should get a turban and tell fortunes at country fairs.'

'I'm serious,' she said.

'I know you are but I'm not. I think you're wacky. I think you and Nora should get together and swap your fantasies first-hand.'

'What does that mean?'

'I've mentioned this to you before. For two people who barely know each other . . .'

'I've known her as long as you have,' Helen said.

'No. You met her when I did. But you don't know her at all and she doesn't know you except from third-person reports. Tell me the truth, have you ever had a conversation alone together for more than five minutes?'

'I don't remember.'

'Of course you don't remember. Because no such conversation ever took place. Outside of family gatherings and sitting at the same dinner tables, I'll bet *all* the time you two have spent together wouldn't total one hour.'

'Are you saying that's my fault?'

'I'm not saying it's anyone's fault. I'm just saying it

astounds me that two women who don't know each other or like each other should spend so much time fantasizing . . .'

'Is that your favourite new word? I have no fantasies about Nora.'

'Of course you do,' Jesse said. 'If you think she and I are having a passionate reunion every time I fly to Paris then *that* is a full-blown fantasy.'

'Maybe it is. But tell me a year from now if it's still a fantasy.'

'I can tell you right now. It will be.'

'We'll see,' Helen said. Then, 'What is Nora's fantasy about me?'

'You know some of it. She thought the first time she saw us together that you and I were room-mates. She thought it all the time she and I lived together, and she still thinks it. Now she believes I'm Floyd's father.'

'You're kidding.'

He shook his head. 'Dead serious.'

Helen smiled. 'Good. I'm glad she thinks that. I hope it makes her miserable.'

'You're really full of surprises, you know that? That's the first really bitchy thing I've ever heard from you.'

'These are special circumstances. Nora deserves special treatment.'

[6]

The following morning Jesse went for a long hike across the moors to visit one of the tenant farmers and Floyd went with him.

'This is a complicated family I fell into,' Floyd said. 'And as I understand it, you used to be as much of an outsider as I am.'

'More so.'

'Let me get this straight. You left your own folks when you were sixteen or seventeen and went to live with Helen's father?'

'That's right. He took me in and I never went back. He and his wife were separated, so the three of us, Raymond and Helen and I, lived there together till he died in 1918.

And the next summer Helen and I came here to meet the Bradshaws.'

'And that's when Helen's grandfather . . . what was his name?'

'Angus,' Jesse said.

'That's when he adopted you?'

'That's right.'

'And then you married Clara's daughter?'

'No. We were engaged for a while but we broke up. Nora married a man named Edmund Bick, Valerie's father.'

'But I thought you and Nora . . .'

'After she and Bick separated, after their marriage was annulled, she and I got together. We lived together for quite a long time. Till 1941.'

'And then you and her daughter . . .'

'That's right. Valerie and I got married right after America got into the war.'

'I guess you didn't have to go into the service. Helen said you got shot up the other time.'

Jesse nodded. 'In 1917. I've had this limp ever since.'

'I used to sit in that lousy ship in the South Pacific and wish I'd get shot so I could get the hell out of there.'

'That must have been rough duty.'

'No, it wasn't. It was just a lot of crap. All wars are a lot of crap. They start waving flags and shooting guns and a bunch of good guys get killed or mangled and after a while it's all over and nothing is changed. The winners give the losers a lot of money to put their country back together again and everybody feels great. Then pretty soon the whole thing starts over again. It's all crap. Some writer said, "Patriotism is the last refuge of the scoundrel." Who said that?'

'Shaw, I think. Oscar Wilde maybe. I'm not sure.'

'You're a writer, aren't you?'

'I work at it,' Jesse said.

'Helen says you're damned good.'

'Mostly I criticize other people's work.'

'Shaw was a critic, wasn't he?'

'Shaw was a lot of things and he was good at all of them.'

'I used to hang out with a guy in California. When I first knew him in San Diego he was a bartender, then he moved to Los Angeles and taught himself to be a bee-keeper. He always said it didn't make a shit bit of difference what you do as long as you like it well enough to be good at it.'

'Pretty good advice.'

'Yeah. I thought so.'

After Jesse had a chat with the tenant farmer, when he and Floyd were walking home, taking a different route, Jesse asked, 'How do you like it so far?'

'You mean England? Or right here?'

'I mean here at Wingate Fields. The whole place.'

'It's too much. It's like a storybook,' Floyd said.

'Had Helen told you much about it?'

'Sure. She talked about it a lot. And showed me a few pictures. But I mean when you come rolling up that driveway and see that house or castle or whatever you want to call it stretched out across the rim of the hill, you think some jaybird in a suit of armour is gonna come galloping out through the gate and stick a lance in your gullet. It's a lot to swallow, I'll tell you that. But you know what I'm talking about. You saw it once just like I'm seeing it now. Has it changed much since then?'

'The family's changed. A lot of people are dead. But the place itself is exactly the way I saw it first. Angus said it hadn't changed in his lifetime and he was born in 1844. The first Bradshaw lived here in the sixteenth century.'

'Jesus. Isn't that something?'

'And now a couple of Midwestern clowns like you and me are part of the whole thing.'

'You look like you were born here.'

'So will you in a few years.'

'I doubt that.'

'What are your plans?' Jesse asked.

'I don't have any.'

'Do you think you'd like to stay here?'

'I haven't even thought about it.'

'You have a girlfriend in the States?'

'Not me. I'm available to the highest bidder.'

'There are a lot of splendid young women here in the county. There always seem to be more young women than young men around.'

'Well, that's something to think about.'

'The name Bradshaw's like catnip around here. You'll see.'

'Well . . . first I'd better get used to *being* a Bradshaw before I put myself on the market. You know what I mean?'

'Sure I do. I'm not trying to marry you off. You know how old I was when I got married? Forty-four.'

'How old was your wife?'
'Twenty-one. She's about your age, I think.'
'I was born in 1920.'
Jesse nodded. 'So was Valerie.'

[7]

On a very warm August afternoon, a few days after Valerie had returned home from Bick House, she was sitting in the shade in a lawn chair just beside the stream that runs along the edge of the deer park, her three children and their nanny were wading in the shallows, laughing and splashing water on each other. She didn't see Floyd come down from the house, wasn't aware of his presence until he sat down on the grass ten feet away from her chair.

'So there you are,' she said.

'That's right. Is it all right if I sit here?'

'Of course. I was just day-dreaming and watching the children.'

'How old are they?'

'Well . . . let's see . . . Rab will be nine in November. Polly was seven in May, and little Bill was six last month.'

'How'd you happen to call him Rab?'

'That's just a nickname. His name is Raymond Angus Bradshaw. We called him Rab when he was a baby and the name stuck.'

'You think you'll have any more children?'

'I don't know,' she said. 'Why do you ask?'

'I just wondered.' Then, 'Did I say something wrong? Is that too personal a question?'

'No, of course not. It isn't a question that somebody asks me every day but I don't see anything wrong with it.'

'That's good.'

'There was a time when I thought I'd have a house full of children but now . . . I think I may be content with the three I have.' Then, 'Do you like children?'

'I don't know,' he said. 'I've never been around them much. Really little kids, I mean.'

'How old are you now?'

'Jesse says you and I are the same age. I was born in 1920.'

'So was I,' Valerie said. 'When's your birthday?'

'March 20th.'

'Mine's 9th October.'

'So I'm older than you are. I'm thirty-one and you're still thirty.' He grinned. 'So if you ever need some fatherly advice from an older man, I'm available.'

'I'll remember that. But I think it's unlikely. You see, I feel as though I'm older than you. I feel like your aunt.'

'Well, that's *your* problem. You're a great-looking lady. You shouldn't feel like anybody's aunt.'

'But I see nothing wrong with that. In ten years I could be a grandmother.'

'Maybe you could. And I could be dead. But I don't think of myself that way. And you shouldn't either.'

'The truth is I don't think about myself much at all.'

'Maybe you should,' he said.

'When you have children they have a way of taking your mind off yourself.'

'I don't believe that.'

'That's because you don't have children.'

'So what? I'm not blind. I don't have to stick my hand in the fire to know it's hot.'

She sat quietly then, looking out at the stream where the children were playing. Finally she said, 'Have you ever been married?'

'No.'

'Any particular reason?'

'Sure. I never saw anybody I wanted to marry. Or if I did they were already married.'

'They say if you fall in love with people you can't have, that means you don't really *want* to get married, you don't really want to commit yourself to one person.'

'Who says that?'

'I don't know. The experts, I guess.'

'I don't give a damn what the experts say. Do you?'

'No. I just think it's remarkable that a presentable young man like you . . .'

'*Presentable?*'

'Does that word offend you?'

'It's just something nobody ever called me before. It sounds like you're talking about a roast turkey.'

'In that case I withdraw the word. Let me put it this way.

You don't seem self-conscious around women and I'm sure a great number of women would like the way you look, as well as your attitude . . .'

'What does that mean?'

'It means that a lot of women like a man who asserts himself. And you seem quite capable of asserting yourself.'

'You don't like me, do you?' Floyd said.

'I'm sorry. Did I say something that . . .'

'I'm not talking about anything you said. I'm talking about the way you are, the way you've acted since you came back from wherever you were the other day.'

'You know where I was. We discussed it at dinner. I was visiting my father in Cumberland.'

'You think I'm a fool, don't you?'

'Not at all. I just think you're somebody who likes a good argument. I don't happen to like . . .'

'If you think I'm not educated you're right. I didn't finish high school and I never went to college. A friend of mine told me I was intelligent but I was ignorant. He said "You know a lot but you've never learned anything." And he's right. But the things I know, I really know. And sooner or later I figure I'll learn something. But if I don't I'll still get by. A lot of people I've met have learned everything but they don't know one damned thing.'

'I agree with you,' Valerie said. 'I think you're absolutely right. So what makes you say I don't like you?'

'I think we'd better just drop it.'

'But I don't want to drop it. You're really angry, aren't you?'

'I don't get angry,' he said. 'I get mad.'

'Good for you. So do I.'

'No, you don't. You get upset. Or impatient. Or frustrated. You don't get mad.'

'What is the matter with you?' she said then. 'What in the world is the matter?'

'Nothing's the matter with me,' He stood up suddenly. 'What's the matter with you?' He turned and walked off toward the house.

She had planned to give Jesse a word-for-word account of her talk with Floyd but when they were alone in their rooms after dinner she simply told him they'd had a conversation that afternoon.

'What do you think of him?' Jesse said.

'I don't know. What do you think?'

'Interesting guy. Kind of a rough diamond. And determined to stay that way. But a lot of potential, I think. Lots of energy. What did he have to say to you?'

'It wasn't what he said. He just seems to have an odd attitude. He seems very young to me. And very angry.'

[8]

The afternoon she arrived at Wingate Fields, Nora announced to the family assembled that on the following day she planned to kidnap Floyd. Then she added in what she felt was a disarming cockney accent, 'You lo' 'ave 'ad 'im ta yaselves fur thray wakes. It's moy turn naow.'

Next morning after breakfast, as soon as they were in her roadster she said, 'In the family portrait gallery there's a painting of me that grows fangs once a month when the moon is full. The servants are instructed to cover it with a drape during those days. I tell you this so you'll know the sort of person you're dealing with.'

'Thanks,' Floyd said. 'I appreciate it.'

'Have you been told ugly stories about me?'

He shook his head. 'No stories at all. Just a few facts here and there. I know you're Clara's daughter and Valerie's mother. You used to be married to a man named Bick and you lived with Jesse for a long time before he married Valerie.'

'Who told you that? The last part.'

'I don't remember. Either Helen or Jesse.'

'What else do you know?' she said.

'Not much.'

'So what did you decide?'

'About what?'

'About me. What kind of a woman did you expect to meet.'

'Well, Helen said you were great-looking and you are. And I got the idea you've always done pretty much what you wanted to.'

'How do you feel about that?' she asked.

'I'm all for it. As long as you're not out to shoot people

down. Everybody wants what they want. Most people just don't have the guts to go after it.'

'Aren't you something?'

'What does that mean?'

'It means I think you and I are going to get along fine.' Then she went on. 'Now . . . I'm sure you have some questions about this family you've fallen into. I'm the person you can ask because I'll tell you the truth. That doesn't mean that everyone else will lie to you but for the most part they are more concerned with appearances and respectability than I am. Don't misunderstand me, I am extremely respectable, but according to my own standards, not someone else's. If anyone has implied that I'm a nymphomaniac, that's not true. Nor am I an alcoholic. I have been known to smoke a bit of hash but cocaine has never touched the delicate membranes of my nostrils. I drive too fast, I'm addicted to chocolate, and I love to sleep in the daytime. But I seldom do it. I have hundreds of women friends but my three best friends are men, all wise and elderly gentlemen who have no impulse to lure me into their beds, although one of them did many years ago. Neither of us regretted it. Have you heard Edith Piaf?'

'Sure. On records.'

'She does a song called "*Je ne Regrette Rien*'. That makes sense to me.'

'It makes sense to *everybody*,' Floyd said, 'but it is not always easy to pull off. Some things are bound to happen to you that you wish hadn't happened.'

'Not me. I make a positive out of everything.'

'You didn't break up with your husband because you were having a great time, did you?'

'No. But that doesn't mean I'm sorry I married him. In the first place we had Valerie. That's the most important thing that ever happened to me. And in the second place I would never have been satisfied not to be married at least once.'

'You don't expect to get married again?'

'Not a chance. Edmund and I separated twenty-five years ago. If I wanted to get married again I'd have done it long since.'

'What about Jesse?'

'What about him?'

'You tell me,' Floyd said.

'I certainly don't regret any of *that* time if that's what you mean. Jesse and I had a great life together. Lots of fun. Lots of good stuff.'

'And then he married Valerie.'

'Not just like that. He and I broke up first.'

'What happened? You told me to ask questions so I'm doing it.'

'What happened?' she said. 'How shall I put it? We had some problems we couldn't solve. I could have lived with them but Jesse couldn't. One problem was that I was jealous of your mother.'

'Jesse and Helen? Where did that come from?'

'From my head. I don't know why I'm being so honest with you.'

'Why are you?'

'Because I feel like it, I guess. And it feels good. You may turn out to be the best thing that's happened to this family since . . .'

'Since Jesse?'

'Better maybe. Jesse did a lot of damage. Not because he tried to or wanted to. Just because he was here and a lot of people had strong reactions to him.

'Like my mother you mean?'

'No. I was wrong about them. It took me a long time to realize it but now I do. I mean they love each other. They've never tried to fool anyone about that. But it wasn't like I thought. I was so crazy about Jesse I couldn't imagine anyone loving him in any way other than the way I did. But I was wrong. My mother loved him and Helen loved him. But nobody loved him as I did.'

'Except Valerie.'

'Not even Valerie.'

Late that afternoon when they returned from their day together, after Floyd went into the house, Nora walked down to the stables and found Jesse there.

'How was your day out?' he said.

'Very enjoyable. He's an unusual young man.' She opened her shoulder bag then, took out a thick envelope and handed it to Jesse.

'What's this?' he said.

'That's the fifty thousand francs I owe you.'

'Does that mean I'm exonerated?'

'Totally.'

'It didn't take you long to make up your mind.'

'You'd never believe how quickly I knew.'

When Floyd came to her rooms that early evening for their ritual pre-dinner drink, Helen said, 'How was your afternoon with Madame Nora?'

'You really don't like her, do you?'

'I wouldn't put it so strongly. Let's just say we've never become close friends.'

'Maybe you ought to give it another try. I have a hunch you two might get to like each other.'

Helen shook her head. 'Too late in the game. Too much water has trickled under the bridge.'

'You never know. People change sometimes.'

'I know. And the mouse eats the tiger.' Helen said. Then, 'Does Nora know you've volunteered as a kind of peacemaker between her and me?'

'No. We didn't talk about you at all. As a matter of fact, I don't discuss you with anybody. And I'm not acting as a peacemaker. That was just a remark. I take it back.'

Helen leaned over and kissed him on the cheek. 'You don't have to take anything back. You made a perfectly civilized suggestion. But for Nora and me, the boat sailed a long time ago.'

'I get the picture.'

'But that's no reason for you not to like her. Or for her not to like you.'

'I'm sure a lot of people feel the same way about her as you do. I can see that she could be a handful to deal with. And maybe when I get to know her better I won't like her any more than you do. But based on what I saw today, I do like her.'

'I'm sure she was trying very hard to make a good impression.'

'Of course she was,' Floyd said. 'I know that. I've seen snow jobs before. Lots of them. But all the same, I *liked* her. She's not afraid to say what she thinks and she seems to have a sense of humour about herself; so we talked a lot — she talked more than I did — and it was a nice day. Mostly she talked about Valerie and her grandchildren. She's crazy about her daughter.'

'Everyone's crazy about Valerie,' Helen said.

'I'm not. And she's she's not crazy about me.'

'What gave you that idea?'

'It's not just an idea. I know what I'm talking about.'

'She told me she thought you were very nice.'

'That doesn't mean anything.' Floyd said. 'I told her mother the same thing about her. I said I thought she was very nice. But the truth is I think she has too much starch in her underwear.'

Helen smiled. 'I'm not sure what that means but I don't think it's intended as a compliment.'

'It's not. She's got herself all tied up in knots and she doesn't even know it. If she ever steps back and takes a good honest look at herself she'll start to unravel like an old sweater.'

[10]

Late that night when everyone had gone upstairs Nora sat with her mother in Clara's second-floor sitting room.

'You are absolutely mistaken,' Clara said. 'I don't know where you get such ideas. I can't understand why you are so eager always to make trouble for Helen.'

'I'm not trying to make trouble for anyone. This is just a conversation between the two of us. Behind closed doors. We're talking about Hugh. You're his mother and I'm his sister. And it's not terrible news, is it? I think it's marvellous.'

'But it's not true. I can't seem to convince you. I *know* the truth. You know how close I am to Helen. You must realize that if such a thing as you're suggesting were true, I would know it.'

'I think you do know it. I believe that Helen would have told you the truth. But I also think that she doesn't want the world to know. I can understand that. But why should you be so frightened to have *me* know? I don't plan to tell anybody. Why would I want to? I'm sure Jesse knows. And now I know. That's four people in the world. I see no reason why anybody else should be told.'

'Nora, I swear to God sometimes you could make a person insane. I don't know what gets into you. I keep telling you you're mistaken, that I *know* you're mistaken, and you go right on talking as if I hadn't spoken. What do I have to say to persuade you?'

'I'm sorry. I'm not trying to upset you. That's the last thing I want to do. But give me some credit. I am neither blind nor simple-minded. I spent the entire day today with that young man. I sat with him in the car. I sat across from him at lunch for two hours. I listened to his voice, I studied his face, I looked at his hands and the way he walks, the way he sits, the way he carries himself.'

'That doesn't matter.'

'It does matter, mother. Listen to me. You know that no other human being knew Hugh the way that I did. No one spent the hours with him that I did. I knew every nuance of his voice, every angle of his face, every move, every gesture. Do you imagine that he could have a son, a mature, grown-up young man who wouldn't bear any resemblance whatsoever to his father?'

'This is all so pointless.'

'No, it's not. What I can't understand is this desperate need for secrecy. Is it just that Helen can't face the truth herself or is she scared to death someone *else* will find out. And why are you so anxious for the truth to be concealed? We're talking about your grandchild. Is there some terrible stigma we're afraid of because Hugh and Helen were first cousins? They had a fine, normal son. That's all that matters, isn't it?'

'No. It doesn't matter at all because it's not true.'

'Can you honestly tell me you've *looked* at Floyd, really looked at him . . .'

'Of course I've looked at him.' Clara said.

'I don't think so. If you've sat across the table and looked at his eyes, you'd know that only two other people in the world had eyes like that . . . Angus and Hugh. Grey and pale and a bit ticked up at the corners. Jungle eyes. Cat eyes. Can you tell me you haven't noticed that?'

'Helen is Angus's granddaughter. Floyd's his great grandson. Why shouldn't he resemble him in some way?'

'No one else has those eyes. No one except Hugh.'

Clara sat looking at Nora, her hands folded in her lap. Finally she said, 'I know how relentless you can be when you decide to go after something. But whatever you're trying to make me say, I won't say it. I'm very tired now and I need my sleep. I'm sure you think you're right about this but you must believe me when I tell you you're wrong.'

'I know you're tired and I'm sorry if I've upset you. But this is important to me too. You know how close I was to Hugh. If he has a son I think it's important for someone to acknowledge it, even if it's only the two of us.'

Nora was a seasoned and brilliant tactician in matters such as these. Experience had taught her that on certain occasions only a lie can bring forth the truth. In this case she had believed and hoped that by sheer energy and conviction she could turn her mother around. But she had prepared an emergency falsehood just in case. Now she saw she would have to use it. 'I have a confession to make to you. I've kept something from you for many years because it was told to me as a secret. Even after Hugh's death I saw no reason to tell you because I thought it would only upset you. But now I must tell you so you'll be convinced that I know what I'm talking about.' She leaned forward in her chair and spoke in a quiet voice. 'You remember when Hugh and Edmund and I went to Scotland together, when Edmund and I got married?'

Clara nodded and Nora went on. 'One afternoon Edmund had to dash off somewhere and Hugh and I had a great deal to drink in a public house behind the castle.' She paused and lit a cigarette. 'And *that* afternoon Hugh told me that he and Helen . . . you know what I'm saying. As I told you, he was quite drunk but from what he told me, in great detail, there was no question in my mind that what he described had actually taken place.'

She sat there studying her mother. Finally she said, 'As I told you before, I think Helen has already told you what I'm telling you now. But the important thing is now you *certainly* know, and you know that I know.'

[11]

As soon as she woke up the following morning, Clara asked her maid to take a note to Jesse. 'Be sure he's quite alone when you give it to him.'

An hour later, the two of them had tea together in Clara's sitting room and she told him in detail about the conversation between herself and Nora the night before. Still later in the morning, when she talked to Helen, when she told her what she'd done, Helen said, 'My God, Clara, what were you thinking of? Why did you tell Jesse? It's bad enough that Nora knows but why pull him into it?'

'I had to. Someone has to deal with her. Someone has to keep her under control. I can't do it and you certainly can't do it, so who else is there?'

'I wish you'd talked to me first. We could have thought of something. Don't you realize that if I'd wanted Jesse to know I'd have told him long ago?'

'There's nothing to be gained by your getting angry with me. I *know* my daughter. She can be like a rabid dog sometimes. She's capable of anything. I assume you don't want her running to Floyd or to Valerie with her little bit of news.'

'What's the difference? Last night when I went to bed only you and I knew. This morning two other people know. Why shouldn't the whole household know by tomorrow?'

'Because I won't permit it. That's why. Jesse will *not* tell Valerie. He doesn't even want her to know. And neither you nor I will tell anyone. Only Nora is the risk. I believed that Jesse could handle her and I still believe that.'

'What did he say when you told him?'

'He didn't say anything.' Clara said.

'I mean what did he say about me?'

'It wasn't that sort of conversation. We were not discussing morality. No one seemed inclined to make judgements. Jesse understood the problem as soon as I presented it to him. He knows how unpredictable Nora can be. We were simply discussing tactics.'

'I can't imagine what he must think. He must have said something.'

Clara sat looking at her. Finally she said, 'I thought I knew you, Helen. Now, all at once, I don't recognize you. I thought you would be concerned about Floyd. I wouldn't have been surprised if you were frantic that Nora would tell *him*. But here we sit, I'm trying my best to prevent that happening and your only worry seems to be that Jesse will think you were a naughty girl.'

'It's not that. I just feel so awful that I lied to him.'

'You lied to everyone,' Clara said. 'You lied to me. I understand that. And so would anyone else. Jesse's had a thorough exposure to life. He knows all about people's weaknesses, including his own. He's the last man in the world to paint a scarlet letter on anyone's forehead. And never on yours.'

'I know that. But I still feel awful about it.'

'Our job is to keep this away from Floyd. At least *I* believe that's the problem. Is that still what you want to do?'

'I have to, don't I? But if someone's going to tell him, then I should do it.'

'That's up to you, of course. But if it was left to me, I'd say this is the worst possible time for it. I think it could be very upsetting for him just when he's getting to know all of us, as he's learning about all of our family histories and entanglements. It's not that many years since you gave him a whole new biography of himself. I think it's much too soon to give him another one.'

'I think *any time* is too soon. I can't imagine ever telling him, if it can be avoided.'

Clara nodded. 'I agree with you. Now you understand why I felt we had to act quickly. That's why I had to call on Jesse.'

'What if he can't persuade Nora? What if she won't listen to him?'

'Let's assume that she will till we hear otherwise.'

[12]

'I've seen some shady manoeuvres from you,' Jesse said, 'but this one is the lowest. What the hell do you think you're doing?'

'And who in the world do you think you're talking to?' Nora said. 'I'm usually sound asleep at this time of the morning. But I got a message from you that you urgently need to see me so I pulled myself together in some chancy fashion, ordered up my coffee and let you come in. However, if you really feel it's urgent at this time of day to point out the flaws in my character, then I can only say "ho-hum" and go back to bed.'

'You know damned well what I'm talking about. I just came from Clara. She told me about the talk you two had last night.'

'What about it?'

'This is not a game of bridge we're talking about. People's lives are involved.'

'That's exactly what I told Clara,' Nora said. 'I said "Just because Hugh's dead doesn't mean . . ." '

'I wasn't talking about Hugh.'

'I know you weren't but I am. It's sad that he died without knowing he had a son. But that's all the more reason it shouldn't be kept a secret for ever.'

'Lots of things should be kept secret. You have a few.'

'So do you, my dear,' Nora said.

'So does everybody else. When Hugh told you all those years ago about himself and Helen, you didn't tell anybody *that*.'

'There was nothing to tell. Hugh never talked to me about his little adventures. He didn't tell me anything about Helen.'

'But you told Clara . . .'

'I lied to her. She was determined not to tell me what she knew and I was determined to find out. So I threw her the hook and she took it. She knew she was on shaky ground anyway. She's studied Floyd just as carefully as I did. She knew that sooner or later somebody would see that resemblance to Hugh. A little genetic characteristic that passed from Angus to Raymond to Helen to Floyd. That's how Clara explained it. And it could have done. But now we all know it didn't. It was a genetic characteristic all right but it passed directly to Floyd from my brother. With Baby Helen as the cooperative intermediary.'

Jesse got up from his chair and refilled his coffee cup. 'I don't understand you,' he said.

'Of course you do. You're the only creature in the world who *does* understand me.'

'I've never understood your odd definition of triumph.'

'Triumph is never odd,' she said. 'It's delicious. Olives and anchovies are odd. Champagne is delicious.'

'You apparently made this trip from Paris just to prove something to yourself.'

'Not at all. I made it to meet my cousin Floyd, who turned out to be my nephew Floyd. But I also expected to win fifty thousand francs from you. I would have bet ten times that much. That's how sure I was. I knew, absolutely knew, that when I looked at Floyd I'd see some give-away feature, some earlobe or dimple that would brand him once and for all as your child. Nobody could have been more surprised than I was when I sat down in front of him and saw Hugh's eyes looking back at me.'

'Why do you think you saw what nobody else saw?'

'Because I'm a witch. Also, I don't believe that nobody else saw it. I'll bet the older servants saw it, the ones who knew Hugh. They don't miss anything. And the three people who knew, you and Helen and Clara, most certainly looked for a resemblance. And when you did, you saw one, just as I did.'

'There weren't three people who knew about it,' Jesse said. 'Just Helen and Clara. I didn't know till this morning when Clara told me.'

'I don't believe that.'

'It's true.'

'All that cloak-and-dagger work you did to help Helen locate her son and she never told you who his father was?'

'I told you. Clara just told me a while ago.'

'That's odd. If it's such a big secret, if it was such a shock for me to find out, I wonder why she'd tell you a few hours later.'

'I don't know,' Jesse said.

'Sure you do. She needed an ally. She wanted someone to reason with me. Somebody I might listen to. So she conscripted you and told you Helen's naughty secret and told you to ask me to . . . what? What am I supposed to do or not do?'

'I hope you'll be considerate of the other people involved and keep this whole thing to yourself.'

'You hope I'll keep it to myself, or Helen hopes that.'

'Helen and Clara hope that and so do I.'

'Maybe I'm being obtuse but what difference does it make to you?'

'I'll tell you the truth. I'd be interested in trying to help Clara and Helen no matter what they wanted or needed. But in this case I have a motive of my own. To look out for the family. However we in the family might understand the circumstances, to a lot of people it would simply be a nice bit of gossip. Raymond's daughter and Clara's son had a bit of a romp and produced a child, that sort of thing.'

'Since when do we care what people think?'

'I'm not concerned at all with what people think of me but I would not like the Bradshaw name and the Bradshaw family to become a subject for smutty jokes. I wouldn't like my children and your grandchildren to have to answer for a lot of mistakes that other people made.'

'You think Helen and Hugh made a mistake, is that it?'

'I'm not judging anyone,' Jesse said. 'That's all ancient history anyway. Now what we're concerned with is information. Public information. Since Hugh is dead, I don't think it's of any value to anyone to know that he was Floyd's father.'

'What about Floyd?'

'Floyd least of all.'

'And Valerie?'

'What possible benefit would it be to her?'

'You don't mind keeping secrets from your wife?'

'In this case, not at all. I wish I didn't know. I wish no one knew but Helen. I'm sorry she even told Clara.'

'But I would have known regardless,' Nora said.

'No, you wouldn't. You would only have suspected. You didn't know for sure, you didn't know absolutely till Clara admitted it to you.'

Nora smiled. 'I hate to tell you you're right, but you are. I *knew* but I didn't really *know*.'

'If Hugh were still living we'd have a different problem, but since he isn't . . .'

'What are you suggesting then?'

'I'm saying that no one benefits if this whole thing becomes general knowledge or county gossip. And everyone benefits if it doesn't. And in my opinion Floyd will benefit most of all.'

'What he doesn't know can't hurt him . . . that sort of thing.'

'Something like that.'

'I've always thought that was a hateful notion. I think what I don't know hurts me a lot.'

'In this case you do know,' Jesse said. 'So that takes care of you. And three other people know. That makes four all together. I think that's enough. I think we should all agree . . .'

'A vow of silence,' Nora whispered.

'No. Nothing dramatic like that. Just a decent agreement . . .'

'One man's decency is another man's vice.'

'You know what I'm talking about.'

'Of course I do,' she said. 'And from your viewpoint, it makes great sense. But I'm curious about what Helen feels.'

'She feels the same as I do.'

'I know. But what does she say?'

'I don't know. We haven't discussed it.'

'You mean you haven't seen her or talked to her since you spoke with Clara this morning?'

'No. I wanted to talk to you as soon as possible.'

'So . . . Helen doesn't know how you've reacted to the forbidden news about her and my brother.'

'I had no reaction. Except what I've told you.'

'Come on, Jesse. This is old reliable Nora you're talking to. You mean you didn't prick up your ears even the slightest bit when Clara told you that while you and I were romping around during that first summer you came here to Wingate, Helen and Hugh were having a little romp of their own. Didn't that surprise you? It certainly surprised me.'

'I don't know anything about it. If Clara knows the details she didn't share them with me. And it's none of my business in any case.'

'But you do have some imagination. And I'll bet you have some curiosity too. We all knew Hugh was a bounder but everybody except me thought Baby Helen was the soul of innocence. How do you suppose she fooled us so? You can't tell me you weren't surprised when Clara told you.'

'Are you grilling me?'

'No. You're asking me for a favour. A pledge of silence. Now I'm asking you for one. I want you to tell me truthfully if you were surprised to find out about Hugh and Helen.'

'Is this a trade-off?'

'No,' she said. 'I'm not promising anything. But I would like to see some evidence that we're negotiating in good faith. Were *you surprised?'*

'Yes,' he said.

'Very surprised?'

'Yes.'

[13]

Only Jesse and Valerie and Floyd appeared at the luncheon table that day. 'Where is everybody?' Floyd asked.

'Eating in their rooms, I expect,' Jesse said. 'Things were a little busy around here this morning.'

'That's an understatement,' Valerie said. 'I've never seen so much hustle and bustle. Everyone dashing through corridors. In and out of Clara's sitting room. What's the occasion? And why wasn't I invited?'

'You're always invited,' Jesse said. 'You know that. But in this case I don't think you'd be very interested.' He had prepared an explanation in advance and now he recited it. 'You know, the bank in London handles all of our business affairs since Angus died but every six months or so there's an elaborate review that requires some family participation. Short proposals to be read through, authorizations to sign, paragraphs to delete or approve. Lots of exciting things like that.' He turned to Floyd. 'We'll be pulling you into some of these sessions before long. Unless you decide to run off and hide.'

'You don't need me. The last business I was involved in was a lemonade stand when I was nine years old. And I used to bank a poker game when I was in the Navy. I never had a cheque book till four or five months ago. If you need a groom I'm pretty good with horses but don't ever expect me to look at a column of figures and make any sense out of it.'

'I notice you're down at the stables a lot,' Jesse said, 'Did you find a good horse to ride?'

'I've ridden all of them. They're all good. Smooth-gaited and a lot of stamina. I'm not much good on those postage-stamp saddles yet but I'm learning. I've always ridden western-style. Or bareback. That's what I like best. But I guess I'd better not try that here?'

'Why not?' Jesse said. 'The roan stallion might like it. He's never cared much for a saddle anyway. You and I should take a long ride some day. I used to ride all the time but now I seldom get around to it.' He turned to Valerie. '*This* is the horseback-rider in the family. She takes after her grandfather. Angus rode like a bandit. And so does Valerie. You should ride out with Floyd some day . . .'

'No, that's all right,' Floyd said. 'If she's a good rider she wouldn't want to mess around with me. I just ride fast and hard. Not pretty. I like to get a horse between my legs and take off.'

'You might get a surprise from Valerie. She can outride

me any day. And she knows some pretty spots around here.'

'He likes to ride by himself, Jesse. Didn't you hear him?'

'I don't mean that I don't appreciate . . . I mean I guess it would be nice to see some of the spots around here that I haven't located myself,' Floyd said.

'Valerie knows *all* of them. She might even show you the place the Bradshaws made famous. It's a spot on the Will River about five miles from here with a ruined castle on the hill above it and a deserted crofter's cottage just beside the stream. Your grandfather, Helen's father, used to meet a lady there . . .'

'You're not going to tell *that* story, are you?'

'I think I've heard some of it,' Floyd said. 'It's sad stuff.'

'It has a sad ending,' Jesse said, 'but it wasn't always sad. They were crazy about each other. I think they had a wonderful time while it lasted. You should take him out there some time, Valerie.'

'That's a good idea,' she said. 'I will.'

'Wait till I put in some more hours on those little saddles. I don't want you galloping away from me out there on the moors.'

Their coffee had just been served when Jesse excused himself and left the table. As soon as he was out of the room Floyd said, 'I'll take my coffee into the drawing room if you'd like that better.'

'Why in the world would I want you to do that?'

'After that conversation we had the last time, I thought . . .'

'You thought what?' Valerie said.

'I figured you wouldn't be anxious to get stuck with me again.'

'But I'm not stuck with you. I can leave the room any time I wish.'

'Well, you know what I mean.'

'No, I don't know what you mean. You are the most defensive young man I've ever met.'

'And don't think I expect you to go riding with me because I don't.'

'You see. There you go again.'

'The truth is I'd just as soon ride by myself,' he said.

'Then that's what you should do. I just made an offer. It wasn't a command.'

'You didn't make the offer. Jesse did.'

'That's true. But I agreed to it.'

Floyd concentrated very hard for a few moments on stirring sugar into his coffee. Then he stood up suddenly, left his coffee on the table, and walked out of the room.

[14]

When Helen came to Nora's rooms in the middle of the afternoon it was plain to see that she'd been crying. When Nora opened the door, however, she pretended not to notice. She said, 'I'm glad you've come to see me. Come and sit down. I'll ring for some tea.'

'Not for me, Thank you.'

'Perhaps you'd rather have a drink.'

'Nothing, thank you.'

When they sat down by the window looking out across the garden, Nora said, 'Last night at dinner I was thinking to myself how strange it is that you and I are cousins, we've known each other for more than half our lives and yet we've spent almost no time together.'

Helen was silent for a long moment. At last she said, 'I've had a difficult day, Nora. I'll be very glad when it's over. So I'm sure you'll understand if I seem abrupt. I've just had a long talk with Jesse and he said you insisted on seeing me. So here I am.'

'Well, that's not exactly the case . . .'

'He said you believe Floyd should be told that Hugh was his father. He said you told him that you might change your mind, however, if I came to you and asked you not to tell Floyd. That's why I'm here. I'm asking you. If you want me to plead with you I will also do that.'

'I don't want any such thing,' Nora said. 'I can't believe that Jesse put it to you that way.'

'Those were his precise words. I listened very carefully. If he misunderstood you, then please tell me what you actually said to him.'

'I can't repeat our conversation word for word, but I assure you . . .'

'Why did you want to see me then? What do you want me to say?'

'I had hoped we could discuss the matter. That's all. I think you know how close I was to my brother. When he was buried I felt as if part of me was being buried too. Now it seems I'm being asked to bury his son as well. And I'm not sure I understand why that's necessary.'

'Maybe it isn't,' Helen said, 'but as I'm sure Jesse explained to you, we think, Clara and Jesse and I, that it's better for Floyd *not* to know, at least not now, and perhaps not ever. He's had enough surprises in his life and we'd prefer not to give him another one.'

'Jesse seemed to feel there was some scandal involved. He felt we should protect the Bradshaw name.'

'I know he feels that way,' Helen said. 'and I understand it. But those are not my concerns. I'm not ashamed of anything I've done. I'm only interested in doing what I think is best for Floyd.'

'Don't you think it's important for a child to know who his father is?'

'Of course I do. Under anything approaching normal circumstances. But these are far from normal circumstances. I also can't sit here and tell you that I know I'm doing the correct thing. Maybe I'm not. But I am certainly doing what I believe is the correct thing.'

'But how do I solve my problem?' Nora said. 'My brother died believing he was childless. Now I discover he had a fine grown-up son. Surely you can understand that I would like him to be acknowledged as Hugh's son, as well as yours. I'd like him to be my nephew. I'd like him to know me as his aunt.'

'I can't bargain with you, Nora. I have nothing to bargain with. Jesse feels that you and I have no way to compromise and I think he's right. As I told you before, I will plead with you if that will help. I am pleading with you. But I don't expect that will persuade you. On the other hand, if you consider what is *truly* best, not for you or for me but for Floyd, I think you may see things differently. At least I hope you will.'

Nora walked to the window and stood there looking out across the deer park. When she turned back she said, 'There are people in this family, my mother included, who think I am an extremely vengeful woman. I don't believe that's true. If it were true I assure you that you and I would not be having this conversation. If it were true I would welcome this opportunity to do something that might make you miserable. Because you have made *me* miserable on more occasions then I can count. Does that surprise you? It shouldn't. That first summer, for example, when Jesse and I became engaged, I have always believed we would have been married then if it hadn't been for you. Instead, I married a man I didn't love, doing severe damage to him as well as to myself. Jesse and I did get together later, of course. Very happily, for the most part. I don't deny that we had some difficulties towards the end of our time together, but all the same the thing that finally separated us was your cry for help, when you'd finally found some clue about Floyd's whereabouts and you felt you needed Jesse's help to find him. Now I discover that you were involved with my brother. I don't know to what extent and I don't need to know. But I can't help wondering why he suddenly went off to Scotland and buried himself there, why he eventually married a worthless woman he cared nothing about and ended up killing himself. I'm not saying I blame you for Hugh's life but I know now that you had some part in it. So you see, no one could expect me to want to accommodate you, to sprinkle rose petals on your path. But I'm going to surprise you. I'm not going to promise you anything, I'm not going to enter some elaborate conspiracy of silence with you and Clara and Jesse, but I will tell you this: for the moment I agree that Floyd would not benefit from having this additional information poured over him. So I do not plan to tell him. In future, however, if a moment arrives when I think he *should* be told, I will tell him without hesitation. You care about what's best for him, you say. So do I. It agonizes me that what's best for him seems also to be best for you, but I will try to live with that.'

[15]

As Helen had indicated to Nora, every aspect of that day had been painful for her, the manipulations and machinations of the moment, the memories that came storming back from the past, and the fearful anticipation of what tomorrow might bring, how it would affect Floyd and alter, perhaps, his feelings for her.

Most painful of all, however, had been her chaotic hour with Jesse. Not *because* of him. There had been no challenge, no disapproval or condemnation in his manner. He had been willing, eager perhaps, to confine their conversation to a discussion of tactics, to discuss the best way to deal with Nora. But for Helen, from the moment he came into her sitting room, it was a grinding session of self-condemnation and regret and tears.

'You have to stop crying like that,' Jesse said. 'You'll make yourself sick.'

'I can't help it. I *can't* stop. I feel so rotten and awful and helpless. I've never felt so terrible in my life.'

'Don't give up so fast. It's not over yet. We may still be able to talk some sense into Nora. If we can, if you can persuade her to keep her mouth shut, then things will work out fine.'

'No, they won't. They can't. I'll never be able to make things the way they were. I'll never be able to make *you* understand. I'll never be able to explain.'

'What difference does that make?' he said. 'You don't have to explain anything to me.'

'Yes, I do. I didn't want to keep lying to you all these years. But once I'd started I didn't know how to straighten it out. With other people, even Clara, I didn't mind so much, but with you, I never could forgive myself. I kept thinking that the right moment would come somehow and then I'd tell you everything. But the moment never came. Or if it did I was too much of a coward to admit it to myself. So everything just dragged on. Even when you went with me to help locate Floyd, when I finally told you *part* of the truth, I couldn't force myself to tell you the whole story. When we were in Crawfordsville and later in South Dakota, and then when we were heading south to where I had to take the train to California, all those times, I can remember as clearly as if it were yesterday, I was just on the verge of telling you everything. The words were on the tip of my tongue. But instead I told you that silly, convenient lie that I'd told before from the first day I found out I was pregnant. Finally I realized that I'd never have the courage to tell you and I told myself it was better that way, better for me to keep it to myself. That way nobody else in the world would know except me. But then I told Clara. And now you've found out everything from her instead of hearing it from me the way you should have.'

'I hope you don't blame Clara. She thought she was doing the best thing under the circumstances. And she was right. Somebody had to try to reason with Nora and there was no time to waste.'

'I know that. And I don't blame her. But that doesn't change the way I feel about myself. I feel small and cheap and I don't like myself at all.'

'Stop it, Helen. You're acting like a child. You did what you did a long time ago. You handled it the best way you knew how. That's all anybody can do. Everybody has something they keep to themselves. It's the way life works. We all do it. And if the truth comes out we all feel like fools. What do you think Raymond did? He invented his whole life. We didn't start to find out the truth about him till after he died.'

'I know that. But if we'd found out somehow when he was still alive, he'd have been as humiliated as I am. He'd have found it as impossible to explain as I do now.'

'I told you, there's nothing to explain. Nobody's judging you.'

'Yes, they are. And I'm judging myself.'

She went to the bathroom then and washed her face. When she came back she seemed tentative and her face was flushed still but she'd stopped crying. She sat down in a chair facing Jesse and said, 'I don't want you to say anything for a few minutes. Please. If you sit there and listen maybe I'll be able to say everything I need to say. I don't promise it will all make sense but it will be the best possible way I can tell you what was in my head that first summer when we came here to England together.'

Jesse didn't answer. He settled back in his chair, crossed his legs, and lit a cigarette.

'In a way this is about you as much as it's about me. Looking back on those days now, I can see how dependent I was on you. I always had been since I was fifteen. But particularly after Raymond died. Maybe I was too dependent. I don't know. But that doesn't matter now. All I know is that you were my best friend. I thought when we left New York and sailed for England that you and I were the best possible friends a man and woman could be. No love and kisses and all that other stuff. Just two people who really knew each other and liked each other and *trusted* each other.

'I remember when we first got here to Wingate Fields,

when we were getting to know everybody and hearing all the stories about the family and about Raymond when he was growing up, we used to make a point of getting together by ourselves at least once a day, taking a walk or something, so we could compare notes about what we'd heard and what we'd learned. I thought I was very grown-up then but I was barely eighteen and it meant a lot to me having you here when I was meeting all these relatives for the first time. And then I started getting to know Clara. We liked each other from the start and we began to spend a great deal of time together. So I didn't see you so much. Also by then you were spending whole days with Angus or dashing around the county with Hugh and Nora. And I thought that was great. I was having a good time and so were you and I figured we'd have a lot of stories to tell each other when we took the ship home together at the end of the summer.

'The first time I got the feeling that maybe things weren't what they had been between you and me was when I teased you one day about Nora and you said you were just trying to be nice or something like that. And the next morning very early I saw her coming out of your room in a nightgown. I didn't care what you were doing but you'd always told me about your girlfriends before so I wondered what was different about this time. Then the next thing I knew you wanted to postpone going home because you'd decided to write a monograph of some kind and Angus was going to publish it for you. So I said, "Fine, we'll go a little later", but I wondered why we'd never talked about it till the whole thing was settled. I began to feel strange. Left out of things. But again I told myself, things would be the same as they'd been before once we were back in Fort Beck.'

She paused for a moment. 'Then came the big evening. The night before you left for London to do your research in the British Museum. I sat there at the dinner table and felt as if I was getting smaller and smaller. All light and gauzy and transparent. First Nora's father stood up and announced that you and his daughter would be married right after Christmas and then, while I was smiling and drinking champagne and trying to get that news sorted out in my head, Angus stood up and announced that he'd adopted you as his son, not that he *planned* to do it but that it had already been done, legal and proper, your name was now Jesse Bradshaw, and you'd been transformed from my best friend into my uncle. I'd never felt so lonely and deserted and unloved, never in my life, as I felt that night while we all chattered and toasted and got drunk and celebrated your good fortune.

'I did think of it as good fortune. Don't misunderstand me. I knew that nothing could have made Raymond happier than having his father adopt you. And nothing could have made me happier. And I didn't think your marrying Nora was a terrible idea either. I didn't know her so well but I thought you made a striking couple and I figured if you loved each other and wanted to get married, why in the world shouldn't you? So the two big announcements of the evening didn't kill me. But something else did. The fact that you'd decided for reasons of your own to cut me out of your life, to make two life-altering decisions and never breathe a word of it to me, that you'd apparently decided to end a friendship that had been the centrepiece of both our lives or, if not to end it, to redefine it in a way that made sense to you but which made no sense at all to *me*. If I told you I was bewildered by all the unanswered questions that were racing through my head, that wouldn't begin to describe the emptiness I felt. As I say, I was only eighteen and perhaps I'd been sheltered in an unusual way. I don't think that's true but it might be true, and whether it is or not that particular night was the first time I had experienced total rejection. Rejection isn't a strong enough word. I felt *discarded*. When I went upstairs to my room that night, after all the laughing and the drinking and the toasts and congratulations were over, as I sat in the bathtub trying to make myself sleepy so I could get into bed and go blank and forget the whole evening, I felt for the first time like a stranger in a strange house. I decided right then that I would go back to America as soon as I could book passage on a ship. But even that decision didn't quiet me down. When I got into bed, my head was spinning, partly from the champagne but mostly from the thoughts that kept whirling through it. Finally I got up and put on my robe. I sat in the chair and tried to read but I couldn't keep my eyes fixed on the page. So I walked around the room then, just wandering like a child, touching things, picking up vases and letter-openers and cigarette-boxes. It was terribly hot and humid that night. Do you remember? It had been the hottest week of the summer. When I stopped by the open window there was no air stirring at all. I took off my robe and slipped my nightdress down off my shoulders and stood there, half-naked like some pagan wench, staring down into the garden. All the plants and trees and bushes semed dead-black but the paths were silvery-white in the moonlight. I felt suddenly that I had to be outside. A walk in the garden would surely calm me down and cool me off. So I put on my robe again, opened my door quietly and slipped out into the corridor. I remember passing by your room and Hugh's room on my way to the central staircase. But when I got there, as I stood at the top of the stairs, I . . . how can I tell you this?'

'You don't have to tell me anything,' Jesse said. 'I understand.'

'No, you don't. And I do have to tell you. You already know what I did. Now I'm just trying to make you see why.'

'It doesn't matter.'

'Yes, it does,' she said. 'It matters to me.' She brushed her hair back from her forehead, she seemed to be struggling to remember, trying to recreate the scene precisely as she recalled it. 'I love this old house at night,' she said, 'after everyone's in bed. I always feel as if the ghosts of three hundred years are strolling around through the corridors. And that night I felt like one of those ghosts, all weightless and transparent. I remember standing at the head of the staircase and looking down into the reception hall. Nothing moved down there. Just darkness and cool floors and Angus's clock ticking quietly far off in the library. I stood there for God knows how long, just poised on the top step in my bare feet ready to go down. But I didn't go. I turned away instead and started back towards my room. But when I came to Hugh's door, I turned the knob, went inside and closed the door behind me. No thought or hesitation. I just went in.

'The light was shining through the window. He'd thrown his pyjamas off onto the floor and he was lying naked on the bed, lying on his back, looking very white in the moonlight. I dropped my robe and nightdress on the floor by the door, walked slowly across the room, and lay down on the bed beside him. I stayed there with him till the sun came up. Then I went back to my own room and went to sleep.'

She paused, then went on. 'I'd never been with him before. I'd hardly talked to him. And I was never with him again. I stayed in my room from then till I left for America five days later.'

[16]

After Raymond's death, several months later, when Jesse was twenty-two and Helen was seventeen, he had been summoned by the chairman of the English department at Foresby, where Raymond had taught and where Jesse, since his return from the war in France, had been an instructor, and informed by that dreary gentleman, a man named Pfrommer, that the school felt — at least Dr Pfrommer and Dean Umbreit felt — that in deference to local mores it would be wiser, perhaps, if Jesse moved away from the Bradshaw home where he had lived ever since coming to Fort Beck and took rooms somewhere by himself in respectable bachelor quarters.

Jesse had refused, of course, and had continued to live in Raymond's house. But the interview with Pfrommer had left a mark on him. The implication that his relationship with Helen might be construed as something altogether different from what it was had not crossed his mind before. But when he'd gone home that afternoon, Pfrommer's self-righteous innuendoes still fresh in his memory, he was disturbed to discover that suddenly, and for the first time, he *did* see Helen differently. When he found her in the library, lying on the couch by the fireplace, her face flushed with the heat, her lips looking pink and swollen, her eyes still misty with sleep, he was aware of a provocative, sensual creature he had never noticed before.

That image, that sensation, had not stayed with him, however. By dinnertime that evening Helen had reacquired the traits he had always associated with her. More friend than woman, more sister than friend. The two of them were what they had always been. They occupied a category they had created for themselves. It had no name, no rules, and no clear definition. But each of them recognized it and cherished it and saw it as unchanging, not as a road to somewhere else but as a destination in its own right.

As Helen sat talking with him that afternoon at Wingate,

however, as she explained what she had done and why she felt she had done it, and her feelings about it all these years later, Jesse remembered very clearly how she'd looked on that winter afternoon by the fireplace in Raymond's house in Fort Beck. As she described that sultry night and her turbulent feelings he felt a throb inside himself that was more painful than guilt. He told himself this feeling could not be jealousy. But the feeling, whatever its name, stayed with him.

Chapter Six

[1]

One morning after breakfast, Valerie said, 'Do you think I've turned into a *hausfrau?*'

'No, I don't,' Jesse said. 'Do you think *I* have?'

'I'm serious.'

'So am I. The popular conception of a *hausfrau* is a woman who cooks and cleans and washes clothes and mops the floor a lot. Walks around in a dirty apron with a kerchief around her head. There's a looking-glass over there. Take a look and see if you fit that definition.'

'I know I don't *look* like one. But maybe there's some subtle transformation that takes place. Other people see it but you don't.'

'*Hausfraus* don't deal in subtle transformations. Boiled cabbage and pig's knuckles . . . that's their speed.'

'I mean when a woman's around the house all the time, when she spends more time with her children than she does with anybody else.'

'What are you trying to say?' Jesse asked.

'I'm not sure. I just get the feeling that people look at me sometimes and slip me into an instant category. Like a card in a file box. They don't bother to find out what I'm like because they think they already know.'

'In your case, maybe they do. Almost everybody you see has known you all your life.'

'Including you.'

'That's right. Especially me. I growed you up. Like a hot-house tulip.'

'Am I suffering the first intimations of old age?' she said then.

'You'd better not be. If you decide *you're* old, what does that make me?'

'I don't think I'm old. And I'm not old, of course. And neither are you.'

'Getting there, sweetheart,' Jesse said. 'A step at a time.'

'I'm talking about perceptions. The way people perceive you. Do you think people look at me and say, "Oh, yes, she looks like a fine mother. Very sweet with her children." '

'I don't know. People may say that. They should. It's time.'

'But do you think that's all they say?'

'I wouldn't think so. But who cares? Why all this sudden concern for what people think of you?'

'I don't know. I guess maybe I'm talking about what I think of myself.'

'I can't help you there. What do you think of yourself?'

'I guess I think I'm a nice mother who's very sweet to her children.'

'There you are. So everybody's right about you.'

'I suppose they are. But I must be a dreadfully boring creature.'

'Not to me,' Jesse said.

'Oh, what a blow. That's like telling a cross-eyed child, "It's all right. Mother loves you." '

'No, it's not. You're either about to get your period or you're fishing for compliments. Which is it?'

'Neither. I just don't want to turn into a concerto of one note.'

'Not bloody likely, my darling. You have infinite variety, sweet breath and beautiful knees. The world is filled with gorgeous women but very few of them have first-rate knees.'

'Wouldn't you like me better if I threw a temper tantrum once in a while? The housekeeper told me the other day that I'm lovely to work for because I'm not emotional.'

'What does *she* know?'

'She's right. I'm not emotional. At least not in public. I've always thought it was inexcusable to run around losing your temper all the time. But sometimes I wish I did. Many people have no respect for people who don't scream and yell.'

'I don't scream and yell,' Jesse said.

'You don't have to. People take one look at those killer eyes of yours and they decide not to get you riled. At least the smart ones do.'

'Good for me. I'm glad to hear that.'

'I can see you don't want to have a serious talk but I'm going ahead anyway.'

'Good for you. Just go ahead without me.'

'Were you very angry when you were younger?'

'How much younger?'

'I don't know. Thirty maybe.'

'You tell me. You were around when I was thirty.'

'I may have been around but I was only seven years old.'

'That's true. Well, let's see . . . I was certainly angrier then than I am now. Most people are.'

'Why is that, do you think?'

'Frustration. Disappointment. Trying to get the things they want. Trying to *decide* what they want and *who* they want. Trying to get the people they want to want them.'

'I'm not angry. Does that mean I have everything I want?'

'Of course not. That's what we're talking about. You want people to understand how complex and interesting you are. You don't want to be mistaken for a nanny or a *hausfrau*.'

'Why do you think Floyd's so angry?' she said then. 'Just because he's at the proper age to be angry or because he can't get the things he wants?'

'You think he's angry?'

'He certainly seems that way to me. Two or three times we've had conversations and he's just marched off in the middle of them.'

'Angry?'

'I assume he was. He didn't slip away or stroll away. He rather stalked away.'

'Maybe you insulted him.'

Valerie shook her head. 'No. He seemed angry with himself.'

'Maybe he's in love with you.'

'You won't be serious, will you?'

'I am serious. Just because you're a *hausfrau* that doesn't mean someone couldn't have a yen for you.'

'I'm sorry I used that word. You'll never let me live it down.'

'Sure I will,' Jesse said. Then, 'Is that who we've been talking about all along? Do you think Floyd looked at you and decided you were one-dimensional and uninteresting?'

'No. It's not that. I don't care much what he thinks, one way or the other. But I care what I think. And when I'm talking with him I feel sometimes as if I'm his mother. Or his aunt. He's like a pin-wheel about to go flying off in all directions and I feel like a well-scrubbed solid woman of a certain age.'

'You're younger than he is as I recall,' Jesse said.

'I know that. So is he very young for his years or have I turned into a matron?'

'No to the last part. Maybe to the first part. You have to remember he's seeing a lot of things and people he's never seen before. A different kind of life. He may feel as if he's being swallowed up and he doesn't like it. He may feel out of place. Whatever he's feeling it's probably something new to him. And a lot of us, when we're dropped into an unfamiliar situation, react by getting angry. It's like a dog barking. An attempt to establish yourself. *You* seem to think people are ignoring you. Or not seeing you for what you really are. Maybe Floyd's thinking the same thing. I don't know what the answer is for him but in your case I suggest you get a grey wig and a whale-bone corset and plunge straight ahead into your middle years.'

'You're very clever. Critics are always clever.'

'On second thoughts,' he went on, 'perhaps we should try to find Floyd a lady friend. I suggested that to him when he first got here but he seemed cool to the idea. Maybe he'd be more receptive now.'

'I have a feeling he's very capable of finding his own lady friends,' Valerie said.

'I'm sure you're right. Time will tell.'

[2]

Even after Nora had returned to Paris, the wreckage of the storm she had created still lay strewn about the house at Wingate Fields. Or so it seemed to Helen. She couldn't help feeling that Clara and Jesse looked at her now in a new way. Even the servants, she imagined, were studying her closely as though fresh and untidy information had come to them and they were searching for confirmation in her face. These circumstances were all invented, of course. In her stable moments, Helen realized this. But some days, and particularly during some sleepless nights, her stable moments were rare indeed. After a week or ten days of struggling to right herself, of trying desperately not to feel self-conscious at meal-times, with Clara and Jesse and Floyd and Valerie all ranged around her in the dining room, she gave up and decided to go back to Fort Beck. Hoping that Floyd would go with her, she told him that of course he could stay on in England if he chose to and he said yes, he thought he would stay a while longer.

After announcing her plans to Clara and Jesse, both of whom, in Helen's shaky state of mind, seemed relieved, she wrote a letter to Frank in Chicago.

> I have not written as often as I'd planned to. Nor have you. But, as I recall, we decided not to flood each other with mail. Isn't that what we said, that we would let the air clear and the sea settle a bit? Well, the settling and the clearing have taken place. For me at least. And I hope for you also. I enclose my travel schedule. I'm counting on seeing you at the airport when I arrive. Don't disappoint me.

When he met her at the airport he said, 'My youngest daughter's due to have a baby any minute at the hospital in Lake Forest. I think I'd better get back there.'

'I thought your youngest daughter wasn't married.'

'She's not. But she's having a baby anyway.' As they walked toward the baggage claim area he said, 'I have a driver waiting for you. He'll take you to the apartment and I'll come along as soon as things settle down at the hospital. The baby should be born by the time I get back. I should be there not later than six-thirty.'

At six-thirty he called the apartment and said, 'The baby's fine but Dierdre's had some complications. I'm waiting to talk to the doctor now. I'll be along as soon as possible.'

At eight-thirty he called again. 'I'm on the outer drive. Meet me at Brocki's. I reserved a table. I should be there in twenty minutes.'

Helen had spent hours when she was in England trying to imagine what her next meeting with Frank would be like. It was inevitable, she felt, that the tone of their conversation the last time they'd been together would be duplicated to one degree of another. Solemn faces, careful proposals, reviews of the past, questions about the future. She had told herself, however, that no matter how she might define her relationship with Frank it was important to her. Whatever his shortcomings, or hers, whatever their shortcomings together, they *knew* each other. There was a warm familiarity between them that could not be easily duplicated. Their good times, she reminded herself, outweighed the bad times. On the other hand, she realized that the mere fact of her listing the plus and minus factors of whatever it was they shared was an indication that some critical ingredient was missing, that her brain was forced to supply the *raison d'être* that her emotions could not deliver.

Ignoring the unquiet insight, however, she assured herself that nothing deserved to be measured in terms of what it isn't, that it must be treasured or discarded for what it is rather than for what it might be or might have been. 'You sought him out because in some way you still needed him. That hasn't changed.'

She was pleasantly surprised, then, by their evening together. Even since their short conversation at the airport a few hours before, he seemed dramatically changed, not to what he had been a few months before, but to the brash and confident young man she remembered from the first years of her marriage. As she had told Clara later, that was the binding force that had held them together until the time came when nothing on earth could have held them so. 'He was an irresistible force,' she had said. 'One that has never seen or *expects* to see an immovable object. He simply would not be denied. I don't mean in relation to me. With me he was very deft and patient. But in relation to the rest of the world he was a pirate, sacking towns and looting palaces. In a way, I suppose, he was like a younger version of Angus. Except Angus was not a big talker. And talking was Frank's best weapon. He was an engine of persuasion. And he could always entertain me. He could always make me laugh.'

As soon as he came into the restaurant and sat down, full of energy and ruddy colour in his cheeks, Frank said, 'Did you ever read Margaret Mead? Quite a lady. I was thinking about her as I drove down here. She said, "Brilliant men are always astonished to find that they have dull and indolent children. They never seem to notice that the slender and beautiful women they married, the *mothers* of those children, are also dull and indolent." ' He laughed, took a long drink from his highball and said, 'I am *not* labelling myself as brilliant. And my two daughters are neither dull nor indolent. Sometimes I wish they were. But they certainly don't seem to be related to me. The genetic process broke down somehow. They have my name but everything else they inherited from Muffy. But as Margaret Mead might have said, "Any man who marries a woman whose friends and family call her *Muffy* should not be surprised by anything." Well, I did and I'm not. With Muffy and Prinny and Deedee in the house, I've always felt like the trainer of an animal act'

'How is she?' Helen said. 'Deedee, isn't it? Isn't she the one who had the baby?'

'I still call her Dierdre, a lovely and respectable Irish name. But she's like a dog who was trained by a Chinese trainer. She only barks and stands on her hind legs when you call her Deedee.'

'Is she all right?'

'Sure, she's fine. She didn't like going through labour. I think her mother had assured her that wouldn't be necessary. But finally everything went well. Her mother had promised she'd have a girl and that's what she had. I'm sure the three of them are sitting in the hospital right now figuring out what kind of dog name to give her.'

'Is this your first grandchild?'

'No. Prinny has a daughter, too. They call her Wisty. But Prinny's two cats are called Norma and Margaret. *You* figure it out.'

'From what you said at the airport, I thought maybe she was having a problem.'

'No,' he said. 'it was *my* problem. You see, my contract with myself is that I am present for all legal or medical occasions. Weddings, divorces, operations, christenings, funerals and the like. And that includes births. All other times I am unavailable. But when a father-figure is necessary, then I am extremely conscientious about my responsibilities. The other three hundred and fifty-five days of the year I am elsewhere. On this occasion I felt particularly responsible because there was no other male in attendance. Aunts and grandmothers and sisters-in-law galore, but no smiling gentleman claiming to be the father.'

'Where is he?' Helen asked.

'Who is he is the first question. But no one dares ask that. You see, as I read the situation, Dierdre had this child as an act of vengeance against her mother. She wanted a new plane so she could fly to Florida to see her boyfriend. She has a plane already but it's two years old already. Anyway for some reason her mother, for the first time in her life, missed a chance to spend some money. She decided not to release the necessary funds. Six weeks later she changed her mind but by then her daughter was already pregnant. So they had a family meeting to which I was not invited and decided it might be fun for her to go ahead and have the baby. So she did. But, as I say, no male parent has surfaced. Her mother chooses to believe that the man in Florida is the one. But I've met him and I doubt it. He's an odd, balding chap in his late thirties who lives with his mother in Palm Beach and spends an hour every morning with his astrologer. There is also a surly young Turk who operates an art gallery on Oak Street in Chicago. Dierdre often has bruises on her face after she's seen him so I'm sure she's fond of him. I suspect that he is the father in question. On the other hand I saw her having a serious conversation with the gardener's son the week before she went into the hospital, so God knows. I haven't heard any talk about a marriage so whoever the baby's father is, I don't expect to see him around the house much. Unless he's the gardener's son. Then he'll be around every day.'

When they'd finished dinner and were sitting with their coffee, Helen said, 'I don't know what's come over you.'

'How do you mean?'

'I was just comparing the way you seem now with the way you were the last time we saw each other and I see an astonishing difference.'

'Why not? I'm one of those weird lizards that change colours all the time.'

'I mean it,' she said. 'What's happened?'

'Let's not talk about serious stuff. I'm having too good a time.'

'Ah, so something has happened to you?'

'Nothing *happened,*' he said. 'not in the sense that you mean. I just got up one morning, shaved, took a shower, had a nice cup of coffee and decided to change direction. The more I thought about it, the better I liked the idea. I spent the morning with my lawyers, then I drove out to Lake Forest, took my wife to lunch and asked her if she'd like to sue me for divorce. She said no, she wouldn't like to. So I said in that case, I was going to divorce her. So that's what I did. The final decree will come in three or four months. What do you think of that for an adventure?'

'I'm surprised.'

'Everybody was surprised except me. Once I decided to do it I knew I should have done it a long time ago. I've been walking around for fifteen years like a man wearing cement shoes.'

'Wasn't it ever any good?' Helen asked.

'Who knows? We all fool ourselves, don't we? I know I did. I was still trying to get over you and not doing a very good job of it. I knew her father because of a land project in Canada we were investing in together, the family was nice to me, and in those days I was still impressed by rich people with dogs and horses and walls around their houses. So the next thing I knew I was married to the daughter and living inside the walls.'

'Don't tell me you didn't *like* her.'

'I did like her. But that was all. And it wasn't enough. And when I got to know her, I didn't even like her. But by then she was pregnant and I thought, "We'll have a couple of nice kids and everything will be all right." But instead we had Prinny and Deedee.'

'And you don't like them either?'

'Not much. Not any more. They were cute little girls and I spent a lot of time with them and I was crazy about them. But then they grew up and by the time they were ten or twelve years old they were both carbon copies of their mother and all her cardboard friends. They're spoiled, insular people, and just because they're related to me doesn't make them *less* spoiled or less insular. You're lucky. You seem to really care about your son. You like him and respect him. But from what I can see that doesn't happen very often. Half of those guys who get drunk every night on commuter trains aren't doing it because of the pressure they had to deal with at the office that day. They're trying to cushion themselves to what they're facing when they get home at night.'

'Bitter, bitter,' Helen said.

'Not me. When you finally tell yourself the truth it leaves a very sweet taste in your mouth.'

'But how do your wife and daughters feel about the divorce?'

'It's like a project with them. Like bandage-rolling or raising money for the Presbyterian Church. They're being very stoic and brave together. Frowning a lot, I'm told, when people ask them what's going on. A friend of mine told me his wife had heard that I was an out-patient at a psychiatric centre in Winnetka. I assume that's the party line, that I'm having some sort of breakdown, the implication being that no one in his right mind would ever leave Muffy. The only one who secretly approves of what I've done is her father. He wishes he'd run off long ago. We have a secret lunch together every week or so and he keeps talking about the great investment opportunities he missed in Australia and New Zealand. What he really means is that he wished he'd escaped like I'm doing.'

As they drove back to the apartment, Helen said, 'Do you remember how carefully you explained to me when you and I got back together again that you would never divorce your wife, and that there was a whole interlocking structure of corporations that could never be disentangled?'

'At the time that was true. At least partially. But also I was protecting myself in some feeble way. I was afraid you'd disappear again as suddenly as you'd showed up so I was trying to convince myself as well as you that there was no future for us in any case. Pretty stupid, huh?'

'One thing you're not is stupid,' Helen said.

'About business I'm not. In all other areas I'm not sure. Anyway . . . the financial stuff was complicated. But it was simplified by the fact that we'd signed a pre-nuptial financial agreement. Her idea. I wasn't protecting my assets. She was protecting hers. So it worked out fine for both of us. Everybody has their own little pile of money. Actually, I don't give a damn about that. I just wanted the divorce. I'd have given her everything if that was the price I had to pay. I can always make money. That's what I'm good at.'

When they were inside the apartment he put his arms around her and said, 'Don't think that this means a big change for us. I didn't get this divorce because of you. I did it for me. On the other hand I think it would be a fine idea if you and I got married again. But I'm not going to badger you about it. If you decide you want to, great. If you don't want to, that's all right, too. So there you are. How can anybody help loving such an agreeable man?'

Later, as she lay awake still, her head on a soft pillow, Frank sleeping somewhere east of her on their great wide bed, she wondered if she had finally discovered a secret that had previously escaped her. Was this how it all worked? Did they give you a menu when you were very young and allow you to select everything that looked good to you in whatever quantity you wished? She decided that perhaps they did. But instead of bringing it to you then in one splendid and sumptuous meal, you had to be content with one bite at a time, or several bites, or long periods with just enough crumbs to keep you alive. In the end, perhaps you would discover that every single thing you had chosen had, at one time or another, been put on your plate. Or you might find that many items had never arrived. Or that orders had been switched and you had received tastes of things you would never have ordered. Or that you had forgotten, through the years, what your precise wishes had been. As she lay there thinking about it, she remembered something Raymond had once said. 'People tell you you can't have everything. That's not true. If you handle yourself right, you can have everything. You just can't have it all at once.'

Remembering the things she had found, the people she had loved and lost and found again, examining the tiny patches of joy and reward and sorrow and anguish that, stitched together, seemed to have covered her days like a home-made country quilt, she felt strangely complete suddenly, in a way that was foreign to her, quiet inside and open to the possibilities of tomorrow. 'After all these years,' she thought, 'is it possible that I finally like myself?' The question alone satisfied her. She felt no need to answer it.

[3]

As he had indicated to her, Floyd felt no strangeness about Helen's returning to America without him. In some way he looked forward to being at Wingate Fields by himself. Up to now he had felt like a visitor. Now he wanted to become a resident, the family member that everyone assured him he truly was. He had felt he was being observed, that people were understandably curious about him, that even the servants, who had been trained to see and hear only what they were meant to see and hear, felt less restricted in their dealings with this loose-gaited, casually garbed American. But now things would change. His continued presence, he was sure, the sense that he was a permanent fixture, would give him a different view of his surroundings and of the people who shared them with him. And their views of him would adjust accordingly.

It had not, however, turned out as he had hoped. Helen's

departure changed things somewhat but not in the ways he had expected. Without her as a catalyst, the remaining family members seemed suddenly shy and quiet and otherwise occupied. Even Clara, the soul of hospitality, was not nearly so visible as she had been before Helen left. Or so it seemed to Floyd. He wouldn't admit to himself that he had misread the situation, had over-reacted, and had, within a few says of his mother's departure, decided to respond by going his own way totally. If few overtures were to be made to him, he would respond by making no overtures whatsoever.

Ironically, the only one who seemed accessible and warm and friendly was Valerie. And she was the person Floyd would not allow himself to see. So he developed a pattern. Early coffee in his room, then out across the moors, either on horseback or driving one of the cars. He was never at home before dinner, sometimes not then. And when he did appear at the dinner table with Clara and Valerie and Jesse, or with just the two of them if Jesse was away, he usually drank quite a lot of wine, made brief answers to any questions he was asked, and went upstairs to his room as soon as dinner ended.

If Clara had not previously allowed herself to see a resemblance between Floyd and Hugh, she now could no longer pretend. Sitting silent across the table from her, his features burned brown by his days on horseback and seeming even darker in the candlelight, he *was* Hugh. It was as though being at Wingate Fields, living there, riding across the same fields, drinking at the same country inns, had accentuated his resemblance to his father. And his new silent self, nothing at all like the outgoing and cheerful young man who had arrived with Helen, seemed to have come directly from Hugh. It disturbed Clara in a way that she could not specifically define. To see such familiar behaviour in a young man who, whatever their blood connection, was still a stranger to her, made her uneasy, unsure of her ground with him. Remembering that she had never been certain what Hugh might do next, she began to feel the same way about Floyd.

Valerie's feelings which she discussed with no one after that one frustrating talk with Jesse, were quite different from Clara's. At first she had been bewildered, as she had told Jesse, unable to understand what had prompted Floyd's attitude toward her. She continued, however, to treat him as she would any other family member. She was pleasant to him, cheerful, and whenever she saw him for more than a few minutes, at dinner, for example, she tried to engage him in conversation. His responses varied from lack of interest to sullenness to specific hostility. The hostility he exhibited only on the rare occasions when they were left at table alone. If he said anything at all before he rose and left the room he made no effort to hide the obvious disdain he seemed to feel.

Valerie's bewilderment changed at last to anger. Whatever benevolent feelings she'd had about Floyd moved gradually from confusion to resentment to budding dislike. At last several weeks of trying to hide her anger, one evening when Jesse was in London, when Clara had left the table early and Floyd had gone immediately afterward, Valerie stood up and followed him into the drawing room, where she found him pouring himself a whisky.

'I don't know what you think you're doing. I have tried to be nice to you, all of us have, but I think your behaviour is absolutely incredible.'

'I don't care what you think,' he said, 'and I didn't ask you to be nice to me. I want you to leave me alone.'

'You're positively rude, why are you being so rude to me?'

'Go to hell,' he said. He set his glass down on the table and walked out of the room. Valerie stood where he'd left her for a few moments, angry tears in her eyes. Then she slowly walked out of the room and through the corridors of the east wing to her own rooms.

The following afternoon, sitting at her window, she saw him ride in across the deer park to the stables. When he walked across the garden towards the house she met him there.

'As you can see, there are at least two of the servants nearby. So I trust you won't make a scene. However, *I* am perfectly capable of making one.' When he didn't answer or brush past her to head for the house, she went on. 'You are a part of this family now. You live in this house with the rest of us. Perhaps no one else minds if you walk around like a surly mute but I do. I am willing to ignore you if nothing else will satisfy you. But I would prefer not to do that.'

'What do you want me to do?' he said.

'I want you to walk over to the summer house with me

and have a civilized conversation for once. I cannot live in a vaccum. I need to know the reasons for things. If I've done something terrible to you that I don't know about, you have to tell me.'

'I don't *have* to tell you anything.'

'That's true. But I'm asking if you will.'

He looked off toward the far side of the garden, then back to her. 'I would advise you not to ask me any questions. You might not like the answers.'

'I'll take the risk.'

'Also, maybe you'll feel better if I tell you I'm going away tomorrow. Your mother asked me to pay a visit to Paris.'

'Do you plan to stay there for ever?' Valerie said.

'No, I suppose not.'

'Then we'll have to face each other sooner or later.'

Again he looked away and didn't answer. Finally he turned and walked towards the summer house. She had a sudden impulse to go back into the house and take refuge in the nursery with her children. But she followed him instead.

He was already sitting down when she got there. She took a seat by the window with the lattice at her back. After a moment she said, 'There must be a reason why you've been behaving as you have. Jesse and I have been kind to you, haven't we?'

'I don't give a damn about Jesse. And don't talk to me as if I'm your maid. I don't need anyone to be *kind* to me.'

'You can't make me go away by being nasty,' she said. 'I want you to tell me why you go out of your way to avoid me and why you never talk to me or to Clara at the dinner table. And why in the world would you say what you said to me last night?'

'What did I say?'

'You know very well what you said. You said you wanted me to leave you alone. What does that mean?'

'It means exactly what you think it means.'

'But why would you say it? I've never given you any reason . . . I mean we barely know each other . . .'

'Shut up.'

'What?' Her voice was very quiet.

'Don't play indignant with me. I want you to be absolutely silent. You want me to tell you why I've avoided you, why I've asked you to stay away from me . . . all right, I'm going to tell you. But I don't want to hear a sound out of you till I've finished.'

Before she could answer, before her lips could form a word, he said, 'Not a *sound*.'

He sat very still then, looking at her, studying her closely with the afternoon sunlight behind her. Finally he said, 'When you get out of the bathtub tonight and see yourself in the mirror I want you to study yourself very carefully. Then you'll know what I see. That's how I've seen you since the first day. When you came back home from visiting your father with your children. I can tell you exactly what you were wearing. A pale blue sun-dress. Your shoulders were brown from the sun and so were your cheeks and there were freckles on your nose. But I saw you then just as I'm seeing you now. Totally naked and warm and beautiful . . .'

She made some small sound in her throat as she stood up and slowly moved towards the door of the summer house. Floyd got up suddenly, pulled her back, spun her around and sat her down firmly in the chair where she'd been sitting. When she said, 'No . . . please . . .' he slapped her so hard her head snapped to one side and his fingers left white marks on her cheek.

'Don't expect me to act like a gentleman,' he said then. He spoke very softly. 'I'm not a gentleman.' He paused. Then, 'You look at me as if I'm describing a chronic illness I suffer from. I assure you it's only been chronic since I came here, since I saw you. I've never looked at another woman and seen her the way I see you. That doesn't mean I'm proud of it. But it won't go away. If I were an artist I could draw you. Every line, every hair, every inch of your skin and fingers and toes, everything that no one else has ever seen I see every time I look at you.'

She sat absolutely still now, looking up at him, her fingers gripping the arms of the wicker chair, her face and neck suddenly pink, the marks of his fingers still white on her cheek.

'In my bed at night,' he said, 'it gets worse. When I close my eyes I see you in every position a woman's body could possibly find. Graceful and beautiful and ugly and awkward. Standing and bending, crouching and leaning and lying down. And when I go to sleep I dream of nothing but you. You and me together. Like two people being tortured. Bound together, twisting and turning, clutching at each other, moaning and crying and screaming. Sitting and lying and standing. In chains, on beds, on the floor. In cars, on the grass, in the water, in the snow, in the mud. There's no place I haven't been with you. There's nothing a man and woman can do together that we haven't done.'

He sat down on a stool beside her chair. They sat silent for a long time, just the sound of the birds in the trees over the summer house and the gardener's clippers snipping across the way beside the wall. At last he said, 'That's why I try to stay away from you. That's why I want you to stay away from me.'

Still she said nothing. Her fingertips gently touched the welts on her cheek and there was a faint stain of perspiration on the front of her white dress.

'I don't know how all this sounds to you,' he said then. 'I don't care how it sounds. I'm just trying to tell you the truth. I'm not telling you I love you because I don't. I don't even know you. It's just this . . . I just have this other life with you. It has nothing to do with love. I don't want to make you love me. I don't want to love *you*. I just need to undress you and hurt you and hear you moan. And feed on you like an animal. I know I'll never do it. I've always known that. Maybe I don't even want to do it. But it's always with me now. And when I see you, it's worse.'

He went outside to the water-pipe then, where the garden hoses connected. He folded his handkerchief into a square pad, soaked it in cold water, and took it back inside the summer house. He put it against her cheek, then moved her hand up to hold it in position. She looked up at him but as soon as their eyes met he turned and walked out through the door of the summer house. As she sat there holding the cool cloth against her cheek she could hear his footsteps crossing the garden on the path leading to the house.

[4]

Clara had not been witness to the conversation years earlier when her father had predicted that Jesse would live to see the wind blowing through the broken windows and empty rooms of Wingate Fields. If she had heard those words they would have made her both sad and angry. But all the same her own state of mind was slowly coming to resemble her father's in the years just before his death. She began to see disintegration and chaos everywhere she looked. She heard hateful music coming from the servant's quarters at night and from her great-grandson's room almost any time of the day. Each year it became more difficult to keep her household staff together. When able people, dear familiar people, died or retired, they were impossible to replace. Her manager reported similar problems with the grooms and gamekeepers and tenant farmers. 'The good ones are eager to go on to some other work and the worthless ones can't be managed or corrected. A lad of eighteen is likely to turn on you with a pitchfork.'

Kitchen help, too, was a continual problem. In one eighteen-month period after the war, she'd employed and discharged six cooks. Young men and girls from the region where almost impossible to hire. The ambitious ones went into the factories or the red-brick universities and the indolent ones refused to work altogether. She had friends in the county who had been forced to hire blacks and Indonesians. Another friend's daughter had been sexually molested by a Sumatran gardner.

Quite apart from the servant problem the quality of life generally in Northumberland, the world she had known as a girl and young woman, had become so changed that she scarcely recognized the surroundings outside her immediate ones. One seldom saw one's neighbours now. There was no sense of community. Many of her friends had died of course and the ones who remained had become as restless, it seemed, as their children and grandchildren. Several women her age, who had once been her close friends, now spent all their time on cruise ships, travelling back and forth across the world with other widows and the small tribes of fashionably dressed homosexuals who seemed always to accompany them. One seventy-year-old woman she knew had married such a one, a Greek boy in his twenties, and had brought him proudly home. They were accompanied by another young person who, although he was a Dane, was presented all round as her husband's cousin.

The younger people in her own family seemed always in transit; so did the entire population of Northumberland. Everyone was constantly off to Salzburg or St Tropez or

Brussels or Oslo. And people had begun to fly to New York as casually as they'd once gone to Newcastle. Even the servants, on their holidays, went to the Algarve or Majorca or Tenerife. The destination, Clara concluded, was unimportant. It was simply necessary, at all costs, to be on the move.

Just as her mother, Louise, had stopped making new friends after her son's disappearance, as she had gradually withdrawn even from members of her own family, so also did Clara begin to feel that she must rely now on her own resources, her own judgements, her own companionship. Watching Helen and Jesse and Nora, and most recently Floyd, casually come and go, she could not help feeling that they all saw her now as pleasant but unnecessary, that Wingate Fields made a comfortable base for them but it was not a place to be regarded as a home, certainly not in the sense that it had been for her parents and their parents, or for Clara herself. It gave her the odd and uncomfortable feeling that all her values had become redundant and that she was the only one who didn't recognize it. She was particularly wounded by Helen and by Jesse. They had been closer to her than her own children, closer that one's children, perhaps, can ever be. When she saw them, they still, out of guilt perhaps, made some effort to revive what had once been but was no longer. But no one was deceived. As Clara criticized them in her thoughts, however, she sensed that she, too, was reluctant to make the effort she had once made, to listen as long or as attentively to Jesse, to tell detailed stories to Helen about her own life as a girl, the pleasure she derived from her children, the look of the moors when it snowed in the winter. These lapses of her own, however, when she marked them, she quickly attributed to some other person. Anything she might perceive as a fault or shortcoming in herself became simply a human reaction to someone else's fault or shortcoming. She could attribute nothing to her age or to her diminished capacity to respond because she refused to embrace or even to recognize such possibilities. The failings she noticed in people her age were non-existent, she felt, in herself. She would never have said that aging was simply an avoidable state of mind but all the same she tended to believe it. When she took herself as an example, she certainly believed it. Her impatience with the changes she saw all around her was intensified by her conviction that no such changes had taken place in her.

One would imagine that Valerie's children, Rab and Polly and William, would have been a great joy to Clara. And they were when they were very small. But later she began to complain, in confidence, to her housekeeper, 'Children grow up too quickly nowadays. The most extraordinary things come out of their little mouths, even the tots. God knows where they pick up these untidy thoughts and sayings. They acquire a vocabulary, it seems, before they've had the time to acquire intelligence. And when you try to explain something to them, they make it quite plain that they're more comfortable with their own misconceptions than they are with your facts. One spends months teaching them to speak and once they've learned, they insist on speaking nonsense that only they understand.' When Valerie said to her as she did quite often, 'They're only children. We mustn't expect too much,' Clara invariably replied, 'We mustn't expect too little. A child is a small grown-up. If you eat with a teaspoon at ten, you will very likely eat with a teaspoon at twenty. Or at best you will be quite clumsy with your fork.'

If Clara saw herself as the last remnant of sanity in a crumbling world, if she saw lunatics everywhere she looked, the exception was always Valerie. If she'd been asked, 'Is there anyone who in any way reminds you of yourself when you were a young woman?' she would surely have said, 'Yes, of course, Valerie.' It was not a question of clinging to one piece of floating wreckage, whatever it's dependability; Valerie's qualities were eminently visible. Even someone who saw her just once could tell that she was kind and patient and composed, sure of her own instincts and rhythms, but slow to criticize those of other people. She was perceptive, particularly quick to spot a fool, but she was not judgemental. The characteristic that served her best as a mother, her ability *not* to notice everything, was also a key to her adult relationships. She knew this about herself and it made her feel older than her years, made her feel, too, as she'd said to Floyd, that she often seemed older to other people.

Valerie had, or seemed to have, that most rare of human qualities . . . balance. She was a long-distance runner. She knew something must be saved. She knew the race would be long. And she seemed to know, also, that the process was more important than the result, that one could lose and still survive, that one could win, or seem to win, and strangle on that success.

Clara knew all these things about her granddaughter. And what she didn't know she sensed somehow. She had come to value her above all the other family members. If there was any link to the future, if the Bradshaws indeed had a future that in any way resembled the past, if Wingate Fields was to stay alive and be relevant and valuable, then Valerie was the key to that continuum. Or so Clara believed. As all her other ikons had developed flaws or had begun to hang crooked on the wall she had found herself turning more and more to the only Bradshaw woman who was constant and available and in residence.

Her sudden perception, then, that Valerie, too, had begun to edge away, was particularly disturbing to Clara. The fact that there was no specific evidence to point to made it even more disturbing. She simply sensed that everything was not as it had been. She did not see any difference in Valerie's behaviour with Jesse. Or with her children. And with Clara she was warm and open as always. But nevertheless some new tide was flowing.

Suddenly, one evening at dinner, Clara realized that the change she had sensed in Valerie was only there when Floyd was with them. Only with him did she behave differently than she did at other times with other people. And *he*, she concluded, behaved differently when Valerie was present.

Seeing nothing between them except that silence at table, however, Clara concluded at last that Floyd's thoughts were elsewhere or that he didn't particularly enjoy dining alone with two ladies. When Jesse was present, the two men did talk freely she noticed, and Valerie, with Jesse to talk to, also seemed herself. So with all the other major and minor anxieties she dealt with every day, Clara decided that the trauma she had imagined she saw in Valerie had been just that — imagination. One afternoon, however, quite by chance, she witnessed the conversation in the garden between Floyd and Valerie. She could not hear what they said, of course, and she would not have listened even if she had been able to hear. But before she got up from her chair at the window and moved away, she could not help observing that there seemed to be a particular urgency in the way Valerie spoke to him.

Clara had gone from her sitting room to her bedroom then and had not seen the two of them walk to the summer house at the back of the garden. Nor did she see Floyd leave the summer house later and cross the garden to the house. Only when she heard him in the entrance hall downstairs talking with one of the servants did she walk to her bedroom window and look out into the garden. Seeing no one there other than two gardeners clipping hedge she was about to turn away when she saw Valerie walk slowly out of the summer house. One arm was folded across her chest. Her other hand seemed to be touching her cheek in an unfamiliar way. She angled across the garden to the west-wing entrance that led directly to the children's nursery and to her own rooms.

That evening the housekeeper told Clara that Valerie was not feeling well and would not be coming down to dinner. But the next afternoon she joined Clara for tea.

'Did Floyd get off all right?' she said.

'Yes, he did. Left late this morning. I thought maybe you'd come down to see him off.'

'I slept late,' she said. 'Awfully tired for some reason. Went to bed early last night and slept almost through the morning. I said goodbye to him yesterday afternoon. Perhaps you saw us, we met in the garden and had a little chat.'

'I did happen to see you,' Clara said. 'I saw you as you came away from the summer house,'

'I thought you might have done. You do your needlework in that east window, don't you?'

'Yes, I do,' Clara said. Then, 'Do you feel just right? You seem rather pale.'

Valerie smiled. 'A bit more powder and paint than usual, I expect.' She touched her left cheek lightly with her fingertips. 'I was having a rough-house with William last night and he accidentally gave me a good hard slap. Left welts on my cheek. I put some ice on them this morning. I should be good as new by breakfast tomorrow.'

Clara had no reason to doubt her story but she did. She had no reason whatsoever to draw a connection between Floyd and the welts on Valerie's cheek, but she did, nonetheless. And for some reason, in her mind, it all seemed connected with Nora. Floyd's leaving for Paris today and Jesse scheduled to return from there tonight. There was nothing rational about the scenarios that presented themselves, one by one, to Clara's mind, but they were, nonetheless, real for her.

[5]

'I'm delighted you're here,' Nora said, 'but I can't understand why you're not staying at my house. I have all kinds of room, I'll give you a key and you can come and go as you like.'

'I know,' Floyd said. 'that's what you said in your letter. And I appreciate it. But I just thought I'd like to knock around by myself for a while. So I found a little hotel room in Montparnasse. I brought some old clothes with me and I'm pretending I'm a poor student.'

They were eating dinner at a small restaurant in Rue Jacob. Floyd had been in Paris for five days but he'd sent Nora a *pneumatique* just that afternoon. 'You should fit in perfectly,' she said. 'Montparnasse and St Germain-des-Prés are crowded with people your age, a lot of them war veterans like you, studying on the GI Bill, living cheap and learning the language from French girls. Do you speak any French?'

'I've learned a few words. I'll get by.'

'I'm sure you will. What's the name of the place where you're staying?'

'Hôtel de Blois.'

She shook her head. 'Don't think I know it.'

'That doesn't surprise me. It's not your style. The room I have costs about five thousand francs a month. That's a little less than fifteen dollars. I've met guys who are living on forty or fifty dollars a month. For a hundred bucks you can live great. Drink wine every night and take a girl to the movies.'

'Sounds dreadful to me,' she said, 'but I'm spoiled. Where is this place exactly?'

'Rue Vavin. Just around the corner form the Café Select. The Coupole's there, too.'

'Oh, yes, I know that section. The Dome is close by. And there's a little night-club called *Les Lilacs*.'

Floyd nodded. 'Right in front of my hotel.'

'*Alors, vous êtes bien placé,*' she said. 'There's a great deal of activity in that quarter. You'll learn all about Paris in a hurry.'

'I'm not in a hurry to do anything. I'm just strolling around, sitting in cafés, soaking it all up. I eat at Wadja's or Chez Rosalie or the Rotonde. I stroll around in the Luxembourg Gardens and I sit at the Kosmos a lot. When somebody talks to me I talk to them. Otherwise I keep to myself.'

'Does that mean I'm never going to see you?'

He shook his head. 'Of course, you're going to see me. You're the one who got me to come here.'

'That's good. I know a lot of people. You'll probably hate most of them but on the other hand you might not. I know a great number of spectacular ladies who would be interested in meeting you. Unless you're planning to live like a monk.'

'I don't think so.' he said.

'Good. Then you must come to one of my Thursday evening salons and I will officially launch you. I'll invite all my sexy lady friends. Some of them are married but they never bring their husbands. I think you'll be able to pick and choose. And I will definitely invite you on a night when Karina won't be there.'

'Who's Karina?'

'She's a crazy young woman who's been my friend since the war but she's death on men. She eats them alive.'

'That doesn't scare me.' Floyd said. 'Maybe you *should* invite her. How old is she?

'Thirty-five, I'd guess. Not too old for you. But too strange for anybody. Jesse can't stand her. For one thing she lies all the time. *Never* tells the truth. Even to me. And I'm her best friend. She even lies if you ask her what she ate for lunch. Or *where* she ate it. When I first met her she said she was Hungarian. Then for a couple of years she was Romanian, then Ukrainian. But the truth is she's German. Comes from Cologne. Her husband, whom nobody has ever met, was a big industrialist before the war. And he may be still for all I know. But he lives in Portugal, in Estoril. Karina goes down to visit him once or twice a year. "Just to keep him quiet." she says. The rest of the time she lives in her house in Neuilly with a girl named Dort, who she claims is her stepsister. Nobody thinks she's quite respectable and she's not of course. But she's welcome everywhere. She makes outrageous comments in the newspapers and the photo magazines like to print pictures of her.'

'Sounds a little rich for my blood.' Floyd said.

'Probably. You might hate her. But she wouldn't hate *you*.'

After they finished dinner they went to a café for coffee. When they sat down on the terrace, Nora said, 'I've decided I'm going to be your aunt. How do you feel about that?'

'I thought you were my cousin. Second cousin, once removed, or something like that.'

She shook her head. 'I'm tired of being everyone's cousin. I've never been an aunt. So I think I'd like to try that. My brother never had children but I'll pretend he did. I'll pretend you're his son and I'm your aunt. That gives me a little more stature. An aunt is the next best thing to a parent. I can buy you warm socks and cough medicine and counsel you about your life. But since I'm only your aunt and have no *real* authority, you can ignore everything I say. It's a perfect situation. I can give as much advice as I like and you can reject it all. How does that sound?'

'It's all right with me,' he said. 'You're going to introduce me as your nephew and if anybody asks me I'm supposed to say your brother was my father. Right?'

She considered that for a moment. Then, 'No. I don't think that's such a good idea. Since I'll only be your aunt when you're in Paris I think I'll say that Helen is my sister. That's probably simpler all round. What do you think?'

'Why not?'

'Or I may just introduce you as Floyd Bradshaw and let people *wonder* who you are. How's that?'

'I'll be a mystery man. We'll have the same last name but nobody will know the connection.'

'That's it. I like that. They may even decide you're Jesse's son.'

'He might not like that,' Floyd said.

'Maybe not. But it wouldn't be our fault, would it?' She paused. 'They might even think you're *my* son.'

'Never. You look too young and I look too weather-beaten.'

'Ah, but you and I know the truth. You and Valerie are the same age.'

'Doesn't matter. You still look too young,' he said.

'Because of that, I will buy you another coffee. *And* a Remy-Martin.'

It was a soft, lovely night. As he walked her along the *quai* towards her house she said, 'How do you see the future?'

'It's very vague.'

'No plans.'

'Nope.'

'Nothing you want to do?'

'Nothing much I can do,' he said. 'I'm one of those people with a great creative urge but no way to express it. I have no gifts.'

She smiled. 'You sound like me. When I first came to Paris after Edmund and I split up, this place was boiling with activity. Great painters and poets and composers working here. The twenties. The war was over and everybody thought everything was possible. I was feeling splendid and independent. I'd broken away from everything and everybody, and brought my daughter to this strange and new and marvellous spot where everyone, it seemed, was an artist. So it seemed inevitable to me that I would be an artist too. I was naive enough to think that with intelligence and industry *anything* could be accomplished. Later I realized that many great, great artists are neither intelligent nor industrious. They're simply artists. They have something that can't be learned or taught. Can't be bought, sold or traded. But . . . in those days I said to myself, "I will study and learn and work hard and then I will be a painter." So that's what I did. In two years I produced a great deal of work. I even managed to arrange a showing of my things. And it was the greatest humiliation of my life. Not because of someone else's reactions but because of my own. As soon as those pictures were outside the cocoon of my studio where my constant exposure to them had made them seem unique and wonderful, as soon as they were hanging on the grey and dispassionate walls of a gallery, I saw that they were empty and derivative and embarrassing. Everything I had learned was of no value whatsoever when one looked at the final product. I simply was not a painter and I realized that if I worked a lifetime I would *still* not be a painter. But I hadn't learned my lesson. I spent another year or two trying to write poetry. With the same results. But at least the poetry led me to buying a little magazine, *two* in fact. And from the wreckage of those publications I started *Icarus*. And then, a little later, I bought the gallery. So I ended up *helping* a lot of artists instead of being one myself.'

'Those things won't happen to me,' Floyd said. 'I know my limitations.'

'That's the most depressing statement I've ever heard. At *your* age, no one should know his limitations. You have to fail at a lot of things before you can start talking like that.'

When he didn't answer, she said, 'Sorry. Am I sounding like your aunt?'

'No. I was just thinking about what you said.'

'Any conclusions?'

'Not yet.'

As they crossed the bridge across the Seine to the island where she lived she said, 'How is it at Wingate?'

'How do you mean?'

'I mean how is it for you?'

'It's a nice place. It's a beautiful place,' he said. 'It's still hard for me to swallow that I'm in any way connected to all that. All that land, all those fields and trees and streams. All that livestock. All the farmers and servants and people coming and going.'

'Do you think you might stay there?'

'You mean permanently?'

'I mean would you like to make your home there? Spend your life there? Be a part of that life?'

'Jesus, I don't know. It's hard even to think of it that way, to think of myself that way. I know it's my home if I want it to be. People have explained that to me. But I still feel like an outsider. I look at Jesse and I tell myself that once he was in the same position I'm in now, but that doesn't help me.'

'Jesse was *never* in the same position you are. Or if he was he wouldn't allow himself to admit it. In some strange way I think Jesse was born to live at Wingate Fields. He and I have talked about it. He says the first time he saw the place he felt as though he'd been there before, as if he were coming home. He had some strange nostalgia for England. Some odd connection with a life he'd never known in a place he'd never seen. It's not just a matter of loving that life, those moors, that county. Jesse *is* that life now. And so is Valerie. I think it's the strongest force that binds them together. If either of them ever left there, and I certainly don't expect that either of them *will*, I don't think the other one would follow. Perhaps I'm wrong. But it's a feeling I have.'

[6]

When Paul Buscatore walked into his office, Mike Rosenthal stood up, shook his hand and said, 'It's good to see you. After all this time I thought maybe you'd scratched me off your list.'

'I had,' Paul said, 'but I had a feeling I was still on *your* list.'

'That sounds like a continuation of the last conversation we had. That night on Fifth Avenue.'

'Some things don't change.'

'Sit down,' Rosenthal said, easing back into his own chair. 'What can I do for you?'

'I'm not sure. We'll have to find out.'

'What does that mean?'

'It means that I came in to tell you I surrender. It means I don't understand the game we've been playing but whatever it was I know I didn't win.'

'I'm still in the dark.'

'Don't try to cock me around, Rosenthal. We're both big boys. Remember the first time I met you? On the aeroplane?'

Rosenthal nodded and Paul went on. 'You put on quite a performance. You told me things about my own operation that really straightened me up. Details I thought nobody knew but me. And maybe my accountant. I fired him, incidentally, not long after that. But that's beside the point. You also told me how much better my business was going to get. And it did. Lots of action. Lots of opportunities, shall we say. It all came true. Just like you said it would. Then all of a sudden it stopped. I don't mean things sort of tapered off. I don't mean I began to lose everything I'd gained. I mean the roof fell in. The phone stopped ringing. When people came into town to throw a little money on the table it wasn't my table any more. And when I travelled around the country all the games I knew had changed locations. Or there was local heat. Or somebody's sister had died. And when I did find a game there was always a sharpshooter I'd never seen before. But after I saw him once, he seemed to show up every time I dealt a hand. Calls himself Perkins. A hayseed kind of a kid. Twenty-five years old maybe. Wearing a Sears-Roebuck suit. Hair slicked back, cheekbones like an Indian, and skinny as a stirring rod. Nothing unusual about him. Not a hard-nose. And no smart remarks. He's just a guy who can't lose. At least he never lost to me. Dice or cards, it made no difference. He just sat there, cool and kind of pale-faced, every place from Stockton to St Louis to Jersey City, and beat my ass. And when I managed to find some action and he wasn't there, I still couldn't win.'

'You hit a bad streak. It happens to everybody.'

'Not me,' Paul said. 'Not like this. I've had bad streaks before. But this is something else. This isn't just losing. This is being shut out. Two weeks ago I got locked out in Amarillo. Do you know Amarillo? You can find a game there on the steps of the Catholic Church. But not me. I couldn't find a kid to pitch pennies with me.'

'I'd never guess it to look at you. You look as prosperous as ever.'

'I am prosperous,' Paul said. 'You know how much money I've made. I've got no complaints about the past. It's the present I'm worried about. I'm out of business.'

'I'm sorry to hear it, Paul.'

'I thought you would be. I thought I'd get sympathy from you. I also figured that a guy who knew how well I was doing before might have heard that things aren't too good now. Have you heard anything?'

'Nothing lately. Someone said a few months ago that you weren't banking games anymore. At least not around New York. Then somebody else said you'd retired, that you were down in Phoenix.'

'Well, now you know better.'

'I wish I could do something,' Rosenthal said. 'Do you need some money?'

Paul smiled. 'No. There's always lots of money around if you're in a bind. What I need from you is something I can't get any place else. I decided I needed someone to advise me. Sort of an adviser. A manager maybe.'

'I seem to remember your telling me you were a solitary operator.'

'Then was then, the lady said, and now is now.'

'I'm afraid I wouldn't be able to give you any advice that would be worth much to you.'

'Goodbye,' Paul said, not moving from his chair.

'What does that mean?'

'You tell *me*. If that wasn't a kiss-off, I've never heard one.'

'You didn't let me finish. I was going to say I'd really like to think of something if I could.'

'You told me once that *that* was your business, *thinking* of something. The first time we ever talked you said you had some clients you wanted me to meet.'

Rosenthal offered Paul a cigarette, then lit one himself. 'Like you said, "Then was then . . ." '

This time Paul stood up. 'Thanks for your time, counsellor.'

'Don't give me that *counsellor* crap. You've been watching too much television. Sit down.'

'I have some other dry-cleaning to deliver. If you're just going to schmooze me, save your breath.'

'Suit yourself, hard-head. I've got just as much dry-cleaning to deliver as *you* have.'

Paul walked over to another chair, circled behind it, slowly unbuttoned his jacket, then sat down.

'What did you have in mind?' Rosenthal said.

'Nothing. I'm looking for somebody who might have *me* in mind.'

'You're not telling me you're looking for a job?'

'Nothing like that. I am open to the offer of an opportunity. If it's an extraordinary opportunity then I might be willing to talk. And ever since I met you, whenever I think of extraordinary opportunities, I always think of you. Am I wrong?'

'Damned if I know. But I never contradict anyone who's giving me a compliment.'

'So where are we?'

'I don't know,' Rosenthal said. 'Nowhere, probably. But let me give it some thought. It may take a little time. If you haven't heard from me in a month, come see me again.'

'If I haven't heard from you in two weeks, I'll know I should look for advice somewhere else.'

[7]

After Floyd had been in Paris for several weeks, Jesse made a trip there. When he came back home, the morning after his return, he said to Valerie, 'It looks as if you were right about Floyd.'

'How do you mean?' Valerie said.

'Remember that conversation you and I had, not long after he came here. I said I thought we should find him a girlfriend here in the county and you said you thought he was capable of finding his own girlfriends.'

'Did *I* say that? I don't remember.'

'No reason why you should. It was a casual conversation, probably just before we went to sleep. Anyway, as I said, it looks as if you were right. According to your mother, he's cutting quite a swath through Paris. Catnip for the ladies, she says. Her French friends say he reminds them of Jean Gabin when he was young.'

'That's silly. Floyd looks nothing like Gabin. Gabin had no lips.'

'They think he looks tough. Like Gabin.'

'Gabin doesn't look tough now. He just looks fat. And he still has no lips.'

'I'm just telling you what Nora said.'

'Is Floyd staying at her house?'

Jesse shook his head. 'He's leading the Bohemian life. Hemingway thirty years after. He's got a room in a little student hotel in Montparnasse. Actually, Nora says the students only live on the top two floors. The rooms on the other four floors are reserved for the *poules*. And each room gets rented about twenty times a day.'

'Are those the French ladies who are so fond of Floyd?'

'Oh, no. Nora says he doesn't have to pay his way. Several of Nora's expensive Right Bank ladies seem to be standing in line, waiting to be noticed.'

'Well, that's very nice, isn't it?' Valerie said. 'You and I have met a few of those ladies who like to meet artists. I think maybe he'd be better off with the *poules*.'

'You might be right. That lot always reminded me of the section in the London zoo where they keep the birds of prey. Instead of you watching them, they're watching you. Like they're reading a menu.'

'Did you see him?' Valerie said then.

'No. Nora said he doesn't come around much. I think she has it in her head that he goes from one bedroom to another like a chambermaid but I'm sure he leads the same kind of life any other young guy in Paris leads. He seemed sort of shy with women when he was here. I can't imagine he's done a full turn-about in just a few weeks. But you never know. Did you ever meet a friend of Nora's named Karina when you were in Paris?'

Valerie nodded. 'Gorgeous. White skin and long black hair. She's Russian, I think.'

'When I met her she was Hungarian. And the latest reports say she's German.'

'Why'd you ask about her?'

'Apparently she had big eyes for Floyd as soon as she met him. She told Nora he was the most authentic man she'd seen in years. But I guess she got a few surprises.'

'With Floyd, you mean?'

Jesse nodded. 'Karina's like a lady in a candy store. She's used to taking home anything she picks out. And she took Floyd home, too, I guess. Bundled him into her chauffeured Daimler and whisked him away to Neuilly with her. She told Nora this story herself so it may or may not be true. The two of them had a little champagne on the way home and everything was going along smoothly, I guess, till they got there. Then Floyd was introduced to Dort, who says she's Karina's step-sister. But after the three of them sat around for a while, he gradually got the idea that when he went to bed with Karina, Dort would be there too. When Dort took off her robe, when everything became unmistakably clear, Floyd stood up, said, "Bonne nuit," and made a clean exit. Karina followed him down to the street, so she told Nora, and tried to reason with him but with no success. Finally she said. "Are you afraid we'll hurt you?" and he said, "No. That's just too many arms and legs for me." Karina thought that was the funniest thing she'd ever heard.'

'So was that the end of Karina?'

'Nora doesn't think so and neither do I. Karina doesn't know the meaning of rejection. Nora says any man who sluffs her off owns her for life. No one has seen her and Floyd together but the theory is that Karina decided to make a separate contract, one that didn't include Dort. She may very well be in residence in Floyd's hotel in Montparnasse, diamonds and all. At least that's what Nora thinks.'

Valerie didn't respond for a moment. Finally she said, 'Well, I'm sure we all wish them well, don't we? Everyone loves a lover. Isn't that the way the saying goes?'

'Something like that. But I've never believed it.'

[8]

Three weeks after their meeting in his office, Rosenthal met Paul for lunch at the Italian Pavilion. He brought two men with him, David Abrams, quiet, attentive, in his late fifties, pale skin and a receding hairline, and Lew Carpenter, tall and rangy, wearing a well-cut suit but looking ruddy and spare and sunburned, as though he would be very much at home on a horse.

During lunch, Rosenthal and Abrams did most of the talking. They discussed Stalin's death, Eisenhower's inauguration and the execution of the Rosenbergs. And what the long-range results of the McCarthy hearings might be. When all their plates had been cleared away, however, and they had ordered coffee, Carpenter, as though by a prearranged signal, took command.

'If you don't mind, I'll call you Paul,' he said, 'because I think we're going to be associates and I know we're going to be friends. As Mike probably told you, David and I are members of a group of Nevada investors, most of us from old families out there. We believe that our area is going to become very important in the next ten or twenty years. A lot of changes are going to take place and we want to be part of that growth pattern. Do we want to make money? Of course we do. But there's more to it than that. We're proud of our state and we want to help it grow and develop. A lot of Johnny-come-latelies have turned up in Nevada since the war and we welcome them. They've brought in new people and new business and because of them the state has made a great deal of money. But on the other hand, looking down the road, those of us whose families went west a hundred years or more ago think we have a role to play. We don't want Nevada to be just an outpost, some sort of colony for a lot of sharpshooters from Los Angeles or Chicago or New York. You know what I mean?'

Paul nodded.

'I'm not a native of Nevada,' Mr Abrams said, 'but I've lived there for several years now and I feel exactly the same as Lew does. We have some well-worked out plans and our support goes right to the State House. And beyond that, to Washington. We're serious people and we're in this for the long haul.'

'Before we go into the details,' Carpenter said, 'I want you to understand that this is not just an elaborate job interview. We don't want to *hire* you. We want you to *join* us. As a member of our team. Because that's what you'll be. And I'm talking about a select group. There are only eleven of us. You'll make twelve if you like the sound of what I will propose to you. In other words we know all we need to know about you and your capabilities. We've already chosen *you*. Now we have to convince you to choose *us*. I've given Mike a memo outlining how you will participate financially. If you decide you want to go ahead you can discuss that area with him later. If it's not satisfactory, I'm sure we can make whatever adjustments are necessary. How does that sound?'

'I'll know more when you tell me the details,' Paul said.

'I have the feeling something's troubling you,' Abrams said.

'No trouble. Just curiosity. How do you know so much about me?

Abrams smiled. 'You're fortunate to have a friend like Mike.'

'I told you we're a group of eleven,' Carpenter said, 'of that group David and I were the only ones who *didn't* know you. That's why we're here. When you meet our nine associates, you'll recognize all of them.'

'And they'll recognize you,' Abrams said. 'They've all lost money to you. Lots of money, they say.'

'You know as well as I do what's happened in Nevada,' Carpenter said. 'In a few years it's become the gambling capital of the world. The state's getting rich from casino taxes. And it's still only the beginning. The building boom never stops in Vegas and Reno. As soon as they finish a landing strip at the airports they have to start another one. We're involved with all of that. We own banks and casinos and restaurants. We've got a bus company, three laundries, a liquor dealership and a commuter airline. We have two of the biggest real-estate operations in the state and our construction companies do thirty percent of the commercial building in Reno and Vegas. I'm not trying to impress you . . .'

'Sure you are,' Paul said.

'That's right, I am.' Carpenter said. 'I want you to see that we have a track record. We're in business to stay. We have deep roots in Vegas and Reno and everywhere else in the state. But now we're going to start something new.'

'And that's where you fit in,' Abrams said.

'We're going to turn Bellwood into another Vegas. We've done a lot of research and we think it's a natural. It's close to Reno, it's just over the line from Tahoe, and it's already a working city. It won't be starting from scratch like it was in Vegas. We've got a thousand-room hotel going into construction next month and two more on the drawing boards. We'll be in business with the first one in a year and five years from now we'll have our own strip. Nine or ten hotels and twenty casinos. We're already booking entertainers. We're paying top dollar and getting dynamite people.'

He took a sip of coffee. 'But all that is down the road a bit. What we're excited about now is what we'll be doing six weeks from now. On June 20th we're going to open the *smallest* hotel and casino in Nevada. Everybody else is thinking *big*, we're thinking small. Small but rich. There's an old hotel in Bellwood, right in the centre of town, called the McKinley. It's been there since the Civil War. It was built to last and it has. It sits right in the centre of a park. A real little gem. But everybody stays in motels now out on the highway. So the McKinley went to hell. The people that owned it went broke five years ago and we bought it cheap just to get the land. Then David got a bright idea.'

'We decided to bring it back to life. When everybody else is trying to cram as many people as possible into their gaming rooms we decided there was a future for a place where *nobody* could get in.'

'It's a private club,' Carpenter said, 'for the biggest gamblers in the world. Everybody makes special concessions to the high rollers. We're opening a whole facility for nothing *but* high rollers. We sent out no announcements. It was all done by word of mouth. Twenty thousand dollars a year to join. And a thousand-member limit. Within three months we had three thousand cheques.

We picked the hottest gamblers in the bunch and sent the other two thousand cheques back.'

'Told them we'd put them on the waiting list,' Abrams said. 'Since then we get a hundred calls a day asking if there's an opening yet. There are guys who have their secretaries call every afternoon.'

'So we know we've got a good thing,' Carpenter said. 'We're keeping the name McKinley and we'll use that name on all our other hotels as well. They'll all be part of the McKinley group. And right at the centre of it all will be this little winner. No rooms. Just suites. One hundred beautiful suites. Everything has to be reserved far ahead. We're already booked solid through the rest of this year and we're not even open yet.'

'What if a guy's laid out twenty grand for a membership and he can't book a suite?'

'Fifty members a day can come into the casino even if they're not living in the hotel. But once that fiftieth card has been logged, the doors close till the next morning.'

'You're gonna have some unhappy people.'

'That's what we expect,' Abrams said. 'We're not trying to make it *easy* for people. We're trading the unhappy people outside for the happy ones inside. We want them to be eager to get inside to lose their money.'

'And feel good about it after they lost it.' Carpenter said. 'What do you think?'

Paul smiled. 'I think you're going to get *very* rich.'

'That's what we hoped you'd say. Because when *we* get rich, *you* get rich. We want you to handle the casino operation for us. It's small-scale, high class, big stakes. You'll be on a first-name basis with every customer in the place. Half of them you know already, I promise you.'

After the two men had left the restaurant and Rosenthal and Paul were alone at the table, Rosenthal said, 'What do you think?'

'You tell me.'

'I think it's the hottest idea I've heard in ten years.'

'So do I. But who are these guys?'

'They told you.'

'No, they didn't. They just waltzed me around the room a little. Are you telling me a bunch of good old boys from Nevada have carved out a gambling empire for themselves among the wolves.'

'What do you think?' Rosenthal said.

'I think they're blowing smoke. I think they're fronting for somebody.'

'You're a smart kid. You're right.'

'So what do they need me for?'

'*I* don't think they do but *they* think they do. Or maybe they don't *need* you. They just *want* you. They want a class act and they think you're it. You know your way around, you know a lot of people and you look good.'

'Are you really talking about a piece of the action?'

'A big piece if I negotiate for you.'

Paul lit a cigarette and watched the bus boys clearing the tables on the other side of the room. Finally he said, 'All right . . . I came to you for advice. Give me some.'

'That's easy. I say grab it.'

'Can I deal with these people?'

'I don't see why not. You're a straight shooter and everybody knows it. They love you now and unless you try to screw them there's no reason why they shouldn't go on loving you. In their business a class guy is hard to find.'

'Are you going to tell me who I'm getting tied up with?'

'I insist on it,' Rosenthal said. 'I'd tell you even if you didn't *want* to know.'

'Is it a New York family?'

Rosenthal nodded and smiled. 'The biggest. The Giulianis.'

'It figures.' Paul said.

'You know them?'

'A little bit. They own the ballroom on Fourteenth Street where I sang during the war. And they own my uncle's candy store on East Ninth Street.'

'There you are. You see, it's a small world.'

[9]

One summer morning when Helen was in her study working at her desk, her housekeeper came to tell her there was a young woman who wished to see her.

'Who is it?'

'Her name's Mrs Tillis. She says she's a friend of Floyd's.'

'Are you sure?' Helen asked.

'That's what she told me.'

'All right. Take her into the library. I'll be there in a minute.'

When Helen walked into the library she said, 'I'm Helen Bradshaw, Mrs Tillis.'

Jeannette turned away from the wall of books she'd been studying, 'Oh, I'm sorry. You scared me a little. My mind was a thousand miles away.'

'I just asked Mrs Clay to bring us some coffee.'

'Oh, I don't want to put you out. I feel silly just dropping in on you like this when you don't have any idea who I am.'

'I know your name now and I understand you're a friend of my son. That's all I need to know. Come, sit on the sofa.'

'We were good friends in high school.' Jeannette said, 'When I knew him then his name was Floyd Simison. My name was Jeannette Kinsman before I got married and that's what it will be again pretty soon. I'm in the process of getting a divorce.'

'Oh, I'm sorry to hear that.'

'It's a mess, all right. But I didn't come here to tell you my troubles. I just wanted to see if I could get in touch with Floyd again. Not because I'm getting divorced, I don't mean that, but just because we really were good friends. I mean, you know — we really *liked* each other. Anyway I've always lived in Crawfordsville, where I grew up, but since this divorce business started and there's been so much trouble with Glen . . . that's my husband's name . . . My daughter has been staying in Crawfordsville with my parents and I've been living over in Lebanon, Indiana, with my friend Amy Briscoe. She was divorced herself a year or so ago, so she knows what I'm going through. Have you ever been divorced?'

'Yes, I have.'

'I don't mean to be nosy but it makes it a lot easier to talk to someone if they understand what you're talking about. You know what I mean.'

'I certainly do.'

'Anyway, I started to tell you how I found you. I haven't seen Floyd since just after he was discharged from the Navy. He came to Crawfordsville to see me and he told me how he'd found out the Simisons had adopted him when he was a little baby. He said his real mother had found him and the two of you had seen each other in San Diego.'

'That's right. That was a happy day for me.'

'I'll bet. But you look so young I'd never believe you were Floyd's mother.'

Helen smiled. 'I'm old enough to be his mother. I guarantee it.'

'He also told me, when I saw him in Crawfordsville after the war, that you lived here in Fort Beck. I remembered the name because Amy's older sister, Sally, went to college for a year here at Foresby. And I guess maybe Floyd told me your name, too. What I mean is, I *know* he told me but I was so excited about seeing him again that it went right out of my head. I remembered your *first* name, Helen, because that's also my mother's name, but that was all. Also, there wasn't much point in my remembering because that time when Floyd came to look me up we decided we couldn't see each other again. I was married with a little daughter — she's not so little now, she's eleven — and there was just no way. If I'd know then what I know now . . . but I didn't. So I never thought I'd lay eyes on Floyd again.'

Mrs Clay came and served their coffee then. When she left the room, Jeannette went on. 'But since I've been living with Amy, we've had a lot of time to sit around and talk about the way things used to be. She knew Floyd from school so naturally his name came up. She asked me where he was now and I told her I didn't have the slightest idea. Nobody we knew in Crawfordsville had heard about him for years and nobody seemed to know where Mr Simison had moved after his wife died. She was a nice woman, not the friendliest person in town but very sweet once she got to know you. I think that's why I said you look so young to be his mother. Because Mrs Simison was really quite an old lady. She always had white hair, from the first time they moved to Crawfordsville. Anyway . . . where was I?'

'I'm not sure,' Helen said.

'I hope I'm not boring you to death.'

'Not at all. This is the first chance I've had to meet one of Floyd's friends. I'm delighted you're here.'

'I remember now. I started to say that Amy is like a little bulldog. She won't give up on anything. Except her idiot husband. Thank God she gave up on him. Anyway, she kept after me, trying to help me remember your name. Because we decided that was our only chance of getting some line on Floyd. She even managed to get hold of a Fort Beck telephone book and every evening she'd skim through a few pages, reading out names as she went. But finally I got her to stop that. I told her it was a waste of time because I wouldn't remember your name even if I heard it. Then one night, just a few weeks ago, we were driving around in Indianapolis and we saw a drug store with the name *Bradshaw* out in front and it rang a bell with me. And then I remembered, there used to be a funeral home in Crawfordsville called Bradshaw's and I'd thought about that when Floyd told me your name. So I told Amy I wasn't sure but I thought Floyd's mother's name was Bradshaw. That got her all excited. As soon as we got back to Lebanon she whipped out that Fort Beck telephone book and sure enough there was a Bradshaw in it. Raymond Bradshaw.'

'That was my father's name,' Helen said. 'I've never changed the listing.'

'I was already starting to get cold feet by then but Amy was on the phone right away. When a woman answered here Amy said she'd like to speak to Helen Bradshaw please and the lady said you were in Chicago.'

Helen nodded. 'Mrs Clay said a woman called several times but didn't leave her name.'

'That's right. That was Amy. Then a few days ago she called again and when your housekeeper said she'd call you to the phone, Amy hung up and said, "She's there." '

'So then you decided to come see me.'

'I didn't decide anything. Like I told you, by then I'd made up my mind it was a stupid idea, just ringing a stranger's doorbell and saying, "Hi, I'm trying to locate your son. Any idea where I can find him?" I didn't know *what* you might think. I'm not sure what you think now.'

'I told you. I'm delighted you're here.'

'Anyway, Amy wouldn't take no for an answer. She kept after me till I agreed to come over and talk to you. And here I am.'

'How far is it from Lebanon to here?' Helen said.

'Eighty-five miles, I guess. A hundred maybe.'

'You must have got an early start this morning.'

Jeannette shook her head. '*Yesterday* morning. I drove over yesterday. Asked directions when I got here and came straight here to your house. Then I lost my nerve. I drove back downtown and went to a movie. After the movie I called Amy from a phone booth and told her I was coming home. She said if I came here without talking to you she'd cut my throat. So I got a room in a motel and stayed over. And this morning I had more courage.'

'If I'd been in your shoes, I'd probably have driven straight back to Lebanon.' She leaned over and refilled their coffee cups. 'Now,' she said, 'What can I tell you about Floyd? How long since you've seen him?'

'Eight years, I guess. As I said, just after the war.'

'Well . . . after you saw him he was here with me for a while. Then he went back to South Dakota and stayed there in the house Mr Simison lived in before he died. And later he went to California and stayed there until last year. We went to England then to see my family. But when I came home he stayed on. And now, for the last few months, he's been living in France. In Paris.'

'Boy, he's really been getting around, hasn't he?'

Helen nodded. 'He's having a good time, I think.'

'I'll bet he is.'

'I'll give you his address so you can write to him. I'm sure he'd be happy to hear from you.'

Jeannette hesitated. 'No, I don't think I'd better do that. To tell you the truth I've been having a tough time with this divorce. My husband used to be a sweet young guy but now he's turned into a maniac. He knows there's no way he can stop me from divorcing him but he keeps trying anyway. Everything he can think of. He's had me followed. He tries to intercept my mail. He's so crazy jealous it scares me. That's why I left Betsy, my little girl, with my folks and moved over to Lebanon with Amy. Her ex-father-in-law's a cop. He lives right next door to her. And Glen knows he can't mess with him. The first time he came over there half-drunk and drove his car up on the lawn, Cliff — that's the cop's name — put a hammer-lock on him and told him in no uncertain terms what he'd do if he came back. But all the same, I've really been behaving myself. It's not hard because there's nobody I want to go out with anyway. I mean I don't even smile at the druggist when I buy aspirin tablets. I just want to get myself disentangled and the sooner the better. So I don't think it's a good idea if I have letters from somebody delivered at the house. From a man, I mean. You understand that, don't you?'

'Of course I do. I'm not sure just when Floyd will be back but I expect him sometime around the end of summer. Meanwhile I'll tell him you were here and we had a nice talk.'

'That's good. Just tell him Amy and I think about him and talk about him a lot. But you don't have to tell him I'm getting a divorce. I try to keep that to myself as much as I can. I was just blabbing to you so you'd understand if I act a little crazy.'

When Helen walked out to her car with her, Jeannette said, 'You've been very sweet to me. You're really easy to talk to. Would you be mad if I called you up once in a while?'

'Not at all. I wish you would.'

'I hope you don't think, just because Glen and I are splitting up and because I said Floyd and I used to like each other, that I'm looking around for my next husband. Because I'm not. The way I feel now I'll never get married again. I just want to make a nice life for my little girl and not go to sleep with a heartache every night.'

Just before she pulled out of the driveway she smiled through the open window at Helen and said, 'You tell Floyd I said he's a lucky guy. He's got a terrific mother.'

[10]

Jesse kept to his usual schedule of visits to Paris — a few days' stay every two or three weeks — during the months when Floyd was there. But they seldom saw each other. When they did it was usually just for a drink at the Select or a coffee at Patrick's and a half-hour's conversation.

It was, in its way, a carefully structured relationship. They seemed to take turns at leaving early. On one occasion, Jesse would have an urgent meeting at *Le Figaro*, the next time they met Floyd would be off to celebrate a friend's birthday at the Cité Universitaire. And when they talked together they seldom spoke about members of the Bradshaw family. All of the women they shared, in one way or another, Clara and Helen and Nora and Valerie, were forbidden subjects, it seemed. Perhaps each of them sensed that their relationships with each of these women were so disparate that no common ground was possible. Or perhaps the reason was less complex. Knowing, each of them, that their conversation together would be brief, they may have concluded that only simple topics, those that could be dealt with in just a few sentences, were appropriate.

In a way it was strange that they continued their charade of comradeship because neither of them felt any need for that kind of superficial, time-killing exercise. Nor did they feel a true family relationship. Each of them, if he were totally honest with himself, would have admitted that he considered the other man an outsider. Floyd, who cared nothing usually for such matters, and who was certainly a family late-comer, was nonetheless aware that Bradshaw blood was in his veins but not in the veins of Jesse. Floyd, on the other hand, was in Jesse's eyes an accidental Bradshaw, a young man who, but for an unlikely series of circumstances, would have lived his life as the wayward offspring of a history professor named Lowell Simison.

They were not contemptuous of each other. Far from it. Each had a grudging respect for the other, which they could not understand totally but which nevertheless persisted. They circled each other slowly, like two stags who were not eager for combat. The device each of them employed, as much as possible, was to keep the other in soft focus, never sharpening the image to the point where a specific judgement or reaction would be required. They avoided accurate definitions of each other as if they felt that something not clearly seen can be more easily ignored.

Privately, however, neither of them could avoid defining the other in terms of the Bradshaw women. Floyd knew about his mother's attachment to Jesse, he knew that Nora had been in love with him and had lived with him for many years, and most important, he was married to Valerie.

Jesse's assessment of Floyd had taken a sharp turn when he learned that Hugh was his father. Helen's open devotion to her son had affected him differently before. Now he saw it as a kind of residual passion for Hugh, something not altogether maternal. By some involved process that Jesse did not pretend to understand, he found that he was jealous suddenly of the mutual affection that Floyd and Helen showed for each other.

There was a seed of jealousy also evident when Jesse considered the friendship between Floyd and Nora. Again, Hugh came into the frame. Nora had always been candid about her feelings for her brother. She was equally candid now in expressing her devotion to his son. Jesse had never questioned Nora's love for him but he had always known that Hugh occupied a sanctuary inside her that was available to no one else. Now, he suspected, Floyd also had access to that special chamber.

And what about Valerie? Was she susceptible also? Here Jesse did not hesitate. He felt that he knew his wife as he knew no other person and as no other person could possibly know her. Since she was eight years old the two of them had been able to communicate clearly and finally with very few words. And often with no words at all. When she was still a child she had said to him, 'We're just one lumpy person actually. Somehow we got split up into two lovely people. But inside there's just one heart and one teeny-weeny brain.'

She'd also said many times, 'Why can't I have secrets? Other people have secrets. Even dogs hide bones where no other dogs can find them. But I'm made of glass. With *you* I am totally manufactured of clear crystal. Everything is visible. I am a woman without mystery. How dull I must be. How predictable. Since I think I *am* you, how in the world could I ever keep anything *from* you? I couldn't of course. And even if the glass got cloudy and for once you couldn't see completely inside and through me, then I would be absolutely sick till I was able to point out to you whatever it was you hadn't seen.'

Jesse believed these things as absolutely as Valerie did. He never wondered how she felt or what she thought. He always knew. He did not expect her to agree with him or to automatically share his opinions but the *pattern* of her disagreements was consistent and dependable. Her convictions never varied, her structure never changed.

Regarding Floyd, Jesse knew precisely how Valerie felt. For Helen's sake she had wanted him to be heroic and special. She had hoped for a particular quality, something precise and recognizable. When she failed to see or find what she sought in him, she had tried to rearrange what she *did* find, to restyle and refurbish somehow. But she'd had no success. Her disappointment, he felt, was evident every time she was in Floyd's company. The social grace that never left her seemed to dissolve when he was around. When he'd told her that Floyd planned to go back to America at the end of the summer there had been an expression on her face that he recognized instantly as a sign of relief.

Floyd's attitude toward Valerie, however, was another matter altogether. Or so Jesse believed. He had sensed it almost from the moment he met Floyd at Wingate Fields when he saw him and Valerie in the same room at the same time. There was some disturbing element he could not define, some unusual attitude, some electricity. Not on Valerie's part but on Floyd's. Jesse noticed that he barely spoke to her. When she mentioned later that Floyd behaved strangely toward her, it only confirmed Jesse's convictions that under other circumstances Floyd would not have been silent with Valerie, would not have been remote or rude.

Did each of these two men suspect that the other one had strong reservations about him? Not at all. Or if he did it was not evident in his manner. On the contrary, when they saw each other in Paris, albeit briefly each time, they resembled two outgoing sportsmen who met once a week for a golf match, enjoyed each other's company for a few hours, but who had absolutely no contact or connection except when they were on the links.

Their last meeting in Paris before Floyd went back to England, and from there to America, was typical of these encounters. They sat on the terrace at Coupole late one afternoon and Jesse said, 'I feel like hell that I can't go back with you and be at Wingate when you leave. I wasn't there when you arrived and now I won't be there when you take off. I'm tempted to make a call to Munich tonight and tell them I can't come over till later.'

Floyd grinned and shook his head. 'No dice, Jesse, I appreciate the thought but I'll only be in England three or four days, a week at the most. It would be good to see you there but don't change your schedule for me.'

'What are your plans?' Jesse said then.

'I don't have any plans.'

'I mean I hope we see you again before too long. How long do you expect to stay in America?'

Floyd shook his head. 'Hard to say. I'm going back to Fort Beck and spend some time with Helen. Then I may go to California for a while to see an old buddy of mine. But nothing's definite. I'll just wait and see what happens.'

'I wouldn't be surprised to see you back here in Paris.'

'Why do you say that?'

'Why not?' Jesse said. 'It's a good life. It's an exciting place to be. After all these years, every time I come back here, it hits me all over again what a fantastic place it is.'

'I don't know,' Floyd said. 'I guess it's different for you. You work when you're here. You have something to do.'

'That's right. But in Paris that's not so important. Half the people here don't seem to do much of anything. They stroll around, eat well, sit in cafés and lead the good life.'

Floyd smiled. 'I know. That's what *I've* been doing. And I had a hell of a good time doing it. But even that gets old after a while. I don't mind being a loafer but I get a little tired of some of the other loafers I see every day.'

'You'll be back. I guarantee it. Maybe you'll decide to settle in at Wingate Fields.'

'Maybe I will. But I haven't decided that yet.'

'Get married, have a family,' Jesse said. 'It's a nice life.'

'I'm in no hurry to do that either. I think I'll do what you did. How old were you when you got married?'

'Forty-four. Almost forty-five.'

'There you are. I've got plenty of time yet.'

'One thing I'm sure of,' Jesse said. 'Now that you've spent some time in Europe, life in America is going to look pretty grim to you.'

'You think so?'

'I *know* it. I went home just like you're doing. And during the war I had to go to New York. Both times I couldn't wait to get back here.'

'Why *is* that, do you think?'

'I'm not sure,' Jesse said. 'I've never been able to explain it to anyone so it makes sense. Usually I say there are more hours in the day when you're here but people just stare at me when I say that.'

'A lot of people don't want more hours in the day. They can't wait to get it over with. Have a few drinks, fall into bed and sleep it off.'

'Let me put it this way. When I lived in Chicago, or Fort Beck, or New York, or Boston, I always knew when I got up in the morning what the day would be like. But when I'm here, or in London, or Munich, or even in sleepy old Northumberland, the only thing I'm sure of when I wake up is that the day will be full of surprises. Not calamities. Just a lot of people I didn't expect to see. Opinions I didn't expect to hear. All kinds of ideas and tastes and smells and colours I hadn't planned on.'

'Most people don't want that either, do they? They want everything laid out neat. They hate surprises.'

'No question about it.' Jesse said. 'But *I'm* not like that. And I don't think you are either.'

Floyd smiled, 'I can't tell you for sure. I'm still trying to find out about myself. And it's a slow process.'

[11]

Any trepidations Clara felt about Floyd's return from Paris disappeared almost as soon as he came into the house. The silent, sometimes surly person of a few months before had been abandoned somewhere it seemed. In his place was a positive and cheerful young man who put his arms around both Clara and Valerie when he arrived and seemed genuinely delighted to be home.

At dinner he and Valerie chattered together like a brother and his sister, reminding Clara of how Hugh and Nora had been many years before. She saw no residue whatsoever of that intense conversation she had witnessed in the garden before his departure for Paris, no evidence that they had quarrelled that afternoon in the summer house. There was, in fact, an energy and a sense of celebration in the dining hall that first night that Clara remembered from another time but which she had concluded she would not see again.

'We thought perhaps you'd go the way of some of the other Bradshaws.' Clara said to him. 'Once they've seen Paris, they seem to lose interest in Wingate Fields.'

'Not me,' Floyd said. 'The longer I stayed there, the more I wanted to come back here.'

'But now you're off to America,' Valerie said.

'Well, you know how it is. A man like me is always in demand. I have to spread myself around.'

Clara smiled. 'I'm sure Helen will be delighted to see you.'

'She'd better be. That's why I'm going back. So *I* can see *her*.'

Two days after he came back he walked into the deer park with Valerie and sat there with her while the children waded and swam in the brook.

'I seem to remember we did this last summer,' Valerie

said. 'It's hard to believe you've been here for almost a year.'

'Yeah. The time went pretty fast.

'Of course you were in Paris for a lot of that time.'

'That's right,' he said.

'I grew up there, you know. I know that city like my pocket. I adored it when I was a young girl and I still do when I go back. But I could never live there again.'

'Why not?'

'I'm not sure. Maybe because I was so connected to it before and because I can't stand to see it change. Not even a little bit. Or maybe it's just that I can't live any place now except right here. Is that a sign of old age?'

'Probably. After all, you're thirty-three years old. Soon be thirty-four. You probably shouldn't be sitting on the damp grass like this.'

She laughed. 'I deserved that. But I think you know what I mean. I'm sure a lot of people would say I've lost my sense of adventure.'

'What's the difference what a lot of people say? If you've found something you like why not hang on to it?'

After a moment she said, 'Have you changed a lot or is it my imagination?'

'It's your imagination. I haven't changed since I was six. I was dull-witted then and I'm dull-witted now.'

'Not true, *mon vieux*. You're different. Did Paris do that to you?'

'I don't think so,' he said.

'Did you lead a wild, carefree life there?'

'I guess so. But I spent a lot of time by myself, too.'

'Thinking deep thoughts?'

He smiled. 'Not me. Just killing time mostly. You know how it is. Just letting your mind wander. Seeing where it goes.'

'Did you reach any conclusions?'

'No.'

'Make any decisions?'

He shook his head. 'I've made some pretty silly decisions in my life. I have better luck when I just let things happen.'

'Don't you get a lot of surprises that way?'

'A few. But not as many as you might think. Most things have a way of working out.'

'Not for me. When I have a problem I always have to

solve it or it drives me crazy. I can't tolerate unfinished business.'

'I'll bet most people look at you and decide you don't *have* any problems.'

'What do you think?' she said.

'I don't think about things like that.'

'You never think about me?'

He looked at her and smiled. 'We don't want to have this discussion, do we?'

'Why not?'

'Because as I remember we already had it. And it didn't work out too well.'

'That's no reason not to have it again.'

'Unfinished business, you mean?'

'More than that. Last time, as I recall, you did all the talking.'

'All right,' he said. 'It's your turn if that's what you want.'

One of the children called to her then and she walked down to the side of the brook, had a short conversation with Polly and William, and then came back. As soon as she was sitting on the grass again, facing Floyd, she said, 'If you think I'm a sophisticated woman, you're mistaken. If you think I'm perfectly organized, all thoughts in order, all elements of my life under control, you're wrong about that, too. I lie awake at night as much as anybody else. I wish I could change things that I know can't be changed. Nobody sees me scream or yell or lose my temper but inside I scream and yell a lot. I know a lot of people think I'm perfect. Perfectly dressed, perfectly controlled, perfectly nice and perfectly happy. But I'm not, of course. Nobody's perfectly *anything*. And me least of all. I asked if you ever thought about me and you didn't answer. I'm not ashamed to tell you that I've thought of you a *lot*. Some days it seems to me I think of nothing else. That half-hour I spent with you in the summer house that afternoon was something new to me. I've never seen anybody open up like that before. I've spent my life with people who are careful to *conceal* what they really feel. I've never seen a man hit a woman before . . .'

'I'm sorry I did that.'

'Don't be sorry. I'm not. I don't mean I enjoyed it. It hurt and I don't like to be hurt. But it taught me something about myself. I've always felt that anything could be talked away, that a proper and reasonable discussion could solve any problem, unravel any situation. But suddenly I saw that wasn't true. I saw something in you that I've never seen before. That's why I thought about you when you were gone. I thought, when have *I* ever exposed myself like that? When have I ever reached a point where I couldn't be articulate or reasonable? The answer is that I never have. And I hate that in myself. Or at least I've come to hate it since that afternoon in the summer house. A moment ago I told you some of the things that people see in me which aren't really there. But if you asked me right now to say what I really am, if you asked me to describe my essential self, I know I would only say that I am a married woman with three children. That would have described me ten years ago and I suppose that will describe me twenty years from now. I will still be married to Jesse, I'll still have three children, and I'll still be wondering . . .'

'Wondering what?'

'I don't know. Wondering how it would feel . . . wondering what it would be like to be as pale and angry and frightening as you were that day, to just stand there and say everything you were feeling, to be different, for a moment, than you've ever been before.'

[12]

Two days later, the morning of the day before he would fly home to America, Floyd found a note on the tray beside his breakfast coffee. It was written on a plain card, enclosed in a plain white envelope and it wasn't signed.

> I'm riding out to the ruined castle this morning. Meet me there.

He sat by the window in his robe. Long after the coffee had gone cold, he stayed there by the window. At last he saw her walk across the garden wearing a white shirt and a blue riding-skirt that hung long below the top of her boots. He sat there till he saw her horse canter out from behind the stables and heard her spaniel barking. Then as he took off his robe and began to dress, he saw her galloping far out across the moors, the morning overcast, with occasional slivers of sunlight slanting through.

He went down for breakfast then and spent a leisurely hour at table with Clara. 'You don't have your riding togs on,' she said as he came into the breakfast room.

'Not today,' he said. 'Too many things to do if I expect to get away tomorrow.'

He was fully prepared to leave, of course, and he had been since his second day back. He had, in fact, planned to ride that morning until he found Valerie's note. As he pottered about his rooms, midmorning, he told himself that he was doing the proper thing, the only thing he could do, and left it there. He made no effort to explore the situation, to clarify what it was, precisely, that he was doing or failing to do. He simply persuaded himself that inaction was the best choice he could make, And until ten-thirty in the morning he persisted in that choice. Then, suddenly, he undressed, put on his jodphurs and hacking jacket and pulled on his boots. In a few minutes he was mounted and riding north across the moors.

Forty minutes later, the sun bright and hot now, as he rode down the long slope toward the river, he could see Valerie lying on a blanket on the grass near the water's edge. When he rode close and dismounted she stood up and came to meet him, her face flushed from the heat, her shirt partly opened. As they stood facing each other, she took his hand and put it inside her shirt. Then she turned slowly and walked away, across the soft grass to the rock-walled remains of the crofter's cottage that stood there over-looking the river. She turned in the shaded doorway to face him, slipped her arms out of the sleeves of her shirt, then disappeared inside. Floyd walked past the grazing horses and the spaniel sleeping in a spot of shade and followed her into the cottage.

Book Three

Chapter Seven

[1]

Although it was unspoken between them, neither Valerie nor Floyd questioned that they had been brought together by a kind of madness. There was no binding force of hope or future, no shared dreams, no feelings of oneness or permanence. Some mute contract made it clear that this one particular chain of moments was all there would be for them. Valerie would not abandon Jesse or her children. Floyd would not make scenes or cry out that he had been misled. He would not redirect his life. They knew they were caught up in a swift current but when it lost itself at last in calm waters, their lives would go on as before. Or so they told themselves.

If Floyd had stayed on at Wingate Fields their resolve might have been tested. But since he left for America as planned only two days after their afternoon together in the crofter's cottage there was no time for second thoughts or changes of heart. They parted, not as lovers, but as civilized members of the same civilized family. As part of that family they would meet again of course but the sweet folly of that summer afternoon would never be repeated.

Valerie felt no guilt for what she had done. Those hours with Floyd had been so remote from the familiar patterns of her life that they could not be judged or measured by the standards she was accustomed to. And even if they could have been she would have felt no sense of responsibility for her actions. She felt rather as if she had stepped out of her skin for those hours and followed a course that she had no memory of having chosen.

With such deft conclusions, Valerie reassured herself. Having changed dramatically, she told herself she remained unchanged. Abandoning all her previous codes and strictures she had succumbed to a jungle impulse and had come away unscathed. Regretting nothing, celebrating, in fact, her splendid courage, she fully intended now to continue the smooth rhythm of her days as though nothing unusual had taken place. She *needed* to do that, so she assured herself it was possible. And for a time it was.

Floyd's departure from England had given her a strong sense of security. She had no wish to forget what they had shared together but she felt obligated to forget *him*, to position him firmly in the past and let matters rest there. There was no place in her structure for a rogue male. She felt no desire to divide herself, even in her secret thoughts, between Jesse and Floyd. So it was critical that Floyd's physical absence should also absent him from her thoughts.

Since she was a wise and aware young woman she should have known better but she did not. Weeks after Floyd left she found him, if anything, more vividly present at Wingate Fields than he had been when he was there. Previously, he had come and gone, had entered and re-entered her consciousness in a normal everyday way. But now the *memory* of him *never* left her, it seemed.

At first she enjoyed it. She carried him with her everywhere like an unborn child, an invisible companion, a precious secret. Any thoughts she'd had of isolating his memory in some small cubicle vanished altogether and at last she became uneasily accustomed to his constant presence. Then she came to enjoy it, and finally she needed it. He became a vital part of her everyday life. She began to believe that his presence must be as visible to others as it was to her. Each day she expected Jesse to confront her with God-knew-what sort of accusation. As time passed and no such confrontation took place she accepted this as solid evidence that he *knew* but for some reason chose not to speak.

Just as her rational self had attempted, by force of will, to isolate Floyd from the main currents of her life, so also was she determined that nothing in her relationship to Jesse would be altered. And nothing was. Every element of their life together remained as it had always been. No tenderness, no intimacy, no passion was lost or diminished. If anything she was more tender, more ardent, more sweetly entwined with her husband than before, more involved with their children, with their home, with all the details that made up her life at Wingate Fields.

All this was in no way a performance. If she had been a selfless wife and mother before, her experience with Floyd seemed somehow to have intensified that selflessness. Also, strange as this may seem, she never once saw herself as a woman divided between two men. She never compared Floyd with Jesse. She saw them as separate in every way. Two unrelated creatures who bore no resemblance to each other either in form or in function. Was this attitude a defence mechanism? Of course. By persuading herself that she had not chosen one man over another, by convincing herself that they were totally unlike in both genus and detail she was able to float along in peace and good conscience putting no accurate or proper name to *anything*.

But a day came at last when she could no longer placate herself. Common sense told her that no one had been deceived. She studied Clara carefully each day, her words and her expressions, her responses and questions; she believed she saw a marked change in her grandmother, a reserve she hadn't seen before, a new attitude. Where all had once been acceptance and approval, she sensed now a climate of judgement.

Jesse's case was different. No amount of scrutiny revealed any change in him. No impatience. No questioning looks. Nothing. To Valerie this meant that he was simply waiting for the proper moment to indict her and condemn her. She had believed at first that whatever she had done, it would never hurt anyone else. Her children would never know, Clara would never know and, most critical of all, Jesse would not know. Now she was convinced that he did know. Or at least he suspected. So everything had changed.

She had told herself that under no circumstances would she ever tell him. Now she believed she *had* to tell him.

[2]

One late night when the house was still and they were alone in their upstairs sitting room Valerie told him. She had planned carefully what she would say but when the moment came she abandoned those plans and recited in simple language exactly what had happened. When she finished he said nothing. He sat in a chair facing her, looking at the brandy glass he held in his hands.

At last she said, 'I know you're very angry.'

He didn't answer or look at her.

'Please,' she said. 'Don't just go silent on me. Can't we talk about it?'

Finally he looked up at her. 'You want to *talk* about it. What do you expect me to say?'

'I don't know. I don't know what I expect. I just can't stand it when you sit there and say nothing.'

'That's too damned bad. Am I supposed to apologize for making *you* uncomfortable?'

'I don't know what to say, Jesse.'

'What kind of reaction did you expect from me? Did you think I'd pat you on the head and give you a sweet?'

'I told you . . . I didn't know what to expect.'

'You must have given it some thought. You've had plenty of time to think about it. I'm surprised you told me at all.'

'I wasn't going to,' she said.

'Then why did you?'

'I've never lied to you about anything. I've known you all my life and I've never kept secrets from you. It made me feel awful. I *had* to tell you.'

'You had to tell me so you could make yourself feel better, is that it?'

'No, that's *not* it.' she said.

'But you *do* feel better now that you've told me.'

'No. I feel terrible. I can't stand the way you're looking at me. I don't recognize you.'

'How the hell do you think *I* feel? Do you think I recognize *you?* We came upstairs after dinner, I put on my robe and pyjamas and sat down with a brandy and you drop a hand grenade in my lap.'

'I'm *sorry*, Jesse. I told you how sorry I am.'

'You're not half as sorry as I am. I feel as if I'd just read a cheap novel and on the last page I found out I was one of the main characters. The stupid one.'

'You're *not* stupid,' she said.

'All right. I'll put it another way. Let's just say I've been made to feel stupid.

'No one was trying to do that. Nobody was trying to make a fool of you.'

'I know,' he said. 'You made that clear. Nothing was planned. It was just something that happened. Nobody in charge, nobody to blame.'

'I think we should talk about this some other time.'

'Suit yourself,' He got up and poured himself another drink.

'Please, Jesse.'

'Please what?'

'Please don't make things worse than they are.'

'I wouldn't know how to make things worse than they are.'

'I didn't mean that nobody was to blame. I suppose we were both to blame. What I meant to say was that it wasn't a plot against you. It wasn't something that was all planned and worked out in advance.'

'I understand that. It was spontaneous and romantic and wonderful. Valerie and Floyd. Captured by destiny.'

'It's not fair to blame it on Floyd,' she said.

'No? Why not? Am I supposed to pat him on the head too? Was he a victim of circumstance just as you were?'

'I didn't use those words.'

'No? What did you say?'

'I don't remember what I said.'

'What kind of an idiot do you think I am? We're not talking about two adolescents. You're both grown-up people. You rode out one afternoon together . . .'

'We didn't go together.'

'That's right,' Jesse said. 'You went first, then he came along later to meet you. Are you trying to tell me that you didn't know *why* you were meeting there, that you didn't know and he didn't know? Do you expect me to swallow that?'

'I told you we'd never planned anything.'

'Of course not. You just knew. You looked at each other one morning across the breakfast table and violins began to play . . .'

'Why are you doing this? You're being deliberately sarcastic and mean. That doesn't make things better.'

'Oh, yes, it does. It makes things a lot better for me. I'm trying to turn a hopeless melodrama into some kind of comedy.'

'Comedy? What's funny about it?'

'Nothing. It's a dreary little tale. But we're stuck with it so we might as well make it less dreary if we can manage it. It's too aimless and arbitrary the way it is. Nobody believes it when things just happen. There has to be a reason. To make this story work we need some new elements. A neglected wife, for instance. Married to an older man, perhaps, who leaves her alone too much. She meets a man her own age who makes her feel important. He reminds her of how young she is, tells her her whole life is before her. She is mesmerized and grateful. To show her gratitude she gives him the ultimate gift . . . herself.'

'Please, Jesse . . .'

'On the other hand you insist that Floyd was guiltless in this whole business. Sort of an innocent bystander. If that's true, and I have no reason to doubt you, that means another scenario is needed. We take a young country wife, living in splendid isolation in the north of England. She has everything she thought she wanted but now she doesn't want it so much. She's restless. Bored with the familiar routine.'

'Stop it, Jesse.'

'Not a chance. You told your story. Now I must have a chance to tell mine.' He took a sip from his brandy glass. 'So what happens? A young man arrives from across the sea. An ordinary chap but inclined to be surly. This intrigues the country wife. She wonders what he's so angry about. One thing leads to another and at last she decided to lure him out across the moors on a summer's day to discover what he's really like.'

'You're being hateful,' she said. 'I was trying to be honest with you.'

'Of course you were trying to do the decent thing. Bullshit, Valerie. You're looking for absolution. You're feeling guilty, guilty as hell, and you want forgiveness. Sorry, but we're fresh out of that. I don't forgive you and I don't forgive Floyd. Are you telling me that it never occurred to you that you were playing Russian roulette with everything that means anything to me, with everything I thought meant something to you? If you are saying that, then I don't believe you. You knew what you were doing and you went ahead and did it anyway. Because you wanted to. Because it meant something to you. I know you. Don't tell me I don't. Nobody can sweet-talk you into bed. Nobody can choose you and sell you a bill of goods. They never could. When there's a choice to be made, you make it. So don't try to tell me you were overcome by the situation, by the gurgle of the River Will or the scent of fresh-cut hay. If you had a romp with Floyd it was because you wanted to. You can deceive yourself if you want to but don't try to kid me. The man never lived who could entice you out to the meadows and persuade you to slip out of your summer dress. If you hadn't engineered it, it wouldn't have taken place. If you hadn't wanted it to happen, you wouldn't have been there that day and neither would he.'

She sat silent for a long moment. At last she said, 'You're right. I did want it. I wanted him. I can't explain it or defend it. I didn't understand it then and I don't understand it now. But it was very real at the time. I didn't love him or even like him very much. All I wanted from him was . . . I just wanted to be with him. It was some craziness I'd never experienced before and I don't expect to experience again. You say I want forgiveness. You're wrong. If I fell off a horse and broke my arm I wouldn't need to be forgiven. And I don't need that now. What I needed was for you to know. Now you do know. As far as I'm concerned nothing has changed between you and me. I know you're hurt and angry but I hope it will go away. I'll do everything I can to make it go away. Beyond that, it's up to you. If you feel you have to punish me in some way, go ahead. I hope you won't decide that you don't want to be married to me any longer but if you do then I promise not to make a nuisance of myself. I love you as much and in the same ways as I always have. I am not tainted merchandise. I belong to you and to nobody else.'

After a moment, Jesse said, 'And what do we do when Floyd comes back to Wingate Fields?'

'I hope we'll treat him as graciously as we treat Nora when she comes to visit.'

[3]

Contrary to what he'd told Valerie, Jesse chose at last to believe she had been blameless. Using as a foundation Floyd's adventurous love-life in Paris, he concluded that he had found a way to manipulate Valerie, that he had taken advantage of her sympathetic feelings towards him and had manoeuvred her at last into a situation she could not escape from.

The more Jesse thought about it, the more sense it made to him. That would explain her need to tell him about it. It was also characteristic of her to take more than her share of the blame. She might very well have convinced herself that Floyd's misbehaviour had been prompted by some misunderstood word or act of hers which had encouraged him.

She knew also, undoubtedly, that if Jesse believed Floyd had forced himself on her he would not let the matter rest there. Or so Jesse reasoned. The more he thought about the things Valerie had told him, the more clearly he saw her as a victim. In spite of her protestations to the contrary. As his respect for her returned, his tolerance for Floyd dissolved entirely. Valerie had come to him with a story of indiscretion. In the following days, in Jesse's mind, it became something altogether different. He saw it as a trespass by Floyd, with Valerie, no matter what she said, as a victim.

As he mulled it over in his mind, as he reviewed the contact he himself had had with Floyd, both at Wingate and in Paris, as he dissected the conversations and discussions between the two of them, he concluded that there had always been an edge of antipathy there. He had always sensed that Floyd resented him. He had never understood why. Nor did he understand now. But it served his greater purpose to accept that antipathy as a fact. It allowed him to believe that Floyd had simply used Valerie as a weapon against Jesse, that she had been duped somehow in what had been, in fact, a vendetta against her husband. Thus he was able not only to forgive her but to feel compassion for what she had gone through.

He shared none of these thoughts, of course, with Valerie. He sensed that she would be no party to his self-deception. And indeed she would not have been. But knowing nothing of what was in Jesse's mind, she was able to judge him only by his actions. And those actions told her, without question, that he wanted their life together to be exactly as it had been before.

Valerie's absolution, however, further intensified Jesse's contempt for Floyd. It gnawed at him, disturbed his concentration when he worked, and kept him awake at night. He longed for a face-to-face confrontation. Or so he told himself. He fantasized about a trip to America, a return to Illinois, an angry meeting with Floyd. He rehearsed scathing speeches in his mind, sought new words to express his defiance and indignation.

He knew, of course, that no such trip would take place

and that he could never risk the truth that might come out of such a confrontation. But his fantasies continued. And at last he wrote a letter to Floyd.

> Since this letter concerns private matters I hope you will have the decency to keep it to yourself.
>
> Valerie has told me what happened just before you left for America and I want you to know that I hold you fully responsible.
>
> I'm sure you realize that you are no longer welcome here. You may explain it to Helen in any way you like but please understand that neither Valerie nor I want to see you at Wingate Fields again.

After he sent the letter off, Jesse felt that he had closed the door on an uncomfortable period. All the splints and bandages were in place now; soon the wounds would heal and be forgotten. He felt as if he had handled the situation in the best possible way.

A few days later however he received a cable from Floyd.

> Go to hell, Jesse. I'll do whatever I want to. When I want to come to Wingate Fields, that's what I'll do.

[4]

Five months after Floyd came back to Fort Beck, Jeannette Tillis obtained her final divorce decree. Ten days later, she and Floyd were married by a Justice of the Peace in Springfield. In a few weeks they knew they'd made a mistake. Each of them knew. But some stubborn masochism kept them together.

Much later, after Jeannette's death in a parking lot in Nevada, Floyd said to Helen, 'I knew it was a terrible marriage. We fought from morning till night. But I never would have left her. And she never would have left me.'

His friend, Abe Rettberg, said, 'Don't think I don't feel sorry for you. I do. I didn't like Jeannette much but I feel sorry for her too. That's a lousy way to die. But it's all over now and there's nothing to be done about it. And you have to admit you two were poison for each other. You told me yourself she wasn't dying to get married. And I swear to Christ you wouldn't have been so hot on the idea either if everybody you talked to hadn't been dead set against it. You're a blockhead, kid. You always have been. Somebody tells you not to do something . . . that's the one thing you've got to do.'

Rettberg was close to the truth, of course. Floyd was stimulated by opposition. Being told he could not or should not do something always caused him to wonder why. And sometimes, depending on his reactions to the person who was trying to persuade him, he was capable of doing, or at least trying, the forbidden simply to prove it could be done. He did not believe, by any stretch of the imagination, that his marriage to Jeannette had followed that pattern but there was no denying that there had been almost uniform opposition to the idea. Even, at times, from Jeannette herself.

When he'd contacted her at Amy Briscoe's not long after his return to Fort Beck, she'd said, 'Oh God, I'm dying to see you but I don't see how I can. I feel as if somebody's watching me night and day.'

Two days later, she and Amy met him for lunch at a restaurant in Decatur, Illinois. At that time they set up an intricate system of communication worthy of an espionage operation, involving Amy, her father-in-law next door, phone booths in Lebanon and Fort Beck, and half a dozen motels roughly equidistant between those two cities. Floyd and Jeannette met in one or the other of those motels two or three afternoons each week.

'If your divorce is practically final,' Floyd said, 'I don't understand why you have to live like an outlaw.'

'That's what I am to him. And practically final is not final. I don't trust the bastard. He's crazy. Wacko. It's all a play about my daughter. He thinks if he can prevent me from getting custody then maybe I won't divorce him. So that's the game. Prove I'm an unfit mother. Bad moral influence. All that stuff. That's why I have to be so damned careful.'

'Do you really think he's having you watched twenty-four hours a day?'

'I don't know. That's the catch. But I feel as if somebody's keeping tabs on me, so that's all that matters. Every move I make I have to wonder if it's something he can use against me to get hold of Betsy. And it won't stop when we're divorced either. He'll still be after her. That's why I put her in that private school up in South Bend. I hate not being able to see her every day but at least when she's there he can't tell some judge I'm a bad influence on her. I'd have to marry a dentist and have three more kids before Glen would believe I'm not a whore.'

'Is that what he thinks of you?'

'Something like that.'

'Then why does he want you back?'

'Because he likes me,' she said. 'He's crazy about me. And I'm his property, for Christ's sake. We've been married for almost fourteen years. What do you think? How does he explain that to his poker buddies at the country club? We're talking about Crawfordsville. When a man's wife leaves him in that town he's got a lot of explaining to do.'

Another time she said, 'Amy's got the right idea. She says she wouldn't get married again for anything. She thinks marriage is the pits and I'm beginning to think she's right. People talk about women being the ones who want to get married but if you ask me it's a game invented for men. Clean clothes, hot meals, a few kids around the house, and a warm body in bed when they get the notion. Look at my mother. You think she has a vote in her own house? Not a chance. Not now. Not ever. She sits around looking at movie magazines and waiting for my Dad to tell her what to do. You call that a life? I don't.'

'Are you telling me that's what your life with Glen was like? Are you saying you didn't have a vote?'

She smiled. 'Are you kidding? Not me. I straightened him out the first week we were married. I said, "I'll be a good wife to you but you don't own me." He bought the idea because he didn't have a choice but he didn't like it. He's like everybody else. He doesn't just want a wife. He wants a disciple.'

'I don't think you have to worry,' Floyd said. 'Nobody's gonna turn you into a disciple.'

'I know that. But I don't want to spend the rest of my time training people. I want to have some fun and it's hard to have fun with your husband.'

'I'll remember that in case I ever get the urge to propose to you.'

'I don't mean you,' she said. 'I always have fun with you. Besides you don't want to get married any more than I do.'

'You never know. I might like to get married for a week or so just to see what it's like.'

Amy, not surprisingly, had expressed similar views. 'If ever I've seen a female who shouldn't be married, it's Jeannette. Don't get me wrong. I don't mean she's a floozy looking for a different man every night of the week. She's not like that at all. Neither am I. But compared to her, I'm a bus-station hooker. For all the bad stuff that was going on between her and Glen, she wasn't fooling around at all. You don't count. I know what happened with you two when you came back after the war. She never could stay away from you and she still can't. But nobody else was in the picture. Plenty of guys wanted to be but she wasn't passing out nothing. But all the same, she's really had her can full of married life. I'm not sure what she wants but it sure isn't that. She wants to break out a little, I think. Live some place besides Crawfordsville and see what the world's like out there. Her old man was like a general all the time she was growing up and Glen tried his best to be a drill sergeant. So I think she's a little tired of that life. She'd like to turn in her uniform and become a female civilian with no bugle sounding every morning. She's like a lot of us. She just wants to take charge of herself.'

Months later, just before the divorce was final, Floyd said to Helen, 'How would you feel about my getting married?'

'I feel fine about it. How do you feel?'

'Jeannette and I have been talking about it.'

'That certainly doesn't surprise me.'

'It looks as if we'll do it after the divorce business is over.'

'I think that's wonderful,' Helen said.

'No, you don't.'

'Why do you say that? I like Jeannette.'

'I know you do. But that doesn't mean you want her for a daughter-in-law.'

'Not true. I want anyone for a daughter-in-law who you want for a wife. Choosing someone to live with is not a democratic process. No one should have a vote except you and the person you're choosing.'

'I'm not asking you to vote,' Floyd said. 'I just asked how you feel about it?'

'I'll be honest with you. If I hated Jeannette I would try not to let you know it. As it happens, I like her. I liked her the first day she came to see me and I like her now. More important you like her and she likes you.'

'You're beating around the bush.'

'No, I'm not. You didn't let me finish. It's up to you to

pick the person you want to marry and I happen to be very fond of the person you picked. Now . . .'

'Now what?'

'If you ask me whether I think you should get married the second the ink is dry on her divorce papers, I have to say I don't think you should.'

'Why not?'

'I'm not sure, It's just an instinct I have. If it makes sense to you . . . fine. If it doesn't, just forget I said anything. All I'm saying is that even a failed marriage stays with you. It's not something you wash away with a sponge and forget about. Maybe Jeannette is an exception but for most people it takes a little time.'

'She hasn't lived with him for quite a while now.'

'I know. But that's not precisely what I mean. I guess I'm saying that when you've been a wife and it hasn't worked out, for whatever reason, you need a while to re-identify yourself, as a person, I mean, before you start to be a wife again. You need to be sure how you feel about yourself before you lose yourself again in somebody else's life. Does that make sense to you?'

'Sure it does. But in this case, Jeannette and I have known each other since we were fourteen. She's known me longer than she's known Glen. We're not starting something. We're starting over. Picking up where we left off. Doesn't that change the whole picture?'

Helen smiled. 'I guess maybe it does. I can see it does as far as you're concerned.'

Some time before, a few weeks after Floyd's return from England, Jeannette had said to him, 'You're going to be mad at me. I did a stupid thing.'

'You never do stupid things. You just do the first thing that comes into your head.'

'This time I did something stupid. I told my mother you were back. I told her I'd seen you again.'

'I thought you didn't want anyone to know.'

'I didn't, but I told her anyway. She promised not to tell my dad.'

'But she told him.'

Jeannette nodded. 'I'd bet on it.'

'Don't worry about it. We're all grown-ups now. Who gives a damn what your old man knows or doesn't know?'

'What if he decides to pay you a visit?'

'Why would he do that?'

'Why does he do anything he does? So he can talk people into doing things his way. You know how he is.'

'I don't know. I haven't seen him for a long time.'

'He hasn't changed,' Jeannette said.

'Good. I hope he does come to see me. I may even send him an invitation.'

A week later, without an invitation, Jeannette's father, Herbert Kinsman, came to the Bradshaw house in Fort Beck. Floyd was in the basement in the workshop when the housekeeper called him on the intercom.

'There's a Mr Kinsman here to see you.'

As Floyd led him into the library a few minutes later, Kinsman said, 'This is a fine home you have. I'm glad to see you've prospered.'

'I haven't prospered. This is my mother's house. I'm the same bum I always was.'

Kinsman smiled, like an old raccoon, and said, 'This isn't the house of a poor man.'

'I didn't say I was poor. I have all kinds of money. But I didn't earn it. It was handed to me.'

'There's nothing wrong with that. All of us try to provide for our children in the best way we can.'

'Yeah, I know,' Floyd said. 'You were ready to send me to jail to keep me away from Jeannette.'

Another lukewarm smile from Kinsman. 'Not exactly. I never expected things to go that far.'

'No? What did you expect to happen?'

'I thought you'd listen to reason. And you did.'

'Reason had nothing to do with it. I was scared of going to jail so I ran away.'

'I always felt bad about that,' Kinsman said.

'I'll bet you did.'

'But, as you said, I was trying to protect my daughter.'

Floyd nodded. 'I know. That's what you told me.' Then, 'And now you're trying to protect her again?'

'Why do you say that?'

'I can't think of any other reason why you'd come here to see me.'

After a moment, Kinsman said, 'It's a different situation this time. I'm here because my wife asked me to come. And Jeannette's husband as well.'

'They want you to reason with me again. Is that it?'

'Not exactly. They think, all of us think, that if I could explain the circumstances to you . . .'

'What is there to explain? Jeannette's getting a divorce. That's not hard to understand.'

'It's not as simple as that. We had just about persuaded her not to proceed with the divorce. Then you re-entered the picture. And since then there's been no talking to her.'

'The way I heard it,' Floyd said, 'She made up her mind a long time ago.'

'That's true. She did make up her mind. But Glen believed he was starting to change her mind.'

'So what are you asking me to do?'

'I realize I'm not in a position to ask anything of you.'

'That's true. You're not.'

'But all the same,' Kinsman went on, 'I am asking you. We're all concerned for my granddaughter. Little Betsy. For her sake, we'd like to hold this marriage together if possible. We know that you and Jeannette have been seeing each other . . .'

'How do you know that?'

'Things like that get around. We also know, at least we believe, that if you'd be willing to cooperate . . .'

'Are you asking me for a favour?' Floyd said.

'I suppose that's what it amounts to. I'm sure you have some influence on Jeannette, more than the rest of us do . . .'

'What makes you think I'd do anything for you?'

'It's not for me. It's for the child. As I said . . .'

'I know what you said. But as I understand it, these divorce proceedings were under way long before I came home from Europe.'

'Technically, you're right. But let's just say the situation seems to have become more urgent since you came on the scene.'

'And now you'd like me to leave the scene. Is that it?'

'I can't force you, of course. I can only appeal to your sense of decency.'

'Decency? What the hell do you know about decency? You think what you want is decent and what anybody else wants is either immoral or illegal.'

'There's no point to our insulting each other.'

'I'm not insulting you. I'm telling you the truth about yourself. You're a pompous pain in the ass and you always have been. You did your best to wreck my life when I was just a scared kid. And you almost pulled it off. I used to lie awake at night trying to figure how I could get even with you. Now here you are, all of a sudden, asking a favour of me. It's too good to be true. But since I never liked to pull the wings off flies I'm gonna be nice to you. I'm gonna give you what you want. I promise I'll stay away from Jeannette. How's that sound?'

'Very encouraging.'

'Wait a minute. I'm not finished. I'll stay away from her if she asks me to. If you can persuade her to stay away from me then I will stay away from her. You can't ask for more than that, can you?'

Kinsman stood up, his face flushed suddenly. 'I should have known better. I should never have come here.'

'That's right. You never should have,' Floyd said.

'You're still second-rate,' Kinsman said. 'You were second-rate as a boy and you're second-rate now.'

'That's right. I haven't changed a bit. And neither have you.'

[5]

Three days after Kinsman's visit to Fort Beck, Glen Tillis showed up. One late afternoon when Floyd came home he was sitting in his car in front of Helen's house. When Floyd turned into his driveway, Glen walked up the driveway behind him, waited for Floyd to get out of his car, and said, 'I'm Glen Tillis.'

Floyd stuck out his hand and said, 'How you doing, Glen? Haven't seen you since high school.'

Glen kept his hands in his pockets. 'This is no social visit. I want to settle a few things.'

Floyd gestured towards the door. 'Come in the house. We'll have a drink.'

'I'll say what I have to say right here.'

'Suit yourself,' Floyd said. He turned and walked towards the door.

'Where you going?'

'I'm going inside to have a drink.'

'I don't want a drink.'

'That's your problem' Floyd disappeared through the doorway. He walked down the corridor to the library and mixed himself a drink. As he sat down by the window looking out over the garden, Glen came into the room, looking rumpled and unsure of himself. He stopped a few feet from Floyd's chair and said, 'I gues you know why I came here?'

'Why don't you tell me so I'll be sure to get it straight.'

'I want you to stay away from my wife.'

'You mean now or after the divorce.'

'There's not going to be a divorce,' Glen said.

'Does Jeannette know that?'

'She knows it all right. She just doesn't want to admit it.'

'I see,' Floyd sipped from his glass. 'Did Mr Kinsman tell you he came here to see me?'

'I don't know. I guess he did.'

'I'm sure he did. And he must have told you what I said when he suggested that I stay away from Jeannette.'

'Yeah, he told me. But that doesn't cut any ice with me. Because I'm telling you man to man.'

'And I'm telling *you* to go to hell. Man to man.'

'Watch your step, Floyd.'

'You watch your step. How many drinks did you need to get up the courage to come over here?'

'You think I'm afraid of you? I don't need any drinks.'

'Then why do you smell like a bar rag?'

'I'm not afraid to fight you if that's what you think. I've been doing karate for over a year now.'

'I don't care if you've got a cannon up your sleeve. You still couldn't lick the glue off a stamp and you know it.'

'I don't feel so good,' Glen said.

'You don't look so good. There's a bathroom right over there. The centre door.'

Through the door, Floyd could hear him being sick. The toilet flushed twice. Then he heard water running in the sink. Finally Glen came back into the room, looking pale, and sat in a wing chair facing Floyd. After a long silence he said, 'I never should have married her. I should have known better. I knew she never got over you. She told me that. I wish I had a dollar for every time she told me. But I didn't listen. I mean I heard her but I didn't listen. I thought we'd have a family and a nice house and pretty soon everything would get straightened out. That's what I wanted to happen, so I told myself it would happen. And it almost did after Betsy was born. I was in the service then but whenever I got home things were great. Everything was just the way I wanted it to be. And it stayed that way till the end of the war when she saw you again. You don't think that was a secret, do you? Everybody in Crawfordsville knew. And when she had a baby nine months later, they all checked their calendars and decided you were the daddy.'

'What are you talking about?'

'Don't play dumb. Didn't she tell you? She had a nine-pound boy. Healthiest kid you ever saw. Ate like a horse. On his six-month birthday pictures he looked like he was a year old. Fat as a butterball. And a few weeks later he was dead. Found him in his bed one morning. Crib death the doctor called it. No reason for it. No explanation. He just went to sleep and didn't wake up. God, how I loved that little boy. A terrific kid he was. Even after I found out he wasn't mine, it didn't matter. I guess I even loved him more then.'

'How'd you find out?'

'How do you think? She told me. Jeannette's not the kind to keep things to herself. Maybe she thought I already knew and I did. At least I had a strong hunch. But I never admitted it to myself. Not till after she told me.' He sat staring at the floor, slumped down in his chair. Then, 'When that little boy died, I thought it would kill Jeannette. And I thought it would kill me too. She thought she was being punished in some way and I guess I thought I was, too. After a while things got better for me, a little easier. But they never got better for her. I told myself that maybe it would bring us closer together. Once I got over the shock I started telling myself how lucky I was to have Betsy. I never really appreciated my daughter till after we lost Duane.'

'Was that his name?' Floyd asked.

'That's right. Duane. After Duane Purvis who used to play halfback at Purdue.'

Floyd remembered then, very clearly, the crazy several days he'd spent with Jeannette, in motels around Crawfordsville. Their last afternoon together she'd said, 'If you ever hear I had a daughter named Tracy or a boy named Duane you'll know you're the daddy.'

'I don't know how other people feel about their kids,' Glen said. 'All I know is how I feel. Betsy and that fat little boy are all I've ever had that I felt really belonged to me. I didn't have any choice about giving him up but I do have about Betsy. No matter what any court says, no matter what I have to do, I'll get her back. If there's any way I can keep Jeannette from leaving me, I'll do that too. But whatever happens between me and her, nothing's gonna separate me from my daughter.'

'Does Jeannette know you feel this way?'

'She ought to. I've told her often enough. But she thinks I'm just gonna roll over and play dead. You'd be doing her a big favour if you told her I'm not about to do that.'

[6]

'He's crazy,' Jeannette said when Floyd told her about his talk with Glen. 'He talks big but when the time comes for action he's hiding in the corner somewhere, sucking on a bottle of bourbon.'

'I wouldn't count on that if I were you.'

'I know him.' she said. 'He'd be scared to death to go head to head with me in a custody case. Glen's scared of everything. But most of all he's scared of me. I never tried to make him that way. That's just the way he is. It's terrible living with a man who's such a chicken. But that's Glen all over. He can't change himself overnight just because he's decided he can't live without his daughter. Besides, Betsy's twelve years old. She won't be home much from now on no matter who has custody. She loves going to school at St Mary's and that's where she should stay till she's ready for college. I can handle Glen and I will handle him. He'll sputter for a while like a wet fire cracker and then it will all be over.'

After Floyd told her everything Glen had told him about Duane, he said, 'Weren't you ever going to tell me about him.'

She didn't hesitate, 'No.'

'Why not?'

'Don't you remember the last time I saw you? I was determined to try to make something of my marriage. We talked about it one whole afternoon.'

Floyd nodded.

'It almost wrecked me, the two of us sitting there and

telling each other we'd never be together again. But I really believed it was the only way. And I think you believed it too. As soon as I found out I was pregnant I knew the baby was yours but it never occurred to me to try to find you and tell you. What good would it have done? At that time I was still convinced I would stay with Glen.'

'But you told him about it. Why did you do that?'

'I was drunk one night. It was after Duane was dead. I was drunk a lot those days. Drunk and angry and crazy. Glen and I were fighting over something or other and all of a sudden I just blurted it out.'

'He says he already knew.'

'No, he didn't. He may have heard some gossip but he didn't know. He didn't know till I told him.'

'I still don't see why you didn't tell me. Sometime during these last weeks when you knew you were getting a divorce anyway, sometime when you and I were alone together.'

'Oh, God, Floyd, don't you think I thought of it? Of course I did. A thousand times. But what good would it have done? Even now, just the thought of that poor cheerful little kid makes me want to bawl. I didn't want to dump that kind of sadness on you. I didn't know how you'd react. I don't know how you're feeling now. As we're talking about it. How do you feel?'

'I don't know. At first I felt awful because I'd never seen him. And then I decided maybe it was better this way.'

She shook her head. 'All this time I thought it was better if you didn't even know about him. But now I'd give anything if you could have seen him just once. It was heart-breaking to lose him but if I had to do it over again I'd still rather have had him for those few months than never have had him at all. He made me smile. He made me the happiest I've ever been. And when he died it wrecked me, some part of me. I lost something I'll never get back. Glen and I always had problems — you know that — but after Duane died, we had nothing, not even problems. We didn't fight any more. We didn't go out much. He drank a lot and I just sat and stared. Or I took sleeping-pills and went to bed at nine o'clock. Finally it dawned on me that I couldn't live like that any more. So I moved out, took Betsy with me, and sued for divorce.'

[7]

Ten days after Floyd and Jennette got married, when they were on their wedding trip to Hawaii, Jeannette fired the first gun in a series of battles that would define their life together. 'Do you know why you wanted to marry me? I'll tell you why. It wasn't because of me. It wasn't because of any way you felt about me. It was just something in your head. Some idea you had. Some notion about yourself. The first time you even mentioned marriage to me was after you found out about Duane. Do you realize that? It was like you felt guilty. Like you had something to make up to me. You wanted to get married because you felt sorry for me. Isn't that right?'

'No, it's not right. What's the matter with you? We've talked about getting married since we were kids.'

'That's different. I'm talking about now. Something snapped in you when we started talking about Duane. You acted like he was still alive, like we had to get married because of him.'

Almost every day something, it seemed, would set her off. And every night, as they lay in bed together, she would say, 'I'm sorry. I didn't mean what I said today. I'm really very happy. It's all too good to be true. I'm still a little jumpy, I guess, because of the divorce and Glen acting so crazy and making threats to everybody. But I'll get settled down after a while and then everything will be great and perfect, the way we always wanted it to be.'

When they came home from Hawaii, they took an apartment in San Francisco. 'Betsy will like it here when she comes to see us and we'll be far enough from my folks so I'll never have to see them if I don't want to.'

Betsy had liked San Francisco but after six months time Jeannette hadn't liked it at all. So she and Floyd took a train to Vancouver, leased a house there with a fine view of the harbour and settled in. 'This is where I went to school,' she told Floyd. 'When my dear daddy was trying to get me away from you. I was miserable when I was here but I always thought it would be a good place to live if you were happy. I think you'll like it.'

Floyd had liked it but Jeannette had been disappointed. It was a wet, soggy autumn and it reminded her too much, she said, of her unhappiness before. So they packed up and headed east on the trans-Canada train. They made stops in Calgary and Banff and Edmonton and Toronto and Montreal, heading, they told themselves, for Boston. 'I've read so much about Boston,' Jeannette said. 'I think I'd *love* to live there.' But after a month in the Ritz Carlton she concluded that all American cities were pretty much the same. 'I mean they all have the same disadvantages. Dirt and noise and too many people. So if you're going to live in a city you might as well pick the one that has the most advantages to compensate for the disadvantages.'

'That means New York,' Floyd said.

'That's right. Let's go there.'

They bought a town house on Gramercy Park, Floyd joined a tennis club and the Salmagundi Club and Jeannette occupied herself for several months with carpenters, plumbers, painters, floor finishers and furniture salesmen. But her mood-swings followed the same pattern that had begun in Honolulu. Back and forth, from black to white, from warm affection to senseless unprovoked attacks. 'I know you'd like me to think it's my fault because we've moved around so much but that's not the way it is at all. If I had my choice I'd be living in South Bend, Indiana. Close to my daughter, so I could see her on some kind of regular basis. And I'd be happy in an upstairs flat. Just because we spend a lot of money doesn't mean we have to. At least I don't have to. You, I'm not so sure of. I think you really enjoy being rich. You enjoy it too much if you ask me. Even the clothes you buy me, and the fur coats and all the jewellery, all those things are reflections on you. When we go out people say, "There's a generous husband," or "That woman's lucky to have a man like him." You know what I mean. It's not for me. It's all for you."

Not long after their arrival in New York she also began to accuse him of being unfaithful to her. 'Don't get me wrong,' she said. 'I know I don't have any claim on you. Just because we're married doesn't mean I own you. Any more than you own me. But don't think you're getting away with anything. If you spent as much time at that tennis club as you say you do, you'd be an international world champion.'

'You're crazy, Jen. I never look twice at another woman and you know it.'

'Oh, no. I don't know it. I know what I say I know. You can't help it, I guess. That's what they say, that men can't help it. But I say they don't want to help it. And you're no different. A little woman at home and a little something on the side. But I'll bet you wouldn't like it if I did that.'

'Is that what you're leading up to?'

'No, it's not. If I wanted to cheat on you I could have plenty of chances. But I don't want to. I take marriage seriously. If I hadn't expected to be faithful to you I'd never have married you in the first place. *I* have standards.'

'I swear to God I don't know where you get these ideas.'

She smiled. 'You see. There you go. It's a science with you. When you get in a corner and can't defend yourself, you change the subject. You try to put the blame on somebody else.'

'I give up. I surrender.'

'Of course you do. Because you're guilty.'

He did feel guilty, of course, but not of the crimes he was accused of. If Jeannette sensed, however, that she was sharing him with another woman she was correct. If it disturbed her, it disturbed him many times over.

When he left England, Floyd had been aware of his vulnerability. The strange blend of ecstasy and heartbreak he had shared with Valerie had shaken him, made him tentative and unsure. Experience had taught him that such internal abrasions were most quickly cured by abrupt immersion into another love affair. For reasons that were not clear to him, however, he was determined not to do this. All the same he could not pretend to be displeased when he learned, on arriving home, that Jeannette had been asking about him. Setting out to find whatever female companionship might be available was one thing. Spending warm afternoons with a passionate friend was something altogether different.

Without scrambling to find someone who might help him to put Valerie out of his mind, Floyd believed that time spent with Jeannette would certainly serve the purpose. And it did. At least he was able to convince himself, for a time, that it did. Until he and Jeannette were married. Then, by some trick of memory or retribution, as he found himself with his wife almost every hour of the day, eating with her, walking, talking, driving, swimming and sleeping beside her every night, he found also that Valerie's face kept drifting in and out of all those waking moments. He saw her clearly, heard her voice, detected her scent. And at night she dominated his dreams so completely that reaching out to touch his wife he believed, in his half-sleep, that he was touching Valerie. He did, indeed, feel guilty and the guilt made him more ardent, more attentive, more considerate towards Jeannette. And baffled as he was by her frequent outbursts of anger and accusation, his guilt made him more tolerant. Although he knew that he had not married Jeannette as a substitute for Valerie she had unquestionably become that. He had given up trying to ignore the fact that the legs and arms that wound around him were, in fact, Valerie's and not Jeannette's. Once their bedroom lights were switched off, his wife ceased to exist for him until the morning light identified her again. The persistent, almost brutal, passion that he showered on Jeannette was always intended for Valerie. His memories of her were so vivid that he could by sheer will and desire bring her body to life on the physical landscape of another woman. Once he accepted this nightly transformation, he enjoyed it, longed for it, lusted for it. Jeannette, who had always secretly believed that no man's passion could be a match for her own, became accustomed to being carried from the dining room to the bedchamber. She took a kind of primitive pride in going the course, in never turning away. But often she heard her own voice in the soft dark. 'You're killing me, honey. You're *killing* me.'

Wherever they moved, whatever unfamiliar house they were living in, whatever quarrels or angry discussions they'd had during the day or at dinner, Jeannette had always felt at home and at peace in their bedroom. And she continued to. To Floyd, however, every bedroom was the crofter's cottage by the River Will in Northumberland. So, in his own way, he was as contented as Jeannette was.

[8]

Floyd's marriage was, of course, no surprise to Helen. He had kept her informed of each development along the way, had asked her advice, and had listened attentively to her answers. She, however, instead of advice, told him precisely what she knew he wanted to hear. Outside of her one suggestion, that it might be wise to wait a bit, she offered nothing but encouragement and applause. Knowing his penchant for swimming against the current, she thought her unqualified approval might slow him down where disapproval would not.

It had not worked, of course. He and Jeannette were married in a civil ceremony in Lebanon with no family members present. Amy and her ex-father-in-law served as witnesses. There was no reception and there were no formal announcements. When Helen told Frank about it, he said, 'That's what we used to call getting married in the dark. Is she pregnant?'

'Why do you ask that?'

'Standard question. When people are in a hurry . . . you know.'

'I'd be surprised if she's pregnant,' Helen said. 'She doesn't seem anxious to have children right away.'

'She's no fool.'

'What does that mean?'

'It means I don't think everybody has to have two point four children to qualify as members of the human race.'

'You had two.' she said.

'That doesn't mean I'm proud of it.'

'Well, *I* am. I'm proud of Floyd. And I hope they *do* have children.'

'Good for you. You'll make a great grandmother.'

'I have a feeling that's not a compliment.'

'Sure it is. What else would it be?'

'I'm not sure,' she said. 'You always get brittle and funny when we talk about Floyd.'

'I may be funny, but I'm not brittle. I'm a flexible young chap in his middle years.'

'No comment.'

'Ouch,' he said. 'That's called damning with no praise.'

'I'm right, aren't I?'

'About what?'

'Don't play dumb. You're not a big fan of my son.'

'Not true. I just don't know him very well. What I *do* know is that you're crazy about him and he has the power to hurt you. So that makes me wary.'

'Floyd doesn't want to hurt me.'

'I didn't say he did. But when you love somebody you're a target. You know that.'

'I'll take my chances,' she said.

'I know you will. But I'm not as reckless about you as

you are about yourself. You told me you didn't want him to get married right away but once he did it you thought it was a grand idea. Or at least that's the way you act.'

'How do you expect me to act?' It was his decision. I always knew that.'

'That's right. But he knew it would please you if he waited a little while.'

'Youth is impatient, I guess.'

'So is middle age. Everybody's impatient.'

'You're not,' she said.

'Sure I am. I have no patience at all. That's why you're crazy about me. There's nothing more boring that a patient man.'

'I can always tell when you want to change the subject.'

'I'm not changing the subject. I don't even remember what we were talking about.'

'We were talking about Floyd,' she said.

'You're right. I do want to change the subject.'

'Why?'

'Because it's dangerous territory.'

'No, it's not. We talk about your two daughters whenever you feel like it.'

'That's different. I have no illusions about them.'

'And I do have illusions about Floyd . . . is that it?'

'It's normal. All mothers are crazy about their sons. And you especially. You've never had him around enough to get tired of him.'

'Why would I get tired of him?'

'Because that's the way people are. Most kids can barely stand the sight of their parents by the time they're fourteen.'

'God, you're cynical.'

'No, I'm not. I'm a student of human nature. Everybody has to hate somebody. And who's a more logical choice than someone in your own family?'

'You don't think Floyd hates me, do you?'

'I'm not sure how he feels about you. That's why I'm suspicious of him.'

'I think he feels the same way about you. Suspicious.'

'Of course he does. He's jealous of me and I'm jealous of him.'

'That's ridiculous,' Helen said.

'No, it's not. I'd be jealous of anybody who spent more time with you than I do.'

'I can't believe my ears.'

'What's the big news? I want you all to myself. Don't tell me that's a surprise to you.'

'It's a surprise when you tell me you resent Floyd.'

'I resent everybody. Sometime when you're asleep I'm gonna have my name tattooed on your forehead. "Property of Frank Wilson — do not disturb." '

'I think I'll pretend I didn't hear that.'

'Why?'

'It sounds like a violation of our agreement.'

'Do we have an agreement?'

'I certainly don't remember anything about tattoos.'

'Small print,' he said. 'Chains, leg irons, and tattoos. Standard equipment in a normal household. Handcuffs, whips, the whole works. Bondage is the answer. Statistics tell us that the happiest women are those who have no control over their lives.'

'You're demented.'

'No, I'm not. I'm very happy. Your son found himself a wife so now I've got you all to myself again.'

'Crazy person.' she said.

'Not me. Eccentric and demanding and possessive . . .'

'Crazy,' she insisted.

'Maybe you're right.'

[9]

In the dining hall at Wingate Fields the news of Floyd's marriage was toasted warmly but not much talked about. Clara, who would normally have led such a discussion avoided it in this case for reasons that were not clear to her. She sensed that Jesse and Valerie weren't eager to explore the subject.

When they were upstairs after dinner, however, Clara having retired to her own rooms, Jesse seemed determined to discuss it. 'I hope he'll be happy,' Valerie said. 'That's what I said downstairs. What else do you expect me to say?'

'I'm surprised, that's all.'

'Why should you be surprised?'

'Well, he is a family member. Our newest family member.

I should think you'd be interested in what sort of wife he's chosen for himself.'

'I imagine he's chosen the one he wants,' Valerie said. 'That's all that matters.'

'That's true. But since he'll certainly be bringing her here . . .'

'I don't assume that. According to Clara he's headed in quite the other direction. Hawaii, I believe.'

'That's just their wedding trip,' Jesse said. 'Helen said they haven't decided where they'll live yet. Didn't Clara show you her letter?'

'Yes, she did. But I just glanced at it. I was busy with something else at the time.'

'Helen didn't actually say they'd be coming here, at least not straight away, but I assume we'll see them within the year. It would be odd if he didn't bring her here. This is the family headquarters after all. I'm sure he'll want her to see it. She's a young woman who hasn't travelled much, it seems. I've been to her home town. Helen and I went there when we were trying to locate Floyd the first time. Ezra Pound once taught at the college there until they sacked him. And the man who wrote *Ben Hur* lived there. But there's not much excitement or variety that I could see. I'm sure Jeannette will be anxious to pay a visit to England. It wouldn't surprise me if they decided to settle here.'

'Why would they do that?'

'Why not? I did. Once I saw Wingate Fields I decided I'd never leave here if I could help it.'

'You're a special case, Jesse. Besides this woman has a daughter, doesn't she?'

'I thought you didn't read the letter.'

'I think Clara said something about the daughter,' Valerie said. Jesse nodded. 'Quite a young lady, I guess. She's Rab's age. So Floyd has a ready-made family. What sort of step-father do you think he'll make?'

'How would I know? The thought never occurred to me.'

'But now that I've brought it up, what do you think? You should be something of an authority. You had the world's greatest step-father.'

Valerie smiled. 'You weren't actually Nora's husband so you weren't really my step-father.'

'Not technically. But didn't I function that way?'

'I suppose you did,' Valerie said. 'But I never thought of you like that. I thought of you as a friend.'

Jesse poured himself a drink, then set off on another tack. 'Since you didn't read Helen's letter I guess you don't know that Floyd and his wife have known each other since they were fourteen years old. Childhood sweethearts, Helen said. Then the war came along and she married someone else and had her daughter. Betsy . . . isn't that her name?'

'I don't know.'

'But now she's divorced and back with Floyd. Quite a tale. Very romantic. Star-crossed lovers. Just like in the movies. Maybe the daughter and Rab will take a shine to each other and we'll have a fancy wedding here at Wingate Fields in a few years.'

'For the love of God, Jesse, can't you leave off?'

'What's the matter?'

'Do you imagine I don't know what you're doing?'

'I'm not doing anything. We're just having a little chat before we go to bed.'

'No, we're not. And you know we're not. You're trying to get some reaction from me. But there's no such reaction to be had. Did you think I was going to dissolve in tears because we've had a letter saying Floyd is married? Can't we put him behind us? Are you going to keep after me for ever?'

'I don't know what you're saying.'

'Yes, you do. Of course you do,' she said.

'I haven't said anything since the night you told me about it. I haven't mentioned him once.'

'You haven't needed to. You've made it clear by your manner that it never leaves your mind. I have the feeling that I haven't regained your approval. Not yet. Still on probation, so to speak. A bit of discipline for the errant wife.'

'If you feel that way it's something you've bloody-well invented. I've gone out of my way . . .'

'Exactly. That's precisely what you've done. You've taken elaborate steps to demonstrate that you've forgiven me and in the process you've made me feel that I'll never be forgiven. It's like water dripping on my forehead. But after a while being forgiven doesn't seem important. You see, I've forgiven myself and I'm contented with that.'

'You seem awfully upset for someone who's so content.'

'Of course I'm upset. You're nipping at my heels like a small dog. Trying to trigger some response. Am I supposed to say I'm heartbroken because Floyd got married? I'll say that if you like but it's not true. I'm not heartbroken. I'm not even surprised. I knew he'd marry someone. Why shouldn't he? I hope he found a nice wife but if he didn't it's not my affair. It's not your affair either, Jesse. I see no reason for us to discuss it again.'

They did not discuss it again. For Valerie there would have been no purpose to such a discussion since she believed she had made her feelings clear. But not surely in the way she had intended. The very vigour and indignation in her denials of a continuing interest in Floyd demonstrated to Jesse that her interest was strong indeed. No longer could he think of her as blameless. No longer could he see her as a victim or Floyd as a predator.

If Jesse believed that Valerie had displayed facets of herself that she was eager to conceal, he would have been astonished if he'd known her true feelings. The truth was that in the months since Floyd's departure for America she had seen a startling change in her attitude towards him. And towards herself in relation to him. When she had told Jesse about herself and Floyd, when she had clearly defined it as a kind of madness that could never be explained or repeated, she believed that. She knew it was true. But it did not remain true. Floyd refused to be labelled or filed away. As her mind relegated him to a specific and isolated past afternoon her senses demanded more. Having once felt there was no possible future for them, she found herself carefully planning such a future. When Jesse was away in Paris or London she rode out often to the site of the ruined castle. Sitting there on the grass by the stream or inside the crofter's cottage, she let her thoughts wander freely, allowed herself to be swept along until at last the impossible became, in her mind, something not only possible but inevitable. At first it astonished her to think that she and Floyd could have a life together and at last it frightened her to think anything else. She felt she was on the threshold of a future she had never planned but could not now do without. Into that fairyland came the news that Floyd was married.

Later she would tell herself that she had been saved by the fact that she had to continue to function. She was an integral part of the daily routine of Wingate Fields. Everyone depended on her. The servants, her children, Clara and Jesse. And she herself was fuelled and nourished by the duties she had chosen as her responsibilities. She had never permitted herself to malinger and she didn't permit it now. For the first few days after Clara's announcement she checked her reflection as often as possible in whatever looking-glass was nearby. Each time she was astounded to see her normal, fresh and lovely face looking back at her. She couldn't believe that the inner torment she felt would not be transmitted somehow to her physical features.

She was tempted to let the tears come and blame them on some imaginary physical pain or sudden migraine but she was afraid that if she let down even the tiniest barricade, if she took even one step backwards, she might crumple completely and find herself babbling to the trees. So she fashioned a survival garment and became, as much as she was able, an automaton. Not a cold and brittle facsimile of herself but the busiest, warmest, most concerned person she was capable of being. No detail was too small to command her complete attention, no complaint too petty. She was everywhere at once, performing all functions for all supplicants, selfless in ways that even she had never been before. Every day was like a forced march through new thickets, leaving her no time for reflection. Night was the enemy. Then there was no more work to be done, no children to instruct or console. But she solved that problem too. Each night just before dinner she took a strong sleeping-draught and after dining went directly from table to her bed. And all the while, some part of her stood to one side and watched, carefully observed her performance, crisp and dispassionate, and marvelled at her ability to be so consistently something she was not. Or, more accurately, to pretend to be something she had once been but might never be again.

She told herself that time would finally accomplish what full resolve and concentration could not, that her inner turbulence would at last subside and she would re-enter her skin again as a single identifiable person. But time failed her. She continued to function like a creature with two souls, one of which could communicate with no one while the other could make contact only with strangers and children and household pets. She had never believed in the condition that is called heart-break. Now she believed in nothing else.

[10]

The French believe that a woman of a certain age, one who is not married and whose gentlemen friends are fewer in number than they once were, will also find herself with very few women friends. It is a notion that the French will explain to you for as long as you are willing to listen. They will supply endless verbal documentation to support that case.

Any friend of Nora's, however, would probably not have defended this proposition. Or if he had, he would certainly not have used her as an illustration of his argument. Since her arrival in Paris in 1924 she had had countless male admirers, most of whom she'd ignored, and countless female admirers, most of whom she'd befriended. Her closest woman friends were always her own age or younger. She believed in image by association; she never appeared in public with a grey-haired or overweight woman. Nor did she ever go about with groups of women. She was quoted in *Paris Match* as saying, "A woman in public should always look as if she's going to an assignation or returning from one. Or perhaps *tous les deux*. Beautiful women have no time to loiter.'

She would occasionally lunch with a woman, but only one, and that one had to be as striking as Nora herself. Also, the lunch had to be at Fouquet's, Chez Marchand, or Prunier's. She had always had great confidence in herself. She felt she would be favourably noticed in any situation, in any company. But she also believed that the wrapping was as important as the gift. She had no impulse to appear first-rate in second-rate surroundings. She needed to be the brightest star in a major constellation.

It was inevitable then that she and Karina Einhorn would become friends. Not close friends perhaps but intimate ones, lashed together by common desires and common follies. Karina was younger than Nora but not as beautiful, not quite so rich but more flamboyant. And like Nora there were no levels of Paris society where she did not have entreé. Even the rumours that her mother was the daughter of a rabbi in Hamburg closed no doors to her. She was thought to be naughty and she herself often implied that she was extremely naughty. But no one, it appeared, was eager to document her naughtiness. In what seemed to be a tribute to her desirability as either guest or friend, no one ever tried to label her as less than admirable. And admirable, desirable people cannot *avoid* being naughty. It goes without saying. Everyone in Paris knew that.

When Nora told Karina that Floyd had gone back to America and married a divorced woman with a child, Karina said, 'What a pity. He was an interesting boy. Great possibilities. He never should have left Paris. We made a pleasant beginning, he and I. I thought he liked me.'

'He did,' Nora said. 'He thought you were gorgeous. But he wasn't fond of your step-sister. Didn't know what to make of her.'

Karina smiled, 'Ahhh, Dort. Who *does* know what to make of her? But she's my little house-cat and I'm fond of her. She manages my life. And she reports to my husband every week so he has an up-to-date list of the men in my life.'

'Why do you put up with that?'

'Why not? It amuses the two of them and it makes no difference to me. Karl has his life in Lisbon and I have my life wherever I happen to be. We manage not to disturb each other.'

'Then why be married?' Nora asked.

'Why not? We're accustomed to each other, neither of us has any desire to marry someone else, and divorce is such an annoyance in any case.'

'I couldn't live with somebody if it was just some sort of arrangement.'

'That's the only way I would live with a man,' Karina said. 'Love is too important to me. Only a fool would ruin a splendid love affair by getting married. And besides, Karl and I never lived together the way you mean. It was always an arrangement as you call it, negotiated between my mama and his lawyers. I became a baroness with more money than I'll ever be able to spend and Karl gained permanent access to his funds in Cologne.'

'What does that mean?'

'He did some disgusting things during the war. He got very rich in the process but now he can't go back to Germany. It's a political matter. The German government isn't really angry with him but they have to pretend to be to satisfy France and England. So the Baron lives in exile in his villa in Estoril and has, in theory, no access to his funds. But the Baroness has free access. Karl's fortune continues to grow in German banks and I am the conduit between those banks and my husband. So you see, we *do* need each other.'

'You mean it's a purely financial arrangement.'

'Not purely,' Karina said. 'Nothing is ever *pure*. Actually, being married is good for me. It keeps me out of silly entanglements. No man imagines he can marry me for my money. And for Karl it is also beneficial. Although I am seldom in Lisbon and I never allow him to come to Paris, photographs of me are often in Portuguese magazines. It's public knowledge that the Baron has a beautiful wife. He tells me this is a lure for other young women. He has two or three in residence at all times.'

'What's he like?'

'Karl? He's quite impossible and fat. And cruel, I think, if he's allowed to be. I've never slept with him and I never would. He boasts that he's made love to hundreds of women but he swears he's never *kissed* one. I'm not sure what that's supposed to mean but I guess it means something to him.'

'Sounds lovely.'

'Nothing lovely about him. Nothing natural. When you look at him you can't imagine him as a little boy. He looks as if he was created just as he is now. Like a George Grosz drawing.'

'You're lucky you don't have to live with him.'

'It's not luck. I arranged it that way. No one loves men more than I do. But I have no time at all for *husbands*. Very few nice men survive the act of marriage. Which brings me back to our sweet Floyd. I hate to think of him being converted to one of those dull American husbands I see walking across the Place de la Concorde pushing a baby carriage. Did you ever notice what beautiful arms he had? Strong brown arms with blue veins. I shouldn't have let him get away.'

'You should have locked Dort in her room.'

Karina smiled. 'I've tried that. No locks can hold her.'

One afternoon as they were sitting in the garden of Karina's home in Neuilly, Dort sun bathing in a wicker lounge-chair beside the pool, Karina said to Nora, 'We have been friends for a long time. Am I allowed to put my nose into your private affairs?'

'Of course you are.'

'You must explain to me what attracts you to Martin Vuko.'

Nora laughed. 'I know you're not crazy about him.'

'It's not important how I feel. What fascinates me, and many of your other friends, is what *you* could possibly see in him.'

'I don't know.'

'For more than five years no one has seen you with any other man. People say you're hopelessly in love with him.'

'I don't care what people say.'

'Neither do I. But I care about *you*. I hate to see someone make a fool of you. Especially a clown like Vuko. If he were clever or very beautiful perhaps I could understand. But he is built like a peasant, he wears odd American clothes, and he speaks a kind of French that no one has heard before. Worst of all, his atelier is like a great bedchamber. He makes love to every mannequin in Paris and boasts about it in a loud voice at the Coupole. Am I missing something? *Is* he the greatest lover in Europe?'

Nora shook her head. 'I'm afraid not. That's why he tries so hard. I don't know why I've spent so much time with him. Maybe because he's unlike any other man I know. Also because he's different from what he appears to be. He's also different from what he *wants* to be. He'd like to be tall and handsome but he's not. He'd like to be well known and wealthy. He's neither of those things. He's not particularly intelligent or well educated and he's not socially acceptable, not in the way he'd like. He was a poor Polish kid from the lower east side of New York who taught himself to use a camera. He was taken up by the fashion crowd in New York and then in Paris because he's like a bear among gazelles. He's a novelty. And until the novelty wears off he'll have a nice career and lots of long-legged girls lying about. Then one day he'll wake up and it will be all over. I'm not sure he knows that but I think he senses it. So he's covering all the ground he can. I suppose I feel sorry for him. But I also like him. He's the only man I've ever known that I have absolutely nothing in common with. He shoots lovely pictures but he doesn't know a good painting from a bad one. For the past five years he's spent at least half of his time here in France but he's never been inside the Louvre or the Jeu de Paume. He doesn't know Bartok from Schumann; he's never read a serious novel; he'd never seen ballet or opera until I took him with me, and he hated every minute of it. I think he feels that all culture was invented to make him feel inadequate. He's suspicious of anything that's foreign to him and everything is foreign to him except his camera and the things he photographs. That means women. That's all he photographs. So he needs to prove to himself that he's expert in all matters that pertain to women. That's his foundation in life and sooner or later it will collapse. But I don't want to be the one to pull it down. If I loved him that would be something else but since I don't I'm willing to ignore all sorts of peculiar behaviour. Vuko doesn't have a great range of choices, you see. He's one of those people who does as much as he can with what he's got. You and I are surrounded by people who don't do much of anything, so Vuko's a nice change. He may be a son of a bitch but he's a genuine peasant. People like him don't show up at my house very often.'

[11]

In December of 1955, Clara celebrated her eightieth Christmas. On her birthday five months before, she had promised herself that she would mount a holiday celebration at Wingate Fields that would be, as much as possible, a duplicate of the ones she had known as a child.

With the exception of Floyd and Jeannette, all the family members were present. Nora came over from Paris to spend a week and Helen flew in from New York to stay a longer time. And Jesse and Valerie and their three children were there, of course. And for the grand events, Christmas Eve, Christmas Day, and Twelfth Night, the tenants and their children and grandchildren, and close friends from the county, all sat down at the dining table laid out in the great hall. The entire ground floor of the house was decorated. A twenty-foot tree glittered in the drawing room, and the scent of cedar and pine pervaded the house. Great silver bowls of egg-nog and Christmas punch were kept filled and a string quartet played afternoon and evening from Christmas Eve through to New Year's Day. Two days before Christmas a heavy snow fell and the ground was white for the next three weeks. 'Did you arrange for the snow, too?' Helen asked Clara. 'Of course,' she said, 'On an occasion like this nothing can be left to chance.'

The driveways, it seemed, were constantly choked with cars, the rooms and hallways crowded with people. Fat geese and turkeys roasted below stairs, haunches of venison and loins of beef. Hock and claret flowed, stout and lager and brandy. Carols were sung, toasts proposed, and ladies of all ages were thoroughly kissed under the sprigs of mistletoe that hung over every doorway. On Twelfth Night, when Clara was toasted and applauded, she rose and said, 'I hope you've all enjoyed these days as much as I have. I tried to turn back the clock fifty years and I think I've succeeded.'

Before coming to England, Helen had stopped in New York for an exchange of gifts and an early celebration with Floyd and Jeannette. On the day after she left, Betsy came on from South Bend to have Christmas with her mother. When she left, to spend the rest of the holiday in Crawfordsville with Glen and two sets of grandparents. Jeannette put her feet up on the *chaise-longue,* opened a bottle of Drambuie and said, 'Thank God that's over.'

'And merry Christmas to you,' Floyd said.

'Don't be cute. I hate Christmas and you know it.'

'Who cares whether it's Christmas or Labour Day? It was nice to have Helen here for a few days. And Betsy had a good time, I think.'

'She should have had. You really showed her the town. Keep that up and she'll be spoiled rotten.'

'No, she won't. She's a good kid,' Floyd said. 'She appreciates everything. I was afraid she'd feel bad because you couldn't come along so I tried to keep her busy. You feeling better now?'

'Not much. I don't know what it is. I just feel punk. My stomach's been all funny for days.'

'I doubt if Drambuie's the best thing to put in an upset stomach.'

'Don't start that again. I like Drambuie. It won't hurt me.'

'I mean it's not something that most people sit down and guzzle like lemonade.'

'I'm not most people. And I like it. We can afford it, can't we?'

'For Christ's sake, Jeannette, what's the matter with you?'

'Nothing's the matter with me. What's the matter with you?'

'You've been acting like a fool since before Christmas.'

'Since your mother was here, you mean?'

'That's right,' he said. 'You acted like a damned fool.'

'You mean just because I wanted to have a little say-so about where we ate dinner that night.'

'No. I mean you acted like a spoiled brat all the time she was here.'

'I didn't say anything, did I? I was polite, wasn't I?'

'I guess you could say you were polite but that's all you were. Helen went out of her way, changed her plane schedule twice so she could spend a few days with us, she brought you enough gifts to fill the back seat of the car, and you act like you're doing her a favour to make coffee in the morning.'

'I made her instant coffee. I got up two hours before I usually do to make her some instant coffee. What's wrong with that?'

'She was a guest in our house. The first time she's ever been here. You could have put yourself out a little.'

'All right. I'll admit it. I don't like people barging in and taking over. You know that. I just don't like it.'

'Taking over what?'

'She was all ready to go into the kitchen and make a big dinner.'

'She was trying to be nice. *Most* people have holiday dinners at home.'

'Well, I wanted to go out. This city's crammed with good restaurants. Why not take advantage of it? But no, she had to make me feel like a fool. She laughed at me.'

'No, she didn't. She said she'd never had Christmas dinner in an Italian restaurant before.'

'It wasn't Christmas yet.'

'But we were celebrating Christmas,' Floyd said.

'I don't care. She made me feel stupid.'

'What do you mean? You got your way. We went to Umberto's, didn't we?'

'We went, but by then she'd already made me feel rotten. And then she did it again in the restaurant. Just because I asked the waiter for some sparkling burgundy.'

'Nobody drinks sparkling burgundy with veal scallopini.'

'I do. I *love* sparkling burgundy.'

'Well, Helen doesn't and neither do I. So I ordered something else for us.'

'Even the waiter looked at me funny. I felt like a damned fool. I was so mad at you I could have screamed.'

'What the hell did *I* do?'

'Nothing. That's it. You're supposed to stand up for me. I'm your wife.'

He sat looking at her as she poured herself another glass of liqueur. Finally he said, 'The first thing you told me when I came back from Europe, when I came over to Amy's to see you, practically the first thing you said was how much you liked Helen.'

'I did at the beginning. But she's different now.'

'How?'

'I don't know. She just seems different. She even looks different. Did she have her face lifted?'

Floyd started to laugh. 'You're really something. The more of that stuff you drink, the funnier you get. Are you going to finish the whole bottle?'

'I will if I want to. And then I might open another one.'

'Listen to me,' he said then, 'You've known me a long time. Do you think I'm going to take the kind of crap from you that you handed out to Glen?'

'Who said I handed him any crap?'

'You did. You told me more than once that you did whatever you wanted to and if he didn't like it, that was too bad. Is that the way you think things are gonna be with us?'

'I never said anything about how things are going to be. What did I say?'

'I'm talking about the way you act.' Floyd said.

'What's the matter with the way I act?'

'Everything. Half the time lately I don't even recognize you.'

'Well, what am I supposed to . . .'

'Wait a minute. Let me finish. We're both thirty-five years old. We've known each other for twenty years. And we've wanted to be married ever since we were old enough to know what marriage meant. Is that right or not?'

'I guess so.'

'Is it or isn't it?'

'Yes.'

'All right. So finally, after a long time, things have worked out. You don't have to put up with Glen any more. Betsy's in a nice school and she doesn't seem bothered because her folks are divorced, and you and I have finally managed to get together. No money worries. No problems at all. We can do what we want to, live where we want to. We can have a good life. It's what you thought you wanted and now you've got it. If you don't want it any more then now's the time to tell me. Because I'm not your father and I'm not Glen. I'll give you anything I've got to make you happy. But if all you want is to be miserable and to make me miserable, then I'm heading for the nearest bus station.'

'Don't say things like that.'

'I mean it. And you know I mean it.'

She sat there looking down at her glass. When she looked up finally, there were tears on her cheeks. 'I thought you loved me,' she said.

'I do. Otherwise we'd have had this talk six months ago.'

'I didn't know I've been so terrible. Has everything been so awful for you?'

'When I look at you and I see somebody who wants to be somewhere else . . .'

'I don't want to be someplace else.'

'I'm telling you what I see.'

'I'm sorry,' she said.

'Sorry's not good enough. I'm trying to find out what's eating you. When you're acting like a stranger there has to be something wrong.'

'I'm not always like a stranger, am I?'

'No. If we could spend twenty-four hours a day in bed I guess we'd have no problem.'

'I wish we could,' she said.

'It's a nice idea. But things don't work that way.'

'I don't know what to say,' she said then.

'Then don't say anything. Just think about what I said.'

'I will, honey, I promise. I hate it when you're mad at me.'

[12]

When she began to plan her elaborate Christmas celebration, Clara, at dinner one evening, told Jesse and Valerie that she was including Floyd and Jeannette on the guest list. 'It will be a fine opportunity for us to meet her,' she said, 'and she'll have a chance to see Wingate Fields at its best, the way it used to be.'

Both of them agreed with her. 'They're part of the family,' Valerie said. 'Of course they must be included.'

'No question about it,' Jesse said. 'On an occasion like this the whole clan has to be here.'

The next day, however, when she and Clara were alone in the morning room, Valerie said, 'I hope we're not going to overpower Floyd's wife.'

'How do you mean?'

'I'm not sure what I mean. But I'd think it would be quite a burden having yourself thrust into a house full of strangers after flying all the way across the ocean. And with the trappings of Christmas thrown in.'

'Do you think so? I have the feeling that the holidays will make it easier for her. Give her an opportunity to look us over when we're all too occupied to look *her* over. Am I mistaken?'

'I don't know. If it were me . . .'

'If it were you, my dear, I'd have no qualms whatsoever. I've never seen anyone with the social aplomb you have. And you've had it since you were five years old.'

'Oh dear, I can't believe you think that.'

'I think it because it's true. Ask you mother or Jesse. They'll tell you I'm right. It's only since your children were born that you've decided to redefine yourself as a shy and retiring soul. But no one who really knows you is deceived. You're a true descendant of Angus Bradshaw. But a slightly different mix. My father was tough on the outside and tender at the core. You, I suspect are the direct opposite.'

'I don't think I'm flattered.'

'You should be. The Bradshaw women are survivors. And each of us finds her own way to do it.' Then, 'If Floyd's wife is a bit overwhelmed I'm counting on you to soothe her. You two are the same age. Helen says she's just four months older than you. I expect you'll be great chums.'

Jesse's approach, when he sought Clara out, was quite different. 'I've given it a lot of thought, this Christmas business, and I think we've got to be selfish. The family has an opportunity to get together so seldom. And we've never done it in such style, not since Angus died.'

'I don't understand your saying we have to be selfish.'

'In the best possible sense,' Jesse said. 'The few of us who are left, who've known each other for all of our adult lives, deserve a chance to be together on our own terms without the pressure of explaining ourselves or adjusting to unfamiliar people. Do you know what I'm saying?'

'No,' Clara said. 'I'm afraid I don't.'

'Let me put it this way. I'm sure you remember what a strain it was, at the time of the memorial services for Ned, when Nora showed up with that exotic young man.'

'You're not drawing a parallel between that creature and Floyd's wife, are you?'

'Of course not. Not directly. I'm just talking about unknown quantities, about spending our holiday season adjusting to someone none of us knows.'

Clara smiled. 'Even if I agreed with you, Jesse, and I *don't*, I can't imagine what possible excuse one could give for not inviting Floyd. He certainly isn't a stranger to any of us. And if he is invited, of course his wife must come too.'

When Jesse didn't answer, Clara said, 'I know that look very well. I expect you have stronger feelings about this than you've told me about.'

'No. Not at all. I was just making a suggestion.'

'Because if you do have such feelings,' she went on, 'then they must be honoured. It's your home as much as it is mine and you are entitled to choose who will be invited here. If we can't find a graceful excuse we will simply use a clumsy one.'

'No, I wouldn't want to do that. We don't want to offend anyone. We certainly don't want to offend Helen.' He paused. 'I just thought if you agreed with me, perhaps we could find a way.'

'We can always find a way,' she said, 'but I do not agree with you.'

'Then let's forget I said anything.'

When Floyd wrote that he and Jeannette would not be able to come because of their plans with Betsy, both Valerie and Jesse seemed genuinely sorry. Clara, however, was not deceived.

'But Helen's coming, isn't she?' Jesse said.

'Of course. She wouldn't miss it.'

Valerie, using her own values and behaviour as barometers, concluded that Floyd would not have told Helen about her. Jesse, using quite different barometers, decided that he might very well have told her. Valerie, trusting her instincts, chose to do and say nothing. Jesse felt that something must be done but he wasn't sure what it should be.

When Helen arrived, he questioned her casually about Floyd. And about Jeannette. He also studied her carefully when Valerie was in the room, involved in the conversation, trying to see some shadow in Helen's eyes, to hear some voice inflection that would tell him what he wanted to know. At last he concluded that she knew nothing of what had transpired between Floyd and Valerie. But it was an uneasy conclusion.

Chapter Eight

[1]

Enid Zoeller worked in the admissions office at Foresby University in Fort Beck. One day she called on Helen, whom she'd known since they went to grammar school together, and talked with her about Doug Slocum.

'We're not sure what we can do with him but we want to do something.' she said. 'Dean Willis has taken an interest in him and he thinks we should bend a few rules if necessary in order to keep him here at Foresby.'

'What's the problem?' Helen asked.

'He's *all* problems. In the first place he didn't finish high school. He went to some one-horse school in West Virginia and after eleventh grade, when he was sixteen, he lied about his age and joined the army.'

'How old is he now?'

'Twenty-two. He was in Korea for three years and since then he's been in and out of army hospitals. So he's not exactly our ideal freshman. Too old and academically unqualified. But he tested well on an IQ test so the Dean thinks that with some remedial reading courses he can make his way.'

'What brought him to Foresby in the first place?'

'He was in an army hospital in Indianapolis and he got to know a young doctor there who's a Foresby graduate. So when they discharged him from the hospital he hitchhiked to Fort Beck, came into my office at the administration building and announced that he wants to go to school here. So that's what we're trying to work out. First of all, he has no money.'

'If he's a veteran, won't the government pay his way?'

Enid shook her head. 'There were apparently some discipline problems. It seems he punched a couple of officers, the last one just before he was released from the hospital in Indianapolis. So he didn't get an honourable discharge and he's entitled to no benefits.'

'Doesn't sound like someone the Dean would be attracted to.'

'I know. That's what I thought. But Willis seems to have decided that Doug is the victim of all the evils of war, all the mistakes that were made in Korea. Also, if you're willing to talk to Doug, you'll see that he has a gift for persuading people. Not by anything he says. He just looks like such a victim.'

'Why do you want me to talk to him?'

'We've arranged a grant-in-aid to take care of his tuition. And he has a job waiting tables in one of the sororities. So that will provide him his meals. But now we need a place for him to stay.'

'I thought freshmen had to stay in residence halls.'

'They do. But he doesn't want to. By the time he left Korea, not only had he been wounded twice but he'd developed some psychological problems. Nothing serious. Just a need for privacy. So we think he shouldn't be in a dormitory with a bunch of rambunctious kids just out of high school. Also, there's such an institutional flavour to a dormitory and we think he's had too much of that. So we're hoping to find a place in a private home for him, a house he can live in. He'll do whatever chores are necessary to pay for his room and he'll have a chance to function like a normal human being again.'

'Are you suggesting that I should take him in?'

'I was hoping you would.'

Helen shook her head. 'Impossible, Enid. I simply . . .'

'Wait a minute. Let me finish. At least take half an hour to talk to him. Then if there's no possibility of his staying here, you might be able to suggest some other place. He's worth the extra effort, Helen. I'm sure you'll agree on that.'

As it turned out, Helen did not agree. As she explained it later to Frank . . . 'I don't know what I expected but it certainly wasn't what came through my door that day. I kept remembering that Enid had used the word *victim* but whatever the word means to me, I didn't see it in Doug Slocum. It's obvious that he doesn't have any money. He still wears his army field jacket and GI shoes. But there's an air about him that makes you thinks he's determined to have something better before too long. I don't mean to say that he's never been a victim, but when I saw him I felt that quality was something he'd learned to use. Twice during our conversation he said, "Don't think I feel sorry for myself. I don't." And maybe he doesn't. But he seems to have learned a few tricks to make sure that other people feel sorry for him.'

'Con artist,' Frank said.

'No, I wouldn't go that far. He really is a kid from the sticks. Where he comes from in West Virginia, it's zero. Nothing grows there, the timber's gone, the mines are closed. He says it was join the army or starve, and I believe him. But all the same I think he's learned a lot since he left home. He has a long way to go but I think he's on the way to becoming a first-class manipulator.'

'Did he try to manipulate you?'

'Not at all. Smooth as pudding. He said Enid had told him there was no chance he could live in my house. So he appreciated the fact that I was willing to meet him anyway. He had good things to say about West Virginia and Korea; he even said some complimentary things about the army. Said it had taught him a lot. He seemed determined to prove to me that his lot in life had been no worse than the next man's, but all the same there was an undercurrent of "poor me". He seemed to be saying that he'd accepted all the bad cards he'd been dealt and that he was determined to play them as well as he could. Courage in adversity. Grace under pressure. "See what a brave young chap I am. Look how well I'm doing." '

'But you weren't impressed?'

'I was impressed. But not in the way I was expected to be. Instead of the faltering creature I'd expected to see, I saw what seemed to be the beginnings of a relentless young man. Whatever he wants I'm sure he'll get it.'

'But he won't be living in your house?'

Helen smiled. 'No, he won't be doing that. But I must say, if I were going to have any student living there, I don't think I'd object to him. There's a lot there that doesn't meet the eye. When it all comes to the surface, if it ever does, he'll be an interesting case history for some psychology student to explore.'

'How'd he take it when you said he couldn't stay with you?'

'It never came up. Not in so many words. Since Enid had told him what I said to her I decided to let it rest there. But I wanted to do something for him so I said we had plenty of yard work and other chores if he needed to pick up some money. He was delighted. So that's the way we left it.'

'You think that's a good idea?'
'Sure. Why not?'
'You know the old story about the camel and the Arab's tent?'
'Doesn't apply here. He'll simply come to my back door when he has some free time, my housekeeper will tell him what needs to be done and he'll do it.'
'And did he find a place to live?'
'No problem. Joe Guinnup, the tennis coach, has a little apartment over his garage. Doug will live there.'

[2]

Among the other delights of the Christmas season at Wingate Fields, perhaps the most surprising one was the change that seemed to have come over Nora. No one failed to notice it. Not Clara, not Valerie, not Helen or Jesse. But perhaps because they thought it too good to be true, no one mentioned it, either to Nora or among themselves.

She was no different physically of course. Her face and her lovely slender body seemed never to change. Her voice rang, as always, with self-confidence, and her personality seemed to reach the far corners of any room. Indeed, she was, in every tangible way, as she had always been.

The messages that came from her interior, however, were radically altered. It was as though she was being driven by a new motor. The fierce energy that had propelled her always seemed to have disappeared or, if not that, to have routed itself through fresh channels. She had always been characterized by conflict and antagonism. Her life, by choice, had been a battlefield. Now, suddenly, the battle seemed to be over. There was a great and unmistakable air of peace about her. Stillness. Contentment.

Clara, who quickly noticed this change in her daughter, and who thought about it most often as she watched her and talked with her during the days she was there, concluded that some event, or series of events, had taken place since the last time she'd seen Nora. Something, some new ingredient, had altered her chemistry. Suddenly she seemed without weapons or defences.

A change had indeed taken place, but not over a period of time. It had occurred quite abruptly, just after Nora's arrival at Wingate Fields, Within an hour after she was delivered to the south entrance by her car, she knew that she and Jesse were going to be together again. It was not a matter of hard evidence. She heard nothing. Nor did she see anything. But the feeling that came over her could not be ignored or denied. It seized her like a tranquilizing drug and brought forth a softness, a tenderness, which she had seldom allowed to surface before.

Once her sensibilities had come to such a splendid conclusion, she accepted it fully and made no effort to shore it up and document it. Like a pauper turned suddenly wealthy she felt inside herself a spirit of generosity she'd never experienced before. And all her family benefited from it.

Before she left England to return to Paris, however, she came to realize that there were concrete pilings under this new revelation. She saw what she believed no one else saw, that some subtle transformation had taken place between Valerie and Jesse. Nothing was missing. All the elements of their relationship were still in place. But the quantities had changed, the proportions, the intensities. They embraced differently now. They waltzed differently together. There was a changed quality to their exit from the drawing room when they went upstairs to bed. Whatever had been instinctive and impulsive seemed learned now. The clear crisp edges had blurred somehow.

Whatever her feelings for Jesse, Nora had promised herself long before that she would not, could not, do anything that would jeopardize his marriage to her daughter. But these were new circumstances, she decided, new developments that had nothing to do with her, that were outside her ring of power. Jesse was coming back to her now, she knew that, no matter what she might say or do or fail to do. Having believed since childhood that all the elements of her existence could be, and must be, controlled by her, she suddenly relinquished that belief and became drowsily fatalistic.

Upon returning to Paris, she decided she must alter nothing, that she must proceed as though her sudden vision of the future had not, in fact, taken place. But when she walked into her house on the Rue de l'Ile, where she had lived so long and so contentedly with Jesse, as she moved through the rooms, she tried to remember exactly how things had looked then, all those years ago, before the war. The next day she searched in old albums for photographs that would jog her memory about furniture and wallpaper and decorations. Before a week had gone by a crew of decorators was making her house, as much as possible, a replica of its earlier self.

In such an atmosphere, where everything that occupied her had a direct connection with Jesse, Nora had no time, suddenly, for Martin Vuko. She had no impulse to see him or talk to him. When he called, the servants were instructed to say she was out. On the two or three occasions when she picked up the receiver herself she told him in detail how busy she was 'My Christmas holiday really threw me. I thought I'd delegated everything before I left. But when I came back it was all in a shambles. I've been working eighteen hours a day and I've still not caught up.'

More than three weeks passed. Almost four. One night at midnight, he appeared at her door, brushed past the butler and came upstairs to her bedroom. She was sitting in bed, reading. When she looked up and saw him, she said, 'No drunken scenes, please.'

'I'm not drunk,' he said. He looked dishevelled but he spoke very quietly. 'What happened to the house?'

'What do you mean?'

'It looks like a different place. Done over. New paint. New furniture.'

'Do you like it?'

'No. I liked it the way it was.'

'I got tired of it,' she said. 'Wanted a bit of a change.'

He sat down in a soft chair beside the bed. 'Tired of me, too?'

'Too late at night for melodrama, Vuko.'

'All right. How about a simple question? What's going on?'

'What do you mean?' she said.

'You know damned well what I mean. We've been together for almost five years and all of a sudden I've got a quarantine sign on my chest.'

'Well, since you brought it up, I'd say that I've been together with you but you have been much less together with me.'

'That's what I figured. You heard about it, didn't you?'

'Everyone in Paris knows what goes on in your studio. One in the bed and one in the air.'

'I don't mean that,' he said. 'You heard about Barcelona, didn't you?'

'What about Barcelona?'

'Don't play dumb, Nora. You must know I went to Barcelona when you were in England.'

'How would I know it if you haven't told me?'

'You must know,' he said. 'It's the only thing I know of that would make you act the way you've been acting.'

'Now I'm getting curious. What is this great piece of news I'm supposed to know?'

'You weren't supposed to know but I'm sure you do. Are you telling me you haven't talked with Karina since you came back?'

'Of course I'm not telling you that. I've seen her several times.'

'Then you know.'

Nora smiled and made a helpless gesture with her hands.

'For some reason you've decided to play cat and mouse with me,' he said.

'No such thing, Vuko.'

'All right,' he said. 'You've apparently decided not to talk about it. But I don't operate that way. Sooner or later things have to be dealt with.' Then . . . 'I went to Barcelona for five days over Christmas. I took Karina with me. I planned to tell you when you got back but when I saw how you were acting I assumed you already knew.'

After a moment Nora said, 'No, I didn't know. Did you have a pleasant time?'

'No. I had a lousy time. Before we got on the plane at Orly I knew I was making a mistake but I didn't know how to wriggle out of it so I went anyway.'

As he talked, Nora tried to imagine how this news would have affected her a month ago, before she went home for Christmas; she tried to summon up the mix of betrayal and anger she would surely have felt. But nothing happened. Only her current feelings presented themselves — a strong empathy for Vuko as he struggled to explain away something that had ceased to be relevant and a slight pinprick of surprise at Karina's role in what was on its way to becoming a bedroom farce. But her strongest reaction was an impulse to laugh. The more serious Vuko became, the stronger that impulse grew.

'What is so damned funny all of a sudden?' he said.

'What do you mean?'

'I mean what are you smiling about?'

'You have to admit there's something amusing here.'

'I don't see it,' He said.

'I know you don't. That makes it twice as funny. You're stumbling all over yourself trying to apologize for something I didn't even know about.'

'I still don't believe that.'

'Believe it or not . . . it's true.'

'All right. Then I'm stupid. Is that what you're laughing about?'

'No. Not at all. I'm trying to figure out if you're apologizing for all the women you've dallied with since you've known me or just for Karina.'

'You know what I'm talking about.'

'No, I don't. That's why I'm asking.'

'We're talking about Karina,' he said.

'And how about the rest of the tribe?'

'You didn't give a damn what I was up to and you know it. If you had . . .'

'What?' she said.

'I knew it didn't matter to you . . .'

'How did you know that?'

'I just knew. And this discussion we're having proves it. We never got into anything like this before. But now, since it's Karina . . .'

'Now what?'

'Now all of a sudden it's a big thing.' he said.

'It's not a big thing with me. You brought all this up. I didn't.'

'I know you didn't. You were playing some kind of a waiting game. Putting the freeze on me.'

She smiled again. 'Why in the world would I be putting the freeze on you, as you put it, if I didn't even know about your Barcelona honeymoon with Karina?'

After a moment, he said. 'That's a good question. What's the answer?'

'There isn't an answer. Like I told you on the telephone, I've been crazily busy since I came back.'

'Redecorating your house.'

'Yes. That, too,' she said. 'Busy with everything.'

'Okay,' he said then. 'I'm starting to get the picture.

Something happened between the time you left here to go to England and the time you came back.'

'A lot happened to you apparently.'

'That doesn't count. Because you say you didn't know about that. Not till I told you.'

'That's right. I didn't.'

'That's what I mean' he said. 'If you're telling me the truth then there's some other reason for what's been going on since Christmas.'

'I told you . . .'

'It doesn't wash, Nora. You're *always* busy. But for five years you've never been too busy to see me. I've never had a problem getting you on the phone. So what happened all of a sudden?'

'Nothing happened.'

'Was Jesse there when you went home?'

'Of course he was there. He lives there.'

'That's right,' Vuko said. 'I forget what a close-knit little family you come from. Very close relationships.'

'Don't be sarcastic.'

'Did you meet somebody else while you were in England? How about your ex-husband. Valerie's father.'

'Oh, for God's sake,' Nora said.

'What's his name? Bick?'

'That's right. And no, I didn't see him. I never see him except at funerals and then he doesn't speak to me. What is all this? Am I giving a deposition? Am I on trial or something?'

Vuko shook his head. 'Not you. Me. It looks as if I was already on trial but nobody told me. Now I've been convicted and I'm about to be sentenced. Have I got it straight?'

'You're being silly.'

'You mean I've made a mistake?'

'I mean you're being very silly.'

He sat still in his chair, looking at her. 'All right . . . I'm sorry.'

'There's nothing to be sorry for,' she said.

'Sure there is. I misjudged you. I thought you were trying to stay away from me. Trying to get rid of me. I'm glad to find out I was wrong.' He stood up then, walked across the room to the liquor table and poured himself a brandy. He turned back to her, still holding the decanter, 'How about it?'

'No, thanks.'

Still standing by the table he said, 'I know I act pretty hard-boiled most of the time. People expect it from me. And I like it, too. It keeps people away. It's good when I'm working. I found out when I'm on location, if I look mean enough the lunatics steer clear of me.' He put down his glass and took off his jacket. Then he walked across the room to a closet and hung it up. 'But the last few weeks I haven't felt like a tough guy at all. To tell you the truth I felt like a crumb. I knew there was something wrong but I couldn't figure out what it was.'

He crossed to the table and sipped from his brandy snifter. Then he sat down in the chair and started to take off his shoes. 'I had all kinds of goblins dancing through my head. I lay in bed every night imagining all kinds of things. One night I . . .'

Nora cut in suddenly. 'What are you doing?'

'What do you mean?'

'I mean what do you think you're doing?'

He looked down at his feet, then back up at her. 'I'm taking off my shoes. A minute ago I took off my jacket and hung it in the closet. Next I plan to take off my shirt and tie. And on and on like that. You've seen me do it hundreds of times. It's called "getting ready for bed".'

'I know what it's called,' she said, 'but I . . .'

'But what?'

'I don't want . . . I mean I don't think it's such a good idea for you to stay here tonight.'

'I think it's a great idea. I haven't seen you since Thursday, December 21st.'

'Please, Martin . . .'

'Martin? You haven't called me Martin since the first time I met you. You said Martin was not a name for . . .'

'I know what I said. I don't want to talk about it.'

He sat up straight in his chair. 'You don't want to talk about that or you don't want to talk about anything?'

'I didn't expect to see you . . .'

'I know you didn't.'

'I'm tired and it's very late . . .'

'Yes, I guess it is,' he said. He began tying his shoelaces.

'What does that mean? What do you mean by that?'

'I mean it's very late. Is it too late?'

'Oh, please. Don't make a big scene.' she said.

'This is a big scene. We're talking about heavy stuff here.

Do we or don't we? Will we or won't we? We're not just picking a name for a pet dog.'

'When I'm so tired and strung out I can't make sense out of anything.'

He stood up, walked to the closet and took his jacket off the hanger. 'Maybe you're right,' he said. 'At least we got a couple things straight. We'll pick up the pieces tomorrow. Why don't you meet me at the Dome at six-thirty? We'll have a nice dinner in Montparnasse.'

'I can't,' she said. 'I can't have dinner tomorrow.'

'Why not?'

'I just can't.'

'Let's have lunch then.'

'Aren't you shooting tomorrow?'

'It doesn't matter. I'll reschedule it.'

'I wouldn't want you to do that.'

'It's no problem. I'll do it.' When she didn't answer, he said, 'I have a feeling you can't have lunch either.'

'I can't.'

After a moment, he said, 'How's the next day look?'

'That's Wednesday, isn't it?'

'That's right.'

'Wednesday's really impossible, Thursday's our deadline for the printer.'

'That means Thursday's out, too,' he said.

'I'm afraid so.'

'I tell you what,' he said then. 'You pick a day.'

'For dinner, you mean?'

'For dinner, lunch, breakfast, cocktails . . . any one or all of those. And if all else fails I'll just come and spend the night. How does that sound?'

When she didn't answer he said, 'No reaction. Does that mean something? Or are you just thinking it over?'

'I feel silly trying to pick a day. I don't have my calendar here or anything. Why don't you call me?'

'Fine. I'll do that. When should I call?'

'Any time.'

'Tomorrow?'

'Fine,' she said.

'We know you're busy for the next few days. Why don't I call you next week? Or maybe the week after.'

'Maybe that would be better.'

'I've got a better idea,' he said then. 'Why don't we

postpone things till your schedule gets a little better? When that happens you call me and we'll make a plan.'

'If you like.'

'What do you think?' he asked.

'I think you're right. I'll call *you*.'

'Good. I'll be waiting to hear from you.'

He walked over and sat beside her on the bed. 'You know, when I was spending all my time in New York, before I started travelling back and forth, between there and here, I had a reputation for ditching girls. And it was true. At least part of it was. I moved around a lot. I was like a kid in the candy store. So people said bad things about me. But let me tell you something . . . compared to you, compared to the dance you're doing on me right now, I was a Christian missionary among the Zulus.'

'I don't know what you mean.'

'Yes, you do. You know exactly what I mean. Some time after you left here to go to England you decided I was redundant. Not amusing any more. But instead of telling me . . . apparently you don't like uncomfortable scenes . . . instead of coming out with it and telling me to my face, you must have figured it was simpler to just let me die on the vine. Was that it? If I couldn't get you on the telephone or manage to see you, I'd finally catch on. Was that the plan?'

'I didn't have a plan. It wasn't that way at all.'

'No? How was it?'

'I don't know. I can't tell you. And I see no reason to. I have nothing to explain and nothing to apologize for. You come storming in here telling me that you and Karina had a little Christmas fling in Spain and the next thing I know you've twisted things about so that I'm the one who's supposed to feel guilty. Well, I don't. And when you've finished your righteous indignation act I still won't feel guilty.'

'That's because you're rich. Rich people never feel guilty.'

'Are you an authority on guilt now?'

'Maybe not,' he said. 'But I know when I've been had.'

'Oh, my God. If you're going to start feeling sorry for yourself then I would like to be excused. If ever a man had free rein it was you. No one could have made fewer demands on you than I did.'

'That's because you didn't give a damn. If you had,' he said, 'a lot of things would have been different.

'Don't make me laugh. Are you trying to say that you were driven into the bony arms of all those skinny models because of my indifference.'

'I wouldn't put in fancy words like that. I knew you didn't give a damn so I pretended I didn't give a damn either.'

'Do you really believe what you're saying? If you do, you're the greatest self-deceiver who ever lived. If you don't believe it, then why in the world would you say it?'

He stood at the foot of the bed looking down at her. Finally, he said, 'Karina's right about you.'

'Since Karina knows nothing about me except what I choose to tell her..'

'She's no fool. She knows more than you think. She says you've been hung up on Jesse for twenty years . . .'

'Longer than that.'

'She says you never cared about any other man and you never will.'

'Karina's very romantic. She believes in endless love and astrology and black silk sheets.'

'Don't try to joke your way out of it. I think she's right.'

'What if she is?' Nora said.

'If she is, then what have you been doing with me all this time?'

'I could ask you the same question.'

'That's no answer.'

'All right. I'll give you an answer. I've been having a very nice time with you. And unless I've totally lost my wits you've been having a good time as well.'

'But now it's over,' he said.

'You said that. I didn't.'

'Oh, yes you did. In a hundred different ways. And now you're painting it on the wall in black letters.'

She spoke very softly then. 'Let's not make a big mess of things, Vuko. We're not enemies, are we? Let's not try to see how nasty we can be to each other.'

'If you expect me to be . . .'

'I don't expect anything,' she said, 'and neither should you. Because we didn't promise anything. We went out of our way to avoid any kind of contract or formal understanding. You know we did. Moment to moment. Some place along the line we used those exact words. So we can't change the rules now. Neither of us can say we were deceived or short-changed. Can you honestly say you gave out more than you got back?'

'I don't like conversations like this where everything's in the past tense.'

'Neither do I.'

'Then why are we having it?'

'I don't know,' she said. 'But we are having it and we can't pretend we're not.'

[3]

'I feel like an idiot,' Karina said.

'That doesn't sound like you,' Nora said. 'I thought your self-esteem was unassailable.'

'Usually it is. But not today.'

It was two days after Nora's late-night discussion with Vuko. Karina had telephoned an hour earlier and said, 'I have to see you. Vuko just called me. He told me what happened.'

As soon as she saw Nora, when she was shown into the library, Karina said, 'God, I was stupid. It never occurred to me that he would tell you. Or even if he did, that it would cause you two to break up.'

'Is that what he told you?'

'He said you had decided not to see each other in future and then he said he'd told you about Barcelona. So it wasn't hard to make the connection.'

Nora smiled. 'But it's a bad connection. I'd made up my mind about Vuko before he told me about his adventure with you.'

'What did he say?'

'No details. You needn't worry about that. He doesn't indulge in storytelling about his lady friends.'

'God, I feel dreadful. You must think I'm a real slut.'

Nora shook her head. 'I'm not a temple of virtue. Why should I expect you to be?'

'Virtue has nothing to do with it. I'm your friend. We're friends. Friends don't do things like that.'

After a moment Nora said, 'Then why did you do it?'

Karina shook her head. 'I don't know. It was just some

kind of craziness. As soon as I was on the plane I knew I was making a dreadful mistake.'

'That's exactly what he said.'

'Well, there you are.'

'So as soon as you got to Barcelona, you got on another plane and came back to Paris.'

Karina smiled. 'You know better than that,' Then, 'What did you say when he told you?'

'I don't remember.'

'You must have been surprised.'

'I suppose I was. But what I felt mostly was . . . I don't know . . . you and I have spent two or three afternoons together since Christmas. And I'd seen absolutely no change in you. That made me feel odd, I guess, when I thought about it.'

'I wanted to tell you,' Karina said. 'I wanted to tell you I'd done a stupid thing but it hadn't meant anything to me or to him.'

'Why didn't you?'

'I'm not sure. I suppose I thought it was pointless. I know you two have a sort of open relationship. At least on his side. I mean no one sees Vuko as the soul of fidelity. Everyone knows about his adventures in the afternoon.'

'That's true,' Nora said, 'But it's slightly different when the adventure is with a friend. Assuming that we understand Vuko's motives, one can't help but wonder what was in the friend's mind.'

Karino looked up. 'You're really angry, aren't you?'

'No. I'm bewildered. It's not long ago that you pointed out to me in some detail that Vuko was not good enough for me, that he was not quite up to standard. So it's surprising to learn that he is suddenly up to your standards.'

'But he's not. I mean it isn't as though I've chosen him or he's chosen me.'

'I know. And that makes it all the more bewildering to me. If you'd both been struck by a bit of passion and stumbled into the first available hotel, that would be one thing. But this was more like a bank robbery. Quite cool and international. If I were a dispassionate bystander I would say it looks more like an act of vengeance than an act of love. But that doesn't make sense either, does it?'

'Not totally. But I think he was a bit put off because you'd toddled off to England for the holidays. And of course he knew that Jesse would be there.'

Nora nodded. 'That's possible. That might have been in his head. But I still can't imagine what was in yours.'

'No, of course you can't. Nor can I.'

'Well, there we are, then. Snug up against a stone wall.'

'I'm afraid so,' Karina said.

They spent the rest of the afternoon together, gossiping and listening to recorded music. As she was preparing to leave, Karina invited Nora for luncheon on the coming Saturday or, if that was impossible, for dinner on Sunday. Nora, it turned out, was not free on either day. Karina, however, was not to be put off. 'You'll just have to play sick. Tell your hosts you're dreadfully ill, then sneak off to my house.'

'I'm afraid I can't,' Nora said.

'It's your loss. I have a lovely group coming, each day. But I'll lunch with you early next week in any case.'

'I don't think so, Karina. I don't plan to see you for a while.'

'What does that mean?'

'Just what it sounds like. I'm not angry with you. And you're certainly not responsible for the break-up between me and Vuko. But for some reason I feel uneasy with you now. It's an unpleasant sensation and I'm sure it will go away at last. But until it does I think we should give it a rest.'

'I can't believe you mean that.'

'But I do mean it,' Nora said.

A few weeks later, Nora heard that Vuko had given up his Paris atelier. Except for occasional location trips to Europe he had announced that he would shoot all his fashion assignments now in New York City.

She also heard that Karina and her step-sister had quarrelled and Dort had gone home to Germany, to Karlsruhe.

Nora saw Karina rather often, at parties, theatre openings, and vernissages. They always had a few moments' conversation together but never more than that. Karina seemed to be experimenting more than usual with new hair-styles and she had affected a very pale make-up and heavy eye-shadow. Twice unsigned postcards from her arrived in the post. One said, 'Must we continue this?' and the other said, 'I miss seeing you.' Once, when they embraced briefly in the entrance hall of the Opera, it seemed to Nora that Karina was trembling under her fur coat.

[4]

One evening when Floyd and Jeannette were having dinner at an Italian restaurant near the Brooklyn Museum, Paul Buscatore came over to their table and talked with them for a few minutes. Just before he went back to his own party on the far side of the room he said, 'It's a pleasure to meet you, Jeannette. You two should come out to visit with me in Nevada. I'll show you a good time.'

'Who is that?' Jeanette said as Paul walked away.

'You're not going to believe this,' Floyd said. 'He's my uncle.'

'Your what?'

'You heard me. He's Helen's half-brother. They had the same mother.'

'Well, I just wish Amy was there to see him. She'd collapse. She loves those dangerous-looking guys. When Bogart died a couple weeks ago she called up and cried for half an hour on the telephone. I'll have to tell her about this one. What did you say his name is?'

'Buscatore. Paul Buscatore.'

'I can't believe he's your uncle. He looks younger than you.'

'He is. Four years younger.'

'I'm telling you, Amy would fall right down on the floor. Slick black hair and a tuxedo. That's all she needs. Where does he live?'

'Nevada. You heard him. He runs a casino out there.'

'Gambling?'

'Sure. What do you think?'

'What's it like?'

'I've never seen it. Tonight's only the second time I've seen Paul. I had lunch with him once with Helen and that was it.'

'You're kidding. Why is that?'

'I don't like him much and he doesn't like me.'

'How do you know that?'

'Trust me.'

'He was very nice just now. He treated you very nice.'

'He treats everybody nice. That's his business.'

'You're an odd duck, Floyd. You don't like anybody.'

'Sure I do. I just don't particularly like Paul.'

'You could live in a cave and be perfectly happy.'

'That's a good idea,' Floyd said. 'Maybe I'll try that.'

'Is he a gambler?' she said then, 'Or does he just run the place?'

'I don't know much about it.'

'Has Helen been there?'

'I'm not sure.'

'We ought to fly out there some time and spend a week. Have a little vacation. Maybe we'll take Amy with us.'

'Are you a gambler?'

'Sure. I love roulette. Glen and I went to Vegas a few times. And up to Calumet City. You talk about *rough*. That used to be a rough place. And over in Danville, Illinois, there used to be some action there. Mostly slot machines. Wouldn't you like to go to Nevada sometime?'

'We'll see.'

'I know you,' she said. 'That means no.'

'You and Amy should go. She'd love it. You two can pretend you're young and foolish again.'

'That's not a bad idea. Maybe we'll do it.' Then, 'I'd never go without you. You know that. I don't like to go any place without you.'

'That's because you're a perfect wife.'

'Don't give me that. I'm a lousy wife and I know it. I sleep too late and I don't like to cook and I don't keep the house neat.'

'Don't worry about it,' Floyd said. 'That's what we have money for. We can pay people to do those things.'

'You're really very nice. You know that?'

'You bet. Men like me are hard to find.'

'I mean it,' she said. 'Sometimes I wonder why you're so nice to me.'

'I'm stuck with you. What else am I going to do?'

'I know I bitch and moan a lot but when I do that it's usually because I don't like myself. So I take it out on you. That doesn't make sense, does it?'

'It must make sense to you or you wouldn't do it.'

'I just do it because . . . well, I have a couple of drinks and I . . . you know how I am.' She reached across the table and touched his hand. 'But it doesn't mean I don't love you. It never means that. It hasn't anything to do with how I feel about you. Or about us. I wish I could be the way you are. You're the same all the time. Like you're really in control of yourself. But I can't do that. I'm all over the place. Up one minute and down the next. I hear myself saying all kinds of ridiculous things and I promise myself I won't do it again. Then something sets me off and away I go. I know how lucky I am but sometimes I forget. I forget how sweet it was when we were kids and how sweet it still is when I just let it be.'

Jeannette had always concerned herself primarily with impulse and direct result. Contemplation of either the past or the future gave her little satisfaction. So when she sensed that there were difficulties between her and Floyd she was unable, and also unwilling, to sort them out. In a conversation with Amy, however, a few days before she and Floyd got married, she touched on a key point that was destined to have a strong effect on their lives together. 'In a way, things are like they always were with us. I mean I just can't get enough of him. I love the way he looks and the way he feels and the way he smells. He's a perfect man. Sweet and perfect. But in another way, things are all switched around now. From the time I met him, Floyd was always an underdog. He was in trouble at school, he was in trouble at home. He didn't have many friends. Then after my dad split us up, Floyd was in more trouble. Stealing cars, getting arrested, going to jail. And when he came to see me after he got out of the service, there he was in his sailor suit. Still floating around. His folks were dead and he wasn't quite sure where he was going. My dad always said he was a loser and I always said I didn't care, I loved him anyway. But dad said I had it all wrong. He said, 'You love him *because* he's a loser.'

'I didn't believe that, not for a minute, and I don't believe it now but all the same I can see that things are different now. I was always the one that had everything. And Floyd had nothing. Now it's the reverse of that. I've lost a lot. The town where I spent all my life, I don't feel like going back to now. My marriage broke up and God knows how that will affect me and Betsy. And I'm certainly not very close to my folks any more. Too much stuff has happened. Too much taking sides and people trying to stack the cards so things would turn out the way *they* wanted them to. So if anybody's floating now, it's me. Trying to figure what went wrong and how things are going to be now. But old Floyd is sitting on top of the world. Dry socks and a tank full of gas. Don't misunderstand me. I don't begrudge him anything. But it is funny sometimes how things work out. You get accustomed to a situation and next thing you know it's all changed. Then you've got something new to get accustomed to. For years I said "Poor Floyd" and now I catch myself thinking, "Poor me".'

Certain minds, once they've isolated and examined a circumstance or condition, can then deal with it. Others can only continue to resent it. In her lucid and charitable moments, Jeannette felt indeed fortunate to be with Floyd. At other times she followed the paper trail of her discontent directly to his door.

[5]

Although Jesse himself was not aware of it, and would have denied it even if it had been brought to his attention, a careful biographer would have discovered a clear pattern in his adult behaviour. The major turning-points in his life had come about, it seemed, not as the result of decisions on his part. On the contrary, circumstances had often forced him into one channel or another. If someone had accused him of being indecisive, however, he would have said, 'Not at all. I'm thoughtful,' and if that was not the total truth it was indeed part of the truth.

Clara, who was able to be objective about him in ways that Helen or Nora or Valerie could not be, had never interpreted Jesse's apparent reluctance to make hard choices or abrupt changes in direction as signs of weakness. She had once said to Angus, 'Jesse is much stronger than people give him credit for. He has the best kind of strength, the sort that doesn't have to advertise itself. He doesn't need to control every element of his life because he has confidence that he can deal with whatever surprises come his way. At least that's the way I see him. Also, he's a kind man. He is truly considerate of other people's feelings. That has become such a rare quality that when we see it we don't know how to label it. Many people see it as something not quite manly. I think it is the most manly characteristic of all. Kindness is everything.'

Did Jesse think of himself as a kind man? Just the opposite. In his work, for example, in the critical articles that he wrote, he knew that he had been labelled as a man of harsh judgements and cruel opinions. When he defended himself, which he did very seldom, he said there was nothing vindictive about critical truth. 'The curse of my profession,' he wrote, 'is that I am allowed to have no friends among the artists and poets whose work I criticize. No artist wants to read anything but praise of his work. And here is the irony. Some of the most hateful men I have met are brilliant artists. They adore me because I praise their work but I avoid all contact with them. On the other hand, some of the most trivial and derivative artists I know are civilized and admirable men whose company I would love to share. But because I do not admire their work they shun me.'

Jesse had no impulse, however, to analyze himself in depth. If he had, perhaps he would have said, 'It's not a question of kindness at all. Nothing so positive as that. More accurately, it's something that I lack. I have no impulse towards vengeance. Never have had. I've never wasted time on plotting how I might get even with someone. That seems like rot to me. Negative and time-consuming and usually not rewarding even if one manages to bring it off.'

Even if he had been vengeful by nature, it is unlikely that Valerie's confession to him about herself and Floyd would have inspired him to respond in kind. His thoughts were totally occupied with what had already been done. There was no room in his mind for the consideration of how he might balance the scales. As angry and bewildered as he was, he was more concerned with setting things right than he was with putting into practice the code of Leviticus, more intent on keeping his family together. If Valerie was to be punished, he was not the one to do it. Or so he told himself.

Are we witness then to an almost unbelievable act of self-abnegation? Not at all. We simply see a thoughtful and reasonable man making reasonable choices. Appearing perhaps to sacrifice himself and his own feelings, he very carefully, in fact, decided how he could best serve his own needs. Then he acted accordingly. Sensing that his life with Valerie would never again be as sweetly perfect as it had been before, he chose nonetheless to continue that life, to preserve the marriage, to move ahead.

Having seen how a single act by Valerie had put everything he valued at risk, Jesse, one would think, would have been very unlikely to have created such a risky situation himself. But he did. Within six months of Clara's Christmas celebration at Wingate Fields, Jesse and Nora were together again. Secretly, discreetly, but unquestionably together.

[6]

In November of 1956, two days after Dwight Eisenhower's re-election as President of the United States, Helen and Frank came home late from a dinner party. As he unlocked the door of his apartment and they came inside from the hall, she said, 'I wish you'd just tell me to shut up. I'm tired of hearing myself talk about it.'

'Why shouldn't you talk about it? It's better than keeping it inside and giving yourself a headache.'

'I get a headache whether I talk about it or not. And a stomach ache, too. It's just such a shame. Two people with no real problems and all they do is make problems.'

'How about a drink?' he said. 'A little calvados to soothe the savage beast.'

'I've been drinking all night.'

'Me, too. And I'm sober as a snowball. Boring people always keep me sober. Are you sober?'

'Completely. Sober with a headache.'

'Two aspirin and a calvados. Fix you right up.'

She kicked off her slippers and sat on the sofa with her feet up. 'I'm not saying that Floyd is a perfect human being. He can be stubborn as a stone. And I'm sure he has a beastly temper. I've never seen him in action but I can guess what he's like. But all the same, from what I've seen, he's done his best to make his marriage work.'

'But it is working, isn't it? I mean they're not about to split up or anything, are they?'

'I haven't heard anything,' Helen said, 'but nothing

would surprise me. From what I can see, they'd be better off if they did split up.'

'Ahh, but it's what you can't see that counts. Some people thrive on chaos, you know. They need a couple of good battles a day to keep their blood pumping.'

'That's her, all right. But it's not Floyd.'

'Don't be too sure.'

'I am sure. I've seen how he is with people. Nothing turns him off like a nice spirited argument. He just pulls into his shell like a turtle. Or else he gets up and leaves the room.'

'That's the best way to end a fight. Especially if you don't want to fight in the first place.'

'It's not a question of fighting,' Helen said. 'They don't have big battles when I'm around. She's too civilized for that. There's just an atmosphere in their house that gives me the creeps. Like being suspended in midair. Like a party where all the people are strangers to each other. You have the feeling there's an ongoing discussion that stops when you enter the room and fires up again as soon as you leave. If you didn't know better, you'd say they were still going through the classic period of adjustment. Getting to know each other, that sort of thing. But they've known each other since they were kids.'

'In the biblical sense?'

Helen nodded. 'Definitely. And every other way. It boggles the mind. At first I thought it was a hangover from her divorce. Married one day. Divorced and married to somebody else the next day.'

'Was it that fast?'

'Not quite. But almost. I know there's no love lost between her and her ex-husband. She talks about him as if he was some kind of a germ. But all the same, you never know what kind of emotional residue is left over after a marriage ends.'

'Look at us,' Frank said. 'Lots of residue.'

'I know you're joking. But I'm serious. I don't mean she still has a little yen for him but even somebody you detest can take up a lot of space in your mind. I certainly thought about you a lot after we were divorced. I never thought we'd get together again the way we have but you were still there whether I wanted you to be or not. So I thought maybe that was Jeannette's problem. Then I decided it was her daughter, Betsy. She's fourteen now, going to boarding school, not really in residence with either of her parents. Dividing her vacation time between the two of them. But apparently that's not the problem either. Betsy's a sensational kid. Sweet and pretty and very grown-up for her age. She likes being independent, Floyd says, and it takes a lot of pressure off her because it doesn't appear as if she's chosen one parent over another. She comes to New York whenever she wants to or she goes home to see her dad and her grandparents. And Jeannette and Floyd fly out to South Bend to see her every few weeks. So everything seems smooth in that department.'

'So where's the rub?'

'That's what I don't know.'

'Have you talked to Floyd about it?'

'God, no. I've never brought up the subject with anyone except you. In the first place it's none of my business and in the second place, even if it were my business, Floyd would freeze up totally if I asked even *one* question. That's the way he is.'

'Do you want some advice?' Frank asked.

'No.'

'I'll give it to you anyway. My advice is — forget the whole thing.'

'Easier said than done.'

'Maybe. But you have to do it anyway. Forget the word *son*. Forget he's your kid. He's a grown-up man who just happens to be your child. All you can be now is his friend.'

'I'm not stupid. I know that. But it doesn't help. Even friends can get you crazy when they're floundering around.'

'I'm floundering around. What about me?'

'You're a hopeless case. Nobody can help you.'

Later when they were lying in bed in the dark she said, 'Every place you look you see people with terrible problems that can't be solved. Really agonizing permanent conditions that just have to be lived with. And then you see people like Floyd and Jeannette who are young and attractive and healthy, who have no money problems, no problems at all as far as anybody can see, and there seems to be some kind of a cloud hanging over them. It just sits there. And they just sit there.'

'The dogs bark but the parade keeps moving.'

'What does that mean?' she said.

'I don't know. What do I know? I live one day at a time.'

Late one night, Jeanette had a phone call from her friend, Amy Briscoe, in Lebanon, Indiana.

'Guess who called me five minutes ago,' Amy said.

'I don't have to guess. What's he want?'

'Said he was just driving through on the way home. Wanted to come over.'

'What did you say?'

'I said, "Nothing doing." So then he asked me to meet him someplace for a drink and I said it was too late. I said, "I'm already in bed." '

'Then what?'

'He hung up.'

When she came back into the study, where Floyd was watching a basketball game on television, Jeannette said, 'The cuckoo bird is loose again.'

'Who's that?'

'Who do you think? Crazy Glen. He's been calling Amy.'

'Who cares? Amy can handle him. That's what she's good at. She can handle anybody.'

'I guess so. But he's so nutsy. I never know what he's gonna do.'

'Sure you do. Nothing. That's what he always does. Glen's all mouth. He was all mouth when he was sixteen and he's all mouth now.'

'I'm not so sure. I saw him take after a guy with a tyre iron one night.'

'He must have been drunk,' Floyd said.

'He was. Clear out of it.'

'That explains everything.'

The next morning at ten o'clock, Glen called Amy again.

'I thought you were heading for Crawfordsville,' she said.

'I was. I drove back here this morning. I need to talk to you.'

'No, you don't. You need to talk to Jeannette. And I'm the next best thing.'

'I'm serious. I've got something to tell you. Can't I come over for a cup of coffee?'

'Sorry. No men allowed over here. I've got a jealous boyfriend. Anybody parks a car in front of my house, he knows about it before the engine gets cool. You don't want to tangle with Harvey.'

After a long pause he said, 'Can't you meet me someplace then? I'll buy you breakfast and we'll have a talk.'

'I don't know, Glen. I'm pretty tied up here.'

'Please. I'll behave myself. I'm at Ralph's drive-in on the bypass.'

'All right,' she said. 'I'll come out there for half an hour. But any of your funny stuff and I'm long gone.'

'I just want to talk.'

He was waiting in a booth by the front window when she walked in. 'You took long enough,' he said. 'I thought you weren't coming.'

'I'm here,' she said. 'Never mind how long it took. I had some phone calls. Clients.'

'What kind of clients?'

'I have a business now.'

'What's that all about?'

'I took an astrology course by mail. Cost me four hundred dollars. But I'm an expert now. I can do charts and everything. Two or three clients a day come to see me. I get twenty dollars an hour. And it looks like I'll be doing a weekly column for the local paper after the first of the year.'

'The only women I know that get twenty dollars an hour don't have anything to do with astrology.'

'One remark from your dirty mouth and I'm gone. Just like I told you on the telephone. Now . . . what did you want to see me about?'

He looked uneasy, as though he'd carefully rehearsed a speech and then forgotten the text. Finally he said, 'It's about Jeannette.'

'What a surprise.'

'Don't get me wrong. I'm not nosing around. I don't want anything from her. I just heard a few stories and I thought she might need some help.'

'Do you have a lot of friends in New York?'

'What do you mean?' he said.

'I was just wondering how you'd be hearing stories about Jeannette.'

'I hear all kinds of things. You'd be surprised.'

'Cut the crap, Glen. What do you really want? If you're trying to pick my brain about Jeannette you're wasting your time.'

'I know that. I just heard . . . this is the truth . . . that she and Floyd were having some trouble . . .'

'Not true,' Amy said.

' . . . heard they might be splitting up and I didn't want her to be stranded there in New York.'

'You mean you want to send her some money?'

He nodded. 'If she needs it.'

'She doesn't need it. She's got money coming out of her ears. Do you know how rich Floyd is?'

'I heard he was pretty well fixed but I don't know whether to believe it or not.'

'You can believe it.'

His face flushed suddenly and he said, 'I guess he bought her away from me. Is that what you're saying?'

'You know better than that. When Jeannette left you she hadn't seen Floyd for years . . .'

'I know what I know.'

'She didn't even know where he was.'

'Well, maybe she did and maybe she didn't.'

'She didn't, Glen. Believe me. I know.'

'I know a few things myself.'

She sat looking at him. Finally she said. 'You look like hell, Glen. Are you taking care of yourself?'

'I'm all right. I've just got a lot on my mind.'

'The graveyards are full of people who thought they could drink all the booze in the world.'

'I'm all right,' he said. Then, 'Betsy says her mother might be moving out to California again. Says they bought a house there.'

Amy shook her head. 'They leased a place on Lake Tahoe. But they're keeping the house in New York.'

'I thought Jeannette hated California.'

'This is different. They're right on the Nevada border. They go to Reno and Carson City and a place called Bellwood. They gamble a lot, especially Jeannette. She loves to roll the dice.'

'What does Floyd do with himself all the time?'

'He manages his money, I guess. And he plays tennis a lot. And Jeannette says he takes some art classes twice a week when they're in New York.'

'Art classes? What's that all about? Does he think he's back in high school?'

'Don't ask me,' Amy said. 'He wants to paint pictures, I guess. Wants to be an artist.'

'He's no artist. You can't just decide to be an artist. Either you are or you're not. He's just got too damned much time on his hands, that's all.'

'You're a great one to talk. You've never worked for anybody but your father in your whole life.'

'So what? We've got a big business to look after. A car agency doesn't run itself.'

'Jeannette told me you spend all your time at the country club . . .'

'What does she know?'

' . . . playing golf all day and drinking and playing cards half the night.'

'I don't give a damn what Jeannette says.'

'Oh yes, you do. That's all you give a damn about. That's the only reason we're sitting here right now. So you can get a report about Jeannette. Isn't that right?'

'Don't kid yourself,' he said.

'Don't you kid yourself. What if I told you that Jeannette's flying into Indianapolis at three o'clock, that I'm gonna meet her there and bring her home with me?'

Glen didn't answer.

'You see what I mean? All of a sudden you're sitting there with your tongue hanging out,' Amy said.

'I didn't say anything.'

'You didn't have to. Your face gives you away. You're like a kid in a candy store.'

'Is she really flying into Indianapolis today?'

'No. She's out in Tahoe.'

'You think they're gonna stay together?' he said then.

'Now we're getting somewhere,' Amy said.

'What do you mean?'

'You know what I mean. Now you're gonna level with me.'

'It drives me nuts not hearing from her,' he said. 'Not knowing anything about her or what she's doing. I keep telling myself this thing with her and Floyd won't last. Even her folks think she'll come home sooner or later.'

Amy sipped from her coffee cup and seemed to consider what she should say next. Finally she said, 'Look, Glen, you and I have known each other a long time. Just because Jeannette and I are good friends doesn't mean I'm your enemy. I mean, whatever troubles you two had is between the two of you. You know what I'm saying?'

'I guess so.'

'So if I give you some advice it's for your own good. It has nothing to do with Jeannette or Floyd or anybody else. It's just between the two of us. Okay?'

'Sure.'

'What I'm telling you is this. I'd hate to see you making any plans for the future that include Jeannette. She's married to somebody else now and as far as I know they're getting along great. But even if that didn't work out for one reason or another, I guarantee you that Jeannette won't be coming back to Indiana.'

'I didn't say anything about Indiana. I don't need to spend the rest of my life in Crawfordsville.'

'I mean she's not coming back to any of us. Maybe she didn't know what she wanted before but from where I'm sitting she sure likes what she got. She loves jumping around from one place to another. From San Francisco to New York to Tahoe. Up to Boston. Down to Palm Beach. She's seeing places she'd only read about and, believe me, she likes what she sees.'

'Anybody likes to travel around I guess. My folks go to Phoenix every winter.'

Amy shook her head. 'I'm not talking about travelling around. I'm talking about a different kind of life. With different people. Jeannette won't be the same now. Nobody should expect her to be the same. She doesn't feel like she left the kind of life she lived here, she feels like she escaped. That's the word she uses. Escaped.'

'You saw the way we lived when she was married to me. You came to our house. Nobody we know had a better place than we did. A new car every year. People to cook and clean and do the yard work. Why would anybody have to escape from all that?'

'I didn't say it makes sense,' Amy said, 'but it makes sense to Jeannette. She's changed now. She's never going back to what she used to be. She couldn't if she tried.'

'So where does that leave me?'

'I can't tell you that. That's up to you.'

'Doesn't sound that way to me. From what you're saying, I can't do a damn thing except go home and forget about it.'

'I didn't say that. At least I didn't mean that. Seems to me you can do anything you want to as long as you don't include Jeannette in your plans.'

He stubbed his cigarette out in his coffee cup and looked out through the window at the parking lot. Finally he said, 'If you're telling me that a person can do anything they want to, that they can mess up other people's lives without giving those people a second thought, then I say you're wrong. Nobody gets to do whatever they want to and to hell with everything else.'

'Oh, no? Maybe it *shouldn't* work that way but it does. Some people can get away with anything. You just have to accept it.'

'Not me,' he said. '*I* don't have to accept it. I don't accept that at all.'

[8]

In one of her regular letters to Helen, Clara wrote —

> I used to scoff at Angus during his last years because each morning when he opened the London *Times* he turned first to the obituary pages. But he always said, 'That's one of the few joys of getting old. Every morning you see a fresh list of the people you've outlived. You'll do it too, I promise you. Once you pass eighty, you start keeping score. It's you against the rest of the world. You can't win the battle but every morning you can persuade yourself you've won another skirmish.'
>
> He was right, of course. I've become a walking log book of who's passed on. Look at the painters, for example. In less then two years we've lost Leger and Peckstein and Utrillo, Feininger and Pollock, Kupka, and Diego Rivera.
>
> Then Thomas Mann died, Brecht and Claudel and Sacha Guitry, Gigli, Toscanini, and Sibelius, Greseking and Honegger. Albert Einstein, the man who changed all our lives. And perhaps shortened them.
>
> Do I draw conclusions from all this concentration on death and dying? Not really. It's difficult, however, not to be cynical when you're old. The absolutes, the lasting values that we've used as reference points while we struggled along, seldom hold up. One can't help believing that everything is transient. *Everything*. All the inspiring and restrictive icons — God, mother, and the flag — reveal themselves as clay-footed, unreliable,

inconsistent, and therefore of little value. They're simply devices for consolation, like rosary beads, snapshots of the children, and stock certificates. Lest these observations make you sad, let me assure you that loss of illusion is the final reward given to the elderly as all other gifts are being taken away. Disillusion is the foundation stone of wisdom. Until you accept that fact it's impossible to *know* anything.

Am I trying to instruct you? Not at all. In fact, I charge you to ignore everything I say. And everything anyone else says. The little bit we manage to learn about ourselves is all we can claim as true knowledge. And in that field of study there are no texts and no instructors. Also no scraps of parchment to frame and hang on the wall. Survival is the ultimate skill and we're told that the cockroach is the only one of God's creatures who has mastered that.

So much for death and profundity. I think of you often in your little corner of America. For all of my reading, poring over maps and looking at the snapshots you send, Fort Beck remains alien ground to me. I used to believe that I would visit you there one day. It never occurred to me that I wouldn't. But now I know that will never come to pass. Not because I am tottering and infirm but just because at a certain age curiosity is the first thing we lose. Only Angus seemed to have unflagging curiosity. He died, as you may remember, returning home from a trip in his fine old limousine. Do you notice how often I mention Angus of late? He *is* very much in my thoughts. I love him more now than I did when he was living. I never imagined that was possible because, as you remember, I loved and admired him without reservation then. On the other hand, the memory of dear Louise, my mother, who was so close to Raymond and me when we were children, almost never enters my consciousness now. Why is that? She certainly withdrew from me, from all of us, in her final years but I'm not sure that explains her absence now. I've concluded that there are all sorts of vengeance patterns within families. Perhaps my forgetting her now is some subconscious act of vengeance for a specific sin that she committed, or that I imagined she committed, long ago. God, what precious time we waste on guilt, ours and others'.

One benefit of letter-writing is that it gives one an opportunity to command, for a few moments, another person's full attention. Or at least it allows me to believe that I have captured that attention. In my daily life that is an uncommon occurrence. You will discover at last, as I have, that the people who used to listen to you so attentively now have trouble concentrating on what you're saying. They strike a courteous listening pose, smile and nod, and sometimes even make a sensible reply, but whatever you're saying they seem to have heard it before. Rather than have a conversation they seem eager to finish it. If I were a garrulous, repetitive old crone I would accept these odd reactions but since I'm not, I don't. I insist on questions and answers and some respectable level of concentration from the people I'm talking with, no matter how glazed their expressions become.

My grandchildren, of course, are exceptions to all the negations I have stated or implied above. They continually gratify, entertain and enlighten me. And how quickly they're growing up. Rab is fifteen now and is indescribably wise and handsome, Polly is thirteen and is a miraculous duplicate of her perfect mother, and young Bill is twelve but seems to have a longing to be age six still. Everything seems slightly off-centre with him. He is awkward and forgetful and slow in his lessons but there is a light behind his eyes that is irresistible. If he is a failure in life he will be the last to know it and the last to care. At this point in my life he is the best friend I have.

One time Angus predicted that Jesse would live to see the winds blowing through the broken windows of a deserted Wingate Fields. That remark disturbed Jesse and it disturbed me recently when he told me about it. But it disturbs me no longer because I think I understood what Angus intended. He meant to say that old eyes see destruction wherever they turn, that we see our own disintegration in our surroundings. Although our fine home here stands as strong and splendid as it did when I was a girl I see broken windows just as Angus did and hear the wind whistling down across the moors and through our deserted corridors.

Another Angus quote: 'God help us if we don't long for things we *don't* have. And God help us if we can't

> find contentment in the things we *do* have.' When I first met you, when you were a young girl, as we came to know each other that fateful summer I had a fantasy that you would stay on at Wingate Fields, that when I became as old as I am now, you would be here and we would enjoy our long talks in the morning room as we did then. I spend a lot of time now thinking about things that never started properly or that started but ended too soon.

As she began each letter to Helen, Clara promised herself that she would explain, as clearly as she could, the changed relationship between Jesse and Valerie. But she was never able to do it. She could not tell her that she had seen passion turn to kindness and love to *politesse*. Nor chould she be sure, in her own mind, that this was precisely what she had witnessed. Her strongest feeling was that having enjoyed the first act of a play she had somehow managed to miss entirely the second act. Now she was watching a tedious third act she did not understand, with no clues as to how the final scenes would play.

[9]

'If you have a servant in the house,' Helen's father had told her, when she was a young girl, 'the worst thing you can do is to treat him like a family member or close friend. Any servant who is worth a damn values his privacy as much as you value yours. He's there to do a job, to do it the way you want it done. But he doesn't want the additional burden of an informal friendship. And you shouldn't want it either.'

'But a servant's not a slave. I couldn't just boss somebody around,' Helen had said. 'If a person's living in your house and you see them every day, you have to treat them like a human being.'

'Exactly,' Raymond said. 'With respect. But respect is not affection. And affection is not familiarity. It's not an easy balance to hit, especially if you're genuinely fond of someone who works for you. But a good servant will help you. If you don't know the rules they'll be patient till you learn them.'

'What about Mrs Esping?' Helen said. Mrs Esping was their housekeeper. 'She treats us both, and Jesse too, as if she's our mother.'

'That's right. Up to a point. But she's *not* our mother and she knows it. She doesn't confide in us and we mustn't confide in her.'

'Why not?'

'Because it puts an improper burden on her. It puts her in the position of doing a job she's not paid to do. She's here to take care of our personal needs. Our emotional problems we have to solve some other way. She's a kind and loving woman, and we're fortunate in that. But those are special personal qualities. She's not paid for such things and we mustn't come to expect those things from her.'

'It's awfully complicated. I don't think I'll ever get it right.'

'Of course you will. Because it all depends on common sense. And you've got plenty of that.'

She had learned of course. And visiting Wingate Fields in the summer of her nineteenth year had helped her to see in practice what Raymond had taught her in principle. Still . . . as a woman who spent a great deal of time in her house in Fort Beck with only her housekeeper, the gardener and the cook, it was a continuing temptation to form friendships with those people that went beyond their household functions.

She had the same impulse toward Doug Slocum. As the months went by she became accustomed to seeing him cutting grass, trimming hedge, raking leaves or shovelling snow. Occasionally she stopped to talk to him in the yard and less frequently she would invite him into the kitchen for a cup of coffee or a glass of lemonade.

She knew from her friend, Enid Zoeller, that he was doing well in school. 'He's in his second year now and we're all pleased with his progress. Dr Hixson in the history department is his faculty adviser and he thinks Doug will be a teacher. He's become an omnivorous reader. Haunts the library.'

'Is he still living above the Guinnup's garage?'

'Yes. I think he's taken root there. We'd hoped he might join a fraternity, and I know several of them asked him, but he wasn't interested. He seems content to spend most of his time by himself. Doesn't seem to have many friends among the students.'

'No girlfriend?'

Enid shook her head. 'He had some dates his freshman year and I guess he went out a few times with a girl from the town but for the most part he keeps to himself. I have a theory that he had some bad times in Korea and he's still getting over them. When he first moved in with the Guinnups they thought he was staying up all night because his bedroom light was always on. But when Guinnup asked him about it Doug told him he sleeps with the lamp on.'

'Did he say why?'

'No. Didn't seem self-conscious about it. He just said he sleeps with the light on and that was it.'

'I can't believe he's scared of the dark. He doesn't look as if he's scared of anything.'

'I know,' Enid said, 'but there you are.'

Sometimes when Helen talked to him, either in the yard or in the kitchen, he was very quiet. Polite, but with little to say it seemed. At other times he would hold forth with great enthusiasm on one topic or another. Jack Kerouac, for example.

'Born in March, 1922. He's almost exactly ten years older than me. It drives me crazy. Makes me feel completely ignorant. I can't believe he was just a little ten-year-old kid when I was born. He's still a young man and he knows everything. I don't mean he's a scholar or a historian. I mean he just knows. I just finished *On the Road* for the fourth time. I've never read a book like that. Some people think it's about a couple of young bums driving around the country, but that's not it at all. It's about somebody exploring himself. It's that kind of a trip. It's internal. What goes on inside a person. It's scary but it's inspiring. You read that book and you say, Jesus, he got it right. He knows what it's like to hurt so much it drives you crazy. He knows how miserable most people are. He knows. That's what I'm saying. He just knows, that's all.'

Another day he lectured Helen about Louis Armstrong and Orson Welles. 'Two great men,' he said. 'Two originals, two inventors. One of them popular all over the world and the other one not very popular at all. You sit down and listen to Louis Armstrong records for two or three hours and you can't help thinking he invented music. At least he invented a way to use it in a way no one ever did before.

He's saying, "This is what it's like to be black." It's heavy and it's painful and it hurts like hell so you have to crank up all the joy you can. You hear all that happening when he's playing and pretty soon there's nothing left but joy. I mean it's like a waterfall of hot chocolate, bubbling and steaming and warm, all good tastes and good feelings and nothing bad is ever gonna happen again. It's not just a man playing a musical instrument. It's pure creation. Pure life. Everybody laughing and hugging and rolling on the grass in the sunshine. And then there's Orson Welles, doing things with his brain, doing technical things, using ideas and machines and constructions and people to make some thing new and to make it so real you think it's always been there. Armstrong makes you feel good and Welles makes you *think* about yourself. And since everybody wants to feel good and nobody wants to think too much about himself, it's not hard to see which man will get his picture on a postage stamp and which one won't.'

One bitter cold afternoon when he'd been shovelling snow on the driveway, he sat with Helen, a steaming mug of coffee in front of him, and said, 'Everybody's sentimental about their families. Not liking your sister is as bad as not liking dogs or babies. But I don't see why anybody should like somebody just because they're blood relatives. Getting born doesn't make you anything special any more than being the father of five or six kids turns you into a first-class human being. I've got three brothers, two of them hopeless drunks and the other one in jail for abusing his wife. One of my sisters is a half-wit and the other one is dishonest and selfish. My dad is the meanest son of a bitch that ever drew a breath and my mom is worse than he is. They detest each other and they detest all their kids. So why should I break my back trying to find something good in an outfit like that? Why should I kid myself? When I was ten years old I thought for sure I was gonna burn in hell because I couldn't stand the sight of anybody in my family. But little by little I got the message. There was nothing wrong with me. *They* were the problem. I mean I'm no blue-ribbon prize. I never thought I was. But I finally figured out I didn't have to be much at all to be a damned sight better than the family I came from.'

'Are they still in West Virginia?' Helen asked.

'I don't know. They tell themselves I'm dead and I tell myself *they're* dead. It works better that way.'

[10]

The following April, one sunny afternoon, Helen made a sudden, unplanned trip to Chicago. Before leaving her house she called Frank at his office.

'I need to see you,' she said.

'That's no problem. I'm easy to see.'

'I mean today. I'm driving up this afternoon.'

'Are you all right?'

'I'm not great,' she said, 'but I'll be better when I've talked with you.'

He was waiting for her in the apartment when she got to Chicago. He met her at the door, put his arms around her and said, 'I made you a drink.'

'Good. I need it.'

When they sat down on the couch he said, 'Should I have brought my lawyer along?'

'What do you mean?'

'I didn't like the way you sounded on the phone. Driving home, I decided you were going to kiss me goodbye.'

'You're crazy.'

'That's what it sounded like. Urgent call, middle of the afternoon, "I have to see you right away." That's the way those things work, isn't it?'

'I don't know how those things work. But I definitely didn't drive up here to kiss you goodbye. I don't want to talk about *us*. This is about Doug Slocum. Remember him, the kid who was in Korea who's been doing odd jobs around my house for the last couple of years?'

'I remember. What happened?'

'Nothing *happened*,' she said. 'I mean nothing really terrible. But I *saw* something today and it really shook me up. It made me think I should *do* something. I just feel as if I should try to do something to help.'

'To help Slocum, you mean?'

'Don't get that look on your face. I remember what you said before. Just let me finish and then you can say whatever you have to say.' She took a sip from her glass, then went on. 'For the last few days, Doug has been spending a few hours each afternoon cleaning up the yard, getting ready for our spring planting. This afternoon he was raking dead leaves out from under that tall hedge on the south edge of the garden, putting them in bags and carrying them back to the trash container behind the garage. I was sitting at my desk upstairs and every so often I'd look up from what I was doing to watch him working. Finally I looked up and I saw he was just standing under that big eucalyptus tree with his back to the house, the rake in one hand, his other arm hanging straight down at his side. I went back to my work but when I looked up a few minutes later he was still standing there. He hadn't moved an inch. I looked away again and when I looked back he was still there. Like a statue. I stared at him for a few minutes and finally I got up from my desk and went downstairs. I went out through the kitchen and crossed the garden towards where he was standing. I was going to speak to him when I was a few steps away but for some reason I didn't. I walked up beside him, then turned around so I could see his face. He was staring at the hedge and tears were running down his face. He wasn't sobbing or making any sound at all. He was just staring straight ahead and crying.'

'What did you do?'

'I didn't do anything. I felt as if I'd invaded his privacy. I felt awful. But he didn't seem to know I was there. He didn't look at me. I couldn't have stood there for more than a few seconds but it seemed like forever. Finally I eased away and walked back into the house. As soon as I got inside I called you. When I left to drive up here I saw he was working again in the side yard.' She drank again from her glass. 'I can't tell you what it was like, seeing someone suffer like that. Just standing there like he was paralyzed and . . . God, it was awful. He's not a child. He's a healthy, grown-up man, and yet there he was . . .'

'He's *not* healthy, Helen. He's sick.'

'No, he's not. Not the way you mean. I know he's upset. He had a difficult time growing up, and I'm sure he had some bad experiences in Korea, but he's not a mental case if that's what you mean.'

'I don't know what I mean,' Frank said. 'All I know about this guy is what you've told me. But I've heard nothing to change my original opinion. I didn't think you should have him living in your house and I don't think you should have him hanging around the place.'

'He's not hanging around. He's working.'

'You know what I mean. I think you should let him go.'

'I can't do that,' she said. 'Why would I even think of doing that?'

'Because it makes sense. His life doesn't depend on raking your leaves and shovelling your walks in winter.'

'How do you know that?'

'Well, if it does, then there's really something wrong with him.'

'Sometimes I don't understand you at all. I wanted to talk to you because I thought you could help me decide what I should do. When somebody is really suffering I don't think you can just turn your back. But that's what you're telling me to do.'

'No, I'm not. I'm telling you to use your head. Whatever problems this man has . . .'

'He's just a boy.'

'You just said he was a man. But whatever he is, he had his problems a long time before he saw you and he'll probably have them for a long time after he's . . .'

'God, what a negative attitude. Are you saying nothing can be fixed?'

'No. I'm saying some things can only be fixed by experts. And in this case you don't qualify.'

'Maybe not. But when somebody's lonely . . .'

'Lonely? You're talking about a twenty-four-year-old guy who's living on a college campus with a couple of thousand young people close to his own age. You mean to tell me he has nobody to talk to or spend time with? It doesn't make sense, Helen. You can't adopt him. You can't move him into your house and make warm cookies for him every afternoon.'

'Why not?'

'Are you serious? I thought we got past that one. You told me yourself he has a place to stay. His own apartment over somebody's garage.'

'That's just it. He's all by himself.'

'So is everybody else in the world.'

'I just feel bad that I can't help him,' she said.

'And I feel bad that you feel bad. But sometimes there's nothing else to do. All you can do is feel bad. Everything can't be fixed. Sometimes people have to fix themselves.'

'And what if they can't?'

'I don't know the answer to that one and neither does anybody else. All of us walk around with scars and flaws and hairline fractures. That's just the way it is.'

'That's what I can't accept. I can't be hard-boiled.'

'I'm not hard-boiled. I bring home stray cats,' he said.

'Objective, then. You can be objective about people. I can't.'

'Nobody's objective about people they care about.'

'Then I guess I care about too many people.'

'There's nothing wrong with that,' he said. 'Long as you've got somebody to protect you.'

'Like you,' she said.

'That's right. Like me.'

Chapter Nine

[1]

Abe Rettberg sat in a canvas chair in the late-afternoon cool of his workshop, rain spattering on the tin roof overhead, a jug of red wine on the table, Floyd sitting opposite him in a battered wicker armchair.

'Five papers a day I take, *New York Times, Washington Post, International Herald Tribune, Christian Science Monitor* and the London *Times*. From three in the afternoon till eight or so when I fix myself some supper, I really digest those suckers, front to back. I don't miss a lick. There's no way to know what's going on till you've read three or four versions of the same story. Then you can start to sort through the lies and pick out the klinkers. After a bit you get to know how a particular paper is gonna handle a particular story. You know what side they'll be coming down on even before you read it. Damned little straight reporting. Newspaper publishing's a big business and anybody with enough money to be involved in it has a few axes to grind for himself and his friends. But if you stay away from the editorial pages you miss a lot of that crap. I hear people talking about "being informed" as if there was some trick to know what's going on in the world. I don't know what they're talking about. The trick is to avoid what's going on. And that can't be done. The only reason I plough through all those papers every day is so I can try to figure out what's coming up next year or five years from now. I don't give a damn about yesterday and it's too late to worry about today. Tomorrow's the problem. That's what a man has to look out for.'

'When I was in jail once in New Jersey,' Floyd said, 'I shared a cell with an old black guy from Kansas. He used to say, "There's no point worrying about tomorrow. It won't be a damned bit different from today." '

'Don't you believe it. I'm no fortune-teller but when I look at some of the things that have happened the last year or so I mother-guarantee you I can see where things are headed. Look at Eisenhower's getting re-elected. What does that mean? I'll tell you what it says to me. It tells me everybody's getting prosperous and cautious. From now on you can forget about politics. It's all gonna be about money. Get what you can and hang on to what you get. It'll be a long time before we see a Roosevelt or a Truman again. Give a man an acre of land or five hundred dollars in a savings account and he'll vote Republican for the rest of his life.'

Floyd smiled. 'Are you telling me you don't like Ike?'

'Sure, I like him. He looks like Daddy Warbucks and he plays golf every day so how can anybody get mad at him? But God help us if he's the best man we got to run the country. And if that bird he's got for Vice-President ever gets control of things then we'd all better pack it in. Don't laugh. I'm telling you. All the signposts are there in the papers if you read the little print. When the Russians have to go into Hungary with tanks, what does that tell you? It means that some place down the line that whole Communist idea's gonna fall apart. It may be fifty years, or sixty, but if they have to use guns on their own people then they're heading for big trouble. And look at that Suez business. I thought Anthony Eden was a good man but he's out of a job now. And that's just the tip of the iceberg. Those rag-heads been fighting each other since the time of Christ so they're not about to stop now. Except now they're rich. More money than they know what to do with. And now they've got Israel to go after. When you and I are dead and buried they'll still be fighting over there. And sooner or later one of those fanatics will get his hands on a big bomb and then we'll really have some fun.'

'Gee, I'm glad I drove down to see you,' Floyd said. 'You're really cheering me up.'

'All right. Let's talk about you. You're not smart but you're lucky. How does everything look to you?'

'Things look good to me. Everything looks great.'

'Bull. Who do you think you're kidding? This is the third time you've been down here in the last two months. I don't know where your wife is but she's not with *you*.'

'I told you. She's up in Tahoe.'

'That's another thing. What are you hanging around that joint for? Everybody in that area's either old or rich. Or else they're trying to make a fast buck off somebody who's old or rich. It's no place for a young guy like you. You'll end up talking to yourself. What's Jeannette see in that place?'

'I told you . . . she likes to gamble. And she likes to wake up and see the mountains outside her window. She's having a great time.'

'I'll bet she is. What's she say about you drifting off down here every few weeks?'

'She knows you and I like to get together and chew the fat. She thinks it's a great idea.'

'As long as she doesn't have to come along.'

'What do you mean by that?'

'What do you think I mean? I saw her giving this place the once-over when you brought her down from San Francisco not long after you two got married. She couldn't wait to get back in the car and lam out of here.'

'That's when you had that family of racoons walking around the place.'

'It wasn't the racoons she objected to. It was me.'

'Not that I know of,' Floyd said. 'She never said anything to me about it.'

'She didn't have to. If her nose had been up any higher in the air, she'd have skinned it on the ceiling-beams.'

Floyd stood up and poured himself a glass of wine. 'I don't know what to tell you, Abe. I'm sorry if she hurt your feelings. She gets on her high horse once in a while. You know how women are.'

Later that evening, after they'd finished supper, Abe said, 'I didn't mean to put the knock on Jeannette. It ain't my job to point out what's wrong with your wife.'

'Sure it is. You and I go back a long way, Abe. I don't hesitate to stick my nose in your business. So it works both ways. If I remember right, you didn't have much time for Luisa either.'

'Wait a minute. You're wrong there. I thought she was cute as a bug. Any guy who didn't want to make a move on her would have to be crazy. What I told you was that I didn't trust that crowd she was mixed up with. I never thought that guy Estéban was really her brother, and when they got into court it turned out he wasn't. I still don't think she was out to get *you* but those guys had her in a bind. I was just trying to warn you about those birds.'

'You were right. I was lucky to get out of that with my head.'

'Well, you got Helen to thank for that. And that uncle of yours. What's his name?'

'Paul Buscatore.'

'That's right. Do you ever see him around New York?'

'He's not in New York. He's in Nevada now. And as a matter of fact we see him quite a bit. He runs a casino in Bellwood and he's got a house in Secret Harbor. We're just around the lake at Carnelian Bay. He found us the house we're leasing.'

'What happened between you two?' Abe said.

'How do you mean?'

'If I remember right, you didn't have much time for him. You thought he was a real pain in the ass.'

'That's right. I did. And he's still not my best friend. But he's gone out of his way to be nice to us. And Jeannette likes to gamble in that fancy place he runs. So we see him pretty often.'

'Well, why not? Like I said, you owe him a lot.'

'That's the way I look at it,' Floyd said.

'So . . . you've got everything going your way. Is that the story?'

'I guess so.'

'You guess so? What more could you want? You've got a house in New York, a house in Illinois, a big place in England where you can drop in any time you feel like it, and now you've got this joint in Tahoe where you can cool your heels and watch the sun go down over the mountains. Am I right?'

'You're right, Abe.'

'I mean you've come a long way since I met you in San Diego. You were a skinny little grasshopper in a sailor suit always looking for a fight. If somebody had asked me then about your future I'd have said you didn't have one.'

'And I'd have agreed with you.'

Abe raised his glass. 'Here's to you, Pal. You've got it licked. No worries. No debts. No problems.'

'Floyd grinned and clinked his glass against Abe's. 'You don't really believe that, do you?'

'Not for a minute. But we have to drink to something.'

[2]

'What the hell is the matter with you?' Floyd asked.

'You know what's the matter with me,' Jeannette said. 'I'm drunk. What's the matter with you?'

'I come home and find you sleeping in your clothes in the living room. All the ashtrays are full and the place smells like a third-rate gin mill on Sunday morning. What do you expect me to say?'

'You can say whatever you want to. I don't care what you say. As far as I'm concerned you can go to hell. You come barging in here at seven in the morning like you're trying to catch me at something. Well, there's nothing to catch me at. Not yet, anyway. But now that I know what you've been up to, it seems to me I'm free to do any damned thing I please. Just remember we're having this conversation because from now on . . .'

'From now on what?'

'From now on you're not going to play me for a sucker.' She lit a cigarette. 'Don't look at me like I just came down from the moon. You know what I'm talking about. You and your trips to Los Angeles to see your dirty-neck friend Abe.'

'What's Abe got to do with it?'

'Not very much, I guess. Since it turns out you never went to see him at all.'

'What?'

'Let me finish,' she said. 'I thought it was a little nutsy that you'd want to drive all the way down there just to sit around in that shack of his and talk about old times. No phone in his place so I couldn't even call you. No way to get in touch with you at all unless you called me.'

'I call you every day when I'm down there. Sometimes twice a day.'

'That's right. Calling from a phone booth. Covering your tracks. But the point is, I couldn't call you. For all I knew, you could have been calling from a gas station two blocks from here.'

Floyd got up from his chair, walked over and sat down beside her. 'Why don't you go take a shower while I make a pot of coffee?'

'I don't want to take a shower and I don't need any coffee. And don't try to change the subject.'

'I'll tell you the truth,' Floyd said. 'I don't even know what the subject is.'

'Oh, yes, you do. You know all right. But you don't think *I* know. No wonder you wanted to have a place out here in Tahoe.'

'That wasn't my idea. It was your idea. You were dying to come out here.'

'Maybe I was,' she said. 'But since I've never been here before somebody must have planted the idea in my head. And the more I thought about it, the more I remembered us talking about it, the more I realized it was you. And now I know why. You were the one who wanted to be out here. So you could be close to your lady friend.'

'Lady friend?'

'Don't act dumb. Remember when you brought home a packet of matches from that restaurant in Stockton?'

'I've eaten at half a dozen places in Stockton. It's right on the main highway between here and L.A.'

'Of course it is,' Jeannette said. 'And another time your car broke down there and you had to stay overnight in a motel.'

'That's right. Two or three months ago.'

'One month and six days. The last time you told me you were driving down to see Abe.'

'All right. I give up. What are you driving at?'

'I'm telling you the party's over. You and your friend Luisa have been making a fool of me long enough.'

'Luisa? What do you mean?'

'I mean Luisa. Your little Mexican tamale.'

'Luisa's in jail, for God's sake. She's down in Bakersfield at the women's correctional facility.'

'No, she's not,' Jeannette said. 'And you know she's not. She's been out for over a year and she lives in Stockton. She sings at a place there called Papagallo.'

'I don't believe that.'

'Then ask Paul. He'll tell you. I saw her picture in his office just two days ago. He has a big book with pictures of all the lounge acts that play this part of California. When I saw her I said "Well, *that's* a pretty girl" and he said, "That's Luisa." At first I didn't catch on. Then slowly it dawned on me. He meant that was *your* Luisa. That's when I started to put two and two together. Your trips to Los Angeles. Three or four days at a time. A *week* once. It never did make sense to me that you could be interested in spending that much time with Abe.'

'Wait a minute,' Floyd said. '*Wait* a minute. Are you saying . . . Are you telling me that you've been sitting here drinking vodka and smoking cigarettes for two days and you've decided that I've been carrying on a love affair with somebody in Stockton . . .'

'Not just somebody. I'm talking about your old girlfriend. You were crazy about her. You told me so yourself.'

'So what? That was all over a long time ago. I swear to God I didn't know she was out of jail. And I sure as hell didn't know she was living in Stockton. But what if I did? Are you saying I pretend to be going to L.A. just so I can stop off in Stockton to see Luisa?'

'That's exactly what I'm saying. And God knows how many times you've driven down there for the day. The way you drive I figure it's only about a two-hour trip from here.'

'Do you really think I'm out looking for women? If I were why would I go farther than Reno or Bellwood. Those towns are filled with beautiful girls.'

'I didn't say you're looking for just anybody. I'm talking about one woman. I'm talking about Luisa. She's not just some tootsie down the block. She was your girl. Like a wife. You lived with her. The two of you lived together.'

'But we're not living together now. We're not doing anything together. I haven't seen her since the trial and I don't expect to see her. I don't want to see her.'

'I don't believe you.'

'You mean your mind's made up? No matter what I say . . .'

'That's right.' she said. 'I didn't expect you to tell the truth about it. Nobody ever tells the truth about stuff like that.'

'Are you telling me that just because I drive through Stockton once in a while on my way to see Abe, and because my car broke down there once, and because I've brought home matches from a couple of restaurants, you've stirred all that together and come to the conclusion that I'm having a red-hot romance with a woman I broke up with years ago?'

'Don't try to make me feel stupid. It won't work. That's what men always do when they're trying to get away with something. I don't have to prove anything to you. I'm just telling you what I know. If it doesn't make sense to you, that's too bad. It makes sense to me. And just telling me I'm dumb won't change anything. When I saw her picture, looking the way she does, and when Paul told me where she lived, I didn't have to sit down and add up a bunch of figures or make a list. I just knew. And I still know. No matter what you say.'

Floyd got up and walked across the room to the window. He stood there looking out across the lake toward the east. Finally he turned back and said, 'All right. Here's what we're going to do. We're going to drive down to Los Angeles and see Abe. We'll ask him how many times I've been there in the last few months and how long I stayed each time.'

'Do you think I'd believe *him?*'

'Wait a minute. Let me finish. Then we'll stop in Stockton on the way home and look up Luisa.'

'Not me. I don't want to see her.'

'Neither do I. But if that's what it takes to convince you that . . .'

'What makes you think that seeing her would convince me? Can you see me asking her questions like we were in a courtroom or something and her swearing to tell the truth and the whole truth?'

'No. But if you saw Luisa and me in the same room you'd know there was nothing between us.'

'No, I wouldn't. I wouldn't believe anything I saw. All I know is how I feel and I trust that. I've known for a long time that there was somebody else in your head. I knew it even before we got married but I just ignored it because I didn't want to spoil anything. And because I hoped that after we were married things would be different. I mean, I wanted everything to be perfect so I told myself it was. But I couldn't fool myself for ever. Even if you proved to me that what you're saying about Luisa is true it wouldn't change the way I feel. I'd still know there was somebody else. I just wouldn't know who it is.'

'What am I supposed to say?'

'Nothing. It doesn't matter what you say. I know you're not going to tell me the truth and I guess I'm hoping you won't.'

'Where's this whole conversation taking us?' Floyd said.

'I don't know. Nowhere, I guess.'

'I keep feeling you're about to say, "So that's it. Let's call it a day." '

'What does that mean?'

'You tell *me*,' he said. 'Are you going to leave me? Is that what you're leading up to?'

She smiled. 'Not me. I'll never leave you. That's not the question. The question is . . . when are you going to leave me?'

[3]

It would have been easy for Jesse to tell himself that Valerie's confession to him about herself and Floyd had been the direct cause of his return to Nora. But such was not the case and he knew it. Moreover, his impulse was not to relate the two circumstances but to keep them, as much as possible, separate. He succeeded in this to such a degree, managed to compartmentalize himself so thoroughly, that when he was at Wingate Fields he was able to mask out completely the life he led in Paris. And when he was in France, Valerie and his children were, for those days or weeks, frozen into silent sculpture far away in Northumberland. Is such mind management, such thorough self-hypnosis possible? Perhaps not, in the abstract. But emotional survival makes its own rules and finds a way to enforce them. Just as he and Valerie managed the details of their lives as though Floyd had never been a consideration, so also did he and Nora pick up the reins again as though they had simply quarrelled, separated, then were reconciled. They did not discuss, nor seem to recognize, either of them, that Valerie had fully occupied that empty space of estrangement. Instinct told them, undoubtedly, that there was no rationalization for the strange triangular relationship they found themselves in, that it could only be dealt with a piece at a time, that any attempt to smooth the jagged, ill-fitting edges would only end in confusion and guilt, any attempt at self-justification, no matter what logic was applied, was destined for chaos.

Passion for a mistress, then, and devotion to a wife need not, indeed must not, be mutually exclusive. For a man like Jesse to maintain his equilibrium, neither element must suffer. Each must be honoured and maintained. But in its own cloister. Colours must not run together, accidental chords must not be struck. When he was with Nora he was a single man and she was a single woman. When he was with Valerie, no world existed for him apart from his home at Wingate.

Likewise with Nora. There could be, in her mind, no connection between Jesse and her daughter. When Jesse left Paris, he simply was absent. She did not envision him with his wife and children in England. She did not connect her daughter or her grandchildren with this sweet, familiar man who had shared her bed for so long and who now shared it again. If anyone said to her, 'How can you?' she would certainly have answered, 'How can I not?'

Although they were many years older than when they had first met that long-ago summer, their life together now was more private and insular and intimate than it had been then. Since many people in Paris knew about their original relationship and how it had changed, they were not anxious to make a public announcement that it had become again what it had once been. They were determined, in fact, that no one in Paris should know what they were about. Jesse seldom visited Nora's house, never by himself, and she never visited the rooms he kept in the hotel in Place St Sulpice. When they were seen together in public, at whatever cultural functions both were obligated to attend, they met briefly, chatted, and parted, smiling and embracing coolly in the French manner.

They managed these public aspects of their life together like two seasoned veterans of the theatre, rejoicing later in private, laughing and congratulating each other on their skills at deceiving an entire city.

Through her lawyers, Nora leased a fine old house in an unfashionable street of the 18th *arrondissement*, hired a small staff, bribed them into total silence, and lived an untraditional but rewarding life there with her gentleman friend who was known to the servants only as Monsieur Gardner. They spent late afternoons and evenings together at that house but never entire nights. Usually Nora was at home in her house by the Seine by midnight. And Jesse was in his hotel. Their friends and associates were not allowed to suspect that either of them was leading a secret sleep-away life.

After so many years apart, what had brought them together again? When they discussed it later, and they discussed it often, it was difficult for them to stipulate how they had gone from one point to another. It had, for one thing, not been a sudden change. They had not simply sighed and fallen into each other's arms. 'It was all quite natural really,' Nora concluded at last. 'We just started talking.'

It was true. After having avoided each other through the years since Jesse had begun coming again to Paris to resume his critical work, they began gradually not to seek each other out but to spend more time together when some business at the magazine, some vernissage or literary event *brought* them together. Bit by bit, these chance meetings were attenuated. They went to convenient cafés for an aperitif or a croque-monsieur. After quite a few months a lunch date was made, and some time after that a dinner date. But always, the topics of conversation were general or professional. They did not reminisce or stumble through the tangled grasses of what-might-have-been. They were simply two adults gradually getting to know each other and finding they had a great deal in common. If their senses had always led the way in their previous life together, they fed now on a different menu. They gradually discovered, each of them, that this familiar person across the table was an extremely sympathetic friend. Topics they had never seemed to have time to deal with before were dissected thoroughly now. He discovered that she was warmer and more thoughtful than he had believed and she found that he was tougher-minded than before. Each of them was pleased by these discoveries. 'It's quite remarkable,' Nora said. 'I used to love you so much it made me angry. Now I discover I like you better than anyone else I know. And that doesn't make me angry at all.'

Jesse discovered also, or rediscovered, the pleasure of being with someone his own age, someone who had been a key witness to most of his follies and triumphs and self-discoveries, someone who had shared in, or contributed to, most of those past experiences. In his journal he wrote, 'How exciting it is, at a certain age or in certain circumstances, to explain yourself to someone, to pour the sum of your wisdom and perception into some attentive ear. But how much more rewarding it is to be with someone who already knows what you consist of, good and bad, who accepts you for your flaws as much as your grandeur.'

They were experiencing, each of them, the joy of rediscovery, taking real pleasure from the past as well as the present, comparing themselves with previous selves and liking what they had become. Using the bedroom now not as a solution to other problems, not as a binding force when other corners threatened to become unstuck, but as a slow and glorious entity all its own, they came together in a tender but more powerful way than they had ever known. Feeling brand-new and splendid, they knew that it was all mysteriously connected with what had gone before, that previous disappointments and guilts and doubts and sins had mixed and mellowed and enabled them to be something quite different now.

'We're really quite marvellous, aren't we?' Nora said. 'I mean, it's a pity that we can't be exhibited or canonized or something very public like that so other people could be inspired. Do you know what I'm saying?'

'Of course I do.'

'It seems to me that our experience might inspire people to poke about in dustbins for odd bits of silver, to look behind badly framed chromos for a Rembrandt etching. *Don't lose heart*. That, I suppose, is the proper motto. Perhaps we should have a great banner made up and fly it here above our illicit house. Does that appeal to you?'

'Why not?' Jesse said.

'Or perhaps it would be in better taste simply to have it embroidered on my towels and bed linen. A pattern of spring flowers in soft colours and "Don't lose heart" in pale blue.'

'Why not a simple monogram instead — the letters DLH in an oval.'

'It's subtle, isn't it?'

'I think so.'

'But won't it look as though we've made off with someone else's sheets?'

'I don't think so. No one sees our sheets except the maid and the laundress.'

'That's true. We lead an isolated life, don't we?'

'Cloistered,' Jesse said.

'But we don't mind, do we?'

Jesse shook his head. 'After all, we've seen quite a lot of the world.'

'And the world has certainly seen a lot of us.'

'Too much perhaps.'

'Do you think so? I don't. I think we've been proper guests. I don't believe we've abused the Lord's hospitality.'

'Who knows?' Jesse said. 'If we have, we have. We shan't fret about it.'

'God, no. No fretting or self-flagellation or dwelling in the past. Although in fairness, you must admit, there were many lovely things in the past.'

'I do admit that.'

'Still, nothing quite compares with *now*. Do you agree?'

'Totally.'

'Do you think we're being rewarded for leading good lives?'

'No, I don't think it works like that,' he said.

'Why not?'

'What I mean is I wouldn't want it to work like that.'

'Why not?'

'If I can be rewarded for past behaviour then I can also be punished for past behaviour.'

'Ahhh . . . but you've done nothing wrong. Neither of us has. We have led exemplary lives. Self-sacrificing. Kindness and generosity all around. Patience, tolerance, all the higher virtues.'

Jesse smiled. '*You* know that and *I* know that. But an objective observer might come to different conclusions. Innocence might look like guilt. Self-sacrifice could be interpreted as self-absorption. We might even be branded as normal, selfish, insecure human beings.'

'They wouldn't dare,' she said. 'That's why duels are fought. That's why people are brought to the bench for slander. Anyone who calls me normal will pay dearly for it, I promise you.'

The greatest change, of course, was in Nora. All her weapons, it seemed, had been converted to household utensils. Her need to do battle, it appeared, had been permanently satisfied. She saw the change in herself and remarked about it. 'I sincerely believed,' she told Jesse, 'that everyone was an enemy or a potential enemy. I felt the person who struck the first blow would surely win the day. So I kept flailing about, slashing away at people who weren't even armed. True, I wounded a lot of opponents who deserved what they got but on the backswing I also cut up some innocent bystanders. I don't mean to say that I have now become an angel of mercy. But at least I don't shoot to kill now and I'm very careful to avoid unarmed people. If I was totally paranoid before, now I am only selectively so. And I'm surprised to find how much more energy I have. Hate and suspicion burn up a great number of calories.'

'Does that mean you'll be plump now?'

'I don't think so. There are enough people around who richly deserve my anger. I'm sure they'll keep me slim.'

As previously noted, they spoke often of the years they had spent together but those reminiscences never included Valerie. She was there, of course, in both their minds, but they never brought her onstage. In the new ambiance they had created, making their being together again something inevitable and final, there was no place for the living contradiction of Valerie. They seemed to sense, each of them, that if she ever entered this new and very private world they had made for themselves, she would never leave. She would have to be discussed and, in one way or another, dealt with. Since neither of them had even the slightest notion of how she *could* be dealt with, since what they really wanted was to have their life together without in any way changing hers, they saw no other solution except to pretend, when they were together, that Valerie did not exist, that her children and Clara did not exist, that indeed there was no one who was, in any way, a threat to them. Nor did Jesse, when he was at Wingate Fields, speak of Nora to either Clara or Valerie. And Nora, when she wrote to her daughter, never mentioned Jesse. Also, she seldom visited England now. And when she did, she managed to arrive when Jesse was not there.

All these subtle changes did not go unnoticed. Certainly not by Valerie. She pretended, however, to give them no importance. Only after she had concluded that Jesse and Nora were together again, only then did she allow herself to list the observations that had led her to that conclusion.

[4]

As Valerie's life and her marriage, her relationship with Jesse and with herself, were slowly being rearranged for her, so also, like a great force moving glacial masses, did Floyd's destiny begin to be redirected.

Adultery comes in all sizes and colours. It is triggered by

a great variety of emotions. One of the most common of these is vengeance. When Jeannette dropped her clothes to the carpet by Paul Buscatore's bed she told herself, very specifically, that she was getting even, getting square with Floyd. Paul's motives were not so expressly vengeful. But all the same he realized he was completing at last an action that had begun for him the first time he and Jeannette were introduced in a restaurant in New York. He knew also that of the six or seven young women he had been introduced to that night, Jeannette was perhaps the least remarkable. But she was the only one who was Floyd's wife.

Paul had no moral restraints about sleeping with other men's wives. He did feel, however, that it was bad for business. In a situation where his power and ability to prevail were dependent on the illusion, if not the fact, of his invulnerability, he was careful to avoid situations which might make him vulnerable. Indignant or angry or self-righteous husbands could be dealt with but they could be an annoyance also. And Paul did not like the gamblers in his casino to be annoyed. Also, from a practical standpoint, in a community that literally bulged with attractive and available women, there was no reason for a man like Paul to turn to a married woman.

This is not to say, then, that Paul, when he met Jeannette, selected her as a future conquest. He did not. His reaction to that meeting, in fact, was centred more on Floyd than on her. Their first encounter, the only other time they'd seen each other, when they'd had lunch together with Helen, came back to him with surprising clarity as soon as the two men shook hands.

Without recalling specific details of that first conversation, Paul did remember, as he talked with Floyd and Jeannette, the resentment he had felt that other time.

Resentment was the operative word. Although he had no proprietary attitude towards Helen, he had become fond of her. He was also in awe of her because he felt she was from a higher station than any he had been exposed to. She was the kind of person he was trying to emulate.

In Floyd, however, Paul saw nothing to emulate. He drew this conclusion even before the two met. From his conversations with Helen and with Mike Rosenthal at the time Floyd was in trouble in California, Paul decided that his nephew was a mongrel, some odd and unpredictable misfit who was taking advantage of Helen and would undoubtedly continue to take advantage of her as long as she permitted it.

Having readied himself for one sort of person, Paul was not at all prepared for the Floyd he met that first day in the restaurant in New York. Having dressed down for the occasion he was surprised to see a trim and expensively-tailored young man sitting across from him at table, seeming more at ease on Paul's own turf than Paul himself was.

When Helen arrived he was even more uncomfortable. She was openly affectionate towards Floyd, asked his opinion on all matters, and found him, it seemed, endlessly amusing. There was a warm and easy relationship between them which fascinated Paul. In short, having prepared himself to meet a young rogue without qualities, he saw instead a man who had, or who at least believed he had, everything.

As he learned, through the years, about the extent of Floyd's wealth, of his acceptance at Wingate Fields and in Paris, as Helen, bit by bit, painted a portrait of her admirable son, Paul's original scorn turned to envy and became then, as envy often does, a kind of hatred.

Recognizing this antipathy in himself and trying for some reason he didn't understand to conceal it, Paul went out of his way to be helpful when Jeannette wrote him a note saying she and Floyd were coming to Bellwood for a visit. When they decided to lease a house Paul made a phone call and found a home for them. And during the months they had lived there he had allowed them guest privileges at his casino and entertained them at small parties at his home and truly grand affairs in the members' dining room of his hotel. He had introduced them to people he thought they would enjoy and had tried to steer them away from people, many of them his friends and associates, who he thought they would be better off without.

All those months he had a kind of easy brother-and-sister relationship with Jeannette. In a guarded way they came to know each other. But he never made any sort of move in her direction, didn't kiss her in some shadowy corner, didn't touch her, stare stupidly into her eyes, or in any way indicate that they should embark on some splendid voyage that did not include Floyd.

All the same, when she came to his house one mid-morning when he was still in bed, when she came into his bedroom carrying a cold bottle of champagne and slipped out of her clothes, he was not surprised to see her there. He knew she was performing an elaborate act of vengeance against her husband. And so was he.

[5]

When Frank was in Chicago and Helen was in Fort Beck, they spoke often on the telephone, sometimes five or six times a day. And they always talked to each other late at night before they went to sleep. When her phone rang just past midnight, one cold night in November, she picked up the receiver expecting to hear Frank's voice. But it was Doug Slocum.

'I hope I didn't wake you up,' he said. His voice sounded thin and distorted.

'No, you didn't. I was just sitting up in bed reading. Are you all right?'

'I guess so. But I'm . . .' His voice trailed off.

'What's the matter?' she said.

'I don't know how to say it. It sounds crazy. But I'm scared. I haven't been able to sleep for three nights. I just sit here listening to the sounds outside and then . . .'

'Then what?'

'It doesn't make sense. I don't know why I'm calling you.'

'I'm glad you called me. All of us need to talk sometimes.'

'I guess maybe I'm by myself too much,' he went on. 'I get an idea in my head and I can't get rid of it. It gets all out of proportion. People who have been very nice to me look like enemies all of a sudden. You know what I'm saying?'

'Of course I do.'

'Sometimes I think I should get a pet. A dog or a cat maybe. Or even some goldfish or a canary if the Guinnups don't want a dog around. Maybe I wouldn't be so lonesome then. Or scared. Or whatever it is I am. Even when I go to sleep I have crazy dreams and they wake me up, dreams about people breaking in here. Really ugly stuff I wouldn't even want to tell you about.'

'Maybe you should move into a dorm for a while. I'll bet if you talked to Enid Zoeller and told her . . .'

'Oh, I couldn't talk to her.'

'Why not,' Helen said. 'Enid likes you.'

'Not anymore she doesn't.'

'What do you mean?'

'I just mean I couldn't ask her for anything because she's got it in for me. Tries to get me in trouble. Told the Dean some stories about me.'

'What kind of stories?'

'I can't tell you. Nasty stuff. Things you wouldn't expect a woman like her to say.'

'I can't imagine . . .' Helen began. Then, 'Why don't I talk to somebody at the school then and see if you can't move into one of the dorms for a while?'

'Thank you. I appreciate it. I knew you'd try to help me if you could. But I don't think the dorm's a good place for me. Too much commotion and fooling around . . .'

'I just thought that if you're frightened of living there by yourself . . .'

'What I really want, the thing that would be best for me is if I could live with a family. In a regular home. In a nice house. Then I'd be all right, I think.' When Helen didn't answer, he went on. 'I know when we talked about it before, when I asked if I could stay at your house, you didn't think it was such a good idea but I thought maybe, now that you know me better, you might have changed your mind.'

She was tempted to say, 'All right. Let's try it for the rest of this semester and see if it works out,' but she could see Frank's scowl suddenly and hear his voice and she said, 'I'm afraid not, Doug. It has nothing to do with you. It's just a situation with the servants here. It would be very complicated and it's a problem I can't handle right now.' When he didn't answer, she said, 'Doug . . .' and he said, 'I'm desperate, Mrs Bradshaw.'

'Don't say that.'

'I don't know what I'm going to do with myself. When I get down in the dumps like I am tonight . . .'

'Don't you have a friend you could stay with?'

'I wish I had. But you're the only person in this town I think of as a friend. That's why I had to talk to you. I mean it, my head was going off in a hundred directions. It still is. If this is what my life is going to be like, then what good is it?'

'Don't talk like that. I won't listen to such foolishness.'

'I don't blame you,' he said. 'I'm sorry. I guess I'd better hang up now.'

'I didn't mean that. I want to talk to you if it makes you feel better.'

'It does, Mrs Bradshaw. It really does. I just wish I could see you.' He paused. Then, 'Could I stay there in your house for just one night? Maybe I could come over and sleep in that spare bedroom back behind the kitchen? It would mean a lot to me, just knowing there was somebody else in the house. I know it's a crazy idea but I'm scared to death to stay here by myself. I'd be ashamed to admit that to anybody but you. But I'm not afraid to tell you anything. Please. Don't say no. Just let me stay there tonight. I'm sure it will do me a world of good.'

Again she almost gave in. But instead she said, 'Let me see what I can do. I'll call you back in ten minutes.'

As soon as she broke the connection with Doug she called Joe Guinnup. 'I hope I didn't wake you,' she said.

'Not quite. Ten minutes later I'd have been dead to the world but now I'm wide awake.'

She told him about her conversation with Doug. 'I'm worried about him. He sounds very upset.'

'Let me take a look. I'll call you right back.'

In a few minutes her phone rang and Joe said, 'I just talked to him.'

'I hope you didn't tell him I called you.'

'No. He's used to me prowling around at night. I told him I needed a typewriter ribbon. So he gave me one.'

'How did he act? How was he?'

'He looked fine to me. He was drinking a bottle of beer, eating potato chips and listening to the radio.'

'He didn't seem upset?'

'He wasn't upset. He was laughing and kidding around. Looks like a million bucks.'

As soon as she was off the phone with Guinnup she called Frank in Chicago and told him what had happened.

'No wonder I couldn't get you,' he said. 'I've been trying to call you for half an hour.'

'I don't know what to do.'

'I'll tell you what to do. Be sure your downstairs doors are locked, then take your phone off the hook and go to sleep. And the next time you see him tell him you don't need him to work for you any longer.'

'What kind of advice is that? We're talking about a kid who's in trouble.'

'He's not a kid,' Frank said. 'And he's not in trouble. He just wants you to *think* he is.'

'Why would he want that?'

'I don't know. Because he's a bird-brain, I guess. And guys like that are dangerous. You never know what wrinkle he'll come up with next.'

'I don't know,' she said. 'I don't think it would do any harm to put him up for one night.'

'Well, I do. I'm telling you. You shouldn't have that guy in the house. I don't want him hanging around there at all. If you can't tell him to stay away then I'll come down there and do it for you.'

'That won't be necessary.'

'No? I think maybe it is necessary. You can't play Florence Nightingale to the world, Helen. The best thing you can do for some people is to stay away from them.'

'You don't even know him.'

'That's right. I don't. And neither do you. If you did, you wouldn't have to call me or Joe Guinnup to find out what you should do. When a guy calls up and says, "How would it be if I come over to spend the night at your house?" the automatic answer is no.'

'I don't believe in automatic answers. I think he's scared to death for some reason, no matter what Guinnup said, and I don't understand your attitude.'

'I'm very easy to understand. All I care about is protecting you. When you tell me about a bird like this one who stands around crying in the yard and who calls up in the middle of the night to tell you he's scared of the dark and wants you to tuck him in then I say that's a guy to stay away from.'

'You make a joke out of everything.'

'It's no joke to me. I think he's trouble and I can't understand that you don't see it.'

'And I can't understand that you don't have a little compassion.'

'Okay,' he said. 'I give up. But next time if you don't want my advice, don't ask for it.'

'I won't. You don't give advice. You give orders.'

'For Christ's sake, Helen, it's one-thirty in the morning. When somebody calls me with a problem at one-thirty I assume there's something urgent about it. So that's how I respond.'

'I have to hang up now,' she said. 'I'm sorry I bothered you.'

'You're not going to call him, are you?'

'Yes, I am.'

'Why, for God's sake?'

'Because I said I would.'

When she called Doug's number there was no answer. She tried three more times before she went to sleep. Still no answer.

When Helen turned out her light and the house went dark, Doug was standing across the street watching. He stood there for a long time staring at her window. At last he turned and walked away and disappeared among the shadows of the elm trees that lined the street.

When he came to do yard work later that week, Helen stayed in her room upstairs. It was more than three weeks, in fact, before she saw him again. One afternoon when she was shopping in a stationery store near the campus he came up beside her and said, 'I'm sorry I called you that night. I shouldn't have done it. But I was a little mixed up and I needed somebody to talk to.'

'Are you all right now?'

'Sure,' he said. 'I'm fine.'

[6]

'The question is . . . when are *you* going to leave *me?*' If one single exchange between a man and a woman could illustrate the core-nature of their relationship that one statement was truly a mirror into Jeannette's soul. All the anger and resentment, the drinking and quarrelling and the thirst for some sweet sip of revenge were connected to that prime truth inside her, that she was not good enough, that Floyd knew it, and sooner or later he would leave her.

It had gnawed at her constantly since their marriage. His generosity and affability only confirmed it in her mind. She told herself that he bought whatever she wanted, took her wherever her whims dictated and put up with her tirades because he knew it was temporary. This conviction only served to make her more wilful, more demanding, more outrageous in her demands and her behaviour. Like a child seeking punishment, she tried to push him farther and farther, hoping for resistance, longing for an explosion of truth that would prove to her that she was right, that would force Floyd to show his hand.

Blundering into an affair with Paul, however, was a grave error. She realized it almost as soon as she'd done it. Because once in she didn't know how to get out. For all of her tough exterior she was still a small-town girl. She quickly discovered, as many women before her had done, that dividing yourself between a husband and a lover is a complex matter indeed. She had no previous experience to guide her. When she was married to Glen she had not experimented with other men. Only when Floyd came home from the war had she allowed herself a three-day lapse with him. Until she turned to Paul, she had been with no one other than Floyd and Glen.

She quickly found that she could not spend the afternoon in bed with Paul and then make love to Floyd that night. So she developed a sinus condition. Then she found a doctor who was accustomed to treating patients with imaginary illnesses. Many bottles of prescription medicine soon studded her bathroom shelves and a machine to purify the air was installed in her bedroom.

Her childlike drive for vengeance against Floyd backfired, however. She had never preferred any man to Floyd. And Paul was no exception. She knew it almost at once. Because she was ingenuous in such matters she decided she would simply end things with Paul, miraculously cure her sinus condition and return to Floyd.

Paul, however, had other ideas. His vengeance scheme had backfired in quite a different way. He fell in love with Jeannette. Until it happened he hadn't realized that it had never happened to him before. This unfamiliar feeling was aggravated by his being forced to share her, further aggravated by his suspicion that her emotions were less profound than his, and made almost maniacal as he came to believe that she would inevitably return to Floyd.

Only a few days after their first afternoon together he said, 'I hope you don't have some idea that things can go on very long like this. I don't like the idea of your leaving me and going home to Floyd.'

Still, at this point, playing the game she said, 'I don't like it either, honey.'

'I know you don't. So the sooner you tell him the better.'

'What do you mean?'

'I mean you can't do the divorce bit till you tell him.'

'I can't divorce Floyd.'

'Sure you can. Once he signs the agreement form, I can arrange it so you're free in forty-eight hours.'

'Forty-eight hours? Nobody can manage that.'

'I can,' he said. 'Trust me.'

'I trust you,' she said, 'but let's not get in a big hurry. We're having too much fun.'

'It's not fun for me. I told you . . . I don't want you to be with him at all.'

'What can I do? I'm married to him.'

'I know you are. But we'll take care of that. And then you'll be married to me.'

Trying to keep things light, she said, 'You're pretty sure of yourself. What if I told you I didn't want to get married again?'

'Is that what you're telling me?'

'No. I'm not telling you anything. But you're like a locomotive running downhill. Give me a little time.'

'I told you. I don't want you living with him. If you don't want to get married this minute that's all right. But leave him.'

'You mean, I should tell him about us?'

'He has to find out sooner or later. If you don't want to tell him, I will.'

'I'll tell him when the time comes.'

'The time's already here.'

At first Paul's attitude simply annoyed her. Then she began to be afraid. One day she said, 'I have to go back East for a couple of weeks. My daughter directed a play at her school and I promised I'd come to see it. And while I'm there I'll go visit my folks.'

'I've got a better idea. Send Floyd to visit your folks. Then you and I will have two weeks to ourselves. We'll fly up to Lake Louise and have a good time.'

'I can't do that.'

'Sure you can. Simplest thing in the world. The doctor'll tell him you have a sinus infection and can't fly.'

'You don't understand. I want to go. I promised my daughter and I don't want to disappoint her.'

'When is it you're planning to go?'

'May 10th.'

'All right. I'm not unreasonable. I'll let you go. But on one condition. Before you leave you tell Floyd about us and get him to sign the divorce paper.'

'You won't quit, will you?'

'What do you expect?' he said.

'I don't know what *you* expect.'

'I told you.'

'I can't do it, Paul.'

'Then you're not going.'

'Yes, I am. Wait and see.'

'I don't have to wait and see. I already know.'

'You're really a bully, aren't you? Do you always get your own way?'

'Somebody has to get his own way. I figure it might as well be me.'

'Did you ever hear of taking turns?'

'Sure. But I'm against it.'

For five days then she didn't see him or call him. On the fifth night he called her at home. Floyd answered the phone, talked to Paul a few minutes, then passed the receiver to Jeannette. When she said hello, Paul said, 'Tomorrow at noon. Yes or no?'

'I don't feel so great,' she said. 'I don't think I can.'

'Suit yourself. I'll be calling your house every hour tomorrow till you show up.'

'Well, maybe I'll feel like it. I'll see.'

When she hung up she said to Floyd, 'There's a fashion show at the casino tomorrow. I asked him to remind me.'

'You want me to take you?'

'That's sweet of you but I think I'll pass.'

The next day at twelve-thirty Paul's car pulled into her driveway. He got out and strolled up the steps to the veranda. She walked out to meet him and said, 'What are you doing here?'

'I expected you at twelve. You didn't show up.'

'You're crazy,' she said. 'You can't just barge in here any time you feel like it.'

'Why not?'

'Because you can't. And you can't call me up in the middle of the night.'

'Sure I can.'

'I don't know what's got into you. What do we say if Floyd comes home now?'

'I hope he does. You don't seem to be able to tell him what's going on so I guess I'll have to.'

'What's the *matter* with you?'

'I haven't seen you or talked to you for five days. How do you expect me to react to that? I told you before I don't want you living here with him and I meant it. I want you to tell him about us and I want you to do it now.'

'You're driving me crazy. Do you know that?'

'That's because you won't face the facts. Once you get away from him you'll feel better.'

After a moment she said, 'What if I told you I've changed my mind?'

'About what?'

'What if I said I didn't want to leave Floyd.'

'I wouldn't believe you.'

'You really scare me, do you know that? I don't want to be pushed and pulled and jerked around. All of a sudden you're telling me what I have to think and what I have to do. If I lived with you is this what it would be like? Because if it is I don't want that. I don't want somebody to own me. Everything you say to me now sounds like a threat.'

'Wait a minute,' he said. 'You say I'm driving you crazy. How do you think I feel? For days I don't see you and I know you're here with him. If you think I'm unreasonable now, you haven't seen anything. But once we get this mess straightened out everything will be good. I promise you. But until that happens, till one of us tells Floyd what the situation is, don't expect me to sit on my hands and smile. That's not my style.'

'You see what I mean? Are you telling me that's not a threat?'

'I don't care what you call it. If that's what it takes to get you moving. I had a rough five days. I don't want any more of that.'

'All right,' she said. 'Here's what I'll do. Floyd's leaving tonight for Indiana . . .'

'I thought you said May 10th.'

'That's when we have to be at Betsy's school.'

'You mean you're going, too?' Paul said.

'Not tonight. I'm meeting him in South Bend May 9th. I'll fly into Chicago and drive down from there. As soon as we come back here I'll tell him.'

'Not good enough. I don't want you to go any place with him. I told you that before. And I want you to tell him about us before he leaves.'

'I can't do it, Paul.'

'Why not?'

'I just can't.'

He stood up and said, 'Suit yourself.' He turned and started across the terrace toward the stairs.

'Where are you going?'

'To the tennis club.'

'He's not there today,' she said.

'Yes, he is. I checked before I came here. He reserved a table for lunch.' He checked his watch. 'I'll be there in time for dessert and coffee.'

When he reached the top of the stairs she said, 'Goodbye, Paul.'

He turned back. 'What does that mean?'

'Just what it sounds like.'

'A little threat from the other side?'

'Exactly. If you're dead set on telling Floyd about us then I guess you'll have to do it. But if you do, don't make any future plans that include me.'

'I don't believe you. You're bluffing.'

'There's one sure way to find out.'

He leaned over and kissed her. 'I'll take a chance,' he said. As he started towards the stairs again, she turned and walked through the open glass doors into the house. When she went into the hallway leading to the kitchen she heard him come into the house behind her.

'How about a compromise?' he said as he walked into the kitchen.

'Why would you compromise? I thought you were holding all the cards.'

'I am. But smart gamblers don't try to win every hand.' Then, 'If I don't tell him, will you promise to tell him tonight?'

'No. We already went through that. Your problem is that you want everything. You don't want me to go meet him in Indiana and you're not willing for me to tell him about us after he comes back? Is that right?'

'That's it.'

'All right. *I'll* compromise. I'll give up something to get something. I won't meet him in Indiana and I'll tell him about us when he gets back. That's the only compromise we have. If it doesn't sound good to you it's still not too late to drive over to the tennis club.'

'It sounds good to me. I'll take it.'

When she drove Floyd to the airport that evening she said, 'Dr Steadman wants to put me in the hospital for a couple of days. See if we can't clear up this sinus infection. What do you think?'

'I didn't know it was that serious.'

'Neither did I. But he says it's dangerous to fly.'

'Will that keep you from coming East?'

'I hope not. But just in case I'll call Betsy tonight and explain the situation to her. If I have to miss her play then I'll see her a few days later.'

'I'll be back in Nevada by then,' Floyd said.

'You don't have to come back here, do you?'

'Where else would I go?'

'Why don't you go home to New York? I'll follow you there after I see Betsy. Then this fall maybe you'll take me on a nice long trip to Europe.'

'You told me you didn't want to go to Europe.'

'I didn't. But now I do. I changed my mind.'

[7]

On his way to Betsy's school Floyd stopped in Fort Beck to see Helen. When they were having dinner together on his first night there he said, 'Did Frank tell you he called me in Nevada a couple weeks ago?'

'No, he didn't. What was that all about?'

'Maybe I'm telling tales out of school. Maybe he didn't want you to know.'

'Did he ask you not to tell me?'

'No.'

'Then he doesn't care. Frank doesn't leave loose ends dangling.'

'That's what I figured,' Floyd said. 'Anyway, it didn't sound very important. I mean he didn't sound upset or anything.'

'So what was on his mind?'

'He knew I was going to stop here to see you. So he

asked me to talk to you about this college kid who does odd jobs for you. Doug, I think he said his name was.'

Helen smiled. 'I don't believe it. Frank really has a bee in his bonnet about that young man. What did he tell you?'

'From some of the things he's heard from you he thinks the kid's unstable. He said he tried to persuade you to let him go but you wouldn't hear of it.'

'Of course I wouldn't. Doug's had enough disappointment in his life. Right now he needs support and understanding. Even the small amount that *I* can give him. Frank doesn't agree with that. He believes in tackling problems head on. If you can't solve them, get rid of them. It works for him but it won't work for me. Most of us don't have Frank's self-confidence. What he doesn't have is a great deal of patience with other people's shortcomings. He's high on energy but low on compassion.'

'And you're just the opposite.'

'Not exactly. I'd be proud of myself if I had accomplished half of what he's accomplished. But on the other hand I have — at least I hope I have — some kind of connection with people I care about, some concern about what happens to them. Frank seems to have lost that along the way. Or perhaps he never had it.'

'Is that what happened to your marriage?'

'Oh, dear,' she said. 'That old thing.' She smiled. 'Sometimes I almost forget that Frank and I were married. We've been together so long the way we are now that it's hard to remember what we were like when we were married.'

'Is he different now?'

'I don't know. I suppose we both are,' she said. 'But, yes, he is different. That self-confidence I mentioned — he always had that — that's what fascinated me when I first knew him. I'd never known anybody before who believed he would come out on top no matter what he tackled. But that was Frank. When he came to Chicago — he was very young then — he just shook that town like a dog with a bone. Every target he shot at he hit. He astounded people. And he astounded me. He simply would not take no for an answer.'

'Was that hard to live with?'

'No,' she said, 'that's what I started to say when I told you just now that he's changed. He was much gentler with people then. He was always wonderfully sweet to me. And even in business he was not known as a shark. He didn't think his success had to be built on somebody else's failure. He's basically a kind man. That's how he was when I met him. And — don't misunderstand me — he's *still* kind now. But not the way he was before. In his business he's achieved everything he ever dreamed of, but, like all the rest of us, he's had disappointments in other departments of his life. I'm sure I was one of them. I can't imagine anyone's going through a divorce and coming out of it with a full supply of self-esteem. And Frank's done it twice now. His children are a disappointment to him, too. And sometimes, if he's lying awake for some reason and can't sleep, I imagine he's a disappointment to himself. None of us get through life without scars. And the worst ones are usually self-inflicted. So we change, usually without realizing it. I'm sure I'm different now, in Frank's eyes, just as he is in mine. He's not as patient now. He can't understand it when things that are perfectly clear to him are not instantly clear to other people. Also, his world is getting smaller, like it does for everyone as they get older. He has fewer friends, fewer activities, not as many outlets for his energy. And — he doesn't talk about this — I think he's very disappointed that he never had a son. Frank is half-pirate and half-pioneer. Pretty good characteristics to pass along to a boy. But it just didn't happen for him and I'm sure he doesn't feel good about it. So . . . he's not as gentle as he used to be. More judgemental now. He thinks all of us have full control of our own lives and he doesn't have much compassion for the ones who don't handle it well.'

'Like Doug, for example.'

'That's right. Frank says I'm a sitting duck for any young person with a problem. He thinks, I'm sure, that I see myself as everyone's mother. But he's wrong about that. I just see myself as your mother. Of course, he may resent that, too — subconsciously, I mean — that I have a son and he doesn't. But whatever he feels, it comes out in odd little ways.'

'Maybe it does,' Floyd said, 'but I got the feeling when we talked on the phone that he was really worried about you, about whether it's safe to have this guy around.'

'I know he's worried. But I've told him over and over that there's nothing to worry about. I'm not trying to be Doug's best friend or a surrogate mother. But if I can give him a little more stability than he's had in the past, then I feel obligated to do it.'

'I'm not sure obligation is the word.'

'I think it is. I feel as if I made a commitment to him when he came here to Foresby. Not a great commitment but something he could depend on. I feel especially strong about it because others here at the school who had made stronger commitments to him seem to have short memories.'

'How do you mean?'

'Dr Willis for one, the Dean of Students. He was Doug's strongest supporter at the beginning. Now, in recent months, he seems to have lost interest.'

'Why is that?'

'I don't know. Enid Zoeller, who works in the Dean's office, told me in confidence that Willis thinks Doug lied to him.'

'About what?'

'She wouldn't say. But she said that she herself didn't feel comfortable with Doug, that she no longer encouraged him to come to her office for advice as she had once done. When I asked her why, she said it was just a feeling she had. She said he looked at her in a way that made her feel uneasy. So that's the situation. Without the Dean's office behind him, Doug will have a difficult time staying in school. He's not a great student. Came here badly prepared. But that's all the more reason why he should be encouraged and helped along as much as possible.'

When they sat in the library later she said, 'Do you get letters from anyone at Wingate Fields?'

Floyd smiled. 'Don't embarrass me. As you know, I am not a letter-writer. I'm not proud of it, but it's painful for me to sit down and write anything at all. Even a page or two. I tell myself I have nothing to say and even if I did I'm no good at putting it down on paper. The truth is it's laziness, I think. I just never got into the habit when I was a kid. So now, if I want to be in touch with somebody I pick up the phone. You know what I mean. I call you ten times for every once that I write.'

'Amen. After we first got to know each other, I decided I would keep all your letters. I bought a lovely teak box to put them in . . .'

'And the box is empty,' he said.

'Not quite. But almost. Let's just say there's a lot of room in it still.'

'Yeah, well, in answer to your question, I've had a few

letters from Jesse and Clara and a couple notes from Nora but I guess they got the message that they weren't going to hear from me very often so they don't write much either.'

'Nothing from Valerie?'

'No,' he said. 'But that doesn't surprise me. We never got to know each other all that well.'

'I thought Clara said you two went riding together.'

'We did. A time or two. But that's not a great way to have a conversation.'

'No, I suppose not.'

'How is everything over there?' he asked then.

'Unchanged, it seems. I hear mostly from Clara, who could teach us all a thing or two about letter-writing. An occasional letter from Jesse and a *very* occasional note from Valerie. She's of your persuasion. No time to write. But still, Clara fills me in on all the details.'

'Is she well?'

'Very well, I think. You'd never guess from her penmanship that she'll be eighty-three this summer.'

'Hard to believe. She's still a beauty.'

'She doesn't think so,' Helen said. 'She writes funny anecdotes about what she calls her "symphony of deterioration". But her doctors say she's in fine shape. And, God knows, there's nothing wrong with her mind. I think she was afraid she might end up like her mother. Poor Louise was as dotty as could be. Angus said she talked to the trees in French and insisted they answered her in Gaelic.'

'You're leaving something out.' Floyd said.

'About Clara, you mean?'

'I think so. I'm getting to know you pretty well. You have a particular way of ending a sentence when you can't decide whether you should go on or just let the subject die.'

Helen smiled. 'Clever, aren't you? But in this instance you're only half right. I have nothing to conceal about Clara because all I have are suspicions. You see she was always the most courageous and optimistic person in the world. The courage is still there but the optimism is severely diluted. I have a feeling that the world hasn't come through at all in the way she had hoped. Clara was always capable of seeing the grand design, of linking the details together and deciding what everything *meant*. She's a religious woman, God-fearing, and all that, but I always felt that her God was a God of order. Clara has always believed in progress and improvement, an ultimate order to things and ideas and people. She found evidence and support for that belief everywhere she looked. Now, I suspect, that vision has failed her. Her letters now are concerned with deterioration rather than renewal or growth or rejuvenation. She thinks that what we call science will destroy us all. She also seems to believe that there's a pattern of internal destruction going on, a loss of direction among the people, a loss of will. In her last letter she said, "I shudder to think what would become of my lovely England if the Battle of Britain were fought today." Also, she's discouraged about the rest of us Bradshaws, I'm sure. And understandably. We *are* a sorry lot. She loves Nora, of course, but she doesn't feel as though she really knows her any longer. Nora's lived so long away from England that she's a stranger to all of us except Jesse.'

'Do you think Clara's disappointed in you?'

'Of course she is. Why shouldn't she be? I'm disappointed in myself. It's not that I haven't fulfilled my promise. I don't think anyone thought I would accomplish great and important things. I certainly didn't. I don't mean to say that Clara doesn't like me. She does. We love each other. Closer than sisters. Closer than a mother and daughter. But I've never become the kind of family person that Clara is, that I think she hoped I would be, someone to take root and spread branches and hold the rest of the family together, to provide shelter and nourishment and a sense of permanence. What Clara couldn't know was that my conception of family was all centred in my father. When he died, it died too. Then after you were born, *you* were what I thought of when I thought of family. By then Jesse had wandered off and everyone else was in England. So you and I were *all* the Bradshaws to me. The fact that I'd never seen you and didn't know how to find you only intensified that feeling. If Clara could hear what I'm saying now she would understand because she understands all human detours and shortcomings, but she still would be disappointed that circumstances prevented me from becoming the new den-mother of Wingate Fields. We skipped a generation, you see, with Nora gone off to France, me to America, and Hugh living in isolation in Scotland. Everything was thrown out of kilter. So the next lady of the castle after Clara became, by default, Valerie.'

'And there was always Jesse.'

Helen nodded. 'That was the idea. That was what Angus

had in mind. But Jesse was a disappointment, too. Like the rest of us. All of us concerned with our individual destinies and no one willing to stand at the centre of the great hall and hold the clan together.'

'But that's how I see Jesse and Valerie and their three kids. The new generation. The Bradshaws in residence.'

'That's what everyone expected, Clara included. But I read things between the lines that make me uncomfortable. Wingate can't run without women, that's true, but there has always been a man at the centre. It's the Bradshaw tradition. The son will replace the father. Like it or not, it's the way things run among the gentry. The servants expect it, the tenants expect it. It's a part of the order that Clara believes in. She needs to have a man in the house, even if he's only a token man. And she doesn't have one.'

'You lost me,' Floyd said. 'You're talking as if Jesse doesn't live there any more.'

'Of course he lives there. But he's *not* there.'

'You mean he's in France all the time?'

'No. I don't mean that. As far as that goes, his schedule doesn't seem to have changed over the last few years.'

'Then I don't know what you're talking about.'

Helen smiled. 'I don't have a great list of facts, my darling. We're talking about perceptions. Foggier than *that*. We're really talking about my perceptions of Clara's perceptions. And since she never writes anything negative . . .'

'You have to read between the lines.'

Helen nodded. 'Exactly. Like I said.'

'If you want my opinion, I think you're borrowing trouble.'

'I hope you're right. But I don't think you are. My instinct tells me the winds have shifted since the last time you were at Wingate.'

'How do you mean?'

'I can't guarantee it, of course, but I have a feeling that Jesse has altered his course in some way, some subtle unspoken way that Clara chooses not to mention but which she reveals all the same by never referring to it. In her last five letters she hasn't mentioned Jesse at all. And she's made almost no reference to Valerie.'

'And that has sinister implications for you?'

'Not sinister. I wouldn't use that word. I simply think that something has gone wrong over there. And I can only think of one area where Clara might not confide in me.'

'Jesse and Valerie?'

'That's correct.'

'You've decided they're having a problem?'

'I haven't decided anything,' she said. 'My witch's instinct tells me something's gone sour and common sense says it's them.'

'All right. Here's what my common sense says. If you're telling me you have no real evidence . . . is that what you're saying?'

'No one's on trial. I don't need evidence.'

' . . . if you're just picking balloons out of the air, then I think you picked the wrong balloon.'

'Maybe you're right,' she said. 'I hope you are.'

[8]

'I'm not surprised she didn't come,' Betsy said. 'I mean, I'm not mad at her or anything. I know why she doesn't like to come here to the school. She always thinks Daddy may be here. She doesn't want to run into him.'

She was sitting in the empty auditorium of the school theatre, mid-afternoon of the day when the play she'd directed would open. She wore sneakers and jeans and a man's work-shirt. Her hair was pulled back and tied with a rolled bandana. Floyd, who had arrived in South Bend an hour before, was sitting in one of the theatre seats beside her. On stage two girls were carefully dressing the set.

'Not this time, Betsy. Until yesterday, she was expecting to come.'

'I can't imagine her being in the hospital. She's healthy as a horse.'

'Nothing serious. The doctor just wanted to keep her in a controlled situation for a few days, try to lick this sinus thing that's been bothering her.'

'Well, too bad for her,' Betsy said. 'She'll miss a great show. *And* the directorial début of a new major force in the theatre.'

'You're disappointed, aren't you?'

'Why do you think that?'

'Because I know your routine. When you act tough and

who-gives-a-damn, that means you're covering up something.'

'Not this time,' she said. 'I told you. I didn't expect her.'

'Why not? She promised she'd be here.'

Betsy shook her head. 'Just a feeling I had. I know her pretty well. I'm seventeen, you know. You spend that many years with somebody, you start to pick up the rhythm. Same thing with Dad. I knew he wouldn't be here tomorrow. He said he'd come next weekend when we do three more performances. But he won't be here then either.'

'I wouldn't be too sure of that.'

'I'm *sure*. They're both a little shaky now. In different ways. And they have been ever since the divorce. Maybe that's what happens to people. And they act funny when they're with me. As if they feel guilty or something. I've told them both that everything's fine with me. But they just nod their heads and go on thinking their own thoughts. They're not sure how to deal with me because they still haven't worked out how they're going to deal with each other. The problem is that Mom doesn't care if she ever sees him again. If it weren't for me, if I didn't remind her that she'd been married before I honestly think she could put it completely out of her mind. But not Dad. I think he believes he's still married to her. Sometimes he talks about her as if she's just off on a trip or something. But other times he gets so mad and crazy he scares me.'

'What does he say?'

'It's not so much what he *says*. It's the way he looks. He'll be talking about her and all of a sudden he gets all white, starts to babble and swear, and really looks scary. When he gets like that I think he'd kill her if she walked into the room.'

'Not Glen,' Floyd said. 'He's not the violent type.'

'You don't think so? I don't know. I wouldn't want him coming after me when he has that look in his eye.'

That evening, when Floyd picked up the ticket Betsy had left for him at the box-office, he found a note from her in the envelope.

Come backstage before the show. I need to see you.

One of the student ushers took him to the backstage entrance and managed, in all the pre-show confusion, to locate Betsy.

'I tried to call you at your hotel,' she said.

'I went out early. I grabbed a bite to eat, then walked round for a while before I came here. What's up?'

She pulled him over to one side in the wings. 'My grandmother called me an hour or so ago. To wish me good luck with the show. When I asked if Dad was there, she said no. She said he flew out to Nevada three days ago.'

'Does he know Jeannette's not here with me?'

'I'm not sure. I may have mentioned she might not be coming the last time I talked to him.'

'When was that?'

'Sunday, I think. I hope I didn't do something idiotic.'

'Not at all. It doesn't matter.'

'Don't you think we should call Mom?'

'That's not a bad idea. Is there a phone booth in the theatre?'

'On the lower level, below the lobby.'

'Good. I'll give her a quick call before the show starts.'

When he called his house in Tahoe, the houseman said Jeannette had gone out but she was expected home before dinner. When he hung up, Floyd looked at his watch. Four forty-five Nevada time.

At the intermission he telephoned again. And after the show was over. And again from the restaurant where he had a late supper with Betsy. But each time he was told Jeannette was not there. Finally he left a message for her to call him at his hotel whenever she came in. When he came home at a few minutes after one, when he unlocked his hotel room, his phone was ringing. It was Jeannette. 'There you are,' she said. 'I've been trying to get you.'

'Just walked in the door.'

'How was the show?'

'Pretty good. Not ready for Broadway but I enjoyed it. And Betsy felt good about it.'

'I've tried twenty times to reach her.'

'She's on the move,' Floyd said. 'She and I had a little supper after the show and then she was off to a cast party. She probably won't be answering her phone till noon tomorrow.'

'Oh, pooh. I wanted to talk to her. Was she teed off because I didn't make it?'

'I don't think so. Didn't seem to be.' Then, 'Have you had any strange visitors in the past few days?'

'Yes, I have,' she said. 'How did you know?'

'Mrs Tillis called Betsy and said Glen had gone to Nevada. Betsy thought we should warn you.'

'Good for her.'

'Have you heard from him?'

'He must have called as soon as he landed at the airport,' Jeannette said. 'He came straight out to see me. He was still carrying his suitcase. Hadn't checked into a hotel yet.'

'So how'd it go?'

'No problem. We sat on the terrace and had a cup of tea. He said he was going to Reno, then to Vegas for a few days, and then head for home.'

'Betsy says he's been acting strange. She was afraid he might give you a hard time.'

'Not at all. We just made small talk for a while, and finally he got up and left. Not very exciting.'

[9]

Jeannette had not told Floyd the truth about her meeting with Glen, but it was not because there was something to conceal. She was in no way protecting herself. She simply had no desire to tell anyone, not even Floyd, how strange Glen had been, how pathetic and vulnerable. It was as though the man she'd been married to for almost fifteen years had vanished and had left behind only a tattered facsimile of himself.

'I've given a lot of thought to our situation,' he said to her. 'At first, as you know, I was mad as hell. But after a while I began to see things as they really are. We've done exactly the same as a lot of other people. We've made a big mistake.'

He paused as if he expected an answer from her. When she said nothing he went on. 'I'm not saying we had a perfect marriage. I guess nobody does these days. I mean I wasn't a perfect husband. I admit that. That counts for a lot, doesn't it?'

'I don't know, It might have meant something if you'd said it when we were married . . .'

'It means something now. I mean if you were to say to me that you realized you'd made a mistake . . .'

'I'm not saying that, Glen. And I think we should end this discussion before it gets out of hand.'

'It won't get out of hand. I promise you. Because I'm in complete control of myself and I know you are too.'

'You don't sound like yourself. You sound as if you'd been reading a tenth-grade psychology book.'

He shook his head. 'Nothing like that. Like I said, I've just had a lot of time to think and for the first time I see things as they are.

'What are you trying to say?'

'It's not complicated,' he said. 'I just think we made a mistake. I think we should get back together again.'

'How do we manage *that?*'

'I mean I think we should get married again.'

'I can't believe my ears.'

'You can believe it. I mean it.'

'I can see you mean it. I just can't believe you're saying it.'

'I told you — I've thought about it a lot and I . . .'

'For God's sake, Glen, did you forget I'm married? I fought you to get a divorce and now I'm married to Floyd. We've been married for four years.'

'That doesn't matter. All I have to do is look at you and I can see you're not happy.'

She sat very still not looking at him. Finally she said, 'Look, I don't want to hurt your feelings but . . . I mean the fact that I'm married to Floyd has nothing to do with it. You and I had decided to separate before he came into the picture. If Floyd left me tomorrow it wouldn't change anything as far as you and I are concerned.' Then, 'We had some good years together, Glen. We have a nice daughter. Can't we just let it go at that?'

He half-rose from his chair then, and suddenly he was on his knees in front of her.

'Please, Jeannette . . .' There were tears in his eyes.

'Stop it, Glen. For the love of God . . .'

'I can't help it. I don't know of any other way to . . .'

'If you don't get back in your chair, I'm going to go inside. I can't stand to see you like this.'

He eased himself heavily into his chair again. He sat there staring at the floor. After a long moment, Jeannette said, 'I'm sorry you're upset. I was trying *not* to upset you. But you must know we can't go backward. We can't just pick up again where we left off.' He didn't answer. 'It's nobody's fault, Glen. It's just . . . that's just the way it *is*.'

Again he didn't answer her or look at her. She stood up and waited there for a long moment, looking down at him. Still he didn't look up. She turned then and crossed the terrace. In the doorway she paused and looked back at him. He was sitting just as she'd left him. She stepped inside and walked across the foyer to the staircase. As she climbed the stairs, she heard him shouting far behind her, his voice raw and breaking, more like a scream than a shout. 'You can't just do whatever you *want* to. Nobody can do that. Nobody gets away with stuff like that.'

When she turned into her room and closed the door behind her, she felt chilled suddenly. Her hands were shaking as she tried to smooth her hair.

Book Four

Chapter Ten

[1]

When Paul turned into the driveway of Jeannette's house on the lake he saw an unfamiliar brown sedan in one of the parking spaces. Jeannette's red roadster was parked at the far side of the area where she always left it. As Paul got out of his car and walked up the steps to the front door a man in a brown uniform came outside and stood in front of the door. Another brown-uniformed man walked off the terrace and joined him. Paul stopped a few feet away and said, 'What's the problem?'

'No problem, sir.'

'You're not Nevada cops and you're not California cops so what's the story?'

'Private security. Working for Mrs Bradshaw. Do you mind giving us your name?'

'Yes, I *do* mind.'

'Our instructions are . . .'

'Yeah . . . okay. I don't have time to argue. My name's Buscatore. Mrs Bradshaw's expecting me.'

One man went inside and picked up the phone in the foyer. The other man stayed outside with Paul.

'I thought I knew most of the security guys from around here. Are you from Tahoe?'

'No, sir.'

'Bellwood?'

'No, sir. Sacramento.'

'You're a long way from home,' Paul said.

'Not too far. We cover northern California.'

The other guard came outside then. 'Mrs Bradshaw said I could bring you up.'

'Don't worry about it. I know the way.'

'She told me to bring you up.'

When Jeannette opened her bedroom door she was wearing a trim blue suit. Behind her near the bed were three pieces of matched luggage. A smaller bag was still open on the bed.

'I'll be right outside,' the guard said as he closed the door.

'What's going on?' Paul said. 'Where do you think you're going?'

'I'm going to New York.'

'Just like that.'

'No. Not just like that. I thought about it a lot. It's the only decent thing I can do.'

'Decent?'

'Yes. There are other people involved . . .'

'You mean Floyd?'

'Not just Floyd. My daughter. My parents. People who care about me.'

'*I* care about you.'

'I know you do. Don't think I didn't consider that.'

'Let me get this straight. You were just planning to pack up and take off and that's it. And later maybe I'd get a Dear John letter . . .'

'Nothing like that. That's why you're here now. That's why I called you and asked you to come over.'

'A fast twenty minutes before you leave for the airport.'

'No,' she said. 'I don't have to leave here for an hour. Look, I'm sorry, Paul. I'm not trying to be a crumb about this. I'm handling it the best way I can,'

'By running away?'

'I don't call it that. I was running away when I came here. Now I'm going back to New York. That's where I live.'

'Did you think I'd try to stop you? Is that what all the bodyguards are for?'

She smiled. 'I knew you'd try to stop me. But that's not why I hired the security people. I told you Glen showed up a week or so ago. As far as I know he may still be hanging around.

'I thought you said you weren't afraid of him.'

'I'm not. I just don't want to be annoyed. I don't want to have to deal with his foolishness.'

'What about my foolishness?'

'There's nothing foolish about you,' she said. 'You have nothing to be ashamed of. I'm the one who made an ass of herself. Now I'm trying to straighten things out.'

'I thought you and I made a deal,' he said then.

'We did. I agreed not to go east with Floyd two weeks ago.'

'And you said you'd tell him about us.'

She nodded. 'That's right. When he came back here to Tahoe. But he didn't come back. He went on to New York.'

'Is this the way you planned things all along? All the time I was telling you I wanted you to marry me, did you know it wasn't going to happen?'

'I didn't know anything, Paul, any more than you did. Things just happened one at a time and finally I knew I couldn't go on trying to be two different people, trying to balance myself between you and Floyd.'

'*I* sure as hell didn't want that.'

'I know you didn't. Neither did I. So, I knew I had to make a choice.'

'So now you've made it. And there's nothing for me to do but lie down and play dead.'

'I don't know what you're going to do. I hope you'll try to understand.'

'If I want to keep you off that plane today, you don't think those two monkeys in uniform are going to stop me, do you?'

'I suppose not.'

'If I pick up that phone and call the sheriff's office, they'll be on their way home to Sacramento.'

'Then what?' she said. 'What good would that do?'

'I'm just telling you that all your secret plans aren't worth a damn if I decide to stop you.'

'But if I want to go, if I've decided to stay with Floyd, why would you want to stop me?'

'Let me get this straight,' he said. 'You made up your mind to come strolling into my bedroom that morning and now you've made up your mind to be a nice wife and go home to your husband,is that it?'

'I'm not proud of anything I've done. I'm not proud of myself. I never have been.'

'Is this what you had in mind from the beginning? A little fooling around and then home in time for Christmas?'

'I didn't have anything in mind. I was mad at Floyd. Don't ask me why. I can't tell you. A lot of craziness. I accused him of everything I could think of. And finally I decided I'd get even with him.'

'So you came to me.'

She nodded. 'That's right. Then I really got in over my head. Because I liked you. And you liked me. So there I was, caught up in the middle between you and Floyd and not knowing which way to turn. I knew it was my own fault but that didn't make it any easier for me. Because whatever you may think of me I haven't passed myself around like a plate of cookies. I've only slept with three men in my life and the other two I was married to.'

'But now you're telling me you want to go back to Floyd?'

'I don't know what I *want*, she said, 'but I know what I have to do. I'm not twenty-one years old any more. In a couple of years I'll be forty. I've got a daughter. And my parents. They're still getting over my divorcing Glen. You see what I mean? There are too many people involved.'

'So that's the whole story,' he said. 'You called me over here to kiss me off. I'm supposed to get in my car and go home and pretend I never saw you.'

'Of course not. Nobody has to pretend anything.'

'But the point is you've made up your mind, no matter what I say?'

'I don't have any choice, Paul.'

'Well, I do,' he said. He walked to the phone picked up the receiver and dialled. 'What airline are you on?'

'United,' she said

Into the receiver he said, 'This is Paul, Sheila. There's a United flight to New York leaving in an hour or so. Get me on it. Book two seats together for me and Mrs Bradshaw. She's already ticketed. If there's any problem, have Norman handle it.'

When he hung up, Jeannette said, 'You're not going to like it. That flight stops in Chicago. I'm getting off there to spend two days in South Bend with my daughter.'

'Then I'll get off, too. I'll buy a brown suit with brass buttons and pretend I'm your bodyguard. I know all about South Bend. I'm a Notre Dame fan.'

'I don't want you to come with me,' she said then.

'I know you don't. But you can't stop me. If I'm gonna get beat in this race I want to at least be at the track.'

'But what good . . .'

'I'll tell you what good. I think you're going back to Floyd because you don't have the guts to tell him about us.'

'So you're going to tell him?'

'Somebody has to.'

'And what do you think will happen then?'

'I don't know. But whatever it is, I don't want to get it second-hand.'

'What if I told you he already knows? What if I've already told him?'

Paul shook his head. 'No good, baby. I don't believe you.'

She turned and walked to a small desk by the window, picked up an envelope, and walked back to him. She slipped two folded pages of writing paper out of the envelope and handed them to him.

'What's this?' he said.

'It's a copy of a letter I sent to Floyd. Read it.'

He slowly read through the letter. When he looked up, she said, 'Did I leave anything out?'

'No, I guess not. When did you send this?'

'Yesterday morning.'

'So he hasn't read it yet?'

She shook her head. 'He'll get it tomorrow or the next day when I'm in South Bend. He'll definitely have it before I see him in New York.'

'Unless it gets lost in the mail,' Paul said. 'That happens sometimes.'

'You don't think I wrote to him, do you?'

He handed the letter back to her. 'I can *see* you did. I just read what you wrote.'

'But you're not sure I sent it to Floyd. I can see it in your eyes.'

'Let me put it this way. If he already knows when we get to New York then I'll see first-hand what his reaction is. If he doesn't know, then either you will tell him or I will tell him.'

'Do you realize what a miserable position you're putting me in?'

'Sure I do. But there's a lot at stake here. I have a choice of doing what I'm doing or doing nothing. And doing nothing doesn't appeal to me. Not when it involves something I want.'

'You mean me?'

'There's no doubt about that, is there?'

'You're a smart guy, Paul. Use your head. If you manipulate me like this, if you force me into a humiliating confrontation with Floyd, with you there as a witness, do you think I could ever have any feelings for you after that, no matter what happens with Floyd and me?'

'I'm not sure,' he said. 'It's a chance I'll have to take.'

[2]

That night in New York, Floyd had an early dinner at his club. On the way home he stopped at the Gramercy Theatre and saw Fellini's *La Dolce Vita*. When he came home it was almost midnight. The houseman had left a note for him on the table in the entry way.

> Several phone calls from Nevada. Man's voice. But no message. Also local call from Mike Rosenthal. Called three times. Urgent. Call him, no matter how late, at Murray-Hill 4-2535.

Floyd took off his coat and hung it in the hall closet. He walked across the foyer to the library, switched on the light, and studied the message as he turned on his desk lamp. When he sat down in his chair, the phone rang. As soon as he answered, a voice said, 'This is Mike Rosenthal, Floyd. I have to see you. I'm in my apartment on Thirty-ninth Street. I'll be at your house in ten minutes. If the telephone rings before I get there, don't answer it.'

'What's going on?'

'I'll tell you when I get there.'

As soon as Rosenthal hung up, Floyd called his house in Tahoe. After five rings, the operator said, 'Sorry, there's no answer.' He called the Drake Hotel in Chicago then and asked for the registration desk. When a young woman answered, he said, 'I'm trying to reach my wife, Mrs Floyd Bradshaw. Can you tell me if she's checked in yet?'

After a moment, the woman said. 'No, sir, she hasn't.'

'She was due to arrive there between nine and ten tonight. Do you mind checking your records again?'

Again she said, 'Sorry sir. We're holding her suite for her but she's not here yet.'

When the bell rang and Floyd opened the street door for Rosenthal, he said, 'Has something happened to Jeanette?'

Rosenthal nodded. 'Did they call here from Bellwood?'

'No. But I tried to reach her in Chicago and she wasn't there. She should have been there three hours ago.'

'She never left Nevada, Floyd. There was an accident at the airport. She was getting her luggage out of the trunk when somebody's car went out of control and slammed into her.'

'What are you telling me? How is she?'

'She was still conscious when they took her to the hospital, but . . . she didn't make it, Floyd. In the emergency room she never came to. Paul's dead too. I guess he'd driven her to the airport. They said he died instantly.'

'Jesus . . .'

'I know the police have been trying to reach you. That's why I told you not to answer the phone. I didn't want some hard-nosed desk cop to give you the news.'

'I can't believe it. We had a long talk on the phone early this afternoon.'

'They still don't know who was driving the car that hit them. The guy spooked apparently. After he hit them he took off. Side-swiped a car and made it out to the highway, heading west toward Tahoe. The police put out an APB but they didn't pick him up. The last time my people out there called, about an hour ago, they said residents on the east side of the lake had reported a car in the water. The story was that somebody had gunned a car right off the end of a long pier, done a flop-over, and into the water. Sounds like the same car that hit your wife and Paul. Probably some coked-up kid, the police think.'

When the phone rang, Rosenthal said, 'Let me get it. I told them they could call me here.' He picked up the receiver and said, 'Yeah, Vinnie, what have we got?' He listened then and said nothing. Finally he said, 'I'll be here for a while. Get back to me as soon as they check the clothes.' He poured himself a drink and one for Floyd. When he sat down he said, 'They fished the guy out. Drowned. A middle-aged guy. Mister nobody. No identification. A rented car. I don't like the smell of it. The accident doesn't look so accidental, all of a sudden.'

'What do you mean?'

'It's the first thing we thought of, that somebody had pinned a target on Paul. If this joker turns out to be a contract guy then we're right.'

'You think somebody was trying to kill Paul?'

'If it wasn't an accident, then it's a cinch somebody was trying to kill *somebody*.'

Next time the telephone rang, Rosenthal sat at the desk and made notes on a pad of paper. When he hung up he said, 'Looks like I'm right. Not a shred of ID on the guy's clothes. Cheap department store stuff that you could buy any place. And a wind-breaker he must have bought in a thrift shop. The churches collect that stuff and ship it all over. This one came from some store in Indiana.'

'Are you sure?'

'I think so. Let me check here.' He looked at his notes. 'Yeah, that's right. Indiana.'

'What town?'

'I can't read my own writing. Do you know anything about Indiana?'

'A little bit.'

'Is there a place called Crawfordsville?'

Floyd nodded. 'It's Jeannette's home town. You can call your friends in Bellwood and tell them the man they pulled out of the lake is Glenn Tillis. And he wasn't trying to kill Paul. Not unless he mistook him for me.'

[3]

Six hours later Floyd flew to Chicago. Betsy met him there at the airport and they flew on together to Nevada. That afternoon Floyd drove to the police morgue in downtown Bellwood and identified Jeannette's body. Then he went back to an office down the hall to continue a conversation he'd begun earlier with a police lieutenant, Sid Reachi. 'As I told you before, we're in an odd situation here,' Reachi said. 'We started out with the notion that we had three accidental deaths. Negligent homicide maybe, leaving the scene of an accident, various nuts and bolts like that. Nobody to prosecute in any case since all the principals suffered fatal injuries.' He paused. 'But now . . . just in the past few hours, things have taken a new shine. Looks like we could have a double murder and suicide on our hands. You know what I'm saying?'

Floyd nodded.

'When a woman is killed by her ex-husband and then he drives his car into the lake without leaving any skid marks on the road we feel obligated to ask questions. I mean anybody else who might have some answers. I know this is a rough shot for you and I appreciate your giving us some time. As I said, we're not trying to build a case. We'd just like to have some better information before we tag these three deaths and drop them in the file.' He looked down at a bound pad with a half-page of notes pencilled on it. 'You've been a big help with the stuff you've told me about Tillis. It sounds as if he had a motive. It happens more often than you might think. We get quite a few cases where somebody says, "If I can't have you, nobody else is gonna have you either," and the bullets start to fly.'

He tapped his pencil against his teeth. 'The thing that bothers us a little is Buscatore. Does he fit in some way or was he just an innocent bystander?'

'Like I told you. He's my uncle. One of the reasons we leased a place out here was because he told us how great it was. So naturally since we've been here, we've seen him quite a bit. We went to his casino once or twice a week. And the three of us had dinner together every once in a while.'

'So he was a family friend?'

'*Part* of the family. Like I said, he's my uncle.'

'Did this man Tillis know Buscatore?'

'Not as far as I know.'

'So he wouldn't have a grudge against him?'

'I wouldn't think so.'

'I don't want to ask you this,' Reachi said then, 'but I have to. Is there any chance that there was some romantic connection between your wife and Buscatore?'

'Why do you ask that?'

'They were together. He'd picked her up at her home and driven her to the airport in his car.'

'I've taken lots of women to the airport.'

'Did you know that Buscatore was booked to fly to Chicago on the same flight and that they were both booked on a flight to New York three days later?'

'No. I didn't know that. What difference does it make?'

'None maybe. But if Tillis knew something we don't know, maybe Buscatore wasn't an innocent victim after all.'

'Look, Lieutenant, I've told you all I know. If you need more information you'll have to get it somewhere else. I'm not going to sit here and play guessing games about my wife.'

'Just tell me one more thing. Did you know your wife hired two security men to guard her house and take her to the airport?'

'She didn't tell me. But one of your detectives did.'

'Why do you think she hired those men if she knew Buscatore was going with her to the airport?'

'She must have had a reason but I don't know what it was.'

'According to those security guys . . .'

'I'm not interested, Lieutenant.' Floyd stood up. 'Now let me ask you a question. Since this case is closed except for putting it to bed in your files, I assume that none of this speculation you've been talking about will get into the papers. My uncle's lawyer is Mike Rosenthal. I think he'd cause a lot of commotion if people started to speculate in public about Paul and my wife.'

'You're not leaning on me, are you?'

'Not at all. You've been asking for information. I just gave you some.'

[4]

Jeannette's father, Herbert Kinsman, was waiting at the lakeside house with Betsy when Floyd came home.

'This is a tragic moment in all our lives,' Kinsman said. 'My wife and I want you to know that you have our sincere sympathy.'

'And you have mine,' Floyd said.

'Heartbreaking as it is, it's a lesson for us all, I suppose. Our lives hang on a thread. A senseless accident can end it all.' He snapped his fingers. 'Like *that*.'

Betsy turned to Floyd. 'When you called from downtown you said you'd been talking with the police. What do they think happened?'

'We *know* what happened, Betsy,' Kinsman said.

Floyd directed his answer to Betsy. 'Your dad could have accidentally run into Jeannette and Paul. And he could have accidentally driven himself into the lake but the police don't think it happened that way.'

'Of course it happened that way,' Kinsman said. 'That's the story we gave to the Montgomery County paper. Accidental death in a car crash.'

'Daddy drowned,' Betsy said to him. Then back to Floyd. 'What *do* they think happened?'

'They have no proof of anything.'

'Exactly my point,' Kinsman said.

'But there were witnesses, weren't there?' Betsy said.

'Betsy, dear,' Kinsman said. 'Policemen have a habit of looking for guilt. They assume that every accident is a crime. I hope you won't confuse yourself with their speculations.'

'But I want to *know*. There were witnesses, weren't there?'

Floyd nodded. 'The two security men Jeannette hired were there in the airport parking lot.'

'I don't believe that story either,' Kinsman said. 'Jeannette had no enemies. Why would she need protection? She wouldn't hire anyone to protect her.'

'She hired them, Mr Kinsman,' Floyd said. 'There's no doubt about that.'

'What did the guards say?' Betsy asked.

'They said Glen's car didn't seem to be out of control. He didn't swerve or put on the brakes. They heard the engine roar and the car went racing past them. It slammed into the back of Paul's car just as he and Jeannette were opening the trunk. Then he put it in reverse, almost hit the two security men when he backed up, and drove like a maniac out of the airport parking lot.'

'If it was an accident, Grandpa, why would he run away like that?'

'No one's convinced me that he did run away. How do we know it was Glen's car that struck Jeannette?'

'There's no question about that,' Floyd said. 'The guards got the licence number. And when the police fished the car out of the water, the front was caved in. And there was paint from Paul's car on the front bumper.'

'Did anyone see the car go into the lake?' Betsy asked.

'Two people,' Floyd said. 'They said he drove straight out to the end of the pier. The car was picking up speed all the way.'

'It makes no sense to me,' Kinsman said.

'The police don't give a damn whether it makes sense or not,' Floyd said. 'They just try to establish what happened.'

'And they're wrong as often as they're right. We're talking about Betsy's mother and father. I don't want her to have a lot of twisted ideas about them.'

'I *don't* have,' she said.' I know exactly what happened. Daddy killed her and then he killed himself.'

'God help us,' Kinsman said. Then turning to Floyd, 'You see what you've planted in her head.'

'He planted nothing in my head,' Betsy said. 'As soon as I heard she was dead I knew it would be something like this.'

'I don't want to hear any more.' Kinsman stood up and paced to the window. Finally he said, 'I hope I can trust you not to talk about any of these theories of yours when you're at home in Crawfordsville.'

'It's nobody's business but ours, Grandpa. I don't plan to discuss it with anyone.'

'Good. I'll depend on that.' He turned to Floyd again, 'I've made plans with a local mortician and he's had a talk with the coroner. Since you're her husband they need your approval to release the body. I assume you have no objections to my daughter's being laid to rest in Crawfordsville.'

'I have no objections as long as Betsy doesn't.'

'This is something for you and me to decide,' Kinsman said.

'Technically that's true,' Floyd said, 'but whatever Betsy wants is what *I* want.'

'What about Daddy?' she said to Kinsman.

'Don Tillis gave me authorization to claim Glen's body and bring it home on the plane with me. And I'll take Jeannette at the same time. We've scheduled the funerals for next Friday.'

'You're not planning to bury them *together*, are you?'

'Actually, your grandmother and I would have preferred separate services. But Glen's family insisted. They're Catholic, you know. In their eyes Glen and Jeannette are still married.'

'You mean you *are* burying them together?'

'They'd always planned to be buried in the Tillis's family plot at St Boniface Cemetery.'

'That was when they were *married*,' Betsy said. 'She's been married to somebody else for years now. How does the Church feel about *that*?'

'I have no idea. Don Tillis will handle all those matters.'

Betsy looked at Floyd, then back to Kinsman. Finally she said, 'I don't think so, Grandpa. The Church may not object but I do. The idea of them being buried side by side as if nothing had ever happened really bothers me.'

'Now, you listen to me, young lady . . .'

'Wait a minute, Grandpa. The other thing is this. Mom didn't *want* to be buried in Crawfordsville. She hated that whole business of open coffins, of people parading past and viewing the body. She wanted to be cremated. And she put it in her will. Didn't she, Floyd?'

Floyd nodded and Kinsman said, 'Her will has nothing to do with it. No one in our family has ever been cremated and if I have anything to say about it . . .'

'She wanted to be cremated,' Betsy went on, 'and she wanted her ashes buried here in Tahoe. There's a little church with a graveyard about twelve miles from here in the mountains. That's where she wanted to be buried.'

'Well, now,' Kinsman said, 'I'm sure Jeannette had a lot of romantic ideas about how things should be. She always did. But this is a serious matter.' He turned to Floyd. 'You're her husband. You're the final authority.'

Floyd looked at Betsy. Then, 'As I told you Mr Kinsman, I'm leaving this decision to Betsy. It's true that Jeannette wanted to be buried out here. And she did believe in cremation.'

'I don't give a damn about that . . .'

'But *I* do,' Betsy said.

Kinsman made a visible effort to pull himself together, then said to Floyd. 'This is your responsibility, young man. It's not something for a child to decide.'

'I'm not deciding,' Betsy said. 'Mom decided what she wanted.'

Kinsman squared himself up then and fixed each of them with a glare that experience had taught him could turn almost any tide in his favour.

'Let's be sure I understand what's happening here. I came all the way from the Midwest, the most heart-breaking trip of my life, carrying with me not only my own grief but that of my wife. I can think of no sadder job for a parent than bringing home a dead child. But it's a job that must be done. Are you telling me that I'm to go home empty-handed and explain to my wife that our granddaughter has decided to bury her mother in some God-forsaken cowboy cemetery in the mountains of a strange state? Is that it?'

Betsy and Floyd looked at each other and said nothing.

'Are you saying you can't see my point of view, that nothing will persuade you to change your mind?'

'I can't. I'm sorry but I *can't*,' Betsy said.

'So be it,' he said then. 'But be sure to make a note of this date. Because it will trouble your conscience for the rest of your life. And as for you,' he said to Floyd, 'I see your hand in all of this. You were a wicked influence on my daughter and now you're using the same tactics on Betsy. I won't speak to you about *conscience* because I'm sure that would mean nothing. But if what I have to say makes no impression on you, perhaps it will mean something to my granddaughter.'

'I know you hate Floyd,' Betsy said. 'Mom told me that a long time ago. But don't expect *me* to hate him.'

'I don't expect anything. I just hope you're wise enough to see through him. You don't owe him a thing, you know. He's not your stepfather any more now that poor Jeannette is gone. Just remember that if it weren't for him, if your mother had never met him, she and your father would be alive today. I know you're a loyal child. Jeannette was the same way. But in this case your loyalty is misplaced. The sooner you realize that he's *nothing* in your life, the better off you'll be.'

She looked at Floyd, then back to Kinsman.

'It doesn't matter if Floyd is my stepfather or not. What matters is that he treats me like a friend. He always has. Sometimes I think he's my only real friend.'

'God help you,' Kinsman said.

[5]

'I know how you feel,' Frank said, 'but you have to try to put it out of your head.'

'How can I?' Helen said. 'It's the ugliest, most painful thing I ever heard of. If that crazy tortured man was trying to get even, trying for some kind of monumental revenge, he certainly succeeded. I can't even count the people whose lives he's tied in knots. His daughter and Floyd, *his* parents, Jeannette's parents, Paul's family, and me. I lost a brother and a daughter-in-law. I've been physically sick ever since Floyd called me. I can't even imagine how all those other people feel.'

'But it sounds as if Betsy handled it well.'

'She's amazing. But God only knows how she's cut up inside. Floyd said she only broke down once, when they buried Jeannette's ashes. But she pulled herself together and went to Indiana for her father's funeral. God knows how she got through *that* scene with her grandparents. But she did. Then she drove up to my house, where Floyd was waiting for her, and spent several days with us.'

'Will she go back to school?'

'Already left. Drove to South Bend this morning when I brought Floyd here to Chicago to catch his plane for New York. He wanted to drive her back to school but she insisted on going by herself.'

'Did she talk about what happened?'

'Not much. I mean she didn't avoid it if something came up but she didn't seem anxious to hash it over. I'm sure she and Floyd covered things pretty thoroughly in the few days they were together there in Tahoe. It seemed she was more concerned about his feelings than she was about her own.'

'She's lucky,' Frank said. 'Some people are born tough.'

'I don't believe that for a minute. Some people learn to conceal how they feel but underneath it always hurts. Nobody escapes that.'

'Maybe you're right. But, like I said, the best thing you can do is try to put it behind you.'

'That's easy to say, Frank.'

'The only thing that works for me is to keep moving ahead. Concentrate on today and forget about yesterday.'

'Maybe you can do that but most of us can't.'

'Albert Schweitzer said, "The secret of contentment in this life is good health and a bad memory." '

'Don't even *say* that to me. I've heard it before. I hate all those crackerbox formulas.'

'But you have to admit there's something to it,' he said.

'There's *nothing* to it except smart-aleck cynicism. Who wants to *forget* everything when you know that people you love are really suffering?'

'All the same, it has to be done. You have to get a handle on it sooner or later.'

'God, I hate it when you use those *business* expressions in circumstances where they don't belong at all.'

He didn't answer for a moment. Then he said, 'Why do I have the feeling that I'm on trial here? How did I get in bad all of a sudden?'

'You're not in bad. It's just that you're . . . never mind, it doesn't matter.'

'Yes, it does. What were you going to say?'

'I don't want to hurt your feelings.'

'Take a chance,' he said. 'I won't hold it against you.'

'You just seem very cold sometimes.'

'To you?'

'No. This has nothing to do with us. I mean you seem to be able to cut yourself off from situations that involve other people.'

'No compassion?'

'Of course you have compassion. But I sometimes wish you had more.'

'Maybe you're right. But to me, compassion is what you tell yourself you feel when you admit you can't *do* anything about the situation.'

'Sometimes *feeling* is as important as *doing*.'

'That's where we differ. A blind man on a corner with a tin cup doesn't need pity. He needs money to buy a meal. The worst thing you can say to somebody is "I'd like to help you but I can't." '

'No,' she said. 'The worst thing is to say "I don't give a damn." '

'You can't give a damn about *everything*.'

'But you have to give a *damn* about *something*.'

'I think we just hit a stone wall,' he said. 'What shall we talk about now?'

'You really don't understand what I'm saying, do you?'

'Of course I do. And I don't disagree with you. We're not talking about whether bananas taste good or not. We have a difference of opinion as to how many you should eat in one day.'

'There you go again. I'll bet you a dollar you've used that same expression in a dozen business meetings.'

'Maybe a hundred,' he said, 'but so what? An idea is an idea wherever you hear it.'

'That's an *easy* answer. Not to be trusted.'

'What about Floyd? How has he handled this whole thing?'

'He hasn't *handled* it. He feels terrible.'

'I'm sure he does. But I'd be surprised if he's not trying, as much as he can, to put it behind him.'

'Like you're telling me I should do.'

'You *have* to sooner or later. We're not supposed to *die* from grief. It doesn't work that way.'

'Oh, for God's sake, Frank. I feel *miserable*, can't you see that? There's no logic to it. It's nothing I can be reasonable about. You either know how I feel or you don't. It's not something you can talk me out of.'

'I just want you to feel better, that's all.'

'But why should I? When people I care about are suffering, how can *I* feel good? I don't *want* to feel good.'

'That's crazy, Helen. Everybody *wants* to feel good.'

She shook her head slowly and there were tears in her eyes. 'Not everybody, Frank. Not all the time. Sometimes you *have* to feel bad. Sometimes you have to feel so bad you think it's going to kill you. If you don't, there's something wrong with you.'

[6]

Floyd found Jeannette's letter waiting for him at his house in New York. The postmark told him she had mailed it the day before she died. He put the unopened letter in his desk drawer.

The following morning he called the servants together in the dining room. 'I want you to know that I deeply appreciate the expressions of sympathy I received from each of you. Betsy asked me to thank you also. As you can imagine, I have not made any plans beyond the immediate future. There are many details that I have to deal with in the next few weeks. One thing I can tell you, however, is that I have no intention of changing anything as far as this house is concerned. Richard is in charge and he will continue to be. Each of you is needed and appreciated here and I hope you will stay on.'

In a private meeting with Richard later on he said, 'I expect to stay close to home for the next few weeks. Anyone who telephones or comes to visit should be told that I'm still in Chicago. Keep a list of names and I'll return the calls when I'm ready. Otherwise, I want the house to function as it always has.'

There were, of course, details that demanded his attention, but the principal reason for his self-imposed isolation was simply that he wanted a cushion of time, a series of silent hours that would allow him to absorb, as thoroughly as possible, the events of the past two weeks. Feeling as though he had been swimming in a sea of other people's emotions, some impulse told him he needed now to sort out his own.

He felt no general sensation of grief or loss. All the abstract elements of death and dying had slipped past him. The details of family and burial, and in particular his continuing concern for Betsy, had almost persuaded him that he was a functionary rather than a principal performer in the piece.

In his mind during those following weeks, all threads connected to Jeannette, not Jeannette mangled and cremated and buried in an urn, but Jeannette alive, as he'd known her for more than twenty-five years. He sat in the upstairs study that adjoined his bedroom and allowed disconnected incidents and dialogues and impressions to edit themselves together in whatever order they chose. Jeannette at fourteen, Jeannette as a woman. As a mother, as a child, as a wife, as a lover. Laughing, weeping, walking, running, swimming, eating, drinking, dancing. And naked on the bed, in the tub, on the floor, on the grass.

By not attempting to direct his memory, he gave it free rein and full power. The images seemed endless. They raced, strolled, and tumbled after each other, fresh and funny, wistful and wry and familiar. Only weeks later, after he'd come out of his cocoon, only then did reflection tell him that some silent censor had blocked the storage centre in his brain that held the unpleasantness. The shrill anger, the screaming, the drunken wails and accusations, the paranoia, the agony and the cruelty, all these had vanished somehow and left behind only the best of Jeannette, the off-beat, sardonic, self-deprecating, irreverent voluptuary, warm and sweet and crazy, quick to laugh, and splendidly generous with the gift of herself.

This creature crystallized for Floyd in a way that her living, disturbing, and contradictory presence had never permitted before. He saw her, not sentimentally but kindly. He fastened on what she had been and permanently discarded what she had *become*. He sat in his chair by the window and made choices. And Jeannette benefited from each choice he made.

How do we understand such behaviour? The explanation is simple. Whatever Jeannette had done, however she'd changed, however she seemed to disintegrate, Floyd felt directly responsible. When she screamed at him that he had never truly been with her, that somewhere there was someone who occupied the place that Jeannette as his wife had expected to occupy, the truth of what she was saying almost smothered him. Without truly *knowing* anything, she sensed everything. And it became, inevitably, the central motif of their marriage. Once he acknowledged that, he could accept *anything* from her, no matter how distasteful. All of her drunken idiocy and midnight screaming had a rationale. She couldn't define it but she knew it existed. And so did he.

His edited memories of Jeannette then were less forgiveness of her than absolution of himself. If he could pretend that she had in no way sinned against him then he could tell himself that he had presented no provocation. He could pretend that Valerie had not, after all, been an always-present third person in his marriage.

Jeannette's true burial, not of her imperfect self, but of the carefully hand-coloured version that Floyd had created in his study, occurred when he emerged at last from his period of isolation and began to make contact with the outside world. Her final eulogy took place when he burned the last letter she had written him without removing it from its sealed envelope.

[7]

Two weeks before the news of Jeannette's death came to Wingate Fields, Valerie telephoned Jesse's hotel in Paris. When he called her back that evening she said, 'I have to go into London on Wednesday to buy some things. I know it's short notice but I thought perhaps you could meet me there and we could spend the day together.'

They met for lunch at Brown's on Wednesday. When he asked if she'd booked a room there she said, 'No. I'm going back on the late train tonight. I assumed you'd have to get back too.'

'Not at all. I was looking forward to a jolly night in some wicked hotel.'

'That does sound inviting,' she said. 'but I promised Clara I'd be back tonight.'

'Let's telephone her. She won't mind if you come tomorrow.'

'I wish I could. But there's too much on the schedule.'

He went with her on a shopping tour that afternoon. They had tea at a shop on Sloane Street and cocktails later at his club in St James's. After delivering her parcels to the railway station and arranging to have them placed in her compartment on the train, they went for dinner to a small French restaurant in Brook Street. When they were shown to their table Valerie said, 'Perhaps this was a foolish choice. You eat so much French food you may be tired of it.'

'No one ever tires of French food.'

'I suppose not,' she said. 'On the other hand our poor English fare can get quite tiresome.'

'Not to me,' Jesse said. 'I never get tired of English food either.'

'You really have catholic tastes.'

'I just know what I like.'

She studied the menu for a moment. Then she said, 'I know you're equally attached to Paris and Wingate Fields but have you ever wondered, if some circumstance forced you to make a choice, which place you would choose.'

'I could never choose,' he said. 'I've thought of it, of course, but I realize I could never select one place over the other.'

'You're a divided man.'

'Not at all. I'm solid, unchanging, and boring.'

'Not boring. You'll never be boring. You have too much curiosity. Curious men are never boring.'

When they finished their meal and ordered coffee, he said, 'We should have chosen more courses. It's still almost two hours before your train.'

'Perfect. We can have a nice chat. I planned it that way.'

As they sipped their coffee and brandy, she said, 'I have something to say to you. It will make it much less difficult for both of us if you let me finish before we have a general discussion.'

'Am I going to be scolded?'

'No, Jesse, nothing like that.' She dropped a lump of sugar into her coffee and stirred it slowly. At last she said, 'I've known you since I was three years old and I'll soon be forty. That's a very long time. You've always been the most important person in my life. We've been married for many years and for me it's been a very happy marriage. But I don't want to be married to you any longer.'

'What in the world does that mean?'

'Exactly what it sounds like, Jesse. I want a divorce. If you won't give it to me, if you decide to make things difficult, I will simply go to live with my father at Bick House.'

'I don't believe what I'm hearing.'

'I'm not trying to upset you. I don't mean to hurt your feelings. But my mind is made up. So I think I must be as honest and direct as I can be.'

'Are you telling me that you came to a final decision about this without even mentioning it to me?'

'There was nothing to discuss. There's not a lot to discuss now for that matter. This is not a bargaining session. I'm not trying to *get* something from you.'

'You're asking me for a divorce. That seems like quite a lot to me.'

'I'm not asking you for a divorce. I'm not *asking* for anything. I'm simply telling you what I've made up my mind to do. You can make things awkward for me perhaps but you can't alter the result.'

'You're angry as hell, aren't you?'

'No. *Angry* is not the word. If I were going to be angry, I suppose I'd be angry at myself. But the fact is I'm not angry at all.'

He sat looking at her for a long moment. 'Does Clara know about this?' he said then.

'Not yet. But she will know when I get home.'

'Do the children know?'

'Of course not.'

After a moment, he said, 'I don't know what to say to you. You're like a stranger suddenly. I don't know how you expect me to react . . .'

'I expected you to be angry and I hoped you'd understand.'

'What is it I'm supposed to understand?'

'That I don't hate you, that I mean what I'm saying, and that nothing you can say will change how I feel.'

'How do you feel? To me it's like sitting here with . . . I don't know. You're like someone who's memorized a speech and then carefully recited it.'

She smiled. 'Not exactly. I did give a lot of thought to what I wanted to say, however.'

'But all you've given me is *nothing*. You must have reasons. You've been thinking about this for a long time, haven't you?'

'Not really. The roots are deep, perhaps, but nothing crystallized until quite recently. I simply realized that we had something very wonderful for a long time but now we no longer have it.'

'Since when?'

'I don't know. If you're trying to make me tie this to some specific event, I can't do that. I won't do it because it wouldn't be accurate.'

'What about Floyd?'

'What about him? If I were going to leave you for Floyd I'd have done it long ago, wouldn't I?'

'But there has to be *something*.'

'If you want me to say that it's because of you and Nora I won't say that either. Why would I have waited till now? I've known about that ever since it started.'

'Known about what?' he said.

'Don't do a dance for me, Jesse. There's no point to it. Did you imagine I didn't know what was going on between you two?'

He smiled and signalled the waiter for more cognac. 'Ahhhh,' he said. 'Now it comes out. Are we having this conversation because of something you've created in your mind? Are you telling me you're leaving me because you've decided I'm having some sort of arrangement with Nora?'

'No, I told you that wasn't the reason. And it's not. But don't make a fool of yourself, Jesse. Don't try to pretend that the "arrangement" as you call it doesn't exist.'

'I don't have to pretend anything. You know why I spend time in Paris. You were the major factor in my decision to work there again.'

'I know that.'

'Of *course* I see your mother when I'm there. We have business matters to discuss. And sometimes we're at the same social functions. It's no secret. I usually mention it to you when I see her. But for God's sake, don't blow that up into something it isn't.'

'Please. It's a good act but it won't work. I know about the house on Rue Bardinet. I'm not imagining things. I *know* what's going on.'

Jesse hesitated. Then he said. 'That's a house that Nora leased for some reason. It has nothing to do with me.'

'It's no use, Jesse, I talked with a solicitor in London. He has associates in Paris. Inquiries were made. Someone questioned the servants. I'm not *guessing* about anything.'

Jesse looked down at his brandy glass and turned it slowly in his fingers. Finally he looked up. 'What do you want me to say?'

'Nothing, Jesse. I don't expect you to say anything.'

[8]

All of the Bradshaws, Clara and Nora, Valerie and Jesse, wrote letters of condolence to Floyd when they heard of Jeannette's death. And a few days later Clara wrote a long letter to Helen.

> What terrible, painful news. The sort of thing one reads about in the papers or hears discussed on the wireless but that you're sure could never happen to your own family. Although I never met Jeannette I felt a bond with her because she was Floyd's wife. I kept hoping he would bring her here to Wingate Fields one day.
>
> How sad it must be for him. And for his step-daughter. I can't imagine what effect that would have on a young girl, knowing her father killed her mother. I hope she and Floyd are close. She'll need all the support she can find now. You say she's gone back to school. That's good. But what about Floyd? Will he spend some time in Fort Beck with you or has he gone back to New York? I've asked him to come here whenever he feels like it. I hope you'll encourage him to do that. Betsy, too, of course. And you know how eager I am for you to come for a long visit. I am an extremely robust and healthy woman of eighty five but I am, after all, eighty-five. And the clock keeps ticking.
>
> We have some sad news here, too. It's so upsetting for me that I hesitate to write about it, even to you. But it's a *fait accompli*, it seems, so you'll know about it soon, one way or another.
>
> Valerie has told Jesse she wants a divorce. I know I've written you from time to time that I sensed things

were not as perfect as they might be, not as smooth and pleasant as they had once been, but it never occurred to me that it would come to this. As you know Valerie and I are very close. But she has told me nothing that would explain what brought all this about. She seems unbelievably cool and contained about the whole affair. She says, 'We were married for a long time and we have three fine children, but now it's over. So far I've devoted my life to other people. Now, I think, I'll devote some time to myself.'

Does that sound like Valerie to you? Of course not, Nor to me. She is so calm and self-assured, it's frightening. No self-doubt whatsoever. Or so it appears. But at the same time she seems as warm and caring, as concerned about Jesse and the children as she ever was. 'Of course I love Jesse,' she says. 'I'll always love him. I loved him long before we married and I expect to love him long after we're divorced. But I'm not *in* love with him any longer and I think it's sinful to spend the rest of my life pretending.'

So here I am. In the centre of all this. One day I'm astonished by Valerie's attitude. The next day I admire her and envy her for her courage. When I remember the charade of a marriage I experienced with Ned I often think how much better off both of us would have been if I'd had the will that Valerie has. But, as you know, those were different days. Different restrictions, different guilts.

As I write this I realize that while you're young enough to be my daughter and old enough to be Valerie's mother you are, in many ways, more of her generation than of mine. You've been divorced and have chosen a pattern of life that was never available to me. And if it *had* been available, I'm not certain that I would have been wise enough or fearless enough to make some of the choices you've made.

And how about Jesse? How has he reacted to all this? It's hard to say. I've seen him just once since Valerie announced to me what she planned to do. He was here briefly when the two of them drove down to the children's schools to tell them they've decided to separate. It's all too dreadfully sophisticated for me. Jesse will have his separate rooms here as he did years ago, he will continue to spend time here and, of course, Valerie will still be here.

Jesse seemed almost removed from the situation when he was here those two days. Now that the die is cast one senses no tension between him and Valerie. On the surface at least, they behave like two people planning a family outing to the seaside. I am not deceived by that of course. There are undoubtedly currents running beneath the surface. But to my eyes at least all is concealed.

There has been no communication whatsoever from Nora since all this transpired. Does that mean she knows less about it than I do? Or more? My instinct tells me that perhaps she knows a great deal. I suspect that if Jesse needs consolation, Nora will be more than willing to provide it. Perhaps she has been providing it all along, but that is no affair of mine.

When I asked Valerie how the children had reacted to the news that their parents would separate, she said she had been astonished. All three of them, Rab and Polly and young Bill, seemed intrigued. Rab said, 'I'm not surprised. It seems quite the thing to do these days.' Polly pretended concern but was obviously titillated by the romantic aspects of the situation, and Bill, once it had been explained to him that his own life and his relationships with his parents would be unchanged, saw no reason to fret. 'Many of my schoolfriends have a stepmother or a stepfather and they think it's quite grand.'

'They seem to have new respect for us,' Valerie told me. 'I'm sure they believed we were too ancient and set in our ways to do anything that might surprise them. They're selfish little beasts and I think they see it as a great adventure for them.'

So there we are, Helen. Further evidence of how the world is rocking beneath us. But in another respect, one thing seems to stay constant among the Bradshaws. For all of our good fortune through many generations in matters of commerce, animal husbandry, and land speculation, we have been less lucky in marriage. Even as a child, I felt my parents had an uneasy relationship. And as they grew older, of course, it deteriorated further. Ned and I tried to put the best possible face on *our* marriage, I more than he, but very few people were deceived. My brother had, as you know, a tragic romance followed by a failed marriage, and both of my children foundered as well, Nora with a nasty divorce, and Hugh with an odd marriage that *should* have ended but endured, unhappily, till his death. You, too, have been plagued, it seems, by the Bradshaw luck. Married once, divorced once, and then suffering the death of a man you truly cared for. Not an exemplary record for any of us. Who would have guessed that Jesse and Valerie would follow in our less-than-laudable footsteps. Not I, surely. In principle theirs was an odd joining, a marriage between a man and a young woman who was in many respects, like a daughter to him. But after my initial surprise, I began to feel that the unlikely nature of their marriage gave it strength. And as the years passed, I believed this more strongly. The rarest thing of all is an alliance that has a foundation of long friendship before it becomes a romance. I can't describe what a pleasure it was to live under the same roof with them for all these years, seeing them together, watching them bring up their children, marvelling at the lovely things I saw in their lives that I had never found in my own. I know of nothing that could have surprised me more than Valerie's announcement that they were separating. Even if I had seen some deterioration, even if I'd sensed that all was not precisely as it had once been — and I did observe small worrisome things — there was nothing to suggest serious problems, no intimation that they might choose to part after all these years.

But it's coming to pass. And the very calmness of the process is almost as disturbing as the fact of it. I haven't heard an angry word, haven't seen a tear shed. It all seems preordained, as though a timer had been set on their wedding day and had been ticking steadily through all this time. But now the ticking's stopped, so they must stop.

I'm sure there are details I don't know. Perhaps many such details. But I'm glad I don't know those things. Still I can't help wondering. It's not a pleasant task, watching something that I assumed would survive me come slowly apart, one bit at a time.

[9]

The day Jesse came back from England, after visiting the children at their schools, he came into Nora's bedroom and found her crying. Sitting in a chair in her dressing gown, silent and immobile, with tears in her eyes.

'Go away,' she said, covering her face with her hands.

'I don't want to go away,' he said, kneeling down beside her.

'I don't want you to see me. I *hate* to cry.'

'I know you do.'

'Don't put your arms around me or I'll really come apart.'

'No, you won't,' he said. 'It's better like this. You'll see.'

He stayed there with his arms around her for a long time. At last, after she stopped crying, he said, 'Are you better now?'

'I don't know if I'm better but I'm all cried out.'

'I thought you were planning to have lunch with me.'

'I was but I can't. I'm a mess.'

'No, you're not. You can go to a plastic surgeon for two hours and I'll meet you at Lipp's at one o'clock.'

When she came into the restaurant to join him he said. 'You see . . . the miracle of surgery. You look great.'

'I don't look great. But at least I look *better*. If I stay in a dim light.'

While they had lunch he told her the details of his meetings with the children in England. When he finished, she said, 'So it went well?'

'I suppose so. I have nothing to compare it to.'

'At least no one had hysterics.'

He shook his head. 'Nothing like that. Everyone was calm and civilized and grown up.'

'Except you.'

'That's right. I was the shakiest one.'

'Are you better now?'

'Not much. I feel terrible.'

'So do I,' she said.

'You weren't even there.'

'Oh, yes, I was. Where do you think my head has been since you left? Nothing is ever as bad as what happens in your imagination. I went through a thousand different hells waiting for you to come back.'

'Was that what this morning was all about?'

'No. That was the after-shock. I didn't start crying till you called from the airport and I knew you were back. Then the floodgates opened and I couldn't stop.'

'How long have I known you now?'

'A long time,' she said.

'I've never seen you cry like that.'

'That's because I've never done it before. There were a lot of tears saved up and they all came down.'

'I'm sorry.'

She shook her head. 'It's not your fault. When you were gone all I thought about was *you* and what you had to do. Once you were back it was *me* trying to come to terms with *me*.'

'And making no progress?'

'None at all. I was walking on cotton wool. The floor kept tilting under my feet. You know me. My whole security is based on being in control. I don't mean I have to control the world or even a roomful of people. But I have to feel as if I'm in control of myself.'

'But not this morning,' he said.

'Not at all this morning. I couldn't think of anything about myself that wasn't hateful. Maybe it sounds funny to you . . .'

'No, it doesn't.'

'God save us all from seeing ourselves objectively. And that's what swamped me this morning. A great drenching wave of ugly objectivity. I felt like a beast. I *still* feel like a beast.'

'I told you this before but I'm going to tell you again. If you think Valerie and I are splitting up because of you, you're mistaken. That was practically the first thing she said to me.'

'I know that,' Nora said. 'And you believe it. But I don't believe it and it's driving me crazy. I'll bet my mother doesn't believe it either.'

'Valerie didn't tell Clara. She doesn't know about us.'

'Clara knows *everything*. Nobody has to tell her.'

'Not this time. She thinks Valerie's gone dotty. She doesn't know what she's up to.'

'And you don't know either,' Nora said.

'All I know is what she says.'

'And all I know is what you say. I don't really know how you feel about all this. I thought about that a lot when you were gone.'

'I told you. I feel awful about it.'

'Too general. Let me ask you this: if Valerie changed her mind suddenly, if she decided not to get a divorce, what would you say?'

'I wouldn't say anything.'

'How would you feel? I mean how would you really feel? And don't just tell me what you think I want to hear.'

'I'd be glad,' he said.

'What if it meant you and I could never . . .'

'You answer that. If Valerie came to you and said she'd stay with me if you'd promise that everything between us was over, what would *you* say?

'I'd promise,' Nora said.

'There's your answer. So would I.'

'We're a fine pair, aren't we? One as loyal as the other.'

'There are all kinds of loyalty,'

After a long moment, Nora said, 'What if we went to her? What if we promised . . .'

'It wouldn't do any good. I already tried it.'

'That means whatever we do or don't do . . .'

'That's right,' he said. 'It won't matter.'

'Except to us.'

He nodded. 'Except to us.'

'So after all these years we're together by default. No opposition.'

'It looks that way,' he said.

'Can we survive that?'

'Life among the wreckage, you mean?'

She nodded.

'I don't know. What do you think?'

'I don't know either,' she said. 'I guess we'll have to wait and see.'

Chapter Eleven

[1]

One morning in July 1960, Helen's housekeeper told her that a downstairs screen had been removed during the night and an attempt had been made to open the window. Two days later, the gardener discovered the lock had been broken on the basement door and someone had tried to pry open the inside door that led upstairs to the kitchen. On both occasions the police were informed. After an inspection of the premises they concluded that an alarm system should be installed.

At three in the morning, July 17th, Henry Barth, a zoology professor at the university, called the police to report a disturbance in the house next door to him.

'I heard somebody screaming. So I put on my robe and hurried right over there. But when I got up on the porch and rang the bell, someone threw a heavy ashtray through the door-glass from the inside and a piece of glass cut my cheek. As I ran back to my own house, I heard a man's voice shouting and a woman screaming again. I'm afraid something terrible has happened to my neighbour.'

Professor Barth's neighbour was Enid Zoeller from the university admissions office. When the police broke down her door a few minutes after receiving Barth's call they found her naked and unconscious on the living-room floor. Her face was bruised and bleeding and her arm was twisted under her at an odd angle.

In the kitchen they found Doug Slocum, crouched in a corner behind the refrigerator, mumbling and whimpering and wearing only a blood-stained shirt. Eye-shadow was smeared around his eyes, there were bright spots of rouge on his cheeks, and his lips were blood-red with lipstick. In his hands he held Enid's torn underclothing.

[2]

'I feel so sorry for him I can't find words for it,' Helen said. She was in Chicago with Frank five days later.

'*I* feel sorry for *Enid Zoeller*.'

'I knew you'd say that. How did I know you'd say that?'

'Because it's logical. I guarantee you the people of Fort Beck are not passing the hat to build up a defence fund for your friend Slocum.'

'He is my friend. That's the point.'

'He's crazy, Helen. Crazy people don't know about friendship. They just know about being crazy.'

'That's ridiculous. If everybody thought the way you do, the world would be filled with crazy people.'

'It is already. And nobody had to make them that way. You don't need lessons to be cuckoo.'

'You're disgusting.'

'You say he was your friend. All right. He was Enid Zoeller's friend, too, wasn't he?'

'Not exactly.'

'Not *exactly* is right. But if I'd asked you two weeks ago you'd have said, "Of course he's Enid's friend." Isn't that true?'

'I don't know. And it doesn't matter anyway. Maybe he didn't know how to be a friend. But I felt like his friend. And I feel as if I let him down.'

'For Christ's sake, Helen, do you know what you're saying? Do you know how lucky you are not to be lying in the hospital with a broken arm and a ruined face like that poor woman?'

'He would never have done that to me.'

'What makes you so sure? How do you know?'

'I just know,' she said.

'Then why did he do it to her?'

'I don't know the answer to that.'

'Of course not. Because there isn't any answer. We're talking about a man who's spent half his life in an institution. Not because he's a criminal. I'm not saying that. But because his mind doesn't work right and he has a history of violence. I'm not blaming him. And I do feel sorry for the poor bastard. But I don't think the thing that ails him can be cured with hot cocoa and a pat on the head.'

'He's disturbed. That's not a crime.'

'He's not just disturbed. From what you said, the doctors at the institution in Richmond consider him dangerous. They didn't come all the way from Virginia just for the ride, did they? They're taking him back there, aren't they?'

'That's just the problem. Once you're institutionalized, people think you should be there for life.'

Frank shook his head. 'You're missing the point, Helen. If he weren't going back to Virginia, he'd be going to prison in Illinois.'

'I don't care what you say. I knew him and you didn't.'

'You didn't know him at all. You thought he was a poor neglected kid trying to make something of himself. It turns out he comes from a good family. His father owns a business in Roanoke. He has a nice brother and sister. Isn't that right?'

Helen nodded. 'But it doesn't matter.'

'You and all the people at Foresby thought he was a war veteran. Went through hell in Korea, all that stuff. It turns out he was never drafted, never put on a uniform, never fired a gun. He lied about everything. So how can you say you knew him?'

'Because I *did*. I'm talking about what he is, not what he said about himself. None of us are finished products. Do you think you're the same now as you were when you were Doug's age?'

'Probably not. But what does that have to do with it?'

'Everything. Most of us change because of the people we're exposed to.'

'For every expert who says that there's another one who says we don't change fundamentally after age six.'

'I'm not talking about theories. I'm talking about life the way we live it. Don't you think you and I have had some effect on each other?'

'No question about it. But if you were mentally deficient when I met you I guarantee you you'd be mentally deficient today.'

'That's like saying, "Life has no meaning." '

'Not at all. I'm saying we face a hundred problems every day. Most of them can be solved. But some of them can't. It's important to know which is which.'

'You're talking like a businessman again. I'm talking about human problems and I don't think they fall into neat categories. If a woman has a rigid idea of what all men are like I suspect that exposure to a different sort of man might have some effect on her beliefs. It's easy to live by your prejudices if no one ever contradicts you or if you never question yourself. Most people who hate avocados have never tasted one.'

'Are you saying that all Doug needed was the love of a good woman?'

'No. I'm saying he might very well have benefited from some civilized contact with an unthreatening woman.'

'Like you?'

'Yes. Like me. I think he was reaching out to me and till the day I die I'll regret that I didn't respond to him.'

'In spite of everything that's happened you still feel that way?'

'I certainly do,' she said.

'In that case I don't think we'd better talk about it any more.'

'If we do, you'll get angry. Right?'

'I didn't say that.'

'I know you didn't say it, but I *know* you.'

'Let's have a drink,' he said then.

'That's a good idea.'

He walked over to the liquor table, poured two drinks and carried the glasses back to the couch where she was sitting. When he sat in the chair facing her, he said, 'It's not a question of anger. Let's just say it's disconcerting to watch an intelligent person trying to make an intelligent case for an absurd proposition.'

She felt her cheeks getting suddenly warm. 'I'd put it another way. I find it disconcerting to try to have an open-minded discussion with someone whose mind is closed.'

Frank smiled and tried to pass it off. 'Thank God you're not talking about *me*.'

She smiled too. 'Yes. That *would* be a calamity, wouldn't it?'

[3]

Three days after coming home from Chicago, Helen flew to Portland, Maine. She told no one where she was going. To her housekeeper she said, 'I need to get away for a little while to clear my head. If anyone asks, tell them I've gone off for a few days but you don't know where. You won't be able to call me but I'll call you.'

In Maine she rented a car at the airport. Before heading north toward Hedrick she drove across downtown Portland and found the building she had come to that autumn in 1919 to arrange for her baby's adoption the following spring.

Pulling into the parking lot, she sat there in her car in the midday warmth studying the entrance to the building, remembering her first visit there, her interview with the director, Dr Kilwinning, and her subsequent talk with him, six or seven years later. She'd begged him for some information about her son and he'd refused, telling her at last only one thing, that the boy's name was Floyd.

She had not planned to go inside the building but suddenly she opened the car door and walked to the entrance. At the reception desk, she asked if Dr Kilwinning was still the director.

The young woman behind the desk smiled and said, 'Dr Kilwinning retired fifteen years ago. Can someone else help you?'

'No. I don't believe so. Thank you very much.'

She drove north through Brunswick and Bath, then through Wiscasset to Damariscotta. Bypassing Hedrick, she drove into Round Pond and parked in the restaurant parking lot. There were summer rental cabins now in the grassy field by the restaurant. And a new house had replaced the Jackovich house that had overlooked the harbour but had burned just a week after Chet died.

The high wharf where the lobstermen pulled in was just as she remembered it. When Chet had worked on the boat engines here as well as the ones in Hedrick, she had spent long summer hours on the soft grass of the slope up the road, reading or doing needlepoint, waiting for him to finish so they could drive home to the house in the woods.

She remembered clearly the first time she'd seen this harbour. It had seemed to her, the harbour and the village, like a forgotten corner, operating on a time scheme that served its own purposes but was in no way connected to the clocks and sun-dials and chronometers of the rest of the world. It seemed that way to her still; she felt a cool thrill of relaxation as she sat there.

Driving back towards Damariscotta she again avoided Hedrick, avoiding more specifically Opal and Bud Feaster who had befriended and served her through the years in more ways than she could count. They had introduced her to Chet and they had shared the short years she spent with him as much as anyone had been allowed to share that time. She couldn't tell herself now why she was avoiding them. She couldn't admit to herself that after all the painful time had passed she was still reluctant, afraid perhaps, to relive those years with the only two people who had been eyewitnesses to that time of joy and heart-break.

Whatever her personal fears, however, she had persuaded herself by the time she checked into the little shingled hotel in Damariscotta that she could not cloister herself there and not see the Feasters. So, as soon as she was alone in her room, she went to the phone and dialled their number.

An unfamiliar voice answered. 'You're out of luck, lady. You just missed them. They left here first thing this morning. They've got a little camp up on Millinocket Lake and I reckon they'll be there till Bud gets his fill of fishing. If you know Bud, there ain't no telling *how* long that's liable to be.'

The next morning she did drive into Hedrick, a village two coves away from Round Pond. Having planned originally to avoid Opal and Bud, the sight of their house overlooking the harbour made her long to sit again in that great open kitchen where Bud and Chet had sat so many nights at the long table, their chairs tilted back against the wall, while she and Opal sat with them.

She parked her car beside their house and walked along the road that circled the harbour, followed it all the way to the mouth, to the small grey bungalow she had rented for those months while she and Chet were performing a deliberate mating ritual that had its finish only when he had completed his careful, almost sculptural, work on the house in the woods and they had moved into it together.

She drove around the area for two or three days, to Boothbay, Bristol, Walpole, and New Harbour. Then north and east to Waldoboro, Thomaston, St George and Port Clyde. She was postponing her first sight, after many years, of the house in the woods. Not from fear, she told herself, but to heighten the pleasure. But she was fearful too. The memory of those months alone there after Chet died, the kind of death that she herself had gone through then, was jagged and ugly for her still, clearer in her mind than the tender times that had gone before. But as she drove along that sharp, unrivalled coastline she threatened and chided herself until the pendulum was nudged heavily to the other side, until she'd worn out the sadness by too much page-turning. At last she was eager to drive to the woods off the Star route and walk back along the rough lane to Chet's house.

The next morning after breakfast she drove to the house. She was surprised to see that the drive-in from the road was mowed and gravelled. By the front door, toys were scattered around and when she walked behind the house she found a young woman hanging clothes on the line. Two small children, a boy and a girl, played on the grass nearby.

'I hope I didn't startle you,' Helen said. 'I didn't see anybody out front so I just came round.'

'That's all right. This is where I am most of the time when the weather's good, back here hanging up wash. You wouldn't believe how many didies I wash in a week.' She patted her stomach, 'And when this one comes I'll have a few more. If you're looking for Marion, he's not here. He's up Rockland way this morning.'

'No. I really came by just to look at your house. A friend of mine built this place. I used to live here.'

'It's not our house. We just rent it off of the Feasters. Marion's folks are moving into Portland this fall and we'll be taking over their place down by Pemaquid. God knows we need the extra room. I just hope we can make the switch before this one I'm carrying comes. But it's doing a lot of kicking so it wouldn't surprise me if I get another preemie like Brucie was.'

'Do you mind if I walk around a little? It's a long time since I was here last.'

'Make yourself at home,' the young woman said. 'Go right inside if you feel like it. The breakfast dishes are still in the sink but outside of that the place is as tidy as it ever is. My kids ain't much for neat. And neither is Marion.'

Helen went inside the house, stood in the big downstairs room and studied the details of beam and floor and wood-work that Chet had carefully wedged and mortised and pegged together. Most of their furniture, worn and battered now, was still here. And the beautiful rug they'd carried home from an auction in Thomaston, stained and frayed now, was still in place on the floor by the fireplace. Upstairs in the loft, the wide bed Chet had built in the corner was still there, too. Carefully made up with soft pillows and a home-done quilt.

After a slow second look at the downstairs she walked out on the screened porch that faced the back yard. 'Is it all right if I sit here for a few minutes,' she called out to the young woman who was still hanging up wet clothes.

'Go right ahead. I've got yard work to do when I finish here. And I can't keep these two outlaws in the house anyhow when the weather's nice like it is today.'

Helen sat on the porch swing Chet had put up and looked out across the yard he'd cleared to the woods. They'd walked there every evening when the ground was dry.

She had prepared herself for sadness. But it didn't come. Rather, as she sat there, she remembered the details of the days and nights she'd spent in this house. Meals she had cooked, radio programmes they'd listened to together, stories he'd told about his life, long conversations on the couch by the fire with heavy snow outside banked high against the windows. She was astonished, as she sat there, to find how clearly the words and the events and the feelings came back to her.

She'd once written to Clara describing this unlikely man she'd found.

> He doesn't own a suit of clothes or a necktie. His entire wardrobe, in fact, except for his winter coat, would fit into one canvas duffel bag. He wears heavy work shoes when he's outdoors and when he comes inside he takes them off and pads about in his sock feet. He doesn't read books, he's never been inside an art museum, he's never heard a symphony orchestra, and he's never owned a car that wasn't a truck. So what am I doing with such a man? I don't know for sure. We've known each other only a short time but I'm really attached to him. How does he feel about it? I can't be sure of that either. He doesn't admit it but I think he needs me. And I hope he loves me. He says he's not a gentleman and I suppose he's not. But he's the gentlest man I've ever seen and I adore him.

For the first time in many years she allowed herself to think about him, to remember details of how he'd looked the first time she'd met him in the Feaster's kitchen.

Chet was not a tall man, no taller than Helen. His face

was lined and weather-beaten, his brown hair streaked with grey, and his body looked as though it had never carried an extra ounce of flesh. All of him seemed, in fact, to be a complex extension of his hands. Those hands were all bones and knuckles and angry tendons. Broken nails and thick calloused pads on palms and fingers. The grease from a thousand engines had been ground through the surface of the skin to a level no soap could reach. His denim jacket and chambray shirt, however, and his corduroy trousers, were worn but clean. And the eyes in his hard face were as soft and brown as the eyes of an Irish setter.

She remembered, too, what he'd said to her that first time they met, as they sat in the Feaster's parlour just off the kitchen. 'Don't make the mistake of falling in love with me. For one thing I'm old enough to be your father. I was fifty years old this year. Number two . . . I've got a wife and daughter floating around some place out in California.And if that's not enough to stop you, I'm dying. Two years to live, they tell me. Three or four at the outside. Not a good bet for any woman.'

Later on, before they'd begun to live together, before they'd allowed themselves to be together the way both of them wanted to be, he'd said, 'I don't want you to think I'm something I can't be. I wouldn't want you to expect something I can't deliver. I'm the same guy now that I was when I was twenty years old. Same as I was when I was in the army. And I'll be like that, I guess, from now on. So if you're gonna get tired of me I hope it happens now. Or pretty soon at least. Before I've swum out so far I can't get back.'

All through the spring and summer she'd watched him put together the house in the woods. At last, near the end of August when even Chet could find nothing more to tighten or loosen or smooth with sandpaper, they stood in front of the fireplace with their arms around each other and Helen said: 'It's finished, isn't it?'

'You never know with a place like this.'

'It's *finished,*' she insisted. She held his face in her hands and kissed him. 'I love you,' she said. 'You're a wonderful man and you've built a wonderful house.'

The next day they moved all her things from her house to his. They ate and drank there, slept and lived there together from that day till Chet died.

One day Opal, complaining that she and Bud never saw

them, had asked Helen what they did with themselves all the time.'

'Well, we sleep late in the morning. Then we take a long time eating breakfast,' Helen told her. 'A little after midday Chet goes to the lobster docks in Hedrick or Round Pond and works on whatever engines need attention till five or so. When he's gone, I do chores around the house or read a book while I keep an eye on whatever I'm fixing for supper. Or I play with the cat or pick ticks off the dog. Lots of exciting stuff like that. Then when Chet comes home he takes a bath. And while he's getting dressed I take a bath.'

'Then you sit there and get swizzled every night.'

'Not every night,' Helen said. 'We eat our supper and listen to Amos and Andy and Lum and Abner. Chet loves the radio. Then we play euchre or Casino or just sort of kid around till we get sleepy and go to bed.'

'And that's it?'

'That's it.'

As the months went by she had begun to hope that Chet's illness was in remission. As more time passed, that hope became a conviction. Then he collapsed one day and was taken to the Portland Hospital. He stayed there for five weeks. On the day he was released the doctor told Helen, 'He must be hospitalized for treatment one week out of four, he must take his medication and injections at home on the schedule we've laid out for him. He must follow his diet and not use tobacco or alcohol. And he must rest in bed except for four hours each day when he's allowed to sit up in a chair.'

'I'm not sure he can live like that,' Helen said.

'Then he won't live at all.'

Sitting there in the swing on the screened porch, the redwood chair she'd found him in that last morning just beside her, Helen relived those final moments. She'd wakened just before dawn. He was not in bed with her and the house seemed silent in an unfamiliar way. When she ran downstairs she found him sitting up in his chair on the porch. Until she saw the empty prescription bottles she thought he was sleeping.

There was a whisky glass on the table beside him, under it a scrap of paper on which he'd scrawled a few words.

> I'm sorry, kid. I'm not cut out to be an invalid and you're not cut out to be a nurse. Just remember that

nobody ever had it as good as we did. It's the only part of my life I can remember.

[4]

As she flew from Portland to Chicago Helen tried to plan precisely what she would say to Frank when she saw him that afternoon. Her thoughts scurried back and forth but didn't settle anywhere. When he met her in the arrival lounge at the airport she said, 'Are you mad at me?'

'Of course not. Why would I be mad at you?'

'Well, it's not very nice to disappear for two weeks and not tell anyone where you are.'

'I know you pretty well by now,' he said. 'You're like a bear. You have to crawl into your cave every once in a while.'

He asked no questions, seemed to expect no explanations. He was totally agreeable. And that agreeableness made her wary. Still she was determined to follow the course she had selected. After dinner that evening she edged her way into it.

'You're right about me. I do have to hibernate from time to time. Add up my debts and try to see if I've collected any assets.'

'Why not? Sounds normal to me. God help those poor souls who can't draw a breath unless there are five or six people in the room. Nothing like a little silence to clear out your carburettor.'

'Do you want to know where I went?'

He shook his head. 'That's your business.'

'I'll tell you anyway. To Hedrick in Maine. The place where I stayed when I was waiting for Floyd to be born.'

'And the place where you lived with Chet.'

'That's right. I wasn't sure you'd remember. It's a long time since I told you that.'

He tapped his forehead. 'Just like a steel vault.' Then, 'How about the assets?'

'What?'

'Did you discover any hidden assets there that you'd forgotten about?'

She shook her head. 'Didn't really expect to. I just thought it might be good for me to sit on a rock and look at the ocean for a few days.'

'Was it?'

'I'm not sure but I think it was. Do you ever say to yourself, "What am I doing? What am I *really* doing?" '

'All the time.'

'Do you ever wonder what you and I are up to?'

'Never. I know exactly what we're up to.'

'I'm serious.'

'So am I.'

'I wasn't really looking for anything in Maine,' she went on, 'but I had a feeling that I was very different when I lived there, different from the way I've been these last few years. I wanted to see if being there . . . you know what I mean.'

'What did you find out?'

'I'm not sure. Nothing maybe. But it's amazing how just seeing a place you knew before can trigger all kinds of strange things inside you.'

'Like what?'

'It's hard to say. I mean it's not the kind of experience where you can sit down and make a list. It's just a feeling. You stand back and see yourself in those familiar circumstances and you start to think, "Oh, yeah. I recognize that creature. I know what she was up to. I remember what made her tick and toddle and move forward." '

'You were very different then, is that what you're saying?'

'Not very different, maybe. But different, all the same.'

'How so?'

'I was trying to be specific about that this morning on the plane flying to Chicago and I decided I was more productive then. Busier. More involved in all kinds of things.'

'That's because you were young and full of beans.'

She shook her head. 'I don't think so. In some ways I was older when you and I got married than I am now. I thought there was a formula for doing everything. I was always looking for the best way. It took me a long time to learn to live in the present, to let my life discover me.'

'And now you've learned that?'

'A lot more than before. Haven't I?'

He nodded. 'No question about it.'

'So anyway, I was looking around and thinking how I used to be and how different I seem now, at least to myself, and I started getting excited about that. Then I said to myself, "Nothing's really happening to you. You're just picking up things from the past." '

'Thud,' Frank said.

'That's right. The wind went right out of my sails. But not for long. Finally I said to myself, "If a place can stimulate you like that, if a change of scene can get your heart pumping, then maybe that's the answer. Spend a bit of time away from Fort Beck. Go back to a few places you saw a long time ago. Be what you were then. Stretch yourself. See new things. Learn new things." You know what I'm saying? Does it make any sense?'

'Of course it does.'

'I certainly don't feel old but I see people getting old all around me and I feel like giving them a push and saying, "Don't do this to yourself. Come to life." '

'Nobody has to say that to *you*.'

'Maybe not. But all the same, I want more. I want to surprise myself. I want to see if there are some secret compartments inside me that I've never opened. I want to use myself.'

'Nobody could quarrel with that impulse.'

'Do you mean it? I wasn't sure what you'd say.'

'I just said it.'

'Then I started thinking about England. I thought, "What a wonderful, rich place that is." And it is of course. And it's all just sitting there, waiting for me. My family are always begging me to come and stay for as long as I like. For ever if I want to. So that's what I wanted to talk with you about. How would you feel if I went to England for a while?'

'I think it's a fine idea. Maybe I'll go with you.'

She hesitated a split second too long. Then she said, 'Oh, that would be perfect. Could you do that? Would you?'

'You know me. I just might do it.' But he said it in a way that made clear what he meant.

'We could have a wonderful time.'

'I'll bet we could. But on the other hand I wouldn't want to spoil anything for you . . .'

'How could you spoil anything?'

'I mean the kind of thing you've been describing to me seems like something that might work better if you're by yourself.'

'You think so?'

He nodded. 'But we don't have to decide right now. Let's see what happens.'

'It's probably a very selfish thing,' she said. 'So if it is, you have to tell me. It's certainly not some elaborate device to get me away from you. I hope you don't think that.'

'Not for a minute. If I did I wouldn't let you go at all.'

'And maybe you will come along,' she said.

'Maybe I will. But I have a hunch the best thing I can do is stay in Chicago so you'll have something to come home to.'

'I never thought of that.'

'You should,' he said, putting his arm around her. 'It's something to think about. When are you planning to leave?'

'I hadn't made any plans. I wanted to talk to you first. But I'd promised to spend some time in New York with Floyd in September. So if I do go to England I'd probably go on from there.'

'It's almost September now,' he said.

'That's true. Maybe I should wait a while.'

'No reason to do that. September's a perfect time to travel. Besides, the sooner you leave, the sooner you'll get back.'

Ten days later he drove her to the airport to catch her flight to New York. As he turned into the O'Hara parking lot, she said, 'How many times have we taken each other to airports?'

He smiled. 'I lost count.'

When they called her flight and he walked her to the boarding station she said, 'Maybe you will come over.'

'Maybe. We'll see what happens.'

He took her in his arms and kissed her.

'That was a *serious* kiss,' she said.

'I'm a serious guy.'

'One way or the other, I'll see you soon,' she said then.

'One way or the other.' He kissed her quickly on the forehead. 'Goodbye, kid.'

'I thought we never said that word.'

'What word?'

'Goodbye.'

'Sometimes we do. When it's a long trip.'

After the attendant checked her ticket at the gate Helen turned back to wave but Frank had already disappeared across the departure lounge.

[5]

'How does Frank feel about this sentimental journey you're making to England?' Floyd asked Helen as they drove to his house from the New York airport.

'Not very good for my ego, I'm afraid. I had a feeling he was glad to see me leave.'

'I don't believe that.'

'I didn't believe it either. But the more I think about it, the more I'm convinced. I've never seen him so agreeable. I just felt he was eager to bundle me off.'

'Doesn't sound like Frank. He's probably planning to fly over to England himself and surprise you.'

'He did mention that he might come over.'

'There you are. I'll make you a bet that you see him in England before you see me again here in New York.'

'Maybe I'll see you in England.'

'I don't think so,' he said.

'Clara keeps asking me when you'll be over.'

'I'll go over some time, I guess. But now's not the time.'

'Clara's not getting any younger,' Helen said. 'Don't wait too long.'

'I never fret about Clara. She'll outlive the sea.'

That night at dinner, Helen said. 'We've talked about everything but you. How are you doing?'

'I'm fine.'

'No stock answers please. It was a serious question. I expect a serious reply.'

'I don't want to be serious,' he said. 'I told you that this afternoon. I'm going to show you New York like you've never seen it before. A different play every night. Midnight suppers. We'll even drive through Central Park in a carriage if you like. We'll dance at the St Regis, drive up to Connecticut . . . the works.'

'High hilarity,' Helen said.

'Something like that.'

'I don't trust high hilarity. Never did. It always seems like a cover-up to me.'

'Not a chance,' Floyd said. 'You're looking at a whole person. No cracks in the plaster.'

'You still didn't answer my question.'

'You're relentless, aren't you?'

'Sometimes.'

'All right,' he said. 'I'll tell you the truth. I've had a rough time. I keep seeing Jeannette the way she looked when I went to identify the body. That was a hell of a way to die. She deserved better than that. Anybody does. I won't try to tell you that everything was roses between us. It wasn't. And I never tried to convince anybody that Paul and I were best friends, but Jesus . . . I wouldn't wish something like that on anybody. He didn't even know Glen Tillis and Glen didn't know him. It was all so bloody senseless. And the weird thing is that sometimes the person I feel sorriest for is Glen. I mean if that's what love does to people, it doesn't make you want to get in line at the marriage licence bureau.'

'Most of us aren't like Glen Tillis.'

Floyd nodded. 'I know. That's what I keep telling myself.'

'How's Betsy doing?'

'Pretty good, I think. She's a sensational kid. And she can be tough when she has to be. I think she made up her mind she wasn't going to let it swamp her. And so far it hasn't. We talk on the phone almost every day and we see each other at least once a month. Either I fly out there for the weekend or she comes here. She's a grown-up now and I treat her like one so we get along fine. She's been accepted at Northwestern as soon as she finishes at St Mary's so she'll be there in the Midwest for four more years.'

'Too bad she couldn't have come to Foresby. Did you talk to her about it?'

Floyd shook his head. 'She likes to make her own plans. I have a hunch she'll do that for the rest of her life.'

The evening before she was to leave New York for England, Floyd said, 'What's going to become of Jesse now?'

'I don't know. I suppose his life will go on pretty much the same. Clara expects him to be at Wingate part of the time and in Paris part of the time.'

'Is the divorce all over now?'

'I'm not sure about the dates. I don't understand how those things work in Britain.'

Floyd gave her a sly smile and said, 'Any connection between that divorce and your decision to go back to England?'

'How do you mean?'

'I always had the feeling that some place along the line you and Jesse might get together.'

'We are together,' Helen said. 'And we have been for

years. We've been friends since I was a young girl. Jesse's probably my best friend.'

'That's not what I mean. I thought you two might decide to choose each other. Wedding bells, maybe. All that stuff.'

Helen laughed. 'Not us. We know each other too well. I don't know what gave you that idea.'

'I'm not the only one who thinks that. When I was living in Paris I had a few wine-soaked luncheons with Nora and she. . . .'

'Nora thinks every woman in the world is sweet on Jesse.'

'Maybe she does,' Floyd said, 'but you're the only one she mentioned.'

Helen smiled. 'Trust me. There's nothing for Jesse and me in that department and there never has been. And now that you've brought up Nora, there doesn't seem to be much doubt that she and Jesse have taken up where they left off years ago.'

'Starting when he and Valerie broke off or before?'

'No one knows the answer to that one except the players themselves. Clara says Valerie was the one who wanted the separation but she's not sure why.'

'Makes sense to me. Can't imagine Jesse wanting to leave her.'

'Why not?'

'Because he was crazy about her. Who wouldn't be?'

'I'm surprised to hear that from you. I seem to remember that you and Valerie didn't hit it off so well.'

'We didn't. But that doesn't mean I didn't appreciate her . . . how shall I put it . . . her finer qualities.'

'Maybe you're the one who should be going to England instead of me.'

'No, thanks, Mom. Not me. That whole Valerie and Jessie and Nora situation is complicated enough without another Bradshaw being stirred into it. And even if I did have a notion to court my divorced cousin . . . she's my cousin . . . right?'

'Third cousin. Or is it fourth?'

'Even if I had an irresistible yen for her, which I don't, it's too late. I guarantee you she's already selected Jesse's successor.'

'Why do you say that?'

'It's the only thing that makes sense. When you first told me they were separating I was as surprised as you were. Since, in my judgement, *nobody* would leave Valerie, then it followed that she was leaving Jesse, as you just said. And why would she do that, I asked myself? Only one reason. If she'd met another man. You said she visits her father up in Cumberland. Isn't that right? Goes there and spends a week or two at a time?'

'So Clara tells me.'

'Then there's the answer. Some charming fellow has turned her head. And once the dust has cleared after the divorce decree we'll all find out who he is. There'll be a fancy wedding at Wingate Fields and Jesse, as head of the family, will give her away.'

'Whatever happens,' Helen said, 'I don't think you'll see Jesse performing that function.'

'Neither do I. That would be a little too intricate even for the Bradshaws.'

[6]

Within days of Jesse's telling her that Valerie had decided to divorce him, Nora made arrangements to meet her daughter in London. Neither Jesse nor Clara were told about the meeting.

Valerie flew down from Newcastle and Nora flew over from Paris and they met at the airport.

'Can we manage this?' Nora said as they sat down across from each other at a restaurant table. 'Or is it all too awkward and painfully stupid?'

'I don't feel awkward about it,' Valerie said.

'But *I* do. I feel guilty and heart-broken. I feel as if I've failed you and Jesse and myself. Your father once told me I was the sort of person who can't help breaking things. I was never sure what he meant but now I am. I feel as though I've broken something that can't be fixed.'

'Something is broken and it can't be fixed. But you are not responsible. You didn't break it. I told Jesse, and I'm sure he's told you, that my decision had nothing to do with what's going on between you two.'

'He did tell me that. But he doesn't believe it and neither do I. You certainly didn't arrange an investigation and have my servants questioned because it didn't matter to you.'

'I have no reason to lie to you, Nora. But you must know that if I were angry with you I wouldn't be able to hide it. I can never hide how I feel. I did want some specific evidence about you and Jesse because I knew it was something he would understand. I thought in a way it might even make it easier for him. But I swear to you I had made up my mind to leave Jesse long before I ever spoke to a solicitor in London, long before he brought me the evidence about your house in Rue Bardinet. You're not to blame, old girl. I told Jesse that and now I'm telling you. I know you love him. Why shouldn't you be with him?'

Nora lit a cigarette and turned her eyes to watch a plane pulling slowly into an arrival bay. Finally she said, 'Either you're a saint or you're the most accomplished liar I've ever seen.'

'Neither one. I'm telling you the plainest truth I'm capable of.'

'You're simply saying you don't want him any more. Is that it?'

'I wouldn't put it that way. That sounds terribly cruel and I don't have cruel feelings toward Jesse.'

'Then what are you saying?'

'I'm saying I don't want to be married. I want to be by myself. Not because Jesse is a bad man or a failed husband. And certainly not because of you or anything you've done. I just want to live alone.'

'Do you expect me to believe, at your age, that you're going to sit in a chair and do needlework for the rest of you life?'

'I don't know what I'm going to do. I haven't made any plans beyond what you already know about. First I have to decide what I don't want to do. And I've already decided that. It's all about me, Nora. Has nothing whatsoever to do with you.'

'Then why do I feel so rotten?'

'Because you're a nice lady and because you can't really believe I'm telling you the truth.'

'That's right. I can't.'

'You will finally. I promise.'

'Let me ask you this,' Nora said then. 'When Jesse left me and married you, did you feel the way I feel now?'

'No. Because in the first place I loved him very much and in the second place I knew that the two of you were breaking up anyway. Isn't that true?'

'It's hard to say. I never wanted to admit it to myself.'

'Can you honestly tell me that you think you and Jesse would have stayed together all these years if he and I hadn't got married?'

Nora smiled. 'I hate to be honest but I have to be once in a while just to see if I can still do it.' Then, 'No, I don't think we would have stayed together.'

Valerie's return flight to Newcastle left half an hour before Nora's flight to Paris. As they approached Valerie's departure gate, Nora said, 'We've had some unusual experiences for a mother and daughter.

Valerie smiled. 'Seems to me that Jesse's the one who's had the unusual experiences.'

'Maybe that's true. But I'm more concerned about us. Have we survived it?'

'No question about that in my mind.'

'Nor in mine,' Nora said.

When they called Valerie's flight, Nora said, 'This is my last try. If I promised you that I would stay away from Jesse, if he promised to stay away from me, would it change anything for you? Or would you still go ahead with the divorce?'

'You haven't been paying attention. I've said from the beginning that I wasn't leaving Jesse because of you. That's the truth.' She put her arms around her mother and kissed her. Then she turned away and walked through the tunnel to her plane.

[7]

For the first showing of the autumn, Galerie Drouant-David on Rue Faubourg St Honoré, presented the new paintings of Bernard Buffet. The gallery was already crowded when Jesse arrived, late afternoon, for the vernissage. As he made his way through the rooms, studying the paintings carefully, Karina joined him and trailed a few steps behind, as intent on Buffet's work, it seemed, as Jesse was.

When they had completed their tour, Karina brought him a glass of wine and steered him to a corner that was not crowded. 'And where is Madame Nora?' she asked.

'She'll be along. She's having a vernissage at her own gallery tomorrow. A few details to look after.' He glanced at his watch. 'She said she'd be here by six.'

'Good. So I'll have you to myself for a while. There are some matters you and I have to discuss.'

'Is your love-life giving you problems again?'

'It's not my love-life that concerns me. It's yours.'

'Why would I want to discuss that?' he said.

'Because it involves Nora. And I am Nora's dearest friend although she usually refuses to acknowledge it.'

'She's very fond of you.'

'Sometimes, but not always. You needn't try to console me. I'm a realist and I've never deceived myself about Nora. Sometimes she likes me, sometimes she doesn't. At the moment I think she *does*. At least she's talking to me again. We've seen each other twice in the past week.'

'Did you question her about her love-life?'

'No. Nor did she volunteer any information. But she did mention that you're ending your marriage to Valerie.'

'I'm not ending it. She's ending it.'

'How gallant you are. Sometimes I think you're the only real gentleman I know.'

'Gallantry has nothing to do with it. I'm simply telling the truth. She ditched me.'

'But she knew you and Nora were living together again. Nora told me that.'

'If you know all the answers I don't see what you and I have to discuss.'

'I'm sorry,' Karina said. 'It's none of my business what happens between you and Valerie. But it matters a lot to me what happens to Nora.'

'Why should anything happen to her?'

'Because she's upset. She feels as if she's in the middle between you and her daughter.'

'That's nothing new. Each one of us has been in the middle at one time or another.'

'But now it's different. Nora's really committed to you now, more than ever.'

Jesse signalled the waiter and he stepped over with two fresh glasses of wine. 'Let me ask you something,' Jesse said then. 'Does Nora know you and I are having this conversation?'

'God, no. She'd kill me if she knew.'

'Then why are you taking the risk?'

'Because I care about her. You know that. I care about what happens to her. If the situation were reversed she'd be just as concerned about me. At least I hope she would. Maybe you don't know what she went through after you and Valerie were married. But I know. That's when I first met her, when she came back to Paris after the war. We spent a lot of time together. She didn't feel like seeing her old friends, people she'd know when you two were together, but she saw me. We confided in each other. I think I know her very well.'

'I'm sure you do.'

'What I'm saying is, I'd hate to see her go through all that again. She had a dreadful time pulling herself back together. I'm not sure she could manage it again.'

'So what are you suggesting?'

'Don't make it difficult, Jesse. This is no fun for me either. I just hope if you're not going to stay with her . . .'

'What makes you think that?'

'I don't think it. I'm just trying to find out.'

'Don't you think that's something for Nora and me to settle between ourselves?'

'I knew you'd say that. I knew you'd think I'm meddling. But I don't care what you think about me. This is all about Nora.'

'Don't you think Nora can take care of herself?'

'Of course she can't take care of herself. She's vulnerable. No woman who feels the way she does can protect herself.'

Jesse looked at her for a moment. Then, 'You surprise me, Karina. This is a side of you I've never seen before. The good Samaritan. Looking out for the best interests of all your friends.'

'Not all my friends. Just Nora.'

'All right . . . let me put it this way. If there's a crisis between me and Nora, I'm not aware of it. But if one should come up, I think you'll have to depend on the two of us to work it out.'

'You're telling me to mind my own business, aren't you?'

'No. I'm saying that I'm just as concerned about Nora's peace of mind as you seem to be. And even if I weren't, I assure you that Nora is very much able to look out for herself.'

'If you think that, then you don't know her as well as I do.'

[8]

That night, when they were at home together, Jesse said to Nora, 'I had a long talk with Karina today before you arrived at the gallery. She gave me quite a scolding. Seems to think I'm going to do wrong by you.'

'Where did she get that idea?'

'I don't know. She said she'd been spending some time with you. What did you tell her?'

'About what?'

'About anything. She was carrying on about me and Valerie and how our divorce is going to affect you.'

'She just knows the facts. That's all I've told her. A lot of people know about your divorce by now.'

'She seems to think she has to protect you,' Jesse said.

'From what?'

'From me.'

'Why on earth does she think that?'

'Don't ask me. I thought you might know the answer.'

'Karina likes to dramatize things. She wants everyone else's life to be as full of strife and deception as hers is.'

'She has an idea that I'm going to leave you at about the same moment that Valerie legally leaves me.'

'News to me,' Nora said. 'Are you?'

'Not much question in Karina's mind. Are you sure you didn't discuss that with her?'

'Absolutely.'

'She doesn't want you to suffer the way you did when you and I broke up before. Did you suffer?'

'Damned right I suffered. What do you think? But that's no affair of Karina's. I can't imagine what she's trying to start by grilling you.'

'She cares about you, she says. And the implication is that nobody else does.'

'Oh, God. She's off again. I wish she'd decide, once and for all, if she adores men or detests them. Right now she's on a plateau of loving all women and hating all men. So you were an accidental victim, I'm afraid.'

'Didn't seem so accidental. She closed the discussion by telling me she knows you much better than I do.'

'What did you say?'

'I was very kind. I said everybody knows you better than I do.'

'Sometimes the only way I can avoid killing her,' Nora said, 'is by staying away from her for a few months. It looks as if she's due for a period of Coventry.'

'I don't think that will work this time. She's determined to stand by you. She wants to make sure you're prepared for the day I pack up and leave you.'

'I'm an old warrior, darling. I'm prepared for *anything*.'

[9]

When Helen arrived in England she found a letter from Frank waiting for her at Wingate Fields.

> I flew out to San Francisco the same day I put you on the plane for New York. That's why you were unable to reach me when you called me in Chicago. I left a message with my answering service and with my office staff that no one was to be told where I'd gone. Does that sound familiar? It's one of the little tricks I learned from you. It's called the disappearing act. If someone's worried about you, too bad for them. They'll get over it.

At this point, Helen refolded the letter and put it back into its envelope. The tone of the first paragraph she had read made her uneasy. She took the letter to her room, put it in the drawer of the bedside table and decided to read it that night, when dinner was over, when the house was still and she was alone.

All through the day she was conscious of the letter waiting for her upstairs. At least once she told herself that the wiser course would be to *not* read it, simply to drop it into the fireplace and pretend it had never arrived. When she was in bed that night, however, she adjusted her lamp, took Frank's letter out of the drawer, and read it through.

> Your behaviour at the airport baffled me. It was as though you didn't realize we were wrapping up whatever was left of all our years together and tossing it in the trash-can. Or perhaps you were disappointed that I knew it as well as you did. You must have known

when you took off on your Maine adventure that I would get the message you were sending me. A little time apart before we closed the door and walked away in opposite directions.

When I was sitting in Chicago waiting for you to come back from Maine I was hoping you'd have the guts to come out and say what was on your mind. I know we've always said we owe each other nothing but I thought that you did owe me that. After all the years we've been together, married and not married, I hoped that if the time came we could make an honest break. But I should have known better.

I'm not trying to be cruel but there's no way I can be truthful, I'm afraid, without hurting you. Ever since we said goodbye in Chicago I've been spending a lot of time, all my time, thinking about you. But for the first time since I met you, I allowed myself to be objective, to let the evidence speak for itself.

A thousand times I've heard you say, 'I never lie to you. I always tell the truth.' I don't question that. But for people who are as close as we've been, withholding information or feelings is the most hateful lie of all. And that's your game, my dear. It always has been. As I sit here with my feet up, going over the details, from the first time we met, I realize that almost everything I know about you is based on assumptions. Because you reveal nothing. You have an instinct for secrecy that seems to be the dominant passion of your life. For years I felt some odd guilt because I knew you so little. I thought it was a flaw in me. Now I know better. Now I see that we had a phantom courtship, an opaque marriage and a mysterious divorce. Your flawless behaviour as a wife, your impeccable attention to appearances and details were not laudable traits as I thought then, not clear evidence of your love for me or your devotion to our marriage. They were simply what they appeared to be and no more — surface manifestations of interior feelings that were, in fact, nonexistent. Scrupulous behaviour on the outside, nothing on the inside.

If you ask me why we've stayed together as long as we have in our second *unmarried* marriage, I'll admit it's hard for me to find the answer. But now I think I know it. There has always been a kind of temporary quality to it, a fragile commitment dressed up as a serious one. A bright shining car with no engine under the hood. Since you were aware that you could walk away at any time, there was no need to walk away. Outside of my occasional suggestions that we get married, I'm sure you felt that my feelings were an exact match for yours, a kind of bland acceptance of synthetic love, a sort of patient and undemanding companionship. Thank God you were wrong about that. Looking back, the only pleasant taste in my mouth comes from the memory of how much I cared about you. I'm grateful for that. No regrets at all about that. Just a sad feeling that you have nothing comparable to remember. You went to the ball and danced every dance but you never heard the music.

I'm sure you've never admitted any of this to yourself. And you won't admit it now. You will probably say to yourself, 'I tried to love him. I would have loved him if I could.' And perhaps that's the whole story. But I think not. I think it's a bit more intricate than that. The question is not whether or not you loved me. The question is why you would spend all these years with me when you didn't.

I don't believe in genetic destiny but in your case I think it may be a factor. Everything you've told me about the magnificent Bradshaws has made me conclude that they are something less than magnificent. True, the only ones I've met are you and Floyd but you've been generous in your descriptions of the others.

I can't help thinking that they are mesmerized by the fact of being Bradshaws, that no other emotional reward can compare with that one. A Bradshaw loves his name, loves himself, and loves, in one way or another, all the others who share that name. It's a kind of spiritual incest that by its forbidden nature makes other relationships seem dull and unworthy.

Consider your own case. Do you imagine that you've ever loved any other man besides your father, Jesse, and Floyd, all members of the clan in one way or the other. I know from certain elliptical and misty-eyed statements you've made that you think of Chet, the boat mechanic, as the sacred love of your life but I suspect that he was no more than a fill-in, just as I've been. If the poor bastard had lived a few more years I'm convinced he would have found a perfumed note on his tool-chest telling him that his faithful Helen was called away on one pretext or another. Does that hurt your feelings? Of course it does. But I don't care. You can be as angry with me as you like.

When I was a schoolboy athlete, my track coach used to caution us about the danger of wet dreams the night before an important race. We were taught how to sleep with a knotted towel around our waists, the knot in the small of the back, so no erotic accident could sap our running and jumping energies.

We were told also that each man is born with a capacity for a specific number of orgasms, the implication being that when that number was exhausted he was finished. At the time I thought it was a chancy scientific conclusion, impossible to prove or disprove. Now I'm not so sure.

Does this relate to you? Of course not. Not directly. But a similar chancy logic tells me that by the time I met you, your full supply of love had already been spoken for. By Raymond, by Jesse, by your son, and perhaps by the nameless soul who was his father. If this is true, then you are blameless. You gave what you could but there simply wasn't very much to give.

There have been times, many such times, when I believed I couldn't live without you. Now those times are over. Only a child believes he can be nourished by a diet of cotton candy.

Helen's first reaction, when she finished reading the letter, was one of anger. When she read it a second time she began to feel a mixture of pity and contempt for Frank. She decided that his attack on her was actually a redirection of his feelings towards himself. His listing of her flaws was in fact an assessment of his own. With that conclusion she turned out her light and told herself the matter was closed. As she lay awake in the dark, however, hearing the small angular night-sounds of the old house and the very different sounds from the gardens outside, Frank's portrait of her became steadily clearer and more detailed in her mind. Failing to see any resemblance to herself, she dismissed it entirely. But it came back. And each time it came back she found it more difficult to deny the resemblance.

[10]

A week or ten days after her arrival in England, Helen drove north to Cumberland to see Valerie, who was staying there in her father's house, living in the wing she had occupied as a child when her mother and Edmund Bick were still married.

'I'm sorry my father's not here,' Valerie said. 'He's off for a month of shooting in Scotland. He tells me you two met a long time ago.'

'That's right,' Helen said. 'In 1919. When Jesse and I arrived in England for our first visit. Nora used to say he was the handsomest man in the county.'

'He still is. The ladies still swoon.'

'Clara says he never married again.'

Valerie smiled and shook her head. 'But he has certainly not lived a celibate life. When he's not hunting or fishing he's really quite naughty. Very busy with the ladies.'

When they had tea in Valerie's parlour looking out on the gardens and the swan pond, Helen said. 'How lovely it is. Will you make your home here now?'

'I'll always spend time here at Bick House. This whole estate will be mine and my children's one day. But Wingate Fields is still my home. Although I spent my early childhood here and the rest of it in France, I know every time my car rolls up that long drive at Wingate that there's where I belong.' She poured tea into Helen's cup. 'For now, however, till all the divorce business is finished, till Jesse and I and everyone else in the family get accustomed to the fact that we are no longer husband and wife, I think it's best for me to be here with my father. Out of sight. Out of the picture.'

Helen stayed for three days at Bick House and until the last morning Valerie restrained herself from asking the questions she'd been longing to ask from the moment she learned Helen was coming to England.

'How is Floyd?' she asked finally. 'You've told me all the

details about what happened to his wife but not how he's dealt with it. He must have been devastated.'

'I'm sure he was. I certainly was. We lost not only Jeannette but my half-brother as well. And poor Betsy lost both her parents in the most painful circumstances one can imagine.' She sipped her tea. 'You asked how Floyd reacted. It's hard to say. I think he was so concerned about Betsy that he didn't allow himself to show how he felt. And he's not a talker. Not even with me. Also, he never feels sorry for himself. And he doesn't allow other people to feel sorry for him either. It's maddening sometimes when you're dying to help someone and you know they don't want to be helped. But at the same time, it's a quality I admire in a man. I really admire Floyd for the way he's gone ahead through these months. And the way he's kept a hand on Betsy.'

'What was Jeannette like?' Valerie said then.

'It's hard to say. She certainly wasn't a typical small-town American girl. She was totally unlike any other young woman I've met. And I'd be surprised if any of the girls you knew in school in Massachusetts resembled Jeannette. There were many contradictions about her. She was attractive but not beautiful. She had an absolutely gorgeous body but if you'd never seen her in a bathing suit you wouldn't realize it. If you passed her on the street you would think she was too slender and angular to be really attractive. She was a great laugher. She had an outrageous sense of humour. But when her face was in repose there was something wistful, even sad about it. Do you know what I'm trying to say? She was difficult to know because there were all sorts of hidden layers.'

'I can't tell if you liked her or didn't like her.'

'I liked her enormously,' Helen said. 'For all her bravado and a kind of sexual self-confidence, she often seemed like a lost child on a street corner. But a tough one. You sensed there was a temper there that could take the paint off the walls if it was turned loose.'

'She and Floyd must have been very much in love. Clara says they were sweethearts when they were still in lower school.'

Helen nodded. 'They'd known each other for a long time. Sometimes that's a good thing in a marriage. Sometimes it's not so good.' She paused. 'I'm being very candid with you and I'm not sure I should be. I've never discussed Jeannette and Floyd with anyone. Not even Clara.'

'I'm sorry. I don't mean to pry.'

'Of course not. I realize that. It's just an odd sensation for me, hearing myself express things that I'd kept to myself before.'

'Shall we change the subject?'

'No. I don't mean to say that. For a moment I felt as though I was violating a confidence. But I'm not. And even if I were I don't think I'd be concerned about telling you. Floyd's a part of your family, too.'

'Yes,' Valerie said. Then, 'Of course he is.'

'What I started to say,' Helen went on, 'when you mentioned how long they'd known each other, is something that never occurred to me till Floyd and Jeannette had been married for two or three years. I got the feeling suddenly that one of them, or both of them perhaps, were trying to keep alive whatever it was they'd had together when they were very young. They had chosen to ignore what each of them had become and had fastened on a person who very probably didn't exist any longer. We all do that of course. None of us want to give up what we had at the beginning. But it's a matter of degree, isn't it? Sometimes I felt that Floyd and Jeannette had tangled themselves hopelessly in the past and they were having a bit of a struggle trying to make the pieces fit together in the present.'

After a moment, Valerie said, 'What do you think he'll do now?'

'I'm not sure. He says he plans to stay in New York. And I know he wants to help Betsy in any way he can. They're very close. He thinks she depends on him and he wants her to depend on him. But he's also wise enough to know that once she's at university she'll need to be as independent as any other girl her age.'

'Do you think he'll marry again?'

'I hope he will,' Helen said, 'but there's no way of knowing with Floyd. If he does I'm sure we'll all know about if *after* it takes place. He is extremely capable of making up his own mind and charting his own course.'

'Does he know about Jesse and me?'

Helen nodded. 'We talked about it when I visited him in New York.'

'Was he surprised?'

'Very.'

'What did he say?'

'He said it must have been your idea because he couldn't imagine anyone divorcing you.'

'Did he really say that?'

'Yes, he did,' Helen said. 'And you're blushing.'

'I know. I can feel it. It's an old habit. Since I was a child. When someone says something nice about me I either blush or weep.'

'He also said that if it was your idea, it was surely because you're in love with someone else.'

'I wonder why he would assume that.'

'I don't know. But he seemed convinced.'

Later in the morning, when Helen's things had been loaded into the car and she and Valerie were walking through the great hall toward the west entrance, Valerie said, 'When you write to Floyd tell him he guessed correctly. There is a man.'

'Ah-ha.'

'No one here knows yet so ask him to keep it to himself.'

'Am I allowed to ask questions?'

Valerie smiled. 'Not yet, I'm afraid. After the divorce, when things fall into place, I will reveal all. If there's anything to reveal.'

'But you said . . .'

'I said there's a man. But I made no predictions. There are rivers to cross.'

When Helen was behind the wheel of the car, just before she drove away, Valerie said, 'Tell Floyd the man is someone I've known for several years. I wouldn't want him to think my head was turned by a passing stranger. I wouldn't want you to think that either.'

[11]

In her letter to Floyd a week later, Helen did not go into detail about her visit with Valerie. She made no effort to reproduce Valerie's remarks word for word. She did however tell him that he had guessed correctly about Valerie's future. 'There is definitely another man in the picture,' she wrote, 'but no one here knows it yet. Except me. And now *you* know it. She says she'll make no announcements till the divorce is final. I have a feeling there may be a problem involved. It wouldn't surprise me if the man in question is married.'

After he read his mother's letter, Floyd went to the bar of the Gramercy Hotel and spent the day there. At seven o'clock he walked to a cocktail lounge called *Sonia's* in Twenty-third Street and at midnight, he walked down Third Avenue, picked up a tired-looking young girl with an Alabama accent and took her home with him.

The following morning, however, he was alone again. The girl was gone, the effects of the alcohol had disappeared, and he was back where he'd started the afternoon before, floating toward the rapids.

Floyd had never attempted to deceive himself about his state of mind when he'd left England a few years earlier. He'd been in full retreat, fleeing a situation he couldn't deal with, trying hard to persuade himself that distance would solve everything. It hadn't worked of course. Nothing had been solved. None of the distractions he pursued, the activities he invented, not even his marriage, had pushed Valerie out of his thoughts.

There had been a temporary respite when he had convinced himself that it was simply not meant to be. That was his state of mind at the time he married Jeannette. But the centre would not hold. Valerie had drifted slowly back again. Fighting to stay afloat, he told himself that whatever might happen in some uncertain future, it was out of his hands. He had no intention of ending his marriage and he had no inkling then that Valerie would end hers.

Nor did Jeannette's sudden death bring Valerie stage-centre in his mind. Quite the contrary. he had never felt more married to Jeannette than he did in the days and weeks following her death. Every detail, every consideration, every arrangement centred on her, on what must be done for her and for Betsy. Floyd reserved little time for his own needs, gave no thought to his own future.

Even the news of Valerie's separation from Jesse did not have an instant effect on him. He did not suddenly see her as an available woman and himself as a seeking man. Jeannette's hard death, in truth, had put a brittle edge on his sensibilities. His thoughts were neither tender nor gentle now. He saw chaos and disappointment and hardship in every corner. If his memories of Valerie had suddenly flooded over him just then he would certainly have chided himself for attaching such importance, for attaching any importance at all, to an isolated long-ago afternoon in a crofter's cottage in Northumberland.

During his mother's visit, however, as they talked about Wingate Fields, as they discussed the Bradshaws one at a time, Valerie slowly came alive for him again. And although he did not allow himself to be linked with her in any way, he could not ignore the fact that her marriage to Jesse, which had once been her prime identity mark, was no longer a factor. Even when he insisted to Helen that Valerie had undoubtedly chosen a new man to replace Jesse, he allowed himself, in his private moments, to question that assumption. In the days after Helen left he even fantasized that he had stayed as alive for Valerie as she had for him. He saw them meeting casually on some future date — Christmas at Wingate perhaps — having a drink together in the library and walking through the garden. Finding perhaps some way back through the years since they'd seen each other. He avoided making concrete plans or factual assumptions but he slowly created an ambiance where he felt comfortable and hopeful, a kind of inflated sphere, temperature-and-humidity-controlled, closed off from fact, logic and contradiction.

Helen's letter when it arrived, punctured this cocoon like a sharp blade. The air escaped, the walls slowly collapsed and Floyd took refuge in the cool, dark bar of the Gramercy Hotel.

After that long afternoon and evening and his night with Arloa, the girl from Alabama, Floyd concluded that there was no whisky bottle large enough for him to crawl into, that no whisky bottle in fact held satisfactory answers for him, and that sweet little dumb Arloa was no answer either. His next impulse was to fly to California and spend some time with Abe Rettberg. That idea seemed so sensible that he rejected it. He knew so surely what Abe would say to him and he was so determined not to hear him say it that he decided not to go.

For several heady hours then he convinced himself that the sensible course, the only course, was to go to England at once. No one would question his coming to Wingate Fields, especially since Helen was there. Since Valerie was away at Bick House he would have time to settle in, to rejoin the family, and learn, bit by bit, precisely what was going on with her. When he had more information he would know what to decide and what to do.

He spent a busy half-day talking with his travel agent and his lawyer, seeing that his passport was brought up to date, and giving instructions about what things he wanted packed for the trip. He booked a plane seat for the following Sunday. He handled every detail and made every arrangement short of calling Helen to tell her he was coming. Something kept him from making the call. It was as though he felt that phone call would be the final commitment, that once he'd announced his plans there would be no chance for reconsideration. So he casually postponed it. First from one hour to the next, then from morning till evening, then from Friday till Saturday. On Sunday morning he called the airline and cancelled his trip.

All the following week he spent in the Museum of Natural History. From opening till closing. In succeeding weeks he was in some museum every day. The Metropolitan, the Modern Museum, the Frick, the Whitney, the Jewish Museum, the Brooklyn Museum.

When he'd exhausted all the museums he concentrated on films. He began going from one motion-picture theatre to another. And at night he'd go to the theatre. For weeks he didn't take a drink, turn on the television set or read a newspaper. He sat in theatres and watched other people perform.

A serious influenza epidemic hit New York that November of 1961. Ignoring all public health cautions, Floyd continued to spend all his time in theatres. He ate heartily, walked in the streets hatless with his coat open and remained healthy. The week after it was announced that the influenza epidemic was over, however, Floyd got sick. For three days, trying to ignore the symptoms, he kept to his regular schedule. On the fourth day he collapsed in the street in front of his house and was taken to the hospital with pneumonia. He was kept there for ten days and was confined to his bed at home for a week after that.

When he was allowed up at last and his nurse was dismissed he was thin and pale and feeling tentative in a way that was foreign to him. When he called Helen in England she said, 'At last. There you are. I've tried to call you a dozen times. Out of town, they told me. Where were you?'

'Had a stupid tussle with the flu and they put me in the hospital.'

'Why didn't you tell me?'

'Nothing serious,' he said. 'Didn't want to worry you.'

'Are you all right now?'

'A little shaky from the hospital food but fine otherwise. How long are you planning to stay over there?'

'At least through Christmas. Maybe longer. Why don't you come over?'

'I'd thought about it. But I want to spend some time with Betsy. Maybe I'll come later.'

'Let me know. I'll stay here till you come.'

'How is everybody?' he said then.

'Healthy and cheerful. Clara's fine and I'm fine. And Jesse and Nora seem to be fine in Paris.'

He waited a moment to see if she'd go on but she didn't. 'How about Valerie. How's she?'

'Haven't seen her since the time I told you about. But we talk on the phone. The divorce is all over now and I know she's relieved about that. She and the children will be here for Christmas. Then the kids go on to Paris for a week or so with Jesse. They think it's a great treat, celebrating Christmas twice.'

When he hung up the receiver he walked to the window and looked out at the light screen of early snow falling on Gramercy Park. Something about the conversation with Helen had unnerved him, something unsaid. On the other hand he had been told the principal thing he'd been waiting to hear.

He left the window and walked to his desk. He sat down, took a sheaf of writing paper out of the drawer, uncapped his pen and began to write. He wrote like a man who had a precise idea of what he wanted to say.

> Valerie,
>
> It occurs to me that I have never written to you before. Not a card. Not a line.
>
> Perhaps I shouldn't be writing now. But I don't care about that. I have spent a great many hours trying to decide what can be done and what should be done. So now I'm simply doing what I want to do.
>
> It seems like a century since I saw you last. I feel as if I've lived a dozen lifetimes since then and perhaps you feel the same. One thing I'm sure of is that no day

has passed that I haven't thought of you. Why has it taken so long for me to tell you that? God knows.

You know that my wife is dead. I know that you and Jesse are divorced. But that's all I know. Helen says you have a gentleman friend. If that's true, use this letter to light a candle and we'll forget the whole thing. I don't know how anybody answers a lunatic letter like this but maybe you'll find a way. If you *don't* find a way I'll figure you had nothing to say to me and I won't be surprised. I've never written a love-letter in my life. So don't be surprised if this doesn't read like one. But all the same that's what it's meant to be.

Floyd

He read through the letter once, put it into an envelope and addressed it. He stuck an overseas airmail stamp on it and propped it against the brass inkwell on his desk.

Each day he saw the letter there, and each day he promised himself he would take it to the Twenty-third Street post office and mail it. But every morning it was still there. At first it was like a mute reprimand but as the days passed he scarcely noticed it and when he did he silently acknowledged that the moment had passed and the letter would never be mailed. He told himself he was glad he'd waited. He convinced himself that on this occasion the proper action had been no action at all.

During the third week in December, he went to Chicago to spend more time with Betsy, to live in splendour at the Drake, the two of them, until she would go along to Crawfordsville for Christmas with her grandparents. When the car arrived to take him to the airport, he picked up the letter from his desk before he went downstairs.

At the airport, as he walked toward the departure lounge he saw a red and blue postbox on the wall. He took the letter out of his pocket and dropped it through the slot.

[12]

Once she had decided to leave Jesse, Valerie never questioned that somehow she and Floyd would find each other again. Long before that, in fact, against all logic and common sense, some child's voice inside had told her that the one day they had spent together could not possibly be the full time they would be allotted. And it never occurred to her that Floyd, in one way or another, didn't share her feelings. She had no specific notion of what events would bring them together but she never questioned, at least some part of her never questioned, that it would happen. All the same when his letter arrived at Bick House, two days before she was to leave to spend Christmas at Wingate, she trembled when she saw it on her breakfast tray.

As soon as she read it through, she got out of bed, put on a quilted robe, sat at her desk, and wrote an answer.

My dear angry Floyd,
I just received your aggressive letter a few minutes ago. God, how I love that about you.

The gentleman friend Helen mentioned is *you*. I couldn't tell her the truth, could I? When I told her to tell you he was someone I knew from several years ago, I thought perhaps you'd guess. When I didn't hear from you I didn't know what to think. Finally I decided that because of what had happened to your wife and what was going on between me and Jesse, you'd decided to wait. So I decided to do the same thing, to wait till the divorce business was finished and I could
— what am I trying to say — till I could be myself.

But I couldn't just wait till I heard from you. When you know me better you'll see I'm no good at games like that. I can show you — and I *will* — a dozen letters I've written but didn't send. It's only a sweet coincidence that you at last broke through at almost the exact time I had chosen to risk everything and present myself to you — ready or not — on a platter.

I don't want to wait any longer, Floyd.I know you're off to Chicago with Betsy and I must do Christmas with the children and Helen and Clara at Wingate, but when that's all past and put away you must meet me and put your arms around me and tell me I am unchanged since our lovely summer day together two thousand years ago.

On St Stephen's Green in Dublin there is an old and lovely hotel called the Russell. I will book a splendid suite overlooking the green. Dublin is cold and wet and grey in winter, a perfect time for people like us. We will sightsee through the shutters and order up sumptuous meals from the elegant restaurant downstairs.

Are you persuaded? You must be. Any fool can go to Madeira or the Canaries in winter. You and I will fly in the teeth of nasty weather and public scorn and nourish ourselves on Dublin.

Only you know of these plans. In case you tire of me quickly it will lessen my humiliation if only the room-service waiter at the Russell knows my scarlet secret.

January 17th, I will be waiting for you in cold and drizzly Ireland. No change of time or place will be tolerated. All future itineraries will be in your hands. This one's on me.

I've loved you for a very long time. I'm desperately eager to see you.

Chapter Twelve

[1]

There was a slashing, swirling rainstorm when Floyd's plane from New York landed two hours behind schedule at the Dublin airport. As he came through the door into the arrival lounge he saw Valerie standing well back from the entrance. She stood there watching as he made his way through the crowd of waiting people and arriving passengers. As he came up to her she said, 'See what I've got you into. You're soaking wet.'

'Just the coat and hat. And the shoes a bit damp. Otherwise I'm dry and fine.'

They didn't shake hands or embrace. She said, 'I've been taken quite shy all of a sudden.'

'That's all right.'

'I've hired a car and a driver. He's waiting just outside. But can we sit for a moment and have a drink? I feel as if I'm the one who was out in the wet. I'm awfully cold suddenly.'

They walked to the lounge bar, sat across from each other at a corner table and ordered whiskies. 'There, that's better,' she said after a sip from her glass. 'I was terribly frightened by the storm. Because your plane was so late. The airline people were quite cavalier about it. They wouldn't tell me anything.'

'It wasn't a bad flight. This is just a local storm. There was a delay at the airport in New York. That's why we were late.'

'You're here. That's the important thing.'

'How did you know which flight I'd be on?'

'I didn't. I arrived in Dublin day before yesterday. I've met all the flights from New York since then.'

'In your letter you said January 17th. Today's the 17th.'

'I know,' she said, 'but once I was here . . . I mean, I didn't want you to arrive with no one to greet you.' She raised her glass, 'Welcome to Ireland.' Then, 'Have I made a shameless fool of myself?'

'No. Have I?'

She smiled and shook her head. 'Can you believe we're here, perched in this frightful little snug? Just looking at each other.'

'Seems sensible to me. Maybe we should just settle in here.'

'I'm sure the publican wouldn't approve of that.'

'We mustn't bother with him. I think we should sit right here until we feel like leaving. I want to make sure your chill has passed. Nobody wants a sick person on his hands.' He signalled the waiter for two more whiskies.

'Are you very changed since I saw you last?' she said then.

'What do you think?'

'You seem awfully thin. Pale and meagre.'

'It's January. Last time we saw each other it was summer. I try to be bronzed and heroic in the summer.'

'Helen told me you were ill just before Christmas.'

'I was. Influenza first. Then pneumonia.'

'In hospital, she said.'

He nodded. 'I was very well cared for.'

'Are you all right now?'

'Underweight still. But I'm counting on the food at the Russell to fix that.'

She smiled. 'We'll both be quite plump in no time. I'm sure of it.'

'How long will we stay here?'

'How long *can* you stay?'

'I haven't made any plans,' he said.

'Did you buy a round-trip ticket?'

'No.'

'Neither did I.'

'We'll become wards of the state.'

'The dole is generous here, they say.'

'Does anybody know where you are?' he asked then.

'I told Clara I'd be in Ireland for a bit. But not in Dublin. I said I was visiting a friend in Sligo.'

'Where's Sligo?'

'It doesn't matter. We're not going there.'

'We're staying in Dublin?'

She nodded. 'Unless the sun comes out. If that happens in Dublin in January everyone leaves the city. It's too great a shock to the system.' Then, 'I want to ask you a question but you mustn't think about the answer. You must say the first thing that comes to your mind. Will you do that?'

'Is it a game?'

'No. Deadly serious. Will you do it?'

'I'll do it.'

'Are you ready?'

'Yes.'

'All right . . . what are you feeling just now? At this very instant?'

'I feel as if I live here.'

'In Ireland?'

'No. At this table. Right here. In this small corner.'

When she didn't speak, he said, 'Was that a bad answer?'

'No.' She looked down at her glass. 'I was afraid you'd be disappointed. I'm still afraid of that. I was afraid you'd look at me and say, "My God. This woman is a stranger." That's why I stood back away from the entrance. So you'd see me gradually as you walked toward me.' She looked up. 'Do you think I've gone dotty?'

'No.'

'Are you disappointed?'

He shook his head. 'I'm not disappointed.'

The rain was still slashing down as they ran from the air terminal to their car. The driver tucked a lap robe around them and they sat silent in the corner of the seat with their arms around each other. As they drove through the countryside, on through the streets of Dublin, and came near at last to their hotel, Floyd said, 'Are you crying?'

'I was. But now I'm laughing.'

'Sure sounds like crying to me.'

'That's the way it is with me. First one thing, then another.'

[2]

When Jesse came to Wingate Fields after the Christmas holiday, Helen showed him the letter Frank had sent her. Before he read it, she said, 'Do you think I'm nice?'

'I've always thought you were extremely nice,' Jesse said. 'Not pretty, not brilliant, but awfully darned nice.'

'I'm serious. Any positive feelings you have about me may vanish once you've read this letter.'

'I'll take a chance.' He slipped the letter out of the envelope and carefully read it through. When he looked up, Helen said, 'You see what I mean?'

'I probably don't see what you see. It's a pretty tough letter but it's a love-letter. Not much question about that. This guy's crazy about you. He feels like you shot him down and he's trying to get even.'

'He did more than get even. He shot *me* down.'

'I don't think so. Tell me the truth . . . you weren't planning to stay with him, were you?'

'That's not the point . . .'

'Yes, it is. As far as you were concerned it was over, wasn't it?'

'Yes.'

'Then you can't be mad at him just because he caught on. And you can't expect him to send roses and wish you well.'

'But this isn't like him. Back in the middle ages, when Frank and I were divorced, it was the most calm and civilized social event of the season.'

Jesse tapped the letter with his fingers. 'It looks as if he's saying some things now that he wishes he'd said then.'

'But what's the point? What does he gain by hurting my feelings?'

'If I know you, kid, you're not hurt, you're mad as hell. Why don't you just burn this letter and forget it?'

'I can't forget it. That's what makes me mad as hell.'

Jesse grinned. 'He really hit a nerve, didn't he?'

'Nobody wants to be told they're cold and empty.'

'He didn't say that exactly.'

'Close to it.'

'Since you know it's not true, why should it bother you?'

'Because it does. Do you know how many years Frank and I were together? Counting married and unmarried, more than twenty.'

'That's my point. If he really felt that way about you, you two wouldn't have stayed together that long.'

'And what is all that business about whatever love I have being spoken for before he ever met me? The idea that I loved Raymond and you and Floyd the way I might have loved him. It's ridiculous.'

'So forget about it.'

'I can't, damn it. What really burns me up is that he must have had these notions in his head for years, all the time he and I have been together.'

'That's no felony. If they prosecuted people for their secret thoughts we'd all be locked up. And nobody would stay married.'

'That's the most cynical thing I've ever heard you say.'

'It's the truth.'

'No, it's not. You've just decided it's the truth.'

'It's true for me. Do you like that better?'

'No. That's what I mean. It's the worst kind of cynicism.'

'If it upsets you, I'll take it back.'

'Taking it back is more cynical than saying it.'

'That's true,' he said. 'Just don't scold me. I couldn't wait to get here and see you, so don't make me feel like a fool, even if I act like one.'

Suddenly she had tears in her eyes. 'Oh, God, Jesse. I'm sorry.' She put her arms around him. 'I really am sorry. Don't pay any attention to me. I don't know what's the matter with me lately. So much has been happening. Everything changing. There doesn't seem to be any solid ground anyplace. People suffering and dying and lying and splitting up. There aren't any rules any more. That's why I wanted to come back here to Wingate Fields. I wanted to be in these stone buildings and walk in the old gardens and across the hills. I needed to be part of something that wasn't about to blow away.'

When she stopped crying finally he stood there for a long time with his arms around her. At last he said, 'Go wash your face and I'll make you a beautiful drink and we'll solve each other's problems like we used to.'

A few minutes later, when she came back into the room, she said, 'I'm sorry. I guess that's been waiting to come out for quite a while. I didn't mean to do it on you.'

'There's an old Navajo saying — "Never waste your tears on strangers." '

'Sounds like a Jesse Bradshaw saying.'

'I accept it. I'll plagiarize anybody.' Then, 'I was thinking about what you said about this place. I feel the same way you do. At least I used to feel that way. There was a time when I thought nothing could ever tear me away from here.

I thought there were no answers I couldn't find in these rooms or on those moors out there. Part of me still feels that way. But . . . circumstances change. And they've certainly changed for me.'

'But you're still the head of this family. You were before you and Valerie married and you still are. Clara certainly thinks of you that way.'

'I know she does, bless her heart, but things have become too entangled now. Valerie and I are not at war with each other, but all the same I don't see the two of us living here in separate wings and having regular family meetings about the tenant farmers. It would be awkward for the children when they were at home and it would be damned awkward for me. And I have to spend a certain amount of time in Paris in any case.'

'It sounds as though you've decided to spend all your time there.'

'Maybe,' he said. 'But I don't think so. I have a notion that I'd like to spend some time in America again. I'd like to do a series of pieces on the American novel in the past forty years. And American painting, of course, since the war, seems to have taken the play away from Europe. So there's plenty to write about there.'

'You'd be in New York then?'

'Part of the time. But there are things happening all over the country. San Francisco, Chicago, the South. This business in Indo-China is stirring up all kinds of new stuff. People are waking up.'

'Not in Fort Beck,' Helen said.

'Not yet maybe. But it will happen. Those Foresby students aren't much different from other kids their age.'

'If they're going to start burning things maybe it's just as well I'm here.'

'Does that mean you're staying for a while?'

'Clara wants me to and I want to, so I think I will.'

'Then maybe you'll let me squat in the house in Fort Beck if I go over. Since you won't be there . . .'

'Whether I'm there or not,' she said. 'But I don't think you'll find life in Fort Beck very thrilling after all these years.'

'You might be surprised. When we were talking about all the things that Wingate represents to both of us it reminded me of how often I've had the same feelings about Fort Beck and the five years when Raymond was still alive and the three of us lived there together. I've always had a fantasy about sitting behind his old desk and working up some of my articles. Almost everything I've managed to learn began with Raymond. I thought it might complete the circle somehow if I did some work there, where he did so much foundation work on me.'

'Nothing would make me happier, Jesse. And nothing would have made Raymond happier. I know it's a long time since you've seen the house but if you go there you'll find that very little has been changed. It's warmer inside in the winter and cooler in the summer and the plumbing works better but I've left everything else pretty much as it was.'

'Well, unless something drastic happens to make me change my mind I think you can count on a part-time tenant before long.'

'You're not a tenant,' she said. 'It's your house as much as mine.'

'There might be one problem. If we're ever there at the same time, the neighbours may gossip a bit.'

Helen smiled. 'I'm sure they will. At least I hope they will. Let's make sure we're there at the same time.'

[3]

In Dublin, Valerie and Floyd were delighted by the weather. It rained every day. One early afternoon as they had lunch by their sitting-room window, still in their robes and slippers and night-clothes, Valerie said, 'Weather like this is supposed to make a person blue and gloomy. Are you blue and gloomy?'

He shook his head. 'Not me.'

'Do you know how long it's been since we've been outside?'

'No idea.'

'Make a guess.'

'Seven years.'

'Sooner or later,' she said, 'we'll have to re-enter the world.'

'Later.'

'Does that mean you feel properly entertained?'

'I don't feel entertained at all,' he said. 'I feel as though I've been creatively occupied.'

'What a lovely way to put it.'

While she removed the serving-dish cover and served the omelette, he poured more wine into their glasses.

'How much has Helen told you about her father?'

'Bits and pieces,' Floyd said.

'Do you know about his tormented love-life? It was the reason he left England and went to America.'

'I *do* know that much. But no details.'

'Most people didn't know the details,' Valerie said, 'but Nora, when she was growing up, made it her business to find out all she could. And many years later, when I was grown up, she told it all to me.' She sipped from her wine glass. 'When Raymond was twenty years old, his parents gave a great dinner and ball to celebrate his birthday. He was in university then. At Cambridge. That night, for the first time, he met Emily Callison. She was young, just a bit older than Raymond, and very beautiful. And she was married. Her husband's name was Oliver. He had a reputation about the county for dishonesty and cruelty — he boasted that he had killed a man in a duel in France — and he was twice her age. No one knows exactly what happened that first night but Nora believed that Raymond and Emily fell in love at once. In any case they began to ride out every morning, she from her home and Raymond from his, and meet at the place where we met that day, at the edge of the river beside the ruined castle. They were planning to go away together as soon as he was old enough to claim his share of the Bradshaw fortune.'

'But his father found out about it,' Floyd said. 'Helen told me that much.'

'Everyone found out apparently. They were not discreet. So her husband took her off to Italy and Angus sent Raymond here to Ireland to complete his schooling. There was no way Raymond could contact her because she was travelling, but she wrote him a series of extremely passionate letters, which seem to have been destroyed but which Nora insists were read by Clara. At last, after a year had passed, she wrote that she had arranged to visit her mother in Wales and she begged Raymond to meet her there. So he crossed the Irish Sea and met her at Holyhead on the day she had specified. He had taken rooms there at the Pembroke Inn. It was a perfect plan except for one detail. Her husband had not been deceived. He broke into their bedroom at the inn. There was a struggle and a shot was fired from Oliver's pistol. It struck Emily and killed her instantly. When he saw what he'd done, her husband walked out into the square opposite the inn and fired a bullet into his own head. Can you believe it?'

'It's a strange story. Strange and sad.'

'It's all true. Most of the details came out at the inquest.'

'And what happened to Raymond?'

'He was in a private clinic for many months, unwilling to see any members of his family. At last he arranged to leave there secretly. He went to America. He married then, your mother was born, and none of his family saw him or heard from him again. After he died, Helen and Jesse came to Wingate Fields. While they were there, Jesse was adopted by my great-grandfather and he and Nora began an affair that is still going on.'

'Is that why you wanted a divorce?'

'No,' Valerie said. 'I made that decision before I knew that he and Nora had discovered each other again.'

'When did that happen?'

'I don't know exactly. Four years ago perhaps.'

'Why do you think he went back to her?'

'Who knows? They were together for a long time. I'm sure in some way they never actually separated.'

'Did you know Jesse wrote me a letter?' Floyd said then. 'A long time ago. Said you'd told him about us.'

'I didn't know he wrote to you. But I did tell him. Does that surprise you?'

'It surprised me then.'

'It surprised me, too, in a way. I hadn't planned to tell him. But after a while I felt as if I had to. I had no regrets about what we'd done. I certainly didn't see it as a mistake. But at that time I was convinced that you and I would never see each other again. I believed that Jesse and I would stay married for ever. So I felt as if I owed it to him to be honest, to tell him what had happened. So I did.'

'How did he react?'

'It seems so long ago now. Like another lifetime. It's hard for me to tell you exactly how it was. He was surprised of course. He certainly didn't like it, but I think he decided to blame you rather than me. As I recall, it was all quite civilized. Once we'd discussed it, it didn't come up again.

It wasn't even a matter of forgiveness. He just seemed to put it behind him.'

'Then he started up with Nora again.'

'Yes, he did.'

'Do you see any connection there?'

'No, I don't. But I may be wrong. I'm sure all kinds of conclusions will be drawn once the family knows that you and I are together.'

'Do we have to tell them?'

'That depends. If you're planning to toy with my affections for a few weeks and then abandon me, I suppose there's no reason for anyone to know.'

'I was thinking of toying with you for a bit longer than that,' Floyd said.

'So was I. Something of a semi-permanent nature.'

'That sounds good to me. Maybe even permanent.'

She nodded. 'Why not? But that means we'll have to tell somebody sometime. Unless we want to keep on like this, meeting in various hotels here and there. How do you feel about that?'

'It doesn't sound bad to me. But all the same, I think we'll have to tell them.'

'Sooner or later.'

'Let's make it as late as we can,' he said. 'It's nice to have a secret.'

'Exactly. We'll keep it to ourselves for as long as possible.'

They stayed there in the hotel on St Stephen's Green for two weeks. When they left at last they hired a car and drove north-west through Westmeath, Longford, Roscommon and County Sligo to Sligo town. There Valerie sent postcards to both Clara and Nora.

'Now I feel as if I told Clara the truth about my whereabouts.'

'Not at all,' Floyd said. 'You've simply documented a falsehood.'

After two days in Sligo, staying in a small hotel for trout fishermen just outside town, they drove farther north to Galway, Raphoe, and Letterkenny. Crossing the Derryveagh mountains then they turned south and drove the intricate western coastline to Ardara, Glencolumbkille and Killybegs. Then farther south through County Mayo, Galway and Limerick to Cork. After five days there, they took the overnight ferry from Cobb to St Malo, where they hired another car. They slowly made their way south then, staying at country inns, eating in renowned restaurants in obscure villages, and joyfully drinking the wine of all regions as they went along.

Arriving at the edge of the Mediterranean finally, they rented a sprawling pink villa with a staff of four just outside St Raphael. Their bedroom with its private terrace looked directly down on the sea. The mistral shook the house every night and caused the sky to be clear and cerulean every morning.

'The only problem is that it's winter,' Valerie said. 'And there's nobody here but us.'

Floyd smiled. 'Isn't that a pity?'

They walked into St Raphael every morning. Visited the outdoor market, and had coffee at a café overlooking the harbour. Some days they drove past the Roman ruins into Fréjus for lunch. Or they drove down the coast road to nearly deserted St Tropez to eat in a fine old restaurant in an historic building at the edge of the water. One day when they were having lunch there she said, 'Did you like Ireland?'

'You know the answer to that.'

'I don't mean did you like me in Ireland. Or us. I certainly know the answer to that. But what did you think of the country . . . the people?'

'I could move there tomorrow,' he said.

'I feel the same way.'

'I like the *size* of the place,' he said. 'I like the way those little walled fields and pastures look in Mayo and Donegal. It looks like a place where people were meant to live. I know it's a poor country and nobody enjoys seeing old beggars or hungry children but they don't seem poor in other ways. I mean, there's something going on. The pilot lights are burning. There's still a visible connection between today and a couple of centuries ago. You get the feeling that they don't have to redefine themselves every ten or twenty years. Outside of Cork, which seems like a European city to me, all the rest of Ireland is of a piece. Lots of courage there. Lots of patience and stamina and poetry.'

'You really do like it,' Valerie said. 'Shall we live there?'

'Why not?'

'What county shall we live in?'

'I like the west. Bare and rocky and severe. County Mayo is hard to beat. But I liked it in Clifden too. And Donegal is like a tough piece of steak. Almost impossible to bite into or chew but with a flavour that's worth it once you've made the effort.'

She smiled. 'Sounds like you're describing yourself.'

'I'm not hard to chew. I'm a mild and tender fellow.'

'Oh, my dear. How little we know ourselves.'

'Are you telling me I'm a tough piece of meat?'

'Almost inedible. Too many tendons and sinews and patches of muscle. Don't you remember when we first met, that summer at Wingate? I thought you were the most contrary human being I'd ever seen.'

'I was in love with you.'

'Not then,' she said. 'I don't think so. Or if you were, it was a kind of love I'd never seen before. Every time I talked with you, every time we had even the beginning of a conversation — and they seldom went past the beginning — I felt as if I was in a life-and-death struggle, some sort of contest I couldn't possibly win. If you were trying to get my attention, you succeeded brilliantly.'

'Nothing fancy or thought-out like that,' Floyd said. 'All I wanted to do was to get you off in a corner and have you to myself for a few minutes. But every time I managed it, things didn't work out right. Either I felt as if you were treating me like a seventeen-year-old or I got such an attack of jealousy . . .'

'Jealousy?'

'What do you think I felt? Every time I saw you and Jesse together, every time I thought of the two of you . . . I got so crazy I couldn't say anything that made sense.'

'Is that why our conversations always ended with you stalking away from me?'

'That's it. And you didn't know it?'

She shook her head. 'Not till that day in the summer house when you told me how you felt. *Then* I knew. And I knew some things about myself that I'd never admitted before. So I lured you away to the crofter's cottage. And then you left for America. Not very good for a young woman's self-esteem.'

'Don't give me that. That was a one-day affair. You never expected it to go beyond that and neither did I.'

'That seems awfully wilful and contrived. I don't much like the sound of it.'

'But it's true, isn't it?'

'I'm not sure. I don't believe I was thinking at all just then.'

'Tell me the truth — did it ever occur to you that you would leave Jesse? Break up your family?'

She shook her head. 'Not then. No.'

'It never occurred to me either. That's why I left.'

'When you did that, when you went back to America, did you think we'd never see each other again?'

'It wasn't a question of seeing you. Not in my mind. When I left I felt the way I'd always felt, that you were tied to Jesse and you always would be. I never thought anything else till Helen told me you were getting a divorce. What did you think after I left?'

'I tried to keep myself from thinking. I was fully occupied with that. And I did pretty well until — this may seem strange to you — until we learned that you'd married someone else, a girl you'd known since you were very young. After that it seemed as though I thought of nothing else but you. You say you were jealous of Jesse . . . I was so jealous of Jeannette I couldn't bear it. Until then, I'd somehow managed to wall off that afternoon you and I had spent together, but once I began to imagine you with your wife, all the details of you and me together crowded into my brain and refused to leave. I was afraid to go to sleep at night, afraid I'd babble out everything that was in my memory. After that, I knew it was only a question of time till I would leave Jesse. And I knew that once I was free I would do anything I could do to get you back.'

[4]

From the time his divorce from Valerie was finalized, Jesse felt as if some unfamiliar mist had floated into the house by the Seine where he was free to live openly now with Nora. This is not to say that there was an abrupt change in his behaviour or in Nora's. Their days went as smoothly as before. They were easy and open with their friends and with each other. As though they had drawn up careful plans, their lives stayed on familiar rails, they stuck with proven routes and tested pleasures. Like experienced actors in a play they had performed together many times before, they missed no cues and kept all stage business exactly as it had been rehearsed and performed previously. But all the same, there was a false note in the performance.

It was difficult to pinpoint what had gone amiss, but there was, unquestionably, some change now in the rhythm; some new cadence, it seemed, had been imperfectly learned.

At last one evening Nora said, 'You feel differently now, don't you? Something's changed, hasn't it?'

'What do you mean? In what way?'

'I don't know. That's why I'm asking you.'

'Is this going to be a serious discussion?'

'That depends on you, I imagine.'

'I don't see how.'

'It depends on you because you have the answers. I have only feeble questions like the one I just asked.'

'And I have no answer,' he said, 'feeble or otherwise.'

'Then let me put it another way. Are you ill at ease with me since you've moved back here?'

'Ill at ease? Why do you say that? Are you ill at ease with me?'

'Very,' she said.

'Since when?'

'Since — I'm not sure I can't put a date to it — but since you've seemed ill at ease with me. That's since your divorce. And maybe a short time before.'

'But I don't feel ill at ease. Even this conversation doesn't disturb me and that must prove something.'

'It proves that you're clever with words. That's nothing new to either of us.'

'You're acting like someone who's eager for a quarrel and that's not like you. You hate to quarrel.'

'I also hate cloudy situations and unanswered questions. Such things don't seem to bother you.'

'If you'll point out a cloudy situation to me perhaps you'll find it bothers me a lot.'

'Here is what I consider a cloudy situation,' Nora said. 'Valerie told me solemnly that her decision to leave you was in no way prompted by the fact that you and I have been together these past few years. She told you the same thing. The question is — do we believe that or don't we?'

'I thought we believed it.'

'I think we chose to believe it,' she said.

'But you don't believe it?'

'At first I didn't. But then I asked myself why she would lie about it.'

'That's easy,' Jesse said. 'So you wouldn't feel responsible. So you wouldn't blame yourself for the divorce.'

'I understand that. But look at it this way. If she divorced you because of us, I can't imagine that she would have been happy about it. So why would she go out of her way to keep me from feeling guilty? Or you for that matter. She would have had a perfect right to be angry as hell.'

'But she isn't angry.'

'That's my point precisely. So to me that means she divorced you for a different reason.'

'Like what?'

'I think she's found another man.'

'I don't believe that at all.'

'I know you don't. That's exactly what makes the situation cloudy. You believe one thing and it makes you feel guilty. I believe something quite different and I feel guiltless.'

'That's your secret weapon. You always feel guiltless.'

'Not at all. You must see what I'm talking about. Why do you think she decided to leave you?'

'I don't know and I'm not sure Valerie knows. But when she says it was not because of us I believe her.'

'She had to have a reason, Jesse. Otherwise, nothing makes sense. Do you really believe she's romping around Ireland by herself?'

'She told Clara she's visiting friends there.'

'What friends?'

'I don't know.'

'Neither do I and neither does anyone else. No one has ever heard her mention friends in Ireland. In Sligo of all places. Yet there she is. Or there she says she is.'

'Valerie's not devious and you know it.'

'We're all devious when we're in love.'

'Not Valerie. It's not her nature.'

'Oh, my dear, I haven't taught you very much about women, have I?'

'You've taught me quite a lot about you.'

'I'm not sure about that either,' she said.

'In any case, I don't see much point in our dissecting Valerie.'

'That's not what we started out to do. I said I think you

feel differently about me now that you're divorced and you had no answer for that.'

Jesse smiled. 'I don't feel differently. The river keeps flowing outside and life goes on.'

'That's the most depressing thing I've ever heard you say.'

'It wasn't meant that way.'

'It sounds as if you've resigned yourself to everything. Am I included in the things you've resigned yourself to?'

'Oh, for God's sake, Nora, let's get off it. We have nothing to quarrel about.'

'I don't agree. We may have something very critical to quarrel about. You and I have been through some bad patches together but I don't recall that we ever bored each other.'

'Those are all your words. Boredom and resignation. I didn't say those things.'

'You didn't say the words but you certainly described the condition. Any man who says "life goes on", and "the river keeps flowing" is bored to death with himself and everybody else.'

'It was just an expression.'

'No, it's not. It's a state of mind, one that you seem to have resigned yourself to.'

'There's that word again.'

'Am I wrong?' she said. 'Can you honestly tell me I'm mistaken? I hope you can. Please contradict me. I'd love to be contradicted. What I see is a man in a holding pattern. Moving along from day to day, waiting for something or somebody to tell him what his next move will be. Am I right? Is that what I have to look forward to? After all these years, now that we really have no obstacles to deal with, am I going to get a big surprise from you some morning? Are you going to explain to me that your destiny is calling you somewhere else? Why are you smiling? Did I say something amusing?'

'No. You just have a magic talent for creating problems where there are no problems.'

'Oh, no, I don't. You're wrong about that. I hate problems and difficulties and misunderstandings, especially between you and me. I don't create them. I don't even like to see them. But I'm not blind. And all my other senses are still in working order. You're my only field of expertise, Jesse, since I was nineteen years old. I know you. If I don't know you I don't know anything. So when I tell you that I'm picking up vibrations from you that are new to me, when I say I can feel a sea-change taking place, you have to believe me. It's not something I want to see, it's something I can't help seeing.'

He sat looking at her and didn't answer. Finally he said, 'I know there's something I'm supposed to say but I don't know what it is.'

'How about "life goes on"?'

'Don't be a bitch,' he said.

'I don't want to be. You'll never know how hard I'm trying not to be.'

[5]

Floyd's birthday was March 18th. As a celebration he and Valerie drove to Cannes and spent three days in a suite at the Negresco. Their last morning there they had breakfast on the terrace overlooking the Promenade des Anglais. It had rained during the night, washing the sky and leaving the morning clear and golden and warm as June.

'Do you think it's a sin to be too happy?' Valerie said.

'No. I think it's a sin to be happy and not realize it till it's over.'

'When I was in school in Massachusetts I used to hear the other girls saying that their main objective in life was to be happy.'

'That's what everybody wants. They have to be happy or else.'

'I always thought it was a foolish thing to wish for,' she said. 'Even when I was very young I had the idea that a person had to try for something else and out of that process he'd gain something that would make him feel good. I decided that pleasure and happiness were two different things. I told myself that happiness could give you pleasure but pleasure wouldn't guarantee happiness.'

'You still think that?'

'No. In the first place I think happy is a crummy word. One of those catch-all words that lost its meaning a long time ago. And in the second place, whatever you call it, I don't think you can work for it or expect it to arrive because you deserve it. It's either genetic like freckles or you find it on the beach. Or in the drawer of an old night-stand. You can't manipulate it or preserve it or tuck it away in a wall-safe. All you can do is recognize it when you find it or when it finds *you*. Taste it and touch it and celebrate it. Gobble it up before it gets away.'

'Is that what we're doing?'

'No. We don't have to. With us it's like a tattoo. Burned into the flesh. We're like a beautiful china egg that got broken into two halves and then after a long time it got stuck back together.'

'When I was a little kid I used to say to my father, the man who'd adopted me, "We're lucky ducks, Daddy." '

'That's us,' Valerie said. 'We're lucky ducks.'

When they'd finished eating and had ordered another cup of coffee, a tall woman in a great white hat with a floppy brim that half-hid her face came across the terrace from the hotel lobby and sat at a nearby table. With her was a young black girl wearing white trousers and a yellow sweater. As soon as they sat down, Valerie, who could see their table clearly from where she sat, said to Floyd, 'We have to leave. Right now.'

'What's the matter?'

'I'll explain later. Don't look around. Just stand up and follow me to the hotel entrance, the one with the striped canopy over it.'

Floyd left some folded francs on the table and followed Valerie into the hotel. 'Are we checked out?' she said.

'All set. The car's just outside.'

As soon as they were inside the car, Floyd said, 'What's the mystery?'

'You know Nora's friend, Karina, don't you?'

'Sure.'

'Apparently she was staying in the hotel when we were there. She came out on the terrace and sat at a table just behind you.'

'Are you sure?'

'No question. Nobody looks like Karina.'

'Was she by herself?'

'She's never by herself. One of her protégées was with her.'

'Did she see us?'

'She may not have recognized you but she certainly got

a good look at me. She seemed to be hiding under her hat. I don't think she was any more anxious to be seen than we were.'

'So maybe she didn't know you.'

'Maybe she didn't,' Valerie said. 'But we can't count on it. And she must have seen you when we walked out. Even if she couldn't see your face, there aren't many men in Cannes who look like you, front *or* rear view.'

'It really doesn't matter, does it?'

'Only in the short run. Just a slight change in tactics. I certainly don't want Nora and Clara and Helen and Jesse to find out about us from a shady lady like Karina. So it looks as though our invisible life is over. I'll write to them as soon as we get back to St Raphael.'

Late that afternoon, after she'd sent letters express mail to Wingate Fields and to Nora in Paris, she said to Floyd, 'Does it make you feel strange now that we're about to be public knowledge.'

He shook his head. 'I liked living in a world with a population of two but we both knew it couldn't last for ever.'

'It won't change anything. Not between us. We've had our sweet time together and we'll have many other times like that. We'll be hermits no matter where we're living. People will see how much we want to be alone so they'll let us be alone. We won't entertain and after a while we won't be invited. We'll have two dogs and three cats and live by ourselves on the moon. You mustn't be worried that things will change now. I won't *let* them change.'

[6]

Clara sat silent in her upstairs parlour, a late-winter storm pounding and streaming outside, the shutters creaking, the great trees punished by the wind. Helen sat in a deep chair facing her.

'I can't believe it,' Clara said at last. 'I simply cannot believe it. Of all the things we feared for Floyd, none of us imagined that this could happen.'

'What did Nora say when she called this morning?'

'She's as baffled as we are.'

'And Jesse wasn't there, you say?'

'No. He'd gone off to Zurich. She expects him back tomorrow.'

'Was Nora's letter the same as the one you received?'

'From what she said, they were almost identical. If anything, Nora was more surprised than we were. She kept saying, "How in the world could it happen? They haven't seen each other for years." '

'They must have found a way to write to each other,' Helen said.

'But I can't imagine that. I can't believe that Valerie was having some sort of liaison, even by letter, when she was married to Jesse and Floyd was married to Jeannette. I know that girl better than I knew my own children. She's incapable of being devious or underhand.'

'She certainly managed to conceal her whereabouts for the past two months.'

'*That* I can understand. Now that I see what the circumstances are, I can see that she would want to have a cushion of time to herself. If, as she says, this is something that started a long time ago . . . what was it she said in the letter?'

Helen picked up the letter she held in her lap, studied it for a moment and said, ' "We have loved each other very much for a very long time." That can mean only one thing. It all started when I brought Floyd here almost ten years ago.'

'If that's true why would he go away and marry someone else? Why would Valerie wait so long to divorce Jesse?'

'You were here all the time Floyd was here. Did you have any hint that something . . .'

'I felt the same way you did,' Clara said. 'It seemed to me that they disliked each other. And that surprised me. Because Valerie is gracious to everyone. But between her and Floyd there always seemed to be a sort of tension. I saw them from my window one afternoon. They were standing face to face on the garden path and they seemed to be having a dreadfully serious discussion. But aside from that, I never saw much evidence that they had anything whatsoever to say to each other. Did you have any indication from Floyd?'

Helen shook her head. 'Nothing. He asked occasionally

if I'd heard from her but it was always connected to some general inquiry about matters here at Wingate.'

'Well, there's not much point to our trying to determine how it happened. We know very clearly now what has happened. Valerie's letter leaves no room for doubt about that. Our task now is to deal with the situation. And I see no easy way to do it. Since it's a family matter of the most delicate sort..'

'It's not your worry, Clara. It's something I have to deal with. If Nora hadn't guessed that Floyd is Hugh's child, no one would have ever known except me and you. If you and Jesse and Nora did not know the truth, it would certainly be my problem to solve. And that hasn't changed. It's a responsibility I can't share with anyone. And one I don't want to share. I sent Floyd a wire an hour ago. I'm flying down to Nice tomorrow morning.'

[7]

When Jesse finished reading Valerie's letter, Nora said, 'You don't seem surprised.'

'Very few things surprise me lately.'

'I talked with Clara on the telephone. She couldn't believe it. I can't believe it either. I like to think that I can spot a romance from across a soccer field but I never dreamed that *this* was going on.'

He tossed the letter on the table. 'Valerie didn't say anything in the letter about something "going on".'

'She didn't have to. She said they'd been very much in love for a very long time. What does that sound like to you?'

'Sounds like a Cole Porter song. Sounds like a newly divorced woman deciding she's discovered romance for the first time. It's a common occurrence.'

'I can't believe what I'm hearing,' Nora said. 'Is that the position you're taking?'

'It has nothing to do with me. Not now. Why should I take *any* position?'

'Are you saying that after her divorce was final, Valerie somehow found herself in contact with Floyd, they made a date to meet in Ireland, and then discovered they were wild about each other? Does that make sense to you?'

'It doesn't have to make sense to me. I'm an innocent bystander.'

'You may be a bystander,' Nora said, 'but you're not innocent. You know how the world works. And you certainly know Valerie. One thing she's not is impulsive. When she seems to act on impulse you can be sure she's been considering the pros and cons for months. It may soothe your pride to think that Valerie and Floyd have discovered each other just since your divorce but my suspicious mind tells me it goes back a bit further, much further in fact.'

'It's a guessing game. I'm not interested.'

'You're interested, all right. You're just embarrassed. You don't want to admit it to yourself that maybe Valerie takes after her naughty mother after all. You know as well as I do that when she says they've been in love for a long time, she means just that. Floyd was at Wingate for quite a while when he came to visit that first time. And you were spending a lot of time in Paris just then. Isn't that right?'

'This is your game. I don't want to inhibit you with the facts.'

'I already know the facts, Jesse, just as well as you do. Only I'm willing to face them and you're not. You've made up your mind that Valerie divorced you for some mysterious, undisclosed reason. Even though you pretend not to be interested, you refuse to concede that your wife could have been having an affair with another man, with Helen's son.'

'Why should I pretend to believe something when I know it isn't true?'

'You mean you hope it isn't true. But I say you're wrong. It's obvious to me that when Floyd was staying at Wingate and you were here in Paris, he and Valerie were having a very serious romp with each other.'

'They were not.'

'How do you know?'

'I know.'

'No, you don't. You have no more information than I do. And I say logic is on my side. They had a lovely affair, they separated for some reason, perhaps because of Valerie's children, but they never got over it. They must have corresponded somehow through those years they were apart and as soon as they were both free . . .'

'Let's drop it, Nora. What's the point?'

'The point is you shouldn't deceive yourself. It's important for you to know why you and Valerie broke up. I know it's not nice to think about your wife sleeping with someone else when your back was turned. Everytime you left home . . .'

'It wasn't that way. Valerie wouldn't have done that. And she didn't do that. It was just . . .' he stopped.

'It was just what?'

'Nothing.'

'Don't tell me that. You started to say something.'

'I don't want to talk about it.'

'But I do,' Nora said. 'This is important to me as well. I don't want you carrying secrets around with you. I don't want to see you deceiving yourself and being hurt.'

'I'm not hurt. It's not that.'

'Yes, it is. You can't talk about it. You can't even bear to discuss it.'

'Of course I can,' he said.

'Then *tell* me.'

'They weren't carrying on an affair behind my back. It was just an incident. And I knew about it.'

'An incident? What does that mean?'

'They went riding together one day. That summer, just before Floyd went back to America.'

'And there was an incident? What an odd way of putting it.'

'What's the difference how I put it? You know what I'm saying.'

'And you knew about it?'

'That's right. Valerie told me. She told me she'd made a foolish mistake and she asked me to forgive her.'

'And you forgave her?'

'These things happen sometimes. I'm not a child. I saw no reason to break up our marriage because of it. Floyd had gone back to America . . .'

'And you decided to come back to me,' Nora said.

'What does that mean?'

'What do you imagine it means? How soon after Valerie's confession did you begin to find me attractive again?'

Jesse smiled. 'I've always found you attractive.'

'Said the snake to the sparrow. Are you trying to tell

me that there was no connection between Valerie's little transgression and our major one? We'd been apart for a long time. Remember? And even after you began coming to Paris again, started writing again, we treated each other like polite strangers. No hint from your behaviour that we had lived together for all those years. I've often wondered how we went from *politesse* to passion after all that time away from each other. What's your theory?'

'It just happened, I guess.'

'That's what I thought, too. But now I'm not sure. Now it seems very possible to me that what I mistook for love rekindled was in fact something else. Like vengeance, for instance. Sauce for the gander. Isn't that the way it goes?'

'No,' Jesse said. 'That's not the way it goes. What are you trying to do?'

'I'm trying very hard not to get depressed. But I'm not succeeding.'

'I never saw any connection between you and me and what Valerie did. And I don't see one now.'

'I know,' Nora said. 'You didn't see any connection between Valerie and Floyd either.' Then, 'No wonder you've seemed different lately. The vengeance is all over, isn't it? There's nobody for you to deceive now. And I won't even be able to deceive myself.'

'I don't know what you're talking about,' Jesse said.

'No, I guess you don't.'

[8]

Floyd drove to Nice to meet Helen at the airport but she gave no hint of why she'd come till she was together with him and Valerie at the villa outside St Raphael. Then she told them, as simply and directly as she could, about herself and Hugh. When she finished speaking there was a long silence. Finally Floyd said, 'What about the other man, the one you said was my father?'

'There was no such man. I made him up. The adoption centre needed a name and I didn't want to involve Hugh and the Bradshaws.'

'But why lie to me about it? When you saw me in San

Diego that first time, wouldn't it have been better to tell me the truth?'

'I've thought about that a thousand times. And I still don't know the answer. You see, at that time, nobody knew the truth except me. I'd almost come to believe the story I told you. Also, if you knew about Hugh, I thought you'd want to meet him. And that would have caused a whole new set of problems.'

'He didn't know about me?'

'Of course not.'

Floyd glanced at Valerie but she was looking intently at Helen. When he turned back to his mother he said, 'You just said, "At *that* time, nobody knew the truth except you." Do other people know now?'

Helen nodded. 'When I brought you to England that first time, as soon as Nora met you, she guessed you were Hugh's child. So the truth came out. Nora knows, and Clara, and Jesse.'

'But still you didn't tell *me*. I don't understand why.'

'I don't have a good answer for that. I suppose I was afraid. Also Hugh was dead by then.I'm sure I told myself it would serve no real purpose to tell you the truth.'

'But you're telling me now,' he said. 'Why now?'

'Because I have to. And it's the most painful duty I've ever had in my life. Under other circumstances, nothing would make me happier than to see you and Valerie together, but now . . . I don't know how to say this.' She took a cigarette from the table beside her and Floyd lit it. Then she said, 'When I found out I was pregnant, it was a happy day for me. The fact that I wasn't married didn't worry me. I had no fears about having a child when I didn't have a husband. At first I had no fears at all. But slowly it began to dawn on me what the consequences might be. I realized — not for the first time but for the first time in relation to you — that I had placed you in terrible jeopardy. Hugh and I were first cousins. My father and his mother were brother and sister. That meant your maternal grandfather and your paternal grandmother were both Bradshaws. If I'd been practical and wise I suppose I would have decided not to give birth at all but I couldn't bear the thought of that. All through my pregnancy I went back and forth from total joy to unbearable fear. I was so afraid you might be flawed in some way. I'd heard such dreadful stories, seen frightening pictures in medical books. I've never been very religious but at that time I was convinced that I would be punished somehow, or that you would be punished because of me. It was a nightmare. It got to be so bad that I was afraid my anxiety in itself would do some damage to you. But no such thing happened. Nothing went wrong. When the doctor told me I had a normal healthy boy it was the happiest moment I'd ever known. If I hadn't prayed before, I certainly prayed then. Prayers of gratitude.'

'What a terrible thing to go through,' Valerie said.

'I know what you're trying to do,' Floyd said. 'And I know why you're doing it. You're telling us not to make the mistake you made. But look at it this way. If you hadn't done what you did, I wouldn't be here today. The world would have been deprived of a sensational human being.'

'Don't try to laugh it off,' Helen said. 'What I did was a dangerous, irresponsible thing that happened to turn out well. But for you and Valerie to have a child would be absolutely disastrous. Hugh and I were first cousins. That in itself is a problem. But you two are also first cousins. That means your child would have *three* grandparents with Bradshaw blood. Do you realize what a genetic explosion that could cause? Do you have any conception of what the result might be?'

Helen took the *rapide* to Paris that night. When they insisted that she stay a few days she said, 'No one can bring bad news as I did and then stay on as a house guest. Next time I'll stay for weeks. Till you throw me out.'

The winds came down from the north-east that night and they had a fire made in the sitting room next to their bedroom.

'Are you all right?' Floyd said.

'I guess so. Are you?'

'I mean are we all right?'

'It wasn't the best day of our lives,' Valerie said.

'It wasn't so good for her either.'

'It must have been horrible for her. Flying down here alone. Going home alone. Feeling the way she feels.'

'Is anything going to change for us?' he said then.

'I hope not. I don't want it to.'

'You don't feel creepy being with me.'

She kissed him on the cheek. 'Never. There's nothing creepy about you.'

'You know what I mean. I don't want you to feel different.'

'I don't.'

'Did it frighten you, what she said?'

'Of course it did. It scares me to death. I'm a woman. I've had children.'

'Would you be afraid for us to have a baby?'

'We *can't* have children, Floyd. Never. It's out of the question.'

'What if you got pregnant?'

'I can't,' she said. 'I mustn't.'

'What if you're pregnant now and don't know it?'

'I don't want to talk about it.'

He put his arm around her. 'You know it doesn't matter to me, don't you?'

'No. I don't know that.'

'It's true. It doesn't matter.'

'But it matters to me. It matters for you. I have three children. You don't have any.'

'I have Betsy.'

'It's not the same.'

'It is to me. And I'll have your kids in a way. They're almost grown-up now but that's all right.'

'All those years I didn't see you,' she said. 'when I thought about you, I always tried to picture what sort of child we'd have. It was something I wanted to give you.'

'I told you it doesn't matter.'

'I wish I believed that.'

'It really doesn't matter,' he said.

They sat silent before the fire for a long time. At last she said, 'Then why does it matter so much to me?'

[9]

The following day and the days after that, it was as though Helen had never come to St Raphael. It was as though the painful subject, past and future, had been exhausted during those hours Floyd and Valerie spent together before the fire. They slipped, with no apparent effort, back into the rhythm they had established in Ireland and had refined in France. Moment-to-moment, sufficient to the day, et cetera. Heavy concentration on wines and food, the quality of the air, the intensity of the mistral, and the softness of the rain when it fell in the garden.

They stayed on in St Raphael through the fragrant springtime, made dilatory trips to Digne, Draguignan, Villefranche, Antibes, Grasse and Vence. And they planned their return to Wingate Fields. 'We'll spend a couple of weeks there with Rab and Polly and Bill,' Valerie said. 'Then, when they get bored with their mother and decide to rattle off somewhere with their school friends, you and I will drive up to Scotland and amuse ourselves in the cool mountains. If the Isle of Skye is too crowded, we'll push farther west and north to Harris or Lewis. There, we'll need a fire even in August. We'll wear heavy Shetland sweaters and drink whisky with honey and butter stirred into it.'

They planned to go north the second week in June. Two days before their departure date, pleading a headache, Valerie sent Floyd to Cannes to buy her a piece of luggage. When he came back he found a note from her stuck to the bathroom mirror.

> No crisis, darling, but I've gone off to see the children by myself. Please don't come to Wingate. I've no stomach for explanations about you and me just now. Stay where you are, *soyez sage*, and I'll write you when to meet me in Scotland.

He persuaded himself that he saw nothing unusual in her decision to go to England by herself. When three weeks passed, however, and he heard nothing from her, he wrote her a note. After ten more days, when he had no answer, he telephoned. Only Clara was there. When Floyd asked about Valerie, she said, 'I don't know where she's gone but she was extremely upset when she left. She said she was going to London but she told Helen she didn't plan to stay there.'

The following day he had an airmail letter from her, postmarked London.

> I'm sure you're dreadfully angry and upset and I'm sorry for that. I've wanted to contact you but I didn't know what to say. I still don't. I only know that I can't hack it, darling. I love you so much it makes me tremble to write the words but I can't face up to giving you less than you deserve. I would end up hating myself so much that *you* would hate me, too. Then we'd both be

lost. I'd give anything if I could find some of that luck you said we had together but I'm afraid it ran out. Not your fault. Not mine. Just a lot of awkward, scary things that we can't change. When I saw you that first day in Dublin I told myself that nothing would ever pry us apart. But something has and it's killing me.

[10]

As soon as she knew what had happened, Helen went again to St Raphael. But when she arrived Floyd wasn't there. The servants said he'd gone off to Ireland. He telephoned every evening, however, while she was there, to see if there had been any word from Valerie.

It was near the end of August before he came back. As soon as he returned, that first evening, he said to Helen, 'I know why you came here and I appreciate your concern but things are under control now. I can handle the situation.'

'I don't mind staying on.'

'I know you don't. But this is something I have to deal with myself. And that's what I want to do.'

'You're really mad at me, aren't you?'

'Not at all. I'm mad at myself. I never should have let her go back to Wingate by herself.'

'But if it weren't for me, none of this would have happened.'

'I don't feel that way,' he said. 'and you mustn't either. You can't blame yourself for things that happened years ago.'

'But where is she? Why doesn't anyone hear from her? She hasn't even contacted the children.'

'Don't worry. I'll hear from her when she's ready. Everything's going to work out, I promise you.'

When she was back in England, Helen told Clara everything she knew about the situation. 'As I told you in my letter, he went back to Dublin because he thought she might be there. He retraced every mile of their trip around Ireland, stopping at every hotel and inn and guest-house where they'd stayed. Then he crossed over to France as they had done and slowly made his way back to St Raphael, visiting every place they had visited together. But no one had seen her since the two of them had been there months earlier.'

'Was he terribly despondent when he got home?'

'That's what I had expected. I had tried to prepare myself for it. But no such thing happened. He was almost cheerful.'

'How can that be?'

'I don't know. He seems to have no doubts about the future. He is absolutely confident that she'll come back to St Raphael or she'll get in touch with him there.'

'Is he really so optimistic or was that a role he was playing for your benefit?'

'I think he really believes what he says. He's convinced they'll be together again soon.'

'What a let-down he'll have if he's wrong.'

'You know Valerie better than any of us. How do you see it?'

'I thought I knew her,' Clara said, 'but since the day she told me she was leaving Jesse, I've seen all sorts of facets to her that are new to me. I decided that perhaps I don't know her well, after all. Each time I make an adjustment there's a new development and I'm at sea again. I would never have thought her capable of disappearing the ways she's done now. No word to anyone. No hint of when we'll see her again.'

'I feel the same way. But Floyd acts as though he understands everything.'

Floyd, of course, alone in St Raphael, did *not* understand at all. He had simply decided to accept the situation and to hope for understanding later. He told himself that his not having found her at any of the places they had stayed together was a good sign. But he did not subject that conclusion to close scrutiny. The fact that she had apparently hidden herself in some new and unfamiliar place led him to believe that she had chosen a temporary haven and would therefore not stay away for long.

St Raphael was crowded with summer travellers and with French families on holiday. The promenade that curled around the harbour of the town and stretched both ways along the sea, north and east toward the edge of the village and west along Fréjus-Plage, was crowded day and night. The restaurants and vendors' stands, the cafés and dancehalls bulged with brown-skinned half-naked youngsters, old men in linen trousers and old women wearing indiscreet sun-dresses. The sands were carpeted with bodies, and sailboats and motor launches moved like lazy insects across the bay.

As if to prove to himself that anxiety was not the major feature of his days, Floyd took an active part in this summer life. Early each morning he swam off the beach in front of his villa and breakfasted in his robe on the terrace. He sailed his small boat, played *boules* in front of the Fréjus *bureau de poste*, played tennis every day, and walked in the late afternoon in the hills behind the town. He drank the lovely Provence wines in the bars and cafés and on the hotel terraces. He followed closely, in fact, the routine that he and Valerie had developed when she was there. Sticking to those old habits helped him to maintain his conviction that she was only temporarily away. He nourished a fantasy that when she came walking up the terrace steps at last, he would be able to say, 'I've been expecting you. I made dinner reservations for tonight at the Toque Blanche.'

September came, however, and St Raphael began to empty. Most of the young people vanished, the Americans and the Germans and the Japanese thinned out. The promenade was returned to white-haired couples and their dogs.

In October, still more people left, all the temporary food-stands along the back of the beach were disassembled and carted away, and hotels and restaurants began to close for the winter. By early November St Raphael had been returned to its year-round residents.

One cool morning, as Floyd had breakfast on his terrace, the kitchen maid asked, 'Will madame be coming home soon? It is sad not to see her for so long.'

Instead of saying, as he would have a few weeks before, 'Yes, she'll be here very soon,' he heard himself saying. 'I'm not certain. Perhaps I will leave and go to join her.'

He realized then that he was preparing himself for possibilities that he hadn't admitted before. This was confirmed for him a few days later when after having drunk seven whiskies in the bar of *Le Grand Breton*, the bartender said. 'It's a long time since we've seen Madame. Will she return soon?' Floyd had answered, 'None of your business,' and stomped out.

He began to admit to himself then that all his apparent confidence had been pretence and self-manipulation. Once he allowed doubt to slip inside his armour he quickly found that he had no armour. When he forced himself to consider facts and only facts he could find no foundation for his assumption that Valerie's absence was temporary, that once she'd had the time and the isolation to weigh the positive against the negative, she would see what he saw and feel as he felt. Very quickly he found that he had made a full turn-around. When he reread the note she'd left when she went off to England and the letter she'd sent later, it was clear to him that her mind had been made up then. However difficult her choice had been, she had chosen. And every day they had been apart, almost five months now, had certainly made that choice more final and permanent. As he saw her accepting a life spent apart, he also began to accept it. One morning as he walked slowly through the villa and through the grounds, he felt no association with the place. He no longer saw Valerie at every turning in the garden, no longer saw her in the halls and the rooms. That afternoon he called his travel agent and booked a flight to London for five days later.

His first impulse had been to go to Wingate Fields. But by the following morning he had begun to have second thoughts. Two things he did not want just now were understanding and sympathy. He had no wish to explain his position or his feelings, or to have those feelings explained to him. Having come to painful terms with the situation he did not want to discuss it or hear it discussed. Nor did he want to be around people who were making a great show of *avoiding* such a discussion. He could not, in fact, think of anyone he wanted to be around. Not even Abe Rettberg.

By that afternoon, however, he realized there was someone he very much wanted to see. He called and cancelled his flight to London and made new reservations, Nice to Paris and Paris to Chicago. Then he wrote a letter to Betsy.

> I hope you're too busy with your life at college, with all your friends and activities, to notice that I've been neglecting you. The steady stream of notes and postcards I send you is no substitute for the regular face-to-face meetings I'd become accustomed to.
>
> So here's the good news. I'm flying to Chicago in a few days. I'll call you when I arrive, and I'll see you as soon after that as you're available. I'll be staying at the Drake so maybe you'll come there and we'll have an extravagant evening together.
>
> I'll fill you in on all the news when I see you. But I

can tell you now that I've had enough of Europe for the time being. So we'll be able to spend some time together now on a regular basis. See you soon.

Floyd became as positive now about returning to America as he had been before that Valerie would come back to him. He was manipulating himself, of course, and he realized it, but he simply surrendered to the manipulation, focused his eyes straight ahead, and permitted no slippage. He did not go so far as to assure himself that things, after all, were working out for the best but he began to be resigned to a set of circumstances he seemed unable to change.

Also, once he had decided what he was going to do, once he'd admitted to himself that he was not the master of the situation, he allowed himself to be angry. First with Helen for not having told him the truth long before, then with the whole Bradshaw clan for the knowledge they'd had and the secret, snotty power it had given them over him. And finally, he let himself admit his anger towards Valerie, not for what she had chosen to do, but for the abrupt, cold, and impersonal way in which she'd done it. In a situation that cruelly affected both of them she had made a separate and solitary choice.

If he had hoped his anger would lessen his torment, he was mistaken. As he made his plans, strengthened his purpose, and set about redefining himself, Valerie stayed as vibrantly alive for him as she had ever been. Bullying himself, telling himself over and over that what they had had together was all they would ever have, insisting that he accept that fact, he could *not* accept it.

As his departure day approached, he had fantasies that the postman would come up the drive with a letter from her just as he was preparing to leave for the airport. When he actually did hear from her, it was not so dramatic as that. Two days before he was to leave, as he was sleeping late one morning, her telegram came.

I'm in Sienna. Hotel Tuscany. Please come and get me. Whatever I'm going to do with my life I can't do it without you.

[11]

All the county residents who had attended Angus' eightieth birthday party and Clara's more recent Christmas celebration agreed that those occasions seemed like plain gatherings indeed when compared with the New Year's Day wedding of Valerie and Floyd. 'It's your second wedding, and mine, too,' Floyd said to her. 'Aren't we supposed to be decorous about this whole thing? Immediate family and a few close friends. Lounge suits for the men and street-length dresses for the ladies.'

'Not at all. This is the major moment of my life and I expect it to be the same for everyone who attends. From now on, people in this county will measure time from this event. Before Valerie's wedding or after Valerie's wedding.'

'Valerie's wedding? What about me?'

'You're just the groom. The marriage may belong to you, but everyone knows the wedding is the sole and exclusive property of the bride. Once the ceremony's over, you may make all my life decisions. Until then, I am the benevolent ruler of your destiny.'

There was some hesitation on Clara's part, too, but she was no match for her fervent granddaughter.

'I won't talk to you about tradition or taste,' Clara said, 'because I know that would be hopeless, but I do think, before we put on this great carnival of a ceremony, that you should consider how your children might react.'

'That was my primary consideration,' Valerie said. 'I consulted them first of all. They decided that Rab should give me away because he's the oldest, Bill will be Floyd's best man, and Polly and Betsy will be my bridesmaids. They're almost as excited as I am.'

'Well, I must say you act like a bride. And you certainly look like one. You don't look a day over twenty-five.'

'That's the way I feel. When Jesse and I were married, I was a sober and serious young woman of twenty-one. We were married in a dim-lit room by a stuffy judge. It never occurred to me in those days that a wedding could be a gay and memorable affair. Now that it has occurred to me, I'm so happy I may explode. And I want the wedding to reflect that. Flowers and wine and music, gorgeous frocks and gentlemen in morning coats. Great lines of limousines creeping up the drive, all the bedrooms filled with guests, a choir and an orchestra and twenty little tots coming down the aisle carrying white roses. And I'll be wearing your mother's wedding gown, my great-grandmother's dress. History, Clara, we'll make some history to start the new year. I am marrying the most splendid man in the world. So no little civilized ceremony will do. We must have a festival! A pageant! An event!'

The occasion turned out to be everything Valerie had hoped for. In both size and splendour. The bridal feast, the music, the dancing, the levels of noise and gaiety and joy and goodwill surpassed everything she had dreamed of. It was truly her wedding, she was the radiant centrepiece. Indeed, with the exception of Floyd and of Valerie's two sons, Rab and Bill, it seemed clear to the guests assembled that the fabled Bradshaw clan had become, in large part, a family of women. Valerie, of course, the regal Clara, Nora and Helen, and the elegant, dark-haired Polly. Spanning four generations, these five creatures glowed like matched stones attached to one chain.

Although each of them was linked in some critical way with Jesse, Helen felt, as she watched the festivities and took full part in them, that only she, of all the family and all the guests, truly marked his absence. At last, however, one deaf and tottering old woman, a cousin of the Bicks in Cumberland, said to Helen, 'I understand Jesse's gone off to America. What a pity he couldn't be here.'

On the eve of the wedding, Rab and Betsy and Bill and Polly stole off into the library with a chilled bottle of champagne. As Rab lifted his glass he said, 'Having made a careful study of the Bradshaw family history, I think the four of us should make a pact, that we will not marry each other.'

They all laughed and drank, and Rab went on, 'To purify our blood lines I plan to take to wife a Zulu maiden, Polly will marry a Polish jockey, Bill, I believe, should find a yellow-skinned girl with bare breasts and sturdy legs, a Balinese perhaps, and you, Betsy . . . although you're not technically a Bradshaw, the three of us have decided to adopt you. So you must be included in this pact. For you, I recommend a great silent Norwegian. And for all of us, a reckless, romantic life. No worries, no heart-break, and lots of handsome, obedient children.'

He laughed and drained his glass. 'Like *us!*'

[12]

The following autumn, near the end of November, Jesse drove from Fort Beck to Champaign to spend three days doing research in the university library. The day Jack Kennedy was shot in Dallas, Jesse was in a private reading room and didn't hear the news till very late in the afternoon. When he called Helen at home she began to cry on the telephone.

'God, I feel so awful I just . . . it's all so senseless.'

'I'm coming home,' Jesse said.

'You don't have to do that. I didn't mean that.'

'I know you didn't. But I'm coming anyway. I'll be there in a couple of hours.'

When he drove into the driveway and put the car in the garage there were no lights on upstairs or in the front of the house. The housekeeper met him in the kitchen when he came in through the back door.

'Is she all right?' he said.

'I think she's asleep. She turned off the television set after you called and went into the library by the fire. I looked in a while ago. She's lying on the couch. I think she's asleep.'

Jesse eased the door open and walked into the room where Helen lay sleeping. He stood at the foot of the couch and looked down at her, curled up on her side like a child, an afghan half-covering her legs, her cheeks glowing pink in the light from the fire. Watching her, he remembered things he thought he'd forgotten long since, moments and sounds and details from those days when he'd lived in this house, when he'd thought of it as his home and had believed he would never choose another home.

He walked behind the couch, came around the end and knelt down beside her so his body blocked the light from the fire. She opened her eyes then. 'You didn't have to come all the way home.'

'Yes, I did.' He lifted her up, sat down on the couch and eased her back down so she rested across his legs, her head on his chest.

'I thought I'd never stop crying,' she said.

'It's not just you. A lot of people are crying.'

He pulled her closer to him and turned her slightly so she could see the fire. They stayed there for a long time, not talking, watching the embers die, the room growing soft and dark around them.